A Much
Married Man

A Much Married Man

Nicholas Coleridge

First published in Great Britain in 2006 by Orion Books
an imprint of The Orion Publishing Group
Orion House, 5 Upper St Martin's Lane, London WC2H 9EA

3 5 7 9 10 8 6 4 2

A CIP catalogue record for this book is available
from the British Library

ISBN-13 978 0 75285 254 6 (hardback)
978 0 75285 255 3 (trade paperback)
ISBN-10 0 75285 254 X (hardback)
0 75285 255 8 (trade paperback)

Typeset by Deltatype Ltd, Birkenhead, Merseyside

Printed and bound in Great Britain by Clays Ltd, St Ives plc

The Orion Publishing Group's policy is to use papers that
are natural, renewable and recyclable products and made
from wood grown in sustainable forests. The logging and
manufacturing processes are expected to conform to the
environmental regulations of the country of origin.

www.orionbooks.co.uk

To my parents
David and Susan Coleridge

Acknowledgements

I would like to thank several people who helped with this book: first and foremost my wife Georgia who read every chapter of the manuscript several times and always gives perceptive advice. I would also like to thank Julia Dixon and Sarah Standing for their thoughtful editing suggestions, and Charlotte Allen who heroically typed long stretches of the story helped by Nina Godfrey, Lucy Musgrave and Megan Walsh. Cristina Monet Zilkha, who has a genius for dialogue, advised from New York, as she has with previous novels. Sally Atkins was essential on the mechanics of organising a rock festival. Vanessa Creedy-Smith was my Paris expert, Geordie Greig my source on shooting.

My editor at Orion, Kate Mills, gave countless invaluable insights and editing points and I owe a great deal too to Jane Wood, Lisa Milton and Genevieve Pegg at Orion, and also to Sophie Hutton-Squire. I am, as ever, enormously grateful to my legendary agent, Ed Victor.

The action in this novel takes place over forty years between October 1965 and July 2005. I would like to emphasise that all the fictional characters are exactly that, and are in no respects based upon real people, either living or dead.

Nicholas Coleridge
Worcestershire, 2006

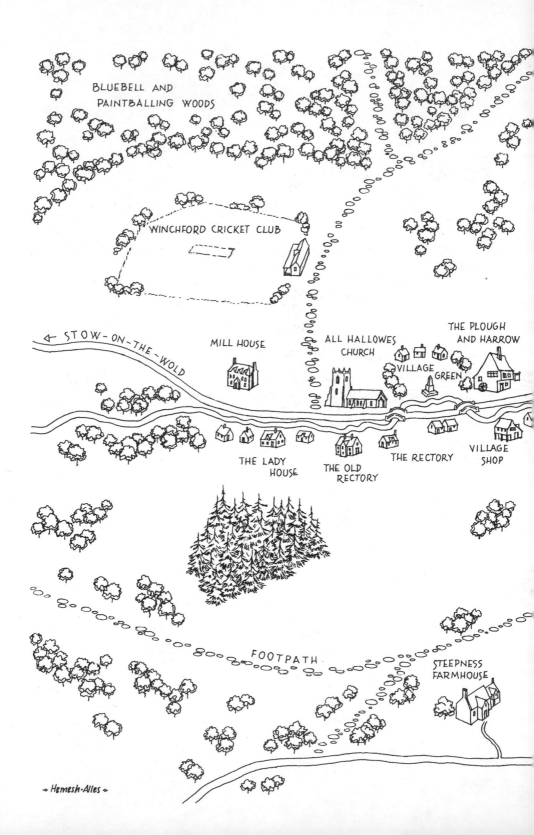

BLUEBELL AND PAINTBALLING WOODS

WINCHFORD CRICKET CLUB

← STOW-ON-THE-WOLD

MILL HOUSE

ALL HALLOWES CHURCH

THE PLOUGH AND HARROW

VILLAGE GREEN

THE LADY HOUSE

THE OLD RECTORY

THE RECTORY

VILLAGE SHOP

FOOTPATH

STEEPNESS FARMHOUSE

- Hemesh-Alles -

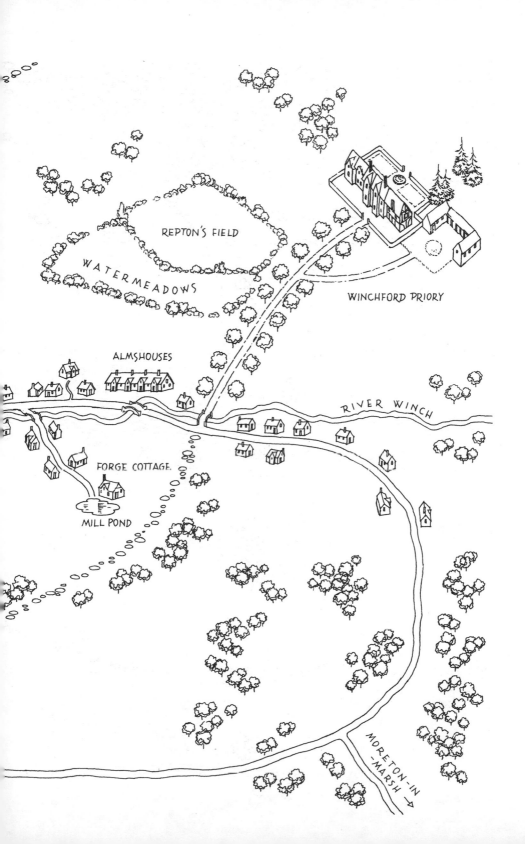

REPTON'S FIELD

WATERMEADOWS

WINCHFORD PRIORY

ALMSHOUSES

RIVER WINCH

FORGE COTTAGE

MILL POND

MORETON-IN-MARSH →

Cast of principal characters in order of appearance

ANTHONY ANSCOMBE: Son and heir to the Winchford Priory estate, Oxfordshire.

AMANDA GIBBONS (later Anscombe): Mesmerising heartbreaker.

GODFREY ANSCOMBE: Anthony's tepid merchant banker father, owner of Winchford Priory.

HENRIETTA ANSCOMBE: Godfrey's powerful, opinionated wife.

CHARLIE EDWARDS: Rodent-faced neighbour of the Anscombes with a notably spotty back.

SIR PERCY BIGGES: Retired British Ambassador living at the Mill House, Winchford.

JACINTHE BIGGES: His busybody wife.

MRS HOLCOMBE: Henrietta Anscombe's ineffectual cleaning lady at Winchford Priory.

WALTER TWINE: Organist at All Hallowes church, hedge-layer and ancient village character.

LEX HOLLAND: Anthony's oldest friend with shared history at three consecutive schools.

'SCROTUM' HOLLAND: Lex's landowner father, reputed to have the biggest dick in Oxfordshire.

ROSIE HOLLAND: Scrotum's long suffering wife.

JASMINE ANSCOMBE: Anthony's daughter with Amanda.

JUDY HOLCOMBE: Barmaid at the Plough and Harrow pub. Daughter of Priory cleaner Mrs Holcombe.

SANDRA POTTS (later Anscombe): Nanny to Jasmine, mother to Richard and Rosanna.

STEVE: Sandra's first fiancé, a very fit soldier.

GERVAISE SABLON: Smarmy Belgian proprietor of the Fox and Terriers gastropub in Lower Oddington.

ARAMINTA NALL-CAINE: Childhood playmate of Jasmine.

RUPERT 'BONGO' NALL-CAINE: Solid, conventional neighbour of Anthony. Gifted amateur cricketer and joint Master of the Heythrop hunt.

MARK AND ANNIE PLUNKETT: Neighbours of the Anscombes at Fyford.

PATRICE BOUILLON: Big, sardonic French movie star. Voted one of the world's sexiest men.

LEONARD POTTS: Sandra's small, matey father, owner of Potts Electrical Services of Poole, Dorset.

MARJORIE POTTS: Len's immaculate, perky wife, mother of Sandra and Ginette.

GINETTE POTTS: Sandra's younger, grossly fat sister.

ARCHIE BIGGES: Dashing, faintly seedy son of Sir Percy and Jacinthe Bigges.

ARABELLA BIGGES: Archie's sister, a secretary at a charity for disabled Maltese donkeys.

MICHAEL ANSCOMBE: Chairman of Anscombe Brothers Bank. First cousin to Godfrey.

REVEREND JEREMY MEEK: Fey parson of All Hallowes, Winchford.

RICHARD ANSCOMBE: Beefy, rugby-loving son of Anthony and Sandra.

ROSANNA ANSCOMBE: Richard's chunky, pony-mad sister.

BRENDON SHEAF: Over-familiar landlord of the Plough and Harrow pub.

NULA STARLING: Paddington-based acupuncturist. Mother of Gaia Anscombe. Ecology activist and hunt saboteur.

DIANE: Immaculate, perky girlfriend of Len Potts.

GAIA STARLING: Nula's daughter by Anthony Anscombe.

JOHN FURLONG: Lugubrious farm manager, father of Tom and Katie.

CONSTANCE FURLONG: Beautiful, pre-Raphaelite first wife of John Furlong.

TOM FURLONG: Clever, smooth son of John and Constance.

KATIE FURLONG: Tom's fragile, artistic, redhead sister.

GRACIDO MENENDEZ: Virile Argentinian nine-goal polo professional.

LADY FITTLEWORTH: Excessively old owner of a West Sussex estate.

SIR HECTOR PLUNKETT: Local Tory MP for Oxfordshire North, father of Mark.

ED GIBBONS: Marsupial, motorbike-riding father of Amanda. A lecturer at the American College in Rome.

DITA EMBOROLEON (later Anscombe): Energetic, strong-minded, collector of millionaires. Anthony's third wife.

CARINA RESNICK: Socially omnipresent interior decorator, Dita's closest girlfriend.

ALECO 'GOLDIE' EMBOROLEON: Multi-millionaire Greek shipping tycoon, Dita's second husband and owner of the island of Kypsos.

JOHN-SPIROS EMBOROLEON: Sensitive son of Aleco and Dita, always immaculately dressed.

AMBROSIA EMBOROLEON: John-Spiros's plump, unhappy sister.

MORAD AHVAZI: Dita's hairy-chested, Rolex-wearing son by her first marriage to Sharif.

JONNY FAISAL: Morad Ahvazi's mega-rich best friend.

REGIS: Dita's French chef at Winchford Priory.

THATCHER: Retriever belonging to the Furlong family.

TEBBIT: Another Furlong family retriever.

DUNCAN: A third Furlong retriever, named after Conservative Leader Iain Duncan-Smith.

PEANUTS: Spaniel puppy belonging to Katie Furlong, shot dead with a paintball gun.

STIGMATA CORBETTA: Spanish housekeeper imported to Winchford Priory by Dita.

SANTOS: Dita's Italian butler.

HENRY ANSCOMBE: Anthony's youngest child, with Dita.

CHALKIE CLIFF: Falklands veteran running Winchford Paintballing.

TREVOR BRATT: Cutting-edge fashion designer.

SHARIF AHVAZI: Dita's first husband, dodgy Iranian casino owner.

DARREN: Dorkish mechanic owner of Winchford Autoparts.

SCOTTY: Darren's business partner.

IRINA EMBOROLEON: Goldie Emboroleon's latest wife, Slavic model with torpedo shaped tits.

SIR RAMNAKRISHNA GUPTA: Software billionaire, reputedly the third richest Ugandan Asian in Britain.

Part One

1

Anthony Anscombe could remember the precise moment he fell madly and irrevocably in love with Amanda Gibbons.

He had been watching the guests arrive at Winchford Priory from the gallery that ran the width of the Great Hall. Originally built for minstrels, the gallery was used by Godfrey Anscombe, Anthony's father, as a handy place in which to store cigars, paper clips and elastic bands in the drawers of an old desk. The reason Anthony was lurking in the gallery, rather than chatting up his parents' neighbours downstairs, was that he wasn't in the mood for this party. Godfrey and Henrietta Anscombe's annual fork supper, held in the same week each October, drew a predictable and, in Anthony's view, thoroughly tedious crowd of local worthies. Three months after leaving school, and two weeks after his eighteenth birthday, he would rather have been meeting some mates in a local pub than doing his bit to entertain the county.

Already there must have been sixty or seventy people milling about downstairs, and continual ascending gusts of icy air as the great oak front door opened and closed heralded ever more guests piling inside from the bitter October night. Fires blazed in the stone hearths at opposite ends of the hall, and dishes of pheasant casserole were being set up on hotplates along a trestle table. One entire wall was hung with Elizabethan portraits of Anscombe ancestors.

The door reopened and Anthony recognised the new arrivals as the Edwardses, who had recently bought Brasenose Farm in Steeple Barford. Several stragglers his own age hovered in their wake, swathed in scarves and overcoats. That was when he caught sight of Amanda. It took him less than a second to realise she was the most enchanting girl he'd ever set eyes on.

She had glanced up to the ceiling with its massive oak beams and spotted Anthony skulking in the gallery, holding his stare in a way he found disconcerting and vaguely flirtatious. Her eyes were huge and black, ringed with kohl, and her hair, also black, was straight and cut into a short bob. She cocked her head to one side in a speculative summons he found irresistible: 'Well, are you coming down here or aren't you?'

He sped down to the Great Hall as though in the pull of some mighty ocean current drawing him towards the sooty-eyed girl. He found her still lingering in a small group with the Edwardses, whom Anthony hardly knew. Charlie Edwards, twenty-one, rodent-faced and smoking, had one arm draped around the girl's back, signalling some kind of pro-prietorial entitlement. Close up, she was even more enticing than she'd appeared from above. Having shed her overcoat, she was dressed like an eighteenth-century highwayman in black frock coat, breeches and gauntlets. Large paste buckles gleamed on her boots.

'Do you normally lurk upstairs during your own parties?' she asked him.

She had high, delicate cheekbones and luminous white skin. Hopeless at estimating girls' ages, having been educated among boys, he reckoned she must be seventeen or eighteen.

'Not normally. I just didn't feel particularly sociable this evening.' He found it difficult to think; her beauty made him anxious.

'I'm Amanda, in case you're wondering.'

'Anthony Anscombe.'

'I know. This is your party and your place.'

'Can I get you a drink or some food?'

'Charlie will do that, won't you, Charlie? No pheasant, if that's what it is. Just vegetables and potatoes, plenty of potatoes.'

'Don't you like pheasant?' Anthony asked.

'No, though red meat is one of my passions. I just loathe game – it's so gamey.'

As Charlie, with evident reluctance, joined the queue for the food, standing in line behind the racing trainers and foxhunting men, solici-tors and stockbrokers who comprised the Anscombes' friends, Amanda leant against one of the two overpowering Italianate marble chimneyp-ieces that dominated both ends of the room. Anthony felt momentarily shy, and wished he was less boringly dressed. Six foot two inches tall, and conventionally handsome with short black hair, he realised he lacked dazzle in his grey suit and dark tie. Heart racing, he tried desperately to think of something interesting to say to this mesmerising girl before Charlie returned with her food. Across the room, he saw his mother staring in their direction, frowning, wondering who this girl was. Then Amanda said, 'Would you show me round your house? Or am I supposed to pay for a guided tour?'

'Er, sure, why not? Of course I can show you, if you want. It's a good excuse to get out of here. But I warn you, it's really not that interesting unless you go in for mullioned windows and moth-eaten tapestries.'

As they left the hall Amanda brushed his arm, and her touch shot through him with an adrenalin rush.

Anthony had led tours of Winchford Priory several times before. The house wasn't open to the public, but there were tours in aid of the local nurses and hospice, for the Tories and the pony club, garden organisations and enthusiasts for vernacular architecture who came to see the linen-fold panelling in the library. He had developed a route around the house which began with the four large reception rooms downstairs, took in the long gallery with its Tudor portraits and a couple of older bedrooms – or 'chambers' as they were known, the Judge's Chamber and the Assize Chamber – and ended up on the roof, with its turrets and distant views towards Warwickshire and Stratford-upon-Avon. He could go into any room and, without even thinking, reel off the facts about soot-blackened armorial firescreens and floorboards refashioned from the decking of British frigates. Tonight he could barely get the words out and heard himself trip over the simplest phrases. Amanda had the sexiest mouth and most provocative smile he had ever seen.

'Are you always so shy?' she demanded. 'You didn't look shy when I saw you up there in the gallery.'

'Me, shy? Not at all. What an odd question. I'll show you the Assize Chamber next, shall I? It's where they used to hold monthly courts at one time; the circuit magistrates convened at Winchford Priory and all the local trials were held here.'

'I'd rather see the roof,' Amanda said. 'It's smoky in this house. I need air.'

'Then we have to go up this rickety staircase. Watch your head – the ceiling gets quite low.'

Anthony stooped at the top of the stone stair and eased open the bolts of the trapdoor. Amanda placed her warm hands on top of his and pretended to help.

They emerged onto the roof, where a leaded walkway, eighteen inches wide, ran round the perimeter of the slates, linking four large turrets. The parapet was castellated, and several precarious pink-brick chimney-stacks tottered above them. Afterwards, Anthony recalled how dark the starless night was, the blackest he could remember.

After some fumbling about, he found the right switches for two or three dusty lights set into walls of the turrets, but Amanda said, 'No, leave them off. I like it better this way. Shhh, don't say a thing; listen to the silence. The wind in the treetops. There's nothing – you can't hear one car.'

Just then the stillness was shattered by a blast of soul music from the Great Hall: The Drifters' 'Up on the Roof'.

Amanda laughed. 'How corny is that? On the roof it's peaceful as can be, and the world below can't bother me.' I think that's how it goes; you can't hear the words clearly. I've always detested that song. It's the pits. Anthony, you didn't lay it on specially, did you?'

'Nothing to do with me, I assure you. It's just the disco. There's supposed to be dancing.'

'Maybe we should go back down.' She gave him a measuring look, as though trying to work out what he wanted. 'Charlie will be wondering where I am. He goes all possessive at parties.'

'Is he . . . ?' Anthony's voice trailed away.

'My boyfriend? Sort of. Kind of. He thinks he should be; let's put it that way. Technically the answer is still no.' She smiled. 'Shall we dance? I've always wanted to do that, dance on a big old rooftop.'

And so they swayed together, awkwardly at first, to the record Amanda said she detested, and to Anthony it felt not quite real, to be dancing with this beautiful girl who made him dumb and powerless with yearning, on the roof of his own house on this arctic October night while the music filtered up through the slates from far below. When the record changed to something slower, Amanda held on to him, so they were properly slow dancing, and Anthony shuddered at her touch.

'If this was my home,' Amanda said, 'I'd live up here all the time in these turrets. One would be our bedroom, another could be our sitting room, a bathroom and . . . kitchen, I suppose.'

Anthony heard only: *our* bedroom, *our* sitting room.

'They're filthy dirty inside, and some of the doors have warped so they're jammed shut. That one at the front's still okay, I used to have it as a hobbies room when I was eleven. But they could probably be repaired.'

'Are they still there – your hobbies, I mean? Can I see?'

So they walked along the leads to the west tower, and Anthony put his shoulder to the door and found the light, and they entered the circular brick room, which had a workbench fixed to the wall. The place still bore faint fumes of paint and turpentine and the floor was littered with bat droppings. Dangling from the ceiling on lengths of cotton were a dozen model aircraft constructed from kits – Spitfires, Stukas and Hurricane bombers – and the workbench was covered with tiny, dried-up tins of acrylic paint, and Anthony's childhood butterfly collecting kit.

'As you can see, no one's been in here for ages,' Anthony said. 'Look at the bat shit everywhere. I'm surprised the bats haven't collided with the planes, actually.'

'It's radar,' Amanda said. 'Bats have this amazing radar. They can find their way in the dark.' Then, with startling speed, she flicked the light switch so they were plunged back into darkness. 'Okay, Anthony, before your eyes acclimatise, you have to find me. I'm going to move about very slowly. All you have to do is touch me. And watch out for your aeroplanes; if you knock into one, it'll give away where you are.'

They edged around the turret, feeling their way in the gloom, listening for any movement that would betray each other's position. Anthony held on to the workbench with one hand while shielding his face from the dangling warplanes, inching his way in the confined space. Sometimes he thought he heard Amanda's cat-like tread, tantalisingly close, but when he moved in that direction she eluded him.

'Amanda? You still in here?'

He heard the softest of whispers. 'I am. But you have to find me.'

'Where on earth are you? I've been round this damn turret twice and you're not anywhere.'

'Then you'll have to persevere. Enjoy it. It's a game.'

This time the voice seemed to come from close behind. Groping in the darkness, his fingers found warm, soft skin. At first he thought it must be her face, then he discovered it was the side of a breast. To his astonishment, it was naked.

'Christ, Amanda. Your clothes . . .'

She laughed. 'Does it shock you?'

'No, just slightly surprised for a second. But, well, great—'

She took his face in her hands and pushed her tongue between his lips, pressing herself against him. Amazed, confused, exhilarated, he kissed her back passionately.

Then he heard the urgency and fierceness of her whisper: 'Fall in love with me, Anthony. I dare you to fall in love with me.'

Before he could reply, they heard footsteps outside on the leads and a male voice calling, 'Amanda? Amanda, you up here?'

'God, it's Charlie.' She cursed, suddenly recoiling. 'Why the hell does he have to show up now?'

Anthony heard her struggle back into her frock coat, and moments later open the turret door, flicking the light back on as she did so. 'Charlie? We're over here. Anthony's showing me his aeroplanes. Come and see.'

Charlie loomed in the doorway, taut with suspicion. 'I've been searching everywhere for you. No one knew where you were. Didn't you hear me calling? You mustn't just disappear like that.' Spotting Anthony, he eyed him with hostility, then flicked a dismissive glance at the plastic models dangling from their threads. 'These are what you and Amanda have been looking at all this time?' he sneered. 'You make them all by yourself from kits, do you? You stick the transfers onto the fuselages yourself?'

'Used to,' Anthony said. 'I haven't made one for ages.' He stole a glance at Amanda, who was standing between them, innocent and noncommittal.

'Anyway, we've got to leave now,' Charlie said, grabbing hold of Amanda's hand and yanking her in the direction of the door. 'We need to be getting back. I still haven't packed.'

Anthony followed them across the roof and re-bolted the door behind him. Charlie and Amanda were twenty yards ahead along the corridor and had reached the top of the staircase that led back down to the Great Hall.

He hastened to catch them up. Hearing his approaching footsteps, Charlie turned and glared, then strode on downstairs.

'Amanda?' Anthony called after her.

She paused, looked back at him and murmured, 'Remember what I told you.'

'What was that?'

'I dared you something.'

'I do remember.'

'Then *accept my dare*,' she whispered. 'I shall be disappointed in you if you don't.' Then she hurried on to join Charlie, who was fuming impatiently by the front door.

2

Anthony woke with the feeling something momentous had happened. Downstairs he heard the sound of hoovering and the drone of an industrial floor polisher in the Great Hall. He had breakfast with his parents who, in their measured way, seemed to think that their party had gone off well enough. 'People seemed to have reasonably enjoyed themselves,' Godfrey Anscombe declared, which was the highest level of satisfaction to which he considered it decent to aspire.

'Who was that peculiar-looking girl who tagged along with the Edwardses?' sniffed Henrietta. 'The one in fancy dress, all in black.'

'She's called Amanda,' Anthony said.

'I didn't at all care for the look of her,' said his mother. 'I'm quite surprised the Edwardses would know anyone like that, let alone bring them here.'

At the age of fifty-three, with a helmet of ash-grey hair, tangerine-coloured lipstick and a large, fleshy, orange-hued face which dimly resembled a Halloween pumpkin, Henrietta was a woman of strongly-held opinions. Anthony had long ago learnt it was easier to tacitly acquiesce to his mother than challenge her directly. Godfrey Anscombe had adopted an identical policy upon marriage.

'She's actually very nice,' Anthony said neutrally.

'I rather doubt that,' Henrietta replied, in a tone that declared the subject closed. 'She didn't look very nice at all.'

There were three telephone extensions in those days at Winchford Priory: one in the drawing room where Henrietta was now ensconced, one in his father's study where Godfrey was reviewing farm accounts, and one next to Anthony's parents' four-poster bed. Slipping into his parents' room, he squatted on the carpet so as not to rumple the bedcover, and dialled the number for the Edwardses.

'May I speak to Amanda please? I believe she's staying with you.' It occurred to him he didn't even know her surname.

'Sorry, she's already left. They set off for France very early this morning.'

'For France?'

'She's gone on holiday with my brother and some other people. Who is this speaking?'

'Anthony Anscombe. Charlie and Amanda were over at our house last night. Amanda told me to ring up for the address in France. I'm probably going to be staying nearby and might look them up.'

'I think they did leave it somewhere,' the girl replied doubtfully. 'Do you want me to hunt for it now?' Anthony heard a great deal of sighing and shifting of papers. Eventually, 'Here it is. It was pinned on the notice board.' She dictated the address of a villa near Sainte Maxime, on the road to Saint Raphael and Frejus.

'Remind me how they were getting there,' Anthony asked. 'Were they flying or driving?'

'On the train. Well, first on the ferry to France, of course.'

Anthony raced upstairs, flung some clothes into a bag, then slipped down the back stairs and out of a side door to the garage yard. His green Triumph, an eighteenth birthday present from his parents, was parked under the arches of the old granary, between a tractor and coils of wire fencing. The ignition turned at first try and, as quietly as possible, he allowed the car to roll outside onto the cobblestones and towards the drive. Had anyone seen him and asked where he was going, Anthony had prepared no reply, though he knew well enough his destination. He glided along the great avenue of horse chestnut trees into the village, past the pub and village shop and medieval almshouses, all built from the same honey-coloured ironstone from the Winchford quarry, then out onto the main road that led to Stow-on-the-Wold. Not until he was well clear of Chipping Norton did he feel sufficiently safe to let rip. In less than five hours he had crossed half of southern England to arrive at Dover, and several hours later disembarked in France.

He drove in a kind of trance, determination tempered by an abnormal calmness. On the ferry, he studied the map, plotted his route along the straight French roads from town to town, estimated the time for each part of the journey that would finish at Sainte Maxime. What he'd do or say once he'd arrived he did not know, or even particularly consider; he would resolve that question when he got there. On that first evening in France he drove for seven hours without stopping, eventually pulling over into the entrance to a field at three o'clock in the morning and dozing at the wheel. It crossed his mind his parents would be worried about him, but he quickly suppressed that thought. He awoke with the thin grey light of dawn, stiff with cold, drove through a dozen village squares before the first café had rolled up its shutters, downed two cups of thick, silty coffee to pull himself together and bought three baguettes to eat in the car. The peculiar thing was, try as he might, he could not visualise Amanda's face; he had no distinct picture of what she looked like, just a fleeting sense of how she was – the highwayman's coat, kohl-black eyes and hair, the memory of the closeness of her lips and the warmth of her breath, whispering, 'Fall in love with me, Anthony. I dare you to fall in love with me.' By the afternoon of the second day he had left behind the dank steeples and war memorials of northern France, and warm breezes were gusting through the open window of the car. At dusk, the sun was so low in the sky he could scarcely see to drive, the leather of the seatback burnt against his bare skin (he was driving shirtless by this time) and the fields on both sides of the road were full of cornflowers and scarlet poppies. Too tired to drive further, he parked next to the chained gates of a modern cemetery and slept in the open on the green tarpaulin he kept in the boot.

Aside from stretching his legs at petrol stations, he had barely left the car in forty hours. Unshaven, unwashed, his only purpose was to reduce the kilometres that lay between him and Amanda. He set targets which he no sooner met than he exceeded them. I will stop and take a break, he promised himself, when I reach Orléans, but arriving at the industrial outskirts of that city he pressed on to Clermont-Ferrand, and then to Saint Etienne, Lyon, Grenoble. 'Is he your boyfriend?' he had asked her of Charlie, and her reply had been equivocal. He had to reach Sainte Maxime before that could change.

He hardly understood the compulsion that propelled him any more than a migrant bird understands why it must journey thousands of miles from the African delta to the eaves of a Sussex barn. Some instinct told him all future happiness depended on being with Amanda. He was mesmerised by her beauty, of course, but it was more than physical beauty; within Amanda, he sensed, lay the key to his whole life. He could see now that his existence to date had been bleak and mediocre; the banality of his parents, of his friends, of Winchford itself. In Amanda lay colour, sexuality, exoticism and the possibility of escape.

Somewhere south of Aix-en-Provence, when he reckoned he must now be within half a day's drive of his destination, he spared a thought to how his imminent appearance on the scene would be received, not only by Amanda, but by Charlie Edwards, last seen glaring with such hostility by the door of Winchford Priory. The scrap of paper on which he had scrawled the address lay on the passenger seat, but he hadn't the vaguest notion to whom the house belonged, or who else might be staying there. He realised how little he knew Amanda. How could he explain his thousand-kilometre journey to see her again?

The villa was difficult to find. It was market day in Sainte Maxime and the centre of town clogged with traffic; it was impossible even to pull over and ask directions. Many of the side streets were shut off by stalls selling melons and cheeses, and their pungent smell, wafting through the car window, reminded him how famished he was.

Eventually he was directed to a road in the foothills above the town, lined with villas surrounded by high walls and covered by trails of bougainvillea. Palm trees were visible above some of the walls, and ornate iron gates bore signs warning against unchained guard dogs. As the road left the town behind, the villas became more widely spaced, interspersed with glimpses of a coast road far below and a sparkling blue sea dotted with sailing boats and motorised yachts.

Three or four miles further on, near to a scrappy arcade of stalls selling fruit and terracotta pots, Anthony located the villa: rendered and pink-washed, set back from the road and screened by lemon trees and a low wall faced with shards of crazy-paving. Three white hire cars, all Peugeots, were parked beneath a vine-covered loggia. To the side of the house was a boules pit, the heavy silver balls abandoned mid-game in the sand, and footprints – large, male footprints – evident around the pitching line.

He had retrieved his shirt, stiff with dried sweat, and wondered whether he should have stopped to wash and shave. Too late now: he pressed the doorbell, and listened with trepidation for approaching footsteps, but none came. The house was silent, the shutters tightly closed; of course, it was siesta time. He dreaded to think he might have arrived too late, and Amanda and Charlie might even now be entwined in the cool of some upstairs bedroom.

He pushed the door and entered a hallway with a grey marble floor like a hotel bathroom. Down some steps lay a sitting room with signs of recent human activity: a backgammon board tilting precariously on a white sofa, open bottles of beer and wine on a table, a half-eaten bowl of black olives with spat-out stones mixed in with the rest.

'Hello? Hello? Is anybody here?' His voice echoed up the stairwell. 'Amanda, you up there?'

'Oh Lord, look what the cat's dragged in.' Charlie Edwards, sporting a towel draped around his bony shoulders, a wet pair of maroon bathing trunks, and legs streaked by sand, appeared at the open French doors from a terrace. 'Now this is what I call a coincidence.'

'I, er, dropped in to see Amanda. I was in the area. She gave me the address the other night.'

'She did? That was clever of her, since she hadn't a clue where we were staying.'

Several other people were surfacing on the terrace from a flight of steps that evidently led up from the beach. Anthony saw two other boys – both slightly older than himself, friends of Charlie's presumably – and two pretty English girls in string bikinis, neither of them Amanda.

'So you "just happened" to be in the area? You didn't say anything on Saturday about coming down to the Côte d'Azur.'

'Aren't you going to introduce us to your friend, Charlie?' asked one of the boys who was wearing white cricket ducks, and whose face and demeanour seemed somewhat less boorish and brutal than Charlie's.

'This is Anthony Anscombe,' Charlie said with a twisted little smile. 'He's a neighbour of ours in Oxfordshire. He tried to pull my girlfriend a couple of nights ago by showing her his collection of model aeroplanes. Amanda was fascinated. Now, by an astounding coincidence, he has turned up at your villa, Mark. Apparently, he was "in the area" and Amanda had given him the address and told him to drop by any time he was passing. That's about it, isn't it, Anthony?'

Charlie sloshed some wine into a glass from the open bottle. His sandy shoulders, Anthony noticed, were spangled with livid red pustules, whether infected mosquito bites or boils, he couldn't tell. From time to time, Charlie adjusted the towel to try and conceal them.

'Where's Amanda?' Anthony asked. 'Is she about?'

'Still crashed out upstairs,' Charlie said. 'We didn't get much sleep on the couchette coming down.' He sniggered, and for the second time Anthony wondered whether he had arrived too late.

'Drink?' asked the friend, Mark. He gestured to the tepid white wine, then said, 'No, don't drink that, it's boiled in the sun. Some cretin forgot to put it back in the fridge. I'll get you something cold. Beer okay?'

The two English girls, introduced as Clarissa and Jemima, perched on the white sofa in their swimsuits. 'So you're a friend of Amanda's?' Jemima asked.

'Yes, though I don't know her all that well, really.'

'You're like Charlie then. He hardly knows her either. She *is* a fast worker.'

Anthony got the impression the girls neither liked nor quite approved of Amanda.

'Where exactly is it you're staying?' Charlie asked.

'Just along the coast,' Anthony replied vaguely. Where was Amanda? He hadn't imagined it would be like this. It was to have been Amanda who opened the door to him at the resolution of this fool's quest.

Mark returned with a Stella. 'We're having a barbecue on the beach. We've been collecting driftwood all afternoon for a fire. Can you stay?'

Anthony sensed Charlie's grimace. 'Is it me or is there a disgusting stink in this room? Kind of like fetid socks?' Charlie said to the room at large.

Anthony coloured. He was increasingly conscious of the smell drifting up from his feet, and had been trying to keep his distance. But Mark's invitation to join the barbecue had thrown him a lifeline, and he grinned with relief.

'Anthony? Is that really you?' Standing on the bottom of the stairs, enveloped in a man's silk dressing gown several sizes too big for her, eyes bleary as though she had just that moment woken up, was Amanda; more ravishing, more captivating than he could have believed possible. She looked so fragile, with childlike bare feet and tousled black bob. He longed to rush over and hug her, but found himself rooted to the spot.

Instead, it was Charlie who hastened over, solicitous and proprietorial, asking how she'd slept and pressing coffee and drinks upon her.

'You know what?' said Mark. 'If we want to get the cooking going before it gets dark, we need to get our skates on and light the fire. Everybody take some things – plates, food, matches, booze. All the food's in boxes on the kitchen table. Charlie, if you could carry the grill, which is quite heavy, and Joe and, er, Anthony and I will take the food, and Clarissa and Jemima, could you grab those plastic salad bowls and plates.'

Amanda, Anthony noticed, was asked to carry nothing. Certain people are automatically excluded from anything so prosaic as transporting picnics. Her role was to trail behind the others in her dressing gown and skimpy leopardskin swimsuit, exuding artless glamour, while each boy sought a reason to hang back and keep her company.

The steps to the beach were steep and winding, descending past the gardens of a dozen small villas and pensions, several with somnolent guard dogs chained to half-laid patios or pawing at bald patches of earth. When the path narrowed to enter a tunnel beneath the coast road, Anthony contrived to be one step ahead of Amanda.

'I knew you'd come,' she breathed. 'I've been expecting you.'

'I hope you don't mind me turning up. I had to see you.'

'It's fate. Neither of us had a choice. You were bound to come.'

Before Anthony could reply, the path widened again and Charlie was waiting for them, buckled under the weight of the iron grill and scowling.

The strip of beach at the foot of the cliff consisted of grey sand above the tide line and smooth flat pebbles below, with a bluff of jagged rocks marking the boundary of the bay. A couple of miles south, towards Sainte Maxime, you could just make out the roped-off private beaches with their coloured umbrellas and tented changing huts, some already closed for the winter. Here, however, the beach was neglected and unraked, the sole attraction being a rusted swimming raft formed from four floating oil drums and a wooden platform, moored fifty yards out to sea.

Mark and Joe started the bonfire, and candles were lit and relit inside jam jars for storm lanterns.

'The sea's getting rough out there; look at the white horses on those waves,' Joe said. 'Do you reckon there'll be a storm?'

'Those black clouds are ominous,' said Mark. 'Probably blow over though – it's moving fairly fast.'

Jemima and Clarissa were already in the sea. Charlie had suggested a swim to Amanda but she'd said no, so now he felt unable to swim himself, since that would mean leaving her unchaperoned with Anthony on the beach, so he sat brooding near her on the sand, like the doorkeeper at a purdah palace, glowering if anyone came too close.

Anthony walked down to the sea and stood in the shallows, cold water lapping over his feet, his mind in a state of confusion. He hardly knew what to make of Amanda with her talk of fate. He'd never met anyone remotely like her. The sky was dark with thunderclouds, and waves were beginning to lash in earnest against the rocks. He waded out up to his waist until it was deep enough to swim. He could feel the swell pulling him this way and that, and the surface of the sea as he ventured further out had a crust of taut ripples. He passed the girls swimming back towards the beach.

'I wouldn't go out much further,' Clarissa said. 'It's really choppy.'

'Just to the raft,' Anthony said. 'No further.'

As he approached the pontoon, he realised it was no simple matter to haul himself aboard. The oil drums were pitching to and fro, and the wooden platform lurched in the water. A short rusty ladder with three metal steps was thrust more than a foot above the waves, before the raft slammed down again with a loud crack. When he reached out for the handrail, he felt the raft jerk away from him and lift half out of the sea, like a flying door above his head.

At the third attempt, he hoisted himself aboard the soaking platform, grasping at the planks for support. He could just make out the others on the darkening beach, black shadows crouched around the fire, their faces illuminated by dancing flames. One of the boys, Mark he thought, was grilling steaks under the beam of a car torch.

'Anthony?' He heard his name from somewhere close by. 'I think I might need a hand up.'

Ten yards from the raft he saw Amanda, heading towards him. 'You're brave,' he said. 'It's rough out here.'

As she came within arm's reach, he yanked her up and was struck by her lightness. They lay side by side on their stomachs on the tilting raft, watching the spray exploding against the jagged bluff.

'Are we slightly crazy, would you say, to be out here?' Amanda asked. 'Or isn't it really that dangerous at all?'

'Probably safer here than on the beach with Charlie around. He isn't going to be too happy when he realises we're here.'

'Poor Charlie. He was quite devoted in his way.'

Anthony, who didn't regard Charlie as a remotely pitiful figure, made no reply. He draped his arm over Amanda's damp, salty back and when she did nothing to remove it, rolled closer and kissed her on the neck. 'So Charlie's not your boyfriend?'

'Not now. Now you've arrived.'

'Why were you so certain I'd come?'

She rolled onto her back and smiled at him. 'I just knew. The minute I saw you looking down from that balcony at your parents' house, I knew what was going to happen.'

'And what is going to happen?'

'Wait and see. Everything.'

'Everything?'

'You accepted my dare.'

The storm, which for a while seemed to be quieting down, now gathered renewed force, and they felt the raft yank beneath them on the barnacled chain that secured it to a concrete block on the seabed. Huge waves, light-struck and broad-shouldered, surged against the oil drums, sending them spinning, before breaking against the beach in a ferocious cascade of spray. As ever-stronger waves broke around them, they clung together on the platform, locked in a salt-kissed embrace so passionate they hardly registered the cries and shouts of warning from the others on the beach.

Mark and Charlie had waded out up to their chests, hollering and waving at the raft. 'Amanda! Anthony! You okay out there?' But their voices blew right back at them.

'It's so damn difficult to see anything,' Mark said. 'Charlie, bring the torch down here, won't you?' Charlie fetched the big rubber torch and directed its beam towards the raft, sweeping like a searchlight across the waves until he found his mark.

For one traumatic moment he held the beam directly on them, before jerking it away. In that instant, the whole raft was illuminated and with it the lovers, fucking for Britain for the very first time.

3

They knew they must leave the villa that night. Charlie was glowering like a wounded bear, humiliated and sullen. Having failed to manoeuvre Amanda away for a reconciliation, he focused his rage upon Anthony. The two girls, Jemima and Clarissa, crept around the living room with sanctimonious expressions, muttering, 'Poor Charlie, but he's well out of it.' Invidiously positioned as host of a divided house, Mark conversed stiffly with Anthony while Amanda gathered her stuff. 'You do have somewhere to go tonight?' he asked.

'We'll be fine,' Anthony said, and he knew they would be fine, not just tonight, but for ever. He felt drained and almost overwhelmed by what had happened, as though he was an actor in a play who had mistakenly turned over two pages in the script and veered out of character, assuming another man's role. How else to explain that steady, predictable Anthony Anscombe had driven halfway across Europe and seized the loveliest girl in the world from the clutches of another man?

Amanda was at the door with the smallest of suitcases. It seemed incredible they would leave together like this. She kissed Mark and Joe goodbye, disregarded the girls and pointedly ignored Charlie who sat sulking in the other room, full of self-righteous indignation.

'Just drive,' Amanda said. 'Let's get as far away from these people as possible.'

So they headed up the coast in the green Triumph, following the road for two hours, then three, as far as Antibes and Juan-les-Pins, until they felt they'd put sufficient distance between themselves and the villa, and drew up outside a small hotel and asked for a room.

'Names?' asked the night porter, for it was after midnight and the door had already been locked. They'd had to knock and knock before he came to let them in.

'Monsieur et Madame Anscombe,' replied Amanda.

'*Passeports, s'il vous plaît.*' He carefully recorded their names and details without comment before handing over a key secured to a fat red tassel.

Safely ensconced in the room, Anthony said, 'What on earth made you tell that guy we were married? I didn't know where to look when we had to hand over our passports. He could see it wasn't true.'

'It hardly matters, does it?' Amanda said. 'By this time tomorrow we really will be married.'

As it transpired, they could not marry the next day, French formalities being too tortuous and prolix for such haste, but two days later, under the great frescoed ceiling of the Hôtel de Ville in Nice, they were married in a civil ceremony that lasted barely twelve minutes. The delicate white lace nightdress Amanda had worn for breakfast on the previous two mornings doubled as a wedding dress, hastily pressed by room service at the larger, grander hotel on the Promenade des Anglais to which they had moved on the eve of their marriage. She carried a posy of tiny white freesias they'd bought in the flower market on their way to the registry office. Anthony thought she looked beautiful, and wondered again how she could possibly have chosen to marry him. He was the luckiest man alive. As they strolled through the town hand in hand, in search of a restaurant after the service, he felt the envious stares of everyone they passed. Even the registrar who had married them had been flirtatious with Amanda, and she had played him along in fluent French. Where, he wondered, had his wife learned to speak French? He was ardently aware he still had an endless amount to learn about her, and ecstatic that he had an eternity in which to do so. As they lunched at a pavement fish restaurant, where the bedazzled owner invited them to drink champagne on the house and produced a long-stemmed rose for the beautiful young bride, teenage boys on Vespas zipped up and down the street, leering and gesticulating and inviting Amanda to hop on the back of their scooters.

At some point towards the end of lunch, feeling a little drunk, Anthony remembered his parents for the first time in five days, and supposed he ought to let them in on his marvellous news. His telephone call forestalled the continent-wide missing persons search that was gearing up to look for him. The Home Office, prodded into action by the Anscombes' local Tory MP, had already established his ferry crossing to France, but thereafter the trail had gone cold.

When Henrietta picked up the phone she sounded furious. 'But what on earth have you been doing all this time, you stupid, thoughtless boy?' she demanded. 'Your father and I have been frantic. You could have been lying dead in a ditch for all we knew. I'll tell you one thing: that car of yours is being confiscated the minute you get home. And I asked you a question to which I'd like an answer please: what in God's name made you suddenly hare off to France without telling anybody?'

'Well, the thing is . . .' Anthony began. From the callbox in the narrow corridor between restaurant kitchen and dining room, he could see Amanda bathed in sunshine at the table outside, laughing with the waiter who was bringing more coffee. 'I'm not quite sure how to tell you this, Mum, but I've got married, actually . . . Yes, that's right, got married . . . I am being serious . . . No . . . No, not to a French girl, to an English girl . . . I promise you . . . She's called Amanda . . . No, I don't think you've met her. Not really. Well, she's been to our house once; that's where we met . . . she came along to your party. That's right, the party on Saturday . . . Yes, I did say that's when I met her. Only last Saturday. She came with the Edwardses . . . Yes, it is that girl – Amanda. When will I be back home?' It was a good question. He had made no plans for the rest of his life. Being with Amanda had seemed like an end in itself. Now, against the background of incredulous disapproval echoing down the telephone line, he wondered what they would actually do, he and Amanda; where would they go and how they would live? He wondered how much longer they could stay in France; at the rate they were getting through his money, it wouldn't last that long.

'Yes . . . yes, I suppose we will be coming home to Winchford,' Anthony said. 'We'll be there by the end of the week, probably.'

'Well, if you think your father will allow you to install this girl, of whom we know absolutely nothing, at the Priory, you're very much mistaken.'

'Then where do you expect us to go, if we can't come home?'

'You should have thought of that before. Hasn't this young woman got parents of her own you can go to? You have *met* her parents, I suppose.'

But Anthony knew nothing about his wife.

'I suppose you could use Forge Cottage, if you really have nowhere else,' he heard his mother concede. 'It is empty at the moment.' Anthony knew Forge Cottage: the thatched workman's hovel at the end of the village by the millstream, where old Tom Tew, the last Winchford blacksmith, had shoed hunters and made fire tongs.

'Thanks, Mum. And don't worry, you're really going to like Amanda when you get to know her. She's the perfect wife.'

*

Had Anthony not been utterly infatuated, he would probably have been more disquieted by Amanda's unpredictability during their journey back to England. They took things more gently than Anthony's frantic dash south, starting late each morning, dawdling over breakfast, driving for scarcely an hour or two before stopping for lunch or drinks in some pretty French village, and often taking a room afterwards in the local hotel, declaring they'd driven far enough already for one day and instead making love on some unyielding, bolster-strewn bed until it fell dark outside and the hotel kitchen was long closed for the night; so they tended to go to bed hungry and needed larger and longer breakfasts on each successive day. Each morning, when he awoke to find Amanda's soft, naked back pressed against him, Anthony blessed his incredible luck. Amanda was his first proper girlfriend and he had been anxious not to disappoint her in bed.

'Did you ever do this . . . with Charlie?' he dared ask her, thinking of her couchette journey with his vanquished rival.

'The answer to that question is no, actually,' she replied, quite sharply. 'But a man should never ask his wife questions like that, especially when she is yours and only yours for ever and ever.' And then she laughed and kissed him with such gentleness and joy, he felt ashamed of his inquisitiveness, and regretted asking.

Similarly, when he asked about her life, her home, family or school, she was deftly evasive, deflecting him with a caress or a shrug.

'You'll meet my parents one day, I'm sure,' she said. 'They're not still together anyway. My dad lives in Rome with his lover. My mum usually stays in Dublin when she's not travelling.'

In a strange way, Anthony felt liberated rather than stonewalled by the sketchiness of information. Living at Winchford, he often felt burdened by an overload of family history pressing down on him from every wall. Every stick of furniture, every rosebush or cedar tree had been bought or planted at the behest of some earlier Anscombe. Amanda, by contrast, was a ravishing, mesmerising sprite, who had miraculously consented to throw in her lot with him as his wife, and whose tantalising elusiveness was all of a piece with the rest. This journey through France was an interlude from real life. They drove as the impulse took them, from hamlet to hamlet. After six days, having covered not even half the distance home, they spotted the walled and towered hill town of Carcassonne from the road and felt compelled to stop for the night. Prohibited from taking the car into the centre of town, they parked outside the walls and Anthony carried their two small bags through the winding medieval streets until they found a hotel, ringed by geranium pots, with a bedroom to rent. From their window on the second floor, you could see right across the sloping rooftops to the arid plain beyond.

Anthony was almost out of cash. Leaving Amanda to unpack, he located a Banque Agricole and converted the last of his English money into francs. Seventy pounds in French bank notes felt like a fortune in his hands, and he walked jauntily back to the hotel. He found their bedroom door open and the room deserted; evidently Amanda had slipped out on some errand. He spread the money on the bedcover and thought about unpacking.

After an hour she had not returned; after two hours he became uneasy and began to pace the streets, ducking in and out of cheese shops and cavernous delicatessens parading wild boar and salami. Every so often he hurried back to the hotel to check whether she'd returned. Her stuff was still strewn about the room, but no Amanda.

It was becoming dark, and he wondered whether to contact the police. Surely she would turn up soon, anyway. Where could she possibly have got to in this tourist-trap hill town? At ten thirty the bars began to shut down for the night. Anthony watched the waiters stack chairs on top of tables and mop the floors. He was desperate. Just before eleven o'clock, returning to the hotel for perhaps the tenth time, he saw her approach from the opposite direction, looking self-possessed and happy.

'Amanda?'

'Oh, hi Ant. Sorry I've been ages.'

'I've been really worried. Where've you been, for heaven's sake? I was about to go to the police.'

'Oh, I went for a walk around the town. Then I got talking to this French boy, and he introduced me to some of his mates. They took me to a bar.'

'But I looked in all the bars. I couldn't find you anywhere.'

'Not in Carcassonne. A bar in the next village. It was great. There was table-football and a jukebox; everyone was dancing.'

'But why didn't you tell me before going off like that? You've been gone *seven hours*. Couldn't you at least have rung the hotel?'

'Sorry, I never realised you'd be worried. Anyway, I didn't know the name of our hotel. Listen, darling, I've said I'm sorry. I was only having a couple of drinks. It was fun – stop fussing. Now let's go up to bed. I've missed you.'

4

As he drove his wife towards the ironstone village of Winchford, Anthony felt an uneasy mixture of pride and dread: pride at introducing her properly to the mellow beauty of the place, of which he knew every cottage, field and footpath; dread at the meeting that must shortly take place between Amanda and his parents, an encounter that would surely be sticky.

'Well, we're almost there now. We're almost at Winchford,' he said as his exhausted car rattled its way to the brow of the hill.

To reach the village, you first drove six miles beyond Stow-on-the-Wold in the direction of Moreton-in-Marsh, then made a sharp turn down a single-track road signposted Winchford Village Only. The track, with its numerous passing places, took you to the rim of a wide, gently sloping valley bordered by copses of oak and horse chestnuts, their foliage a dramatic orange and yellow on this crisp October afternoon; far below, in the bottom of the valley, lay the slate and thatched rooftops of forty cottages and barns, the square steeple of a Norman church, and a shallow river, the Winch, which meandered beside a cobbled village street. There was an old stone trough opposite the almshouses erected by Anthony's five-times-great-grandfather, and a memorial to the fallen of the Great War, where stragglers from the village pub, the Plough and Harrow, congregated after closing time on Saturday night, leaving the stone plinth littered with empty glasses and bottles. Nestling into a cleft of the hillside, a quarter of a mile above the village, stood the great mongrel facade of Winchford Priory, the mullioned windows of the Elizabethan hall glinting in the sunshine, flanked by the solid Victorian wing and the Georgian coach house, covered in Virginia creeper. The Winchford Estate, it was generally agreed, with its two thousand acres surrounding its own picturesque village, and perhaps the finest high-pheasant shoot in the country, was one of the most magical spots in England. It had belonged to the Anscombe family, of Anscombe Brothers merchant bank, for three hundred and seventy years.

In addition to the cottages and Priory, there were two other large houses at opposite ends of the village: the Rectory, the only building that didn't belong to the estate, being the property of the local diocese; and Mill House, which was let by Anthony's parents to the retired British ambassador to Islamabad, Sir Percy Bigges, and his wife Jacinthe. Lady Bigges presided over all those village institutions – WI, harvest supper, church flower rota – that were not the ex-officio preserve of Henrietta Anscombe. On account of their surname, and position as second most important household in the village, the Biggeses were widely known as 'the number twos'.

'Those cottages are beautiful,' Amanda said, as they drove past the medieval almshouses. 'Can we live in one of those?'

'Sadly they're lived in already,' Anthony replied. 'My parents' cleaning lady, Mrs Holcombe, has one, and an amazing old guy called Walter Twine, who must be about seventy but still lays all the hedges for the estate, has one of the others. You'll meet him; he's a real character. His father fought in the Boer War, the only time he ever left Winchford in his life, apparently. He hated being abroad and told his son not to bother going. Walter took him at his word and has never been further than Stow-on-the-Wold. He hits the village pub every Saturday night and drinks everyone under the table.'

'How weird never to go anywhere,' Amanda said. 'To never leave this village. Maybe it would be rather a marvellous feeling, actually belonging somewhere. I've never experienced that; we never stayed anywhere for long. Does it feel very different having roots in a place like this?'

'I've never really thought about it. Sometimes it gets a bit claustrophobic, actually, everyone knowing what you're doing all the time. They gossip about everything in Winchford. I expect they've been gossiping about us non-stop, once the news got out.'

'About *us*? What's interesting about us?'

'People don't have that much to think about round here, and with my parents sort of owning the village and everything, they do get quite interested, God knows why. It's not that we're so fascinating. I warn you, the first time we go to church, they'll all be scrutinising you from behind their psalters. Hope you don't object to being stared at. They're lovely people in this village mostly.'

'How would anyone even *know* about us getting married? You don't have a town crier, do you, announcing it on the village green? Oh yea, Oh yea . . .' Amanda laughed. 'From what you've told me about your parents, they don't sound exactly overjoyed about me. I'm surprised they even told anyone, hoping it would all blow over.'

'Don't worry about them. I was only warning you they can be tricky sometimes. They're very square. Once they get to know you, it'll be fine. They'll love you. Everyone will. How could they not? I'm just so happy, darling, it's ridiculous.'

'Don't overdo it, Ant. I might actually believe you.'

'I *want* you to believe me. I want you to know how happy I am.'

'Well, anyway,' she said. 'You were about to tell me how people would know about us.'

'How? Well, for one thing, since we're going to be living at Forge Cottage, the place will have been got ready for us. Mrs Holcombe will have been sent down with her dustpan and brush to give it the once over. And if Mrs Holcombe knows about it, then everyone else will, too – she's the biggest gossip. Her daughter, Judy, works behind the bar at the Plough and Harrow, so the whole pub will have been in on it in five minutes flat. And I've just remembered Mrs Holcombe is one of the flower ladies at the church, which means Jacinthe Bigges will have heard, which means the vicar will know too, and will probably be feeling miffed we didn't get married in his church. But we don't need to bother too much about him – he's a closet poof and always has his knickers in a twist about something or other.'

'God,' said Amanda. 'Is that really what goes on in villages? You sure I'm going to be cut out for country life? I haven't got a clue about churches or flowers or village fetes.'

'You'll be fine, I promise. My mother can advise you if you need any help – she's been doing it for years.' But, even as he mentioned her, he wondered how Amanda would get on with his formidably conventional mother, and the thought of them together filled him with misgivings. As the Triumph rattled across the cobblestones in the direction of Forge Cottage, Anthony felt an extraordinary surge of love for this strange, ravishing, beguiling girl sitting in the bucket seat next to him, and longed for her to be happy in Winchford; but, at the same time, he couldn't help seeing Amanda through the eyes of Henrietta, and knew that his kohl-eyed wife, in her velvet coat and buckled boots, was about as far removed from his mother's idea of a suitable daughter-in-law as was humanly possible.

Like so many Cotswold village houses, Forge Cottage had clearly been constructed specifically with tourist board calendars and biscuit tin manufacturers in mind. With its four-foot-thick gables, flannel-sized windows and imploding thatched roof, and with two of its four outside walls rooted ankle-deep in the babbling waters of the millstream, it epitomised everything charming and desirable in English domestic architecture, until you stepped inside. Having found the door key beneath a brick on the front step, Anthony and Amanda ducked into a narrow, cold stone passageway with a bare lightbulb dangling from a wonky plastic ceiling rose, and were assaulted by an overpowering stench of rat poison and damp.

'Christ,' said Anthony. 'We'd better open some windows and air the place.'

So they wrenched open the tiny latched panes, which made little impact on the smell, but caused the temperature to plunge a further few degrees. They explored downstairs with its low sitting room and kitchen, an icy ground-floor bathroom with black mould sprouting from the grouting, and a lean-to at the back still littered with the remnants of Tom Tew's trade, including several decaying cardboard boxes of iron tacks.

'I'm sure we can fix it all up,' Anthony said doubtfully. Having never previously ventured further than the farrier's yard behind the cottage, he felt daunted by the clammy reality of his first marital home.

'Of course we can,' said Amanda, who seemed almost childishly delighted by it all. 'I love it here.' Then, sniffing, she said, 'Is it my imagination, or is there a smell of pig?'

'Probably. Until about sixty years ago, they would have had livestock living down here during the winter. The people lived upstairs. The hogs would have kept the place warm – hot air rises and so forth.'

'Maybe we should get some ourselves. Pigs, I mean. Is it always going to be this cold?'

Anthony shrugged and walked towards the stairs. 'Let's see what's up here. God, it's awfully low. I can't stand upright without banging my head.'

They edged around the two sloping bedrooms beneath the eaves, Anthony stooping as he dodged the beams. In each room, at floor level, a tiny window was fringed by thatch, admitting a thin grey light. In the first bedroom were two narrow single beds made up with sheets and covered by candlewick covers; in the second, smaller room was a bare, wooden double bed, apparently hewn from two enormous tree trunks, with what looked like a five-bar farm gate as a bedhead. 'I adore this bed,' Amanda said. 'We must sleep in here; it's much nicer.' So, together, they made up the bed with the single sheets and mattresses carried from next door and then they made love, in that freezing cold room, with their breath leaving vapour trails like bonfire smoke. After they had come, and Amanda was lighting up the last of the Gauloises she'd brought from France, there was a rapping on the door downstairs.

'Who the hell is that?' Amanda asked. 'Let's not answer. Pretend we're not here.'

But Anthony, naked, was crossing the floor to peer down from the window. 'Oh Christ, it's my parents. We'd better go down. Get dressed quick as you can.' He pulled on his trousers and a jersey and bounded downstairs as the knocking resumed.

'Anthony? Anthony?' A woman's voice, hectoring and imperious, echoed through the letterbox into the empty cottage. 'Anthony, are you in there?'

Anthony opened the door, suddenly sheepish. 'Hi, Mother.'

'We saw your car outside, so knew you were back. And incidentally, you must know you can't leave it parked there where it blocks the turning-place; it's so thoughtless. Your proper parking space is down by Long Barn.'

Henrietta Anscombe had had many long years to refine her ability to intimidate. Having married late in life but advantageously, she had evolved from a slightly gauche, horsey girl into a woman of implacable confidence with an unshakeable belief in the infallibility of her own opinions. The conviction that anyone who crossed her path, and most particularly anyone who chose to inhabit the village of Winchford, should instantly fall in with her worldview was never challenged, least of all by her unassuming husband. Today, she marched into Forge Cottage, a thick tartan overcoat filling the narrow passage, while Godfrey shuffled in behind carrying a bottle of Tio Pepe and a box of Ritz crackers as a cottage-warming offering.

'We only got back half an hour ago,' Anthony said. 'It's a much longer journey than I'd realised."

'That depends whether you go all out for it or dawdle about,' said Henrietta. 'Your father and I once drove from the Hotel Eden Roc back to Calais in under two days, and we weren't using the toll roads either, which I categorically refuse to pay for. Not until the French start paying to drive on *our* roads, anyway. Have you ever seen a Frenchman being charged to drive along the A40?' She strode over to the kitchen window, and Anthony watched while she pulled it shut. 'Don't let the heat escape, for heaven's sake, you booby. It's early frost outside or haven't you noticed?'

'We were trying to get rid of the smell.'

'What smell? I can't smell anything. Anyway, we've come to meet this girl you say you've married. So where is she?'

'Amanda's just coming down. She's . . . unpacking.'

'Unpacking into *what* I'd like to know. There's no furniture here, you realise. Tom Tew rented the cottage unfurnished, and of course his children stripped the place the minute he died. Even took the loo-roll holders, which I'm quite certain belonged to the estate and they had no business touching. So what she's unpacking into, I can't imagine.'

Godfrey was saying something about there possibly being some furniture to borrow in one of the outhouses up at the Priory, when Amanda appeared in the kitchen, hair tousled, fag aloft, velvet tailcoat pulled over a pair of men's striped pyjamas; Anthony's own pyjamas, in fact, given to him for Christmas last year as a supplementary present by his parents. From the look of disapproval on Henrietta's face, it was obvious that she recognised them too.

'Amanda, you haven't met my parents.' The pathos of the introduction was lost on nobody.

Henrietta stood rooted to the spot, next to the buzzing Electrolux fridge, waiting for her daughter-in-law to cross the kitchen floor to greet her. But Amanda remained precisely where she was, not moving, but thrusting out a languid hand to shake. The distance between the two women was less than ten feet. For several long seconds, they stood assessing one another, locked in some unspoken power struggle. Then Godfrey placatingly hastened across the tiled floor, saying, 'We're delighted to meet you, Amanda. We've heard so much about you,' which was scarcely true, but the moment of confrontation passed, and Amanda was leaning forwards to kiss Godfrey on the cheek and he was complimenting her on her scent – 'French, is it?' – which she had hurriedly applied to disguise the lingering aroma of their lovemaking.

'Well, I am sure we shall all be seeing rather a lot of one another,' Henrietta said. 'Winchford is hardly a very large place. I don't know what you plan to do with yourselves down here. Do you hunt, Amanda?'

'I've never tried. But I'm prepared to try everything once.'

'No doubt,' she replied, sniffing. 'And you'll need to run up curtains for this cottage. Bare windows look so depressing on a winter's evening. I take it your mother did teach you how to make curtains?'

'No. But I've never really liked curtains anyway.'

'Mercifully the windows here are very small.' And with that Henrietta headed for the door, while Godfrey carefully placed the bottle of sherry and the cheese biscuits on top of an ice-cold night storage heater before trailing after her.

5

As predicted, the young squire's arrival in Winchford with his teenage bride provided weeks of gossip and speculation, though Amanda could hardly be described as immersing herself in village life. In fact, she was seldom spotted from week to week. Once or twice she was encountered with Anthony walking – reluctantly, some felt – through the kale fields at the top of the estate, picking her way along sodden tracks in stiletto-heeled boots. Or she would arrive at the village shop half an hour after closing time, and push against the door, apparently surprised not to find it open, explaining to passers-by that she only needed milk and cereal for supper.

It was decided, in an awkward interview with his parents, that since Anthony had got himself married, there was no longer much point in his going up to university since he would presumably need to support his wife. And since, at eighteen, he was too young to be imposed upon Anscombe Brothers (twenty-two being the recognised joining age at the bank for family members), he had better make himself useful helping on the farm.

Forge Cottage underwent a gradual transformation. While Anthony, with the assistance of the estate plumber and carpenter, did up the bathroom and foraged furniture from attics and outhouses, Amanda draped armchairs with Indian bedspreads and tablecloths dangling with mirrored decals. Scraps of old lace were drawing-pinned from the beams, and posters of Indian gods, of Shiva and monkey-faced deities, hung in the sitting room. There was no question but that she had an original eye. Spotting an old Victorian washstand in the gunroom at Winchford Priory, with its cracked china jug and bowl that had been used for ever to store old dog leads, she had it brought to Forge Cottage, stripped and painted it, and put it in the corner of their bedroom. Anthony was entranced by her every addition. She covered the kitchen table with an old gold brocade curtain, which was quickly covered by coffee rings and dried candle wax, but the general effect, especially at night, was thrillingly bohemian. Even Anthony's shooting prints and school photographs, which he insisted on hanging in the hall and cloakroom, were enhanced by the lengths of purple velvet ribbon Amanda twined around the wire.

He was bedazzled by his wife. Not only was she the most beautiful girl he'd ever seen, there was an edge of danger to her he relished. She was very impetuous. She'd ask to be driven into Stow but would abruptly change her mind and demand to go to Wales instead to see the Black Mountains she'd been reading about. On a whim, she would beg Anthony to drive her to the sea (Winchford, it so happened, was about as far from the sea as it is possible to be in Britain); or, after supper, she would yearn to visit a friend or a club in London. Anthony was thrilled by this unpredictability. Growing up in Winchford, nothing was ever spontaneous. Plans to attend a particular point-to-point or agricultural show would be made weeks in advance and inscribed unbreakably in the diary. When they went out together, she looked so striking that passers-by often stopped to gawp; in bed, she was wilful and passionate, and Anthony was perpetually amazed she had chosen him.

'I love the way you've got so muscly,' Amanda said one night.

He laughed. 'Must be working on the farm; it makes you fit.'

'You look like an overgrown schoolboy. A schoolboy's face, but so tall, and now these great biceps.'

'You make me sound like a bit of a freak.'

'Not a freak – handsome. I love it.'

As a housekeeper, Amanda left everything to be desired, but Anthony felt this was a small price to pay. Of course, she seldom shopped for food or everyday essentials, so they ran out of lavatory paper and their larder was empty; his supper after a long day driving the tractor often consisted of toast and a mug of powdered soup. The floors of both bedrooms were covered by her clothes, until you could barely see the boards beneath the heaps of damp brocade and velvet, and you picked your way to the bathroom around open suitcases. Matters deteriorated further when Mrs Holcombe, who came in twice a week to clean, gave notice. As she told her daughter Judy, who told everyone else, 'I can hardly change the sheets if that girl's still sleeping like the dead in them.' The sink was soon erupting with saucepans encrusted with scrambled eggs, and saucers defaced by fag ash. From time to time, Anthony scoured his way to the bottom of the heap, but it quickly reaccumulated.

At Amanda's prompting, Anthony began to dress more flamboyantly himself. Although he was working full days on the farm and never abandoned his cords and jerseys for estate work, in the evenings he took to embroidered waistcoats and purple velvet trousers. His mother complained his hair needed a good cut and was spilling over his collar: 'I shudder to think *what* the farmhands make of you got up in that extraordinary fashion – you look like a circus clown.' On their ever more frequent trips to London, Amanda encouraged him to wear lace jabots and velvet frock coats, into which he surreptitiously changed when they were well clear of Winchford.

Their trips to London became Amanda's chief raison d'être. They went to parties and nightspots in every part of the capital, and the more parties they went to, the more invitations flowed in. At first they would always drive back to Winchford at the end of the evening, for Anthony needed to be up and about on farm business by seven o'clock, but then Amanda took to staying overnight in town – dossing down wherever she could – while her husband hit the road alone, trusting his wife to follow by train to Kingham the next day. Soon it made better sense for her to remain up in London for a few days at a stretch, and for Anthony to bomb up the A40 after work to join her at innumerable happenings, hooking up at a gallery or at some Kings Road flat. He was impressed by Amanda's capacity for appropriating new friends, people so different and so infinitely more fascinating than anyone he'd encountered before in his life. When she started doing publicity shots for a boutique in Savile Row and got paid in free clothes – a dove-grey frock coat – he felt proud to be married to a real model. He was invited (or more accurately Amanda was invited and he tagged along) to parties given by the trendiest of hipsters just returned from Morocco, reeking of patchouli oil or about to set up shop as cutting-edge tailors. He met girls who had reputedly slept with several members of the Rolling Stones; at another party he was introduced to a Negro singer whose halo of frizzy hair had actually adorned the chorus line of *Hair*. It occurred to him they were moving on the periphery of the permissive society he had read about in the newspapers, and which Sir Percy Bigges discussed so disparagingly over Sunday lunch with Anthony's father. One evening he managed to bunk off early from the farm and joined Amanda at a church hall behind Redcliffe Square for a freak-out, at which psychedelic patterns of oil were projected onto a white wall while people read aloud their own poetry. Afterwards, queuing up for a much-needed drink, Anthony was approached by one of the poets.

'I saw you sitting with Amanda during the performance,' said the poet.

'She's one hot chick. Do you hang together, you two?'

'Well, I am married to her, if that's what you mean.'

'Married to Amanda Gibbons?' The man looked astonished.

'Strictly speaking, she's Amanda Anscombe now, but don't let it worry you.'

As time went by, Anthony came slightly to resent the time Amanda spent away from him. For one thing, he found the constant round-trips to London – ninety-two miles each way – exhausting at the end of a long day, particularly when spring gave way to summer and the light evenings meant longer hours on the farm and he couldn't leave Winchford much before eight o'clock. And whilst he never actually suspected his wife of sleeping with anyone else, he was conventional enough to wish that she was at home with him at Forge Cottage.

'And will we be lucky enough to have your lovely Amanda with us at the harvest supper this year, or will it just be you?' asked Jacinthe Bigges, beadily.

'Just me this time, I'm afraid,' Anthony was forced to reply. 'Amanda needs to be up in London on Thursday.'

'She *does* spend a lot of time in London,' said Lady Bigges. 'Poor Amanda. I do dislike London, especially when the weather has been as kind as it has been recently. Remind me, what exactly is it Amanda does in London? I did ask your dear mother, but Henrietta wasn't sure. So unlike her not to know.'

'This and that,' replied Anthony. 'She's been doing some modelling and, er, that sort of thing.'

Anthony resented these Winchford probings as to the movements of his wife, from his parents most of all. What possible business was it of theirs and, anyway, why shouldn't Amanda spend time in London if she chose? It wasn't as if Winchford was exactly the most swinging village in Oxfordshire. In fact, if they were handing out prizes for the dullest, Winchford would certainly contend for top honours. At such moments, Anthony felt affronted on behalf of his wife, who was after all only nineteen and would scarcely want to bury herself alive at the end of a country lane. The more he thought about it, the more enraged he found he could become; in his head, he railed against neighbours who had not even raised the subject of Amanda's frequent absences, simply because he sensed (or thought he sensed) their disapproval. He cursed the Jacinthe Biggeses of the world for assuming that a free spirit like Amanda should opt to join their harvest supper with people fifty – no, make that sixty – years older than herself, rather than living it up a little in London! How proud he felt – and how lucky – to be married to the sort of beautiful, interesting wife who actually knew where London was, which was more than could be said for most of the straw-sucking bumpkins of Winchford.

Nevertheless, there were times when he keenly wished Amanda was around more, and that he didn't have to do quite so much for himself. It wasn't that he was incapable of frying eggs or grilling bacon for his supper, but over time he found it slightly lonely. He would have invited himself to dinner at the Priory could he have borne his parents' incessant questioning; he would have eaten at the Plough and Harrow had he not felt awkward about Judy Holcombe behind the bar, who must have heard so much bad stuff about Amanda from her mother. Nevertheless, something made him reluctant to raise the topic with Amanda herself. For some reason, whether fear or politeness he couldn't say, he hesitated, and by the time she began skipping whole weekends in the country, he had left it too long to start making a fuss.

He was, in any case, no stranger to loneliness. As an only child of distant parents, he had spent more time alone than other boys of his own age. He had become a collector, first of fossils and flint arrow heads which could still be picked up on parts of the estate, later and most passionately of butterflies. By his ninth birthday, he knew the names of every species of butterfly and moth in the British Isles. He hunted for caterpillars in the old walled garden and watched them turn into chrysalises and eventually hatch under glass domes. In the long summer holidays, he would set off for whole afternoons alone with net and killing bottle, searching for butterflies to catch and set. Once, he had spotted a Purple Emperor in the oak copse above the Priory, which was the very last time that species had been seen in North Oxfordshire. Sometimes, during these days without Amanda, he was reminded of how he had felt then – self-sufficient but starved of company.

All this happened before they had been married much more than a year, and by the time their second Christmas together arrived, Amanda was spending all but two weekends a month up in London. In Winchford, she had long ago become an object of conjecture, seldom glimpsed but widely discussed.

Her startling appearance at the August bank holiday village fete, dressed in black leather leggings, scarlet silk jacket and thigh-length boots, and stationed by Jacinthe behind the tombola, was chewed over for weeks afterwards, and there wasn't a teenager for miles around in whose dreams Amanda Anscombe did not feature.

Anthony was respected in Winchford, and better liked than either of his parents. When he had arrived back from France with this peach of a girl, without his haughty mother or henpecked father knowing the least thing about it, old Walter Twine had raised a glass or two to the young so-and-so in the Plough and Harrow. But, gradually, happiness for Anthony had been replaced by headshakings of concern and sympathy. 'That little minx,' Walter proclaimed in the public bar. 'I wouldn't mind giving her a piece of my mind, I tell you I would not, that's if ever she was around to speak to, and I mean that with no disrespect to anyone at all.'

As Christmas Day approached, it was tacitly assumed that Anthony and Amanda would after Christmas morning church go up to the Priory for lunch and to exchange presents, as they had the previous year. Although not naturally hospitable, the elder Anscombes well understood their duty, as owners of the village, to set an example and celebrate Christmas as traditionally as possible; after all, if they did not, then the Biggeses would surely fill the void, which would be inappropriate. So Henrietta went to endless lengths to have great evergreen boughs dragged into the Priory, and the tops of the Elizabethan portraits decked with holly and holly berries. The old Victorian crib, with its oversized lead Magi, Christ child, one-winged angel and wonky donkey, was arranged with real straw in the manger. Tenants and neighbours were separately commanded up to the Great Hall for carols and mince pies in the run-up to Christmas. Anthony showed up at both these gatherings, increasingly annoyed at having to justify Amanda's absence to all and sundry. 'No Amanda this evening then?' asked Judy from the pub, with a meaningful look.

'She's up in London, actually.'

'So long as she's not still tucked up in her bed. My goodness, she does need her sleep that one, I hear.'

Since Amanda had no fixed place to stay in London, constantly shifting from chum to chum, Anthony could seldom ring her and waited for her to ring him at Forge Cottage. As Christmas Day came closer, he began to worry about Christmas presents – who exactly would be buying them, and what and for whom. But Amanda was annoyingly disengaged. 'Oh, Christmas,' she said vaguely. 'I've never seen the point of Christmas. Your parents overdid it like mad last time. I felt so overstuffed with food, I was almost sick.'

'Well, we have to get them presents. They'll certainly have them for us.'

'Listen, I'll probably be down on Tuesday, maybe Wednesday; we can pick up something then.'

'Isn't that cutting it a bit fine? Half the shops won't be open on Christmas Eve, not even in Cirencester. Amanda, I do need you to be here sometimes, you know. It's quite hard with you away all the time.'

'Do you think I don't miss you myself, every minute of every day? Do you imagine it isn't a problem for me too? But you keep saying you want to help on your estate, so you can't be with me. I'd far prefer us to be together all the time, but it's your choice.'

'Oh God, darling, you're making me feel awfully guilty about working on the farm. I know it's hard on you, but I don't really have much choice.' He sighed. 'Everything is just so difficult with you up there and me stuck down here.'

'Don't feel guilty. Never feel guilty. Physical separation doesn't actually matter that much, because even when you're not there you're always there in my head. That will never ever change, because of our special bond. Remember: you accepted my dare.'

As it happened, Amanda couldn't leave London on Tuesday and Anthony couldn't join her at a party given by a photographer in Camden Town which clashed with the Winchford Estate drinks. Then, throughout Wednesday, having woken with a splitting hangover and feeling quite sick, she kept changing her mind about which train to catch, and after half a dozen changes of plan it made sense to forget travelling on Christmas Eve altogether, and to get a really good night's sleep and catch an early Christmas Day train to Kingham via Oxford. It meant missing church, which would irritate the Anscombe parents, but she'd been ill, poor girl, and what else was to be done?

And so, around teatime on Christmas Eve, Anthony drove alone into Cirencester to buy presents for his parents; and in WH Smiths in Corn Market, where shop assistants were already hustling shoppers out into the cold and switching off the lights, he managed to scoop up a humorous loo book about shooting for his father (it was called *Yonder Pheasant, Who is He?*), a picture book about the Labrador in English art for his mother, and a Stones LP, *Aftermath*, for his wife.

Christmas morning found Anthony in Kingham station car park, waiting for the 11.05 train. It was a bright, frosty morning; carols leaked from the car radio, and the heater blasted tepid air and petrol fumes at his feet. The car park was practically deserted, the waiting room shut and padlocked until New Year. The back seat of the Triumph was covered with his inexpertly wrapped presents. Every so often, he got out to stare up the empty track, where the signal seemed permanently stuck on red.

At last it turned green, and three carriages behind a locomotive creaked and squealed to a halt. One door, then a second, opened and slammed behind alighting passengers. But neither of them was Amanda.

Anthony began to worry. Where the hell was she? He could exactly imagine the scene at Winchford Priory. After Christmas church, his father felt an obligation to invite the vicar, Jeremy Meek, up for a quick festive drink, along with Percy and Jacinthe Bigges to make it more of a party, and even now he would be tapping the little drops of angostura bitters into the champagne cocktails that were part of his Christmas ritual, and circulating the china dish of cheese footballs. 'Now whatever can be keeping Anthony and everybody?' Henrietta would be asking. She tried, as much as possible, not to use Amanda's name. 'He *promised* to be here by half past eleven at the latest.'

The next train was due to arrive at 12.37 and Anthony didn't see he had any choice but to wait and hope she was on that – but the carriages came and went with no Amanda. Now he was seriously panicked. He rang the Priory from the station telephone box and was luckily answered by Mrs Holcombe, who was preparing Christmas lunch, and he warned her there had been a slight delay, and they'd be home as soon as humanly possible. Meanwhile, with mounting anxiety and creeping pessimism, he awaited the 13.31.

The train arrived, a solitary door opened . . . and there stood Amanda on the empty platform. Anthony was transfixed and gawped in awe – his wife had never looked more alluring than at that moment, bathed in crisp sunshine. She was dressed in an ankle-length purple kaftan with gold embroidery around the neck, and was clutching a bottle of champagne.

'Amanda, thank God. What on earth happened to you?'

'Have you been waiting a long time?' She sounded surprised.

'You said you'd be on the five past eleven train.'

'Did I? I'm sorry. It all took so long, crossing London and everything. Anyway, I'm here now. Happy Christmas, darling.' She kissed him. 'By the way, I haven't had any breakfast. I'm desperate to stop somewhere and buy a snack.'

'Look, jump in the car quick. We were meant to be at my parents two hours ago. My mother's going to go mental; she hates people being late for lunch.'

'Don't drive too fast,' Amanda said. 'I have something amazing to tell you.'

Meanwhile, at Winchford Priory, Henrietta was incandescent with fury. 'It's too much. This time, Godfrey, you have to agree with me. It's the absolute limit. It's a *quarter to two*! I'm livid. Poor Mrs Holcombe; the turkey will be completely overcooked – she put it in at six o'clock this morning. Where can they be, for heaven's sake? That damn thoughtless girl. She's unbearable. And I shall tell her so too when she condescends to turn up.'

'Quite sure they'll be here soon,' said Godfrey, more in hope than conviction, as he bent over his tray to refill the vicar's and the Biggeses' glasses. The guests were all too interested by the unfolding drama to leave and were becoming quietly sozzled.

At that moment, Amanda and Anthony threw open the door, eyes sparkling.

'Hi, Mum, hi Dad. Sorry we're late. But we've got the most wonderful news.' He looked adoringly at his wife. 'Amanda, do you want to tell them or shall I?'

Amanda, radiant in the purple kaftan, contrived to look bashful and defiantly sexy at the same time, and Percy, who had always had an eye for a pretty young thing, snorted in his drink at the sight of her.

'I'm pregnant,' Amanda announced. 'I've only just discovered, but I'm going to have a baby.'

A gasp of surprise rose in the room, quickly followed by expressions of delight in varying degrees of warmth and sincerity. Godfrey shook his son by the hand, as did Percy, who moved rapidly on to Amanda to give her a congratulatory kiss. The vicar, who always found mention of pregnancy indelicate, looked on uncertainly, confining his gaze to tall, handsome young Anthony and away from the disconcerting mother-to-be. Henrietta congratulated her daughter-in-law with a thin, icy smile, and inwardly cursed that they were now bound to the damn girl for ever more.

Now, of course, there could be no question of recriminations for lateness. More champagne was fetched up from the cellar and Amanda's bottle put into the fridge, and everyone pretended not to mind about the turkey as dry as balsa wood and watery, overcooked Brussels sprouts. And, after lunch, when presents were exchanged, Henrietta thanked Amanda for being so clever and choosing the exact book she'd been longing to read, while Amanda barely blanched when she unwrapped her own gifts from Anthony's parents: a fawn-coloured Barbour jacket and the new Constance Spry cookbook.

Amanda, at the urging of Anthony, agreed to spend more time in Winchford; feeling sluggish in any case as the baby grew inside her, she took to staying in bed until eleven or twelve o'clock each morning, and generally napping after lunch as well. Anthony felt so happy having her there with him, and so proud of her pregnancy, he would permit her to do nothing to help. If he saw her so much as picking up a teacup, he rushed forward, saying, 'No, leave that to me, darling, I can do that. You shouldn't be stacking plates in your condition.' And Amanda was quick to submit.

Having led a hermetic existence, Anthony now made a conscious effort to renew old ties with country neighbours. His oldest friend, Lex Holland, with whom he had been at three consecutive schools, came over for supper at Forge Cottage to meet Amanda properly for the first time. Anthony fried steaks in the kitchen while Amanda dragged herself downstairs wearing his dressing gown and focused on zinging up Anthony's prosaic salad dressing with garlic, lemon juice and hot harissa sauce.

As it happened, Anthony had always been slightly envious of Lex, who he felt was better-looking and easier around girls than himself. Lex's father, 'Scrotum' Holland, owned nine hundred acres to the west of Winchford and reputedly possessed the biggest dick in Oxfordshire; his broad-shouldered son had inherited the family pheromones, and generally ended up with the pick of the crop at local dances. Tonight, to Anthony's amusement, Lex was clearly besotted by Amanda. He hung on her every word, trying harder than Anthony had seen him try with any girl before. And Amanda, responding to the flattery, flirted back, while contriving to describe Anthony as her husband as frequently as possible.

'When my husband and I were in the south of France . . .' or 'I was at this party the other night with my husband when . . .'

After supper, pleading exhaustion, Amanda retired to bed and Anthony and Lex walked together through the village for a quiet pint at the Plough and Harrow.

'I must say, you've fallen on your feet there all right,' said Lex. 'Amanda's a cracker. I don't know how the hell you pulled it off, but I have to hand it to you.'

'Thanks,' said Anthony. 'She is pretty, isn't she?'

'She isn't pretty, she's bloody jawdropping, incredible. Is it true you drove down to France to nick her off her boyfriend?'

Anthony shrugged. 'I suppose you could put it that way, if you must. We got married in Nice.'

'The other bloke's still devastated, that's what I heard. He lives somewhere round here. A spotty-looking guy. I met him playing tennis.'

'His name's Charlie Edwards. He wasn't exactly Amanda's boyfriend as a matter of fact; it wasn't serious.'

'That's not what he says. I heard he was desperate to get her back.' They walked on in silence while Anthony digested this piece of information. 'Anyway,' said Lex, 'it's academic now. You've married her and got her up the duff. She's off the market for good.'

The baby was due in late July, and as the time approached, Anthony felt they should be doing something to prepare for the birth. 'Oughtn't we to be getting a bedroom ready?' he asked his wife. 'I don't know, but shouldn't we buy a cot or a potty or feeding bottles or whatever it is you need?' But Amanda, shrugging, told him not to fuss. 'It can sleep in our bed with us. I don't want to fill the cottage with plastic junk.' Having one of those metabolisms which deny weight-gain, even in pregnancy, Amanda at eight months barely showed at all, and it was easy to imagine the due date was still distant and hardly to be considered.

The summer of 1967 was abnormally hot, harvest came early and Anthony found himself working ten-hour days behind the wheel of a combine. For three consecutive weeks all leave was suspended as every farmhand hurried to bring in the crops. The heat made it a stellar year for butterflies, and the wheat and hedgerows were alive with meadow browns, small tortoiseshells and peacocks. Having ploughed and scattered many of the fields in the first place, Anthony took personal satisfaction in seeing all his efforts come good, with the bales stacked high in the aluminium barns on top of Steepness Hill. Gazing down from the summit across the wide valley, with Winchford Priory more than a mile away on the rising slope, Anthony realised it formed a natural amphitheatre, like something used by the Romans for gladiatorial games, only several times bigger. 'You could have a Roman games here,' he said to old Walter Twine, who every year rallied round to help with the harvest. 'You know, Romans versus Christians, something gory like that.'

'If you're asking my opinion,' Walter replied, 'oi'd hold a stock car rally over that anyday. Now that would be something interesting for the village.'

That evening, with the harvest all but home and dry and the fine weather set to hold for several more days, Anthony took the men for a celebratory drink at the Plough and Harrow. As the ten of them lined the counter, and Judy drew the cider and bitter, Anthony was surprised to spot Amanda next door in the private bar. She was rapt in conversation with a man sitting with his back turned to Anthony. She was staring intently into the unseen face, looking serious and sympathetic, as though listening to something infinitely sad.

'Excuse me a moment,' Anthony told the farmhands, slipping through to the other bar. Seeing his wife among the horse brasses and Jubilee jugs of the pub was odd enough in itself, because she professed to hate the place, and it was with a feeling of dread that he now approached her table.

'Amanda?'

'Oh, hi Ant.' Was it his imagination or had she looked momentarily guilty? If so, she recovered quickly. 'You remember Charlie, don't you?'

Anthony was face to face with Charlie Edwards, who certainly did look uncomfortable, which wasn't altogether surprising since he had last been seen standing at the door of the villa near Sainte Maxime, impotently watching while Anthony drove away his girlfriend in the green TR4. Today, Charlie was wearing a hairy grey sweater with a rollneck, and smoking a Marlboro. His sideburns – bugger's grips – had grown two thirds of the way towards his lips.

'I'm, er, just having a jaw and a jar with Amanda for old times' sake. You know, we're catching up; we haven't seen each other for ages.'

'Then you've probably heard our news, about the baby I mean.'

'Er, sure, she was telling me about it. That's great news, really great.'

'We're thrilled. It's due quite soon actually, just a couple more weeks to go.'

'Yeah, that's what Amanda said.' Then, rallying, he said, 'Can I buy you a drink or something? That's if you need to pay for your drinks here. Amanda says you own the place.'

'My parents have the freehold, but we don't run the pub ourselves,' Anthony replied. 'So we pay for drinks like everyone else. But, actually, I've got a glass of beer waiting for me over there, and I'd better get back to the men. So I'll say goodbye if you don't mind.'

Hardly an hour later, when he returned to Forge Cottage, he found their bedroom in darkness and Amanda underneath the bedclothes asleep. Stepping gingerly between suitcases and scattered shoes, and drawing the drooping bedroom curtains Amanda had left wide open, he slipped into bed beside her and ruminated on the return of Charlie. It wasn't that he objected to his wife seeing her old boyfriend, but he wished she had mentioned it beforehand, and he wondered whether she would ever have mentioned it at all, had he not chanced on them by accident. Sometimes he wished Amanda was more open with him, though he imagined all beautiful women needed their secrets. Nevertheless, he was determined to say something about it in the morning, without seeming heavy-handed.

As it happened, however, at slightly after three o'clock in the morning Amanda shook him awake to complain of stomach cramps, which quickly developed into full-blown contractions, and by breakfast time they were installed in Cheltenham General Hospital celebrating the birth of a healthy baby daughter.

6

Jasmine Henrietta Anscombe, seven pounds four ounces, was widely considered to be the spitting image of her mother, except by Henrietta who could identify in her minuscule and unformed features traces of every Anscombe living or dead, but nothing whatever of Amanda. When Mrs Holcombe mentioned that 'baby Jasmine and Anthony's wife are alike as two peas in a pod,' Henrietta became quite frosty, declaring she could see no resemblance and that, if anything, Jasmine's sweet little mouth came straight from her great grandmother, Marguerite Anscombe, whose formidable, thin-lipped portrait glowered above the dressing table in the Judge's Chamber.

In triumph, Anthony brought his wife and daughter home from hospital. The previous day, he had bought electric blow-heaters in Stow to ensure Forge Cottage was sufficiently warm for a new baby, and these ugly grey tin boxes, with their trailing black wires and rattling fans, soon filled each room with a stifling dry heat. Anthony was besotted by Jasmine. He grinned inanely in her face and talked to her in soppy singsong voices: 'Hello, little Jazzy. Who do you think I am, Jazzy? Am I a great big grizzly bear? No-oooo, I'm not a great big grizzly bear, am I, Jazzy? I'm your special Daddy, aren't I? Can you say 'Daddy', Jazzy? No – silly Daddy – of course I can't say Daddy yet, I'm only four days old, aren't I? Silly, stupid Daddy. Isn't Daddy a silly, Jazzy?' and so on, until Amanda began to feel exasperated and claustrophobic, and implored him to go downstairs and do something useful, such as the washing-up.

With the fretful anxiety of a new parent, he marched around the tiny cottage, adjusting the temperature from room to room. Sometimes, declaring their bedroom draughty, he pressed down all three switches on the fan, which became noisier than a grain-dryer, blowing clouds of dust mites into the air. Or he would say, 'God, this room's stuffy. Poor Jasmine, she'll die of suffocation,' and fling open the windows to beckon fresh air inside with the palms of his hands.

Before she was a week old, Anthony had strapped his well-wrapped daughter into an Edwardian pushchair he'd found up at the Priory, and insisted on wheeling her around the village, introducing her to the lady in the village shop and Judy at the Plough and Harrow. Everyone agreed she was the prettiest baby they had ever seen, and 'small wonder seeing as how she's her mother's daughter.' The Reverend Jeremy Meek peered anxiously at the muffled bundle, felt he perhaps ought to kiss her, puckered his lips and was mortified when Jasmine burst into terrified tears. 'Oh dear, oh dear,' he fretted, polishing the lenses of his spectacles with the hem of his cassock. 'I fear I've never had much luck with small babies. Anyway, I do hope she will join our little Sunday School classes when she's old enough. Mother fit and well, I trust?'

'She's fine,' replied Anthony. 'On excellent form.' But in truth he was uneasy about Amanda, who appeared permanently tired and strangely uninterested in their daughter. She was feeding Jasmine herself – a procedure that seemed never to end, as one feed ran into another, with Jasmine nuzzling around her mother's small breasts – and at night the tiny baby dozed between them in the five-bar-gate bed, waking every hour to suck and grizzle. Amanda was somnolent, as if all vitality had been sucked out of her. She lay listlessly in bed, explaining it was pointless getting dressed since she'd be feeding again in no time. So she drifted between bed and bathroom in her nightdress, seldom leaving the cottage. When the district nurse turned up to weigh Jasmine and check how everything was going, it was Anthony who let her in and answered her questions; Amanda wandered away upstairs mid-visit, which Anthony found embarrassing, especially since the district nurse knew everyone in Winchford and had called on every newborn for more than fifteen years.

The remarkable thing about Amanda was that, for all her exhaustion, she remained hauntingly beautiful. Looking at her, you would never have guessed she'd given birth only eight weeks earlier. There was no question of regaining her figure, for she had never lost it; it was as if Jasmine had been born without the indignity of pregnancy. Perhaps it was the very ease of it all that made Amanda so disengaged. To Anthony, she appeared neither enchanted nor particularly absorbed by her baby, as though the two did not belong to one another. He perched on the low windowsill of their bedroom, which was practically like sitting on the floor, and watched mesmerised and dismayed while his tiny daughter clung to her mother, almost desperately it seemed to Anthony, as though by some instinct Jasmine recognised their love was one-sided. Amanda said, 'Ant, don't sit there gawping at us all day. You look like Walter Twine with your mouth hanging open. Put on a record, can't you?' So Anthony put on a Doors album – which was the music that for ever afterwards defined this period for him – and wondered whether it was his fault that Amanda did not completely adore their child. He considered his own mother, and the degree to which he had been doted on as a baby, concluding that Henrietta was hardly likely to have been more demonstrative than Amanda, but was doubtless more efficient and organised. He watched Amanda constantly, wondering what he could do to make her happier. He took her unhappiness as a personal reproof. Meanwhile, his love for her was undiminished. He consoled himself that, given time, nature would do its work and all would be well. He pulled on a wax jacket and set off in the direction of the Estate Office where they kept the keys for the tractors.

Winter afternoons in October were short and dark, and by a quarter past four the day was as good as over. Anthony ploughed half of a great sloping field beneath Ironstone Hill, a field in which, so legend said, a detachment of Prince Rupert's advancing army had rested under a great oak tree following the Battle of Edge Hill, and buried two sacks of gold plate. There was always a slight excitement when ploughing this field, in case you struck treasure. The oak was long gone, and Anthony wasn't holding his breath.

Half the windows in the village were lit up as he walked home. Winchford never looked more beautiful than on a winter's night like this, with the ironstone of the cottages and barns melding in the twilight. He passed the almshouses, almost monastic with their plain stone lintels, the war memorial and pub. There was a smell of bonfires and cattle in the air, and from the Norman church the sound of a choir practice in progress. At this point in his nightly stroll, Anthony would grow sentimental at the thought of his little family awaiting him in the cottage by the millstream. In his fantasy, a simple but nourishing dinner would be awaiting him on the table – some sort of sustaining game concoction with a pie crust – but he was sufficiently realistic to know he would soon be rummaging about in an almost empty larder, choosing between tinned tomato soup or canned tuna and sweetcorn.

He arrived at Forge Cottage and found the key beneath the stone; it lived there because, since Jasmine's birth, you never knew when Amanda might be resting. Tonight, the cottage was very quiet. There was a light on in the hall, but not in the sitting room or kitchen. Having hung his jacket on a hook, Anthony crept upstairs; he guessed his wife and daughter would be asleep together in the five-bar-gate bed. He crossed the bedroom through the usual obstacle course of suitcases and clothes, and was confronted by an empty mound of discarded sheets and blankets. He went back downstairs, turning on lights and drawing curtains. Maybe Amanda had taken Jasmine for a stroll. A wind was blowing up, and a drumming of raindrops started up against the kitchen window. It hardly seemed the night or the time for a walk, and the pushchair was parked in the washroom at the back. Well, no doubt they'd be home soon, and Anthony went into the drawing room to make a fire. There was a basket of dry logs and kindling and Anthony knelt at the hearth arranging tapers of old newspaper; it was a point of pride that he never needed to resort to firelighters. He was listening with approval to the first deep crackle of the kindling, which meant the fire had taken, when he heard a snuffling noise from somewhere behind him. On the sofa he noticed, for the first time, a strange arrangement of pillows and cushions covered by a tablecloth – like a dog-basket with a canopy – and there was something moving about inside. Then the bundle began to cry.

'Jasmine?' He raced across the room. 'Is that you under there?' He tugged at the tablecloth, and there was Jasmine, crusted sleep in the corner of her eyes, bawling her head off.

He picked her up and tried to comfort her, but it was obvious she was hungry. He jiggled her about a bit and showed her the fire, hoping she'd calm down, but she seemed furious and ravenous in a way only her mother could do anything about.

'Now, where *is* Mummy?' he asked her rhetorically. 'Where's lovely Mummy gone? Has she forgotten Jazzy's special teatime? Silly Mummy, because you're so hungry aren't you Jazzy, you need your lovely milko.' Momentarily, it occurred to him Amanda might be back in the Plough and Harrow with Charlie, then he remembered the pub wouldn't be open and cursed his suspicious mind.

Then he saw the envelope. It was tucked between two of the pillows, and his name was written on the front in Amanda's spidery handwriting. Probably it was the fact it was a sealed envelope and not just a sheet of paper that made him sense danger. Gingerly he opened it and read the message, and then his whole world fell apart.

Part Two

7

Amanda's abrupt flight from Forge Cottage – to where or why, he had no idea – left him devastated. For a week, he could bring himself to tell no one, hoping she would quickly return and life resume as before. He rang every number in London where she had ever stayed, but if anybody knew where she was, they weren't saying. Pretending to have picked up filthy flu, he took time off work and did his best to care for Jasmine. Avoiding local shops where he was known, he bought feeding bottles and formula milk and a brown plastic sterilising kit at a chemist in Moreton-in-Marsh. But, accustomed to the taste and reassurance of her mother, Jasmine rejected the substitute with scorn and her weight began to drop alarmingly. At night, she bawled her head off for hours on end, so sleep deprivation compounded Anthony's despair. A dozen times a day, hearing a car door slam somewhere in the lane, he ran to the window, praying it might be a taxi bearing Amanda. He missed her so intensely, craved her with a yearning so consuming it made him ill. Her note had been so final, so inadequate: 'Darling Anthony. Our life just isn't right for me. I need to get away. I hope you understand. Never forget I will love you until the sun burns up in the heavens and the oceans run dry. I bequeath Jasmine to you as a sign of our unbreakable bond. Always, Amanda.'

Eventually, faced with the realisation that his wife would not be returning any time soon, he was forced to tell his parents, and thus to endure the jubilant consolation of Henrietta, who had known from the start Amanda was quite the wrong sort of girl. Her sanctimonious triumph barely touched him, however, for he knew that Amanda was precisely the right girl – that was the tragedy – and it was, in fact, he who was evidently the wrong sort of man for Amanda.

With the selflessness demanded of the situation, Henrietta agreed that

Mrs Holcombe should give up some of her hours at the Priory and allocate them to Anthony instead, to help care for Jasmine; so a routine was established whereby Mrs Holcombe devoted a few hours each morning to Forge Cottage, smoking over the baby, then passed Jasmine on to her daughter Judy at the Plough and Harrow, who kept an eye on her in a basket behind the bar. Anthony, meanwhile, advertised for a nanny to look after her on a more permanent basis.

Having heard the news, Lex Holland drove over to commiserate with his friend. He found Anthony in the lowest spirits, white-faced and gaunt, attempting to soothe his howling daughter to sleep.

'Can't we just leave her here for a tick and go to the pub?' said Lex. 'She can't walk yet, so she can't come to much harm.'

But Anthony said he couldn't leave Jasmine, and since the cottage was completely out of booze, Lex drove up to the Plough and Harrow and returned with six bottles of beer and two bottles of wine, and they tried to drown out the bawling baby by downing the lot.

'And you've really no idea where Amanda is?' Lex asked. 'She just did a bunk?'

'Not a trace. I've rung everyone I can think of.'

'You rang Charlie?'

'Charlie Edwards? No, I didn't ring him.'

'Maybe you should. Remember what I told you?'

'You really think it's possible?' The idea horrified him.

Lex shrugged. 'He's away at university. Bristol, I think. And he's playing in some rock band down there, or so my sister tells me.'

They sat in silence for a moment, while Lex opened the second bottle. 'Would you take her back?' he asked.

'Take Amanda back? You kidding? I'd do anything. Anything.'

'Even if she's been with another bloke?'

'Lex, you've met Amanda. You know what she's like. Do you honestly think there's anything I wouldn't forgive?'

Lex thought. 'No, I think that's fair enough. She's not like most women you meet.'

'You know something – and I don't mean this to sound pretentious – but I really do believe we were destined for each other. Amanda agrees. She said that the first time we met.'

Lex glanced at him, to check whether or not his friend was serious. 'Well, how come she's gone and done a runner then?'

'That's what I've been trying to work out. I haven't been thinking about much else.'

'You'll get over her,' Lex said. 'That's if she doesn't come back. Which she probably will. I mean, it's one thing to walk out on you, mate, but who'd walk out on Winchford? She'd have to be crazy.'

'Thanks for that, Lex. That makes me feel a lot better. You're saying she'd dump me, but might come back for the village?'

'No offence meant. But you've got to admit, there aren't many estates like Winchford around. That's what Dad says, anyhow. It has to be a factor.'

Anthony did not give up hope of Amanda's return; in fact, he half expected it every day. With each post, he waited for a letter, and in the sixth week was rewarded with a postcard. The stamp was French, postmarked Paris, the picture of a monumental bronze sculpture from the Musée Rodin called 'The Gates of Hell'. The message read, 'Thinking about you all the time. Jasmine too, but you above all, who daily crowd my thoughts. Love without end, Amanda.'

The advertisement for a nanny, placed in *The Lady*, drew five replies. It might have got more, but the wording Anthony chose was too circumspect for that. He was worried that 'lone father of newborn baby' would attract only the desperate or the opportunist.

Sandra Potts, from Poole in Dorset, was twenty-five and had been working at a daycare centre close to her parents' home. It was her dream, she wrote, to look after a small baby full-time. She was driven to the interview by her boyfriend, Steve, a fit young corporal in the Logistics Corps who, when she accepted the position, returned with her luggage, pictures, cushions and soft toys, which he carried up to the bedroom with the two single beds and candlewick covers.

It was a relief to have found someone, especially since his mother had been so sure he would not. 'Who could possibly be willing to accept a position where they have to share a bathroom with their employer? And especially with a man. It isn't really very nice at all, nor very suitable either. And such a *horrid* little bathroom, especially with the only lavatory in there, too. Such a pity there isn't a separate cloakroom. I do so hate downstairs bathrooms. I shall be quite surprised if anyone takes the job, once they've seen the set-up.'

Sandra Potts, however, had eyes only for Jasmine, with whom she instantly bonded. Anthony was astounded by the whole thing. When he tried to give Jasmine her bottle himself, she screwed up her face and turned her cross little mouth away from him; but this perfect stranger – this slightly plump, blonde, soft, bosomy girl – walked straight into Forge Cottage, hoisted his daughter up from the floor, and within minutes Jasmine was sucking away at the bottle, content as anything. Soon, Jasmine was clutching at Sandra's neck and bosom, not wanting to let go, and eventually fell asleep on her lap while Anthony, Sandra and Steve were talking together in the sitting room.

You couldn't have described their conversation as an interview. Knowing nothing about babies, Anthony was only too willing to go along with anything Sandra suggested. She asked him about Jasmine's routine, quickly established there was no routine, and explained her own for a baby's day. It all sounded more than fine to Anthony. He had immediate confidence in the attractive, considerate girl sitting opposite him; she exuded competence, and a pleasant openness it was impossible not to like. Steve, the boyfriend, while paying a visit to the bathroom, returned saying 'that cistern in your toilet is filling slowly' and asked where Anthony kept his tools. Anthony located a drawer of random screwdrivers and spanners, and within minutes Steve was on his knees fixing the cistern and a dripping tap in the basin. By the time they left, Anthony had offered Sandra the job and encouraged her to start as soon as possible.

Of the various changes that overtook Forge Cottage, it was the new smell Anthony noticed the most. Previously, there had been a lingering whiff of damp and stale cooking. The kitchen had been impregnated with bacon fat and burnt toast, which seemed to have sullied every pot and pan as well as the blackened oak beams of the ceiling.

Quite suddenly, the cottage smelt instead of talcum powder and fresh ironing. Each evening, when Anthony got back from the farm, he encountered a large blue plastic basket of neatly folded baby clothes on the kitchen table, and the soothing prospect of Sandra stationed behind the ironing board, pressing and spraying with a steam iron.

'How's Jasmine been?' he would ask, looking round the kitchen for his daughter.

'Oh, she's sound asleep upstairs in her cot, bless her,' Sandra would reply. 'She was so sleepy this evening, she could hardly keep her eyes open during her bath. We had our little walk to look at the cows in the big field. She does love those cows. It's a treat to see how her little face lights up. She's a very bright little person, that one.'

Then Anthony would tiptoe upstairs to peep at Jasmine, who now slept in a big Edwardian cot Henrietta had disinterred from the attics of the Priory. It was the cot that Anthony had slept in himself as an infant, and his father before him. Sandra had put the cot in her own bedroom, which was transformed from the days that Anthony and Amanda had rejected it for their own use. The bare, uneven floorboards were now covered by small, colourful, shaggy rugs with pom-pom borders, and the second single bed, with its pink candlewick cover, had been pushed back against the wall and arranged with Sandra's extensive collection of smirking pink cats, rhubarb-coloured caterpillars and centipedes, pandas, zebras and plump yellow gonks. She asked Anthony if he'd mind if she painted the old pine chest of drawers, and soon it was a dazzling gloss white, stencilled with a pattern of poppies and sunflowers, and covered by a pretty lace cloth. Suspended above Jasmine's cot was a colourful mobile constructed of wire and pieces of orange and yellow paper, which Sandra had made herself, and which Jasmine reputedly loved to stare up at while dropping off to sleep.

Then, having kissed his own fingers and transferred the kiss between the bars of the cot to Jasmine's soft cheek, Anthony would return downstairs, pour himself a large whisky and offer a drink to Sandra. 'Thank you, but not when I'm working,' she invariably replied. 'But I wouldn't say no to a small white wine to keep for later on.'

At first, Anthony had found it awkward living in such close proximity to a strange female, especially in a cottage where every sound was so clearly audible. He was conscious of his shoes clumping across uncarpeted floorboards; through the walls of his bedroom, he could follow Sandra's progress around her own room as she stepped from rug to floorboard to rug and into bed. In the morning, he occupied the bathroom for the minimum time so as not to inconvenience her. If he heard her step on the stone passage outside, he loudly splashed the water about, to make his presence known, then got out as rapidly as possible. Sandra in turn took immense pains to ensure her co-occupation of the bathroom was almost imperceptible. While Anthony's shaving foam, razor and toothbrush lived on permanent display on a shelf, Sandra kept her washing kit stored underneath the basin in a Pyrex container. A bright pink box of tissues on the windowsill was the only permanent clue to a female presence.

'I'll put your clean shirts in the airing cupboard overnight, because they're still slightly damp,' Sandra said, taking five ironed shirts to the shelves beside the boiler. That was another revelation. With Amanda, there had never been any question of her involvement with his laundry; in their two years together, he had never worn an uncreased shirt unless he pressed it himself. But Sandra insisted she loved ironing; she asked whether he'd mind if she did Steve the boyfriend's washing too, and late into most evenings she worked her way through a basket of Steve's shirts and underwear, and a basket of Anthony's.

His long days on the farm were ushered in by hearty cooked breakfasts, prepared by Sandra and eaten in the kitchen with Jasmine. Anthony's days now followed an unchanging pattern. He discovered heavy physical labour was the only way he could later get to sleep, so he volunteered for the most strenuous jobs, repairing fences, cutting hedgerows and thinning out the new plantations his father had established along the Winchford–Moreton road. At lunchtime, he tried to drop in at Forge Cottage, even if only for half an hour, to check Jasmine was OK and to eat the cheese and homemade soups Sandra had ready for him. By the time he got home again in the evening, Jasmine was generally already down for the night, so he carried a whisky into his bath, which he hoped would take the edge off his unhappiness, but it only seemed to make him sadder. He bought headphones for his stereo, so he could listen to records without disturbing his daughter or her nanny.

He remained as obsessively preoccupied with Amanda as ever. He kept the French postcard with him at all times, frequently pulling over in the car or tractor to finger it like a talisman. Why was she in Paris and, more to the point, was she alone? Anthony had visited Paris only once on a school trip, and his impression of the place hardly extended beyond the Eiffel Tower and the Seine on a bateau mouche. He remembered an embankment beside the river with stalls selling prints and old books. He read the postcard so often he knew it by heart: 'Thinking about you all the time . . . you above all, who daily crowd my thoughts.' The words struck him as poetic, but also slightly irritating and unilluminating. If she kept thinking about him, as she said she did, why didn't she get in touch? The sign-off – 'Love without end' – gave him grounds for optimism, but what actually did it mean, if anything at all? Whatever he'd done to alienate her (and, over those weeks, he thought of many possibilities, beginning with keeping her cooped up in an Oxfordshire labourer's cottage, which now struck him as almost insane), he wondered how she could bear to be apart from Jasmine, who became sweeter and happier every day. Had he any idea where to look for her in Paris, he would have gone immediately. He had half a mind to go anyway and scour the cafés as he'd done in Carcassonne. But he was reluctant to leave Jasmine, and still hopeful Amanda might yet turn up in Winchford; he wanted to be there when she did.

'Don't those parents of hers have any idea where she is?' asked Anthony's mother. 'Have you actually spoken to her mother and father? Surely they can't be quite so casual that they're not worried about her too? If you ask me, the whole thing is most peculiar.' But Anthony could hardly ring Amanda's parents, since he had never met them and hadn't the faintest idea where they lived.

Then, at the beginning of December, he received a second postcard.

8

This time, the picture was of a French hotel lobby. It wasn't the lobby of a large or grand place; the photograph showed a modest reception desk with room keys dangling from a keyboard and miniature flags of several nations standing along the surface of the counter. The edges of the postcard were perforated with a wavy pattern like pastry. The caption said it was the Hôtel Petit Trianon in the Rue St Denis; the postmark showed it had been franked five days earlier in the second arrondissement.

The message, as before, was tantalisingly brief. 'Darling Anthony. I can understand why people fall in love with/in this beautiful city. Do you ever think about our drive back through France from Nice? Sweet memories. Masses of love to Jasmine – and to you, dearest one. Always, Amanda.'

Anthony scrutinised the words for every nuance; he felt his heart racing with excitement and anticipation. Amanda's reference to their journey home from the south of France – surely the happiest, most romantic and passionate ten days of their time together – could only be interpreted as a sign that she was wavering towards wanting to get back together. What other possible meaning could be attached to it? And she had told him where she was staying. The postcard from the Hôtel Petit Trianon had to be the unsubtlest of hints.

By lunchtime, he had negotiated Friday and Monday as holiday from the farm and Sandra had agreed to work the weekend. (Steve the soldier would stay over, and Jasmine's cot be shifted temporarily into Anthony's own bedroom.) He hastily packed a case, left a stash of cash on the kitchen table, and made the overnight boat-train from Victoria by the skin of his teeth.

Having sat up half the night on the ferry, and dozed ineffectually on the train into the Gare du Nord, he arrived feeling dazed and a little daunted. Paris was larger and greyer than he remembered, with its wide, windy boulevards extending from the station. For the first time since the arrival of the second postcard, he felt anxious about his quest, and realised he had no idea what to say to Amanda if he found her. He had imagined them returning on the next train – fetching her home to Winchford – but now that he was here, in this alien city, he wondered if it would actually be that simple. Maybe she would refuse to come. Maybe their marriage really was over, and the postcard held no significance. He reflected that it was just over two years since he had first set eyes on her at his parents' party from the gallery of the Great Hall. Two years. Already, the time that he'd known Amanda seemed infinitely longer in span and significance than the sum total of his previous life. It struck him this was the second time he had travelled to France to retrieve her.

A cab cruised by and he asked to go to the Hôtel Petit Trianon, which turned out to be less than fifteen minutes away on another wide street lined with apartments and office buildings. Across the road from the hotel was a bar-brasserie with a glass-enclosed café on the street, and Anthony crossed over with his bag, feeling a beer might help bolster him up for an encounter with Amanda. He was conscious his palms were sweating. He ordered a Stella and sat in the café with its wicker chairs and wonky metal tables, peering at the entrance to the hotel.

The Hôtel Petit Trianon boasted five white-stuccoed storeys and a steep mansard roof. The rooms on the first floor had elaborate iron balconies, but above that level the balconies were narrower and plainer. Anthony was on the watch for any sign of life, but at this time of the day (shortly after eleven o'clock in the morning) the place was very quiet. Now he considered it, he guessed Amanda would probably be out; it was probable she might even have a job. The likelihood of her having this whole other life, from which he'd been excluded, was disheartening.

Re-crossing the street, he passed passed beneath an archway into the hotel. The reception was by now so familiar to him from the postcard he could have entered a competition about its design and fittings; in reality, it was smaller than the photograph implied. A listless woman with peroxide blonde hair asked whether he needed a room. 'No,' he replied in faltering French. 'I am looking for Amanda Anscombe. Amanda Gibbons. Is she staying at the hotel?'

The woman consulted the register and pointed towards a lift. '*Chambre* seventeen. Fourth floor.' Anthony saw the key to room seventeen was missing from the keyboard, indicating Amanda was upstairs.

The lift was small and narrow as a coffin, with grey sliding metal doors on both sides of the car; you entered through one set of doors and exited from the other. Had a second person tried to fit inside, it would surely have been impossible. He pressed the button and felt the lift begin its ascent in a series of slow jerks. As the rubber-cased wires twitched and creaked above him, he felt almost sick with fear and longing at the thought of seeing her. For the briefest of moments, the grinding of the lift mechanism reminded him of Amanda on the raft at Sainte Maxime, and the rasp of the shingle being dragged across the beach by the waves. He now knew exactly how he would play it, this reconciliation: they would stay in Paris for the weekend, they needed time alone together, they'd find a restaurant serving plateaux de fruits de mer like they'd had the whole time in Nice, and only then return to Winchford and Jasmine. The lift jolted to a halt and the doors jerked open. Next to the lift was a staircase and a chrome ashtray on a stand, with sand in the lid and a collection of old cigarette butts. Room seventeen was at the end of the passage. He paused for a moment outside the door to pull himself together. Inside, he thought he heard bathwater running.

He knocked. Then, hearing nothing, knocked again more loudly. This time footsteps crossed the floor.

He heard a key turning, then a male voice saying, 'Amanda? You were quick.' The door opened, and there stood Charlie Edwards wrapped in a bath towel, as he had stood once before in a towel at the villa in the south of France.

Anthony stared at him for a second before turning away. He heard Charlie say, 'Anthony? Oh, fuck,' as he headed for the stairs. He was running now, taking the stairs four at a time, desperate to get shot of the place. Charlie's bony shoulders had been covered by hard red boils like barnacles clinging to a rock, his stomach and chest hairless as Formica. Anthony felt nauseous. Reaching ground level, he sprinted through the lobby and out into the street, then on and on without stopping, still clutching his bag, down the Boulevard Sebastopol towards Châtelet Les Halles. His one emotion now was fear: fear of running into Amanda. Of course, he could never see her again; it was all irretrievably over. Charlie Edwards: who had never given up, who had come to Winchford and presumably planned all this, planned it at the Plough and Harrow, right under his nose. Well, Lex had been right; nobody could say he hadn't been warned. Charlie – spotty, boorish, insufferable Charlie – had always been determined to get her back – and now he had her, and there was an end to it.

By three o'clock that same afternoon Anthony had boarded the train to London, and by lunchtime on Saturday was back in Winchford. As he drove into the village, he saw Sandra and Steve taking Jasmine for a walk in her pushchair. He slowed down and said hello through the car window.

'You're back early,' Sandra said. 'We weren't expecting to see Daddy until Monday, were we, Jasmine?'

'I found it didn't take as long in Paris as I expected. So I'm back, I'm afraid.' It was almost the first time he'd spoken since leaving the hotel, and his voice choked with emotion. He dared not look up in case the nanny or her boyfriend saw the tears in his eyes.

'Well, don't look at the mess in the kitchen,' Sandra was saying. 'I mean the crayons and paints on the table. Jasmine and I have been making a little surprise for you. We've been stencilling a frieze of bluebells right round the kitchen to cheer the place up, haven't we, Jasmine? We think Daddy's going to be ever so happy when he sees what we've been up to.'

9

Defeated, Anthony resumed his life as best he could. The finality of his break with Amanda filled him with an all-consuming despair. Try as he might, he could not prevent himself from reliving, over and over again, the image of Charlie standing in the doorway of room seventeen, draped in a bath towel. It was extraordinary the additional details his brain retrieved from that single, devastating moment; now, he could see Amanda's open suitcases on the floor beyond Charlie's shoulder, and a pile of her clothes thrown across a chair and draped over a radiator. Even the thought of her made him flinch. He knew that inside his wallet, tucked behind some French banknotes he could not bring himself to reconvert, were two treasured photographs of his wife on their honeymoon, the first taken during lunch immediately after the wedding ceremony: Amanda in her white lace nightdress; the second during the long drive back from the south of France. The pictures lay like undetonated bombs, too dangerous to extricate from their pigskin sheath, capable of unleashing misery if he so much as glanced at them.

His one consolation was Jasmine. He adored her, though as her first birthday approached, she became clingy and fractious when he was around. Perhaps responding at some instinctive level to the disappearance of her mother, she alternately hugged or rejected him, which to someone as straightforward and uncomplicated as Anthony was bewildering.

'Don't worry about it,' Sandra always told him, whenever Jasmine pushed him away. 'She's quite the manipulative little monkey this one; it's only her way of getting your attention. She loves you to bits really. She gets ever so excited when she hears you coming home. You do love your Daddy, don't you, poppet?'

A few weeks before Jasmine's first birthday, Henrietta rang her son and asked what plans he had made for a birthday party.

'Er, none actually, Mum,' Anthony replied. 'I hadn't thought about a party.'

'Well, that's very thoughtless of you. Poor Jasmine, of course she must have a birthday party. If you're not intending to give her one, and I'm quite sure her vanishing mother isn't either, I'll just have to organise one myself up here at the Priory. It'll be nice for her to have some little friends for tea. And that nanny of yours can make herself useful – I'm sure she's got plenty of time with only one baby to mind. Meanwhile, what you can do is send me a little list of Jasmine's friends, so we can get invitations into the post.'

Having resolved to give a party for her granddaughter, Henrietta rapidly drew up a list of tasks for Sandra, including buying and sending out a dozen Peter Rabbit invitations to the guests, drawing up a suit-able tea menu for her approval, shopping and making the sandwiches, cakes and jellies, and purchasing the paper plates and cups as well as the going-home presents. By the time she had also discussed the party with Mrs Holcombe, insisting she switch some of her hours at Forge Cottage back to Winchford Priory in order to prepare for the festivities, and had furthermore asked her to ensure Judy was available to help on the day, Henrietta felt quite the martyr. As she said to Godfrey over dinner, 'I can't imagine what would have happened if I hadn't stepped in and done the whole thing myself. I don't know of any other grandmothers who are expected to organise an entire children's tea party!' She sighed in a put-upon manner. 'What a simply ghastly mess Anthony has made of everything. That beastly girl he married! I hope I shall never set eyes upon her again. You'd have thought she might have the good manners to telephone and thank me for all this extra work I'm being put to for her daughter. It's outrageous she isn't here herself, doing her part.'

For Anthony, the prospect of his mother's birthday party for Jasmine provoked mixed feelings. Of course he was pleased Jasmine would have a party, and he hoped she would enjoy it. At the same time, the protracted preparations inevitably sucked him back into the orbit of Winchford Priory, which he had done his best to avoid since Amanda's disappearance. He resented, too, the way that his mother was bossing Sandra around, arbitrarily rejecting her suggestion of honey sandwiches and insisting upon egg and cress bridge rolls. Furthermore, he was expected to magic up nine babies for this great birthday tea, when he knew nobody with babies. None of his schoolfriends or contemporaries were anywhere near having families, so he had to spend hours tracking down suitable children of the right age, the offspring of tenuous acquaintances.

Sandra, impervious to his mother's nitpicking, carried on as if nothing could rile her, happy to rethink the colour of the icing on the fairy cakes several times ('I do find pink icing awfully common,' Henrietta declared at one point) and to return the paper napkins to the shop when Henrietta winced at the cartoon characters.

'I'm so sorry about my mother,' Anthony said one evening. 'I know she can be a nightmare.'

'No problem at all,' Sandra said. 'I like your mother. She knows what she wants and I'm fine with that.'

Anthony's admiration for his daughter's nanny grew from day to day. Not only was she endlessly patient with Jasmine, but considerate and kind to him, too. After the mesmerising chaos of life with Amanda, there was a lot to be said for cohabiting with someone so dependable and stable. Although he had barely discussed his wife with her, beyond explaining she was away in France, he guessed Mrs Holcombe and Judy had lost no time in briefing her on his disastrous marital situation, and Sandra was sensitive to his abrupt shifts of mood. When he seemed overtaken by despair, she left him comforting soups in saucepans on the cooker, and took Jasmine out for long walks to give him some peace. If he seemed in better spirits, Sandra encouraged him to play with Jasmine or to join them on their twice-daily walks around the village. Anthony found himself becoming acquainted, through Sandra, with locals whom previously he had merely glimpsed in church on Christmas Day and, once he had overcome their pitying stares, he enjoyed the experience. Soon he felt that, for the first time since moving into the cottage, he was starting to become part of the wider village. One sultry afternoon, while pushing Jasmine up by the old dairy towards Steepness Hill, Anthony and Sandra met an elderly woman out walking with a spaniel puppy. They stopped to show Jasmine the baby dog, and the old woman returned their compliments by admiring the baby girl. 'What a pretty little baby – she looks the spitting image of you,' she said, approvingly patting Sandra's arm. Sandra, reddening, hastily explained the mistake, before resuming the walk in some confusion.

The day of Jasmine's party arrived, and Sandra spent the morning rootling round the Priory for suitable chairs and stools to be placed around the table in the Great Hall (Henrietta had declared the Sheraton dining chairs too precious to be subjected to children or their nannies). Two bunches of brightly coloured balloons, inflated by Sandra and Anthony, now dangled from the gate piers at the top of the drive, and trestle tables had been carried up from the cellar and covered with table cloths and tea cups and jugs of orange and lemon barley water. Children and nannies and some parents, mostly ten or more years older than Anthony, were climbing out of cars with their little wrapped presents for Jasmine. If truth be told, most had been slightly surprised to be invited to the party, but came out of curiosity, partly to meet Anthony, about whose glamorous teenage bride there had been so much gossip, and partly to see inside Winchford Priory.

Henrietta and Godfrey were receiving guests in the Great Hall. Henrietta was whispering conspiratorially to each arrival, 'I've had to organise this entire tea single-handed, but you've heard I'm sure about poor Anthony's troubles with his ghastly wife. We haven't heard one squeak out of her for months.'

Sandra was supervising a game of pass-the-parcel, directing the children to sit in a circle and unwrap one layer of tissue paper at a time. Most of the babies, being too young to understand, simply dropped the parcel onto the ground, until a three-year-old grabbed it, ripped off all the layers at once and shot off behind a sofa clutching the present.

Anthony, who had legged it up to the minstrel's gallery with Lex, whom he had coerced into coming, watched proceedings from above while Lex smoked a cigarette.

'Well, old boy, I bet you never would have predicted all this two years ago,' Lex said. They could hear Sandra clapping her hands for attention, and telling everyone that tea would shortly be served, once all the children had washed their hands nicely in the cloakroom just through those big doors and to the right.

'Predicted all what?' asked Anthony. 'The children's party you mean?'

'All of it, everything. Having a kid and bringing her up on your own. Not going to university. Meeting Amanda. I'm just saying I never would have predicted it – not of you. You seemed too conventional.'

Anthony shrugged. 'You make it sound like I've really screwed things up. Maybe I have; my parents certainly think so. I keep half expecting Amanda to show up again.'

'Really? I thought you said . . .'

Lex was the only person Anthony had told about the disastrous visit to Paris.

'I know, you don't have to remind me. I can't seem to get her out of my mind, that's all.'

Down below, Henrietta was marshalling everyone up to the long tables where the tea was laid, and looking round for Anthony. Sandra was gathering up the torn wrapping paper on the floor.

'You know what they say is the best way of getting a bird out of your system?' Lex said.

'What's that?'

'Screw another one, quick as possible.'

Anthony gave his friend a withering look.

'I'm serious, mate,' Lex went on. 'This is high-quality advice. I've tried it myself and it works every time. A girl gives you the shoulder, you bed the next one pronto. Doesn't matter who, she can wear a paper bag over her head if need be. The point is, you fuck the old one out of your system. Next day, you never want to see the girl again – either of them. But you feel a lot better and you're back in business. It's like hair of the dog.'

'Thanks, Lex. I'll bear it in mind, but to be honest I'm nowhere near ready for anything like that yet. Maybe never, actually. It's different for you; it just wouldn't be me to do that.'

'Oh for God's sake, Anthony. Amanda's gone, okay? She's never coming back. She's a great-looking bird, no question, but she's big trouble and always will be. Also she's a nymphomaniac in case you've forgotten. Even if she turned up now, she'd be off again in a matter of months. It's in her nature.'

'That's unfair. You don't know Amanda well enough to make those assumptions.'

'Maybe, maybe not. But I've got a pretty good idea, and so have you. If I were you . . . know what I'd do?'

'I dread to think.'

'I'd screw the nanny, mate.'

'Sandra?' Anthony sounded shocked.

'Sandra, if that's what she's called. Why not? She's very tasty, all on her own, right under your roof. I was watching her when she was playing those games with the kids. Good body, great tits. Go for it. I bet she's just waiting for you to make the move.'

'Quite apart from anything else, she's got a boyfriend. A soldier. They're probably about to get engaged.'

'So? I'm not suggesting you marry her. I'm recommending a remedial fuck.'

'You, Lex, are outrageous. You don't know anything about anything. You only met Amanda a couple of times, and you don't know Sandra at all. We're so different you and me, I don't even get why we're friends. Now we'd better go downstairs and watch the children having tea or my mother will go apeshit.'

Jasmine blew at her candles, 'Happy Birthday' was sung and the tea was coming to its end. Sandra was going round the table transferring the dozens of uneaten egg and cress bridge rolls onto paper plates to take home to Forge Cottage for Jasmine to eat all week. Judy Holcombe was furtively removing leftover cheddar cheese cubes to place on the bar of the Plough and Harrow. Anthony was avoiding Jacinthe Bigges who wanted to involve him in the village fete 'and dear Amanda too, of course, if she's around that weekend.'

As the guests began to make their way home, Sandra helped Jasmine open some of her presents, whilst compiling a list of who had given her what. They had unwrapped some wooden bricks and an Ant and Bee reading book when there was a ring on the doorbell. A postman from Oxford was outside, requesting a signature for special delivery. He handed over a parcel addressed to Jasmine Anscombe at Forge Cottage; having found no one at home, he had been directed by a neighbour to the Priory. Covering about half the parcel were forty French stamps in long grey strips.

'How very extraordinary,' declared Henrietta, looming above the sofa where her granddaughter was propped against cushions. 'Special delivery! So extravagant. What could possibly be so urgent that one would pay double for it to arrive one day sooner?'

Recognising the handwriting, Anthony blanched and tore off the outer packaging, before bringing the tissued bundle over to Sandra and Jasmine. Cocooned in several layers of paper were three party dresses, two voile and one velvet. The voile was exquisitely hand-smocked and embroidered, the velvet black with a pale satin sash festooned with a pink satin rose. The labels showed they came from a boutique in the rue du Faubourg St Honoré.

'Now those really are *very* pretty,' Henrietta said. 'Totally impractical, of course, impossible to launder. Still, the French *do* make delightful children's clothes, always have. Now, who sent Jasmine these lovely things?'

'Well, isn't that nice, Jasmine?' Sandra was saying. 'These come from your Mummy. The card says, "Happy Birthday darling, with lots of love, Amanda".'

'"Amanda" indeed,' snorted Henrietta. 'I simply can't stand it when parents sign themselves to their children by their first names. So over-familiar.'

Returning to Forge Cottage from the farm the following evening, Anthony found Sandra preparing supper.

'Sorry, I'm running late,' she said. 'I hope you don't mind but we're finishing up leftover party food. I was at the Priory clearing up today, so there hasn't been a lot of time.' She was standing at the kitchen table, wearing a blue apron and a white blouse, which suited her.

'Sounds great,' Anthony said. 'The supper, I mean. I hope my mother wasn't making you do too much.'

Sandra laughed good naturedly. She has such a pretty smile, Anthony thought. 'Oh, you know your mother. She had Mrs Holcombe and me hard at it most of the day, polishing furniture in the drawing room and doing the silver and everything.'

'For heaven's sake, we didn't go anywhere near the drawing room. Or use her silver. She's too much sometimes, she really is. I'm so sorry.'

'Honestly, it was no trouble; I was pleased to help. Now, you do like anchovies, don't you? I'm making a savoury with all those egg rolls – we've got about a hundred in the fridge and they won't keep for ever. Jasmine ate four for her tea.'

'Sandra, I must thank you for everything you did to pull that party together. I know it was all down to you. You were a complete hero.'

'Oh, don't mention it. And Jasmine seemed to enjoy herself, that was the main thing. She really played well with a couple of the little girls yesterday. I'm going to phone up and see if we can get them round for tea. It would be nice for her to have some play-friends.'

'That's a good idea. Please do that. I don't want her to grow up entirely on her own. It's all a bit difficult, as you know, with her mother away.'

'Jasmine seems much happier in herself than she was a few months ago,' Sandra said. 'She's a highly strung little thing, but that's understandable, and she's sleeping much better too. She still occasionally wakes up in a bit of a state, but then I get up and give her a cuddle and she soon drops off again. I try not to let her disturb you too much.'

'That's very thoughtful of you, but it seriously doesn't matter. I'm just so grateful for all this extra work you do. Would you ever like to take a long weekend or a holiday with Steve or something? I'm sure Jasmine and I could manage on our own for a bit.'

Sandra coloured. 'Actually Steve and I aren't together any more. But thanks just the same.'

'Well, something else then. Could I buy you dinner at a pub one night? There's a great one that does food in Upper Oddington. We could ask Judy to babysit.'

'Well, that would be really nice. I'd love to see more of the area. And my birthday's coming up soon. It'd be a real treat.'

'When's your birthday?'

'Next Thursday.'

'Great, let's do it then. I'll book a table and ring Judy. A birthday dinner at the Fox and Terriers.'

*

The power of suggestion works in mysterious ways, and Anthony was still quite unaware that he had started to think of Sandra in a new light. Maybe it was Lex's ribald recommendation that first planted the seed, or it could have been her smile or the white blouse stretched tight across her breasts; but, little by little, he became conscious he found Sandra distinctly attractive. Perhaps he had always fancied her (he remembered his first sight of her, climbing out of Steve's car) or was this simply revisionist lust? There was something clean and uncomplicated about her; her thick blonde hair smelt of lemon shampoo, and she was always cheerful and optimistic. On sunny days she exclaimed at how much she adored sunshine, and gave Jasmine her tea at the garden table in the suntrap behind the cottage; when it rained, she said she loved rain, and took Jasmine for walks through the puddles. She loved the narrow strip of garden between Forge Cottage and the millstream, erected a fence to make it safe for Jasmine to play and filled the flowerbeds with seeds bought in packets from the post office. Soon, all kinds of brightly coloured blooms – delphiniums, pansies, holy pokers – sprang from the carefully hoed earth, and miniature radishes and carrots were growing in tidy rows. Jasmine clearly worshipped her, and her first steps were taken that summer on the lawn, tottering towards Sandra's open arms. Several times, as she bent over to tidy up coloured plastic bricks from the grass, Anthony was acutely conscious of Sandra's generous curves, and tantalising glimpses of the lacy white bra, just discernible beneath her shirt. For the first time in months, he felt stirrings of lust.

The Fox and Terriers in Upper Oddington was the only pub for miles around with halfway decent food. While most of the pubs still served up scampi-in-a-basket or gloopy ladlefuls of shepherd's pie, the Fox and Terriers was an embryonic English gastro-inn, owned by an effete Belgian who prided himself on his cellar of French wines and steak with garlic butter, considered daringly exotic at this time. Anthony had eaten there before with Lex and Lex's parents, Scrotum and Rosie Holland, and Lex often declared that if you only got a potential girlfriend across the threshold of the place then you were three-quarters of the way to swinging a leg over.

The car park of the pub was crowded with expensive cars and dirty Land Rovers, and a roar of voices from the bar could be heard from outside. They entered through a stable door covered by a thatched porch, into a low flagstoned room with a crackling fire and fifteen wooden tables. The walls were decorated with foxes' masks mounted on wooden shields and glass cases of stuffed partridges and woodcock, and set along a picture rail were pewter platters and a collection of ornamental boot-scrapers in the shape of hounds, hares and huntsmen.

'What a lovely atmosphere this place has,' Sandra said. 'It's so cosy. It reminds me of a pub near Mum and Dad's called the Ship's Chandler. We went there on Mum's last birthday for a family celebration. They fried your steaks for you at the table in brandy, with flames and everything.'

Anthony and Sandra were shown to a table at the back of the restaurant, set inside the inglenook of a huge disused fireplace. All around them, on the exposed brick walls of the chimney, were copper bedpans and horse brasses. A waitress brought a breadbasket and lit a candle on the table, then invited them to view a blackboard above the bar which featured the day's specialities. As they re-crossed the restaurant, weaving between closely packed tables, Anthony sensed the other diners scanning Sandra with approval.

There was no question, she really did look very fetching that night. In the candlelight, her face glowed soft and rosy, and he hadn't fully appreciated just how good her figure was until she tripped down the cottage stairs in a salmon-pink belted coat, high-heeled boots and a mini skirt, all of which she'd bought specially in Oxford. She had piled her hair up on top of her head in some clever way, and Anthony had never noticed how graceful and slender her neck was; he loved the way the hair at the nape had been drawn upwards, in long golden strands, so her shoulders (which he was fairly certain he'd never seen before) were on show; and the hint of cleavage was alluring too, seeming to offer a preview of things to come. That, anyway, was what Anthony reckoned by the time he'd polished off his second gin and tonic, and had ordered, on the agonised advice of Gervaise Sablon, the proprietor, an expensive bottle of Bordeaux for Sandra's birthday.

'Sandra, I truly don't know how I'd manage without you,' Anthony said, the wine helping loosen his tongue in a torrent of heartfelt gratitude that overrode his English reserve. 'Jasmine and I owe you such a lot. You're so brilliant with her. I can tell she adores you; I'm sure you realise that.'

'She's a sweet little thing, a joy to look after. It's very rewarding.'

'It's not been easy with my wife . . . with my wife leaving me and everything. You being with us, as part of the family, I don't know how we'd have managed otherwise, seriously. You've been like a second mother to Jasmine.'

Sandra went pink, and stared down at her trout with almonds.

'I can never be a substitute for her biological mother, you know, and one shouldn't even try. They taught us that at NNEB – it was part of our coursework. You have to talk about the real mother in these situations, not cut her out. So, you know, when we're out on our little walks together to visit the sheep and the ponies, I always say something to Jasmine about Mummy – to keep her alive inside her little head, and make sure she remembers her.'

'And does she? Remember her, I mean.'

'I think so. Not clearly, of course, but there's a memory there somewhere. She was only a few months old, wasn't she, when your wife . . .'

'Walked out? Yes, Amanda left when Jasmine was three months. She left her on the sofa in a pile of cushions, but you've probably heard about that. More wine?' He tipped the bottle towards her glass.

'I really shouldn't. It goes to my head and especially not with Jasmine to look after tomorrow morning. She wakes so early, little angel.'

'Go on, it's good for you.' He refilled the glass and also his own.

They ate in silence for a while, suddenly awkward, and then Sandra said, 'I don't mean to pry or anything – I know it's none of my business – but I was just wondering about Mrs Anscombe. Your wife, I mean, not your mother. I was wondering when she's going to . . . come back.'

Anthony shrugged. 'Your guess is as good as mine. To be brutally honest, I've no idea. I've spent months wishing she would; it's coming up for a year now, ten months anyway. It's been very difficult.' He drained his glass. 'Sorry, I don't mean to bore you. It's not something I usually talk about.'

'I don't mind if you do. At NNEB they taught us how important it is to share . . .'

'God knows, I don't know what to think half the time. The whole thing's been extraordinary . . . meeting Amanda, getting married so quickly and now this.'

Sandra gazed at him so sympathetically, so full of concern, her eyes seemed to be pricked with tears. 'Were you very much in love with her?'

Anthony smiled ruefully. 'I was, very. It's difficult to describe, quite embarrassing in fact. But if you'll believe me, I *knew*, the minute I saw her . . . it really was love at first sight.'

'Can I ask how you met?'

'Up at the Priory. Most improbably, at a party given by my parents. She walked through the door and . . . I was totally smitten. Even before we'd exchanged one word.'

'That is so romantic,' she exclaimed. 'I love stories like that. Did . . . did Amanda feel the same way too, straight away I mean, like you did?'

'That, Sandra, is truly the million-dollar question. I've mulled over that one endlessly. It was like being in a film, not something I'd ever imagined happening to me. Two people meet at a party and that's it. Instant infatuation.'

'And you started going out together.'

'It wasn't quite that easy. Nothing about Amanda is ever that easy. First I had to follow her down to the south of France. She was on holiday with . . . some boyfriend.' He felt himself flinch. 'So I drove down to . . . claim her.'

'Oh my goodness,' said Sandra. 'That's the most amazing thing I've heard in my whole life. How romantic.' She looked suddenly wistful. 'I only wish something like that could happen to me one day, not that I'm holding my breath.'

'You know something, Sandra? Here's a piece of free advice – if your life is suddenly hit for six by a whirlwind, like mine was with Amanda, proceed with caution. That's the one thing I've learnt from all this. Getting knocked sideways for love is miraculous, amazing, but it might not mean so much in the end. It's like petrol on a bonfire – you get this great blaze of passion, but the fire might not have taken at all, not properly. The logs, I mean. Oh to hell with it, sorry, I'm talking rubbish.'

'But you're still in love with her?'

'Well, yes. Maybe. I think so, probably. Or maybe not. As you can see, I'm hopelessly muddled. I haven't confided this to anyone before – and I'm not sure why I'm telling you now – but I actually thought of killing myself a few months back, I was missing her so much. There didn't seem a lot of point soldiering on without her. But, of course, I could never have gone through with it because of Jasmine. Amanda behaved so strangely sometimes; she was completely unpredictable. You never knew what was going to happen, or even if and when she'd turn up. It's hell being married to someone like that.'

Sandra's face, softened by the candlelight, looked aghast at Anthony's confession, and her voice held real feeling as she murmured, 'I feel so awful you've been going through all this, and here I've been living under the very same roof, never dreaming how you'd suffered or trying to do anything to help. If only I'd known.'

'Actually you've been a star. Just having you around as a normal, well-adjusted, beautiful woman . . .'

Sandra, blushing, said, 'I'm sure I'm very boring compared to Amanda.'

'You're not boring, not boring at all, and even if you were, I prefer it. That's another thing I've come to appreciate – stability, normality. Just waking up in the morning and knowing there's going to be milk in the fridge, and not worrying all the time about Amanda's moods when she's around, or when she isn't around worrying about where she is and what she's up to. I used to spend hours every week on the telephone just trying to track her down. She hated Winchford, you see, hated living there.'

'Mrs Holcombe did mention she was up in town a lot.'

'She was very keen on parties – London parties that is, not Winchford ones. When we were first married, we went to some amazing ones. Everyone wanted to invite her. She has that effect on people . . . on everyone really; that was a big part of the problem.'

They had left the pub and were driving back through Stow-on-the-Wold. Suddenly Anthony was acutely conscious of Sandra in the bucket seat beside him, and so grateful for her sympathetic presence. It seemed to him she was the antidote to everything Amanda represented. Her wholesomeness, loyalty and good sense struck him then as something rare and precious, a White Princess to Amanda's Black Queen. And he knew with an almighty certainty that his life must gravitate towards good values, not bad. In marrying Amanda, he had bound himself to a lifelong commitment, tethered to anxiety and tortured by trickiness, when all the time he should have been teaming up with someone like Sandra.

It was just before the traffic lights outside the White Hart Inn, alongside a bow-fronted antiques shop selling Victorian grandfather clocks, that he leant over and gently began to kiss her.

Sandra's mouth and rounded cheeks felt as soft as butter. Accustomed to Amanda's angularities, for Anthony it was like attaching his lips to a bowl of pink Angel Delight. Her hands and arms, when she wrapped them around his shoulders and tenderly stroked his face, smelt of Johnson's baby lotion.

'We shouldn't be doing this; it's not right,' Sandra whispered, as their kisses became more passionate.

'It feels fine to me, more than fine.'

'But you're my employer. I work for you and I'm older than you.'

'Only three or four years. Nothing.'

'Five, actually. It's my birthday today, remember?'

'Happy birthday, beautiful.'

Then the lights changed to green, and the cars behind began honking at them to move on.

10

There was an awkwardness in the air at Forge Cottage, but it was an awkwardness based upon suppressed expectation, not regret. After their long snog at the traffic lights, Anthony and Sandra had arrived home to relieve Judy the babysitter, and Sandra had said a polite goodnight and retired to her bedroom, firmly shutting the door behind her. Anthony had not attempted to follow. He had been startled by the speed and intensity of events, and wanted time to think it through.

Emerging from the bathroom the next morning, he passed Sandra wearing her baby-blue dressing gown made of some fleecy material, with its dozens of buttons reaching down to the floor, and matching fleecy slippers. She smiled sheepishly. At breakfast, they twice caught themselves staring at each other, blushed and turned away. While helping Jasmine into the straps of her pushchair (a procedure requiring two people since she wriggled so much) their hands touched, and they both pulled back. Instantly regretting it, they allowed their hands to meet again as they tightened her buckles, this time more lingeringly. Over lunch, they smiled openly, and their great secret filled them with a sickening, anxious joy.

Sandra spent much of the afternoon arranging play dates for Jasmine, and Anthony, who had bunked off early from work, watched her with admiration. He liked the quiet, efficient way in which she rang all his neighbours, conferring either with mother or nanny, inviting them over for tea with their children. Amanda had never once made any arrangement for the social life of her daughter, but here was Sandra calling the Nall-Caines at Long Barton to secure Araminta, and the Plunketts at Fyford for Edward, the Elliots at High Dean for Emmy, the Fanes at Steeple Chadlington for Max and the Loxtons at Picton-under-

Wynchwood for the redheaded twins Benedict and Charlotte. Each time she'd set something up, she said, 'We'll look forward to seeing you on the day then. Jasmine will be so excited when I tell her Araminta [or whoever] is coming to play.'

When he took Sandra's evening glass of wine to her in the kitchen, she said, 'Anthony, do you mind if I have a word?'

'Sure.'

'It's about last night. And what happened.'

'I hope you're not about to say you regret it.'

'Nothing like that. But I did want to ask where it leaves us. What I mean is, I'm not sure where we stand now, that's all.'

Anthony looked at her, and at that moment felt not the slightest doubt over where he stood. But he answered, 'All I can say, Sandra, is that I think you're a marvellous girl, and I adored what happened last night, even though it caught us both completely unawares. It all feels so right.'

Sandra said, 'I hope it won't be a bit strange, the two of us living here in the same cottage.' She looked suddenly awkward. 'Anthony, there's one thing I have to make clear.'

'Yes?'

'This is a bit difficult to say, because we don't know how things will develop, but I'm not promiscuous . . . you have to respect that. I never let Steve touch me before we got engaged.' She blushed.

It took Anthony a moment to understand what Sandra was saying.

'I hadn't even realised you and Steve *were* engaged. You never said anything.'

'We kept it a secret. Mum and Dad thought we were too young.'

'Well, listen, of course I won't embarrass you. What matters is that Jasmine is happy, and we'll just see what happens with the other thing. If it's meant – as I think it is – there's no hurry. I wouldn't dream of imposing myself on you. And I hope I'll never do anything to embarrass you, either.'

Sandra stepped away from the oven where she was cooking, eyes shining. 'You're so honourable.'

Anthony laughed. 'Honourable, indeed. I don't think a married man groping the nanny at the traffic lights is particularly honourable, even if he is separated. Well, not exactly separated, more abandoned. Anyway, at least you're not rejecting me out of hand.' He poured himself a drink to join Sandra, and raised his glass. 'To us and to the future – let it be an honourable one.' And they laughed and drank and he kissed her again.

*

It was a Wednesday morning and Anthony had taken some rare time off from the farm. Araminta Nall-Caine, sixteen months old, had come over from the Manor House in Long Barton with her nanny, Joan Warren, known only as Nanny Nall-Caine, to play with Jasmine at Forge Cottage. The two little girls were crawling about on the lawn while the two nannies, with covert competitiveness, coaxed their charges onto their bandy hind legs. Sandra had told Nanny Nall-Caine about Jasmine taking her first steps when she was barely a year old, and Nanny Nall-Caine, determined not to be shown up as the nanny of a late developer, towered over Araminta, hauling her to her feet and attempting to balance her before she collapsed in a heap. With her flame-red curly mop, stroppy emerald eyes and a stubbornness about the jaw, Araminta was a miniature distillation of both halves of her parentage: a Joint Master of the Heythrop hunt and a former beauty assistant on *Queen* magazine.

As he lolled in his deckchair with a can of Carling, the drone of the bees in his ears as they hovered above Sandra's marigolds, Anthony felt more contented than at any time for several years. Surreptitiously, he watched Sandra encouraging the two baby girls to interact. Sandra was an ardent advocate of interaction as a key stage in the development process. Anthony thought how pretty her soft, sweet face looked as she crouched on the lawn between the children, and how good her legs were in shorts.

Sandra was saying, 'Why, hello Miss Jasmine! Have you met Miss Araminta yet? Have you two young ladies been properly introduced? Now why don't you shake hands with Araminta, Jasmine; there you are, I'll help you. Say "How do you do, Araminta." And, "How do you do, Jasmine." That's right.'

Nanny Nall-Caine, who had imagined the play date would be up at Winchford Priory, and was distinctly unimpressed by Forge Cottage, which reminded her of the cottage in which she had grown up outside Kettering, had slipped into the farrier's yard for a furtive cigarette.

At the front of the cottage, Anthony heard a car door slam. It crossed his mind that it might be his mother; recently, Henrietta had taken to dropping in unannounced. He wondered whether she was on to anything between himself and Sandra (her antennae for unsuitable matches in Winchford was acute) or whether she had simply found in Sandra a pliable new audience. He knew Henrietta had a high opinion of her, because she recently declared, 'Your new nanny is quite a success; you must try not to lose her. She's not a bad-looking girl, either. I was watching her in church, and was thinking that if one didn't know better, she really looks quite good class.'

'Anthony? Ant? Is anyone about?'

He knew that voice. With a frisson of fear and excitement, he darted to his feet. 'Amanda?'

And there she stood, on the strip of lawn outside their nuptial nest . . . and she was glorious: bathed in sunshine, with her back to the cottage, gazing about her with her huge kohl-rimmed eyes. She looked younger and sexier than ever in tight white cotton trousers and a white lace kaftan top. She exuded an exotic beauty and sexiness that seemed out of place in the neat cottage garden. She smiled, and he knew in that second that nothing had changed.

'Amanda? This is amazing – I had no idea you were coming. You didn't tell me.'

'We were in Oxford. We just decided to come over on the spur of the moment. I wanted to see you – and Jasmine, of course.'

We? She couldn't have brought Charlie Edwards to Forge Cottage, could she?

'Patrice drove me over. He's parking the car, re-parking it I should say. We'd parked outside but your mother saw us and made him move it.'

'My mother's here too?'

'Don't worry, she's not staying. She took one look at me, snorted, and stormed off. Didn't even say hello. *Plus ça change*: she always hated me, the old boot.'

Anthony felt half paralysed with love. His breath quickened and he could think of nothing to say. He stared dumbly at his wife, overwhelmed by the violence with which he had missed her. Eventually he said, 'You must say hello to Jasmine. She's over there on the lawn. She has a friend over to play.'

'*That* is Jasmine? She's so big, I didn't recognise her. You never said she'd grown so much.'

Anthony wanted to say, 'How could I? You disappeared.' Instead he said, 'She's one now. We had a birthday party for her. Oh, and thank you for those lovely dresses you sent.'

'She isn't wearing one, I notice.'

'Not for playing. Sandra says they're too good for every day.'

'That's exactly when you should wear them. Every day. It's only the bourgeois who keep clothes back for special occasions.'

Then she strolled over to where Jasmine was playing with Sandra and, ignoring the nanny, asked, 'Have you missed Mummy, Jazz-pot, while she's been away in Paris? No answer. Well that's not surprising, I suppose.' Turning to Sandra she said, 'Can she speak?'

'A few words. She can say Da-da and baa-baa, which is her word for the little lambs she loves visiting.'

'And you are, by the way?' asked Amanda. 'I'm Amanda, Anthony's wife.'

'Sandra Potts. Jasmine's nanny. I look after her.'

Observing the exchange, Anthony saw Sandra stiffen. Her hostility to Amanda was obvious, to Anthony anyway, and presumably to Amanda too. Worse than that, he could feel Sandra diminishing before his eyes. Next to Amanda, her English rose prettiness seemed commonplace and bland. It was like seeing a sugary watercolour next to a vivid oil painting. Everything which, only twenty minutes earlier, he had found wholesome and appealing in Sandra now seemed wishy-washy and insipid alongside his smouldering wife.

Just then, a tall and self-consciously rugged male appeared in the cottage garden. He looked thirty-eight, perhaps forty, Anthony reckoned, a strikingly big man with big shoulders, a big head covered by thick black hair, a sardonic lived-in face and heavy lidded eyes. In profile, his nose was huge and Roman, his face suntanned and unshaven; he wore jeans and some kind of combat jacket with numerous small pockets. For some reason, Anthony felt he had seen him before.

'This is Patrice,' Amanda said lightly.

'Anthony Anscombe.' Anthony crossed the lawn and shook hands.

The man – Patrice – said something in French and exhaled loudly, as though expelling some slight boredom at being there.

Anthony regarded him, wondering what he was to Amanda. Her driver? Friend? Lover?

'You were in Oxford, I hear?' Anthony said.

Patrice looked weary at the thought of answering such a dull question and blew. 'Yes, from Oxford. We are staying at some old Brit-eesh hotel, not so special. The Randolph, I think it is called.'

'The Randolph's meant to be quite good. Oxford's best, apparently.'

Patrice shrugged, implying he could just about tolerate it, though no more than that, and had no wish to pursue the conversation.

Anthony longed to be alone with Amanda; there was so much he needed to say to her, though at that precise moment he couldn't think what. He could see Sandra sitting at the tea table with Jasmine, Araminta and Nanny Nall-Caine, glowering at Amanda, who was standing some distance away on the garden path, lighting up a Gitane. Anthony felt disconcerted, too, by Patrice's mention of the hotel, with its implication that he and Amanda were travelling as a couple.

Amanda said, 'Is there such a thing as a cup of tea, or better still, a drink?'

They went into the kitchen and she said, 'You've had the painters in.

The place looks different. Ant, tell me you're not responsible for that hideous bluebell frieze? Promise me you're not.'

He laughed. 'Not guilty. That was Jasmine. Well, mostly Sandra actually. She's very keen on that sort of craft thing, she's forever making things with Jasmine.'

'It really is a shocker. Rather you than me having to see it every morning.'

He found an open bottle of wine and poured her a glass. 'Does your friend want one too?'

'Patrice? Sure. Though he won't think much of the vintage,' she said, looking at the label. 'He's French, ergo a wine snob. Best not give him much in any case; if he drinks one glass he'll want ten. He's virtually alcoholic.'

'His face is familiar. He wasn't at one of those London parties we went to?'

'You've seen him at the cinema – he's an actor. Patrice Bouillon. Quite well known, in Europe especially. You remember the movie we saw that time in Camden? *L'Oiseau d'or*. He was in that.'

'The French film with subtitles? The one I kept nodding off in. God, yes, he played the homicidal farmhand obsessed with the Viscount's niece, or her reflection in the lake or something. That awful film – no wonder I remember him; he was almost the only actor in it.' Anthony felt momentarily bucked up that Patrice Bouillon had been part of such a crashingly dull entertainment, then remembered Patrice was probably sleeping with his wife.

'Amanda – you and Patrice. Is there anything I ought to know?'

'Is he my lover, you mean? Honestly Anthony, I've only been here ten minutes and you're cross-questioning me. Well, what do you think? He's old enough to be my father.'

Anthony felt a rush of relief.

Amanda went on, 'He isn't my type, darling, not in the long run. I might be getting a small part in his next film; there's a possibility, anyway. And we're kind of together for now. That's all.'

'Last time I heard, you were back with Charlie.'

'Oh, Charlie.' Amanda dismissed him with a roll of the eyes. 'That was never really anything. He's a pest. I heard you turned up looking for me in Paris, by the way.'

'And found Charlie instead.'

'I wish you hadn't just turned up,' Amanda sighed. 'If you'd told me you were coming, I'd have organised something. Shown you some of the hotspots.'

'For heaven's sake, Amanda, I hadn't the faintest idea where you were. You walked out, remember – on me and our daughter – you didn't even say where you were going.'

She came up to him and pulled his hands into her own. 'We can't talk about this here, not now. Not with Patrice skulking around and that nanny of yours, the one who looks like she wants to murder me. What's Elsie the Cow's problem, anyway? Have you been spreading malicious stories about me?'

Anthony shook his head. 'You know I'd never do that.'

'I do know,' Amanda said. 'Neither of us would ever betray each other, because of our special bond.'

'Our special bond.' Anthony repeated the words ironically. 'So much for the special bond. You left me.'

'I had to get away. I needed space; I told you that. But I never stopped loving you, not for one minute, and I never will. Just as you will never stop loving me. We made a pledge – you accepted my dare.'

There was a sound of clanking china in the passage, and Sandra and Nanny Nall-Caine came into the kitchen carrying tea trays.

Amanda whispered urgently, 'What are you doing tomorrow? In the morning. About eleven o'clock.'

'Nothing particularly.'

'Come to the Randolph. Room sixteen. It's on the first floor. Up the main staircase, turn left, and right down to the end of the corridor. Then we'll be on our own.'

Before Anthony could reply, Sandra was banging down a tray piled with plates, teacups and the remains of a coffee and walnut cake, and Patrice's big French head was looming at the kitchen window.

'I have to go,' Amanda said. Then, without further words with her husband or any farewell for her daughter, she hurried off with Patrice.

The room seemed darker and colder after she'd gone, as though the sun had been covered by cloud, and Anthony went upstairs to fetch a jersey.

11

He set off for the Randolph determined to resolve things with Amanda. Her reappearance at Forge Cottage had provoked an intense inner turmoil that left him exhausted; he had found his reaction irresponsible and almost mad. What did he think he was doing, falling for her all over again? She had walked out of their marriage, barely leaving a note. She hadn't spoken to him or Jasmine for more than ten months. He must be insane to imagine they could have any future together. All evening he had endured Sandra's unspoken disapproval.

The drive to Oxford took him through some of the loveliest villages in Britain; the trees and hedgerows were bursting into life. He had drawn back his bedroom curtains that morning and counted sixteen hen pheasants in the oilseed rape field across the millpond, and at least four cock pheasants strutting along the grass margins of the copse. Sandra had looked a little wistful at breakfast, and Anthony regretted his mean-minded comparison of her with Amanda. Watching her feed Jasmine with spoonfuls of banana, he was reminded what a kind, maternal person she was, and recognised with a stab of self-reproach that her pretty modesty was worth far more than Amanda's self-centred histrionics.

And yet, as he approached the outskirts of Oxford, he felt giddy with anticipation. He parked in a car park behind the hotel and walked round to the main entrance. The lobby was full of people, mostly men, wearing plastic name badges; delegates at some medical conference. A table laid with coffee cups and percolators had been set up on a swirling patterned carpet. Pushing through the throng, Anthony found the staircase and headed up to the first floor. Following arrows towards number sixteen, through half a dozen fire doors that whooshed shut behind him, he found the room and knocked. For a moment, he was reminded of the

Hôtel Petit Trianon in Paris, and half expected Patrice Bouillon – or indeed Charlie – to open the door in a bath towel, but this time it was Amanda, wearing men's pyjamas and a hotel bathrobe with the words Randolph Hotel and the badge of Oxford University emblazoned on the breast.

Precariously balanced on a coffee table was the remains of a hardly touched cooked breakfast for two: scrambled eggs, a basket of croissants and several miniature pots of apricot jam and honey. Elsewhere, Anthony could see further evidence of dual occupancy, including two large leather bags, presumably Patrice's, and a sturdy pair of laced hiking boots which looked size twelve or fourteen.

Following his gaze, Amanda said, 'Don't worry. He's out visiting some people. He won't be back till three or four at the earliest. Later if he drinks.'

Anthony sat in an armchair and said, 'Amanda, we need to talk.'

She smiled. 'I love it when you become all serious. You look seven years old – so sweet. I'm sure we don't *need* to do anything, but let's talk if you want. What do you want to talk about?'

'Well, us. And Jasmine. What's going to happen to her – and to us?'

Amanda stared with a quizzical innocence that made his heart lurch. 'To us? Like what exactly?'

'Well, our marriage, of course. You walked out. You disappeared to Paris and never got in touch. I've been trying my best to look after Jasmine, but it can't go on like this, all this uncertainty. Either we're married ... or we're not married. Then there's Charlie and this French movie star or whatever he is. You can't just go off with other men; it doesn't work like that.'

Amanda, who had been sitting on the bed, came to him and perched on the armchair and draped her feet across his thighs. 'Darling Ant, do you remember that raft at the villa in France? During the storm? The waves crashing over us, and the raft tipping, and we thought it might flip over completely or be lifted out of the sea and blown into the middle of the ocean?'

'Yes.'

'And how afterwards – after the storm was over – we felt closer than ever. Making love on the raft, knowing how dangerous it was, the waves pounding and the taste of salt and everything, just screwing on the raging ocean.'

Anthony nodded. He was remembering how the raft had jerked against the rusted chain, and Amanda's glistening skin, as she had tugged down her swimsuit and pulled him inside her for the first time.

'You see, we'll never forget that, not in our whole lives. So when you ask, "What's going to happen next?" I don't know the answer to that question. Don't ask for things I can't give you. Don't ask me to come and live with you again in that musty cottage. Not now. Maybe some day in the future but, Christ, not now. It'll never work, we both know that. Ask me for things I can give you.'

'Such as?'

'Such as . . . anything you like. We have four hours until Patrice comes back. We could have lunch somewhere. We could walk along the river and see the colleges. Or we could make love.'

Anthony looked to see if she was joking, and she stared at him, like a challenge. 'I'd like . . . the third option,' he replied. 'I'd like that a lot, if that's really okay.'

'Why shouldn't it be okay? We *are* married.'

In the passage they heard the rattle of the housekeeper's trolley approaching to service the room, so Anthony put his arm round the door and hung the Do Not Disturb sign on the handle, and by the time he turned round again Amanda was naked on the bedclothes. The sight of her made him gasp – she was so ravishing.

For three and a half hours they made love in room sixteen and it seemed to Anthony that he had never felt closer to his wife than during that time. He was seized by an intensity bordering on madness. He adored her. Afterwards, sensing that Patrice might shortly return and that his status as Amanda's husband was insufficient excuse to get caught in their room, he hurriedly dressed and gathered up his car keys.

'Amanda, you sure you won't come back to Winchford? I really would love you to.' He was imploring her.

She shook her head. 'Anything else, but I can't live with you.'

'And Jasmine?'

'Take good care of her for me.'

'On my own?'

'You need a wife.'

'I have a wife.'

'You should get married to someone else. I was never the perfect wife, we both know that. Choose someone more suitable next time. I'm sure your mother can help.' She laughed. 'I'm not joking, I'm being helpful.'

Anthony looked at her and said, 'I'll never, ever find someone like you.'

'You don't need to. You have me already.'

Part Three

12

The engagement between Anthony John Fenwick Anscombe of Winchford Priory, Oxfordshire, and Sandra Lauraine Potts of Poole, Dorset, was announced in both *The Times* and the *Daily Telegraph.*

There were several at the time who voiced misgivings about the match, among them Percy and Jacinthe Bigges, who felt it was only the other day that Anthony had produced his first wife for general inspection, and Lex, who told his friend straight out that marriage was a ridiculous over-reaction, and if he intended marrying every girl he went to bed with he'd end up with untold numbers of wives. On the plus side, Anthony's parents came out strongly behind the marriage, as did Mrs Holcombe and Judy, who considered Sandra to be 'streets better than that lazy scrubber Amanda,' and said as much to everyone in the Plough and Harrow. Detecting a certain disapproval from Jacinthe, Henrietta insisted to her neighbour she was 'delighted' by the turn of events. 'I don't suppose we shall have a great deal in common with Sandra's parents,' she conceded, 'but she's the sweetest girl, in her lovely, unaffected way, and of course it's going to be such a godsend for Anthony having a supportive little wife around who is actually prepared to take on the first one's child. Not everyone would do that.'

Elsewhere in the county, the engagement provoked diverse reactions. The Rev. Jeremy Meek, having missed out on Anthony's first wedding, was hugely excited at the prospect of conducting the second one at All Hallowes; he hand-delivered a postcard to Forge Cottage, offering his services and reassuring the happy couple he could see no reason not to sanctify the union in church, whatever the unfortunate prior circumstances. He eagerly looked forward to seeing Anthony in his morning coat, and anticipated many cosy pre-nuptial tutorials, with or without the bride-to-be. Old Walter Twine commented 'that young Anthony has quite an eye for the ladies,' and that 'this latest one, the blonde, with a little more flesh on her than the other one, is not a bad looker either.' From the county neighbours – the Nall-Caines, Plunketts, Elliots, Loxtons and Fanes – messages of congratulations poured in, for everyone instinctively liked Anthony, though they did confide to one another that it was all a little hasty, and they did hope it would work out this time with, er, Sandra. The word 'rebound' was uttered more than once. Nanny Nall-Caine, taking the bull by the horns, declared it was all wrong Mr Anscombe becoming engaged to the nanny, and said she had always had her doubts about that Sandra, the scheming little minx, who had set her cap at him from the beginning.

For Anthony, the greatest obstacle lay in telling Amanda, whose latest telephone number in Paris he had had the foresight to obtain on that torrid afternoon at the Randolph. Even while he was proposing to Sandra during a picnic on the summit of Steepness Hill, with Jasmine strapped into her pushchair to allow them some peace, he was wondering how best to break the news to his present wife. It had been an extraordinarily still August afternoon, with the temperature way up into the eighties and no hint of breeze. Not a leaf fluttered on the boughs of the oak; nothing seemed to move apart from a pair of pale-yellow Brimstone butterflies darting between clumps of nettles. Sandra was wearing a yellow sundress, the fine hairs on her arms bleached golden by sunshine.

'Is Jasmine sleeping?' Anthony whispered. His daughter's dark head was slumped forward against her chest, restrained by the straps of the pushchair.

Sandra went to look. 'Yes, fast asleep in her buggy, bless her heart. It's this hot weather; it makes everyone drowsy. I've put her little sunhat back on, but she does hate it so – she keeps pulling it off.'

They leant back against a fallen tree trunk, overlooking the valley which stretched for a mile to the rising slope. From here, Winchford village was almost hidden, with only a few rooftops and the spire of All Hallowes marking the place; nestling halfway up the hill lay Winchford Priory, bathed in late-afternoon sunshine. They could see the mishmash of Elizabethan elevations and chimneys, and the flat section of the roof with its four corner turrets, then the brutal Victorian additions that housed the kitchens and billiards room, and the drive with its avenue of horse chestnuts sweeping down to the village.

'I always think the big house looks rather dramatic from up here,' Anthony said. 'Better at this distance than closer up.'

'It's a beautiful place,' Sandra said. 'So much history.'

'It's always seemed a bit of a monstrosity to me. And freezing in winter. Of course it didn't help we were never allowed any heating.'

'That's one thing Mum and Dad really insist on,' Sandra said. 'Our home is always toasty – they turn the dial right up. Dad re-plumbed the whole property himself, top to bottom. We have the biggest electric-fired boiler in Poole, Dad says.'

'Maybe one day, if Winchford comes to me, I can cheer it up a bit. It's a house that needs people to bring it alive. Big log fires and, as you say, a lot of central heating.'

'It must cost a fortune heating a place like that. I dread to think.'

'That's why my parents never do. They wear three jerseys and an over-coat instead. I'm not joking. I've seen my father sitting down to Sunday lunch wearing a jersey, jacket, Barbour and old tweed coat on top. He can't bring himself to shell out for oil. A few times they've turned up the radiators for a party and you can see the oil gauge going down. You can literally watch the level nose-diving.'

'If you do move in to that house, it needs a good lick of paint, too,' Sandra said. 'I hope you don't mind me saying, but your parents like the gloomiest colours. All those greys and browns in the living room.'

'They've hardly changed the place since my grandfather's time and I don't think he did much either.' He made a face. 'Is it me, or are you totally boiled? I've never known it this hot in England, ever. It's like the south of France.'

'I'd like weather like this all year round,' Sandra said. 'There's some really good beaches round Mum and Dad's. We used to take a picnic dinner over to Sandbanks and spend the whole day there in a heatwave.' She lay back on the grass with her face towards the sun, and closed her eyes in rapture. Watching her, and the dappled sunshine playing across her cheeks, Anthony again thought how lovely she was, and how relaxed he felt around her. There was no pressure, no anxiety. Here they all were at the top of Steepness Hill on a perfect English summer's day, with Jasmine dozing peacefully under the tree, and Sandra sunbathing sweetly on the grass. It was idyllic. He was sufficiently self aware to recognise that whenever he was with Amanda, any fleeting moment of joy was rewarded by months of despair; with Sandra, a sustained level of low-key happiness was the natural order of things.

'Sandra?' He said her name tentatively, in case she had dropped off.

'Mmm?'

'Sandra, there's something I want to ask you.'

She rolled onto her side and opened her eyes. 'Yes? What is it?'

'Does the idea of getting married to someone who's been married already, and made a complete hash of it first time round, hold any appeal?'

For a moment she stared at him dumbly, trying to work out what he meant, before replying, 'Is that . . . a proposal of marriage?'

Anthony nodded. 'Look, if the idea fills you with complete horror, I won't be offended. It just seemed . . . rather a perfect idea, that's all. Certainly from my point of view . . .'

'Shouldn't you be going down on one knee first to ask for a lady's hand? Steve went down on one knee when we became engaged. We were in a Harvester restaurant and everyone in the place applauded.'

Anthony, who had never been able to summon much curiosity about Sandra's stint with Corporal Steve, and hardly regarded him as the benchmark for correct etiquette, nevertheless knelt down between the sheep droppings and said, 'Sandra, I would really love it if you would marry me.'

'Thank you for your proposal,' Sandra replied, rather stiffly. 'And after due consideration I accept with great pleasure.'

Anthony gave a whoop of delight and seconds later opened the bottle of warm champagne he'd concealed, earlier that day, inside the hollow tree, and they toasted their future while Sandra's eyes filled with tears of happiness.

'I can't wait to phone up Mum – she's going to be over the moon,' she said. 'I've been telling her all about you, but she kept warning me not to get too excited. Dad thought you'd never ask.'

'Well, that just shows how wrong your parents were,' Anthony said. 'And I shall tell them so when we meet. By the way, do you think I should be asking your father's permission or something? You don't think he'll object? He might not like the idea of his daughter marrying a divorced man.'

'We can phone them up tonight,' Sandra said. 'Dad's going to be really happy for us; they'll be off celebrating. Knowing Dad, he'll open up a very special bottle of champagne. He loves his bubbles, any excuse.'

Seizing the moment while Jasmine remained asleep, and the permission implicit in their sudden engagement, Anthony and Sandra made love for the first time behind the fallen tree. Having only ever done it before with Amanda, whose underwear was habitually a dingy shade of grey, Anthony was almost dazzled by the snowy whiteness of Sandra's; her whole body was so clean and pink and smooth, like an inflatable boat, only soft and pliant. With Amanda, sex had been earthy and dirty, with an edge of danger. With Sandra, it was marvellously wholesome and sanitary. Her face became pinker and pinker like a boiled langoustine, and her skin, which had been soaking up sunshine, radiated heat. Afterwards, for the first time in his life, Anthony felt no trace of sleaziness; making love with Sandra was exactly that, an act of love, the most natural and untainted experience imaginable. At long last, he felt himself free of the shadow of Amanda.

Nevertheless, the following morning, when Sandra nipped out to the village shop with Jasmine in her pushchair, Anthony dialled Amanda's number in Paris to break the news. He heard the French ringing tone for almost a minute and was about to give up when Patrice answered. Soon afterwards, Amanda came on the line, sounding sleepy.

Nervously, Anthony told her about his engagement, and explained he would need to ask her for a divorce.

'OK,' Amanda replied. 'If you want me to sign any papers or anything, Patrice and I should be coming back to Oxford soon. Maybe we can meet up at the Randolph.'

Anthony had no intention of meeting Amanda alone at the Randolph, but felt a shiver of excitement at the prospect.

'Who are you marrying?' Amanda asked.

'She's called Sandra Potts.'

'Well, come on, what's she like? Prettier than her name, I hope.'

'Yes, very pretty. What can I tell you? She's blonde, kind, loyal, really good with Jasmine – and that's important.'

'Where did you meet?'

'Actually at Forge Cottage. She's been looking after Jasmine.'

'Not the big blonde nanny who stencilled those flowers round the kitchen ceiling? Heavens, Ant, you sure this is such a good idea?'

'Utterly sure, actually. Sandra's fantastic. She's one of the nicest people I've ever met.' Anthony was affronted Amanda should question his choice of wife; it wasn't as if she'd exactly excelled in the position herself. 'She's going to be perfect. I can't think of anyone I'd rather be marrying.' He realised he sounded defensive.

'Don't get me wrong, I think she sounds like a . . . very sensible choice,' Amanda said. 'I hope she knows how lucky she is, marrying you. Will you invite me to the wedding?'

'Come off it. That wouldn't be very appropriate.'

'I don't see why not. I am probably your closest friend. But I realise my delightful mother-in-law, ex-mother-in-law I should say, would have kittens if I showed up. So I'll just have to be there in spirit, won't I?'

*

Henrietta understood it was her duty to ask Sandra's parents, Leonard and Marjorie Potts, to Saturday lunch at Winchford Priory at the earliest suitable opportunity. Although she had no expectation of enjoying the visit, she wanted to get her invitation in quickly, ahead of Sandra's parents, since she had no wish to cross half of England to the Dorset coast, which was so inconvenient for Oxfordshire. To invite the Pottses to Winchford was the lesser of two evils, and certainly more interesting, in any case, for them to come here than vice versa. She knew nothing about Sandra's parents, beyond the fact that Leonard Potts owned an electrical business. In her haughty way, Henrietta looked forward to putting them at their ease, as the full extent of their daughter's advantageous marriage sank in. She duly received a charming notelet from Sandra's mother, Marjorie, with a line-drawing of a hedgehog on the front, thanking her for the invitation and asking if it would be all right if Sandra's sister, Ginette, came along too, since she would be home that weekend from nursing college.

At quarter past twelve on Saturday, a highly polished maroon Ford Zodiac pulled up outside the mullioned façade of the Priory. Anthony and Sandra were already at the big house; Sandra had been helping Mrs Holcombe lay the dining room table with the better silver and armorial sauceboats Henrietta insisted upon. At Henrietta's suggestion, Jasmine had been parked on Judy for the afternoon. 'I can't believe Sandra's poor parents want to see your children from previous marriages,' Henrietta remarked. 'Not the first time they meet us all, anyway. Agree with me, Sandra.'

'Well, I'm sure they wouldn't mind,' Sandra said. 'They've heard so much about Jasmine from me.'

'No, it would be entirely inappropriate,' Henrietta said firmly. 'Much better leave her with Judy. She's not ready to eat with us in the dining room in any case.'

Sandra looked particularly juicy that day, Anthony thought, in a new summer dress they'd chosen together in Cheltenham. With each hour that passed, he felt more sure of his decision to remarry quickly; to have so dependable and good-natured a fiancée, who made everything so pleasant for him, was a wonderful and novel experience. Although slightly apprehensive about the impending parents' lunch, he looked forward to meeting Len and Marjorie and Ginette, all of whom Sandra so evidently adored. As the Pottses' car drew up outside, they hurried out to greet them.

Len Potts could not have been taller than five foot three; Anthony towered a good thirteen inches above him. Nevertheless, there was something unmistakably impressive about him. His shoulders were wide and strong, and his hair, which Anthony at first suspected might be a toupée, was thick, black and springy; the parting, spirit-level straight, reminded him of the plastic rim of a car seat. His teeth were enormous and unnaturally white, quite unlike Henrietta's or Godfrey's teeth, which were slightly yellow and broken down.

'Now, you must be the lucky young fellow who wants to wed our Sandra,' Len said, extending a meaty hand. He was dressed in a well-pressed pair of grey flannel trousers, shirt and tie, and a caramel-coloured suede jerkin with a zip.

'And you must be Sandra's mother,' Anthony said, greeting an immaculate, perky lady with blonde hair in a neat beehive, a smart blue suit and matching handbag and shoes.

Extracting herself with difficulty from the rear seat of the Ford Zodiac was an ample twenty year old, evidently Ginette, who was the spitting image of Sandra, only grossly fat, with a swollen pink face, swollen ankles and swollen fingers. Delighted at seeing her family, Sandra hugged them affectionately, as endless congratulations were exchanged on their engagement. Len said, 'Your mother and I couldn't get over it when you phoned and told us. We had no idea anything like this was on the cards. What a dark horse you are, Sandra; you kept it all very quiet.'

'It has all happened rather quickly,' Anthony said. 'I hope you're not too shocked. I feel incredibly lucky to be marrying your daughter.'

'Ah, you say that now,' Len replied jovially. 'But will you still be saying it in twenty years' time, when you've discovered what she's really like?' And then Sandra said, 'Oh, Dad,' and punched him lightly on the arm, and Len said, 'Only kidding, princess. I'm sure Anthony knows exactly how fortunate he is. Now, where's that champagne I brought as a gift for Anthony's parents?' And he produced, from the boot of the car, a bottle of Cristal in a special cellophane-wrapped box.

They trooped inside to the Great Hall and through into a room known as the white drawing room. North facing, sun-starved and rigidly formal, it was seldom used from one year to the next. A pair of silk-covered sofas were arranged on either side of an Adam fireplace, at such a distance from each other it was impossible to talk naturally between them. Most of one wall was taken up by a Georgian breakfront cabinet, containing a collection of bone china plates with maroon and gold edges. The shelves of the cabinet were, in theory at least, lit up by a dozen oblong electric lightbulbs, but half had blown long ago, and several others flickered disconcertingly. The six Victorian sash windows were flanked by brittle-looking blue moiré curtains, in which the fabric had sheared away from the lining, exposing bald areas of netting. These curtains could never be drawn since they would have crumbled like perished parchment. Dotted elsewhere around the white drawing room were numerous spindly pieces of mahogany furniture – chairs, nests of tables and stools – some wildly valuable, others too fragile to be used – their legs buckled and splintered by the antique Hoover with which Mrs Holcombe cheerfully biffed them twice a week.

Henrietta and Godfrey stood graciously at the furthest end of the room to receive their son's future in–laws. With her hair puffed up like a guardsman's bearskin, and a fixed, slightly condescending smile, Henrietta took two small steps in the direction of the approaching group, a gesture towards meeting them halfway. Godfrey, meanwhile, who had a lifelong prejudice against meeting new people, began messing nervously around a tray of drinks, double-checking there was ice inside the ice bucket, and inspecting the numerous small bottles of Britvic tomato juice and tonic water.

Len bounded across the room, almost crushing Henrietta's bony outstretched hand in his own. 'Well, this is a nice excuse for a celebration, isn't it? Marjorie and I are tickled pink about the whole thing. I've only this minute met Ant for the first time, but he seems a pleasant young man. I reckon he's going to do for our Sandra. I think he passes the test.'

Henrietta, who hadn't exactly imagined that Anthony, the eventual owner of Winchford, was about to be turned down by the nanny, smiled thinly. 'I hope the journey didn't take too long, Mr Potts. The traffic can be quite busy at weekends, I believe.'

'Oh, please call me Len. No formality now we're to be family. We're Len and Marjorie to all and sundry. We were on a cruise recently up the Norwegian fjords. I don't know whether you've ever done one, but I can recommend it – excellent food, lovely staterooms. Anyway, the captain of this floating gin palace, he started up with all this 'Mr Potts this, Mrs Potts that', and I told him firmly we were Len and Marjorie. I don't mind whether it's the Queen of England, it's first names from day one.'

Registering a nano-second of pain, Henrietta replied, 'I do agree, it's all becoming much less stuffy these days. And by all means call me Henrietta, if you would prefer to. And my husband is Godfrey.'

'Hello, Godfrey,' said Len. 'That's a very serious-looking bar you've got set up over there. Marjorie and I have brought along a little contribution.' He handed over the gift box of Cristal, in which the bottle sat like a yellow missile in its satin-lined trench. 'I don't know whether or not you're a big Cristal fan, Godfrey, but for me it's the king of champagnes. I was first introduced to it at a little local hostelry where we were celebrating our wedding anniversary. The sommelier said, "Go on, Len, try this one. I personally recommend it." One sip and I wouldn't touch anything else. For me, it's got to be Cristal every time.'

Anthony and Sandra circulated with dishes of peanuts and Cheeselets while Ginette, having asked for a white wine and been told there was none open, sipped at a Cointreau on the rocks. Marjorie was telling Henrietta about a recent holiday to Reid's hotel in Madeira, and how two pieces of her luggage had never turned up on the carousel, so the next morning Len had told her to replace everything at the hotel boutiques, but at least it had all been in escudos and the insurance company reimbursed most of it.

Henrietta quickly understood that the Pottses' electrical business was more successful than she'd imagined, and wondered whether this was a good or a bad thing. Across the room, she could hear Len telling Godfrey about it. It seemed he had the exclusive right to sell Creda and Hotpoint dishwashers and ovens across large swathes of the south-west of England – he was referring to them as 'white goods' – and apparently employed more than two hundred people 'on the books'. Half listening to Len, and half tuned into Sandra's fat sister, Ginette, who was describing her course as a student paediatric nurse, Henrietta wondered whether they quite appreciated how fortunate they were to be forging links with Winchford.

They went into lunch, where Godfrey set about carving a leg of lamb at the sideboard. Len expressed amazement he wasn't using an electric carving knife. 'I'll tell you what I'm going to do, Godfrey, I'm going to have one sent over to you first thing next week. You tell me if it isn't the business. You're going to kick yourself you didn't get one years ago.' Henrietta, who had a hatred of the chainsaw whirr of electric carving knives, gritted her teeth.

Sitting on Godfrey's right, Marjorie was confiding her delight at the engagement. 'When Sandra told us she had met this man who'd been married before, and had a child already, of course we had our reservations. No mother could help feeling a little disappointed. But having met Anthony, he's such a charming young man, all my worries have just flown away.'

Godfrey, psychologically unequal to intimate conversations or soul baring, nodded perfunctorily, and passed around the sauceboats of mint sauce and redcurrant jelly.

'Don't get me wrong,' Marjorie went on. 'I'm not saying we were unhappy about the situation, even before we met Anthony. Sandra's a lovely responsible girl, and anyone she produced would be fine by us. But we got on like a house on fire with her former fiancé, Steve, so we did wonder what the new one would be like.'

Recoiling slightly at Len's unselfconscious account of his recent cosmetic dentistry, which had involved capping all his upper teeth ('I could give you the number if you like. Lovely little surgery – nothing's too much trouble'), Henrietta turned the conversation to the wedding itself. 'I hope you won't mind very much if it takes place here at All Hallowes in the village. It would be so disappointing for our local parson if it didn't; I feel it's so important we all support the parish.'

Marjorie said, 'We're not great churchgoers as a rule, but I do enjoy a nice wedding. And Ginette's set her heart on being a bridesmaid, haven't you, Ginette? We were just saying in the car, "This is your big chance, Ginette." She's always wanted to be maid of honour to her sister.'

Henrietta, who had envisaged rather younger bridesmaids and pages of her own choosing, rather than the lumpy paediatric nurse, said, 'Yes, that might be a lovely idea,' in a syrupy noncommittal voice.

'If the ceremony is to take place up here,' said Len, 'and very nice too, I do insist on paying for the wedding breakfast. That's for the bride's family to do. So all you good ladies need to put your heads together – Marjorie, Henrie and Sandra – and let me know what you're planning, and I'll take it from there with the suppliers. We do a lot of business with caterers, so I'll get trade terms on everything.'

Marjorie said, 'I can't get over the thought of Sandra as a married lady. It seems only yesterday Len and I were going up the aisle ourselves.'

'Which year did you and Godfrey tie the knot then, Henrie?' Len asked Henrietta.

'We married in nineteen forty-eight, June, here at Winchford,' Henrietta replied. 'Godfrey was just out of uniform.'

'We were nineteen forty-seven,' Len said. 'One year ahead of you.' Watching his future father-in-law across the table, Anthony realised Len was competitive in everything, and began to wish the lunch would not go on for much longer. He felt a sensation of being trapped, something he had often felt before in his parents' dining room. He tried talking to Marjorie, but found it hard to concentrate. Her perky, bright face was telling him things, he nodded and laughed, but his mind kept drifting away to Amanda's room at the Randolph. Taking a firm grip on himself, he tuned back in while staring at Sandra across the table, who looked so sweet and dependable. No, he was certain he had made the right decision. Sandra was wonderful with Jasmine and, besides, he loved her.

At the end of lunch, Henrietta pressed a bell fixed to the underside of the table, and Mrs Holcombe came in, pushing a trolley, to clear away the plates. Henrietta replaced a pair of silver salt and pepper shakers on the sideboard, and asked everyone to carry something through to the kitchen. She gave Ginette the remains of the treacle tart and Len and Marjorie jugs of custard and cream.

'Whoah, this I have to see,' said Len, entering the vast unmodernised kitchen. 'This place is priceless; I've never seen anything like it. A real museum piece. It can't have been touched for a hundred years.'

Having never given much thought to the Priory kitchen, which had been like this since he was born, Anthony scrutinised it properly for the first time. It was true: the room – or rather series of rooms, for there was a scullery and various pantries and coldrooms – was defiantly decrepit and entirely lacking in what Len would call 'mod cons'. Upon an uneven stone floor, worn by centuries of use, stood numerous pieces of sturdy, Edwardian furniture; a slate-topped table and massive dresser with chipped paint, from which dangled old teacups with tea-stained rims on dozens of plastic-covered hooks; the wooden draining boards around the two Belfast sinks were streaked and blackened by water; sticky flypapers covered with old dead insects hung from the ceiling. There was a tower of rusty biscuit tins, and a muslin cloche on a marble stand containing small lumps of cheese. A second, Victorian dresser with drawers either rammed shut or jammed half open displayed a selection of serving dishes, many cracked and riveted back together again with metal staples. There was no fridge, but a cold larder with slate shelves, on which butter and milk bottles congealed gently against an exterior wall. Several ancient hairy dog baskets, lined with scraps of blanket and corduroy cushions, lay on the floor. The only daylight came from three skylights set into the twenty-foot ceiling, the glass of which was partially obscured by a thick lather of pigeon droppings.

'I'm telling you, it's a piece of living history, this place. A museum would love to take it away just as it is and put it on display. I've half a mind to bring some of my salesmen along – with your permission, of course, Henrie – and show them how people used to live.'

'I suppose it is rather old fashioned,' said Henrietta, who couldn't have cared less about the kitchen since she seldom went near it. 'One day we shall probably have to think about bringing it more up to date.'

'Well, if you ever do, you know where to come,' said Len. 'I could get you thirty, forty per cent off everything, no problem. That's for the units and appliances, not the installation, though we should be able to do something on that too. It would be a big job in a space like this, but nothing adds value like a kitchen; the value stays in the property. Breakfast bar, nice built-in units, slide and glide cutlery drawers, a proper cork tiled floor. Could be an idea to lower the ceiling with sound-absorbent tiles, and run some spots along a track. Tell you what, if you want to get the job finished before the great wedding, I could call in some favours, so let me know when you want to push the button.'

Henrietta smiled icily. 'How very kind of you, Leonard. I shall bear that in mind.'

13

Now Anthony and Sandra were engaged, a search began for somewhere larger for them to live on the Winchford estate. Apart from the Mill House, home to the Biggeses, and the Rectory which belonged to the diocese, the remainder of the village consisted of thirty-three cottages, variously too small or already tenanted; however, on the periphery of the estate were several possibilities, including Steepness Farmhouse, which had recently become vacant but was in bad repair.

Situated close to the old quarry near the top of Steepness Hill, the farmhouse was barely half a mile from the Priory by a footpath through two large fields, but almost two miles by road, which Anthony saw as an advantage. Lately, he had become tired of his mother's unannounced visits to Forge Cottage, and he doubted these would continue at the farmhouse, which lay at the end of a rough track. Furthermore, Sandra instantly loved the farmhouse, which she considered a perfect first married home. A two-storey building of local ironstone, with four sash windows across, it struck Sandra as 'the perfect size, with a nice bedroom for us, a lovely little bedroom for Jasmine, and two others we can use as guest bedrooms for now, but which will one day be ideal for any little people who might come along.' To Anthony, remembering how long it had taken him and Amanda to make Forge Cottage half habitable, it seemed a daunting challenge. For thirty years home to the estate dairyman, the place had subsequently been let to a procession of local tenants, none of whom had stayed long. It had a decrepit air. The rooms were dark and cold, the garden a jungle filled with rotting hen houses collapsing into a neglected orchard. Sandra – and Len when he came to case the joint – did not share Anthony's misgivings, and announced the place could be put right in just a few months. Rejecting the local Stow and Moreton builders as too slow and expensive, Len said he knew some émigré Poles who would move into the property and get the job done by Christmas, cash in hand.

'Dad's a real star; he always knows what to do,' Sandra said.

At the same time, it was agreed by Henrietta and Godfrey that Anthony must start a proper job. 'All this helping out on the farm has gone on long enough,' Henrietta declared. 'If he's old enough to be getting married for the *second* time, he's certainly old enough to join the bank and get down to it.' And so, at the age of twenty–two, Anthony began travelling into the City each morning with his father; Godfrey greeting his son on the platform at Kingham station before separating on the train (Godfrey travelled first class, Anthony in second) and meeting up again by the barrier at Paddington, from where Anthony caught a lift in the big black car sent to meet Godfrey and drive him into Anscombe Brothers bank in Lombard Street. Being the youngest member of the family working for the bank, there was not a great deal he could usefully do, but Anthony soon became familiar with the sandwich bars and pubs of the area and, if he made no actual decisions, he at least absorbed the atmosphere of the cautious, private and old-fashioned family concern. Founded by a direct ancestor, Ishmail Aaronson of Vienna, whose son Jacob changed his first name to Harry and his surname to Anscombe and was knighted soon afterwards, the bank was one of only half a dozen still in family hands. Godfrey's cousin, Michael, the present chairman, and five other Anscombes, mostly rather old, served as directors. For Anthony, the greatest advantage of being an Anscombe at Anscombes was that everyone was unfailingly nice to him, and didn't say anything when he rolled back from lunch after three o'clock. Things became even more fun when Lex started work at Cazenoves in Moorgate, and then Archie Bigges, Percy and Jacinthe's son, who had left Cambridge, rolled up at Anscombes on a postgraduate trainee scheme, and was always up for a long, boozy lunch. The three Oxfordshire musketeers were soon meeting up two or three times a week; Anthony, as the only married member of the trio and the tallest, was deferred to as older and wiser, but often felt himself to be the least sophisticated.

Meanwhile, the farmhouse came on with astonishing speed. Every Saturday morning, Anthony and Sandra drove up for a site inspection. Sandra had appointed herself a supremely efficient works manager, and no detail was too minor for her to notice. While Lech and his team of Polish builders stripped out the old lean-to kitchen and demolished an internal wall to double its size, she was choosing fitted pine kitchen units from a shop in Cheltenham, and replacing the Belfast sinks with gleaming new stainless steel ones. Within weeks, a gingerbread-coloured Formica 'peninsular' breakfast bar had been assembled for the new kitchen, and this now jutted into the enlarged room surrounded by matching stools. An olive green bathroom suite replaced the rusting iron white bathtub upstairs. At the same time, the dingy bedrooms were repainted in the muted pastel colours Sandra loved – oatmealy pinks and cornflower blues. Downstairs, everything was yellow and egg-shell white and wonderfully clean and organised. No sooner was the kitchen installed than special ceramic jars for pasta, rice and flour were placed in readiness on the shelves, each jar having the word PASTA, RICE or FLOUR stencilled in big blue letters.

As an engaged couple, Sandra had moved out of the bedroom she had shared with Jasmine at Forge Cottage, and into Anthony's bedroom next door. She insisted it 'didn't feel quite right' to be sleeping there in the five-bar-gate bed, where Anthony had slept during his marriage to Amanda, so Anthony had the bed removed and stored, and Sandra chose a new double bed with quilted headboard at the Cavendish House department store in Cheltenham. Matching white bedside tables with fluted legs followed, and matching bedside lamps with oatmeal lamp-shades, and a pink bedcover and valance in a spriggy rosebud pattern from Laura Ashley. There was no question, having proper bedside lights that turned on and off and didn't flicker was a big improvement, and the cold little bedroom was soon barely recognisable. One evening, return-ing from work, Anthony noticed Amanda's old Victorian washstand, the one she had retrieved from the gunroom and stripped and painted, had disappeared from the corner of the room, replaced by a bamboo basket chair. Secretly prefering the washstand, but not wanting to hurt San-dra's feelings, he hoped he might find a place for it one day at Steepness Farmhouse.

Plans for the wedding were a constant topic between Sandra and her mother. Both spent endless time poring over bridal magazines, but no decisions could be made until Anthony obtained his divorce from Amanda. They had been separated for two and a half years, and Amanda agreed to admit to abandoning her husband and child for another man. She would make no financial claims against Anthony, which Henrietta described as 'the greatest relief of all', and would sign all necessary papers. The problem lay in getting her physically to do so. Having mentally moved on from the marriage long ago, she regarded its official dissolu-tion as a matter of no urgency, and was in any case hard to pin down. For four months, she followed Patrice to Ouarzazate in Morocco where he was making a film; later, they changed their Paris telephone number and forgot to tell Anthony the new one. Although the Anscombes' solicitor said this must be regarded as a deliberate delaying tactic, Anthony knew it was simple vagueness.

Sandra took great pains to keep Jasmine feeling happy and secure about the forthcoming marriage, but in the weeks following the engagement, she became progressively withdrawn. Her little face clouded with anxiety, and she became clingy and fretful, sometimes refusing to talk to Anthony, sometimes ignoring Sandra. 'If Nanny Sandra is going to be my new Mummy, does that mean Mummy is going to be my new Nanny?' she asked Anthony in the car. Anthony wasn't even sure Jasmine remembered Amanda. Unless he mentioned her himself, Jasmine never did. It was Sandra who read to her every night and Sandra who took her to the playground in Stow and to feed the ducks in Bourton-on-the-Water. It was Sandra, too, who chose and bought all her clothes, and took her to see the bluebells in the bluebell woods and the snowdrops in Winchford churchyard. It didn't help that Amanda made no contact for months at a time. Jasmine's third birthday came and went, but no birthday card or present from her mother arrived. When, out of the blue, a postcard turned up from Ouarzazate, with a picture of camels crossing sand dunes and a message saying Amanda had sent Jasmine a pair of magic slippers, no slippers ever turned up. In the end, Sandra had to buy her a pair of fluffy ones herself in the local shoe shop and pretend. Often Jasmine woke up crying in the night, and then either Anthony or Sandra would go into her bedroom and sleep in her bed. They felt it was wrong for her to sleep in their own bed, while they were still unmarried.

As time went by and the divorce papers remained unsigned, Sandra became rather despondent, and even questioned how hard Anthony was trying to obtain this divorce at all. Once, in the middle of Saturday lunch, she dissolved into tears, saying she did realise she wasn't as pretty or interesting as Amanda, but she was trying so hard to make him happy, and if he didn't want to go ahead with the marriage he should tell her now – she'd rather know than have all these delays and prevarications. This made Anthony feel so guilty, he spent the whole weekend telephoning Amanda's apartment. To make matters worse, Len rang him the following Monday morning at the bank, something he had never done before, and made it clear, in a civil but uncomfortably firm way, that he and his wife were both unhappy about the way things were going, and he expected Anthony to get it sorted by the end of the month.

In the end, against the advice of his solicitor, Anthony realised the only sure way of getting Amanda to sign the papers was to go to Paris himself and stand over her until she did. Imagining Sandra would be impressed by his decisive plan, he was puzzled and dismayed when she took it badly, saying she had always been suspicious of Amanda, and didn't like her at all, and could see no reason for Anthony to be running around France after her. Rallying to the defence of his first wife, he pointed out that Amanda was actually a very talented person, which was exactly the wrong thing to say to Sandra, who took umbrage ('Meaning I'm not, I suppose'), and it quickly escalated into a major row. So when he set off for Paris the next morning he did wonder, as he studied the divorce papers on the boat-train to double check exactly where Amanda and her witness were supposed to sign, exactly why he was so deeply in the doghouse, since all he was doing was clearing the way to marry Sandra.

He checked into a hotel on the Left Bank, close to the apartment where Amanda lived with Patrice. He dumped his case by the bed, showered and changed, then walked the two streets to the Rue de Verneuil for his rendezvous with his wife. When they had spoken on the telephone, she had promised to be there. In his briefcase was the envelope containing the divorce papers and a bottle of duty-free Chanel eau de cologne he had bought her on the ferry.

The apartment building was enormous: a grand entrance with engraved brass bell plates flanked on both sides by expensive-looking boutiques. Anthony had pressed the bell marked Bouillon before noticing a scrap of paper, in Amanda's handwriting, taped just beneath. It said, 'Hi, Ant. Hope you've arrived safely in this city of fading dreams. We are in a restaurant, the Voltaire, not far, by the river. Join us there.'

The restaurant was on the Quai Voltaire and the kind of deeply romantic neighbourhood place that tourists travel to Paris in the hope of finding. There was a smell inside of scent and seawater, and the couples at the tables nearest to the door were sharing plateaux de fruits de mer. Anthony looked around for Amanda, but could see no sign of her. A massive spray of blue flowers stood in a vase on a plinth. A waiter in a white jacket appeared and, knowing the place was full, prepared to turn him away. He said he was looking for Mademoiselle Amanda Anscombe or Patrice Bouillon.

At the mention of Patrice, the waiter's attitude altered and Anthony was shown into a second room. Patrice and Amanda were sitting together on a banquette next to the window. It took him a moment to recognise them. Since he had last seen her in room sixteen of the Randolph, Amanda had grown her hair, and this was now worn up on top of her head in a lacquered chignon. The effect was to make her neck seem almost impossibly long; her shoulders, in a strapless black dress, added to the impression of a young French starlet. Patrice, meanwhile, had had his head shaven into a crew cut, the result, Anthony soon learnt, of a part in a film about the French Foreign Legion.

'Amanda.' He felt suddenly shy approaching the table. Shy and bedazzled. He wished he had not been carrying the briefcase – the leather briefcase he took each day on the train into work, the briefcase with their divorce papers inside. It seemed momentarily unlikely he had ever been married to this beautiful girl.

'Ant!' Her face lit up, genuinely pleased to see him. 'It's been ages. I'm sorry I've been useless about everything. We've been away a lot.' She kissed him across the table.

'You were in Morocco, I hear. You sent Jasmine a postcard.'

There was no spare chair at the table, so he remained standing, looming over them. Patrice looked displeased to see him, even hostile. He was conscious of another table directly behind him – his arse was practically in their faces – and he felt conspicuous and too tall. With evident reluctance, a waiter produced a chair which was squeezed into the space opposite the banquette.

'How's Jasmine?' Amanda asked.

'Fine. She's a happy little girl. And getting pretty, too. You should come and see her.'

'I want to. Maybe after New York.'

'New York?'

'Only for a week or two. There's some people Patrice needs to see, for business.'

He could feel Patrice regarding him in a bored way, and then he said, 'So, Antoine, you would like maybe some drink?'

'A glass of wine would be great. Red, preferably.'

'Have you eaten?' Amanda asked. 'Why not order something?'

Feeling suddenly ravenous, Anthony asked for a steak and pommes frites, to which Patrice said, 'We are the same, Antoine. I also choose the big steak and cheeps. It is good, no? We enjoy the same meat, same women . . .' Then he roared with laughter and draped his big, brawny arm around Amanda's fragile shoulders. 'You have nice taste, Antoine, same as me.'

'For heaven's sake, shut up won't you, Patrice,' Amanda said. 'Sometimes you're too crass. I don't like it.' At which Patrice puckered his big lips at her, and shrugged as if he didn't care that much about what Amanda thought, and exhaled in a French way that managed to imply excess sexuality.

'You're in Paris for just the weekend?' Patrice asked.

'Just tonight, really. I'm heading back tomorrow morning.'

'You should stay longer. Paris is beautiful in springtime.'

'Perhaps another time.' The conversation struck Anthony as surreal. Did Patrice even realise why he was there? It would have been typical of Amanda not to have explained. His food arrived and he tucked in hungrily.

'When do you next expect to be over in England?' he asked her. 'As I said, Jasmine would love to see you. She talks about you.'

'Maybe this summer, I'm not sure. We were talking about going back to Oxford.' Turning to Patrice, she said, 'Oxford. Our idea of visiting this summer.' Patrice shrugged. 'You must remember, Patrice, when we stayed at the Randolph, next to that museum?'

Looking meaningfully at Anthony, she said, 'Ant came to visit me at the hotel. It was a memorable afternoon.'

Turning crimson, Anthony said, 'Amanda, I've got those papers to sign. They need your signature and then they have to be witnessed. Maybe Patrice could do it.' He flicked open the briefcase and laid the papers on the tablecloth, where they looked shabby and official. 'This is the important page, down at the bottom where it says "Spouse". The rest has already been filled in for you.'

Amanda borrowed a pen from the waiter and wrote 'Amanda Gibbons (Anscombe)', and Patrice scrawled his signature on the witness line.

Suddenly Anthony was seized by an impulse to set the papers ablaze; he longed to pick up the Voltaire matchbox and send them up in flames. But, having obtained his signatures, he stood up and kissed Amanda goodnight, shook hands with Patrice, and made his way out between the noisy tables. As he left the restaurant, he caught a final glimpse of his soon to be ex-wife, and wondered when he would next see her.

Back at the hotel he remembered the bottle of duty-free scent, and resolved to give it to Sandra instead.

Three months later, four days before his wedding to Sandra, Anthony arrived home from his evening commute from the City to find a local taxi parked outside Steepness Farmhouse. Inside, sitting at the kitchen table, was his first wife drinking coffee with his second.

'Hi, Anthony,' Amanda said, crossing the room to kiss him hello. 'You look very serious in that pinstripe suit.' In a floaty pale-blue kaftan, she was sunburnt, beautiful and absurdly young. Her hair, shorter than it had been in Paris, reminded him of the first time they met.

'Amanda! Good Lord, what on earth are you doing here?'

Anthony had several reactions to finding his ex-wife in his kitchen, all vaguely unworthy. The first was how much older Sandra looked than Amanda; since their engagement eighteen months earlier, she had become daily more grown up, while Amanda remained forever eighteen. Sitting opposite each other at the pine table, drinking from Sandra's big oatmeal-coloured cups, they belonged to different generations.

Seeing himself and his house through Amanda's eyes, he wished he hadn't been wearing a suit, hot and smelly from the train, and that their kitchen wasn't quite so child-focused or lacking any trace of originality. Although he had come to intensely dislike the neglected bohemian kitchen of Amanda's period at Forge Cottage, he could easily imagine what she thought of the new Formica and pine units; above her shoulder, he saw the procession of yellow ceramic dormice climbing the tiles, flinched, and hoped Amanda would not turn round and notice them too.

'What am I doing here? Really, Ant, that's not very welcoming of you. Actually, I'm over in England for the summer and making plans with Sandra. I'm going to take Jasmine off her hands for a few days and give her some space to get ready for your wedding.'

For the first time, Anthony noticed his daughter sitting behind the laundry basket in the kitchen, apprehensively watching Amanda. It was scarcely surprising since, at three and a half, Jasmine had seen her mother only twice in three years. She was a virtual stranger.

'Amanda's going to take Jasmine to stay with some friends of hers at Fyford,' Sandra was saying, 'and then drop her back here again at nine o'clock on Saturday morning. So you'll have plenty of time to get changed into your pretty bridesmaid's dress, Jasmine, with all the other children.'

'We have some friends at Fyford,' Anthony said. 'The Plunketts, Mark and Annie.'

'We'll be staying with a guy in the music business,' Amanda replied vaguely. 'He's living on a kind of commune over there.'

'Well, I'd better get going and pack for you, Jasmine,' Sandra said. 'Let's go up to your bedroom and choose lots of pretty clothes for staying with Mummy, shall we? I did a whole basket of your ironing this morning, so you've got lots of lovely clean things to choose from.'

Alone in the kitchen, Amanda said, 'I see you've got the sort of home life you always wanted, Ant. I'm pleased for you. You must love living with someone who irons and cooks and keeps things nice. That was never my forte.'

'No, it wasn't exactly your thing.' He laughed. 'I was just thinking about our old kitchen at the cottage. Do you remember when we had mice that time? And I bought those traps in Moreton you said were cruel, and you wouldn't let me put them out. So the mice bred more and more, and in the end we had to call in Rentokil.'

'It was cute, that cottage. We weren't unhappy all the time, were we? I don't remember being.'

'I think we were quite a bit happier than we realised, actually.'

Amanda held his gaze for a moment. 'Probably we were too young. We didn't know how difficult it is to be happy. We didn't realise how close we'd got.'

'A pity, then,' said Anthony.

'Yes, pity,' Amanda replied, and then they heard Sandra and Jasmine coming back downstairs with Jasmine's overnight bag. Jasmine had been changed into fresh clothes for the outing: pink gingham dungarees, a white shirt embroidered with flowers, and a matching white cotton sunhat.

Anthony noticed Amanda grimace, and then she said to Jasmine, 'You look sweet, darling. Like one of those photographs of child models in the windows of C&A.' Sandra, who had bought the whole outfit there, couldn't tell whether this was meant as a snub or a compliment.

'I hope Saturday is beautiful,' Amanda murmured to Anthony. 'Saturday and beyond.'

'Thanks.'

'I notice you've got mice in this house too,' she said as she was leaving. 'You hated them at Forge Cottage, but here you put them on tiles all over the kitchen walls.'

'Don't forget we need her back here by nine o'clock,' Sandra said as they watched Jasmine climb into the back of the taxi with her mother. 'It's going to be chaos come Saturday morning, and we need lots of time to get the little people organised.'

14

Deftly declining Henrietta's suggestion that the bridesmaids and pages should get changed at Winchford Priory, Anthony and Sandra decided Steepness Farmhouse would make a less stressful centre of operations. It was here, in the sitting room and master bedroom, that the hairdresser and make-up artist, wedding dress designer and lady who made the bridesmaids' dresses, congregated with the various attendants, their mothers and nannies, to get everyone ready for the twelve o'clock wedding service.

Anthony had woken, alone, in the best possible spirits. He and Sandra had decided, in a nod towards convention, that they would sleep separately on the eve of their wedding, so Sandra had joined her parents and Ginette at the Royalist Hotel in Stow. Anthony woke to the sound of church bells tolling out across the fields, and went downstairs to find Sandra already returned in full organisational mode. A table was being laid under a tree in the garden for the children to have snacks and squash before the wedding, and the furniture in the sitting room had been replaced by dressing tables and mirrors. Marjorie was bustling about in an excited, efficient manner, clutching armfuls of clothes.

Anthony poured a cup of coffee and carried it outside. It was barely eight o'clock but already the sun was becoming quite fierce. The weather forecast predicted a blisteringly hot day. The garden, once desolate, had been transformed by Sandra into a wonderfully neat oasis of cheerfulness and colour; there were beds of sweet peas and marigolds, geraniums and carnations, several of which had been cut for buttonholes for the ushers and stood in readiness in the kitchen in small cream jugs. The old mud path to the front door had been re-laid with crazy paving, the derelict hen houses dismantled and burnt, and the long grass beneath the apple trees strimmed low by Walter Twine for the great day. As Anthony sat there, a cloud of white butterflies were swept up in a gust of wind, and danced around the treetops.

He sipped his coffee and turned his face towards the sun. He could hardly believe how relaxed he was feeling. Although it was going to be a big wedding, the process had been miraculously stress-free, largely because his bride-to-be and her mother had taken every decision. Marrying Amanda in Nice, it had been Anthony who had done the rushing about, hassling French bureaucrats, photocopying passports and changing money to purchase the marriage licence; this time he had taken a back seat. Although it would have been unjust to describe Anthony as lazy, he was the sort of Englishman who was perfectly happy going with the flow. He was not a person of entrenched opinions. Instinctively preferring the countryside to the town, Cavaliers to the Roundheads, Tories to the socialists, savoury to sweet, he was otherwise free of fixed tastes and prejudice. If Sandra wanted peach-coloured bridesmaids' dresses that was fine by him, even if they weren't precisely the shade he would have chosen, left to himself. If Sandra wanted her sister as her chief bridesmaid, well why not? That was fine too. When Henrietta had taken him to one side and urged him to veto the Ginette idea ('I do detest older bridesmaids. So common. So much nicer to have lots of lovely little children coming up the aisle'), he dismayed her by saying, quite truthfully, that he really couldn't care less one way or the other. Similarly, when the Pottses wanted a full sit-down wedding banquet, and the Anscombes preferred a stand-up reception, Anthony again insisted he didn't give a damn, and they might as well go with the Pottses' preference since they were paying for everything. This reference to money did the trick, being one commodity for which Henrietta had enormous respect, having plenty already, and no more was said about canapés on trays.

As the sunshine warmed his face, he drank his coffee slowly, cradling the brightly coloured ceramic mug, delaying the moment he must begin to think about getting changed. He reflected on how incredibly lucky he was to be marrying Sandra. In extricating himself from Amanda, he felt he had miraculously fallen off a death-defying rollercoaster ride, bruised but alive, and begun a fresh life in a perfect cottage garden. In Sandra, he had at last found loyalty and constancy; he could easily envisage the two of them, fifty years hence, leading useful, happy, reassuringly predictable lives. At that moment, there was nothing in the world he craved quite so much. Her thoughtfulness – the continual little acts of kindness and affection – never ceased to amaze him; he had woken up to find a jug of sweet peas on the bedside table, which she must have placed there while he was still asleep. Hearing footsteps on the path, he saw her approaching with a tray of croissants, jam and butter, three slices of grilled bacon and a fresh pot of coffee. 'Ah, there you are, sweetheart. I was looking everywhere for you. I've brought you some wedding breakfast.'

'Thank you, darling. I was just sitting here thinking how much I love you, and how lucky I am.'

'I'm the lucky one; you know that.' She kissed him on the top of his head. 'Now, when you've finished, it would be helpful if you could bring the tray back inside, and get going a bit. All the little attendants will be arriving soon, and I ought to start getting changed myself.' Sandra's wedding dress, still unseen by Anthony, had been hanging in the cupboard in a special suit bag. 'It's not for you to see – that's considered unlucky,' Sandra had told him. 'I don't want Jasmine's sticky little fingers all over it either.'

Soon after nine, a succession of bridesmaids and pages were dropped off at Steepness Farmhouse, and the place was overrun by little boys and girls tearing from room to room, with mothers and nannies trailing after them, imploring them to come back and calm down. Araminta Nall-Caine and Emmy Elliot were bouncing happily on Sandra's bed, on which her wedding dress had been carefully laid out, and Edward Plunkett and Archie Fane, tough little five-year-olds, had shot straight through the house and out into the garden and were climbing the lower branches of a sweet chestnut tree. The Loxton twins, Benedict and Charlotte, had somehow found their way into the kitchen, where Benedict was smearing his face with chocolate spread, watched with horrified fascination by his sister. Sandra, being brilliant with children, somehow contrived to be everywhere at once, settling them all down, tidying them up and telling them how impressive and smart they would soon appear in their special bridesmaids' and pages' outfits.

Despite being far more friendly with some of the young nannies than with any of the mothers, Sandra nevertheless managed to organise everyone and everything with equal authority, and in a miraculously short space of time they were compliantly putting on their buckled shoes and having final adjustments made to their peach-coloured dresses, before being ushered outside for crisps, sandwiches, squash and a quiet story. Meanwhile Ginette, already kitted out in peach ruffles, lumbered around the sitting room like an Indian elephant decorated for a religious festival. When Anthony's best man, Lex, caught sight of her, he pretended to shiver and shake, telling Anthony he thought he might be trampled underfoot. 'That's Sandra's sister? Blooming hell. I thought the best man was meant to get off with the chief bridesmaid, but no way am I going there. It'd be like inserting your knob into a bouncy castle.'

It seemed to Anthony that every room in the farmhouse was occupied by someone or other in some stage of preparation. Len and Marjorie had taken over Anthony's little study, and Len was now striding about the house in pearl-grey tails with a pearl-grey cravat and a top hat, offering glasses of Cristal. Several of the nannies, already slightly tiddly, had locked themselves en masse into the bathroom to doll themselves up. Shrieks of laughter drifted out through the door, and the Loxtons' nanny, Hayley, briefly broke cover in a very short skirt to refill their glasses. When Marjorie eventually emerged from the study in a tangerine-coloured twinset with tangerine boots, false eyelashes and a tangerine hat, looking years younger than Ginette and totally amazing, everyone broke into spontaneous applause.

Then Anthony's ushers turned up with much banging of car doors, the hairdresser was putting the final touches to Ginette's and Marjorie's hair, and there was so much coming and going that nobody noticed how the time had sped by, or that Jasmine still hadn't been dropped home by Amanda.

Naturally it was Sandra, halfway through being helped into her full-skirted, rustling white taffeta wedding dress, who remembered. 'Is Jasmine back? I haven't seen her all morning.'

Anthony was alerted, and everyone was asked whether they'd seen her, and it was soon established nobody had. Her peach bridesmaid dress was the last one left hanging forlornly on the rail. It was ten past eleven and they'd have to start leaving for the church in twenty minutes. Panicked and silently cursing Amanda, because this was so typical, Anthony realised he had no idea where they were staying. Amanda had mentioned some commune near Fyford, but he had no telephone number, assuming the place was even on the phone. Annie Plunkett, Edward's mother, thought she could guess which house it might be, but hadn't the vaguest notion what the people there were called.

'Someone must know where Jasmine is,' said Lex, trying to be helpful. 'Doesn't her nanny know?'

'Her nanny is Sandra, you ass,' Anthony said. 'My wife-to-be, in case you've forgotten.' He was standing by the gate, listening out for an approaching car. He could have murdered Amanda; it was just so predictable. He blamed himself for letting Jasmine go off with her in the first place. Where the hell were they? Even Amanda couldn't have forgotten about the wedding, could she? He would have driven over to Fyford, but it was twenty-five minutes each way. It couldn't be done in time.

It was twenty-five to twelve. He drove to the church with Lex and the ushers, still hoping they might pass Jasmine on the road. Her bridesmaid dress was on the back seat. If she missed the wedding, he'd never forgive Amanda. Jasmine had been longing to be a bridesmaid.

All Hallowes, Winchford, was one of the oldest Norman churches in Oxfordshire. As Archie Bigges remarked, 'It certainly smells like it is, in any case.' With its narrow arched doorway surrounded by zigzag banding, Pevsner dated the entrance to 1150 AD, though the chancel and south aisle were considered to be later. A wide stone area of floor in front of the altar was covered with brasses of knights in armour, which Henrietta smothered with scraps of old carpet to deter brass rubbers, and which the vicar surreptitiously removed. A crumbling stone wall was covered by Baroque wall tablets, many to assorted Anscombes, and a bay window contained a stained glass memorial to Anthony's great uncle Peverel, who fell in the Great War; angels hovered about his uniformed corpse in a field of primroses and, bizarrely, Winchford Priory itself was inserted in the background on a rocky Palatine hill. As Anthony arrived, still in a flap about Jasmine, he saw the church was already half full of guests. Old Walter Twine, who had played the organ at All Hallowes for thirty years, was installed in his organ loft, pounding away on the pedals. Not wanting to take up his position at the front in case Jasmine turned up, Anthony hung around by the door with Lex while the congregation drifted in. The Biggeses arrived with their gawky twenty-three-year-old daughter, Arabella, who had been viewed as a perfect future wife for Anthony, despite being shockingly plain. Anthony knew that Arabella was living these days in Fulham, working as a secretary at a charity for Maltese donkeys. Her handsome and raffish brother, Archie, Anthony's friend from the bank, sloped in behind his parents, looking hungover.

Anthony spotted his parents in a front pew, his mother wearing a severe, navy-blue three-quarter-length jacket with matching dress underneath, and a large, ancient family brooch pinned to the lapel; Godfrey was in the same tailcoat in which he had himself been married, and regimental cufflinks. Henrietta was glaring across the aisle to the bride's side, where Sandra's gregarious nanny friends were making a lot of noise.

'Can't you tell them to shut up?' she asked Godfrey. 'It's so rude to the vicar.' Godfrey bowed his head and pretended not to hear.

The church was almost full, the congregation fidgeting with anticipation. Two minivans of Sandra's old college friends had arrived from Poole, and her side of the church was nearly as packed as the Anscombes'. Her ex-fiancé Steve and several of his army mates, all out of uniform in baggy suits, commandeered the rear pews and were busy eyeing up the nannies. So, across the aisle, was Archie, who suddenly looked a lot perkier.

Anthony was pacing around at the top of the lane, still hoping Jasmine might turn up. Her little outfit was ready in the porch, and if she arrived now they could quickly change her and begin the service a few minutes late. Walter Twine was improvising an anthem on the organ, which sounded like 'One Man Went to Mow'.

Now the chauffer-driven white Bentley with white leather upholstery that Len had hired for the big day was drawing up, and Sandra was being helped out by the dressmaker, who arranged the billowing train behind her. Through the open door of the church, gusts of heat drifted into the chilly knave, and birdsong competed with the organ music. It was ten minutes past noon and the vicar was agitating to get started. Four small bridesmaids, two pages and Ginette formed up behind Sandra, then Walter struck up 'Here comes the Bride' and the procession began.

Still fuming, and feeling his wedding had been sabotaged by his ex-wife, Anthony finally conceded defeat and joined his best man at the front of the church. The congregation rose, and Sandra and her father were walking down the aisle towards him. As they craned forward to catch a glimpse of her, everyone whispered what an exceptionally pretty girl the bride was, with her hair swept up in a blonde bouffant, and two little fake plaits wound round it. Len was a picture of pride, beaming like the genial compère of a variety show. The bridesmaids and pages, so serious and angelic, brought tear pricks to their mothers' eyes. Only the vast form of Ginette, galumphing along and blocking the view of the children, made people shake their heads.

Jeremy Meek was preparing himself for his words of welcome, when the roar of a car engine was heard outside, and a Joan Baez tape blaring at maximum volume. A moment or two later there was the sound of running footsteps, and a little girl's voice shouting, 'Daddy, Nanny, I'm here. Don't start without me, pleeeease.'

Jasmine was tearing up the aisle towards them. She was still in her pink gingham dungarees, now very grubby, and a borrowed cheesecloth shirt dangling to the floor. Around her forehead was some kind of beaded headband. Dimly, at the back of the church, Anthony could see Amanda, Patrice, a second girl in denim dungarees and a long-haired man in patched Levis. 'Don't start yet, Nanny,' Jasmine pleaded. 'You promised I could be a bridesmaid, you *promised*.' Throwing her arms around Sandra's waist, smearing the dress with dirty handprints, she burst into tears and clung on for dear life.

'Come on, let go of Sandra, darling,' Anthony said. 'There isn't time for this; the service has started.'

But Jasmine, inconsolable, wouldn't let go. She clung tighter, and couldn't be prised away. 'You *promised* I could be a bridesmaid. You *said* I could.'

'Listen, darling, of course you can be a bridesmaid,' Sandra said. 'Just give us a couple of minutes, vicar, and I'll have her changed in two ticks.' Then she lifted Jasmine into her arms, and carried her back up the aisle to where the peach frock was waiting.

'For better or worse, for richer, for poorer,' intoned the vicar, as Sandra repeated her marriage vows and Jasmine buried her snotty little face deep in the folds of her wedding dress.

15

Thirteen months after their wedding, Anthony and Sandra's first child was born in Cheltenham General Hospital. They named him Richard Godfrey Leonard, thus making both grandfathers feel included and flattered. The birth had been uncomplicated, and Anthony felt elated as his strong, healthy wife pushed out their strong, healthy, nine-pound son. Richard was born at lunchtime, so Anthony was able to drive home to Steepness Farmhouse to collect Jasmine (Mrs Holcombe's daughter Judy was minding her) and bring her to the hospital to be introduced to her half-brother. Sandra, ever thoughtful, had a little present waiting for her 'from the baby', so she wouldn't feel jealous of him; Jasmine took one look at the knitted doll, burst into tears and crawled underneath the hospital bed. It had taken twenty minutes to coax her out.

To nobody's surprise, Sandra turned out to be a natural mother. Ecstatic yet tranquil, she took to Richard immediately, and joyfully immersed herself in caring for a newborn baby. Anthony loved to watch her as she gently patted his son to sleep and gently patted him awake again, establishing a routine, basting him with baby oils and clouds of powder and sponging him with such care in a plastic bath of perfectly tepid water. At the same time, she was punctilious about lavishing equal attention on Jasmine, so her stepdaughter wouldn't feel excluded; while Richard slept, Sandra would play games with her, brush her hair, and do everything to make her feel secure in their newly enlarged family. One of the many things about his second wife that filled Anthony with gratitude was the way she tried to love Jasmine as her own. Not that it was always easy; with her dark hair and skinniness, and her sallow skin, Jasmine increasingly resembled Amanda in appearance, and there was also something awkward and all too familiar about her behaviour. Pitifully oversensitive, the slightest thing could upset her and she would withdraw into herself for hours. When she fell into one of her 'Jasmine moods', no sympathy or diversion could snap her out of it, and Anthony became uneasy, sensing her slip away to a faraway place inside her head. He recognised too many characteristics of her mother, and wished he didn't.

In other respects, Anthony felt his life to be more complete than ever before. He was twenty-five years old, married to a girl who adored him, living in a happy house with two healthy children. Furthermore, he was at last being given some responsibility at the bank, and found he actually enjoyed the work and was reasonably good at it. He played a small role in the disposal of two manufacturing businesses, and in the refinancing of a Derbyshire foundry, and got on easily with clients. If anything had held back the Anscombes over the years, it was a certain stiffness of manner, which made customers prefer to look elsewhere for their advice, but Anthony – tall and handsome and unobtrusively informal – put them at ease.

Each evening he caught the 18:13 train from Paddington to Kingham, where he kept a car at the station, and was home by eight o'clock for supper. Sandra was a keen cook with a particular love of pastry, and always made sure some wholesome hot meal was waiting for him. Boeuf en croute was one of her favourites; if they had friends over for supper, she produced soup as a first course with cheese straws made from puff pastry floating on top. For pudding, she loved to make apple crumble from windfalls gathered in their orchard. When Anthony, at Len's suggestion, bought one of the first Westinghouse deep freezers in North Oxfordshire, she became passionate about cooking 'for the freezer'. If you lifted the lid, you found icy blocks of shepherds pie and fish pie, enough to last for years.

Visitors to the farmhouse commented on how it was the most child-friendly home they had ever been to. Paintings and crayon drawings by Jasmine, and soon by Richard too, covered every wall of the kitchen, the walls above the freezer in the annexe, and then all around the dining room. On the mantelpiece were framed handprints and footprints of month-old Richard.

Upstairs, Sandra's gift for arts and crafts found a further outlet in Richard's bedroom. She made his curtains herself, and then a frieze of stencilled shapes – apples, drums and toy boxes – and finally, over many evenings, a wall hanging in the shape of a circus clown, with dangly hair from scraps of wool, and patchwork pockets with giant buttons and giant numbers cut out of fuzzy felt. As Sandra said, 'It is so important to have a bright focus for a baby to look at.' Anthony felt he would rather stare at a blank wall than the hideous, demented clown, but kept these thoughts to himself.

The garden was turned over in its entirety to the pleasure of the children. Len started the ball rolling by giving Richard, as a first birthday present, a Wendy house made of orange-coloured wood with a grey shingle roof and plywood chimney. It was the largest playhouse anyone had ever seen and Sandra had it erected directly outside the kitchen windows so she could keep an eye on everyone while cooking. Richard adored it and, as he learnt to crawl and then to walk, was forever heaving himself upright from the low windowsills. Jasmine, too, loved the Wendy house, and regularly disappeared inside to sulk.

The Wendy house was soon joined by a swing and a sandpit, and then by a big colourful climbing frame and a paddling pool, with its full compliment of plastic spades and buckets. Soon, every part of the garden was colonised by a different activity. Annie Plunkett, when she brought Edward over to play, later told her husband Mark she thought it was 'quite killing' and that 'there's actually more stuff to play on than at Fyford playground.' Mark said he thoroughly approved, and that 'probably everyone should marry the nanny. They're far better at keeping the kids entertained, and cheaper too, not having to pay them. They always were a shrewd lot, those Anscombes.'

At weekends, Anthony felt like the young father in an American TV sitcom: pushing his kids on the swing, filling and emptying the paddling pool, making castles in the sandpit. When Lex and Archie came over to see him, they called him Bert after the chimneysweep in Mary Poppins.

Although a large part of him was contented by domestic life, he sometimes proposed more exciting adventures to Sandra. He had an idea they should go to the Isle of Wight pop festival for the weekend and sleep in tents (Genesis were playing that year) but Sandra worried about leaving the kids for so long. He suggested they should go, on their own, to Biarritz for a week's holiday, and either get his parents or hers to take the children, but Sandra felt anxious, so the idea was quietly dropped. Even locally, Sandra was happier staying at home than going out. She found the formality of the Oxfordshire dinner party circuit daunting, and Anthony was ambivalent about it all in any case, so their life increasingly centred upon their own cosy kitchen.

Unlike Amanda, Sandra did become absorbed into village life. Jasmine started going to the little local school behind All Hallowes and Sandra made friends with the other young mums, who brought their children up to play at the Steepness Farmhouse amusement park. In due course, she became ensnared in Jacinthe Bigges's church flower rota, where her enthusiasm and openness made her instantly popular with the group. As Jacinthe said: 'She's not the most sophisticated bunny, but such an improvement on the first one, I can't tell you. I think in the end she'll do very well. Anyway, Henrietta's going to go on and on for years; I can't see her letting go of anything in a hurry. So Sandra's got plenty of time to polish herself up.'

One Sunday morning, having collected his *Sunday Times* from the village shop, Anthony's eye was caught by an article in the colour magazine. It was an interview with Patrice Bouillon, five or six pages with photographs of him filming on location in Luxor for a movie about ancient Egypt. Patrice was playing the part of Anubis, the jackal-headed god. Two of the photographs included Amanda, described in the text as his 'stunning long-term girlfriend'. One picture was of the two of them sitting with the director of the film beneath the awning of a tent. Amanda was dressed in some kind of Palestinian keffiyeh and heartbreakingly beautiful. The second picture, filling an entire page, showed Patrice and Amanda lounging in bed together, in an enormous white bedstead festooned with mosquito netting. Patrice was bare-chested, Amanda tugging the bed sheets up above her breasts. The picture was the sexiest he had ever seen of her. The pain shot straight to his heart.

His first thought, on returning home, was to find Jasmine and show her the new pictures of her mother. But the prospect of Jasmine and Sandra poring over them, and Sandra's certain disapproval, made him hesitate, and in the end he thrust the magazine into the top drawer of his desk. Over subsequent days and weeks he found himself studying it when no one was around; it became obsessive, his need to turn to pages seventy-two to seventy-nine. The images of Amanda invaded his dreams. He awakened thinking he was still married to her, reached out for her and found Sandra instead.

Over a drink at the Plough and Harrow, Archie asked, 'Was that really your first wife in that colour mag? My mother said it was, but I said, "Not a prayer. A bird that tasty would never go for Anthony".'

'Actually, Archie, that *was* Amanda, thank you very much. But, look, do me a favour and don't say anything about it to Sandra. It'll only upset her.'

The following weekend, having again dreamt half the night about the pictures, Anthony woke up with a massive erection. Making love to Sandra, he thought only of Amanda. Four weeks afterwards, Sandra said, 'This might be a false alarm . . . it could be nothing, but I think I could be pregnant again, darling.' Eight months later to the day, Rosanna Henrietta Marjorie Anscombe was born at Cheltenham General Hospital, weighing in at eight pounds and ten ounces.

The arrival of a second grandchild was greeted with such elation by Len and Marjorie, and such equivocation from Godfrey and Henrietta, it left Anthony slightly deflated. Len arrived in a van from Poole with two of his mates, and delivered a gigantic plywood doll's house. Five feet high, with a hinged front, it was a perfect miniature version of Steepness Farmhouse, with all the rooms recreated including the kitchen with its peninsular breakfast bar and the freezer annexe. It turned out Len had been working on it for six months, 'though I can't claim credit for the fiddly bits – those I handed over to the boys in the workshop.' The doll's house was so large, and plainly too precious ever to be touched by any child, that it was stored in the dining room under lock and key, rendering that little-used room more superfluous than before.

Anthony's parents told him they were privately rather horrified he'd had a third child. 'Haven't you considered the crippling expense of all those school fees? You must have read what that ghastly Denis Healey keeps saying about soaking the rich. You probably won't even be able to afford to *feed* them all, you know.'

'I'm sure we'll manage somehow.'

'Well, you say that, but don't rely on us being able to help. Winchford is burden enough already.'

Rosanna's christening took place, as Richard's before, at All Hallowes with Jeremy Meek officiating. Richard had been allocated Lex and Ginette as godparents at his own christening, so Rosanna was entrusted to Archie and to Annie Plunkett. The two godparents, plus Sandra and Anthony, Jasmine and Richard, Henrietta and Godfrey, Len, Marjorie and Ginette duly assembled in the church for morning service, in the middle of which the baptism would take place. It was on the way to the church, with Anthony driving and Sandra holding Rosanna in the ancestral Anscombe christening dress, that Jasmine began fussing about never having been christened herself. 'It's so unfair,' she wailed. 'Everybody else gets christened, and gets presents from their godparents – everyone except me. I'm the *only person* in my class not to have any godparents, not one single one.'

It was perfectly true, Anthony thought; they never had christened Jasmine. For the simple reason that her mother had done a runner by then.

'Don't worry, precious,' he said. 'It really doesn't matter. Plenty of people don't get christened.'

'But they *do*. And their godparents send them presents for their birthdays and Christmas. Tom in my class got *two pounds* from his godfather. Everybody does. And now Rosanna's going to too, and she's only a baby and it's *so unfair*, and the only reason is because you love Rosanna and Richard more than me.' They had arrived outside the church, where the two sets of grandparents, the godparents and half a dozen villagers, including Sir Percy and Jacinthe Bigges, were waiting to go inside.

'Darling, that just isn't true about loving the others more,' Anthony said. 'We love you all equally.'

'No, you don't. Sandra isn't even my real mother, and she loves her own children better, and *so do you*, because you don't even like my mummy, you hate her.' The little group of onlookers, realising they were witnessing a family drama, variously tuned in or stared politely away, according to character. Jacinthe and Marjorie drifted closer.

'Truly, Jasmine,' Anthony assured her. 'Of course I don't hate her. She's a wonderful person.'

'Then why did you stop being married to her, if you loved her? And why did you hide those pictures of her in your drawer? I saw you. The pictures in the magazine. You hid them where nobody would see them, because you hate her.'

Sandra was not the first mother to discover that three small children under the age of seven is a lot more work than two. And Anthony was not the first father of three to find himself demoted in the family pecking order to a distant number four, whose requirements for feeding, laundry and stimulating conversation ranked low.

Where once he had returned from his long commute to a prettily laid table and a casserole simmering on the hob, he now found a frazzled wife struggling to get everyone bathed and into bed. Jasmine would be sitting at the kitchen table, surrounded by the remains of tea, whingeing over her homework; Richard was waiting impatiently for his bedtime story, while Sandra was busy rocking Rosanna, who wouldn't settle. By the time the children were asleep, it was nine o'clock and Sandra was ready to crash out and in no mood to start cooking her husband's dinner. 'I'm sorry, darling,' she'd say, 'but I'm at the end of my tether. Jasmine's been a nightmare all day. I *wish* she'd stop being so mean to Rosanna; she's quite spiteful. I don't know why. Anyway, would you mind finishing up the children's tea for supper? There's half a shepherds pie in the fridge if you want to heat it through. I'm off to bed.' Anthony soon fell into a routine of helping himself to ladlefuls of mince from the remains in the big earthenware dish, or fish fingers left on the grill – stuck to the bars – and eating them in front of the *Nine o'clock News*.

Not that Anthony complained. He knew at first hand from his weekends how exhausting it could be looking after the brood, and he was sensitive to the fact that Jasmine wasn't Sandra's own child, and it was generally Jasmine who lay behind any domestic drama. When Rosanna woke abruptly from her sleep, bawling her head off, you could be fairly sure Jasmine had slyly pinched her through the bars of her cot; when Richard crushed his fingers in the hinged door of the doll's house, suspicion fell on his half-sister who had unlocked the door to the dining room and drawn him inside to play. It was scarcely surprising Sandra was shattered.

Nor did it help that Sandra seldom got any unbroken sleep. It seemed that every single night one child or other turned up in their room and clambered into the bed, or else stood trance-like in the doorway complaining of hearing scary noises. At pains not to disturb him – the working husband – Sandra would creep out of the bedroom (but never quietly enough) to change a wet sheet. As often as not, he woke up alone in the matrimonial bed. After five years of marriage, Anthony and Sandra's sex life had diminished into a perfunctory reprise.

That Sandra was a perfect mother was acknowledged by everyone. Her devotion to all three children was absolute. The annoying expression 'unconditional love' had not yet passed into common usage, but nothing better described the selflessness and patience Sandra lavished upon Richard, Rosanna and Jasmine. She read and reread their favourite books without a trace of boredom; their clothes were immaculate and perfectly ironed. When Anthony, disheartened by leftovers for the third night in a row, suggested they could probably afford a nanny or au pair to lend a hand around the place, Sandra wouldn't hear of it, saying she couldn't bear the idea of a stranger looking after their children. 'I know what nannies can be like, remember. I wouldn't trust one anywhere near my own kids.' It would, in any case, have been difficult to find anyone who measured up to Sandra's standards of tidiness and hygiene. Rinsing his plate under the kitchen tap, Anthony frequently found a plastic washing-up bowl in the sink full of plastic dolls and duplo left to soak overnight in Dettol.

Anthony worked and sometimes succeeded at being a good father. At weekends, he dutifully pushed Rosanna on the swing and played football with Richard in the garden (Len had delivered miniature goalposts with proper nets) and tried to make sure he did something with Jasmine on her own, even if it was just taking her up to the Priory to visit her grandparents. Henrietta tried to get Jasmine interested in riding, without success, and Jasmine was afraid of the Priory dogs, which yapped and snarled whenever she approached them, but Anthony felt it was important she should have contact with his parents. Within the limits of the very minimal interest Henrietta manifested in any of the grandchildren, Anthony thought she favoured his children by Sandra, and hoped to redress the balance.

Richard, now four, joined his half-sister for mornings at Winchford school, and Sandra felt she spent her life driving to and from the village, collecting first her son, then back again for Jasmine. One afternoon, waiting outside the schoolhouse, Sandra was chatting to one of the other mothers, a newcomer to the area, married to the postman. 'I hope you don't think this is cheeky,' the postman's wife said, 'but I only recently heard the lovely tale about how you and your husband got together.'

Sandra smiled modestly.

'You know, how you met at this big bash up at the Priory, and he fell head over heels for you, and drove non-stop all the way down to the South of France just to see you again. I did think it was romantic. I couldn't get over it. I don't think my old man would ever have done anything half so gallant for me!'

Sandra simply replied, 'I wouldn't believe everything you pick up around the village, if I were you.'

'It was ever such a romantic thing to do,' went on the postman's wife. 'I'm not the least bit surprised either, having met you, because you're such a lovely lady and he knew you were worth going after.'

One summer evening Anthony returned from the City to find Len and a couple of men at work in his garden. They were erecting a treehouse in the copper beech, in the little sheltered bower Anthony had begun referring to as the 'grown-up garden', being the last remaining patch without a children's amenity. It was the place to which he sneaked away with the Sunday newspapers for a few moments of peace.

'Hello, Len. This is a nice surprise finding you here.'

'Wait till you see what we're up to,' Len said. He was halfway up a ladder, lopping off the lower branches of the beech with a saw. 'The children are going to love this. You'll climb up to the playhouse by this rope ladder, see, and then there's going to be a wooden walkway right across the garden to the big yew. Up one tree, across the planks, down the other; what do you reckon?'

'It sounds rather big,' Anthony said doubtfully. He felt a flash of indignation as an ancient branch crashed onto the lawn. Only a surfeit of good manners prevented him from protesting.

'As I said to Marjorie,' Len went on, 'you can't take it with you. May as well give some pleasure while you still can. Anyway, Ant, I'm glad I've run into you because I wanted a word.' He was climbing down the ladder in his dungarees and lumberjack shirt, leaving the others to carry on building the platform. 'The thing is,' he said, 'I'll be fifty-five next birthday and don't want to go on working for ever. Thirty years I've put in to the business and I reckon it's time for someone else to have a go. Fellow I know with a dealership half my size outside Basingstoke sold up recently for three million quid. Well, that got me thinking. And what I thought was "I'll ask Ant for a bit of advice. This could be right up his street, selling off a business." See anything in it, Ant, or is your father-in-law whistling in the wind? Tell me honestly if I am.'

Anthony said he thought he might be able to help, and would be happy to take a look, and he'd ring Len first thing tomorrow from the bank. Ten weeks and four visits to Poole later, Anthony and a roomful of assistants were working on a trade sale prospectus, valuing Potts Electrical Services at four and a half million pounds.

With the involvement of Anscombes, the trade sale went even better than expected. Anthony managed to engineer a small bidding war between Thorn and Creda, both of which wanted to extend their service capabilities, and Len trousered, as he put it, five big ones. Godfrey congratulated his son on his first self-generated deal, which brought with it more than four hundred thousand pounds in commission and fees. Thereafter, Anthony was permitted to sit in a first class carriage on the train, and to read the *Financial Times* after Godfrey had done with it. Only Henrietta, who felt that Len had no business having that sort of capital, was displeased by the turn of events.

A peculiar aspect of Anthony's life was that, surrounded by so many children, he nevertheless felt lonely at weekends, and took to meeting Lex and Archie at the Plough and Harrow for a Sunday evening pint. Anthony felt that, without the prospect of a drink and a bit of amusing chat, he might actually have gone insane. From Friday night until Monday morning, he otherwise exchanged not a single intelligent word with anyone. If he attempted conversation with Sandra, they were constantly interrupted; two or three sentences was the longest they ever went without one child or another butting in. When Sandra taught Rosanna to put her hand up when she wanted to say something, as she did at school, she sat throughout lunch with her arm in the air, trying to catch their eye and murmuring, 'My turn, my turn'.

'For Pete's sake, Rosanna, *put* your bottom *back* on that chair and *stop* hopping up and down like a jack in the box,' Sandra said sharply.

'Daddy's telling me something important about the government. What was it you were saying again, Anthony?' she asked vaguely.

As the children grew older and were deemed sufficiently well behaved to have lunch at the Priory, a routine was established whereby they would go to the Anscombes and the Pottses for regular Sunday lunches. Following Len's lucrative early retirement, they had sold their home in Poole and bought a large gabled mansion at Shipston-on-Stour, twenty-five minutes from Winchford, to be nearer to the grandchildren, and thus became regular visitors to Steepness Farmhouse, to Sandra's great delight. For Christmas, Len gave Anthony one of the first gas-fired barbecues to be imported from the United States; when, by May bank holiday, he showed no signs of assembling it, Len came over for the afternoon, laid out the hundreds of parts across the lawn, and built it from the manual in four hours flat.

Anthony's loneliness was inexplicable. Here he was, rapidly approaching his thirtieth birthday, with a pretty wife and three healthy children, and a good job, and yet much of the time he felt dissatisfied. He wondered whether the rest of his life was destined to be like this. For eight years he had caught the same train, two hundred and thirty-something times a year, from Kingham into Paddington, and chances were he would be riding that same train for thirty-five years more. He was a lifetime commuter. Maudlin with self-pity, he realised he merely went out, earned money, came home and went to bed. What excitement, what magic was there any longer in his life? What passion and danger? Apart from Lex and Archie and a handful of neighbours, whom did he ever see? Other than the view from his window at the bank, and through the smeared windows of a moving carriage, and three or four market towns in North Oxfordshire and Warwickshire, where did they ever go? Unbelievably, he had never once travelled out of England with his wife. There really was nothing to choose between him and Walter Twine – the man who never left Winchford! All this and more passed through Anthony's mind as he gnawed on a cold corncob, left over from the children's tea.

Somewhere upstairs, he could hear Sandra reading *Babar* to Rosanna. Once he had loved to listen to her read aloud to their children. Sandra's soft voice, and the sight of the children in their pyjamas snuggling up to her on the bed, had provoked in him overwhelming feelings of love for his little family, enveloping him with sentimentality and goodwill. Lately, however, he heard in Sandra's droning tone only further evidence of her banality. Would the damn story never end? Through the drawing room ceiling he heard her finish one chapter, then a second, then start on a third. 'Please, Mummy, just one more page,' Rosanna was pleading.

'And then it's my turn for a story,' cheered Richard. 'Hooray! And I'm allowed a long one too – like Rosanna.'

Was it really too much to expect that, after a long day at the office, he should be able to sit down with his wife, have a drink, and chew over the events of the day for ten minutes? That very evening he had gone to the freezer to fetch ice cubes for his whisky – ice from the metal trays he had personally filled the previous night – and found both trays had been removed to make way for home-made ice lollies. Sometimes it seemed to Anthony that his children and their predilections were deployed as a weapon specifically to exasperate him.

Furthermore, it annoyed him that he was annoyed. He did not like this new, sour person he was turning into. When he compared himself to the man he had been only ten years earlier, he was filled with self-pity. He thought of the wild parties and nightclubs he'd been to with Amanda, and those long vanished days seemed like the happiest he had known. He remembered his embroidered waistcoats and velvet trousers, which Sandra had discovered hanging in the back of the wardrobe and given away to Jacinthe Bigges's bring-and-buy sale, and wondered whether he would ever again feel carefree or remotely glamorous.

Each night at Paddington Anthony bought a copy of the *Evening Standard* from the newsvendor next to the station buffet. Beginning with the business pages, he took a quick look at the sport before glancing at the gossip column, which invariably featured people and places that meant nothing to him. One evening he spotted a photograph of Amanda. The accompanying paragraph contained several startling facts. Describing Amanda as the 'gorgeous lover of French movie heart-throb Patrice Bouillon', it went on to say that she had joined Proust's Handmaidens, the all-girl rock band, as lead singer and was being tipped as the new Patti Smith. The paragraph concluded that 'the sultry chanteuse and former teenage bride of Anscombe banking scion Anthony, 29,' was carrying Patrice's baby, but did not expect the pregnancy to affect Proust's Handmaidens' imminent appearance on *Top of the Pops*.

It was Sunday evening, and shortly before seven o'clock Anthony, Lex and Archie congregated outside the Plough and Harrow, waiting for Judy to shoot the bolts and let them in.

The pub was seldom full on Sunday nights, which was why Anthony liked it. Brendon Sheaf, the publican and Judy's boss, was changing over the barrels of Hook Norton bitter. Walter Twine dozed gently in front of the hearth.

'Evening gentlemen,' said Brendon Sheaf. 'And what can oi get the

young squire and his merrie men this fine evening?' One of several irritating things about Brendon was his insistence on making a big thing
about Anthony's family owning the village. Another was his mock Oxfordshire accent.

'Three pints of Hookie, please.'

'Oi trust you'll find moy beer well kept, fine sirs, otherwise you'll put
me in the village stocks. Oi know moy place.'

Before taking on the landlordship at Winchford, Brendon had been
banqueting manager of a big hotel in Colchester, and the new Lucky
Nugget fruit machine by the pub door and novelty condom dispenser in
the gents were his two gifts of civilisation to the country yokels.

Having endured further banter from Brendon, the three men carried
their drinks to the most distant table. 'Now,' Archie said. 'Level with us,
Anthony. Amanda from Proust's Handmaidens. Are we really supposed
to believe she was actually once married to you, of all people?'

Anthony guessed what was coming. Ever since her Thursday night
appearance on *Top of the Pops*, dressed in leather basque and suspend-
ers, Amanda had been the principal topic of conversation, not just in
Winchford but everywhere else. The Friday and Saturday papers had
been full of articles about Proust's Handmaidens, and their catchy track
'Remembering (Things Past)' was shooting up the singles charts. But it
was the 'wild child' lead singer, Amanda, with her smudged kohl-black
eyes and luminous white skin, who had caught the public imagination.
That very morning in the *Sunday Express*, John Junor had railed against
the BBC in his weekly morality column for 'broadcasting provocative
and salacious images of a scantily-clad so-called pop star prancing about
like a Glasgow streetwalker, before the nine o'clock watershed' and called
for their charter to be revoked.

'Actually, Archie, yes. Amanda and I *were* married, strange as it may
seem to you.'

'You mean she actually lived here, in Winchford, with you? Amanda
from Proust's Handmaidens?'

'Of course we did. We lived in Forge Cottage, the end cottage by the
millstream. You know that; everyone does. Jasmine is Amanda's child.'

'Fuck me, you mean you've actually *had sex* with Amanda from
Proust's Handmaidens?'

'Give it a rest, Archie. And stop calling her Amanda from Proust's
Handtowels or whatever their name is. Strictly speaking she's still
Amanda Anscombe, seeing as she hasn't remarried, or Amanda Gibbons
if she's reverted to her maiden name. Or Amanda Bouillon, I guess, if
she ever gets round to marrying that Frog she's with now. I don't know

what she calls herself, actually. Unlike you, I'm not that obsessed.'

Here, Anthony was not being entirely candid. He had in fact left the City at Thursday lunchtime to be sure of catching *TOTP*, and had watched it with Jasmine on the big colour set in the sitting room. Sandra, to his immense relief, had been reading to Rosanna upstairs, and he decided not to tell her what was coming. It seemed easier not to.

Proust's Handmaidens came on one act in from the end and were captivating. The song opened with a burst of furious drumming, followed by a banshee shriek as four girls in black leather beat the hell out of guitars, keyboards and bongo drums. Amanda smouldered hypnotically at the front, snarling and pouting, before belting out the chorus: 'Remember, remember, remember, remember . . . things past, baby.' If she was pregnant, as the papers kept saying, it certainly didn't show.

Jasmine, curled up on the sofa, asked, 'Is that really my mummy?'

'It certainly is. Isn't she a good singer?'

'She looks weird.'

'I think she looks great.'

'You are joking,' came a voice from behind them: Sandra's. She was standing at the door holding a basket of washing. 'Is that Amanda in that outfit? How horrid. I don't actually think this is a very suitable programme for Jasmine. Can we please switch it off?'

Archie was continuing to shake his head in wonder at the thought of Anthony with Amanda.

'I don't know why you're making such a big thing of it,' Anthony said defensively. 'We were only married for two years. Your parents met Amanda. Your mother didn't approve, because she didn't pull her weight at the fête.'

'Amanda at the Winchford fête-worse-than-death . . . unbelievable.'

'Lex met her. too. You came over to the cottage that time.'

'She had this really sexy little mouth. Archie would have gone mad. I'm surprised you didn't see her at Ant's wedding to Sandra. You were there, weren't you?'

'Amanda was at that?'

'She wasn't invited,' Anthony said. 'She turned up at the church with Jasmine, three hours late. Sandra went ballistic.'

'Fuck, wish I'd known,' Archie said. 'I was too busy trying to get off with those nannies.'

'Not just trying,' Lex said.

'Yeah, well, the one called Hayley was a good laugh. Her friend Stacey wasn't bad either, though Dad wasn't happy when she used his razor on her legs.'

'You're such a sleazebag, Arch.'

'You haven't heard the worst bit. I was dropping Stacey at Kingham station the next day when this huge bloke comes over, built like a brick shithouse. Turns out he's her boyfriend, a squaddie called Steve, rippling muscles, tattoos, bloody terrifying. I thought he was going to wring my neck.'

'What did you do?'

'Shoved Stacey out the car and sped off. She seemed to like him. Actually I've remembered something: she said he'd been engaged to Sandra before her – to your Sandra.'

'Well, there you go,' Anthony said. 'Stacey, Hayley, Amanda . . . if you hang out in Winchford long enough, they all come by in the end.'

'You know what?' Archie said. 'It's only just come to me, this. You're a bit of a dark horse, aren't you, Ant? A bit of a secret ladies' man in a standoffish English kind of way.'

'I hardly think so.'

'Think about it. First you elope with Amanda from Proust's Handmaidens and she's how old at the time? Sixteen – that's what I heard. Practically cradle snatching. And then, the minute that one's over, you shack up with a blonde nanny you've nicked off some tattooed para. You're insatiable. And how old are you? Twenty-eight?'

'Twenty-nine.'

'There you are then. Twice married and not yet thirty. Keep it up at this rate and you'll have ten wives.'

'You are so ridiculous. Sandra and I are together for life.'

But, even as he said it, the prospect filled him with a sort of dread.

16

Rosanna, pony-mad, spent every possible moment up at the Priory where her nine-hand chestnut Shetland, Bubblegum, lived in the stables in the old coachyard. Disappointed at the total lack of horsiness from Jasmine and Richard, Henrietta overcompensated wildly with her third grandchild, obliging Anthony to buy her a pony, then a fitted riding jacket, hacking jacket, jodhpurs and a velvet hat. 'After all,' she pointed out, 'I shall be providing stable and tack, so I hardly think riding kit and a mount is beyond you.'

As she approached her sixth birthday, Rosanna emerged as one of the most promising riders of her age in North Oxfordshire, with a board full of rosettes and confidence way beyond her years. Watching her grim determination as she jumped multiple cavalettis at the Heythrop gymkhana, Anthony, who had always hated gymkhanas, was astonished he could have produced such a hardy little star. Not having ridden herself as a child, Sandra took to the Pony Club with a convert's fervour and could be found at everything, proudly leading Rosanna and Bubblegum in the collecting ring; Rosanna's success boosted Sandra's social confidence, as she realised the other 'horsey' mums were less intimidating than she'd imagined, and even seemed to look up to her for being an Anscombe. She was a quick learner, and soon stopped referring to 'horseriding' and dressed herself in quilted jacket and snaffle-buckled shoes. With almost five million pounds burning a hole in his pocket, and time on his hands, Len was turning up at half the shows and talking about buying a horse-box and trailer for his granddaughter.

Immediately beyond the haha at the Priory lay a large paddock known as Repton's Field, laid out as parkland with three mighty horse chestnut trees said to have been planted by Humphrey Repton himself. It was here

Henrietta had erected a miniature cross-country course where Rosanna could practise before the forthcoming Turkdean gymkhana.

Anthony was at work when the terrible accident occurred, and the first he knew about it was when Godfrey burst from his own office next door, stammering that an ambulance had arrived in under twenty minutes and was rushing her to the Radcliffe Infirmary in Oxford.

What had happened was this: Rosanna and Bubblegum were struggling at the water hazard. Each time they approached it, Bubblegum refused, pulling up abruptly and sending Rosanna tumbling over his head. Every time she fell off, she became more frustrated and tearful.

'For Christ's sake, child, use your *heels*. Loosen the reins.' Henrietta in her tartan coat was issuing orders from the sidelines. '*Show* her the jump; that's it. Now take her round and try again.'

For the fifth time, Rosanna rode furiously towards the jump, felt Bubblegum stall and was thrust forwards and down onto the grass. Henrietta snorted. Rosanna wept. Sandra, easily flustered in the presence of her imperious mother-in-law, ran forwards to hold Bubblegum, who was munching buttercups.

'What we're going to try this time,' Henrietta announced, 'is screening the jump. Sandra, you stand on one side, closer than that, with your arms out, and I'll stand on the other. At the approach, we move in behind, look, waving our arms. If necessary, I'll give her a good thwack with my riding crop.'

Sniffling bravely at her sixth approach, Rosanna galloped towards the fence. 'Keep going, *keep going*,' Henrietta commanded. They were less than a yard away now, Henrietta and Sandra flapping furiously to make them take off. Suddenly, they stopped dead. Henrietta brought the silver-topped crop down sharply on Bubblegum's hind quarters, the pony reared and kicked, there was a sickening sound of shattering bone and Henrietta was out cold.

Henrietta's long hospitalisation was followed by a longer convalescence at Winchford Priory. Painstaking reconstruction work on her jaw and cheekbones by one of the country's foremost maxillofacial surgeons eventually made it possible for her to make herself understood, though the effort of speaking exhausted her, and she mostly communicated by terse notes scribbled in the margins of the *Daily Telegraph*. The surgery could not, however, entirely remove the imprint of a well-shod pony's hoof from her face, nor could any amount of orange-based foundation conceal the crescent-shaped crater.

Instinctively wanting to make herself useful to her injured mother-in-law, Sandra became an invaluable nurse and companion, heading up to the Priory after she'd dropped the children at school, changing bed linen, preparing and carrying meals on trays, running baths and retuning Roberts radios between Light Programme and Home Service. With Henrietta out of action, Godfrey needed constant supervision, and Sandra soon found herself organising all his meals as well as any washing Mrs Holcombe considered too much for her. 'How we'd manage without your wife I do not know,' Godfrey told his son, when Anthony was returning the cardigans Sandra removed from Godfrey's dressing room to darn and hand wash.

'She's an incredibly kind person,' Anthony agreed. 'She loves being busy.'

It could not be expected, with his wife on full-time nursing duty, that much could be done for Anthony in the way of meals or attention, and he frequently felt he was leading an independent existence between Anscombes and Steepness Farmhouse. He scarcely spoke to Sandra all week. By the time he got home, she was already crashed out in bed; when he woke up, she had disappeared to a child's bed during the night (Rosanna suffered nightmares about her grandmother's smashed face). Wearing yesterday's shirt and an old pair of boxers retrieved from the bottom of the linen basket, he set off to the station without saying goodbye. Some days, for the first time in his life, he began to feel older and weary. He felt constricted in his three-piece pinstripe City suit, and slightly stooped. He had lost fitness since quitting the farm, and often looked pale from the train and a lack of fresh air. It was hard to credit that this was the same Anthony who had pursued Amanda so impetuously across France.

As domestic life contracted, his working life became more stretching. On his thirtieth birthday, he was summoned into the boardroom by Godfrey and his cousin Michael, the chairman, and in the presence of half a dozen Anscombe cousins was formally made a partner in the family bank. Beneath the three-quarter-length portrait of their founding forebear Ishmail, which hung above a sturdy claw-footed sideboard, a tepid speech of congratulation was made by Michael, and soon afterwards everyone returned to their respective offices to get on with the day's business. Which in Anthony's case meant the disposal of the assets of a bankrupt Birmingham boiler works to a Japanese corporation, and the part-financing of a forty-storey office block in Holborn, which would rival Centre Point for modernity and function. Taking a taxi with Archie through central Birmingham, past the new state-of-the-art Bullring shopping centre in which Anscombes had been a lead investor, a familiar pop anthem drifted from the cab radio: 'Remember, remember, remember, remember . . . things past, baby.' For almost a year, you hadn't been able to get away from that song. The record had spent fifteen weeks in the hit parade and only Abba's 'Dancing Queen' kept it off the top spot. Each time he heard it, Anthony felt his stomach clench. To make matters worse, there had been endless interviews with Amanda in which she had said very little that made sense, but the interviewers had been besotted; you could practically hear them drooling as you read their copy, in which she invoked Jean-Paul Sartre, Jean-Luc Godard and Nico of the Velvet Underground as influences on her work. A style section piece in the *Sunday Times* referred to her 'adolescent marriage' to Anthony ('of the super-rich Anscombe banking dynasty') and included the whole story of his mad dash to Sainte Maxime and the registry office wedding. Anthony found it difficult to recognise himself; they made him sound like a playboy with a creepy thing about young girls. Henrietta wrote an indignant margin note, pronouncing it 'very vulgar and unnecessary' and said she hoped no one in the village would see it.

A newspaper reported Amanda had given birth in Paris to a baby girl, but when Anthony told Jasmine she had a little half-sister, she merely shrugged. Anthony felt depressed for the next few weeks, at the finality of Amanda having Patrice's child. His depression increased further when he read that Amanda and Patrice had married quietly in St Tropez.

So, too, his anxiety about Jasmine grew. That she was unhappy, and probably disturbed, was plain to see. She was painfully uncommunicative, not just with adults but other children too. If visitors came to the house, she hid away in her bedroom; forced to come downstairs and join in, she refused to talk. She had a way of creeping slyly around the house, peering out from behind sofas. Her school reports were discouraging, noting that she was dropping behind the year group, and had difficulties fitting in. When they watched television as a family, while Richard and Rosanna snuggled up to their mother on the sofa, Jasmine chose to sit on her own, signalling her isolation.

Recently she had shown signs of being asthmatic, so the doctor prescribed an inhaler which had to be with her at all times. When Anthony pictured his daughter these days, he saw a tense white face reedily exhaling, and pumping her puffer into the back of her throat.

Ironically, the one area in which Jasmine seemed to show genuine talent was as an actress. Uncomfortable in her own skin, she blossomed when assuming another character, seemingly liberated from awkwardness and even from her asthma. Her only positive reports came from her drama teacher; you could have been reading about a different child. When Anthony and Sandra watched her in the senior school play in Winchford village hall, they could scarcely believe their eyes. Her near-perfect and highly precocious solo of 'Remember (Things Past)' stole the show.

Meanwhile, Henrietta's recovery stalled and even the most optimistic specialists no longer predicted she would resume life as before. She came to hate the idea of being seen by her neighbours or by anyone in the village. Reluctant to leave the house or even her bed, she first lost first muscle tone, then mobility. Eventually it made sense for her to sleep downstairs, and a bed was installed in the white drawing room.

Henrietta's incapacity meant Sandra became more familiar with the big house. Prior to the accident, she had seldom even been upstairs. With her freedom to roam came the realisation of how much needed to be done. She could hardly believe how the house had been neglected. Half the bathrooms on the top floor had damp patches on the ceiling and limescale around the plugholes. As for the kitchen, her father had been quite right: it was completely insanitary. She felt weak at the thought of using the old blackened pots, and the first thing she did was to drive into Moreton and buy a set of non-stick pans, scrubbing brushes and a plastic spatula.

Although she had dimly understood that she and Anthony and the children might one day move into the Priory themselves, Godfrey and Henrietta had seemed so physically formidable, and so completely the masters of their domain, that it had been a distant notion. Now she saw their vulnerability, and the prospect of bringing her small family to this crumbling, unmanageable house became suddenly all too real.

But Sandra was not dispirited. The more time she spent at the Priory, the more she saw its potential, increasingly sure she could turn it into a child-friendly home that actually worked. As each improvement occurred to her, she carefully wrote it down in a notebook and became quite excited. One afternoon, when she and Anthony were up at the house visiting the sick, Sandra took him into her confidence; she was sure he'd be pleased she was taking her job as future chatelaine of Winchford so seriously. So she sat him down in the Great Hall on one of the hard-as-rock sofas (they would be going for a start) and took him through her ideas, room by room.

It was when Sandra proposed replacing the mullioned Elizabethan windows with heat-saving double-glazed sashes that Anthony began to feel irritable.

'Darling, there isn't a hope in hell we could change the windows, even if we wanted to. We're Grade Two listed. The planners wouldn't allow it in a million years.'

When she suggested covering the flagstones with wall-to-wall carpet, he became testy. 'Sandra, the flagstones came from the original priory, from when the Cistercians were here.'

'But they're so uneven. Anyone could trip up over them. Think of Richard tearing about all over the place; he'd be forever falling over and grazing his knees. And they're so cold underfoot.'

'Seriously, darling, it isn't something we could even consider. People come here specially to see them. It would be sacrilege.'

'What do you mean, "People come here to see them"? Which people?'

'Architectural historians. Groups interested in historic houses. They were always coming before my mother got ill.'

'I'd hate that. People wandering all over our home. I want this to be a proper family home, Anthony, not a museum.'

'Look, they don't come *that* often. It's by appointment in any case – they don't just turn up. Just like we open the gardens on August bank holiday Monday in aid of the nurses, and for the local Conservatives.'

'I've had some ideas for the garden too,' Sandra said. 'It isn't practical the way it is; there are too many hidden-away bits. I wouldn't know where the children were with all those yew hedges. I wouldn't feel it was safe.'

'We can hardly tear up the yews. Those hedges have taken ninety years to grow like that. Some of the topiary is Gertrude Jekyll.'

'We wouldn't have to remove it all,' she said doubtfully. 'All we need is a proper enclosed area for the children where I can keep an eye on them from the kitchen. So if Rosanna needs me, I can be there in a second. If we dig out those little low hedges outside the drawing room, that would probably be enough play space.'

'Which low hedges? You don't mean the knot garden?'

'The ones below the patio. You could turf it over and put the sandpit and climbing frame there. I know they're getting a bit old for the sandpit, but other little people do come over to play, and even Richard still makes his water channels.'

'You do realise you're talking about uprooting an original Elizabethan knot garden? There are only about six of them left in the country. There are different medicinal herbs growing in each section – it's an apothecary's garden. The knot garden predates the house. Half the bricks are Tudor, but they reckon the slate is actually medieval.'

'The pathway's a worse hazard than the flagstones. I talked to Dad about it, and he says we'd be liable if any visitors came a cropper. People sue the council all the time – there was this big case in Poole marina.'

'I'm sorry, but it's out of the question. People would think we'd gone completely mad.'

'Only people with no children. I've talked to some of the other mums, and they agree with me.'

'Well, the answer's no. And that's final.' Anthony sat crossly on the sofa, refusing to look at her. 'Anyway, even if we did dig it all up, you still wouldn't be able to see it from the kitchen. The kitchen's on the other side of the house.'

'I was coming to that. I had the idea we could put in a new kitchen where the white drawing room is now. You'd get natural light from the big windows, and it would lead right off the hall, which would work much better. After all, a kitchen *is* meant to be the heart of the home.'

Realising he must take some initiative to repair relations with Sandra, who was acquiring a permanently martyred air, Anthony booked a skiing holiday in Courchevel and somehow persuaded her to come. Naturally this was very difficult since Sandra was reluctant to leave the children or his parents, even for one week. Many complicated arrangements were put in place for the school run, meals and care, involving not just Mrs Holcombe, Judy, Marjorie and Ginette, but the Plunketts and the Elliots and half the mothers at Winchford School. Even the week before departure, Sandra was asking, 'Wouldn't it be better if we took the children with us? After all, Richard is old enough to start learning to ski. And Jasmine's twelve and has never been either.' But Anthony was immovable. He knew he and his wife needed time alone. The Sandra who occupied Steepness Farmhouse, the mother of his younger children, the busy woman in a quilted jacket he saw driving Rosanna to and from her gymkhanas, had become a virtual stranger. One evening, sitting in front of *Panorama* with a plate of cheese, his eye settled on their framed wedding photograph on top of the television. He knew it had been taken only a decade ago, and yet it seemed much older. He picked it up and examined it. The picture was awkwardly posed, because Sandra had been standing at an angle to hide Jasmine's dirty handprints which daubed one panel of her dress, and she was holding her bouquet at bosom-height to cover snotty smears from Jasmine's face. She had been twenty-eight when they married, and Anthony was reminded how happy she had been that day. Her eyes sparkled with contentment. She looked like . . . a nursery school teacher, radiating kindness, and he realised how passionately he wanted to reconnect with the lovely, tender girl he had married.

They rented a self-catering apartment in the village, and each morning took skiing lessons in a class in which they were the only pupils aged over nine. From the first day it became obvious Sandra was a natural skier and Anthony was not; by the third afternoon Sandra was weaving down red runs at breakneck speed, leaving him far behind. Like many tall beginners, Anthony had difficulty with posture and, as he said to Sandra, 'further to fall'. After two years on the gymkhana circuit, leading Bubblegum at events, Sandra was also fitter than her younger husband. Enjoying his first experience of skiing less than he'd expected, Anthony was nonetheless heartened by a change of mood in Sandra. The mountain air, the skiing, the break from Winchford, all cheered her up, and Anthony saw glimpses of the old Sandra. Each morning and evening she rang the children to make sure everything was fine at home, and when she actually forgot to make the call one night he knew the holiday had been a good idea.

One evening in a fondue restaurant, mellow from a second glass of glühwein, Sandra said, 'Can I ask you a question? And I want you to tell me the honest truth.'

'Sure.'

'Do you ever still think about Amanda?'

'About Amanda?' He sounded purposefully vague. 'Amanda Gibbons, you mean? Well, obviously one couldn't get away from her when that awful record came out, but apart from that, no. Why do you ask?'

'Just curious.' She looked down at her plate. 'It's just that . . . you realise you sometimes call me Amanda by mistake?'

'I do?'

'In your sleep. I thought I'd misheard the first time, but it's happened quite a few times.'

'Well, I'm very sorry. It's the first I've heard of it.'

'You do always seem rather fascinated by her; it's annoying, actually.'

'Seriously, I don't give a damn about Amanda. I don't know why you think I do. I never even mention her.'

'Your friends do. Lex and Archie are always talking about her.'

'As far as I'm concerned, Amanda was years ago. I can hardly even remember her. We got married too young; it was all a stupid mistake. We were different people.'

Sandra looked troubled. 'I know it was years ago, but I feel she's still in our lives, somehow. It's probably just people talking about her, because she's famous from the record and this film she's doing.'

'What film?' Anthony spoke too quickly and keenly.

'There you are, you see, you *are* fascinated. That's precisely what I mean.'

'I am not fascinated. Anyway, what is this film?'

She shrugged. 'There was something about it in the paper. I didn't read it that carefully. Some French film; it sounded boring. Her husband's in it. I'm sure they won't show it in Cheltenham anyway.'

'Let's not talk about Amanda. It's history. She doesn't mean anything now.'

'Then don't keep saying her name in your sleep.'

On the fourth day of the skiing holiday, Sandra said she wanted to try a black run. Anthony didn't want to be a wet blanket, so they took the bubble to the top of Vizelle, had lunch and prepared to ski back down. Sandra set off with sleek competence, with Anthony trailing behind.

Anthony was almost at the bottom, and had got through the worst of it, when he fell at the foot of the piste and felt an immediate sharp pain in his right shoulder. Thinking he'd broken it, they struggled into hospital for an X-ray. He hadn't broken anything, but the doctor diagnosed a badly trapped nerve and prescribed painkillers, anti-inflammatories and more pills to help him sleep.

Anthony hobbled about in agony. The flight back was a trial, and when the stewardess accidentally biffed his arm with the edge of her duty-free trolley, the pain was excruciating. A week after arriving home, and showing no improvement, he visited his local GP in Moreton-in-Marsh in his grand Georgian surgery in the Woolmarket. More and stronger pills dulled the pain for as long as he exceeded the recommended dose. After three weeks he still couldn't drive, and Sandra was delivering and collecting him from Kingham station. The daily commute became an obstacle course. His posture was alarmingly contorted.

It was one of Sandra's new horsey friends who recommended acupuncture, which had worked for her when she trapped a nerve at a hunter trial. Sceptical about being stuck all over with needles like a porcupine, Anthony eventually consented and found an acupuncturist in Praed Street, behind Paddington Station, that he could visit on the way home.

The acupuncturist's name was Nula Starling and her consulting rooms were in a second-floor walk-up above a branch of Victoria Wine. Anthony's first impression was that the flat was entirely purple, with purple walls, a purple-painted wooden floor and a purple ceiling decorated with tiny silver stars. Along the windowsill were numerous droopy plants with varnished prickly leaves. Pinned onto the walls were anatomical charts and Chinese scrolls showing the meridians of the human body; the whole place smelt of joss sticks. Most of the space was taken up by a wooden massage table covered by towels and blankets.

Nula reminded Anthony of the people he used to meet with Amanda at parties in Camden Town. She had long wavy brown hair, parted in the middle, and a black and yellow brocade kaftan. In the gloom of the flat, with the curtains half drawn, it was difficult to tell her age, but he guessed she was about thirty. Her face was notably calm and unstressed, and she moved across the floor in a serene, gliding way. When she picked up a pencil to take his details, she held the pencil reverently, as though it was a precious object. All in all, he found her rather disconcerting.

After she'd taken down his medical history and told him something about the twelve primary Qi channels along the eight meridians, and Anthony had explained about the skiing accident to his shoulder, Nula asked him to strip down to his boxer shorts and lie on his back on the table. Gently covering him with a blanket, she sat on a little stool and held his pulse. Her fingers felt remarkably light, as though barely connecting with his skin. Close up, she was surprisingly pretty, Anthony felt.

After a while, he asked, 'Can you feel anything?'

'Too much stagnation.' She spoke practically in a whisper. 'The energy is blocked; nothing is moving.'

'Must be my frozen shoulder. The nerve's wrapped itself round the bone, apparently. Can you do anything for it?'

'Oh yes, I can unblock the energy lines. That is simple to do.' Then she said, 'You are a very complex person.'

'I am?'

'I feel a lot of repression. Repression but also passion. You have a great capacity for love locked up inside you.'

'Really?' Anthony was strangely pleased by this information.

'I feel it in the spleen and the stomach – the Yin and the Yang. The stomach is related to the emotion of pensiveness. You have a lot of troubles in your life – some anxiety.'

'That's certainly true.' Swaddled in blankets, Anthony was rather enjoying the conversation. It wasn't at all what he'd been expecting. He'd imagined an inscrutable Chinese doctor plunging needles into his shoulder, but instead here was this loopy, attractive woman telling him about himself with uncanny accuracy.

'The spleen and stomach are paired organs,' she was telling him. 'They belong to earth in the Five Phases, the season of long summer, the climatic condition of dampness, the colour yellow, the taste of sweetness, and the sound of singing. Their opening is the mouth and they control the flesh and the limbs.'

She was continuing to press – so lightly – on his pulse, but the fingers of her other hand moved to his chest.

'I can feel your heart,' she said. 'It is very strong, but I feel sadness here too. A sadness of parting. Have you some sadness present in your life?'

'Well, I don't know about sadness exactly. I suppose we all have our good and bad days.'

'The heart and small intestine are paired organs, corresponding to fire in the Five Phases. They represent the southerly direction, the summer season, the climatic condition of heat, the colour red, the emotion of happiness, the sound of laughter, the taste of bitterness and the odour of burning. The point of entry is the tongue.'

'Good Lord,' said Anthony. 'That one sounds like a bit of a mish-mash – happiness and laughter, but bitterness in there too. I don't think of myself as a particularly bitter person, actually.'

'What I can feel is a body out of balance. You strive for balance in your life, but cannot achieve it. There is an absence of Qi. There is a yearning and passion unfulfilled.'

'All this passion stuff is a bit embarrassing, I must say.'

'You cannot feel the passion?'

'Well, I've had three children. But, recently . . . I mean, I have to catch a pretty early train into London every morning, and I'm knackered by the time I get home. It's more weekends and holidays . . . and not always that, actually.'

'I am going to make a start in releasing the Qi and getting the energy moving,' Nula said, 'but I cannot do it all in one session. We will need a course: six treatments, maybe twelve.'

'And it will cure my shoulder?'

'Your shoulder, of course. That will begin to happen in only two or three treatments. But I need to work on the whole of you.'

Then Nula opened a red lacquer box with Chinese letters and retrieved three sharp, silver needles. 'For the first treatment, this will be sufficient,' she said, twisting them into the top of his forefinger, halfway up the arm and into the Ah Shi points in his shoulder. Then, very gently, she twiddled the needles until he felt a dull throb.

'That was actually quite painful.'

'That is good,' Nula said. 'That means it's working. The Qi around your shoulder was stagnated, but it's begun to move freely again. Next week we can go deeper.'

It was Anthony's routine on Sunday afternoons, before meeting up with Archie and Lex at the Plough and Harrow, to stride around the fields with a shotgun hoping for a pot at a rook or rabbit. Generally Richard accompanied his father, and was allowed a couple of shots at the rook colony that swirled around the ivy-clad coppice near the Moreton road. Since his trapped nerve, Anthony found it too painful to shoot, so

Richard was getting a lot of practice and improving fast. The Winchford shoot was one of the best in Oxfordshire, second only to Lockinge and Compton Beauchamp, and the days rented out to syndicates covered the salaries for three gamekeepers. Godfrey kept half a dozen of the best days back for himself and his neighbours, and had promised his grandson that, once he was twelve, he could join the guns for his first proper shoot. Anthony shot at Winchford a couple of times a year, but it hadn't been viable during the Amanda period, and Sandra liked him to be at home on Saturdays to supervise the children. 'After all, you've hardly seen them all week.'

Anthony watched as Richard took careful aim at a sinister-looking rook gliding on bat wings from its twig-lined nest. His concentration was total. Sometimes, in his hooded brow, Anthony recognised something of Godfrey in his son, but there was no getting away from the fact that Richard was a stocky, miniature version of his grandfather Len. With his sturdy legs and springy black hair, he had inherited none of the Anscombe diffidence. The word from school was that he wasn't especially bright, and Anthony hoped he'd get through the entrance test at Broadley Court, Anthony's old prep school, where Richard was meant to be heading in a year next September.

The shotgun went off and the rook crashed through branches into the undergrowth with a thud. In no time Richard had retrieved it and dangled it by the neck from a fence with a length of binding twine.

'Well done, Richard. That's your fourth rook, isn't it?'

'Fifth! I shot four before, remember. Two up at Grandfather Anscombe's house, one in the garden and one in Repton's Field, so it's *five.*'

'You're becoming a good shot.'

They were walking back towards the farmhouse across a spooky area of pastureland covered by ancient barrows, which some people reckoned were the remains of a Black Death settlement, and others said was medieval strip agriculture. Richard said, 'Dad, can I ask you a question?'

'Sure.'

'You know Grandfather's house and the farm and everything?'

'Winchford, you mean?'

'Yes, Winchford. Well, I was just wondering, when Grandfather Anscombe dies, who is going to actually live there then?'

'Well, that's a bit of a hypothetical question because he isn't going to die for a long, long time. But, when he does, it will probably be us.'

'That's what Mum says too. But what I was *really* wondering is, when *you* die, then who's going to have it?'

'Now that really is a long way off. At least I hope so. When I die, goodness knows. Probably the Labour government will have confiscated it long ago and sold it to Sainsbury's for a car park.'

'Be sensible, Dad. Who *will* get it?'

'Seriously? You, probably.'

Richard's face lit up. 'I *hoped* you'd say that. You promise it'll be me and not Jasmine?'

Realising he was straying into dangerous territory, Anthony said, 'Obviously all the children will get a fair share. Everything will be shared out . . . and it's not very good manners to talk about things like that.'

'It would just be *so unfair* if Jasmine got it,' Richard went on. 'I mean, her mother isn't even your *wife*. She was just an early mistake, and she's a bad mother. That's what Mum says. And, anyway, I'm a boy and she's a girl, and the eldest boy is *supposed* to inherit an estate, that's what Mum says, and Grandpa Potts agrees.'

Anthony was startled, on returning to the farmhouse, to find his fat sister-in-law Ginette in the kitchen hugging Sandra and both of them in floods of tears. Ginette's shoulders heaved with misery. Sandra was trembling. Jasmine and Rosanna sat dumbly at the table, watching the sisters comfort each other.

'Sandra, Ginette, whatever's happened?'

His wife turned to him, and he saw her eyes were bloodshot.

'It's . . . it's *Dad*,' she blurted, dissolving into violent sobs.

'Len? Whatever's happened to him? Is he OK?'

The question triggered a further eruption, and Ginette actually began howling with grief, which Anthony had never witnessed in real life before. His first thought was that Len must have driven his red Maserati – the latest treat from the sale of Potts Electrical Services – into an oncoming lorry, something he'd been anticipating for several weeks.

'He's left Mum.' Sandra calmed herself for long enough to speak. 'He's walked out on her and gone off . . . with someone else.'

'Grief. When did all this happen?'

'This morning. Ginette's just driven over from Shipston. After breakfast he just came into the conservatory where Mum was watering the plants and told her he'd found someone and wanted to leave. And then he did, just like that.'

'I can't believe it. I thought Len and Marjorie were so happy.'

'So did we,' wailed Ginette. 'Dad's forever saying how much Mum means to him. It was their anniversary last week and he sent her fifty long-stemmed red roses.' And then she broke down again at the memory of it.

Anthony suggested they might all need a drink and fetched a glass of white wine for Sandra and a Bailey's for Ginette. 'Do we know who this other woman is?'

'She's called Diane,' Sandra said. 'She's a complete bitch, only thirty-three. It's disgusting. She's younger than me.'

'How did they even meet?'

'She lives in the village, just down the lane from Mum and Dad's. I've met her up at the house, and Ginette says she was always round there, the scheming cow. She was helping Dad choose his boat.'

'His *boat*?'

'He's been on about buying one of those Sunseekers. He always wanted one; he was forever looking at them in Poole marina. Diane said she'd help him because Mum suffers from seasickness.'

'God, what a mess,' Anthony said. 'Do we know where your father is now? Where they've gone, I mean.'

'That's the worst thing,' Sandra said. 'He refused to say. He wouldn't tell Mum anything. He just said he'd bought a yacht and is going to live on it with Diane, somewhere abroad in the sunshine.'

'Your poor mother. She must be devastated.'

'She's driving over right now,' Sandra said. 'I've asked her and Ginette to stop with us until we know what's happening. Jasmine's going to double up with Rosanna, and Mum will move into Jasmine's room with a put-me-up for Ginette.'

17

A nthony came to look forward to his weekly acupuncture sessions in Paddington. There was no doubt about it, Nula's needles were doing wonders for his shoulder. After three treatments, it was no longer painful to lift up his briefcase, and by the eighth he was able to play a gentle game of tennis with his father. As he progressed physically, Nula expanded the scope of the treatments, until the sole purpose of the needles was to unblock aspects of Anthony's personality. As she explained it, Anthony was a soul in arrested development, emotionally stagnated. In some dextrous way which was oddly appealing, Nula inferred his trapped nerve hadn't been the result of the Courchevel skiing accident but of some deeper malaise, physical manifestation of an inner turbulence and his body's way of signalling distress. 'Your energy, your Qi, is smothered. I am going to set it free,' she said, tossing her hair. 'Like releasing a dove from its cage.'

The routine of subjecting himself to Nula's needles, and of answering her increasingly probing psychological questions, no longer caused him either pain or embarrassment. Face up on her treatment table, bundled in towels and blankets, he felt strangely liberated. As Nula held his pulse, or gently massaged his feet as a prelude to her quivering needles, he began to confide in her.

He talked about Anscombes, his small successes and disappointments; he told her about Winchford, the house and the village, and how his love for the place was tempered by feelings of responsibility and obligation and the expense of keeping it all going, and how he dreaded being the last Anscombe to live there: the one who let it go.

Nula had a way of gently nudging the conversation from the factual to the emotional. How had growing up in a place like Winchford moulded him as a person? How had it affected his relationship with his parents? Had he ever felt, as a small child, they might care more about Winchford than about him?

Sometimes, in the middle of their treatments, which had begun as one-hour sessions but now ran to ninety minutes, Nula appeared to have left the room altogether, leaving Anthony in a suspended state, half waking, half sleeping, with only the murmur of traffic from Praed Street below, and the wail of an ambulance pulling up outside St Mary's Hospital. And then, somewhere behind him, he would hear her soft footsteps – she was generally barefoot – and realised she had been there all the time, awaiting the auspicious moment to resume the treatment. 'I am your guardian angel,' she said. 'You need someone to watch over you.'

She worried about the pericardium channel of Anthony's hand. She detected in it a fatal blockage of Qi, dissipated by a yearning for love, first in childhood, now adulthood. She told him that, in her years as an acupuncturist, she had never encountered such a capacity for passion or such deep sadness.

For the first ten treatments, some English reserve prevented him from talking about his domestic life. He had, of course, told Nula he was married to Sandra and had three children, but had not elaborated, and certainly never mentioned Amanda. One evening, however, while easing a particularly stubborn needle into his calf, Nula said, 'There is something I don't understand, Anthony. I have sensed this before in you. Your channels are divergent. Like tributaries of a mighty river, your heart splits in two directions.'

Then he told her about Amanda, how he had fallen madly in love and what an unmitigated disaster it had been, and how he'd put her completely behind him now. And how he was so lucky being married to Sandra, because she wasn't crazy for one thing, and was wonderful with his children, even Jasmine who wasn't her own. Nula listened sympathetically, hardly interrupting as it all came tumbling out, only prompting him slightly from time to time, and Anthony felt a wonderful release being able to talk about his troubles to such an interesting, intuitive person. He realised it was the first time he'd talked honestly and openly about himself. Thinking about it afterwards on the train, he reckoned it was the first intelligent conversation he'd had with anyone on an emotional level since Amanda left.

Having breached his defences, Nula kept on the scent like a bloodhound. As they revisited every nuance of his relationship with Amanda, Anthony came to see that Nula and Amanda had a lot in common; there was a directness about them, a readiness to challenge and provoke.

Where Sandra soothed and left well alone, Nula rummaged in his psyche, distressing him by reopening old wounds, but making him stronger by confronting them.

'It sounds to me,' Nula said, in her soft, mellifluous voice, 'you loved Amanda because she expanded your soul.'

'Expanded it?'

'The soul is like every other organ of the body. When you take exercise, the muscles in your legs and the capacity of your lungs strengthen and expand. So it is with the soul. Without sustenance, a soul withers. With the correct nourishment, it expands. It's like Yin and Yang. In order to soar, each soul must pair with a true partner.'

'And you think Amanda was more right for me than Sandra is?'

'It isn't for me to answer those questions. Only you can do that. There are partners who nourish our Qi and partners who stagnate it. For every soul, there are other souls with the capacity to pair with them. The purpose of the journey is to find your soulmate.'

18

After a fortnight of cajoling by Sandra, Anthony agreed to fly down to Nice at the weekend and confront his father-in-law, who had surfaced at a marina at Villeneuve Loubet near Cagnes-sur-Mer in the Baie des Anges. The prospect of turning up uninvited at Len's floating lovenest – on a mission to reunite him with the wife he'd so recently abandoned – filled Anthony with dread; on the other hand, the alternative of spending a third weekend in a row at Steepness Farmhouse with Marjorie, Sandra and Ginette, variously tearful and indignant, was on balance slightly worse, so he acquiesced and caught a Friday evening flight to the south of France.

Arriving too late at night to drive down the coast and embark on a deck-to-deck search of the several hundred yachts moored around the Baie des Anges, he found a hotel in the centre of Nice and set out for a quick dinner. It was the first time he had returned to Nice since his doomed wedding at the Hôtel de Ville thirteen years earlier, and it cannot merely have been chance that found him striding through the deserted flower market and then past the great civic edifice where he and Amanda had got married. And, later, having rejected a dozen plausible restaurants as too quiet or too noisy, he had ended up at the pavement fish restaurant, scene of their post-wedding lunch.

Having secured, after a lengthy wait, a table for one overlooking the boulevard, Anthony proceeded to get quietly plastered. He had bought a newspaper and a couple of French magazines to leaf through while he was eating, but the sensation of being back in that seminal restaurant almost overwhelmed him. Aside from the prices, the menu seemed un-altered. Waiters scurried by balancing *plateaux des fruits de mer*. Teenage toughs on Vespas cruised past gesticulating at pretty girls. In the narrow corridor between kitchen and restaurant, he could see the callbox from which he had rung Henrietta at Winchford Priory to break the news of his marriage. The sight of the telephone reminded him he really ought to ring home, to tell Sandra he'd arrived safely and say goodnight to the children, but he couldn't quite face it. With his fourth glass of wine, nostalgic melancholy gave way to something perilously closer to regret. The actual table once occupied by himself and Amanda – the table at which the restaurant owner, bedazzled by the nubile bride, had presented them with a bottle of champagne – was within arm's length from where he sat now. He could remember precisely how Amanda had looked that day in her white lace nightdress, and tears pricked his eyes. What would he not have given to rewind time, and begin things again with the girl whose soul was paired with his own?

He finished off the bottle and ordered coffee and a brandy. Normally he never touched brandy, but the sight of an oversized balloon glass deposited on to a neighbouring table seemed in keeping with his maudlin mood. Idly, he flicked through the *Paris Match* he had bought at the kiosk. There were fuzzy pictures inside of the Monagesque princesses topless sunbathing at Jimmy'z beach bar, and pictures of Brigitte Bardot shopping for melons in the Des Lices market in St Tropez. Then he saw Amanda . . .

In fact, it was Patrice he noticed first. With his big Roman nose and heavy-lidded eyes, he was unmistakable. Amanda was standing next to him, holding a baby. They were on a beach with palm trees and a blue sea – it looked Caribbean – in a big crowd of people. Then he saw Mick Jagger and Jerry Hall, and Princess Margaret under the shade of a white and gold parasol.

Gingerly, painfully, he translated the text as best he could. Amanda, Patrice and the uncaptioned baby were staying on Mustique. Whether they were actually staying at Mick Jagger's villa, or merely partying with him on the island, Anthony could not be certain. Amanda looked breathtaking. He held the photograph close to his face and, half sloshed, kissed the page until his lips were coated by rotogravure ink.

The following morning, somewhat the worse for wear, he took a cab along the coast to Cagnes-sur-Mer, where Len's newly acquired yacht was reputed to be moored. He arrived at an immense development of high-rise apartments overlooking a man-made harbour, with sea walls formed of huge boulders, and half a dozen concrete jetties. From these bobbed several hundred craft of all shapes and sizes in murky black waters that smelt faintly of diesel. He ordered a strong cup of coffee in a café and stared out at the lines of fibreglass boats glinting in the sunshine, wondering where to begin. The biggest ones, with tinted windows and mahogany-lined cabins, were exuberantly vulgar, and he felt sure his father-in-law would have loved one, but even his recent windfall wouldn't quite have run to that. There were yachts with panthers painted on their sides, and yachts with doormats at the bottom of their gangplanks on the quayside announcing their names: Costa Packet, Costa Fortune, Floating Asset. Most had national flags dangling from their sterns, and Anthony decided to start at one end of the basin and work his way along to the other, checking out every boat displaying a White Ensign.

It was coming up to three hours later when he did a double-take. There, surely, was Marjorie, her perky face and neat beehive appearing through the hatch of a gleaming Sunseeker. Len, in billowing khaki shorts, was handing her a glass.

It took Anthony a moment to realise it wasn't Marjorie at all, but a streamlined, younger reissue, groomed and nimble and eager to please. Diane – it could be no one else – hopped up onto the deck and perched herself on a plastic sunlounger. Her legs in shorts were long, white and slightly bandy, and she placed a straw hat on top of her immaculately made-up face.

'Len?' Anthony approached the yacht. 'Len? Can I come aboard?'

Len did not appear particularly surprised by the sudden arrival of his son-in-law, and flashed a big toothy smile of welcome. 'Perfect timing as ever, young man,' he said, seizing his hand and shaking it violently. 'I've just cracked open a nice cold bottle of Cristal, which is the only way to start the day round here. Do you know, you can buy this stuff in the Monoprix for three quid a bottle? About a quarter what it costs at home. That's one reason I've given the Chancellor the old one finger salute. One of many, I should say.' Then he said, 'Don't think you've met Diane. God knows why she's thrown in her lot with an old chap like yours truly, but she has, God bless her. Come on over here, gorgeous, and meet my son-in-law. Don't worry, he doesn't bite. He does talk like he's got a couple of plums stuck up his back passage, but don't let that put you off. He's a good bloke is Tony, even if he doesn't know how to assemble a barbecue from a flatpack. Remember that, Tone?'

Anthony smiled appreciatively at the old joke. 'Knowing you, you probably built this boat from a kit.'

Len roared with laughter. 'That would be beyond even me, though I did replumb the shower yesterday, didn't I, Di? Couldn't stand the drip, drip, drip.'

'Len's so clever with his hands,' Diane said. 'He has natural aptitude.'

She even talked like Marjorie. 'He's going to do all the routine maintenance himself, aren't you, Len?'

'A power shower they called it,' Len went on, 'though the pressure wasn't up to much. Took four hours all told – works like a dream now. I love a strong shower. Have one yourself if you're feeling hot, Tone. This sunshine's a bit of all right, isn't it? Twenty-four days in a row we've had, all blue skies. I've forgotten what a cloud looks like.'

'It's been filthy round us,' Anthony said. 'Not much of a summer at all. Marjorie and Sandra asked me to see you. And Ginette.'

'Thought they might of,' Len said, topping up everyone's glass. 'You've been dispatched, have you, to tell old Len what a bad dog he's been?'

'Something like that. As you can imagine, everyone's very upset.' He looked uncomfortably towards Diane, wishing she wasn't there.

'Oh, don't mind Diane,' Len said, reading his mind. 'There's nothing we can't say in front of you, is there, gorgeous?'

Diane pursed her lips in a manner that reminded Anthony vividly of Marjorie, and said, 'It's not a very nice situation, Anthony, because nobody likes to upset anybody, but Len says it will all blow over with time, and he's always right. He's such a clever man, aren't you, lover boy?'

There was something sick-making and disarming about their constant flow of endearments. Len and Diane were evidently crazy about each other, and it certainly didn't look like he was about to scuttle home. Anthony noticed Len was wearing a thin gold chain around his fat neck, which he'd never done before.

'Can I ask what your plans are?' Anthony asked.

'Plans? No plans! That's the beauty of living on a yacht. We might run her down to Monte at some point; then again we might not. We've got some mates sailing over to the Costa Smerelda who asked us to come along for the ride, but we haven't decided, and we won't till we do. And do you know the best bit? No taxes! Everything's offshore, no forwarding address. First sign of a taxman and it's anchors aweigh and off we go. Can't stand England now. Whole place is going down the toilet. When I was running my own business, I wouldn't have left Callaghan in charge of the warehouse. So it's goodbye and good riddance.'

'You can't just walk out on your family. They're devastated.'

'I know, I know – guilty as charged; you don't have to remind me. It's all a damn shame. Marjorie's a nice lady, and I worship the girls, even if they can be Little Miss Madams on occasion, but life moves on. You know that yourself, Tone – you've been hitched before. Sometimes things don't feel right any more. With the business sold I was just hanging about the house with nothing to do. Then Diane came into the frame, and the whole picture changed, and here we are.'

'So you're planning on living for ever on this boat?'

'I've had it up to here with lousy weather, filthy streets, unions guzzling beer and sandwiches with the PM at Number Ten, all cosy-cosy while the country falls apart. Don't want any part in it. We'll be all right, won't we, Diane? The prices in the restaurants out here, they're incredible. You can have a four-course meal with a nice carafe of a decent little vino for, what, thirty francs? Barely three quid!'

'And what about Marjorie?'

'Never you worry, I'll see her all right and tight. I'm going to make her a hefty settlement, very generous. My lawyers are on the case. She knows we never had much of a marriage, not for a long time. She'd admit that, if you put it to her.'

For the briefest of moments Anthony was filled with a sneaky admiration for Len, who'd clearly decided to please himself at this late stage in his life. Len certainly seemed to be relishing his newfound freedom.

'Won't you get bored? I know how busy you like to be,' Anthony said.

'Bored! Never! There's always things to be messing about with on a boat, and you couldn't be bored with Diane here. And there's always people passing through for a jaw, commercial blokes like myself who've taken early retirement and don't fancy England any more. And there's the casino.'

'The casino? You're not a gambler, are you?'

'Only the odd game of roulette now and then. I go for the atmosphere. But I'll tell you what, old Len's been working up a system where you can't lose. It's got to be logically impossible.'

'Really?'

'I won't say I invented it, because I didn't, but that doesn't mean it isn't the goods. I've banked a lot of winnings already, haven't I, Diane?'

'Len's brilliant at the tables,' Diane said. 'The croupiers cringe when he comes in, he's that lucky.'

'I'll let you in on the secret,' Len said, 'providing you keep it under your hat. Always bet on red. Start with a fiver; if you lose, double the stake. If you lose again, double it. If you lose six times in a row, doesn't matter, carry on doubling on red. Eventually red's got to come up, and you get it all back, everything. And half the time you're going to win anyway. As a system, it's bloody foolproof, you take my word.'

19

The trains to Kingham were cancelled for the third night running, and the pavements overflowed with pedestrians affected by the wildcat Tube strikes. Godfrey was refusing to travel into London until things settled down, and stayed put in Winchford. Anthony's uncle Michael, Chairman of Anscombes, looked grave and warned the partners that, unless the Prime Minister got to grips with the situation soon, he expected a devaluation of sterling and the stockmarket in freefall. 'Callaghan's a walking disaster. At this rate, the so-called winter of discontent will go right on into the spring.'

To reach Praed Street for his weekly acupuncture, Anthony had walked from Oxford Circus and arrived twenty-five minutes late.

'I'm sorry, Nula. The ruddy Tube's stopped running and most of the bus drivers have come out in sympathy too.'

Nula looked startled by Anthony's report from the front line. She was cross-legged on the massage table, practising deep breathing. 'Sympathy with whom? Is there a problem?'

'Only a national strike, virtually. The train drivers are out in support of the steel workers. The coalminers joined in. Now their comrades the Tube and bus drivers are out too. The hospital porters will be next, followed no doubt by the nurses.'

'I didn't know. Well, I'm sure they all deserve some more money; they all work so hard.'

Something Anthony found exasperating about his spiritual guru was her total ignorance of anything beyond her treatment room. It was entirely in character for her to be oblivious to the industrial unrest paralysing Britain. He had never seen a newspaper in her flat and was fairly certain there was no television either. He reckoned if the Red Army ever rolled across the frontier into the West, the first Nula would know about it was when they burst into her purple chamber.

Paradoxically, it was her detachment from world affairs that made her so appealing. Her ability to pick up on his frustrations and insecurities was uncanny. When she leaned across him on the massage table, her long brown hair brushing against his shoulders, he blushed that she might guess what was passing through his mind. Numerous small Rajasthani mirrors hung on the walls, and he studied her face while she slid her thin silver needles in his stomach and chest. Sometimes she worked in silence, sometimes probed him with questions. Frequently, she made him recount his seminal experience on the storm-tossed raft, when he had made love to Amanda for the first time. The therapy sessions left him maudlin and horny.

Acupuncture reawakened longings he thought had vanished for ever. Through Nula, he remembered the bold, impetuous Anthony who had travelled halfway across Europe in pursuit of a girl. After the domestic claustrophobia of life with Sandra, Nula rediscovered his soul. When she twiddled a silver needle in the Ah Shi point above his groin, he felt a rush of heat to his balls and the stirring of an almighty hard-on.

After the session on the night of the train strike, Anthony said, 'You don't feel like a quick bite to eat, do you? That's if you don't have another patient arriving.'

Nula said, 'That would be nice. I haven't eaten today. I've been fasting.'

'Great, there's a curry place I keep passing opposite the station. They do tandooris, that sort of thing.' Nula said she was vegetarian, but felt sure she could find something suitable on the menu.

She changed out of her loose treatment clothes into tight black jeans, black jumper and boots, which made her grow in height by three inches. It was the first time he had seen her without bare feet. Walking alongside her to the Star of Bengal, he felt inexplicably shy, because she knew more about him than any person alive, including Sandra. In everyday clothes, she looked like a student.

The Star of Bengal was the kind of Indian restaurant then common-place, with red velveteen flock wallpaper, starched white tablecloths, five lurking waiters and no customers. There were more than one hundred dishes to choose between on the tasselled menu, all smothered in the same thick, brown, masala sauce. Anthony said, 'It's really nice to be able to look at you properly for a change. Normally I'm lying there under the blankets with my eyes shut, while you do all the work.'

Nula laughed, and her face lit up in a way Anthony found attractive.

It was the first time he had ever seen her laugh.

'Anyway,' he said, 'this supper is to thank you for everything you've done for me. My shoulder's completely cured and you've given me lots of great advice.'

'It has helped you?'

'Definitely. I can play tennis, squash, even shoot again.'

'I meant, has the treatment helped you grow in yourself?'

'In myself? God, I don't really think about that much. No time. Not with my job and three children and everything.'

'Don't joke, please, Anthony. You always try to avoid serious questions, but it is good to be serious sometimes.'

'I'm sorry, I just find it slightly embarrassing talking about personal things. It's hard enough at your flat when I can't see you. But across the table . . .'

'Then shut your eyes,' Nula said. 'Close your eyes and tell me what you want from your life.'

'Well, that is difficult,' he said slowly, closing his eyes as she asked. 'What do I want? I'm so lucky already in so many ways, with the children and the house, and Sandra of course.'

'But you have told me you don't feel happy, not fulfilled.'

'It's true, I do sometimes feel it's all a bit predictable. That isn't a criticism of Sandra or anything; she's a fantastic mother and all that.'

'But you don't connect spiritually. Or sexually.'

'Steady on – we've got two great kids together, you know. And do you mind if I open my eyes now? I'd like some more of that sag paneer aloo before they take it away.'

He reopened them to find Nula staring intently at him as though reading his mind, which was disconcerting because what he was thinking was how much he fancied her. Whether it was the effect of the needle in his groin, or her provoking references to sexual compatibility, Anthony longed for her. More than any other woman, Nula understood him as a person. They responded to each other on a far deeper level than he had ever managed even with Amanda, and as for Sandra, it was hopeless: they were chalk and cheese.

They lingered in the restaurant while Anthony talked about Amanda and Sandra and Henrietta and Winchford against a background of piped sitar music. He told Nula about seeing a photograph of Amanda in a French magazine, and how it had meant nothing to him, like looking at a picture of a stranger.

'I'm sorry,' he said. 'I shouldn't be talking about myself all the time. I'd much rather hear about *you*.' But when he addressed any direct question to Nula, she turned the question back on him, encouraging him to open up even more.

The place was closing for the night, and they were standing on the pavement in Praed Street. Suddenly it seemed inevitable that he should accompany her back to the purple room, and that they should make love on the wooden massage table.

20

Anthony and Sandra were standing on the touchline at Broadley Court preparatory school in Berkshire, watching Richard play in his third team match against St George's. It was nine weeks into the Michaelmas term and, so far, he was settling in fine. Academically it was always going to be a stretch, and had Archie Trumper, Anthony's old headmaster still *in situ*, not been lenient in his admissions policy, Richard would probably not have passed into Broadley at all; but on the games field he was a natural. As he watched his son pounding down the wing, sending his opponents flying, Anthony recognised more of Len in him: confident, stocky and stubborn.

'Come on, Broadley Court! Good pass, Tom. Well done!' Sandra, in quilted Barbour, was cheering frenziedly. Having conquered the church flower rota and Pony Club, she would soon be leading the Broadley Colts Supporters' Club too. Already, Anthony noticed, she knew the names of all the boys in the team, and most of their parents too. Always rather reserved himself in school situations, he watched his wife with a mixture of admiration and disdain.

The heavens opened, as they always seemed to, the minute the whistle blew to start play. Now it was sheeting down and forming in muddy puddles across the pitch. Rosanna, in her Winchford school anorak, shivered at Anthony's legs. Jasmine, who had come to watch the match under protest, was sitting in the car listening to Kate Bush. Sandra was chatting away to some other parents, John and Constance Furlong, whose son Tom was Richard's best friend. Sandra was saying, 'We must get you all over to Winchford at long exeat. It would be lovely to get the boys together, since they've become such mates.'

Anthony hoped the invitation didn't extend to the parents, since Mr

Furlong struck him as a particularly dull stick. He couldn't imagine what Mrs Furlong – Constance – saw in him; she looked far too lovely, like a fragile pre-Raphaelite with her pale skin and long red hair.

Sandra was discussing the various members of staff with John Furlong. Something else he found astonishing and faintly irritating about his wife was the way she could recognise every teacher – not just the ones who taught Richard, but every teacher in the school. She knew the names of their wives, which subjects they taught, using which textbooks and in which classrooms. She had also taken to using school slang. She would ask Richard, 'Do you need to use the backs before Godders?' (the lavatory before evening chapel). Anthony, who had been at the place himself, felt he knew less about Broadley Court than Sandra did.

He also observed, and disliked, her growing snobbishness, which was especially obnoxious at the school. As they sat in chapel she would whisper, 'That little chap with brown hair in the choir is Viscount Arbroath's grandson,' or 'That's Lord Parkes's son, Adam.'

Since taking up with Nula he had redoubled his efforts at being a supportive husband. He realised Sandra had never been the ideal choice of wife, but he owed her a lot. In the past year Godfrey's health had deteriorated, and Sandra now had two invalids to care for at the Priory. It didn't help that Henrietta saw Godfrey as a rival for Sandra's room service, and insisted she take precedence in everything. Meanwhile, Len was still holed up with Diane on the Sunseeker, and had as yet made no financial provision for Majorie or Ginette, both of whom continued to live at Steepness Farmhouse. All they could discover was that Len had relocated from Cagnes-sur-Mer to a marina in Monaco, where he spent the afternoons in the Casino Parc Panoramique de Monte Carlo.

Anthony felt that if it wasn't for his weekly visits to Nula, where the insertion of silver needles was the prelude to lovemaking on the massage table, he would surely have gone mad. After every treatment, when he paid Nula her thirty pounds before taking her out to supper at the Star of Bengal, he momentarily puzzled over the nature of their relationship, before dismissing all such metaphysical musings as irrelevant.

Godfrey's death in February 1979, during weather so cold that the water at the Priory froze solid inside the pipes and the great Edwardian boiler finally packed up for good, took everyone by surprise. It had been assumed it would be Henrietta who would be the first to go, but instead the villagers gathered at All Hallowes for the funeral of the diffident squire of Winchford. There was not a damp eye in the church as the village heard Jeremy Meek commend a life that had touched so few of them. Godfrey Anscombe was a man who had lived in the thrall of three crushing responsibilities: his village, his bank and his wife. As Percy Bigges, who was an acute old boy in his way, put it, 'The tragic thing about poor Godfrey was that he never seemed to enjoy anything as much as he should have.' He gave the impression that the house, village and estate were millstones around his neck, bringing nothing but bother and expense; the bank was an irksome obligation, casting him into daily contact with cousins he would prefer to have seen less frequently; his marriage had compounded this feeling of being constantly put-upon, and he expended great ingenuity in contriving to hide away in his gun room or in the minstrel's gallery, lest Henrietta ask him to do anything.

The frost that was desiccating the snowdrops as they struggled to push through the frozen earth crunched underfoot as Anthony wheeled his mother from the nave into the churchyard. Brendon Sheaf, as a mark of respect, had opened the Plough and Harrow an hour early, and it was there the village now headed, while the local gentry converged on the Priory for a duty drink. The fact was, Godfrey had been a challenge as a neighbour. As the owner of Winchford and a former Lord Lieutenant, he must certainly be included in all large gatherings and drinks parties of seventy people or more, and be invited with Henrietta to dinner once every twenty-four months, but his presence at a party could not be relied upon to ensure its success. Many were the hostesses with Godfrey coming to dinner who fretted in their Floris-scented baths over whom he could possibly be seated next to. Before dinner, it had to be quietly and firmly explained to his neighbour exactly who Godfrey was – his money, Anscombe Brothers, Winchford Priory and the village – so they might fully appreciate what a terrifically significant fellow he was. Otherwise, they would never have guessed.

In selecting the hymns and readings, nobody could remember any that he had particularly favoured. So, in the end, they went for the old standbys: 'Dear Lord and Father of Mankind' and 'Guide me, O Thou Great Redeemer', which had the added advantage of being two tunes Walter could play on the organ. As for the readings, Anthony found an old prayer by Bishop Brent which began, 'You can shed tears that he is gone, or you can smile because he has lived'; but even as he read it, he realised that few in the congregation would do either. Sandra had agitated for Richard to read a poem, but Anthony insisted it should be Jasmine, as the eldest grandchild, who fulfilled that duty; and when she chose instead to sing a traditional Oxfordshire folk song, the *Ballad of Rollright Henge*, her beautiful, reedy voice soaring around the Norman church stirred the only moment of genuine emotion at the funeral.

From the day of her father-in-law's death, Sandra began to exhibit unexpected character traits. Until now she had taken pains not to appear presumptuous about her eventual occupation of Winchford Priory, but with Godfrey gone she became proprietorial, and began pressing her husband on when they would move into the big house. 'It's not that I want to put any pressure on Henrietta,' she said, 'but everybody keeps asking when we're moving in. It would be great for the kids to have the space, somewhere for Richard to kick a football about.'

'I don't want my mother to feel we're breathing down her neck. It's been her home for so long, and she might want to stay on.'

'You can't have one old lady living in a place that size. Can't she move into one of the cottages, or even Steepness Farmhouse after we move out?'

'Darling, Dad's only been dead ten days. I wouldn't dream of discussing it. It's far too early.'

Sandra's renovation plans were seldom far from her thoughts, and it slightly irked Anthony, when calling on Henrietta to discuss some detail of the probate, to find Sandra there with John Furlong, the father of Richard's schoolfriend Tom, discussing her scheme to lay Amtico flooring across the flagstones in the Great Hall. Both looked embarrassed to see him, and Sandra explained John was farm manager at a large West Sussex estate near Midhurst and Petworth, and had a lot of experience updating old houses. Several times Sandra commented on what a tragedy it was that Len wasn't around, 'because Dad would know exactly how to plan a really nice, functional, family kitchen in the white drawing room. With all those sash windows, it's difficult to fit in enough wall units.'

Sandra had reckoned without Henrietta. When Mrs Holcombe foolishly let slip that Sandra had escorted a planner from a specialist kitchen company into her drawing room, Henrietta summoned Anthony. 'You may tell your wife that her mother-in-law, who has lived in this house for more than thirty years, has no intention of leaving until she is finally carried out in a box. It may be very inconvenient, but if Sandra imagines I will make way for her, not to mention her mother and that common-looking sister of hers, she had better revise her ideas.'

Although not normally interested in *The Times* arts pages, Anthony immediately spotted the prominent five-column photograph of Amanda. The accompanying caption said she was appearing in a new French film showing at the Paris Pullman in Drayton Gardens, called *La Lune et Le Soleil Noir*. The leading actor was Patrice, Gérard Ossard the cult underground director. Amanda was described as 'the thinking man's Isabelle

Adjani, whose violent rages as her character's mental illness spirals out of control are nearly as diverting as her numerous scenes of full-frontal nudity.' Instantly determining not to watch the film, by lunchtime that same day he felt himself relent, and by 6.50 p.m. was seated in a virtually empty cinema waiting for it to begin, having told Sandra he was detained in meetings and would stay in London overnight.

As he sat in the small, smoky auditorium, Anthony kept his coat collar up and his head down. He was relieved that the audience consisted only of a few students and goatee-bearded film buffs. Somehow, he didn't want to be spotted watching a semi-blue movie starring his ex-wife.

The film began and he realised it was precisely the kind of dark, pretentious, subtitled production Amanda would love. It reminded him of the painful art house movies she had dragged him off to in Camden Town. If there was a plot to *La Lune et Le Soleil Noir,* he certainly didn't get it. The film was set in a provincial French town with Patrice playing a local priest who lusted after Amanda. Every so often she stripped off her clothes and wafted around the priest's house in the buff, though whether this was meant to be happening in real life, or was a figment of the priest's imagination, there was no way of telling. What was certain was that Anthony was seeing more of his ex-wife's body than he'd glimpsed for twelve years, and she looked incredible. For one thing, her figure was better today than on their honeymoon. Her breasts seemed larger, but she was as lean and toned as a teenager. Accustomed to seeing Sandra wandering about their bedroom at Steepness Farmhouse, with stretch marks from Richard and Rosanna, and soft pouches of cellulite on the backs of her thighs, he was transfixed. More than once he wondered how he could ever have been married to her. Long before the film's inconclusive conclusion, he realised watching it had been a colossal mistake. He was as madly in love with Amanda as ever, and next to her all other women were pale substitutes.

He left the cinema damp with sweat and too revved up to contemplate going straight to Archie's Fulham flat, where he stayed whenever he needed a bed in London. Instead, he decided to drop in on Nula. In recent months, their acupuncture sessions had lost some of their initial allure, and he had been wondering how to end the arrangement without offending her. The fact was, although he still enjoyed their weekly sex fixture, the dinners at the Star of Bengal had become something of a trial; their opinions on practically everything from marijuana to nuclear weapons to foxhunting were diametrically different. Having just watched Amanda in *La Lune et Le Soleil Noir,* his relationship with Nula seemed unworthy, and he determined to finish it right away.

He took a taxi to Paddington and pressed the intercom. Nula sounded pleased to hear from him, buzzed him up, and opened the door with shining eyes.

'I knew it was going to be you. I had a premonition. I've been thinking about you; you probably felt the psychic energy.'

'Er, probably. I've been at the cinema. There's something I need to talk to you about.'

'I'm so glad you've come,' she said. 'I've got something wonderful to tell you. I only just found out. I'm carrying your baby.'

21

Nula's wonderful news plunged Anthony into despair, made worse by the fact he could tell no one what had happened and, furthermore, he felt compelled to pretend to Nula he was delighted. He could hardly believe he had been so stupid as to get her pregnant. He cursed himself a hundred times a day. It wasn't even as if they'd been in love – their relationship had simply happened, engendered by the intimacy of the accupuncture. How it had ever tipped over into a sexual affair, he couldn't now recall. He must be stark staring mad. He was going to become a father for the fourth time.

A strange development was that the moment Nula announced she was pregnant, he ceased to find her physically attractive. He could now see she wasn't his type of woman at all. With her greasy brown hair and grubby kaftan, she was the kind of person he would under normal circumstances have avoided like the plague, and yet she was pregnant with his child. He saw at once that the whole thing was his own fault, and that he must at all costs behave honourably towards mother and child. Obviously he couldn't leave Sandra to marry Nula but he understood it was his duty to take care of her. Over the next fortnight he called on her in Praed Street every evening on his way home, and each time found the visit more disconcerting. He had not appreciated how unpleasant the flat was, with its nauseating smell of joss sticks and fried aubergines. With the curtains open and overhead lights on, it hardly seemed habitable, and Nula's tiny bathroom, with its cracked basin and pink plastic shower hose she attached to the taps, was no place to bring up a baby.

Nula began to ask whether he knew of anywhere she could move to. Something she'd been contemplating, she said, was a move out of London to the countryside. As a healer, she could take her gift anywhere.

On the fifth visit, she asked whether there was a spare cottage on his estate.

Now Anthony regretted the hours he had poured his heart out about Winchford. Over more than a year of treatments, there was nothing he hadn't told her. Not only had he described the big house, but most of the cottages and farmhouses, and the almshouses where Mrs Holcombe and Walter Twine paid peppercorn rents. He remembered Nula had always been curious about the details of the estate, and now she played it all back to him with impressive recall, asking who would be living at Steepness Farmhouse after he'd moved into the Priory.

When he finally escaped to the train, he felt drained from prevarication. The idea of Nula moving anywhere near Winchford filled him with a hyperventilating panic. As he knocked back a whisky in a plastic glass from the trolley wheeled through the first-class carriages, he reproached himself ceaselessly. If only Sandra had been the kind of wife he could talk to, he wouldn't have become involved with Nula in the first place, but he knew he had been a complete bloody idiot for not keeping his trousers on.

It was characteristic of Anthony that he never once blamed Nula. Of her motive in becoming pregnant, he gave scarcely a thought. The only time he asked her about it, she replied, 'It's a cosmic thing. When a new soul is ready to come into the world, it always finds a way.'

If Sandra noticed Anthony's anxiety, she said nothing. Frequently, having raced home from Kingham station, he found John Furlong in the kitchen with his wife, along with Marjorie and Ginette. Too consumed by anger against her father to return to work, Ginette abandoned her job as a paediatric nurse, and devoted herself to looking after Marjorie. This activity, so far as Anthony could tell, involved only bitching and wailing about 'Dad' over plates of mini rolls and milk chocolate digestive biscuits. Sandra, meanwhile, had a diversion of her own in the Furlongs' marriage, which had hit the rails, Constance having run off with an Argentinian polo player, Gracido Menendez, whom she had met at the Veuve Clicquot gold cup at Cowdray Park.

Tom Furlong being Richard's best friend, Sandra felt personally involved in the drama, and went out of her way to invite John, Tom and his five-year-old sister Katie to stay. Steepness Farmhouse was now so overcrowded, there was no single corner unoccupied by droopy, emotional guests. At night, Rosanna, Katie and Jasmine were shoehorned into Rosanna's room, Tom was in with Richard, Marjorie and Ginette were still sharing Jasmine's bedroom and looked like settling in for ever, and John dossed down on the sofa in Anthony's tiny study.

Amidst the chaos, Anthony's soul-searching and self-reproach passed unnoticed. When he tried to slip off alone for a quiet walk to mull things over, Sandra asked him to take the Furlong children with him. 'They could do with a good blow. Don't make a face, Anthony, and help little Katie put her wellington boots on.' When he tried to slope off to the Plough and Harrow for his Sunday night pint with Archie and Lex, Sandra said, 'Do take John with you, darling. He's feeling so low, poor man. He'd love to go with you.' And so Anthony and his friends had to endure John Furlong banging on about how Constance had, quite literally, upped sticks with the polo gorilla and bolted off to some farm near Buenos Aires. The fact was, Anthony found John a colossal bore and longed for him to go home and leave them all alone. He could see he was attractive, in a tall, thick, repressed English way, but as a companion for a Sunday night drink, he was deathly dull.

'You're being very unfair,' Sandra said, when he shared some of this with her. 'Poor John. He's a real gentleman, and his wife has behaved atrociously. I don't know how he's going to cope. I do despise people who betray their married partners. Don't you ever try that or I'll kill you.'

'I'm only saying he's rather ponderous. He sits there in silence half the time.'

'So did you when I first met you. You were exactly the same when that horrid Amanda left you; I had an awful job drawing you out of yourself.'

'Admit it, he wasn't much fun even before his wife ran off.'

'I don't agree at all. John's a very intelligent man. He must be, otherwise he wouldn't have that job. The Fittleworth Estate is three thousand acres you know – quite a lot bigger than Winchford. Apart from Cowdray Park, it's one of the largest estates in West Sussex, John says. And he manages the whole place himself. Old Lady Fittleworth is eighty-something years old and relies on him for everything.'

'You're probably right. I know he's a sound man. I just hope he won't be staying here much longer; it's getting very cramped.'

'That's why I keep saying we should move into the Priory. I was talking to Mum and Ginette about it earlier on, and they agree with me. It's ridiculous all of us squashed like sardines down here, and just your mother with all that space up there.'

It took a month after his father's death for Anthony to appreciate the full extent of his inheritance. He had, of course, been aware all his life that he had been born into a rich family, and that Winchford was a remarkable set-up, but he had never given much thought to what proportion of the family bank might belong to his particular branch of the Anscombes. A fortnight after the funeral, however, he was summoned by the family solicitor, Aubrey Whitton, to the boardroom at Lombard Street, and there the details were disclosed to him. Aubrey's delivery was so measured, and included so many caveats about provisions of family trusts, it was only towards the end of the meeting that Anthony grasped how vastly rich he really was. As the only child of an only child, the Winchford Anscombes' inheritance had been less widely distributed than other branches of the family. Furthermore, Godfrey had lived so parsimoniously that capital had accumulated. Where Anscombe cousins had bought yachts and racehorses, and villas in the Bahamas, Godfrey and Henrietta had led their lives under the perpetual expectation of bankruptcy, convinced the socialists would confiscate Winchford if they so much as raised their heads. To Anthony's astonishment, he found himself the bank's majority shareholder. 'In the fullness of time,' said his uncle Michael, 'it is anticipated you will take your turn as chairman. Obviously that is a decision to be taken by the whole board of family members, but I think we may anticipate your candidacy will be well starred.'

Later that evening, when he called on Nula in Praed Street, he was still reeling from the shock of inheriting more than forty million pounds in shares, land and property. Instead of feeling elated, the news had the effect of rather exhausting him, and he would have liked to head straight home on the train. But recently Nula had taken to leaving messages for him at the bank, and something in their urgent tone made him fearful of ignoring them. A disconcerting edge had crept into her conversation, and she explained that, being too knackered to give treatments, because of the baby, she had cancelled her appointments and was consequently skint. Anthony felt he had no option but to pay her rent for the next quarter, and to lend her a hundred pounds to tide her over. Soon these hundred pound loans ceased being loans, but became gifts. As his spiritual guru gained weight, and a discernable bump appeared beneath the yellow and black kimono, he became desperate that Sandra would find out, and the handouts became larger and more frequent.

Once, Anthony asked in an apologetic voice, 'Nula, you are quite sure you want to, er, have this baby?'

She stared at him for several withering seconds, as though he had offered her a bleeding rump steak, and replied, 'Anthony, it isn't my decision whether a new life re-enters this world from the lagoon of souls. That is determined by a higher power.'

'Blimey,' said Anthony, who would shortly assume Godfrey's hereditary position as sidesman at All Hallowes. 'You really believe in all this rein-carnation lark?'

'I have incarnated many times,' said Nula. 'First as a cupbearer in the temple of Queen Hatshepsut. Later as a novice nun at a convent on Iona, and a Mayan doctor of herbal remedies.' Then she said, 'If you want, I can trace your past lives with regression therapy. I can tell you are an old soul; you have been here many times.'

But Anthony said he had to rush for the train, and quickly thrust five twenty-pound notes into her open palm.

With his inheritance of the Winchford Estate came more duties than he had ever imagined, all previously carried out with forensic caution by Godfrey. Anthony soon found all his Saturday mornings, and often his Sunday mornings too, taken up with meetings and farm reviews in the estate office. Overnight, Anthony was expected to determine which fields should be sown with barley, wheat or kale, and which should be left fallow. For many years Godfrey had vacillated over whether or not to plant oil seed rape, and Anthony, pressed for a decision, rang Lex's father, 'Scrotum' Holland, for advice before agreeing to a fifty-acre experiment. There were rent reviews to be conducted on the cottages and farmhouses. The local Church of England diocese announced its intention to sell the Rectory, having built a pebbledash bungalow in the kitchen garden for the vicar, and would Winchford Estates like to buy the freehold? Then there was a scheme, long deferred, to introduce more forestry to an area close to the Moreton road, and Winchford quarry needed new stone-cutting equipment. There were decisions too about the shoot, and how many pheasant chicks should be reared for release in the numerous copses. All these responsibilities pressed down on An-thony as he pored over the wall-sized ordnance map in the estate office, with the Winchford boundaries delineated in green ink. More than once Anthony blessed his luck he hadn't gone to university but had worked on the farm, otherwise he would have been even more confused. At least he knew the names of all the fields, and the whereabouts of the barns and grain silos that peppered the estate. But even as he adapted to his new tasks he fretted about Nula and the impending birth of their child.

March became April, April became May, and John and his children re-mained firmly entrenched at Steepness Farmhouse along with Marjorie and Ginette. During term time, at least, Richard and Tom were away at Broadley Court, which meant John could vacate the sofa in Anthony's study and move upstairs into the boys' bedroom. Sandra had managed to wangle a place for Katie at Winchford School, which implied they would be staying at least until the summer. John began commuting between

Fittleworth and Winchford, a journey of three hours, and resumed his role at the Fittleworth Estate part-time, but he still found the prospect of sleeping at home impossible, with all its painful associations, and preferred to return to Oxfordshire each night, where he could depend upon a sympathetic audience. 'It's actually going to be a godsend having John here with the General Election coming up,' Sandra said brightly. 'He's promised to go round the whole village canvassing, which you'll never have time to do with the farm and everything.'

Anthony privately doubted John Furlong would swing many unde-cideds to the Conservative cause in a village which in any case returned a ninety-nine per cent Tory vote. But he felt it would at least keep him occupied and out of the house, so was grateful for it. He realised having a woman as the new Conservative leader was going to require selling to the older Winchford inhabitants, and John, who would himself have preferred Willie Whitelaw to Margaret Thatcher, could spend hours on doorsteps, chewing it all over.

As the May election loomed, all the sad inhabitants of Steepness Farm-house were soon corralled by Sandra into supporting the Tory effort. John and Sandra set off evening after evening, delivering blue literature and posters to the cottages. Marjorie, too, was a conviction Conserva-tive and spent days constructing a wooden placard to be erected on the Moreton road, displaying a poster of the local candidate, Sir Hector Plunkett, father of Anthony's friends Mark and Annie of Fyford. 'If only Len were here,' Marjorie sadly observed, 'we could have finished the job much quicker. He's so good with his hands.' Even Ginette got caught up in the excitement, teaming up with Arabella Bigges, the charity worker for Maltese donkeys, and providing tea and cake for a rally in the village hall.

Despite being an intuitive Tory for reasons so primal he never bothered to analyse them, Anthony had never regarded himself as a Conservative activist. He voted Tory in the same spirit that he supported the parish church and local hunt: because they were there, and he recognised the institutions as forces for good in the community. It amused him to watch Sandra and John's mounting outrage at the two Winchford residents who did not intend to vote Conservative. Walter Twine, who had never voted Tory in his life, announced in the Plough and Harrow he was a 'radical like the old Tolpuddle Martyrs' and would 'do away with the monarchy and the landlords, the whole lot of 'em, like those Frenchies did, given half a chance.' Shocked to the core, Sandra asked, 'But aren't you happy living in your cottage, Walter? My husband's been very kind over your rent, you know.'

'Oi know that, Mrs Anscombe,' Walter replied. 'And oi'm not complaining about anyone as such. But oi'd rather be living up at the Priory than in my cottage, which is why oi won't cast my vote for your Landlord's party, for who's to say the day won't come . . .'

Sandra, who would like to have been living up at the Priory herself, could think of no appropriate response.

John, meanwhile, was appalled when Jeremy Meek revealed himself as a Labour supporter, and stuck a provocative red poster in the window of his new, pebbledash rectory.

'I find it outrageous, actually,' John stormed. 'For one thing, parsons shouldn't be allowed political opinions; it's completely unethical. And they certainly shouldn't be allowed to be socialists. I wonder if his bishop knows?'

'Our new bishop moved here from Southwark,' Anthony said. 'I'm sure I read that in one of the papers. They call him the Pinko Prelate.'

'Good grief,' said John. 'Jesus would be turning in his grave if he knew what was going on.'

When a Conservative administration was returned to power with 339 seats, John and Sandra refused to attend morning service for two Sundays in a row to signal their disapproval of the vicar's disloyalty.

Soon the schools were breaking up for the summer. Constance Furlong would be returning to England with Gracido, who was contracted to play in various tournaments at Smith's Lawn and Cowdray, but their schedule was too packed to allow Constance to see much of her children, so Sandra invited John to stay on at Steepness Farmhouse with Tom and Katie for the holidays. 'It will be so much more fun for Richard and Rosanna to have friends their own age to play with,' Sandra told her husband when she saw his expression. 'The holidays are *eleven weeks long*, you know. Everyone will be bored to tears.'

Anthony had no issue with Tom and Katie; it was their father who filled him with a terrible gloom. Anthony recognised Tom was a good influence on Richard, being brighter and lighter in spirit than his son. Left to himself, Richard would have vegged out in front of the television; Tom encouraged him to build elaborate camps in the copse, and even to make a start on Broadley Court's compulsory summer school project, which Richard would otherwise have left until the last day. As the boys worked side by side at the kitchen table, tracing pictures of Crusader knights and their castles, Tom was clearly more motivated, the natural leader. At Broadley he was invariably top of the form, and Richard somewhere close to the bottom.

With Rosanna and Katie it was different. Theirs was a more complicated friendship. In many respects, six-year-old Katie had more in common with Jasmine, and certainly preferred her company, than with Rosanna, her exact contemporary. Like Jasmine, Katie was fragile and dreamy, and had inherited Constance's beautiful pale skin and red hair. Next to Rosanna – the Pony Club champion, hardier and tougher every day – Katie was a nymph, who loved walking through the meadows below the Priory gathering wild flowers. Sandra and John were perpetually worried about her, confused by her feyness. Sandra had a theory that, if only Katie got into competitive riding like Rosanna, it would take her mind off her mother's disappearance. But Katie made it perfectly clear she had no intention of getting into the Pony Club, so Rosanna set off to camp alone, leaving Katie to listen to pop records with Jasmine in her bedroom.

It seemed to Anthony, who didn't pretend to understand psychology, that the person most damaged by Constance's rejection wasn't Katie but her father. Four months after the fact, John still found it difficult to speak of anything else. Anthony came to dread the Sunday night drives from Winchford to Broadley Court after short exeats, when the two fathers shared the journey to deliver their sons back to boarding school. It was all right on the outward trip, with Richard and Tom in the car imitating the weirder members of staff, but on the way back John became morose and recriminatory, constantly asking Anthony why he thought Constance had left him.

'Am I so dull?' he asked. 'Was I such a rotten husband?'

Anthony would reply, 'You seem to have been a model husband, actually. You shouldn't dwell on it. There aren't always simple explanations for these things.'

'You must have *some* idea. Why would she go off like that? With no warning. I had come back home for lunch as usual – she always used to have something ready for me: a casserole, or a slice of cheese and French bread – but that day there was nothing. Not in the Aga, not in the Belling; I hunted everywhere. No lunch, no Constance. I went upstairs to the bedroom to see if she was there, and thought the place looked a bit different, then I realised half her stuff was missing from the dressing table. Her pots of creams and potions, women's clutter. Then I saw her clothes were gone too, and the suitcase on top of the cupboard.'

'It must have been a shock,' Anthony said for the hundredth time.

'She didn't leave a note. No letter, nothing. I only heard afterwards she'd bolted with this Dago fellow. I hope she knows what she's doing. He's had affairs with half the women round Midhurst,' John brooded, while they drove round the Oxford ringroad in the rain. 'She's a cracking-looking girl, Constance. God knows why she'd want to run off with a greasy foreign bounder like that.'

'At least your children seem OK, especially Tom. When my first wife Amanda walked out, it was Jasmine I was most worried about.'

'It's Sandra I have to thank for that. She's been an absolute brick with Tom and Katie, she really has. Sandra's one in a million and you're a very lucky chap to be married to her.'

22

John Furlong had an idea, and Sandra agreed, that they ought to hold a fathers and sons cricket match at Winchford during the summer holidays. The players would be Richard and Tom's friends from Broadley Court, plus as many of their fathers as were available, with the rest of the teams being made up of Oxfordshire neighbours and villagers. 'The crucial thing,' John said, 'is to have a mixture of ages and classes, everyone mucking in together.'

Never much of a cricketer himself, and already stretched by commitments to the farm and at the bank, Anthony was discouraging, but Sandra insisted. 'Really, Anthony,' she said, 'I don't know why you're being a wet blanket. The boys will have such fun. John is volunteering to organise everything, so you won't need to lift a finger. Anyway, we've already chosen a date and the pitch is free that Saturday. I've checked.'

The Winchford village cricket field was situated in a large flat meadow beyond the Mill House, home to the Biggeses. For much of the year sheep were left to gnaw at the grass, though the square was enclosed by a temporary fence that was removed before matches, and rolled by the Winchford estate. The cricket pavilion, a mock Tudor structure of beams and wattle, had been erected by Anthony's grandfather as a gift to the village, loosely based on designs for the Bembridge Yacht Club, of which Seymour Anscombe had been an enthusiastic member.

Although he had no reason to be anything but grateful to John for arranging the match, Anthony found the build-up to it profoundly irritating. Each night when he arrived home from the City, he found Sandra and John drawing up lists of players and houseparties. Henrietta made it perfectly clear no one could stay at the Priory ('We have nobody to give them breakfast'), and Sandra had arranged for players to be billeted with the Biggeses at the Mill House, with the Plunketts in Fyford and the Fanes at Steeple Chadlington. The remainder of the teams would camp out in tents at Steepness Farmhouse, and Sandra asked everyone to bring sleeping bags.

Regarding himself as a natural organiser, John soon roped in everyone in the neighbourhood. Lex and Archie had both already been signed up to play. Brendon Sheaf sloped over from behind the bar at the Plough and Harrow to say how much he was looking forward to the game, as was his son Gareth. Walter Twine was persuaded to umpire, and Ginette would team up with Arabella to do the teas. Richard and Tom spent all day practising in the cricket nets that had been Len's final gift. Their thirteen-year-old neighbours Max Fane and Ben Loxton came over for nets too, as half the county limbered up for the match.

Nula's due date came nearer and nearer. Although Anthony didn't have the courage to ask her exactly when the baby was expected, in case she asked him to be present at the birth, he realised it couldn't be long now. He had managed to reduce his visits to once or twice a week, and consequently over-compensated with his donations, handing over hundreds of pounds at a time. What she was doing with the cash, he didn't feel he could ask.

He became expert at anticipating when Nula would begin pestering him for a cottage in Winchford. So he always pretended he was in a tearing hurry – rushing off to a meeting – and scarpered when he felt a cottage conversation brewing. More than once he considered consulting Aubrey Whitton to find out where he stood legally in this ghastly mess. But to confide in Aubrey would have formalised the scandal, which Anthony still hoped might somehow blow away like a bad dream.

It was a particularly busy period at work. Anscombe Brothers was lead bank in a doomed initiative to refinance the Clyde shipbuilding industry, and Anthony found himself shuttling between London and Glasgow and staying in the old Caledonian Terminus Hotel for several nights at a time. Nagged by guilt that he hadn't visited Nula for a fortnight, he found it easier to sleep with a distance of four hundred miles between them. A packed schedule of meetings with the Board of Trade allowed him to put her from his mind for hours at a stretch. Then he became paralysed with fear, as images of the pregnant acupuncturist swam into his head. Hitherto he had envisaged the baby strictly in the abstract; now he couldn't help speculating on whether it would be a boy or a girl, and he flinched at the prospect of Nula giving birth, probably alone, in some National Health maternity ward. Waves of cold fear swept over him until he could barely place one foot before another. He would be halfway down a corridor and quite suddenly freeze, mortified by the horror of it all. He would set up a trust fund for the baby – a really generous one, so it wanted for nothing. But how could this ever be achieved without Sandra finding out?

Negotiations on the Clyde continued late into Friday evening before being abandoned. The new Conservative government would no longer subsidise the loss-making Scottish industry, and without government guarantees there was no role for Anscombes. Exhausted and disappointed, since he had put a lot of energy into the scheme, Anthony rang Sandra to say he would be back very late; he would take the train as far as Birmingham and a taxi on to Winchford. With luck, he'd arrive home by two o'clock in the morning. Sandra sighed. 'It is slightly thoughtless of you to be so late, Anthony; we have fourteen small boys here already, and they're running wild all over the house. I could have done with you to take control. At least John's here being saintly.'

'I'd have been there if I could. The meetings dragged on and on.'

'Couldn't you have explained you've got a houseful of Broadley Court boys for a fathers and sons cricket match? It's just a question of priorities.'

'Look, I'll be home as soon as I can, OK?'

'Well, while you're sitting in your lovely comfy first-class carriage, you can think of me and John trying to settle down all our little players in their tents. And please creep in quietly when you get here, because we're all going to really need some shut-eye before the big day tomorrow.'

The day of the cricket match dawned with blazing sunshine, and the weather forecast confirmed it was going to be the hottest Saturday of the summer. The Broadley Court boys, billeted in scout tents behind the farmhouse, all woke up at five a.m. as light streamed through green canvas, and by a quarter past six Anthony and John were grilling bacon and frying eggs in the kitchen. Once Sandra had made them brush their teeth and roll up their sleeping bags, the boys had some last-minute practice in the nets. Richard was Captain of the Winchford Wanderers, comprised of seven Broadley pupils plus Anthony, Lex, Mark Plunkett and Ben Loxton's father, Nick; Tom Furlong had six Broadley boys, John, Archie, Brendon Sheaf and his son Gareth, and Rupert ('Bongo') Nall-Caine in his team, the Moreton-in-Marsh Mercenaries.

By half past ten everyone was down at the field changing into their whites. Outside the pavilion, small boys were running about practising their bowling actions. Lines of cars had formed up around the boundaries, and spectators were erecting deckchairs and assembling picnic tables. Long before the two captains tossed to bat or bowl, there must have been a hundred and fifty people there, good-naturedly complaining about the heat. Anthony had to admit that John and Sandra had done a fine job in getting the word out. Most of the village had come along to see what was happening; Brendon Sheaf had set up a long bar for the day, with barrels of Hook Norton and plastic containers of home-brew cider, and Judy was doing brisk business serving pints. Delicious picnics were already being laid out on tartan rugs. Several people had brought golfing umbrellas to shade their dogs from the sun, and everywhere labradors and king charles spaniels were dozing with their tongues hanging out or lapping thirstily at dishes of water.

Anthony could now see that the cricket match was an excellent idea, and exactly the sort of initiative to breathe life into Winchford; as the new thirty-two-year-old squire, he was glad it was taking place so soon after he had taken up the reins.

Tom's team won the toss and elected to bat, so Anthony was fielding on the far boundary as backstop. It was a long time since he'd played cricket at Winchford, and he had forgotten how idyllic it all was, with the Mill House standing four-square between two enormous copper beech trees, and a herd of Jersey cows all in line, watching the cricket from an adjacent meadow. On two sides of the field, Ironstone Hill sloped towards its hazy summit. The atmosphere was so still you could hear the droning of bees and horseflies from the long grass, and when Walter Twine in long white laboratory coat called for an over, his voice echoed around the valley. Anthony could see Percy Bigges sitting in front of the pavilion as scorer in a panama hat, recording every ball in microscopic hieroglyphics. Jacinthe, whose ancient tea dress sported a pattern of muted herbaceous annuals, was busy talking at Henrietta, who had been wheeled down from the Priory by her latest Australian agency nurse.

From his position near the boundary, Anthony saw his wife strolling from car to car with John Furlong, thanking everyone for coming and telling the Broadley parents how charming and helpful their sons had been last night at Steepness Farmhouse. 'If only Richard was always so helpful,' she exclaimed. 'Perhaps he is in other people's homes.' Sometimes Anthony found it difficult to match the girl he had married with the woman Sandra had become. By no means fat, she was nevertheless noticeably stout, an impression enhanced by her choice of a too-tight pink blouse with piecrust collar and two strings of pearls. Her breasts strained against the thin cotton and a discernable roll of flesh rested above the hem of her pleated skirt. Recently Sandra had taken to buying more expensive shoes and bags. For the cricket match she wore a pair of Gucci snaffle-buckled loafers and carried an Hermès beach bag printed with prancing circus ponies. As they walked behind the cars, Anthony watched John talking to Sandra, and Sandra pealing with laughter at something he'd said; it only emphasised how little Anthony felt he had left to say to his wife these days. As they introduced themselves to each new set of parents, John tipped his panama and handed out duplicated lists of the teams.

At half past one the match broke for lunch, Winchford Wanderers having dispatched the Moreton Mercenaries all out for 147 runs. Everyone said Richard had been the man of the morning, clean bowling six players, and Lex had electrified spectators with a brilliant one-handed catch; his other hand had been stuffed down the front of his whites, easing a stuck testicle. Gareth Sheaf, Brendon's ten-year-old, scored a half-century and Archie was bowled out for a duck. As the two teams huddled in the shade of the pavilion's veranda and relived the action, Marjorie Potts and Mrs Holcombe circulated with plates of sausages on sticks and cold chicken legs, and Anthony and John distributed glasses of wine to the grown-ups and Fantas for the boys. Anthony could see the Plough and Harrow bar doing brisk business, with punters queuing three-deep for a pint; better certainly than Ginette and Arabella's tea and cake table, where the two stallholders looked rather dejected.

'Anthony? Remember me?'

Hearing his name, he turned to find a rat-faced man about his own age, with bad skin and bugger's grips. It took him a second or two to place him.

'Charlie?'

Charlie Edwards grasped him by the hand. 'I hope you don't mind me being here. I'm with the Elliots; they brought me along.'

Anthony hadn't clapped eyes on Charlie since the fateful morning at the Hotel Petit Trianon. For many years he had daydreamed of punching his smarmy face, but now the opportunity presented itself he felt strangely passive. Charlie looked older than he had at their last encounter, though his neck was still covered by small scabby spots.

'I still feel bad about what happened,' Charlie said. 'That was a bad scene. I wanted to say something.'

'It was a long time ago,' Anthony replied. 'My marriage to Amanda was pretty much over in any case.'

'She was an amazing chick. Tough to be married to, I should imagine.'

'Well, yes . . .' Suddenly, Anthony felt extraordinarily curious about Amanda, and whether Charlie kept in touch. 'Have you seen her lately?'

He shook his head. 'Not for a few years. Actually that's not true – I went to watch her band play a pub in Hammersmith. That's when she was with Proust's Handmaidens. They were fucking brilliant by the way; they'd have been mega if she'd stuck with it. That single was a classic.'

'The "Remember" song . . .'

'I didn't expect you to know that somehow.'

'Why's that?'

'You're the big country squire these days, aren't you? Tilling your acres and slaughtering pheasants. I wouldn't have had you down for following the rock scene. We actually tried to sign Amanda up, but it never happened.'

'You work in the music industry?'

'It's a grubby business but it pays OK and the girls are plentiful and willing. Not generally as good in the sack as Amanda, but that's another story.'

'Yes,' Anthony replied. 'Another story.' And then he said goodbye and hurried quickly away.

Perambulating between the cars, Anthony felt half the people he'd ever met had turned out to watch the match, and he began to feel anxious about his impending innings. It was ridiculous to be nervous about batting in a fathers and sons match, in a prep school team captained by his own nine-year-old, but he could just imagine Tom Furlong bowling him out for a duck or, worse, being caught in the slips by John.

'Wish me luck,' he said to Jeremy Meek, who was mincing by with a half pint of Pimms overstuffed with mint.

'I can't take sides, you know,' murmured the vicar. 'I don't believe in competitive sport.'

Down at the scoreboard Anthony spotted Rosanna, who was diligently updating the tin numbers with a group of friends. Jasmine and Katie were sitting on the giant roller in the long grass, ostentatiously listening to Radio One. Even Gervaise Sablon, proprietor of the Fox and Terriers, had come along to support the occasion; ever since Anthony and Sandra's first date at his pub, he flattered himself he had a special bond with the presiding family of Winchford.

Lunch over, the Winchford Wanderers went in to bat. Anthony was slated to bat eighth, and sat with Percy on the veranda, waiting his turn. There was no question, Tom Furlong was a lethal bowler and wickets were tumbling. Lex was despatched for three and Mark Plunkett, who had once played semi-professionally, was given LBW by Walter Twine in his first over.

Sooner than he'd expected, it was Anthony's turn at the crease. A ripple of applause went up from the spectators as the young squire strode out, pads buckled and swinging his bat. The heat in the field was stifling. Somewhere overhead, an orange-tip butterfly furiously flapped its wings in a breezeless sky. Anthony took his position at centre stump and the fielders fell into their crouching postures.

Tom was beginning his run-up when the commotion started. Anthony was dimly conscious of a woman's voice calling him from the boundary, and then someone striding onto the pitch in the direction of the square. He saw Walter signalling to suspend play.

He could see the woman through the haze now, stumbling towards him, clutching some sort of bundle. In a moment of horror, he recognised Nula.

The fielders, and most of the spectators, looked on in astonishment as she approached him and thrust the bundle into his arms. 'I thought you should meet your daughter.' Her words echoed around the field, and you could hear the sharp intake of breath.

Anthony gazed at his newborn child, squinting up at him in the bright sunshine. Her hair was brown like her mother's. As he stared at her she began to cry, and the fingers of a tiny pink hand closed around his own finger.

He looked at Nula, who was standing on the square, hot and defiant in the black and yellow brocade kaftan she'd been wearing the very first time they'd met. 'How did you get here?' he stumbled.

'By train. Then a taxi from the station. You owe the driver four quid because I didn't have enough cash.'

Sweat trickled down his face and he wiped it away with his sleeve. His daughter's soft little fingers were still firmly clenched around his, and he felt an overwhelming desire to kiss her.

'Has she got a name?'

'Gaia.'

'That's a new one on me. I haven't heard that name before.'

'It means "one-ness". The fruits of the earth.' Then she said, 'I asked the taxi man to drive me round the village for a look-see. There are several nice cottages that look vacant to me.'

Before Anthony could reply, he spotted Sandra striding purposefully across the pitch in her piecrust blouse, followed by Henrietta in her wheelchair, urging the Australian nurse to push her faster.

Part Four

23

A fter such deep and public humiliation, Sandra said it was impossible for her to remain in Winchford, so she went to Fittleworth to stay with John, taking Richard, Rosanna and Marjorie with her.

For the three days it took to arrive at this solution she holed up at Steepness Farmhouse with the curtains drawn, comforted alternately by her mother and by John, before emerging downstairs to rail at Anthony. Her bitterness, hurt and incomprehension were terrible to behold, as she struggled with her husband's betrayal. It wasn't merely that he had had an affair with a grubby woman in a kaftan, though that was in itself devastating, but that the whole village knew about it. 'How can I ever hold up my head again?' she kept asking in a plaintive voice. 'Bringing that baby here . . . I thought I'd die of shame.'

Anthony felt honour-bound to take time off work to endure her assaults at close range. He acknowledged he had behaved abysmally and made no excuses. That he had so deeply wounded his wife filled him with terrible remorse, and he would have done anything to turn the clock back. Every minute, every second of those early days cooped up inside the darkened farmhouse was unbearable. It did not help that there was no place to hide himself away. John was again occupying his study, sleeping on the sofa, and Anthony moved downstairs to the sofa in the sitting room. If he went into the kitchen, he faced the recriminatory stares of Richard and Rosanna. Marjorie bustled about, tight-lipped, handing out cups of sugary white tea, but kept her distance from her son-in-law, leaving his teacup on the breakfast bar rather than bringing it over to him. Only Jasmine went out of her way to be affectionate, though he knew she was hurt and confused. She sometimes found Sandra infuriatingly dull as a teenager, especially compared to Amanda. But she knew that her stepmother had loved her, and had provided consistency and reassurance throughout her childhood.

His unmasking as an adulterer – with an illegitimate baby – had happened so suddenly, and before such a large crowd, it was inevitable the whole world would soon know about it. Mercifully nothing appeared in the newspapers, but in Oxfordshire and Gloucestershire, and the adjacent counties of Northamptonshire and Warwickshire, the talk was of little else. The parents of every cricketer told the story half a dozen times by Sunday night ('The whole match had to be called off when this *extraordinary*-looking woman in a *dressing gown* appeared on the field carrying a *baby*') and, down in the Plough and Harrow, the village was agog. Even the vicar, who never entered the pub on principle, felt compelled to make an appearance for a ginger beer shandy to take the moral temperature of the parish. The Biggeses declared themselves 'totally astonished' by the whole business, and wouldn't have believed it had not Anthony clearly known the woman. Lex and Archie had their regular Sunday-night pint on their own, and discussed nothing else. Lex advanced the opinion that Nula was 'a complete dog' and couldn't see the attraction. Archie said he found her quite sexy in an odd way, though agreed she looked rough close up. Word got out that Nula was an acupuncturist, and Archie almost choked over his joke: 'First she put her pricks into him, and then he put his into her.'

Walter Twine repeated his old observation that Anthony had 'always had an eye for the ladies, and good luck to him too, the dirty dog'. He reminded the saloon bar that the first Mrs Anscombe had been a looker herself, and Sandra 'had a great pair of knockers on her, even if she has become a bit of a Lady Muck.' The vicar felt himself compelled to remind Walter there were ladies present, at which Judy jeered raucously and told him not to be such a prude.

Isolated and sleep-starved, Anthony was a walking wraith. Having let so many people down, he hardly knew where to begin in making amends. In the back garden, the row of tents so hastily evacuated by the prep school cricketers still stood there, a constant reminder of his shame. Had it not begun tipping down with rain, he would have moved outside to sleep in a tent himself.

Over and over, he relived Nula's hideous appearance at the match, registering a confusing variety of emotions: fear, self-loathing, shame and love for the baby, Gaia. He had fallen for her the minute he set eyes on her, enveloped in the blankets and towels he recognised from the treatment room in Paddington; in all likelihood she had been conceived on those very towels. Even as Sandra and Henrietta had moved resolutely in his direction, eyes ablaze, Anthony made a private vow that whatever pressure was placed upon him, he would stand by this child. By his selfishness and stupidity he had brought her into the world, and he had a moral obligation to take care of her.

On that stifling afternoon of the cricket match, under the censorious gaze of family and neighbours, and the wounded incredulity of Sandra, he had gently escorted Nula from the field. In the lane behind the Mill House, they had found the waiting taxi, and Anthony had asked the driver to take the three of them to Forge Cottage. The key was underneath the brick, where it had always been, and Anthony took mother and daughter upstairs and showed them into the bedroom – Sandra's nanny bedroom – with the two single beds with candlewick covers. Then he had gone around the cottage, switching on the immersion heater and checking that the electricity and fridge were working, and opening windows. The smell of damp had returned with a vengeance, reminding him of the first time he went inside with Amanda on their return from France. Sandra's frieze of stencilled bluebells was covered by cobwebs. Then he had walked up to the village shop and bought eggs, bread, tea and milk, and left instructions that anything the new tenant needed was to be charged to his account.

He returned to the cottage to find Gaia already fast asleep in one of the beds, and made a cup of Tetley for Nula, apologising that the village shop didn't sell any herbal teas.

'Is it really all right for us to stop here?' Nula asked. 'The thing is, the landlord at my flat wants us out. He's going to rent the place out as a knocking shop.'

'You can stay as long as you like. And in case you're wondering, there won't be any rent to pay.'

Nula looked suspicious, as if there must be some catch. 'That's a genuine offer?'

'You have my word. Some people might think my word a slightly devalued currency at the moment, but it's still worth something, I promise.'

Then he had hurried off to face the music at home. As he left Forge Cottage and walked up the village street he loved so well, he blanched at the unimaginable ghastliness of it all. Whatever the repercussions – and he already knew that Sandra would be unforgiving – the thing that puzzled him most about the whole business was this: what on earth had he ever seen in Nula in the first place?

*

Sandra removed herself to Fittleworth and suddenly Steepness Farm-house was almost empty of children. Richard and Rosanna had gone with their mother, and Tom and Katie with John, so only Jasmine was left. Sandra had offered to take her too, but Jasmine said she preferred to remain with her father. Anthony had been at pains to put no pressure on her one way or the other, but was nonetheless pathetically cheered by her decision, and grateful for her silent presence. Neither father nor daughter could bring themselves to discuss the turbulent events of recent days, and spent their time cooking nourishing meals as a means of avoiding deeper conversation. Having never cooked with his daughter before, and his own repertoire hardly extending beyond steak and oven-ready chips, Anthony was fascinated to discover she was a natural. They shopped together at the delicatessen in Moreton-in-Marsh (Anthony preferred to avoid the village shop where the place fell silent when he entered, and where he might run into Nula, judging by her liberal use of his account), buying special olive oils, exotic salamis and cheeses from which Jasmine constructed Mediterranean salads from Sandra's Elizabeth David cook-book. Anthony later believed that had it not been for Jasmine's watchful presence, he might have cracked up completely. Unable to face friends or neighbours, he watched television and drank too much. But with Jasmine there, he had less opportunity to lapse into introspection, and they had an unspoken pact to keep each other's spirits up.

Not long after Sandra left, Henrietta rang Anthony and told him to come and see her at the Priory. He arrived with Jasmine, who was sent outside while they talked privately.

'Well, Anthony. You have now managed to get through a second wife.'

He nodded glumly.

'To lose two wives is extremely careless,' she said. 'I take it there is no prospect of the nursery nurse returning to you?'

'It's too early to say what's going to happen. Sandra and the children are staying over in Sussex with John Furlong.'

Henrietta sniffed. 'Both your marriages have been hopeless. Has it crossed your mind why that might be?'

His mother was seated in her wheelchair in front of one of the great stone chimneypieces; her ravaged face, seen without make-up, reminded Anthony of an archaeological site with its hoof-shaped amphitheatre flanked by brittle, crumbling remains. 'You probably think I'm very old-fashioned, but you must stop choosing these unsuitable women. That first girl you married, we knew nothing about. She was pretty I suppose, but hopeless as a wife and would have been worse than hopeless running

Winchford. That should have been perfectly clear to you from the start, but you raced ahead, never pausing to think, and married her. You were very fortunate she didn't take you to the cleaners. Plenty of girls like her would have done.'

Anthony began to say something about Amanda not being like other girls, but his mother cut him short.

'As I have said, you were lucky that time, and I doubt you will be so lucky with Sandra. Has she asked you for money yet?'

'Of course not.'

'You say of course not, but she will. How is she supporting herself and your children in the meantime? Is her friend Mr Furlong paying for everything?'

'Well, we have a joint bank account, a household account, so I'm sure she's using that when she needs anything.'

'So she *is* relying upon Anscombe money! You told me just now she wasn't!'

'Mother, I am still married to Sandra. She only left last week. Naturally we haven't finalised anything yet. In fact we haven't even thought about it.'

'You can be quite certain *she* has, even if you haven't. And it's perfectly ridiculous she's gone off in a huff like this in the first place. Such a middle-class reaction, and somehow typical of her. No, I'm not being critical; she's a very kind little person in her way, and you're going to miss her when the children are around, because I don't see you coping on your own. But you have to admit she's being awfully feeble. Your great grandfather turned out half a dozen little bastards, so one always heard, and nobody batted an eye. Wives used to accept these things. Certainly not something to leave home over. You have installed your mistress and bastard in Forge Cottage, I gather.'

'She isn't my mistress. And I wish you wouldn't call the baby a bastard.'

'That's what she is, is she not? And if that extraordinary-looking woman isn't your mistress, what is she doing here in Winchford? I don't even know where you met her.'

'Mother, I had an affair with her. I'm not even sure that affair is the right expression, actually. Anyway, it happened and it was very stupid and she became pregnant. She's got nowhere else to live.'

Henrietta shuddered. 'Do we even know who or what she is?'

'She's an acupuncturist.' His mother looked bemused, so he explained. 'You know: they stick pins and needles in you. It's medical. I went to see her for my shoulder.'

'Oh Lord, it's even worse than I imagined. She's another nurse like Sandra. Anthony, what is it about you? Don't you ever meet normal, nice girls of your own background?'

'Now you *are* being old-fashioned.'

'There are perfectly sound reasons, you know, why people marry other people like themselves. Now if you had only married Arabella Bigges as I've often suggested—'

'Arabella? Now that is an extraordinary idea.'

'Jacinthe can be trying on occasions, as these diplomatic wives often are when they return home, and Arabella's no beauty, I grant you, but she's longing to get married, poor thing, and Percy was such a loyal friend to your father.'

'This is an absurd conversation. I'm not looking for a wife; it's the last thing I need. I'm still married to Sandra and in all likelihood we'll get back together eventually. We just need time.'

'If you really want to know,' Henrietta said, 'I rather hope that you don't get back together. If you do, it'll only be because of the house. She's been desperate to move into the Priory for years.'

24

Anthony was dismantling the tents in the back garden when he received a visit from Percy Bigges. Although not predisposed to see anyone, he had always been fond of the retired ambassador, a man of diffident charm and tact. Tall, silver-haired and knighted for long and distinguished service in a succession of Islamic hardship posts, he was a free thinker who delighted in advancing contrary opinions, always with an amused gleam in his eye.

'If this is a bad moment,' he said, 'for heaven's sake tell me. But I thought you might appreciate some moral support.'

Anthony smiled ruefully. 'The past week hasn't been great. I've made such a hash of things. Can I get you a drink?'

'Only if you're having one yourself.'

'It's good to see you, Percy. I thought I couldn't face anyone, but now you're here . . .'

They went into the house and made gin and tonics, then carried them back outside into the garden and sat down on a bench beneath Len's treehouse. 'So this is your father-in-law's famous treewalk? I've heard reports.' Percy gazed about him, taking in the enormity of the structure.

'Len never does things by halves. He lopped half the branches off this copper beech.'

'We were introduced at your wedding. An intriguing character. You know we have his younger daughter staying with us at the Mill House?'

'Ginette? I hadn't realised.'

'She's become quite chummy with Arabella. She didn't want to go off with her mother and sister, so she's come down to us instead.'

'That's very kind of you. She was devastated when her father walked out.'

Percy's eye focused on a large bush of white buddleia. 'Isn't that a painted lady settling on the top there? You should know, Anthony, you were the great butterfly collector.'

'It is a painted lady. There have been quite a few about this year. And there's a small tortoiseshell on that patch of sunlight on the path.'

'We used to have spectacular butterflies at the consulate in Peshawar. There was quite a big garden there at one time, until they sold half of it off.'

'I didn't know you'd been in Peshawar. I knew about Islamabad.'

'Ah, it was a long time ago, one of my first postings. I was in the visa section, lowly stuff.' Percy stared towards the summit of Ironstone Hill, and Anthony had the impression he was deliberating about something. 'I am going to tell you a story I've never told anyone before, not even my wife, especially not my wife in fact. I must ask for your word nothing I say will go any further.'

Anthony promised with a heavy heart. He was not in the mood for more secrets.

'The reason I'm telling you is because it may be helpful; you may find certain parallels. It doesn't put me in a good light I'm afraid, though attitudes were different back then. Anyway,' he went on, 'I spent two and a half years in Peshawar. There weren't many of us British there, certainly not of my own age, which was eighteen when I arrived. There were some soldiers stationed outside the town, and perhaps a dozen of us in the consulate all told, but not a great deal going on, especially in the evenings, and time hung rather heavy. To cut a long story short, I met a girl, a Muslim girl, very pretty. She had been married already as a teenager, an arranged marriage of course, to a much older man, but it hadn't worked out and in the Muslim manner he had divorced her. Well, I took up with her and we began to see more and more of one another, and after a month or two she moved into my bungalow. It wasn't something we could be open about, because that sort of arrangement was frowned upon, so it all had to be rather clandestine, which was far from ideal but that was the situation. She was a sweet thing, and I think we were very happy together. Then one day she told me she was pregnant. It surprised me very much at the time – God knows why. I must have been a very innocent young man in those days. It simply hadn't entered my head such a thing could happen, so I was in a dreadful flap, not knowing what to do, and with nobody I could talk to. In the end, I summoned up the courage to confide in my superior. He was unequivocal about what should happen, which was that I should clear out of town as rapidly as possible. Before I knew it, a transfer had been organised. I hope you will believe me when I tell you I was very uneasy about the whole thing, and my only possible excuse was that I was still very young. I didn't even dare face the girl and tell her what was happening. I left her a letter instead, which was unforgivably cowardly, and as much money as I could spare. Three days later, I was on a boat sailing from Bombay. What happened to her and our baby I have never been able to discover, though I did try quite hard to trace her some time later. Over the years, I've thought about it all more than you might imagine. I still feel enormous guilt. That child was my responsibility, every bit as much as Archie and Arabella are. As it is, I don't even know whether she's alive or dead. If alive, she'd be fifty-two now. Anglo-Indian. Not a great hand in life. If I only knew where she was, there's very little I wouldn't do to help and support her. Covertly, of course. I've often been tempted to tell Jacinthe, but in the end I know she wouldn't understand, so there's no purpose in pointlessly upsetting her.'

He took out a large white handkerchief, blew his nose briskly, then took a long sip of his drink. 'Reason I regurgitated all that ancient history was my roundabout way of telling you you've done the right thing standing up to your responsibilities with your child and her mother. No doubt that there are those, my wife included, who think you should have turned your back on them, and they will find an opportunity to tell you so too. But they are wrong. Take it from an old man, long out to pasture, who took the other path and still bitterly regrets it.'

Weeks passed with painful slowness, and many of Percy's predictions came to pass. Jacinthe was not alone in inferring that Winchford would be a more respectable place without the presence of Nula and Gaia. It did not help that Nula made so little effort to acclimatise to the village; she prowled about the lanes, sometimes pushing Gaia in the Edwardian pushchair she had retrieved from an outhouse, wearing the grubby robes that had looked peculiar enough on the streets of Paddington, yet more so in Winchford. Sometimes in addition she wore big hairy jerseys, like Yeti skins, and open-toed sandals from which long, curling toenails protruded. Everyone considered her very peculiar indeed. Anthony made a point of calling at Forge Cottage after work, sometimes taking Jasmine, who had developed a fascination for her tiny, surprise half-sister. It soon emerged Nula was incapable in all matters related to DIY, so it fell to Anthony to repaint the stairwell in bright yellow and to cover Sandra's bluebell frieze with auspicious purple and silver stars. When Nula took against the gleaming sprayed courgettes and carrots in the village shop, which came from Mrs Holcombe's highly fertilised cottage garden, Anthony found himself digging over Sandra's neglected vegetable patch and sowing a late summer crop. Nula's shop account, meanwhile, continued to find its way to Steepness Farmhouse, with Anthony settling quite large bills for olive oil, vitamins, pulses, brown rice and soya milk, none of which he had realised they even sold.

One evening he arrived home from the bank to find a letter waiting at the farmhouse from Amanda. It was postmarked Paris, and inside was a scrawled note in her familiar hand. It said she had heard 'on the grapevine' about Anthony's troubles, that she was very sorry and hoped to catch up with him before too long. She mentioned she had been spending four months in the Reunion Islands where Patrice was making a movie, and that they would shortly be shooting another movie in Calcutta. Would Jasmine like to fly out and stay with her while they were there 'in the City of Joy'?

Anthony's immediate reaction on reading the letter was extraordinary elation at hearing from her at all. It had been such a long time that he had begun to think of Amanda as strictly part of his distant past. Watching her in *La Lune et Le Soleil Noir* had somehow placed a further barrier between them, casting his ex-wife into an elevated stratosphere of movie stardom.

The logistics of caring for Jasmine, with no Sandra there to help, became daily more complicated, particularly when she moved on to her big school, Cheltenham Ladies' College, as a daygirl in September. As he had done before when a previous wife left him, Anthony threw himself on the mercy of Mrs Holcombe and Judy, who came in to give her breakfast, drive her to school, collect her again and cook her tea. Anthony hated to think of his thirteen-year-old daughter's lonely evenings at the farmhouse, eating turkey drummers and arctic roll (Judy's favourite shop was Iceland) and struggling through her homework at the kitchen table. He considered sending her to Cheltenham as a boarder, but couldn't face the thought of being alone at weekends. His work at Anscombes was becoming very demanding; he did everything to resist overnight absences, but this was sometimes impossible. Deprived of Sandra's home cooking, Jasmine began to lose weight, first slowly, then dramatically, until Anthony began to wonder whether she was suffering from an eating disorder he'd read about in *The Times*. But when he took her to see their GP in Moreton, the doctor said there was nothing whatever to worry about, and he didn't believe in anorexia anyway.

Still undecided whether or not to allow Jasmine to stay with Amanda in Calcutta, he took her out for dinner at the Fox and Terriers. The pub, which held so many ambivalent memories, had become a favourite treat for his daughter, and they had often celebrated birthdays and exam results there as a family. Tonight, Anthony felt maudlin as he entered the flagstoned dining room, with its mounted foxes' masks and boot-scrapers. A fire blazed in the hearth, and the place smelt of woodsmoke and leather polish. When she had appeared downstairs, ready to go out, Anthony had been amazed to see Jasmine wearing one of her mother's old black frock coats, which fitted her near perfectly.

'God, Jasmine, where did you find that?'

'I've had it for ages in the cupboard in my bedroom.'

'Isn't it one of your mother's old ones? I'm sure I recognise it.'

She looked momentarily furtive. 'Yuh. I found it when we were moving, a long time ago. Sandra wanted to chuck it out.'

'Well, you look great. It suits you. And it shows how tall you've got, because Amanda used to wear that when we were married.'

During dinner he found Jasmine eager to talk about Amanda, which was surprising because she had never previously shown much interest in her mother. She asked how he and Amanda had first met, and he found himself telling her how he'd glimpsed her from the minstrel's gallery and followed her to France, entranced by her beauty, and how they'd married only two days later.

Jasmine fell silent, and then said, 'I hope that happens to me one day. It would be so romantic, to just run away and get married to a secret lover.'

'Really, Jasmine, I hope you don't. I hope you'll be much more sensible than your mother and I were. First you should go to university and afterwards get a job for a few years, and then, when you're really sure you've met the right man, the one you really love, *then* get married. That would be far better.'

Jasmine's serious little face furrowed with concentration. Seeing her in Amanda's clothes, Anthony began to see resemblances to her mother he'd never noticed before. Having always considered her awkward-looking rather than beautiful, he suddenly saw that his daughter at seventeen might be a heartbreaker.

'And you really do want to go to India for Christmas?' he asked. 'It's entirely up to you. If you want to go, I'll arrange it for you. But if you want to stay here, Amanda will understand and I'm sure she'll ask you another time.' This last part wasn't strictly true, of course, since Amanda had no track record of issuing invitations; this was the first time in years she'd invited Jasmine anywhere.

Jasmine looked at her father. She had chosen asparagus risotto and, to Anthony's relief, had eaten more than half a dozen forkfuls of the stuff, which was the most he'd seen her swallow in as many weeks.

'Wouldn't you be lonely at Christmas if I did go, Dad?'

Anthony, who knew he'd be very lonely, said, 'I can spend Christmas with Granny. We'll have Christmas together at the Priory so I won't be lonely, darling. And I'll see Lex and Archie, all my friends. And I expect I'll see Richard and Rosanna one day over Christmas as well.'

'And Gaia?'

'And Gaia. You'll have to help me choose a Christmas present for her, something she'd really like.'

'I think I *would* like to go to India,' Jasmine said at last. 'I don't really know Amanda that well, and I see you all the time, well most of the time, when you're not at work.'

'OK, darling. I'll write and tell her. It'll be very exciting; I'm sure you'll enjoy it.'

'Dad, you know you said earlier about me not marrying too early? And waiting until I find the person I *really* love.'

'Yes.'

'Does that mean you didn't really love Amanda when you got married to her? I don't quite understand, because you said you did.'

'I adored your mother, really adored her. I was so in love, you can't imagine. But in the end we just weren't the right people for each other, and probably we should have waited a bit longer before getting married, and then we'd have found that out before.'

Jasmine toyed with another forkful of risotto. 'Who did you love more, Amanda or Sandra?'

Anthony furrowed his brow. 'That's a difficult question, because I loved them in such different ways. Sandra's such a kind person, and she looked after you so well.'

'I don't really like her that much, actually.'

'Oh, come on, darling, yes you do. And she's always loved you, ever since you were a tiny baby.'

'I bet Amanda loves me more.'

'Well, Amanda's your real mother, which makes it a bit different. But you couldn't have wished for a kinder, more loving stepmother than Sandra.'

Jasmine thought some more. 'So who do you prefer out of Sandra and Nula?'

'That's enough difficult questions, Jasmine. But since you ask, the answer is Sandra.'

'So each of your girlfriends you've loved less than the one before. First Amanda, then Sandra, then Nula.'

'I didn't say that at all. Now, Jasmine, finish that risotto or leave it – I don't mind which – and order a pudding if you want one; you love the treacle tart here.'

She made a face. 'I am *not* eating treacle tart.' Then, with a deep breath, she said, 'You know what, Dad, I think you should get back with Amanda. She was your best one, and you were really in love with her, which you weren't so much with Sandra or Nula.'

'*Enough*, Jasmine. Stop. I'm serious. Anyway, your mother has a husband, Patrice, who you'll meet properly in India, *and* a new baby. So there's no way anything like that is going to happen.'

'OK, I won't go on about it. But if I don't think she's happy with this Patrice man, I'm going to remind her about you, and maybe she will come back to Winchford. That would be so good, because she could do up our house in a really cool way, like you said she did up Forge Cottage, with Indian fabrics and Moroccan cushions and amazing stuff, and we could get rid of all Sandra's boring old furniture and curtains.'

25

A letter arrived from Sandra asking for a divorce, followed by a second letter from a firm of London solicitors, saying the same thing but this time more expensively. Sandra said she had been talking things through with John, and he agreed with her she'd been placed in an impossible position with all Anthony's carrying on behind her back, and that all things considered it made sense to go for a clean break. She went on to say that she would, of course, be seeking custody of the children, 'since they are both very upset, and can hardly be expected to grow up in the same village as your mistress and your illegitimate child, who I gather are installed in Forge Cottage, which is a calculated insult to me personally and very hurtful.' She mentioned she had 'received several supportive letters from people in Winchford, all of whom are as horrified as I am that you would bring that woman to the village. You can imagine how upset Richard and Rosanna are, thinking of her living there. John thinks it's one of the most extraordinary things he's heard in his life.'

Sandra's barb about people in Winchford sending supportive letters had the desired effect, and Anthony found himself pondering on who they might be. At All Hallowes for morning worship the next Sunday he reviewed the sparse pews for likely candidates. Not Percy, obviously, but Jacinthe seemed a high possibility, and Arabella, the donkey saver, was another. Today, Arabella and Ginette, who was evidently still at the Mill House, were identically dressed in black reefer jackets and both had cut their hair very strangely with James Dean quiffs. When he tried to say hello to Ginette in the aisle, she glared and cut him dead. It was a despondent Anthony who wheeled Henrietta back to the Priory, where Mrs Holcombe was overcooking a roast for them both, plus Jasmine and the newest Australian nurse, Shireen.

By November, it was becoming obvious that the living arrangements for Jasmine were unworkable. It was therefore decided that Anthony and his daughter would leave Steepness Farmhouse and move permanently into the Priory with Henrietta. There were several sound reasons for the move: Anthony was working longer hours at the bank and often arrived home after Jasmine was already asleep; neither Judy nor Mrs Holcombe had proved to be reliable chauffeurs, frequently turning up late at Cheltenham and writing off three cars in two months; Judy couldn't drive without a cigarette in her mouth, and kept veering off the road while trying to extract new fags from the packet. Furthermore, a move to the Priory would resolve two problems at once: Henrietta's Australian nurse could keep an eye on Jasmine, thus giving her slightly more to do, which might make her stay longer, and both Henrietta and Jasmine would have companionship of sorts. The chauffeuring to and from school would be taken over by Walter Twine.

Sadly and methodically Jasmine packed up her belongings from Steepness Farmhouse into boxes, and unpacked them in a large, cold spare bedroom at Winchford Priory. The room had two single beds in it, a William and Mary oak bureau and, on the walls, several small Victorian watercolours. Spotting her struggling upstairs with a pile of posters of pop stars, Henrietta made her promise that nothing would be stuck up on the walls in case it marked the wallpaper, and when Anthony came to see how his daughter was getting along settling into her new room, he found her in tears. They quickly agreed that, since Henrietta's wheelchair meant she couldn't go upstairs, they would ignore her completely and tell Mrs Holcombe to keep her mouth shut too. In no time the watercolours were taken down and stacked up in the back of a wardrobe, and Blondie posters Blu-tacked in their place. Jasmine's stereo was set up on the oak bureau.

Henrietta took it for granted that Anthony would move back into his childhood bedroom at the top of the house, but he asserted himself and commandeered the room next to Jasmine, the Assize Chamber, with its canopied bed and heavy Elizabethan furniture. When unpacking, he found the four-picture photograph frame that he'd brought up from Steepness Farmhouse, with snaps of Sandra, Jasmine, Richard and Rosanna smiling out from four ovals. It was a frame he had often carried with him on business trips to put by his bedside. Today he removed the picture of Sandra, shifting the other ones up a space and leaving a vacant oval for Gaia. His marrying days were behind him. He decided all his energy and love would be dedicated to the happiness of his four children.

He had feared that, in moving back into the Priory, he'd be back under his mother's thumb. As it turned out, her wheelchair was a godsend, rendering large areas of the house inaccessible to her, which could be co-opted by Anthony and Jasmine for themselves. Her rule extended only to the white drawing room, Great Hall, library and cloakroom, which had been converted into a primitive bathroom. Her progress between these downstairs rooms was marked by the tracks of her wheels across carpets and rugs.

The steep terracing of the Priory gardens was another godsend. Pushed by the Australian nurse, Shireen, Henrietta could penetrate only as far as the knot garden, or to the old grass tennis court where she was parked beneath the shade of the four-hundred-year-old cedar. The croquet lawn was put out of reach by a too-steep bank of grass, and the old kitchen garden, long overrun by gone-to-seed rhubarb bushes, became a favourite retreat of Anthony's. It was here he brought his farm documents and bumph from the bank. Grumbling because he had banned her tinny rattling Walkman from the kitchen garden, Jasmine often kept him company, bringing books or homework instead.

The old butterfly enthusiast in Anthony began to reassert itself in that wild garden, and he introduced butterfly-friendly plants like buddleia, hesperus and sedum which attracted clouds of new species. Pale Clouded Yellows, Red Admirals and Peacocks became commonplace, and to his great delight a rare Silver Washed Fritillary flitted over the wall from the great oaks above the house. He took it as a good omen. After so many reverses, maybe his life would settle into a comfortably predictable path again.

26

It did not take Anthony long to realise Nula's permanent presence in Winchford was a grave mistake. For all her ecological protestations, it was hard to imagine a less countryish soul. The smell of manure from Winchford dairy, which drifted towards Forge Cottage when the wind was in the wrong direction, nauseated her, and she worried about the effect on Gaia of methane gas. On Sunday mornings the pealing of church bells disturbed her sleep and she wrote a sarcastic letter to Jeremy Meek, copied to Anthony, demanding they cease immediately. As it happened, the vicar was rather sympathetic to the request, regarding church bells as symbolic of outdated feudalism, but hardly dared say so, since Jacinthe was a fearsome chair of the Parochial Parish Council. The hunt offended Nula's every sensibility, and when the meet was held in Repton's Field, as it had been held every year for as long as anyone could remember, she was spotted in the lane with Gaia in her pushchair, muttering loudly about ritualised murder and shaking her fist at the hounds. Scrotum and Rosie Holland, who were out that day with the Heythrop, were intrigued to see the much-discussed acupuncturist for the first time, having missed her famous debut at the cricket match. Scrotum serenaded her with a long blast of his hunting horn. Instinctively despising the handsome, sneering landowner with his pink coat and red face, Nula yelled up at him, 'How would you like to be ripped to pieces by a pack of trained killer dogs?'

Scrotum replied, 'More than being stuck with needles like a hedgehog by a dog like you, dear heart.'

It was in his dual capacity as farmer and banker that Nula was most severe in her criticism of the father of her child; she found it hard to know which she disapproved of more. Recently, she had read that 'agribiz' was poisoning the countryside with pesticides and chemical fertilisers, and that every acre of arable land would be turned into a barren wasteland within ten years. Each time he called at Forge Cottage, Anthony was greeted by a barrage of apocalyptic statistics. As Nula told it, if he persisted in spraying the wheat crop against weeds Winchford would soon become a Gobi desert of shifting sands and howling jackals.

'Honestly, Nula, I do think you're being unnecessarily alarmist,' Anthony said, as he dug over the onion patch for her at Forge Cottage. 'We're not heavy users of pesticides here in any case. They are very expensive and I don't like to use too much because of the pheasant chicks.'

Nula shuddered. The pheasant rearing pens were another of her bête noires.

'I don't understand why your farm isn't fully organic.'

'I've told you before, because the yield drops so much if we don't spray, and anyway the supermarkets won't buy organic because people don't like misshapen tomatoes and carrots.'

'Well, you'll only have yourself to blame when the next Ice Age arrives.'

As his patience wore thin, Anthony floated the possibility to Nula that she might be happier living somewhere else. But she became so angry with him, accusing him of trying to cast her out 'like some little Victorian housemaid who's got into trouble with the son of the big house – which is exactly our situation, isn't it?' that he quickly backed off. In any case, his love for Gaia was real and deep, and he didn't trust Nula to look after her properly on her own. In Winchford, he could at least ensure they had a roof over their heads, and hot water and heating. Once they were settled in, Anthony encouraged Nula to take up her acupuncture again. He was continuing to settle her bills at the village shop, as well as handing over regular top-ups of cash, and it was all surprisingly expensive; it didn't help that Nula proved to be a hopeless gardener and Sandra's old vegetable patch, once bristling with orderly lines of potatoes and chard, leeks and four different varieties of lettuce, was soon abandoned and organic produce ordered from a neighbouring farmer instead.

It became routine that on Thursday afternoons, when Walter drove into Cheltenham to collect Jasmine from school, Nula would hitch a lift in the car, having first deposited Gaia at the Priory. In Cheltenham, having done some shopping, she attended an adult education course on fair trade for the Third World at the technical college before catching the late bus back to Winchford. Having done his best to escape early from the City on Thursdays, Anthony looked after Gaia for the evening, playing with her and giving her her bath before settling her down in

Nula's special carry-cot woven from dried bulrushes. He then tried to stay awake until Nula arrived home to collect their baby. Generally, she would insist on coming inside. There she harangued him on the iniquities of the international banking community, whose policy of loaning money to developing countries that could never afford the repayments was creating a culture of dependency and debt of which he should be personally very ashamed.

27

As Christmas loomed, and with it Jasmine's trip to visit Amanda on the film set in Calcutta, Anthony rang Sandra to invite Richard and Rosanna to the Priory. It was five months since either of them had set foot in Winchford, and Anthony's contact with them had, for all his efforts, been intermittent and strained. At the Broadley Court production of *Macbeth*, in which Richard played the non-speaking part of a Scottish clansman, and Tom Furlong captivated as Duncan, Sandra had pointedly refused to sit next to him, inserting John as a barrier between them. When Anthony asked to attend Rosanna's end-of-term carol concert at Petworth church, close to her new school, Sandra said Rosanna was still feeling 'funny' about him, so he had stayed away. The prospect of Christmas at the Priory with just Henrietta and Shireen (who consented to work over the holiday for double money) was so dispiriting that he swept aside Sandra's various attempts to deflect him and insisted both children stay with him for at least two nights. Eventually, in a voice filled with sanctimonious misgivings, Sandra agreed they could come from 27 to 29 December while informing him that 'both children are very unsure about staying with you, especially Rosanna, who still has nightmares about that dreadful woman turning up at the cricket match.'

Anthony drove Jasmine to Heathrow and handed her over to Amanda at the terminal. They were flying to Calcutta via Bahrain and Delhi with a group of other film people, and Amanda arrived so late that she practically missed the flight and Jasmine was in tears of panic. Patrice was already in India for six weeks' pre-production. All the hand luggage was tagged with special labels printed *Mrs Gupta's Trip to Paradise*, which was the title of the movie. What with Jasmine's tears and Amanda's vagueness, Anthony left Heathrow doubtful they'd ever arrive in Calcutta at all, and cursing his ex-wife for her casualness and beauty. The day before in *The Sunday Times*, she'd been described as 'a raven-haired Marianne Faithfull lookalike.'

That first Christmas without Sandra was the worst of his life. He woke up on Christmas morning in the Assize Chamber feeling unbearably lonely. Deprived of all four of his children, the seventy-two hours from Christmas Eve to Boxing Day seemed to last a month. Anthony felt it was up to him, for his mother's sake, to uphold the Winchford traditions established by Godfrey, so he dragged evergreen boughs into the Priory, spiked the tops of the Elizabethan portraits with holly branches, and organised fruit punch and mince pies in the Great Hall. As he set out the lead figures of the Victorian crib, Anthony wondered what he thought he was doing, erecting a crib in a house without children. At the tenants' drinks, he roused himself to make a speech wishing them all a very happy Christmas. Percy Bigges told him afterwards it was one of the best speeches of its kind he'd ever heard, being warm, sincere and short. The only silver lining was that Nula had made it clear beforehand she wouldn't be attending the party herself, disapproving of the condescending idea of treating the serfs to a drink at the big house, having fleeced them for rent all year. Anthony felt like reminding her that she hadn't contributed a shilling in rent herself, but he kept quiet, because he wanted to stay on good terms for Gaia's sake.

After church on Christmas Day he made champagne cocktails for Henrietta and Shireen, and they were joined by Percy, Jacinthe and Archie, but not Arabella or Ginette, who preferred to stay behind cooking lunch together at the Mill House.

'Is Ginette intending to say with you for ever?' Anthony asked Archie under his breath. 'She's been there for months.'

'Search me,' Archie hissed back. 'It's all highly suspect. They're inseparable. If you ask Bella about it, she clams up.'

'Ginette won't talk to me. She did it again in church just now. She must still be blaming me for the whole Sandra thing.'

'Probably blaming you for being a bloke, actually. But let's not go there.'

Since Judy was working at the Plough and Harrow over Christmas, where Brendon had introduced a special eat-as-much-as-you-like Yuletide buffet for £4.99 a head, half-price for kids, Mrs Holcombe was having to cope with lunch at the Priory on her own. Panicked, she put the turkey in the oven far too late and eventually served up an almost raw bird at three o'clock, by which time Henrietta had been wheeled off to bed, full of champagne cocktails. Anthony was so hungry that he took Shireen down to the pub at four o'clock for a crack at the buffet, where they piled their plates high with turkey breast, bacon and chipolatas, and a choice of six kinds of potatoes and four different stuffings, washed down by two bottles of Australian chardonnay. Afterwards, feeling suddenly maudlin about his life and absent children, he walked back to the Priory and rang Fittleworth to wish Richard and Rosanna a happy Christmas, only to be told they'd gone skating with some friends. He then dialled the number he'd been given for Jasmine in Calcutta, but all lines to India were permanently engaged. Feeling he had to speak to someone or die of loneliness, he went to Forge Cottage to see how Gaia was getting on with the xylophone he and Jasmine had chosen for her at the toyshop in Moreton. He arrived to find Nula complaining of a migraine, brought on by church bells and Gaia's constant banging on the xylophone, and could he please give her two hundred quid she needed for her next term's course fees?

By the time his middle two children arrived from Fittleworth, delivered by Sandra who refused to get out of the car, Anthony was so wretched he almost dreaded them coming, fearing it might be another disaster. It was a new experience for him, feeling awkward around his own children, and he hated it. The first evening, having supper together in the Priory kitchen, Anthony felt it was like meeting them for the first time. Rosanna was painfully quiet, occasionally staring at him when she thought he wasn't looking. Richard replied to Anthony's questions about football and what presents he'd got for Christmas rather formally, as though his father was a master at Broadley Court. A couple of times he addressed him as 'sir' by accident. When Anthony said goodnight to them in the bedroom they were sharing, and sat on the edge of their single beds to kiss them, Rosanna covered her face with a sheet and refused to kiss him back. Richard was happily reading an old *Dandy* annual brought from the farmhouse, said 'Night, Dad' and gave him a fleeting peck before returning to the comic. If it's this bad tomorrow, I may as well give up, Anthony thought. He wished Jasmine had been there too, instead of in India. Since Sandra's departure, he had grown to rely on her company and Rosanna might have been more forthcoming with her elder sister around.

The next day, as it happened, was much better. Anthony had arranged for Bubblegum to be tacked up ready for an after-breakfast ride, and Rosanna headed off on her own across Ironstone Hill for three hours. When she got back she was in much better form and even smiled once or twice during lunch, when she thought no one was looking. While she was riding, Anthony took his son on a long walk round the estate, showing him the new sheep dip and sawmill and the newly-installed stonecutting equipment at the quarry. As Richard had grown taller, he had also grown stockier; he said he was looking forward to the rugby term, because he was better at rugby than soccer. They dropped in on Walter at his almshouse and sat in his gloomy back kitchen, and Walter reminisced about the old days on the estate when every single field was harvested by hand, 'using only scythes, which is something people today can't imagine. We used to start on the outsides of the fields and work our way in towards the middle, until there was only a small square of corn left. Then some of the men fetched their shotguns because the square was full of rabbits and they'd all come running out at once, helter-skelter, with everyone taking pots at them.'

'They must have been very different days, Walter,' Anthony said. 'Amazing memories. Were they better or worse days back then, do you reckon?'

'Far worse.'

'Worse *then?*'

'Oi'd say so. You'd be considered lucky to get paid two shillings for a whole day's work in them days. Mean as mustard the squire was.'

'That would have been who exactly? Seymour, I suppose.'

'Mean old bugger he was and all, begging your pardon. A goose he used to give us at Christmas time, and we were supposed to be grateful too.'

'Not a goose fan, are you, Walter?'

'Oi don't mind goose. Nothing wrong with goose. But oi'd prefer to have a nice Christmas dinner all paid for down the Plough and Harrow, never mind any blasted goose.'

Anthony felt his day with the children had been reassuringly bonding, and they were a merrier family sitting down to supper that night in the Great Hall, where Grandmother Henrietta joined them in her wheelchair along with Shireen. Rosanna opened up about her new school in Petworth, which she appeared to be enjoying, and said she'd made some friends, and there was a craze at the school for collecting My Little Ponies. Richard said he watched a lot of sport on TV with John Furlong in John's study. 'He knows so much about racing and cricket – he's like this walking encyclopedia.' Shireen volunteered that she'd once been out with a cricketer – 'he wicket-kept for Adelaide' – and Henrietta sniffed, signalling her lack of interest in Shireen's old boyfriends. Rosanna mentioned that John 'can be a bit annoying and boring sometimes' (which pleased Anthony), but Richard seemed to have bonded with him well enough.

On their last morning, before Anthony was due to drive them back over to Fittleworth, he took the children down to the village shop with the promise of a pound each to spend. So soon after Christmas, the choice of goods was even more limited and tacky than usual, and it was frankly a challenge to find a pound's worth of anything amongst the plastic spinning tops and whistles, school rubbers, balsa wood gliders, bendy snakes and tin yoyos, all made in Cambodia and imported to Winchford by heaven knows what supply chain of novelty wholesalers. They were pawing over the cardboard boxes of trash when a figure in long brown robes appeared at the doorway, pushing a baby in a buggy. Her hair was wild and uneven, as though self-cut with pinking shears, and dyed purple at the ends. On her feet were a pair of very old, dirty hiking boots over rainbow-striped socks.

'Hey, that looks like *our* old pushchair,' Richard said.

Anthony froze. Nula had spotted him and was heading right towards them. Gaia, at least, appeared pleased to see him, her tiny mouth displaying a definite smile of recognition.

Anthony considered vaulting across the wooden counter and escaping out of the back door of the shop, but of course it was impossible. Already Rosanna had spotted Nula and was glaring from the toys section with a mixture of hatred and fear.

'So these must be the posh side of the family?' Nula said. 'The privileged children born on the right side of the blanket.'

Anthony couldn't help thinking it was a hideously inept expression, remembering the musty blankets in Nula's treatment room, on top of which Gaia had certainly been conceived.

'Er, Richard, Rosanna, come and say hello to Nula, who lives in Forge Cottage. Her little baby is called Gaia.'

'You can call me Auntie Nula if you like,' she said, bearing down on them. Rosanna reversed towards the chill cabinet, desperate to get away.

'*Don't* you look like your father, then?' Nula said to her. 'The same nose and chin. Gaia has the same nose too. Look at you both – you could be sisters, which you are, sort of.'

Dissolving into floods of tears, Rosanna pushed past her father, past Nula and Gaia, past the little queue of Winchford pensioners who had been watching the unfolding drama, and ran outside into the street, wailing hysterically as she went.

Sandra wrote a stinging letter, as he knew she would, saying Rosanna had been 'traumatised' by her visit, and the children would never again be allowed to come to Winchford so long as 'that woman' was living there.

She went on to say she wanted their divorce to go through as quickly as possible, because John had asked her to marry him when his own divorce became absolute, and she had accepted his offer. There followed a long paragraph on the merits of John Furlong, with the clear inference that he was everything Anthony wasn't.

'You will be pleased to hear,' Sandra said, 'that I have told my solicitors I want very little for myself from the divorce, and will only be asking for proper maintenance for Richard and Rosanna. John's job with Lady Fittleworth is quite well paid and comes with a nice house, and he is also a Member of Lloyd's so we don't need to be beholden to you. You may, of course, continue to have access to the children, but in future it will have to be strictly on neutral ground.'

28

Jasmine returned from Calcutta on 5 January and it was with mounting excitement that Anthony waited for her to come through into the terminal. The Priory had been lonely without her, and eerily silent without the constant background beat of her music. He was intrigued, too, to hear what she'd made of Amanda. It took very little to prime his fascination for his first wife and he was eager for news.

Jasmine appeared in the arrivals hall as brown as a betel nut, carrying a glass and brass hookah of the sort used for smoking ganja. Customs officers peered at her suspiciously as she passed by.

'Hi, Dad. This is for you. It's a present from Amanda.'

'It's a marijuana pipe, isn't it?'

'A chillum. People were smoking them all the time on the set.'

They drove straight back to Winchford from the airport, Anthony questioning her about everything she'd seen and done. Most of the cast of *Mrs Gupta's Trip to Paradise* had been staying at the Tollygunge Club, a colonial-style set-up with a golf course and polo fields, in a series of bungalows in the grounds. Jasmine had been given her own bungalow, but seemed to have spent most nights sharing Amanda's, with her mother and her half-sister, which she had loved. Like everyone who came into her orbit, Jasmine had fallen under Amanda's spell, entranced by her beauty and wilfulness. 'I just could hardly believe she was my *mother*,' Jasmine said. 'She never told me to do *anything at all*. You could just do whatever you liked. If you wanted six Coca-Colas, you could have them. In fact they don't actually have Coca-Cola in India, they have Thumbs Up, which is the same thing really, but more sugary. Sandra would have hated it. And another really cool thing about Amanda is you never have to go to bed. There was no bedtime. You can stay up all night if you want; she doesn't mind. When she had parties in the bungalow I stayed up till four o'clock in the morning, and then went to sleep on the sofa with Amelie with the party still going on.'

'How old is Amelie now? I've lost track. She must be three or four, isn't she?'

'She's five. She's really sweet and pretty, but so-oo naughty. And Amanda never tells her off or anything. And she comes out to dinner every night in restaurants.'

Anthony thought the whole set-up sounded typically Amanda, and was reminded of the last time she had left Jasmine asleep on a sofa. On that occasion she had disappeared, abandoning her daughter for good.

He heard about their visits to Chowringhee market and to a botanical garden, but mostly it sounded like Jasmine hadn't done much sightseeing, instead hanging about at the Tollygunge Club or playing with her sister on the film set in BBD Bagh.

'Did you have a nice Christmas lunch?' he asked her.

'Christmas? Oh yeah, they don't really have Christmas in India, because it's a Hindu country, so they don't celebrate it.'

'So there was no Christmas lunch? No turkey?'

'We actually forgot all about it, during the day anyway. They were filming on set all day and nobody even mentioned it. And then we went to this big luxury hotel called the Oberoi Grand for dinner, and we suddenly noticed all these decorations and pretend snow everywhere and said 'Oh right, it's *Christmas Day*! Happy Christmas everybody!' And the director bought champagne for everyone, which is so expensive in India – it costs a hundred pounds a bottle or something – and all the actors were getting really drunk and everything.'

'And did Amanda give you a nice Christmas present?'

'Well, she was *going* to. We were going to go back to a sari shop we'd seen in the market, where they had these really beautiful saris, but there was never any time. She doesn't wake up until quite late, and then we usually had to go to watch the filming.'

Anthony noticed the name Patrice hadn't been mentioned once during their conversations, and he found himself becoming curious at the omission. It occurred to him Amanda must have been all over her French actor boyfriend, and Jasmine was sparing his feelings.

'And how about Patrice?' he asked, bracing himself. 'Was he nice to you?'

Jasmine looked uncertain. 'He was OK.'

'Were he and Amanda on good form together?

'Well, Patrice is a bit strange.'

'Strange?'

'I don't think he's that nice to Amanda. He has lots of other girlfriends too – that's what some people were saying. He's always sitting in his dressing room with the actress who plays Mrs Gupta's daughter, Anaradha.'

'Does your mother know about Anaradha?'

'I *think* she does, but she didn't really say anything. Sometimes she looked a bit sad. That's why she kept asking me to sleep in her bungalow, because Patrice wasn't there much.'

Why did Anthony feel a rush of joy that filled every part of his being? 'Poor Amanda. You think she might be a bit unhappy?'

'Only sometimes. When she's writing her songs, she's happy. She had a guitar, and every day she practised for a few hours. She's written lots of new songs and they might come out as an album.'

'But she and Patrice aren't that happy, you say?'

'Only because of his girlfriends. I think they do like each other really. But Patrice can't be in a room alone with a lady without making a pass at her; that's what I was told.'

Anthony was driving home from the station one evening when he passed Arabella Bigges and offered her a lift.

Ginette was in a terrible state, Arabella said. She was sitting in the Mill House kitchen, crying, and Arabella had been dispatched for extra supplies of Jaffa Cakes.

'Why, whatever's happened?'

According to Arabella, Len Potts had lost every penny. He had declared himself bankrupt and put the Sunseeker up for sale. Diane had left him. Then, the day before yesterday, he had moved in with Sandra and Marjorie to John Furlong's house in Fittleworth.

'Christ,' Anthony said. 'He's lost the *whole lot*? How did he manage that? He had several million not long ago.'

'In the casino, apparently.'

Anthony groaned. 'He told me he had a system.'

'From what I can gather from Ginette, he always bet on red and kept doubling the stakes whenever he lost. Well, black came up nineteen times in a row, and by then he was betting three million pounds. The casino stopped him going any higher. They said he'd reached the house limit.'

'Jesus.'

'When he had to settle up, it turned out he couldn't. The police were called and he spent the night in the cells. In fact they wouldn't let him out for three days, and he had to do a deal with the casino. It was partly their fault, because they shouldn't have given him so much credit, so they couldn't make him pay the whole lot.'

'That's something at least.'

'Not really, because he'd spent so much money on the boat and everything, he's been getting through it at a rate of knots. Apparently he bought masses of jewellery and clothes for Diane.'

'And now she's left him, you say.'

'The minute she realised he'd nothing left. What a mercenary cow! Ginette says she's going to hunt her down and kill her. I don't know whether she hates Diane more for running off with her Dad or for leaving him,' she went on. 'She's such a loyal person, Ginette; she believes love should be for life.'

'Poor Ginette. I'm sure she's taking it hard.'

Arabella shrugged. 'Yes, she is, poor love. I'm doing my best to look after her, but it's difficult. At least she enjoys her new job.'

'New job?'

'She's teaching martial arts at Moreton High. She's become a sports teacher.'

Back at the Priory, Anthony rang Sandra to say he'd heard about Len. They were, after all, still married, and he felt a lot of residual affection for his soon-to-be-former-father-in-law.

He found Sandra in a resigned mood. 'Dad's very down in the mouth, as you can imagine. He knows he's been a fool, not just about the money but Diane and Mum and everything. He's being very tough on himself. You know Dad; he likes to win all the time. He can't bear the thought of people feeling sorry for him.'

'Well, give him my best wishes. I've always liked your father and it's rotten for him. How's Marjorie taking it?'

'Pleased he's back, I think. Not that she's saying much. It'll take her time to forgive him, but I think she will in the end. He's such a big personality and she's used to having him around.'

'Listen, Sandra, there's something I want to say, to do with Len. It's sort of to do with our divorce, too. When you said you didn't want any money in the settlement, that was before your father lost all his. You must have been assuming at least some of it would come your way one day, and if there isn't any . . .'

He could sense Sandra on the other end of the line, weighing his offer against her considerable pride.

'It's a kind thought, Anthony,' she said at last, 'and I genuinely appreciate it. But we don't need anything. John has enough of his own, and I was never relying on Dad's. John's so clever with money and he's got himself on to some really good Lloyd's syndicates. He's so kind; he's taking me and all the kids to Tenerife for my birthday.'

Jasmine remained the only child living at home. With each year, she became prettier and less awkward. Shortly after her fifteenth birthday, she went into Cheltenham one afternoon with a group of friends and had her hair cropped. Anthony couldn't believe how trendy she looked. It horrified him to realise that, in only a couple of years' time, she'd be the same age Amanda had been when they'd got married.

He had been drawn to Amanda all those years ago precisely because she was complicated and intriguing. In his daughter, he wanted only for her to be straightforward. The more 'normal' Jasmine became, the happier her father. He encouraged her to invite her friends to Winchford, and liked them best when they were blonde and giggly. He had the old swimming pool at the Priory renovated, ripping out the slime-covered wooden steps and frog-infested filter, and installing heating. He loved the way the pool gave so much pleasure and provided such a focus for Jasmine's friends, who messed about in the water for three or four hours at a stretch. Anthony's first job each evening when he came home from work was to dive down to the bottom and retrieve all the masks and goggles they'd left there.

It infuriated him that Sandra still refused to allow Richard and Rosanna to come to Winchford. 'Come and see them here whenever you want,' she said. 'You can take them away on holiday, anything, but they may not go to the Priory, not while *that woman* is living down the lane.'

Whenever he attempted a calm, rational conversation on the subject, it quickly turned confrontational, with Sandra reminding him how atrociously he'd behaved, and how mortified the children were, and he couldn't expect her to relent when he insisted on installing his mistress so brazenly in their old cottage. 'I suppose you're visiting her whenever you feel the urge,' she complained. 'I can't imagine what the villagers think about it, having a virtual brothel in the middle of Winchford.'

Sandra's occupation of the moral high ground was absolute and unchallenged. The fact she was cohobating with a married man herself counted for nothing, since it was poor John who had been left by Constance. On the infrequent occasions Anthony saw the Furlong children at Fittleworth, he got the impression that Katie, in particular, was badly messed up by her mother's vanishing act. Constance now lived eight months a year in Argentina, and was by all accounts happy with Gracido; she had all but forgotten her children in West Sussex.

'I bet she's drinking herself to death,' Anthony heard Katie say bitterly, 'and I hope she does, too. I hate Mummy.' At which Sandra had said, 'Now, now, Katie, don't speak about your mother like that. You know she loves you all very much.'

Anthony had heard before from John that Constance was a bit of a drinker. During their marriage, she had taken to boozing in the afternoons at the Fittleworth Arms with the polo set who congregated there, and she drank too much at the numerous polo lunches given by sponsors in marquees. Anthony reckoned that if he'd been married to John Furlong, he'd probably have turned to the bottle too.

The Furlongs' divorce, so difficult to finesse at long distance, finally came through and John was a free man, ready and eager to marry Sandra. Anthony was secretly very relieved because he hoped that, with a new ring on her finger, she might relax a bit and let him have his children to stay. They married one Saturday afternoon in Fittleworth parish church, where John had persuaded the local vicar that, as two blameless divorcees, they should be allowed a full church wedding. Arabella, who was the only person from Winchford to be invited, apart from Ginette of course, reported that it had been a lovely, happy wedding, with Katie and Rosanna as the only bridesmaids, looking sweet in daisy dresses made by Sandra, and Tom and Richard as ushers in little rented tailcoats. Arabella did mention, to Anthony's quiet satisfaction, that Sandra had overdone it in electing to wear a full white meringue second time around. Now Sandra was remarried, Anthony felt less obligation towards her. In the future, Sandra and John would play an ever diminishing role in his life. Eventually, if he was lucky, he'd hardly have to see them at all. It was a wonderfully liberating prospect.

Gaia had recently started nursery school in Winchford and, according to reports, was thriving, despite the obvious eccentricities of her home situation. As Mrs Round, who had taught all Anthony's children, put it, 'Mrs Starling is rather an *unusual* lady, and some of her ideas are very strange, but Gaia's a bright little spark. I wish you could talk to her mother about her diet. We've tried ourselves, but nothing makes a blind bit of difference.'

Anthony was acutely conscious of Nula's cranky views on food. Lately, Nula had placed herself and Gaia on a macrobiotic diet, which meant they could eat virtually nothing. No longer were only meat and fish banned, but milk and eggs, wheat, pasta and practically everything else. 'About all she's allowed, poor little girl, is soy beans and sorrel,' he told Lex when they discussed it in the Plough and Harrow. 'Nula won't even let her have her school milk at breaktime, in case the cows ate grass sprayed with chemicals.'

'I have to hand it to you,' Lex replied. 'When it comes to choosing certifiable lunatics as bedmates, you win the prize every time.'

'Hold on, that's very unfair. Only Nula's like that.'

'Not Amanda? I've never forgotten her at the fete, parading about in that scarlet tailcoat. Anyway, she stars in blue movies.'

'It wasn't a blue movie, actually.'

'That's not what Archie and I thought when we saw it.'

Anthony blanched. 'Well, Sandra isn't mad.'

'Just maddening. But you've palmed her off on Britain's Dullest Man, so that's OK.'

'I do worry about Gaia,' Anthony said. 'I saw her the other day in the village shop. There's no colour in her cheeks; she looks anaemic. It's this ridiculous diet.'

'Can't you ask her to tea at the Priory, and fill her up with cakes and buns?'

'I keep inviting her up to swim, but Nula won't let her come. She says it's because of the chlorine, but I think she doesn't want her to come to the house. It's a shame, because Jasmine's great with her and I'd love to do more for her.'

'It was slightly mad of you to give Nula a cottage here in the first place; that's what most people think. You could have paid her to live somewhere else.'

'You're right, I could have. But if I'd done that, I wouldn't ever know if Gaia's OK. At least I can keep an eye on her here. I don't trust Nula on her own. I dread the day she decides to take Gaia back to London.'

29

Anthony started dreaming again about Amanda.

Ever since Jasmine's remark that Amanda and Patrice's marriage was in trouble, he had found himself thinking about his first wife. So far as he knew, she was still living with Patrice at the apartment in the Rue de Verneuil, and it was to there he posted birthday cards with suitably innocuous messages, and more cards at Christmas. None elicited any response. The next birthday he sent off a selection of rock music cassettes, carefully chosen with Jasmine's help at Our Price, with a friendly inscription 'from Jasmine and Anthony'. When there was no reaction, he wondered whether she could have moved or was away filming.

It was shortly afterwards that Patrice, hitherto employed only in French art-house productions, surfaced as the male lead in a Hollywood remake of *The Count of Monte Cristo*, one of the highest grossing movies of the year. There were articles about him in all the papers, and Patrice Bouillon's name began to crop up in lists of the world's sexiest men. Each time he saw anything about him, Anthony scrutinised the piece for any mention of Amanda. Often there was nothing about her at all, which fed his unspoken hope that the couple might have split up. After the British premiere at the Odeon, Leicester Square, however, a large photograph of Patrice appeared in the following day's *Daily Mail*, with Amanda at his side, being presented to Princess Margaret. Patrice and the Princess were beaming at each other – old friends from Mustique – while Amanda looked cool and almost disengaged, as though meeting royalty was way beneath her. Sitting on his commuter train, Anthony studied the body language between Patrice and his ex for several minutes, looking for clues that all might not be well between them.

When *The Count of Monte Cristo* opened at the multiplex in Cheltenham and Jasmine was invited for a schoolfriend's birthday, she quickly accepted, but instinctively knew not to mention she was going to her father.

One evening Jasmine arrived home with a letter from the school asking whether her parents wanted her to be confirmed. Most of the girls in her year group would be prepared for confirmation, the letter said, and the school's Visitor, the Bishop of Gloucester, was scheduled to conduct the ceremony in July. 'What do you reckon?' Anthony asked her. 'Do you *want* to be confirmed? I've never thought of you as religious, but maybe it would be a good thing to do.'

'I don't even know if I'm allowed to be confirmed,' Jasmine said. 'I haven't been christened, remember.'

'That's true. Hmm. Well, I'm sure a christening isn't that hard to arrange. I can ring the vicar if you like.'

'Does that mean I'd get to have godparents?'

'I suppose it could,' he replied doubtfully. 'Richard and Rosanna already got most of our best friends, but I'm sure we'll think of someone. Maybe you'd like to choose them yourself.'

In the end, Jeremy agreed to hold a private Saturday morning baptism at All Hallowes, having first assured Jasmine she needn't be submerged naked in the font, and that she could be blessed with a dab of holy water on her forehead instead. Jasmine's choice of godparents, to her father's surprise and Henrietta's strong disapproval, were Mrs Holcombe and Gaia Starling, who was now three.

'That is the most ridiculous idea I've heard in my entire life,' Henrietta protested. 'Both are totally unsuitable. You must put your foot down, Anthony.'

But Jeremy had already endorsed the idea, saying there was nothing in the prayer book to prohibit younger sponsors. 'I find it refreshing,' he told Anthony. 'It is important for the church to embrace youth with open arms.'

Nula, to no one's surprise, was sceptical about Gaia taking part in any ritual that wasn't pagan, but Jasmine was so guileless she eventually acquiesced. She knew Gaia adored Jasmine, who always referred to her as 'my little sister' and dropped in at Forge Cottage to play with her.

The christening out of the way, Jasmine embarked on her preparation for confirmation. Mostly this seemed to consist of listening to *Tubular Bells* in her bedroom while wading through the New English Bible. One evening she announced her intention of becoming a nun, and asked for advice on convents, but the next evening she was glued to *The Sweeney* on TV as usual, and the danger seemed to have passed.

Further communications arrived from the school, including an allocation of seats which was 'strictly restricted to ten per confirmand. This should allow sufficient places to accommodate parents, grandparents and up to four godparents per pupil.'

'Is Amanda coming?' Jasmine asked.

'Would you like her to?'

Jasmine nodded. 'And what about my other grandparents? I've never even *met* Amanda's parents in my whole life, you realise. All the other girls have four grandparents coming, if they're still alive.'

'I've never met Amanda's parents either. Your other grandpa lives in Rome, I think.'

'Can't you ring him and invite him? I can't *just* have Granny Anscombe. She's scary in her wheelchair.'

It occurred to Anthony that Jasmine's confirmation gave him the perfect pretext to track down Amanda and renew contact, and the next morning he threw all the resources of Anscombes Bank behind the task. Within forty-eight hours, he'd obtained a current telephone number for the Rue de Verneuil apartment, which was ex-directory but apparently remained their Paris address.

He dialled the number, which was answered by a maid who sounded Algerian, and after a long wait Amanda came on to the line. It was the first time they had spoken for more than three years, and he felt a shiver of excitement on hearing her voice.

'Hi, Ant. It's been ages. How many more kids have you had lately? You're probably up to six or seven by now.'

'None, actually.' He laughed. 'Still on four. How about you?'

'No new ones either. We're obviously not getting enough action.'

'And everything's all right in Paris . . . with Patrice and so on?'

He sensed her miss a beat, before replying, 'He's fine. He's in LA. He's up for about twenty movies after *Cristo*. It's changed his life.'

'But you stay in Paris.'

'I'm writing. Trying to. There's meant to be a new album.'

'So Jasmine said. She told me you'd written some great new songs in India.'

'I always think they should be better. How about you? You're still a banker, right?'

'Fraid so. And I'm meant to be running Winchford these days, too.'

'How is Winchford? I was thinking about it the other day. I never liked the place when I was living there, but it was probably quite beautiful. That stone the cottages are built of, it's a good colour.'

'You should visit,' Anthony said. 'That's what I'm ringing about, actually.' He told her about Jasmine's confirmation and how much their daughter wanted both parents to be there, plus her grandparents too if that were remotely possible.

'Christ,' Amanda said. 'Confirmation? I don't think I even know what that means. But, sure, when is it? If I can come, I will. It might help my writer's block.'

'And your parents?'

'I wouldn't bank on it. Mum was in Fez, last I heard. I've got a number for Dad somewhere, but it might be out of date.'

Almost seventy girls had been prepared for confirmation that year and the whole of the nave was taken up by their families and supporters. The confirmands were seated on long benches before the altar, in tidy dresses, and Anthony, who recognised several of Jasmine's friends, pointed them out to Amanda.

Amanda's appearance in the church in a black Saint Laurent gypsy coat had drawn stares from the congregation, and other parents were surreptitiously turning round in their pews to catch a glimpse of her. It was more than five years since her hit record, but news of the blue movie had filtered around the school, and she was an object of curiosity, particularly since it was the first time she'd turned up at anything.

She had arrived at the Priory the previous evening by London taxi, two hours later than expected, but there nonetheless. They had supper in the garden under the cypress tree: Anthony, Amanda, Jasmine, Henrietta and the new Australian nurse Danii. Henrietta, who hadn't set eyes on her former daughter-in-law for nearly fifteen years, was prepared to be icy, but was disarmed at being presented with an enormous box of Fauchon truffles; she sniffed disapprovingly at the extravagance before eating several and handing the box to Danii to hide away inside.

'I understood your father was joining us. We do have a ticket for him for tomorrow, you realise,' Henrietta said to Amanda.

'I think he's on his way,' Amanda said. 'He's driving over from Rome on his motorbike.'

Henrietta, who had never met anyone who actually owned a motorcycle, other than youths in the village, shot her a look of amazed disapproval.

After dinner Anthony took Amanda for a walk around the village in the twilight, though he made sure they turned back before getting too close to Forge Cottage. It was bad enough that the mother of his first child was going to meet the mother of his fourth tomorrow at the confirmation, to which Nula insisted on escorting Gaia. He couldn't face a premature introduction in the lane. Although Anthony had once seen close parallels between the two women, he could no longer remember what these might have been, and felt only dread at the prospect of them meeting. He felt embarrassed at Amanda seeing how low he had fallen with Nula.

As they passed the old almshouses where Walter and Mrs Holcombe lived, Amanda said, 'I always loved those cottages. Do you think if we'd lived in one of them instead, things would have been different?'

'We'd still have been us, and you'd still have found Winchford stifling.'

'I don't know. Different houses and places make such a difference to how you feel. I've found that with Patrice, too. We always get on particularly well in Morocco and Algeria, all those North African countries. But we fight like cat and dog in the States every time, because we hate American hotels.'

'How about in Paris?'

'Fifty-fifty. He can be a difficult man to live with, but you probably guessed that.'

'Jasmine did suggest something of the sort.'

'He drinks too much, and stays out all night without saying where he is. I used to worry, but now I don't bother. It's not worth it. Usually it's better not to know.'

Anthony said nothing and she went on, 'I learnt long ago there's *always* a girl. On every film set, in Paris, wherever, it doesn't matter. It's a question of how much one cares at any particular moment.'

'I'm sorry. I didn't know.' He spoke gravely, but a part of him soared with joy.

'It's not as if I didn't walk into it with my eyes wide open. He was the same with Sabine – that was his first wife. Except then I was the bit on the side and she was the deceived wife.'

'Will you stay together?'

They were walking past the Plough and Harrow, and Brendon Sheaf's jukebox was pounding out *A Whiter Shade of Pale*, which was a village favourite, on the permanent playlist. Gales of laughter spilled out onto the lane.

'I do think about leaving sometimes. But then I decide to give him one final chance. I love him, you see. Not all the time, but enough, just enough. We have our good times. And there's Amelie to consider. She'll be six soon; she adores her Papa when he's around. So it's not an easy call.'

'Well, if you do ever decide to call it a day, you can always come here for a bit. Jasmine would love it.'

'I don't think your mother would be too happy. She hated me enough the first time round. I notice she's given me the worst bedroom in the Priory.'

'You could borrow a cottage.'

'An almshouse? My life ambition fulfilled at last.'

'Not one of them, I'm afraid, not until Walter or Mrs Holcombe keels over. Walter's going to be ninety next year, I think. Something like that. But a cottage, definitely.'

Amanda gave him a long, meaningful look. 'You're a good man, you know that. I was right about you all those years ago. The first time I saw you, I knew we had a special bond.'

The Bishop of Gloucester gave an address of excessive length, welcoming the schoolgirls into the adult community of the church and speaking about the responsibilities of Christian life, before proceeding to the altar to lay his hands on the head of each one, saying, 'Confirm, oh Lord, the servant of your Holy Spirit' and 'Defend, oh Lord, this thy servant with thy heavenly grace.'

Anthony spotted Jasmine looking out for them as the bishop worked his way down the line towards her, and waved at her encouragingly. Looking along his pew, he couldn't help thinking their own party was particularly eccentric, consisting in addition to himself and Amanda of Mrs Holcombe in her everyday tweed coat, her daughter Judy who'd rolled up in black dungarees without an invitation and somehow got in, Nula looking more the Earth Mother than ever in a garment seemingly made from old farmyard sacks, Gaia in one of Rosanna's cast-off party dresses, Henrietta in the navy-blue jacket and diamond brooch she'd worn at his wedding to Sandra, and Danii the nurse in a big pink sunhat and lace gloves. The only disappointment was that Amanda's father had still not made it. Jasmine would be sad about that – she'd been telling her friends he was coming by motorbike all the way from Italy.

'May she continue thine for ever,' intoned the bishop, placing his hand on Jasmine's dark head, 'and daily increase in thy Holy Spirit, until she comes to thy everlasting Kingdom.'

At that moment Anthony became conscious of a commotion in the aisle, and a small, bald, brown man in biking leathers, carrying a black motorcycle helmet with visor, was pushing his way into the end of their pew.

*

Anthony had booked a table for lunch after the service at a restaurant called Bumbles, which was three minutes walk from the cathedral. He had chosen it partly for its wheelchair access, so Henrietta could get in, and partly for its menu, which majored on upmarket hamburgers and Caesar salads. His aim was to feed everyone as quickly as possible and send them on their way.

Danii was soon negotiating her boss's wheelchair across the glazed terrazzo floor, and Henrietta was scrutinising the other customers disdainfully, making it clear that Bumbles wasn't her idea of a suitable venue for a post-confirmation family lunch. Jasmine, still in her smart dress and carrying a presentation prayer book, was being congratulated by everyone, while Anthony struggled to work out a seating plan with the best prospect of averting disaster. In the end, accepting nothing was going to be ideal, he placed himself between his mother and Mrs Holcombe; Jasmine between her two grandparents; Nula on the other side of Amanda's father, Ed, with Gaia next to her mother; then Judy, Danii and Amanda, who had Mrs Holcombe on her left. The plan had the advantage of keeping Nula and Amanda spaced well apart, so they couldn't discuss him, and he'd partially neutralised Henrietta by taking her himself.

As a waiter with spiky bleached hair took their orders, Anthony became conscious of several drawbacks to the scheme. Mrs Holcombe had never approved of Amanda since giving notice at Forge Cottage and looked unhappy. Danii was telling Amanda in a low voice what a peculiar lady Nula was, and how no one in the village could think why Anthony had ever got involved with her. Across the table he could see Ed Gibbons, Amanda's father, getting on well with Nula, which was a relief since he'd feared she might be tricky. Ed struck him as a surprising figure. He didn't know what he'd been expecting – someone taller and more handsome probably – not this tiny, marsupial man in bikers' leathers with bronze bracelets round his wrists. Amanda had once mentioned her father taught English at the American University in Rome, though whether he still did, Anthony didn't know. All he'd heard was that he'd been married several times, most recently to one of his pupils, half his age.

Partly as a strategy to avoid talking to his mother, who was complaining the napkins at Bumbles were made of paper, Anthony proposed a toast to Jasmine. 'I cannot tell you how happy we are that you could all be here on Jasmine's important day. For Jasmine to have her mother here too, who has travelled all the way from Paris, and two of the grandparents – Ed, you really do deserve a medal for coming such an incredible distance from Rome *by motorbike* – plus both her godparents – Mrs Holcombe and Gaia – is a great honour, and something Jasmine will remember all her life. So thank you *all* for making such a tremendous effort, and let's drink a toast to Jasmine – my holiest daughter.'

Everyone raised their glasses, and Jasmine groaned, '*Oh, Dad,*' and Anthony felt that, on balance, things could really have gone a lot worse. It struck him that the future was going to be full of gatherings like this one, with different combinations of his children's mothers all there together, celebrating weddings, birthdays and the rest of it. Maybe it would work out better than he'd feared. After all, they were all adults, and there was no reason they shouldn't rub along. Maybe even Sandra would come round eventually.

Having made no effort to address a single word to Amanda's father, Henrietta was now put out that he was engrossed in conversation with Nula and ignoring her. They did seem to be fascinated by each other, and Anthony heard Nula say, 'Your Qi sounds like it might be smothered, Ed. You must give me a chance to set it free.'

When lunch ended Anthony went up to his former father-in-law and said, 'It's been so good to meet you at last. I'm afraid we haven't really had much of a chance to talk. You are coming back to Winchford now, I hope? We've got a room ready for you at the Priory.'

'That's very hospitable of you,' Ed replied genially. 'But I've already accepted an offer of accommodation from Nula. She's asked me to stay over at her cottage; we have a mutual interest in the healing arts.'

30

D espite his confident prediction that Sandra, now Mrs John Furlong, would fade away to the margins of his life, two events propelled her back to centre stage.

The two years following Jasmine's confirmation were relatively untroubled ones for Anthony. At the bank he prospered and was now a member of the three-man chairman's committee which ran the place. The deals he oversaw became bigger and more complicated, and he had almost complete autonomy in his handling of them. Business took him to Germany and Scandinavia and occasionally to New York, and he often found himself scrutinising the Winchford farm accounts sitting in a plane. There were so many different aspects to the estate, what with the farm, the forestry, quarry and cottages. These days he carried two briefcases: one for documents related to Anscombes Bank, the other for estate bumph.

He had seen nothing of Amanda since the confirmation, and whatever yearnings he still had in that direction had been suppressed. To the best of his knowledge, she was still with Patrice, for better or worse, and sticking it out. Nula, meanwhile, had finally set up a business practising reflexology and energy healing she called reiki. The influence of her new boyfriend, Ed Gibbons, Amanda's father, who had moved into Forge Cottage after Jasmine's confirmation, had generally been beneficial, Anthony felt, although the weekly food bills from the village shop had increased noticeably with three mouths to feed instead of two. Ed did at least exert a calming influence, and was kind to Gaia. In the summer, he brought her up to the Priory to swim, having somehow convinced Nula that chlorine was less toxic than she'd supposed; he also talked her out of the macrobiotic diet and Gaia was consequently looking a lot healthier.

Whenever his daughter came to visit, Anthony delighted in making her a large Nesquik strawberry milkshake and a plate of marmite toast, having first sworn Ed not to breathe a word.

Anthony reopened the conversation with Sandra about their children coming to stay at Winchford but, to his mounting frustration, she remained obstinate. More than once he was reduced to talking to John to see if he could help bring her round, but despite his plodding promises to do his best, Sandra wouldn't budge. 'Not while *you know who* is there. I'm not going through all that trauma again, thank you very much.'

It was all the more surprising, then, when she rang him one Friday, very agitated, and asked whether she could drive over to the Priory the following morning for urgent advice.

'Sure,' Anthony replied uncertainly. 'What about?'

'Not something I can talk about on the phone. It's too awful; I need to see you.'

'It's not the children? No one's been hurt?'

'They're fine. It's not them. Listen, I don't even want John to know I'm coming. I need to see you privately.'

Anthony was rather intrigued by Sandra's secret mission. All evening he speculated on what it could be. Something outrageous involving John, he hoped; she'd discovered a stash of pornography in his golf bag, or he enjoyed dressing up in her knickers. Neither seemed terribly plausible. Yet she had sounded desperate, and it had to be something important for her to come to Winchford.

Bang on time, Sandra's dark green Ford Fiesta nosed into the stable yard and there she was at the kitchen door. Jasmine was sitting at the table in pyjamas drinking a mug of coffee, and clambered up to kiss her former stepmother hello.

'Gracious, haven't you grown!' Sandra exclaimed. 'You're taller than me now. You'll be seventeen next month, won't you?'

They exchanged stilted pleasantries about school and A-levels, then Anthony took Sandra through into the library. He was shocked by his ex-wife's appearance; in the years since she'd left Winchford, she had aged. She must be in her early forties now, but looked older, with deep crow's feet and ash-coloured strands in her hair. From the dark circles under her eyes, it was clear she wasn't sleeping well.

No sooner were they alone than it all came tumbling out. It had been a devastating month for John Furlong. First, he had been dismissed from his job as estate manager to the Fittleworth Estate.

'I'm astonished,' Anthony said. 'I thought Lady Fittleworth adored him.'

'She does,' wailed Sandra. 'She's always saying she couldn't manage without him. It isn't her; it's her nephew, who's one of the trustees. He's a horrible smug man. I've never liked him and I warned John he wasn't to be trusted. Anyway, he insisted on an audit of the farm accounts, and it turned out John hasn't been putting in for all those awful EEC subsidies, he's never bothered filling in the forms. He says most of them are gobbledegook in any case. Anyway, Adrian – that's the nephew – is saying John missed out on thousands of pounds worth of rebates, and it was his responsibility. He's made such a fuss about it, complaining to all the other trustees, and they came to a meeting with Lady Fittleworth and forced her to sack him.

'He's devastated,' Sandra went on. 'It's not only the job, it's our house too. It goes with the position and we've been given twelve weeks to move out. We haven't told the children and they're gong to be so sad – they love that house. We've only just done up Katie and Rosanna's bedrooms with new curtains and matching dressing tables and everything.'

'I really am so sorry, Sandra. Tell John if there's anything I can do . . .'

'Well, that's why I'm here,' Sandra said. 'John doesn't know anything about me coming to see you. He's such a proud man, but I don't know where else to go. I haven't even told you the worst bit yet, but a letter has come from Lloyd's, saying we owe them over a hundred thousand pounds.'

'Oh dear.'

'We can't understand it. John's on all these brilliant underwriting syndicates, that's what everyone said, and we've had some lovely cheques every year. We've been relying on them to pay Tom's school fees. And Eton's going to be a lot more expensive than Broadley from next September. I don't know how we'll cope, let alone how we're going to pay the Lloyd's losses. We haven't got that sort of money sitting around.'

'Obviously I've been following all the coverage in the press. It's been hard to miss it.'

'John rang his agency to say there must be a mistake, and this horrid man said there wasn't a mistake at all and we have to send a cheque before Christmas.'

'Do we know why? What's led to the losses, I mean. Was it asbestos?'

'This man said we had a tiny share in insuring some tin mine in Mexico. John didn't know anything about it. And the mine has collapsed, killing lots of people, and now the miners' widows are all suing the mining company for compensation, and we're being told it's up to us to pay part of the cost. It's all so terrible. Nobody warned John anything like this could happen, or he'd never have got involved. We were told you got a big cheque for nothing every summer. That's why he joined.'

'What a dreadful mess.'

'We'll have nowhere to live by September, and I don't know how John's going to find a job; it could take ages. And then there's this huge bill hanging over us.' Sandra began sniffling into a tissue.

'Has John negotiated anything with his bank yet?'

Sandra shook her head. 'He wouldn't know about that. He's not like you – he's an outdoors sort of man.'

Ignoring the unwitting insult, Anthony said, 'Well, I think he should talk to them as soon as possible. He must explain the situation, and they may be able to help with a low-interest loan. The crucial thing is to keep them in the picture.' Sandra nodded, but seemed unconvinced.

'Anthony, you know what you said about doing something to help? I hate asking, but I've no one else to turn to, and you *are* Richard and Rosanna's father.'

'Of course. Anything.'

'Well it's a bit embarrassing, but I was wondering if there might be a spare cottage for us to move into. Here in Winchford. Just for a while until John finds a new job.'

Anthony blanched. Sandra back in Winchford. It wasn't appealing. Then he thought: if the children were here, I could see them all the time. 'No spare cottages,' he said, 'not at the moment anyway. But I'll tell you what is free and that's the Old Rectory. The people who've been renting it just moved out. You can have that for a bit if it helps.'

Sandra leaned over and kissed his cheek. 'Thank you, you've saved our lives. John's going to be so grateful. I know he'll ring you himself.'

'No need. Glad to be able to help.'

'Could I ask you one more teensy favour? It's more for John's sake really.'

Anthony shrugged. 'Sure.'

'He won't be happy, poor man, about taking charity. Not after everything he's been through. I know he'd like to do something in return. Couldn't he make himself useful on the farm, give you some back-up?'

'Well, I suppose we could always use a bit of extra help,' Anthony said doubtfully.

'I'll tell John, then; it'll make such a difference. He hates being beholden. I'll tell him he's got a job in your estate office and it comes with a tied house.'

It was not many weeks afterwards that a horsebox packed with furniture drew up outside the Old Rectory, and John and Sandra Furlong and their four respective children moved back into the village they had left so abruptly three and a half years earlier.

For Anthony it was a mixed blessing. He was thrilled to have Richard and Rosanna in Winchford again, and on the first afternoon invited them up to the Priory to swim with Jasmine. One of the most rewarding sights was their happiness at all being together again. The children seemed delighted to be back in the village and moreover to be there with their father. They were received by Henrietta in the white drawing room, and dutifully kissed their grandmother on her powdered, subsiding cheek, then dropped in with Anthony to say hello to Mrs Holcombe and Walter Twine.

Afterwards he took them both for a drink in the beer garden of the Plough and Harrow, where Richard insisted on ordering half a pint of cider, claiming that, as an almost-teenager, he was allowed. Although Anthony never would have wished misfortune on the Furlongs, it was a fact that it had brought his family back together. That night, in his bath, he happily reflected that tonight was the first time since Sandra walked out that all four of his children would be sleeping in the village.

The downside was that he had now to contend with John's presence in the estate office. On his first morning John had commandeered a large table as a desk for himself, and set about a thorough overhaul of working practices. Where Anthony had always set an easy-going but deceptively effective regime, with the various farmhands given a high degree of autonomy, John fussed over timesheets. He had an infuriating ability to create tensions where none had existed before, and almost every Saturday morning Anthony had to smooth ruffled feathers in the team. Although John was depressed by the recent turn of events in his life, he had lost none of his self-confidence when it came to farm management. Seemingly oblivious to his recent dismissal for incompetence, he referred constantly and approvingly to his stewardship at Fittleworth. 'At Fittleworth,' he announced, 'I introduced a system whereby every piece of farm machinery – tractors, combines, sprayers – were parked up in line at the end of each day facing in the same direction. Not only does it look more professional, but it helps create a climate of efficiency which permeates the entire business.'

Sandra's return to the village, to a different house and with a different surname, must have caused her some mortification, which she did well to disguise. In terms of prestige, her new status as wife to the temporary farm manager ranked some way behind her former position, and Anthony was not alone in observing a renewed bossiness in Jacinthe, who instinctively understood how it affected her own ranking in village affairs.

The one obvious omission in the Furlongs' prodigal return was Marjorie, no longer part of the family package. Marjorie and Len were giving their marriage a second chance, and had been attending marriage counselling in Wisborough Green, close to the adult education college where Len had enrolled on a course in pub management. Having lost every penny, he and Marjorie were toying with the idea of running a pub together, which would have the added advantage of providing accommodation. According to Richard, who had seen Grandpa Potts recently, Len had become fascinated by the process of keeping beer in peak condition, and by the complex hydraulics of pumping it from barrel to bar. Marjorie was preparing herself for her new life by learning to make bar snacks; already she was capable of running up two hundred cheddar cheese and pineapple nibbles on toothpicks in less than one hour, which is a rate of more than one every twenty seconds.

By the time the new school terms began in September, Rosanna and Katie had both been happily enrolled at senior school in Moreton which, if larger and less academic than their school in Petworth, was at least full of friends they remembered from before. Gaia was still at the junior school, and so far there had been no awkward confrontations between Sandra and Nula at the school gates. Nula's acupuncture business was finally beginning to take off, and she had expanded her repertoire to embrace Indian cranial massage and kinesiology, which she advertised in the back of the All Hallowes parish newsletter. Tom Furlong had made a strong start at Eton, where he had been placed in high divisions and was enjoying the field games. At the request of Sandra, Anthony agreed to pay his first term's fees. 'It really is just a loan,' Sandra assured him. 'John hates me even asking, and I wouldn't normally, but for Tom's *education* I just have to. I know you understand.' Sandra said Tom looked so handsome in his Eton tailcoat.

Anthony consented – he could hardly have done otherwise, Tom being Richard's best friend and extended family – but did ask whether Tom's mother and her Argentinian polo friend were contributing. Sandra looked uncomfortable. 'John wrote to Constance asking if she could help, but we haven't heard a squeak. I'm spitting, because Gracido spends a fortune on polo ponies every season.'

Richard was off to his own new school, Radley, where he had got into one of the best 'socials' – school slang for houses. Having scraped through Common Entrance, and been placed in the bottom class for every single subject, it was going to be a struggle. Anthony was just relieved that he'd got in at all. Eton had never been an option academically, and they'd toyed with Stowe, so Radley was really a very good result, and good for sport too, which was Richard's thing.

Jasmine was starting her final year at Cheltenham and doing a lot of acting, at which she was the school star. Anthony knew he was biased, but her performance as Tallulah in Bugsy Malone really did show talent, and he had more or less agreed she could give up on university and go to drama school next year instead. The only disappointment for Jasmine was that Amanda, who had promised to come to *Bugsy* with Patrice, failed to show up on the night, wasting two front row tickets and devastating the entire cast, who were desperate to meet a real movie star. Instead, she had had to make do with Anthony, Rosanna and Katie, and Mrs Holcombe and Judy, who applauded wildly each time she came on stage. Much to everyone's relief, Henrietta said she had no intention of watching a musical set in an American bordello.

There were times when Anthony wondered how it had all worked out like this; he felt he had ended up at the epicentre of an enormous adhesive spider's web, upon which legions of ex-lovers, ex-wives, children and extended families were stuck for ever, all looking to him to feed, house and educate them. As he walked through the village, every corner invoked a different episode from his past; he felt like a garden snail that has left a slime trail behind him, marking its progress along an algae-covered path. He couldn't decide whether he was incredibly fortunate or incredibly unfortunate. He had four children, all of whom he adored. Obviously it was far from ideal that, of the four, only one actually lived in the same house as him, but he must make the best of it. It was unsatisfactory too that, in owning one of the prettiest villages in England, he still did not have a house of his own, but lived with his mother. Winchford Priory had become a source of worry; it was increasingly obvious that it needed a lot of work; the plumbing and electrics hadn't been touched for fifty years, and the place could go up in flames any time. Part of the balustrade around the minstrel's gallery had toppled down into the Great Hall, and he suspected the panelling was riddled with dry rot. But nothing drastic could be done while Henrietta was *in situ*.

Anthony had vowed to steer clear of women and devote himself entirely to his children. Not once since the Nula episode had he even permitted himself to be alone in a room with a single woman, let alone taken one out to dinner. His social abstinence was much commented upon, and several attractive Oxfordshire divorcees became quite agitated about it, for Anthony was the most eligible catch for miles around.

As for Amanda, he could never hear or read her name without a frission of fear and excitement. He did not seriously believe they would ever get back together, and yet he never entirely suppressed that hope.

Whenever Jasmine asked about her mother, he felt himself tense up. If a neighbour referred to her in conversation, he was impassive, betraying nothing. And yet he knew it would have taken only a postcard, a single word, to reignite his passion, a dormant volcano waiting to erupt.

Anthony's regular Sunday night drinks with Lex and Archie had recently shifted from the Plough and Harrow to a wine bar in Moreton-in-Marsh owned by Archie. Having given up on the City as too much like hard work, Archie had sunk the proceeds of his Fulham flat into buying the lease on the old Woolmarket, where the doctor's surgery had been. This he had converted into a cavernous bistro-cum-wine bar called Marshmellows, which quickly became a magnet for local businessmen and sixth-form babes from Moreton comprehensive.

'You should bring Jasmine with you,' Archie said. His day consisted of sitting at a table close to the bar, though not actually serving or participating in any other way, so far as Anthony could see.

'Jasmine? This is the last place I'd bring her.'

'What's your problem? Jasmine's looking knockout – I saw her at the village shop on Saturday.'

'She's barely seventeen. I don't want her hanging out in places like this. Not yet, not never.'

'Exactly, Anthony. She's *seventeen*. How old was Amanda when you eloped with her?'

'I didn't "elope", as you put it, and it was completely different in any case. Amanda was much more sophisticated. There's no comparison.'

'What do you reckon, Lex? One rule for the Sheriff of Winchford, another for his comely maid?'

Lex laughed. 'I'm not surprised he's keeping her under wraps. She's looking more like the first Mrs Anscombe every day.'

'Let's hope she isn't taking part in any skin flicks up at the Priory, then. You have to admit it's the perfect location. I'm surprised you don't rent the place out, Ant.'

'Listen, you two. This is my daughter you're joking about. And if you think I'm bringing her to Marshmellows to be pawed at by you, think again.'

'Talking of people pawing one's relations, turn round very slowly,' Archie said. 'In the corner by the cigarette machine.'

Anthony stared into the gloom, where two heads were glued together in a passionate snog. Both had very short hair, but he couldn't see their faces.

'Arabella and Ginette,' Archie said. 'Does that make us related, do you reckon? My sister necking with your ex-sister-in-law?'

'That's *them*?'

'It's lurve. They don't bother hiding it any more. Except at home, though even there it's hard to miss. After four years, I think even my mother's getting the message.'

'Does she mind?'

Archie shrugged. 'She'd always had Bella marked down for *you*, actually. That was her big hope. So I doubt she's exactly thrilled. But what can you do? She'll probably try and get Bella off with Jasmine next.'

Part Five

31

One warm June evening, in the upstairs bar of Mark's Club in Charles Street, Mayfair, where Anthony had been hosting a business dinner for clients, he met the woman who would become his third wife.

Dita Emboroleon, recently estranged wife of Aleco 'Goldie' Emboroleon, the Greek shipping tycoon, had been dining with friends in the panelled restaurant downstairs. Afterwards they had returned to the sofa-filled first-floor bar for more drinks and coffee. Anthony and Dita found themselves perching on adjacent sofa arms.

Even before they had exchanged a sentence, Anthony found himself intrigued. The first thing he noticed was her scent, which enveloped her in a musky, luxurious mist. He was struck, too, by a sense of energy and fun. She had bright, snappy eyes. Her tawny, bronzed skin was unusually plumped, like the quilting on a Chanel handbag. Her wrists were festooned with wide gold bracelets that clanked opulently whenever she gestured, and her hair was an expensive panoply of shades of honey-blonde. On the carpet, next to her perfectly polished crocodile mules, stood a perfectly polished crocodile evening bag.

He could not help overhearing snatches of her conversation, which was about holidays and friends and yachts. Her voice was gravelly, deep and efficiently sexy. He reckoned she was approaching forty.

Anthony had moved to the corner of a padded stool arranged with art books, newspapers and magazines. His back was turned against her, but he was conscious of her proximity. When she leant forwards and asked him, 'Have you any objections to my smoking a cigarette?' he felt himself shiver.

Her eyes were an unusual and piercing cobalt blue. If others detected a steely glint to them, Anthony did not. With her even white teeth and bright pink gums, and a slightly supercilious pout to her lips, Anthony found her captivating, and gladly held out the ashtray while she breathed smoke towards his face.

'Dita Emboroleon,' she said. 'Mrs Aleco Emboroleon, but not for much longer, thank God.'

'Anthony Anscombe.'

Dita's eyes flickered imperceptibly. 'Anything to do with the bank?'

Anthony smiled. 'Actually, yes. How very clever of you.' He was oddly pleased. Normally nobody had heard of Anscombes. Not like they knew Barings or Flemings or Hoares, let alone Rothschilds or the other really famous ones. Occasionally Anthony wondered whether his family's obsession with maintaining a low profile counted against them.

She said she had recently met some Anscombes while dining with the Weinstocks – 'An older man with a wife who adores Scotland' - and they established it had been Anthony's uncle, Michael, the chairman of the bank, and his aunt Bridget. Dita seemed impressed that Anthony had recently been promoted to deputy chairman, and fired off several shrewd questions about their short-term investment strategy. There was no doubt about it, Dita Emboroleon was a clever woman, as well as a very attractive one.

As they were saying goodnight Dita asked whether Anthony would mind if she rang him. 'I don't know if you're a fan of the opera,' she murmured.

As he left the club and strolled towards Berkeley Square in search of a taxi, Anthony felt quite exhilarated: he had met someone rather interesting for once.

Dita rang him at the office the very next morning. On the telephone she sounded wonderfully competent, as though everything in her life was seamless and achievable. Diary in hand, she suggested a couple of dates for operas and ballets to which she was already holding tickets and taking small parties of friends; she mentioned the names of several prominent bankers and socialites. 'Afterwards I thought we'd have supper at that new restaurant of Nico Ladenis's. Nothing too late, as we all have to work the next day.'

They met in the crush bar of the Royal Opera House, where it turned out that Dita was a patron, her husband having given a serious cheque towards the renovation of the Grand Staircase. She looked ravishing. She was dressed in a long, pink, diaphanous evening dress with a pattern of exotic birds, draped from one shoulder, exposing a nut-brown back and toned arms. Around one wrist was a thick gold cuff studded with emeralds, sapphires and topaz.

When she saw Anthony, she exclaimed, 'Ah, my absolute *favourite man.*' As she guided him around her little group, introducing him, she held on to his upper arm in a gesture he interpreted as warm and reassuring. When she made introductions, she added a sentence or two of flattering explanation about each person: 'I'm sure you know Boobie van Haagen, who everyone says is the cleverest banker at Lazards', or 'This is one of my dearest girlfriends, Carina Resnick, who has the prettiest house in Cap d'Antibes' or, in Anthony's case, 'I want you to meet Anthony Anscombe. Of course you know his family bank, Anscombe Brothers, and he has the most ravishing estate in Oxfordshire, or so I am told.'

'But you must come and see it,' Anthony replied at once. 'You must come down to lunch.' But even as he issued the invitation he wondered what Dita would make of the rapidly disintegrating Priory, with his wheelchair-bound mother and the kitchen full of sprawling children. When he had quit the house before dawn this morning he had left Richard and Rosanna plus Tom Furlong asleep in the Great Hall; they had come over to watch TV with Jasmine and afterwards dossed down on sofas.

The opera itself, Anthony found a trial. He had never understood opera, with its random tunes and implausible plots. This one was by Mozart and told the story of a birdcatcher and his magic flute. The actor playing the birdcatcher had a remarkably long nose, which made Anthony think of Patrice Bouillon and ruminate on the latest state of his marriage to Amanda. He had heard nothing from her for more than eight months, though Jasmine had received a postcard from Capri. Several times during the performance he sensed the closeness of Dita sitting next to him. Her scent, which was different from the one she'd been wearing at Mark's Club, was almost overpowering; when she fanned herself with her programme, clouds of it gusted towards him in a sweet petro-chemical haze. He was conscious of an almost electrical energy emanating from her. He had never experienced anything like it. When he'd been married to Sandra, he had recognised that she had higher levels of energy than Amanda, but with Dita it was on an altogether different scale. He reckoned she must have been a perfect wife for Goldie Emboroleon, who owned the second largest container fleet in Athens and was notoriously social. In profile, her face didn't look Greek at all, and he wondered where she came from originally.

After the opera they travelled to the restaurant in a convoy of black Mercedes, whose chauffeurs were waiting at the kerb outside the Opera

House. Anthony and Dita travelled together in the first car with Carina Resnick, and Dita and Carina regaled him with gossip about the rest of the party following behind. Anthony was surprised by how many of the others he had read about, though he had met none of them before. Dita expressed astonishment that he knew neither the Hindlips nor the Daniloviches. 'What have you been *doing* all these years, Anthony? Really, I cannot believe it; it cannot be true. You are teasing me. Or have you been hiding yourself away?'

'I'm afraid that's country life for you,' he replied. 'I'm really quite a country bumpkin.'

'Well, we all adore the countryside,' Dita said. 'It is such fun to visit for weekends, essential in fact. But during the week – *impossible*. Nobody can live in the country during the week. No, I cannot imagine it.'

As dinner progressed, Anthony found himself in the unusual position of centre of attention. Having never thought of himself as remotely interesting, he was surprised, and rather gratified, by how attentive Dita's friends were to him, and how much they seemed to know about investment banking and the deals that were currently going on. Carina Resnick said she had recently stayed with Anthony's neighbours Scrotum and Rosie Holland for the weekend, and they had driven back through Winchford from a lunch party. 'It is simply the most *divine* village,' Carina said. 'Really, so charming. Those little cottages, they remind me of the ones in Woodstock you pass on the way to Sonny and Rosita Marlborough's. Truly, you have been so clever to keep it so unspoiled.'

'Thank you,' said Anthony. 'Though, to be honest, my parents were always too stingy to modernise anything. I've been slowly renovating the cottages one at a time. I'm glad you don't think it looks too garish.'

'No, I *adore* it,' Carina assured him. 'It's a magical place. And to own the whole village – that is quite unusual in England, no? It must be worth a fortune.'

Anthony noticed Dita smiling at him across the table, and he smiled diffidently back. She really was the most fabulous-looking woman.

'All I know,' he replied to Carina, 'is that farming is a perpetual struggle, and if we break even on the property lets at the end of the year, we're happy. We have a lot of tenants who've been living there for years, and I can't really put their rents up.'

'I fell quite in love with it,' Carina insisted. 'I was telling Dita that it's a special place. Probably you know the Bamfords, who cannot be too far from you at Daylesford. That is another house I simply adore . . .'

At the end of dinner Dita suggested her driver would drop Anthony where he liked and, once in the car, invited him for a nightcap at her flat in Cadogan Place. 'I promise you, we will not be late,' she said, forestalling his protests. 'I know how you bankers like to arrive at your offices so early.'

Dita lived in a second-floor flat, which she referred to as an 'apartment', in a redbrick building with a pillared porch on the corner of Cadogan Place. A uniformed porter, dozing behind a desk, got up to unbolt the front door and summon the lift. The communal hall, with its white-veined marble floor, Robert Adam-style chimneypiece and enormous spray of white lilies, reminded Anthony of his Wigmore Street dentist.

Upstairs, Dita let him into her flat. It was one of the most comfortable flats Anthony had ever seen. The drawing room, corridors and dining room were a mass of competing chintzes, with cabbage roses and ribbons cascading on every side. Glazed chintz fabric hung from the walls on battens, and enormous four-seater sofas were covered in gardenias and rosebuds. Dozens of small oil paintings of dogs and leopards, thickly framed and individually lit, were displayed on each wall. Numerous thickly-clothed and fringed tables were strewn with china and silver knick-knacks, ivory-handled letter knives, magnifying glasses, Herend china baskets containing china strawberries, and silver-framed photographs of children, yachts and container ships. Anthony noticed a picture of a neat, slim young boy in a blazer with gold buttons. 'My son,' said Dita. 'John-Spiros. Goldie is very tough on him; too tough really.'

'He looks like a civilised chap.'

'That is partly the problem. My husband feels he may be homosexual. He is very unhappy about it.'

'And this is?' Anthony picked up a framed photograph of a twelve-year-old girl sitting glumly in the back of a motorboat. From the picture, she looked plump and more obviously Greek.

'Ambrosia. Our daughter.' Dita shrugged. 'She still has a lot to learn, that one. She is not really happy, which is a nonsense since she has all the advantages. All except looks. There is too much of her father in her, Goldie's genes. I keep telling her, "Wake up, Ambrosia. You have everything – money, staff, boats. Enjoy it. You may be no beauty, but anyone can look passable if they smile".'

Dita opened a bottle of champagne which she poured into two long-stemmed glasses. 'I bought these last weekend in Venice,' she said. 'When I saw them, they reminded me of the glass in Harry's Bar, the London one, I mean. They are quite pretty, no?'

Anthony agreed that they were. Looking around, he felt that everything in the flat was pretty. The lamps (and there were dozens of them) were perfect and gleaming: glass ones, and china ones with little butterflies and moths painted on them, wooden lamps like Trajan's column, all with silk lampshades and working lightbulbs. Every weekend at Winchford Priory, Anthony struggled round the house, changing bulbs and realigning wonky lampshades, but when he'd finished it never looked remotely like this. Everything in Dita's flat was in perfect working order. The wide floorboards ran seamlessly from room to room without the abrupt differences in height you got at the Priory. There was an ice-making machine in a cupboard in the study along with several shelves of gleaming tumblers, wine glasses and cocktail glasses. There was a chrome bucket full of ice, and a variety of small glass jugs with squeezed lemon juice and bowls of olives. Anthony thought how glorious it must be to live as comfortably as this.

On several of the tables were photographs of a dark-skinned teenager wearing a leather jacket with a big Rolex watch on his wrist. On his upper lip were wispy traces of moustache. Anthony instinctively didn't care for the look of him.

'Ah, I see you are looking at Morad,' Dita said. 'He is handsome, no? The girls find him so attractive, I am dreading how it will be in a year or two.'

'He's yours? Morad, I mean.' Anthony was surprised Dita could have such a grown-up son.

'He is my first baby. I *adore* Morad, even though he can bring so much worry to his mother.'

'Does he live here with you?'

'In the holidays, yes; we are here sometimes. Only for a few days, to visit the dentist. Usually he is at boarding school in Switzerland – Le Rosey.' Dita looked momentarily troubled. 'I hope he is behaving. I keep telling him, "Morad, they will kick you out if you continue this way. Truly. They will send you home".'

'What does he say to that?'

'Oh, you know how boys are. He does not listen to his mother. Or he thinks, if he is sent away, he will come to London and go to night-clubs every night. That is what he is hoping. Girls, girls, girls. He is girl crazy.'

They sat side by side on a glazed chintz sofa, which was so well plumped that Anthony felt he was sinking into a cream cake.

'So, tell me about you, Anthony,' Dita said. 'We have barely spoken all evening; there were far too many people as usual.'

'About *me*? I'm not sure what there is to say, really. I'm at the bank all week and then, at weekends, there's a tribe of children to entertain at Winchford.'

'Your first wife was Amanda Bouillon, no? Patrice's wife. She is a beautiful woman. I have always thought that.'

Anthony was surprised. 'You know Amanda?'

'Not so well. I have seen her many times at things. In Paris, mostly. Goldie and I used to go there all the time. He loves the Bristol hotel; it is a favourite for him.'

'And you used to see Amanda.'

'At parties, at cocktails. She is beautiful. Not well dressed, not so chic, but men find her quite sexy. I had to tell Aleco: "No, no, no, Goldie. She is spoken for already, that one." Otherwise I think he would have been quite interested, truly.'

'Well, she is pretty.' Anthony blushed.

'We had her pop record one summer on the boat,' Dita said. 'It was good for dancing: "Remember, Remember . . . things past, baby", wasn't that how it went? That summer we played it all the time. I told the crew, we *love* that song, so they played it each night for us.' Then she asked, 'Why did you let her go, Anthony?'

'I didn't. She left me.' He smiled. 'It was a long time ago. Our daughter, Jasmine, is eighteen and going to drama school soon.'

'Amanda left *you*? I'm surprised. Then she is more foolish than I realised.' Dita gazed at him appraisingly. 'You have other children too?'

'Three. Two by my second wife, and then a younger one, another daughter. She's called Gaia. I'm afraid she was born, er, out of wedlock.' Why was he telling her all this? He felt suddenly embarrassed.

Dita shrugged. 'It happens. All the time, it happens. Some women are calculating like that. With a man like you, in your position, with everything you have, you will be an obvious target. It is not significant.'

'That's very broad-minded of you. It's been quite awkward in the village, actually, with everyone knowing.'

'That is the English countryside for you. The people are not sophisticated. You cannot blame them; they have been nowhere to learn better.'

'It's all a bit complicated, with my children from my various marriages et cetera, but it's working better recently. They all get on well together, which is great.'

'The children, they live with you at Winchford Priory?'

'Only Jasmine. She's the only one who's there all the time, though she'll be off to college any minute. The others come at weekends, to swim and play tennis and sometimes stay over. I try to see them as much as possible.'

'And you have good staff at Winchford?'

'Staff? Well, sort of. A nice lady in the village, Mrs Holcombe, comes up three mornings a week and pushes a Hoover about. Sometimes her daughter helps out too, if she's got time.'

'But you have a proper housekeeper? And a butler?'

'Er, neither actually. I'm afraid we're not so well organised as that.'

'Then all I can say,' exclaimed Dita, 'is that you must be even more of a saint than I imagined. To manage all that by yourself, with no help, is something incredible. It must be a tough job.'

'I suppose it is sometimes. I'm a bit worried about the house, actually. It needs a lot of work. Chunks of plaster keep dropping off the ceiling.'

'I must come and see it,' Dita said. 'I have a lot of experience of these things. When I was with Goldie, I redid three large houses for him: on Kypsos, in Provence and in Connecticut. His mother had let them go – she had done nothing for thirty years. They were all completely un-touched. I had to do everything myself.'

'Well, I'd be eternally grateful for any suggestions. It's hard to know where to begin with a house like the Priory.'

'Let us begin this Saturday,' said Dita. 'First you will take me to lunch in London. Then we will drive together to Oxfordshire for dinner and on Sunday I will give you my best advice.'

32

nthony felt that Dita's visit to Winchford was, on balance, a great
success. Until he viewed the Priory through her fresh eyes, he
hadn't appreciated how much needed to be done, but her confidence and clarity made it all seem possible, and for the first time he felt
less daunted.

They had lunched together at San Lorenzo, where Dita greeted friends
at almost every table, and later were driven down to Winchford in a dark-
blue Mercedes by a chauffeur from Dita's regular car service. Anthony
had suggested the train (his car was parked in readiness at Kingham
station) but Dita said she disliked railways ('All that hanging about') and
her driver, Makepiece, had already planned the route to Winchford.

For her first two hours at the Priory, Dita rapturously exclaimed at the
beauty of the place. Everything delighted her. The Priory was one of the
loveliest houses she had ever seen; the Great Hall reminded her of the
medieval banqueting room at Hatfield House. She loved the Elizabethan
knot garden, the flagstones and the cedar tree, and Anthony couldn't
help thinking that, if Sandra had got her way, all three would have been
destroyed by now. It was a wonderful relief to be showing the house to
someone who appreciated it, and really understood about beautiful old
buildings. The two great Italianate chimneypieces made her think of the
Villa Rotunda. The view from her bedroom window across the estate
was 'very special', and she adored the feeling that everything in the house
had accumulated over time, 'as though it has just been left behind by
previous generations, with no careful thought. It is so English, I adore
it.'

She was more casually dressed than before, and Anthony thought
she looked younger than she had at Mark's Club and at the opera. In

her short suede skirt and nip-waisted tweed jacket, her honey-blonde highlights glinting in the sunshine, she looked closer to thirty than forty. Before dinner he took her on a tour of the estate by Land Rover, and was touched by her observant flattery. He showed her the new plantations, the dairy, quarry and avenue of horse chestnut whips he had recently planted near the Moreton Road, which would reach their full potential in forty or fifty years' time, 'long after I'm dead and gone.'

'Oh, no, don't say that,' Dita scolded him. 'You are young; you shouldn't talk about dying. You are only just starting.'

Henrietta insisted on joining them for dinner in the Great Hall, and Anthony invited Richard and Rosanna to come over to supper too, as well as Jasmine, who was busy learning the part of Cressida for a Fringe production of Troilus and Cressida at the Edinburgh Festival in August.

Dita had gone up to change for dinner, and from time to time messages were sent downstairs, requesting items she could not find in her room: a padded coathanger so she could hang up her jacket; later, an iron and ironing board, and a hairdryer. She eventually emerged with combed wet hair, having found no plug for the hairdryer within reach of the dressing table.

Anthony could barely believe how attractive or how smart she looked in a red knee-length evening dress, which she said came from the Valentino boutique. She stood at the doorway of the Great Hall waiting to be offered a drink, and staring with beady disapproval at the three teenagers, none of whom had bothered to change. Richard was watching a game show on TV, Jasmine lying full length on the sofa in an old sweater with holes in the elbows, reciting her lines to Rosanna.

Anthony now slightly wished he'd put on a smoking jacket for dinner, and hissed at his children: 'For heaven's sake, stand up when a lady comes into the room. And go and smarten yourself up – quickly – it'll be dinner in ten minutes.' To Dita he said, 'Sorry about the hairdryer. I'm afraid the house is an electrical nightmare; it needs major rewiring.'

'More sockets, I think,' Dita said. 'And shaving sockets in the bathrooms.'

'I'm making a list of things like that, for when we one day get round to doing it all. Mrs Holcombe keeps saying we need a microwave in the kitchen.'

Dita shuddered. 'Microwave indeed! Beastly things. Goldie had a chef once in Zurich who started to use one. We dismissed him immediately we found out.'

Dita having asked for a kir royale before dinner, Anthony disappeared to the kitchen to hunt about for cassis; he dimly remembered spotting a bottle in the old larder. But the cassis could not be found, if it had ever existed, so he made her a champagne cocktail, following the traditional Winchford Christmas Day method, with sugar lumps and angostura bitters. Seeing him pour the champagne on to Tate & Lyle sugar lumps, Dita asked to have hers without the sugar. 'So fattening, you know. And so bad for one.'

They heard the approaching whirr of a wheelchair, and there was Henrietta, who had roused herself from bed and drawn a navy-blue bedcoat over her nightdress for dinner.

'How do you do, Mrs Emboroleon,' she said, shaking her hand and glaring at her suspiciously. 'I understand you have been driven down from London by your chauffeur. I hope you weren't imagining we could put him up here for the night. We used to, of course, in the old days, but it is no longer practical.'

'It is not a problem,' Dita replied. 'The driver went back to London. He will return tomorrow afternoon to collect me.'

'Good gracious, what extravagance! All that petrol. I dread to think.'

'It is awful, I know,' Dita replied, in a tone which suggested she didn't find it remotely awful. 'But what I always feel about petrol is that once you've seen a private jet refuelled for even a short trip, it hardly seems worth worrying about cars.'

For dinner, Mrs Holcombe produced a mixed grill, one of her faithful stand-bys, incorporating lamb chops, Wall's sausages, grilled bacon, dried-out kidneys and grilled tomatoes, served with mashed potato and frozen peas. Henrietta, who must have eaten this same dish once a week for twenty years, cleared her plate in two minutes. Her gimlet eye settled on Dita's plate, which was barely touched.

'Is the food not to your liking? I see you have hardly eaten a thing.'

'It's fine. I am not so hungry,' Dita replied. 'We had lunch at San Lorenzo.'

'Did you indeed?' said Henrietta. 'I do so dislike restaurants. So much nicer, I always think, to eat at one's own table, with all one's own things around one. Where do you live yourself, Mrs Emboroleon?'

'Mostly in London at the moment. Cadogan Place. But until very recently, I travelled a great deal. My husband has several homes in Greece, and we spent different parts of the year in the States and in Switzerland.'

'How perfectly ghastly for you,' Henrietta sniffed. 'I should hate to be flitting about from place to place. One would never know where anything is.'

'It was not such a problem,' Dita replied. 'Aleco, my husband, bought everything in triplicate. One for each of our main houses. He hates to travel with anything besides hand baggage. A small bag and my jewellery case – that is all I took anywhere.'

After this combative start, in which Anthony felt that his mother and Dita instinctively loathed one another, he observed a surprising development. Slowly but surely, Dita began to charm Henrietta. She questioned her about the history of the Priory, and praised her for her understated decoration. She talked to her about horses, and some of their grander neighbours, and the big houses of the county that Henrietta had known in the previous generation, but which had now passed down to her friends' children. Dita listened to Henrietta's long stories, and always got the point, even when she rambled so far off it that the thread was lost. Anthony was filled with admiration for Dita, and so grateful to her for making an effort with his poor old mother. At the same time, he couldn't avoid seeing the Priory through her eyes, and felt slightly embarrassed by the succession of chipped plates and serving dishes that emerged from the kitchen, and the dirty cutlery and serving spoons. Her wine glass had a crack in the rim and had to be exchanged for a new one, the salt cellar was empty of salt and the silver pepper grinder broken. The napkins in their tarnished silver napkin rings clearly hadn't been washed for weeks.

Henrietta, for her part, began to feel less hostility towards Dita. Of course one could not feel completely sanguine about having a rich Greek stranger staying under one's roof, particularly one who had so recently separated from her husband. Henrietta felt uncomfortable about the idea of rich foreign people, unless they were either Italian or American, in which case one could respectively place them or accept them for what they were. With Greeks, as with Russians or Persians, one could never be quite sure. It upset Henrietta that such people might conceivably be richer than her, or might not recognise her, chatelaine of the Winchford estate, as their social superior. Nevertheless she saw in Dita Emboroleon a person who at least inhabited the same universe as herself. Soon she was reflecting that Dita was the first woman Anthony had ever brought home who might be said to fit in. Amanda, she remembered with a shudder, had been utterly unsuitable and hopeless. The second one – Sandra – was a nice enough girl, but had never been on the right wavelength to run Winchford. Then there had been that unspeakable mad woman who had borne Anthony's child. Now it was a Greek divorcee! Well, she was an improvement on the others – Henrietta would concede that. There was a preciseness about Mrs Emboroleon that she respected.

Jasmine and Rosanna were watching Dita across the table. Jasmine had put on a denim skirt for dinner, but was still wearing the jersey with the holes, and Anthony didn't feel she was making much effort to be friendly to their guest. In fact she was sulky and monosyllabic. Rosanna, meanwhile, was wearing jodhpurs, but with a striped shirt pulled over her T-shirt. Recently, Anthony felt Rosanna was too much of a tomboy: she had given up dressing like a little girl and strode around the place in riding kit and boots. She had announced she wanted to be a vet, and had started to put on weight.

From time to time Dita tried to draw the children into the conversation, but the two girls glared sullenly back at her. Daughters, Anthony thought. It was the first time in ages he'd brought a girlfriend home (was Dita a girlfriend? Not technically, but already it felt like a possibility), and maybe all daughters reacted like this to their father's women. 'I must introduce you to my son Morad,' Dita told them. 'He is so handsome, you will adore him. All the girls go crazy about him; he has to fight them off.'

Richard, at least, was his usual hearty self, telling Dita about the Under Fifteen rugby colts at Radley, in which he played prop forward. Last season they had won nine out of their eleven games, including a grudge match against Wellington – the first time in seven years.

Straight after dinner, Dita announced she was going to bed. 'Would you have a little bottle of water I can take up to my room?' she asked Anthony. 'I couldn't see any on the night table.'

'God, I'm so sorry,' Anthony apologised. 'I'm fairly sure we're out of mineral water. You're quite right; I should get some. Can I fetch you a jug of tap water to take up with you?'

'You are so sweet,' Dita replied. 'I found a carafe in my room, and I will fill it up myself.'

Immediately after breakfast, Dita embarked on her tour of the house. She carried a leatherbound Smythson's notebook and a gold propelling pencil. Anthony was impressed by her stamina. The tour lasted more than three hours, beginning with the water tanks in the attics where Dita fished a decomposing bat from the unlagged cistern. They clambered out onto the roof, inspected each turret and made a note that some slates needed replacing. They visited every bedroom and every bathroom, apart from Jasmine's room in which she was still asleep. In each bedroom, Dita insisted Anthony shift the dressing table and bedbacks away from the walls, so they could look at the state of the wallpaper behind, and the round three-point plugs dangling dangerously from their sockets.

Dita had a gift for entering a room and immediately suggesting half a dozen ways to improve it. Soon Anthony had rung Richard at the Old Rectory, who arrived with Tom, and together the three of them dragged sofas and chests from one end of rooms to another, as Dita rearranged the furniture. Walnut tables that had sat in the same corridor for a hundred years, unnoticed, were humped into the library to incredible effect. Lamps were moved into gloomy corners.

'The secret of decoration,' Dita declared, 'is that it need have nothing to do with expense. Everything is about correct placement. You have so many beautiful things in this house, it is a simple question of making the best of them.'

As she strode from room to room, Anthony was issued with a stream of ideas to follow up in future weeks and months. 'If you just placed a pair of lamps on that refrectory table,' she said, 'it would draw attention to that painting above. It is quite pretty, no? I love equine paintings.'

'If you rehung those small watercolours closer together, all massed on one wall,' she said, 'and moved the pretty little Constable from the white drawing room, this could be charming.'

'I'm not sure about moving the Constable,' Anthony replied doubtfully. 'My mother loves that picture, and the white drawing room is her bedroom these days.'

'Yes, so it is,' Dita replied. 'That is also unfortunate. It has the potential to be one of the best reception rooms in the house.'

By the time her car and driver returned to whisk her away, Anthony felt exhausted, but also exhilarated. Walking around his own house, reviewing the improvements, he could hardly believe they'd achieved so much in only one day. The whole place had come alive.

When he went to see how Jasmine was feeling, since she had earlier sent word she was too ill to come down to lunch, she groaned and told him to go away and leave her alone.

33

Three days after her successful visit to the Priory, Dita and Anthony spent the night together for the first time.

At Dita's invitation, Anthony had accompanied her to a drinks party at Boucheron in Bond Street, where several hundred socialites were drinking champagne between cabinets of jewellery; afterwards, they dropped in on a stiff and formal cocktail party at the Italian embassy in Grosvenor Square, which Dita described as a 'duty drink'; afterwards, they joined two other couples for dinner at a restaurant named Drones in Pont Street where they ate asparagus and grilled calves liver and, had Anthony not been rather tipsy by this point, he would have been even more shocked by the enormous bill; afterwards, Dita and Anthony headed back to the Cadogan Place flat for a nightcap, which they quickly decided to forgo in favour of bed.

Anthony had only hazy memories of that first passionate coupling in Dita's huge, canopied, lace-covered bed. He remembered helping her to remove half a dozen big white pillows and bolsters, some with the entwined initials D and A embroidered upon them. He remembered kicking off his brogues, and Dita folding his suit trousers across the seat of a rosebud-patterned chair. He remembered noticing what a marvellous figure she had, toned and lean, and a flash of trimmed pubic hair with blonde highlights. He remembered grunting his way through a variety of basic sexual positions, and Dita's greedy energy when she clambered on top. After that, he quickly dropped off to sleep.

After what seemed like only the shortest of nights he awoke to a knock on the door and breakfast being delivered by a uniformed Filipino maid. Overcome by embarrassment, he turned to Dita who was sitting bolt upright in bed, cocooned by pillows, looking immaculate and reading the *Daily Mail*. The maid, Lina, was now setting up a bedtray across his knee and smoothing the eiderdown. Then she placed the breakfast upon the bedtray laid with a white linen cloth, with a cafetiere of coffee, a pretty bone china coffee cup, a plate of scrambled eggs and smoked salmon, and a silver toast rack with brown granary toast. A moment or two later she returned with a second breakfast tray, this time for Dita, with half a grapefruit, a glass dish of plain yoghurt and honey, and a cup of herbal tea. Lina handed him a copy of the *Daily Telegraph* and the *Financial Times*, and placed his black brogues – the ones he had kicked off last night in his haste to undress – on the floor next to the dressing table. The shoes were freshly polished and the laces untied.

'Heavens,' Anthony said, when the Filipino had at last departed. 'That was embarrassing, her finding me here. How did she even know? This amazing breakfast and everything?'

'I told her, of course,' Dita said matter-of-factly. 'Lina arrives each morning at six o'clock. We always have a little discussion when she gets here, to plan the day. I hope you like your eggs scrambled.'

'You bet I do. But, seriously, Lina won't mention this to your husband? I don't want to cause problems.'

'Tell Aleco?' Dita laughed. 'Of course not. Lina is devoted to me. Last winter I paid for a new school in her village at home – only a simple place, of course, but she is so grateful. She will say nothing.'

'That's a relief.' Anthony laughed. He looked at Dita and could scarcely believe what had taken place last night. This morning she was impossibly serene. He was no expert, but it almost looked like she was wearing full make-up already. She was unbelievably attractive.

'Quickly, eat your breakfast,' Dita said. 'I have ordered a car for you for half past seven. The traffic can be slow to the City, so you need to get going. Your bathroom is the one beyond my dressing room. I think the shower is strong enough, though you can never depend on that in England. You will find razors and everything on the shelf.'

Anthony leant across the bed to kiss her good morning and slipped his hand inside her white lacy nightdress. Dita shook him off. 'Not on a weekday morning, Anthony, we are all too busy,' she said sharply. 'There will be plenty of time for that tonight, after the Palumbo's drinks for the Serpentine Gallery. I have refused the dinner afterwards. Truly, we cannot be out every single night; it is a kind of tyranny. I hope you are not disappointed.'

Anthony embarked on a new routine of spending Wednesday and Thursday nights up in London with Dita at Cadogan Place; Dita, in turn, began coming down to Winchford Priory every second weekend. Initially occupying a spare bedroom close to Anthony's own, they soon abandoned any pretence and she moved openly in with him, keeping her country clothes in his cupboards and civilising his cold, decrepit bathroom with bottles of bath essence and expensive pots of face cream. Arriving on Saturdays in time for lunch, she was never empty-handed: her driver struggled from the car with armfuls of fresh flowers and cachepots filled with jasmine and orchids. Often she brought whole sides of smoked salmon, Parma ham and melons and baskets full of pungent goats' cheeses from Partridges in Sloane Street, close to her flat. These were delivered to Mrs Holcombe in the kitchen, who was quick to take offence, and Anthony had to reassure her it was absolutely no reflection on her cooking, and that Mrs Emboroleon was simply being a thoughtful guest. It was noticeable that Dita barely touched Mrs Holcombe's well-cooked pies and roasts, preferring to carve a sliver of salmon from the sideboard.

Anthony's London evenings soon coloured his life. Until Dita took him under her wing he had had no idea what he'd been missing by catching the train home to Kingham each night. With Dita, he went to more cocktail parties in their first twelve weeks together than he'd been to in the previous twelve years. They went to gallery openings in Cork and Albermarle Street, shop openings the length of Bond Street, parties in big white stucco-faced houses in Chester Square, dinners in restaurants, dinners in private members' clubs, dinners in aid of charities held in hotel ballrooms and in the soaring foyers of museums. It seemed to Anthony that every minute of every evening he was being handed a glass of champagne. His dinner jacket, which he'd had made in his early twenties by a tailor in Cheltenham, and which he had worn barely four times a year ever since, now became a mainstay of his wardrobe; on its fourth or fifth outing, Dita pronounced it old and shabby and sent him to a shockingly expensive tailor in Mount Street for a new one.

Anthony was awed by the number and range of people Dita knew. Never naturally gregarious, he found that, in Dita's wake, it was much easier to get on with his new acquaintances than he would have imagined. At dinner at Cecconi's – a restaurant where a single lamb cutlet cost more than the market price for a full-grown ewe – Anthony met the governor of the Bank of England for the first time; at a fundraiser gala in the Elgin Court of the British Museum, he was placed between the wife of the senior partner of Hoare's Bank and the wife of the new chief executive of Coutts; at dinner with the Rocco Fortes in Cheyne Gardens, he discussed the economic outlook with not one but two Thatcherite monetarist advisors, as well as the chairman of Cable & Wireless. To Anthony's amazement, all these distinguished figures took him seriously and seemed eager to hear his opinions. 'I hope we can get you more involved with the Party,' said a Tory cabinet minister. 'I'm going to have them ask you to one of our City lunches with the treasurer's department.' Sometimes, from the corner of his eye, he glimpsed Dita explaining him to her friends: he saw the words 'Anscombe Brothers, his family merchant bank' form upon her lips. He was amazed that, out of all the men she knew, Dita should have chosen him as her lover.

'You are too gaunt,' she told him in bed. 'Carina agrees with me; you need to gain a little muscle tone. Not too much – it suits you being tall and slim, and you are really quite handsome.'

'Hardly. I'm beginning to go grey, look.'

'I like that. It's distinguished. No, you look quite good, seriously. But you must work out more. I know a good gym you must join.'

Not since that first turbulent year of marriage to Amanda had Anthony been to so many parties, and yet this time it was different. At Amanda's parties in Camden Town he had felt like an outsider, admitted on sufferance as an appendage of his ravishing wife. With Dita, he felt himself to be amusing and substantial. At a party at Verdura, the jeweller, Dita's friend Carina told him, 'I can't tell you how much we all love having you around. A new heterosexual man on the scene! It's unheard of.'

As time passed, Anthony felt under pressure to spend more than two nights in London. Dita lured him with invitations to dinners she really wanted him to accompany her to, and Anthony had to be strong-minded to refuse. When he declined to stay up in London on a Tuesday night for dinner at Kensington Palace, it led to their first big row. But Anthony was immovable. 'I'm sorry, darling, you can't change my mind on this one. I have to get home and see Jasmine. It's not fair to leave her alone with Mrs Holcombe all week.'

'Really, Anthony, you can be very peculiar sometimes,' Dita said. 'She is not eleven years old any more, she is eighteen. Of course she can be left. I find this incessant pandering to your children unnatural.'

'Well, that's my decision,' Anthony said. 'Even if it was the Queen of England asking us to dinner, I wouldn't change it.'

'Actually, it is her sister,' Dita replied. 'There will be a fun crowd there; it is always amusing at K.P. Ned Ryan is going.'

And so, leaving work punctually to catch the train from Paddington, Anthony abandoned his demanding girlfriend and spent the evening in front of the television with his eldest daughter. Whenever he addressed a word to her, she barely replied. When he asked whether she'd like him to test her on her script, she shrugged. When Mrs Holcombe produced a lasagne and broccoli, Jasmine said she wasn't feeling hungry.

'Oh, for goodness' sake, darling,' Anthony said at last. 'What is this all about? Come on, out with it. Is it about Dita?'

Jasmine made a face.

'Look, darling, I know you don't really like Dita. I can tell that. But you've got to be a little bit understanding and see it from my point of view. You know, fathers are allowed to have girlfriends too. It isn't fair otherwise. I have to have a grown-up life sometimes.'

Jasmine screwed up her nose. 'It's not that I exactly *hate* Dita. It's just that it spoils everything having her here all the time. She's so bossy and always telling everybody what to do, when it's got nothing to do with her.'

'She's only trying to be helpful. It's very kind of her, the way she's helping us sort out the house. You have to admit it's much more comfy now she's changed things about.'

'But why does she have to keep interfering with *us*? It's nothing to do with her what I wear to have supper in, or what time I get up. And how dare she tell me to tidy my room? It's not even her house.'

Anthony sighed. 'I know, darling. I'm sure it feels strange having a grown-up woman here again, when we've been on our own for such a long time. And, you're right, Dita shouldn't be telling you what to do, and I'll talk to her and ask her not to. But you've got to remember she's only trying to make everything nicer for all of us. I know she has high standards and expects us all to be neat and tidy.' He laughed. 'Even with me, she's always telling me to brush my hair and put on a clean jersey. But she's a very kind person really, and she's always saying how much she likes all you children.'

'She's just so . . . in your face. That's what I can't stand about her, Dad.'

'Well, try and be civil to her for my sake, if nothing else. Promise me you'll try, darling? It would make me so happy.'

Jasmine nodded doubtfully and kissed him on the cheek. As far as she was concerned, the day Dita disappeared off the scene wouldn't be a day too soon. If she was honest, she admitted there wasn't anything exactly evil about Dita, but she frightened her. When she was around, the entire pace of the day speeded up; it was like having the clocks brought forward by an hour. Dita was an irresistible force, whose energy and strong will made Jasmine feel like a sapling buffeted by the wind. How could her father stand to be with someone so exhausting? Surely he would be happier with someone more laid back and bohemian: someone like her own mother, in fact.

One of the many things Anthony liked about Dita was her fondness for long walks. Every Saturday and Sunday afternoon, straight after lunch, she put on her walking clothes and they strode out together across the estate for a couple of hours. Dita was the first woman he had known who could walk at his own fast pace. The first time she appeared in the Great Hall in her country kit of immaculate walking shoes, cashmere scarf and dark orange quilted jacket, Jasmine and Richard sniggered, but were later impressed when they heard exactly how far she'd got, and how quickly. For Anthony, who was never happier than tramping the perimeter footpaths of his farm, walking with Dita was revitalising. During his Amanda days, walks had largely been solitary, since she seldom set foot out of doors. With Sandra, they had been a frustrating stop-start experience, as she moved at the pace of their slowest, smallest child, and kept pausing to point out cows or pick blackberries. He had never gone walking with Nula, but periodically spotted her in the copse behind Forge Cottage, hugging the trunks of beech trees or breathing in very, very slowly and saying she was connecting. How satisfying, then, to stride out with a girlfriend who loved to walk. Sometimes Dita carried two miniature silver dumbbells with her, to improve the muscle tone in her upper arms.

On one of their earliest outings, when they were cutting back into the village via the little picket gate behind the church, they ran into Sandra and John, out walking a retriever. Momentarily uncomfortable at this first encounter between his new love-interest, ex-wife and estate manager, Anthony stumbled through the introductions.

Dita, however, was marvellously assured. 'I'm so delighted to meet you,' she told Sandra, who was herself slightly flustered in the face of this awkward convergence. 'Having met both your lovely children, and your equally charming stepson Thomas, who was heroic in helping us move furniture about. Those young men are so handsome and soignée, I adore them.'

'I'm pleased to hear it,' Sandra replied, almost cowed by Dita's overpowering civility. 'So long as my children are polite and helpful, I'm happy. And both of their colleges put a lot of store by manners.'

'No, they are charming,' Dita insisted. 'Richard was telling me about his rugby games. The stamina of these boys, incredible!' Then she said, 'I hope you will both come and visit us soon at the Priory, before the builders begin work. It is a beautiful house, but needs attention now.'

Sandra was about to say she'd had plenty of schemes of her own, which she'd never been allowed to take further, but thought better of it. Instead, she said, 'Yes, Anthony has always loved that house. Well, the whole place, actually.'

'Aah, dear Anthony,' Dita exclaimed, squeezing his hand. 'I should thank you too, Sandra, for the fantastic job you did on him when you were married. You trained him up to be the *perfect* man; I'm for ever grateful to you. You did all the hard work and I am the beneficiary.' After they had gone, Sandra and John were left in the lane, almost speechless at their first experience of Dita. For the first time in ages, Sandra truly had nothing to say.

One of Dita's escalating complaints about the Priory was that it was so dirty. She would run her finger along a mantelpiece, or across the tops of pictures, and hold up a dusty digit as incriminating proof. Or she would beat a cushion and purse her lips as clouds of dust rose into the room like smoke from a bonfire. 'Do you know,' she announced, 'I hardly dare sit down anywhere in this entire house. I cannot even wear a light-coloured frock, because it will mark from the sofas. I'm not convinced anyone is doing any cleaning from one month to the next.'

'Poor Mrs Holcombe tries her best,' Anthony replied. 'It isn't easy with my mother in her way all the time. In any case, she's getting on a bit and has only nine hours a week.'

'Most of which she spends drinking coffee in the kitchen. Just look at the state of these curtains.' Dita slapped them violently and stepped back coughing. 'It's totally unacceptable; agree with me. Doesn't she consider dusting part of her job? What does she actually think she *achieves* in return for her four pounds an hour?'

'This is a big house for one elderly lady to keep clean. I don't even think she particularly does it for the money; she's being kind to us and loyal to my mother.'

'If it's too much for her, why don't you get some extra help? You probably need two cleaners at least, both full time. There must be plenty of people in the village who'd leap at the chance.'

'If only that were true. We put a postcard in the shop advertising for help when Mrs Holcombe hurt her back, but got no replies at all. None of the young women want to do domestic work. They prefer working in Tesco.'

'Well, it's perfectly ridiculous,' Dita snapped. 'I don't know what the problem is with the English. Actually I do know: they're paid too much and lack respect. You should simply *order* some of them to come and help, the villagers I mean, if they want to live in your cottages. I don't mean they should work for no money, of course not, but they should have more of a sense of duty. They can't expect the owner of Winchford to manage without proper help.'

'I'm sure you're right,' Anthony replied patiently. 'But sadly things don't work like that any more. Not in Oxfordshire anyway.'

'I can assure you they do on Kypsos,' Dita replied. 'All the girls on the island were available to help, and were proud to, too. Aleco knows all their parents, and they sent their daughters to us when they turned sixteen. The laundry was always immaculate, better even than in New York.'

The very next time she came to stay, Dita arrived in convoy with a second Mercedes containing her Filipina maid, Lina, and Lina's two friends, Concepcion and Pura. They emerged from the back-up car with a vast arsenal of cleaning equipment: brand new bright-green plastic buckets, J cloths, mops, sponges, squeezy mops, chamois leathers, an industrial carpet cleaner and two turbo-suction vacuum cleaners. For the next seven hours, under Dita's supervision, they scrubbed and sucked at every corner of the Priory. The ancient fridge was defrosted and sponged down for the first time in years; rugs and runners were carried outside into the garden, hoisted onto the washing line and vigorously beaten; loose covers were stripped from sofas and valances from beds, and folded up for delivery to a dry cleaner in Belgravia.

Soon the whole Priory smelt of beeswax, as the three cheerful, Tegula-speaking maids polished every piece of furniture in the house. 'I don't believe this desk has been touched in years,' Dita complained. 'Not with beeswax, anyway.'

'I have seen Mrs Holcombe having a go at it,' Anthony said in defence of his old retainer. 'She uses a spray, I think, Mr Sheen or something.'

'She should be shot,' said Dita. 'Mr Sheen indeed! It's worse than Pledge! Silicon spray is a disaster for proper furniture.' Then she said, 'The next thing I'm going to do is open that chaotic cupboard where she keeps her cleaning things, and chuck the whole lot into the dustbin. No, no protests, that's what I'm going to do. All of it: *out*. All those beastly aerosols and nasty blue detergents she puts down the lavatory. Gone! I shall leave her the beeswax and the rest of the stuff I brought down, and you must tell her to use it properly from now on. Which reminds me, you need a good window cleaner. The panes in the kitchen are so grimy you can scarcely see through them.'

'As a matter of fact we've been looking for a window cleaner for months. They're hard to get hold of round here. Walter Twine used to do all the windows, but he's afraid to go up a ladder now.'

'Really, leave it to me then. I'll find you a window cleaner. There are plenty of big houses around here, and the others seem to manage; it can't be so difficult. I thought there were meant to be two million un-employed. There must be someone who isn't work-shy with a sponge and a stepladder.'

As was often his reaction during Dita's whirlwind descents upon the Priory, Anthony felt anxiety, even anguish, while they were actually happening, as she stormed the tranquillity of his home, issuing orders, changing everything, challenging decades of inertia. But afterwards he felt intensely grateful. In dozens of different ways, large and small, crea-ture comforts improved out of recognition. For the past eight months, since Dita's arrival on the scene, he had had the sheets on his bed changed twice a week; previously, Mrs Holcombe had changed them only every second or third week, and they had usually been replaced straight from the dryer, crumpled and unironed. Dita had insisted ('Believe me, An-thony, this is quite inappropriate. You are the owner of an important bank') and, with a shrug of bemused compliance, Mrs Holcombe con-sented to the new routine. Anthony was amazed how much he enjoyed the experience of sleeping between crisp, clean sheets.

After listening to him enthuse about how civilised it had become at home, Lex said, 'The thing about you, Ant, is you just love being looked after. You loved it when Sandra was feeding you all that nursery grub. Now it's the same with Dita the Greek.'

'That's not true, in actual fact. I'm not interested in Dita for her food.'

Lex laughed. 'I'm sure she's great at other things too. She must be, or she'd never have held on to her husband for so long. You know his reputation. They don't call him Goldmember for nothing.'

'Ha, ha,' Anthony replied flatly. 'I don't know why you always think of women in terms of sex and food. No wonder you've never married. The thing about Dita is she's a lot of fun to have around. She's intelligent and organised, which is great for the Priory.'

It was the following weekend, while having the best hot bath of his entire life, that Anthony realised with a flash of inspiration what had to happen next.

Thanks to Dita, the Edwardian boiler had been stripped down and overhauled, and now worked perfectly. For the first time ever, Anthony was soaking in a bathtub of boiling water, right up to his neck, and it felt glorious. In fact, looking around the bathroom, he could hardly believe it was the same dank, chilly room he'd been washing in for years. Next to the tub was a new little round table covered by a white cloth, on which stood a vase of flowers, a pretty china soap dish and two new biographies of a politician and a financier, both presents from Dita. The chrome taps and bath plug had both been descaled and gleamed brightly from regular polishing. Across the bath rested a new chrome bathrack, with a clean flannel and a cake of Roger and Gallet Vetiver soap. Over the heated towel rail were draped two enormous thick white towels. The windows were cleaned and the curtains freshly washed. All this, he knew, was the work of Dita, who had initiated and supervised every step.

At that moment Dita entered the bathroom, changed for dinner and immaculately made up. She handed him a whisky and soda for the bath.

His heart swelled. 'Dita, this may well be the last question in the world you want me to ask you,' he said. 'And, if it is, just forget I said anything. But would you ever consider marrying me?'

34

It was the Tuesday morning following his weekend proposal to Dita, and Anthony was at his desk at Anscombes. Shortly before lunch, his PA, Charlotte, said that an Amanda Bouillon was on the line and insisting on speaking to him. 'She sounds a little upset, but says you know who she is.'

'Yes, that's fine, put her through please.' Briefly, absurdly, Anthony felt a twinge of guilt, as though by proposing to Dita he had somehow betrayed his first wife.

'Hi, Ant.' She sounded spacey and slightly depressed.

'Amanda? It's great to hear your voice. It's been ages.' He realised he was gabbling; extraordinary she still had this effect on him.

'I need to talk to you. I really need your help. I have to see you.'

'Sure. Of course. Where are you anyway? Paris?'

'London.'

'London? That's fantastic. When did you arrive?'

'I've been here since the summer. Since August. Eight or nine weeks.'

Why did this information deflate him? Amanda had been here all that time and not rung him. 'What's brought you over?'

There was a long silence, as though the connection on the line was fading.

'Amanda? You still there?'

'I really do need to see you. Can you come over?'

'You mean *now*? Not possible, I'm afraid. I'm meant to be having a business lunch with a client.' But the next moment he changed his mind. 'Actually, I suppose I could come now. Where are you?'

She gave an address in a mews behind Beaufort Street in Chelsea, off Elm Park Gardens.

'I'll be there in forty-five minutes, traffic permitting.'

The taxi dropped him at a cobbled mews of cottages painted different colours. The number Amanda had given him had a black front door; a single storey flat above a double garage. He pressed the bell and waited almost a minute before hearing footsteps descending the stairs. The door opened and there was Amanda: thinner and barefoot, in jeans and a black T-shirt. Her hair, which had grown longer, was worn up on her head. He had a fleeting impression she looked older, but this evaporated when she smiled. 'Thank you for answering my distress call,' she said. 'I knew you'd come.'

'I was so pleased to hear from you.'

'I didn't have anyone else to call. Not in London. Only you.'

They went upstairs into a small sitting room painted magnolia with a leather sofa in front of a fireplace and matching armchairs. The carpet smelt new. Leaning against one wall was a framed film poster for *La Lune et Le Soleil Noir*.

'Whose flat is this?' Anthony asked, looking around.

'Rented. I wouldn't have chosen it, but it was the best I could find for the money.'

'Is Patrice with you?'

'It's over with Patrice. That's why I'm here. We're not together any more.'

'Oh, Amanda. I'm sorry.' She looked so vulnerable, he hugged her, and was shocked to feel her spine and ribs beneath the T-shirt. 'When did all this happen?'

'Over the summer. It's been bad for a long time, but then it got worse. He stopped bothering to pretend.'

'What do you mean?'

'The girls. He always had them; I wasn't under any illusions. But at least he had the good manners to lie to me. He'd swear on his mother's grave he wasn't seeing anyone, and it suited us both if I believed him. Then he stopped bothering, and started taking them to dinner in the same places we went to together. I think it was his way of telling me it was finally over.'

'I'm so terribly sorry. You've been together for ages – it seemed to work so well.'

'It never worked, not really. Patrice doesn't have the right temperament for marriage; we shouldn't have tried.' Anthony felt the bitterness in her voice. 'Too much of a tomcat.'

They sat on the leather sofa and Anthony did his best to console her. 'Can I get you a drink?'

'I'd love one. More than I can say. There's nothing in the flat. I've drunk the place dry, drowning my sorrows. There's an Oddbins on the Fulham Road if you can face it.'

Anthony returned with a couple of bottles of wine and they drank them together in the underfurnished flat. He had never known Amanda like this: fragile and fatalistic. She told him she knew she'd lost her looks. Her music career was over – her record company had decided not to release the new album. She doubted she would ever get another part in a movie, her agent had withdrawn representation. Slowly it all came out: how Patrice had brought women back to the Paris apartment while she was away in Capri. She had found a packet of sanitary towels, not her own brand, in the bathroom cabinet, and Patrice had confessed with a shrug. 'He didn't even pretend it mattered.' Amanda was crying into Anthony's shoulder, snuggling up against him as warm tears dampened his shirt. His arms were wrapped around her, comforting her. He could smell her hair, her skin felt soft against his.

'What about your daughter?' he asked. 'Where's she?'

'Paris. Patrice wouldn't let me take her. She's with the Algerian maid.' She sighed. 'I'm missing her so much, but it is better for her there. What is there for her here? Living with a has-been in a dump like this?'

'She must be seven or eight now.'

'Eight. She goes to big school every day now.' Then she began crying again, this time more violently. 'I am such a bad mother. I keep leaving my children. First Jasmine, now Amelie. I'm so selfish, I know that's what you think. I should never have left Jasmine; she was only a tiny baby. How could I have done that?'

'Amanda, don't torture yourself; it doesn't help. And actually I don't think you're selfish or a bad mother. And you look great too: you're beautiful.'

He was holding on to her so tightly, as though the firmness of his grip might reassure her. She was staring back with her big kohl-lined eyes, and suddenly they were kissing. Her lips pressed against his own and he felt the salt from her tears on his tongue.

'I knew you'd help me,' Amanda murmured as their kisses became more passionate. 'I knew you'd come. You remembered our bond.'

35

'I have to go now, Amanda. Seriously, I've got to go to work.'

It was Wednesday morning. He hadn't returned to the office on Tuesday afternoon, but spent it in bed with Amanda. It was the first time they'd slept together since the Randolph Hotel, and he could hardly believe how wonderful it had been, or how natural it all seemed. It felt like they were still married, or more precisely how it had been when they first married, except that Amanda was softer and more vulnerable. He felt himself to be stronger than her for the first time. He saw now that, throughout their marriage, he had acted like the weaker partner, mesmerised by his quixotic wife, too anxious to please and appease and grateful for each small gesture of love and attention. Now he sensed the balance had shifted, that it was he who was the confident one, and she needy of his approval.

She was too thin, like a patient in convalescence from a long illness. But to Anthony, who saw Amanda through old eyes and the intense mist of their history, she was as beautiful as ever, perhaps more so, because she existed for him as a composite of all her earlier selves. She was the girl he had glimpsed from the gallery in the Great Hall; the girl on the roof and the storm-tossed raft; the mother of Jasmine and ethereal starlet of *La Lune et Le Soleil Noir.*

'Stay with me.' She was sitting up in bed, naked, sheets pulled up round her face.

'Darling, I really do have to go. I'm already late. I have meetings.'

'Stay.'

'Honestly, I'd love to – believe me I'd love to. But I've got to go.'

'You'll come back tonight? You will come back?' She was begging him.

Anthony swallowed. He was meant to be going to a dinner with Dita, something to do with the Royal Academy.

'I'll try my hardest.'

'Not try. Come. Promise.'

'All right, I promise.'

'What time will you get here?'

'Six o'clock? Six or six thirty.' He might have time to fit in a quick drink and still make it to Cadogan Place with time to change. The dinner was black tie.

Amanda in bed reminded him of something, but he couldn't think what. Then he remembered: the photograph in the old *Sunday Times* magazine of her in Egypt with Patrice, under the mosquito netting. What would he not have given then to be there with her? Yet here he was deserting her to go to the bank and out to dinner with Dita Emboroleon.

'Take this,' Amanda said. She handed him a key. 'Then I won't need to come down to let you in.'

'See you later, darling,' Anthony said, kissing her.

'Remember your promise,' she replied.

Anthony spent much of the day advising a publicly quoted department store conglomerate on the acquisition of a frozen foods cash-and-carry business. The burly American chief executive of the stores group, which already owned 1,700 high street fashion outlets, was anxious to take over the ninety edge-of-town hypermarkets. The rationale, which Anthony knew would play well with institutional investors, was that the Freeza-Kwik sheds could retail fashion lines alongside their frozen crinkle chips and pizzas, driving margin through synergy.

For six hours Anthony and his team of analysts sat in the newly renovated boardroom of Anscombes, in which the portraits of dead partners had been replaced by projectors and whiteboards, crunching strategy with the client and his legal team. Not once did Anthony miss a beat or fumble a number, and yet there was never a moment when he was not thinking about Amanda.

Waves of confusion washed over him. Even thinking about her made him breathless. He wanted to stand up and leave the meeting and run to her. Having found her again, he must never let her go. It was miraculous, like the fairytale conclusion to a romantic movie.

But there was also Dita to be considered. There was no question about it: he did love Dita, and was a little scared of her too. Perhaps not scared exactly, but respectful of her energy and character. Why hadn't he told Amanda about Dita? He should have announced his news straight away: 'Something exciting has happened: I'm getting married again.' But the opportunity had passed; he had been too quickly reabsorbed into Amanda's parallel world.

Most pressingly, what should he do about tonight? It was logistically feasible to get to Elm Park Mews, have a twenty-minute drink and then double back to Dita's flat. But he was realistic enough to guess what might happen if he saw Amanda – in fact he longed for it – and Dita's fury if he was late didn't bear thinking about.

The conference resumed over sandwiches at lunchtime, followed by a telephone and loo break. Anthony raced to the sanctuary of his office and dialled Amanda's number. Suddenly it was very clear what he must do.

'Amanda?'

'Ant.'

He took a deep breath. 'Listen, I've only got a few minutes before my meeting starts again, so I have to be quick. There's something I should have told you yesterday, and I'm feeling guilty. The thing is, I'm actually engaged to someone. I'm getting married again. So, everything that happened . . . I behaved very stupidly, and I'm terribly sorry. There: I've said it now. I felt I had to tell you, or it wouldn't be fair.'

As he spoke, he was reminded of ringing his mother from the restaurant in Nice to inform her about his marriage to Amanda.

The silence down the line was excruciating. He could hear her breathing but she did not speak.

'Amanda? You still there?'

Eventually, a heartbreaking whisper. 'You're getting *married*? But you were married to *me*.'

'Amanda, that was a long, long time ago. God, I've been an idiot. Look, I really am sorry about everything; it was completely my fault. I've been thinking about it non-stop, and it wouldn't be right if I didn't tell you. Not fair on Dita either.'

'Dita?'

'Dita Emboroleon. My fiancée. She used to be married to a Greek guy.'

'I know who she is; I've met her.' Amanda spoke in a shocked, flat voice, almost without emotion. 'Her husband's an arsehole. He kept sending me roses. You want to be with *her* more than me?'

'Darling, I'm engaged to her. I've given her a promise.'

'You gave *me* a promise. Our special bond.'

'Oh God, this is so difficult. We only got engaged a few days ago. She's been telling everyone and, anyway, it's the right thing to do. For me and for Dita. For you as well, I'm sure. We can't turn the clock back – it would never work.'

But he was thinking: maybe it *would* work. In being loyal to Dita, was he destroying Amanda's only chance of happiness? And his own?

'You *are* still coming round?' Amanda asked.

'I don't think I should. It would be better not.'

'I've been out and bought wine.'

'I can't. I mustn't. There won't be enough time, in any case.'

'Time,' she said fatalistically. 'It's always about time, isn't it? If I'd called you before you got engaged, just a few days earlier . . .'

'It wouldn't have made any difference. Honestly, I love Dita. We'd still be getting married.'

He felt the need to be absolutely firm on that point. But he had an uncomfortable feeling she could be right: had Amanda reappeared one week earlier, would he have become engaged to Dita?

'I've got to go,' he said. 'My meeting's about to start. But – Amanda – I promise I'll ring you. Tomorrow. Tomorrow or later in the week. And if there's anything I can do to help, anything at all . . .'

He heard the click as she replaced the receiver.

It was after six o'clock the meeting ended and Anthony went back up to his office.

His PA said, 'Amanda Bouillon wants you to ring her urgently. She's called quite a few times.' From the look on her face, Anthony got the picture.

'Amanda? It's Anthony.'

'You have to come *right now*.' She sounded groggy. 'I've taken some pills. I'm going to kill myself.'

'For God's sake, Amanda. Don't do anything. I'll be right over.'

'There's nothing left to live for. I may as well be dead.'

'*No.*'

'Goodbye, Ant. You were the only person who cared about me. The only one.' He heard the receiver drop to the floor. When he redialled the number, it was off the hook.

He found a cab in Lombard Street and told the driver to step on it to Elm Park Mews. The traffic was gridlocked and it took almost an hour to get there. Desperately, he fumbled with the lock. He wished he'd rung an ambulance before leaving the bank.

'Amanda? Amanda? Where are you?' His feet stumbled on the treads as he raced upstairs. 'Amanda?'

'Hello.' A faint voice from the bathroom. He threw open the door and there she was, naked in bathwater dark red with blood. Both wrists were slashed at the veins, and blood was seeping into the warm water. A razor blade lay on the tiled ledge by the bath, and an open bottle of pills.

'Christ, no!' He leant over the bath, plunging his arms into the milky red water and began hauling her out. Her head flopped as he lifted her, and he took the weight of her body against his own, dragging her upright. His suit was soaked, and blood dripped onto his shirt and over the bathroom floor. He thought, 'Thank God, she's still alive.'

Somehow, he heaved her over the side of the tub and onto the floor, now swampy with blood and water. 'I've got to get your arms above your head,' he said, yanking them up. Her face, drained of blood, was white and surprisingly ugly, a death mask.

He found hand towels hanging from a chrome ring next to the lavatory, and bound them round her wrists as tourniquets. The cheap pink towels quickly became sodden with blood. 'Sorry, darling, I have to leave you here for a second. I'm calling an ambulance.'

Even before it had arrived, he made a second call, this time to Dita.

'I'm at my ex-wife's flat and she's tried to commit suicide,' he blurted. 'Yes, of course I mean Amanda – not Sandra. I'm waiting for an ambulance to get here.'

Dita said something and Anthony winced.

'Ok, darling, you go on ahead. I'll try and join you later at the Royal Academy. Yes, I know who's on our table. I know it's important. I really will make it if I possibly can, I promise. I can't just leave now, the ambulance is on its way . . . Yes, yes, I know I didn't say I was seeing Amanda this evening, she only just rang up . . . I was meeting her for a drink . . . Yes, I do know how tricky she is, I do realise that . . . She just tried to *kill herself* . . . No, I don't know why she did that, no idea at all . . .'

36

It was going to be tremendously important, Dita and Anthony agreed, that all their children should get on well together, so a weekend was scheduled at Winchford Priory for Morad, John-Spiros and Ambrosia to bond with Anthony's own extended brood. A date was chosen in June when the three oldest Anscombe children would all be around and the weather was likely to be good, which would make it all much easier, with the swimming pool in action and tennis for anyone who wanted to play. 'I really do need you to be friendly to Dita's children,' Anthony told his lot. 'I want them to feel part of the family.'

Jasmine made a face and sighed. 'Yes, Dad. We'll be nice to them.'

'Imagine how *you'd* feel,' he went on. 'It'll be quite an ordeal for them, meeting you all. Dita says Ambrosia's painfully shy. So please do be kind to her.'

'Dad, we already *said* we will be.'

Four weeks after his engagement, Anthony realised his children still hated the whole idea, Jasmine and Rosanna especially. But he was hopeful that, if the weekend went well and everyone got on, it would become a lot easier. His strategy was to make the weekend as action-packed as possible; Tom and Katie would come over for swimming and supper. With eight children around, it would surely go OK.

Anthony was hopeful, too, that Morad would be an asset. Dita was clearly besotted by her elder son, home for half term from his Swiss boarding school, and talked constantly about his charm, sophistication and good looks. Anthony thought Morad might hit it off with Jasmine, being close in age, which could soften her hostility to Dita.

Anthony had recently learnt, slightly to his surprise since his fiancée had never mentioned it, that Morad wasn't her son by Goldie Emboroleon, but by an earlier marriage to an Iranian businessman, Sharif Ahvazi. He hadn't realised Dita had been married twice before, and the knowledge was disconcerting. But when he raised it with her, she laughed it away. 'Oh, darling, it was so long ago I can hardly remember it myself. I was seventeen, for God's sake. Sharif was so attractive, but much older than me. He died of heart failure when Morad was almost still a baby. So sad, but quite soon afterwards I met Aleco.'

'How awful about Sharif. The heart attack, I mean. I'd love to hear about him.'

Dita gave a dismissive little wave of her hand. 'What is there to say? He was a lovely old gentleman who lived in Monaco, that is all.'

'What did he do? For a living, I mean.'

'Questions, questions. He was involved in many businesses, import-export, casinos, clubs,' she replied vaguely. 'Why do you want to know?'

'Well, only because he was your husband. If he was an important part of your life, I'd like to know about him, that's all.'

'Sharif was OK. A bit of a bullshitter. Everyone imagined he was rolling rich, but when he died there wasn't much there at all. Only debts.'

'It must have been difficult for you.'

'We managed. Money has never been so important to me, not like for some people. It is only Morad I am sorry for.'

'Why Morad?'

'John-Spiros and Ambrosia will both have so much one day, but Morad has nothing. Sometimes he feels it, poor boy; it wasn't easy for him having Aleco as a stepfather. So much wealth around, and nothing for himself.'

'I do see.'

'Maybe one day you can help him, Anthony. Not now, of course not, but when you come to love him as a son. He is a fine boy really, even though he can be trying at times.'

In good time for Saturday lunch, the black Mercedes containing Dita and her three children drew up outside the Priory. Anthony had insisted his three be ready and waiting in the Great Hall, which wasn't easy since Jasmine never got up before lunch, and even Richard had taken to lying in on weekends home from school. Anthony had to ring Sandra at the Old Rectory to wake him.

'Here they are now,' Anthony said, as Dita's chauffeur leapt out to open the car door. 'Now, remember everyone what we agreed. Richard, you can help me do the drinks and, Rosanna, you hand round the nuts and crisps, please.'

Through the mullioned windows they saw Dita striding towards the front door, dressed in one of the new country tweed suits she had recently had made in Paris. Trailing behind was a neat young boy in a double-breasted blazer with gold buttons, tassled loafers and large, dark, sensitive eyes.

'God, he looks a bit of a weed,' Richard said.

'Shush, Richard. Stop that,' said Anthony, sharply.

Behind John-Spiros came a pudding-faced girl with long, brown hair tied in a ponytail. This, presumably, was Ambrosia.

Bringing up the rear was Morad: squat and dark-skinned with tight curly black hair, a brown leather jacket and a bolshie expression. He stared up at the Priory with a disdainful curl of the lip, as if he'd been expecting something bigger and better.

'Come in, come in,' Anthony was saying, kissing Dita and shaking her children warmly by the hand. 'I've heard so much about you all; it's marvellous to actually meet you at last. Now, you must be John-Spiros.' Painfully polite, John-Spiros gave a little nod of his neatly combed head, and glanced towards his mother for reassurance. Ambrosia could not make eye contact at all, and lurked behind Dita, a big unhappy lump.

Morad struck Anthony as one of the most unsettling sixteen-year-olds he'd ever set eyes on. There was an air of repressed sexuality about him as he gazed superciliously around the room. When he saw Jasmine, he gave her an appraising stare. Jasmine scowled back.

Soon Anthony and Richard were busying themselves doling out Cokes and glasses of cider for the older teenagers, and Dubonnet for Dita, while the children stood around in awkward silence.

Morad was still staring at Jasmine in a knowing way, and Anthony thought he seemed a lot older than his daughter, even though Jasmine was in fact a couple of years older than Morad. He was wearing a white voile shirt under his leather jacket, through which you could see tufts of black chest hair; on his wrist was a large Rolex with a steel strap.

'I hear you're at Le Rosey, Morad,' Anthony said. 'How is it? You must get a lot of good skiing out there.'

Morad rolled his eyes. 'It's a crap place. The teachers are useless and there's nothing to do.'

'Oh, Morad,' Dita twittered. 'That isn't what you told me yesterday. You said you're having a wonderful time. You've made so many friends, and you love all the girls.'

'Actually, I hate the girls. They're all slags and hookers. The only person I like is Jonny Faisal, even though he's allowed flying lessons and I'm not.'

'Darling, you're just being silly now. Morad loves to tease,' she explained to Anthony. 'He has the best sense of humour – everything with him is so amusing.'

Morad scowled at her.

'I've got an idea,' Anthony said to everyone. 'Lunch isn't for another hour, so why not take our guests on a tour of the garden? I'm sure you'd all like some air after your long drive. Richard, show John-Spiros and everyone the swimming pool and the walled garden. I'm sure you'd like that, wouldn't you, John-Spiros?'

But John-Spiros said he had forgotten to bring any outdoor shoes, so perhaps it would be better if he remained inside.

'Don't worry, we have plenty of spare boots. Come on everyone, take John-Spiros and his sister and Morad to the boot room. I'm sure you'll find something that fits.'

Slowly and reluctantly, the children headed for the boot room, and later Anthony saw them through the window, trailing stiffly across the lawn. 'I'm sure they'll warm up soon,' he told Dita. 'This often happens with new children. For the first half hour it's agony, and then they suddenly click.'

'With Morad there it will be fine,' Dita predicted. 'He loves the company of girls. They adore him.'

Before lunch, Anthony showed Dita's children to their bedrooms. He had suggested putting them in with his own children – Richard and Rosanna would stay up at the Priory overnight – but Dita said they would feel more comfortable in proper spare rooms on their own. When he took Morad up to the Judge's Chamber, he was surprised when the teenager stopped at every mirror on the way, to pat his hair.

Lunch was an awkward meal. In his button-down pink shirt with his initials woven on the chest, John-Spiros was the neatest, politest boy ever to have visited the Priory, but looked stricken whenever Anthony addressed a word to him.

'I hear you go sailing on a marvellous yacht every summer with your father,' Anthony said. 'That must be fun.'

'Er, yes sir,' he replied stiffly. 'Great fun.' But he looked mortified, and straightened the cutlery on either side of his plate.

Ambrosia didn't say one word all lunchtime, and Anthony felt both his own daughters might have tried harder in that respect too. Jasmine appeared to have withdrawn inside herself, making no effort. She was still wearing the grey jersey with holes he'd particularly asked her to change out of, with the sleeves tugged down over her hands.

Ever since her mother's attempted suicide, she had been in a dreadful mess emotionally, and Anthony now regretted telling her about it, though he still believed it was the right thing to have done, for Amanda's sake as much as Jasmine's. Jasmine had at first refused to discuss it, less still visit Amanda in hospital. She was probably in denial because later she became terribly upset, crying for days on end. Then she became furious with Amanda, as her hurt turned into anger. Now, she lapsed into long, moody silences.

Rosanna too was very quiet, though she agreed to show Ambrosia the horses after lunch when he asked her to. Richard, thank goodness, was his usual boistereous self, telling Morad about the inedible food at Radley. 'On Thursdays for supper it's spam in batter with sweetcorn. Nobody eats it; we just use it for food fights.'

'Jonny Faisal sends out for food from restaurants,' Morad said. 'He gets his bodyguards to drive into Gstaad for caviar.'

'Yuck, I *hate* caviar,' Richard said. 'I had some once; it's *disgusting*. It's raw fish eggs, you know.'

'The beluga at Tramp is the best,' Morad said. 'Jonny Faisal had it at his birthday party.'

Anthony hoped the atmosphere would become less sticky when the Furlong children arrived to swim. Their father might be a crasher, but at least Tom and Katie were bright sparks.

After lunch things improved slightly, though it was hard to assimilate Dita's children into the family group. The pool temperature had been pumped up to eighty-eight degrees, and Tom and Katie, who loved swimming, were soon belly-flopping off the diving board into the dinghy with Richard and Rosanna, and playing a home-grown version of waterpolo using the long-handled nets meant for scooping leaves off the sump.

'Come on, you lot,' Anthony said to John-Spiros and Ambrosia, who were sitting on the sunloungers, watching. 'Aren't you going to swim? I've had the heating on all week for you. There are plenty of spare trunks in the hut if you need to borrow some.'

But John-Spiros said he wasn't that fond of swimming, and Ambrosia said she didn't want to either. Dita chided her children: 'You two are such drips sometimes. Really, what is the matter with you? I suppose you're sensitive about wearing a bikini, Ambrosia. Well, if you're fat, you're fat; you've got to get on with it.'

Morad, meanwhile, was loping round the pool like a panther on the prowl. He seemed to be taking an indecent interest in Katie who, at fourteen, had recently turned rather pretty, and developed small satsuma-sized breasts. Luckily for her, she had inherited her mother's looks and not John's, and her thick copper-coloured hair hung halfway down her back.

Morad disappeared into the changing hut and reappeared in an old pair of Anthony's trunks. His body was oddly triangular and shockingly hairy: a broad matted chest supported by short, muscular legs.

'Oh, bravo!' Dita exclaimed, as her son stood on the diving board, flexing a bicep. 'You look gorgeous, darling.'

He gave an arrogant smirk before diving smoothly into the water. When he resurfaced at the far end of the pool, his mother applauded.

Something Anthony had found laudable about Dita over recent weeks, since Amanda's suicide attempt in Elm Park Mews, was the way she had made so little of it. She had not blamed him, nor been angry with him, nor criticised nor cross-questioned him. She took the entire episode in her stride. Of course, she had made the point, several times, that Amanda Bouillon was insane and always had been. She said that in Paris everyone realised it, and felt quite sorry for Patrice who had been placed in an impossible position. 'It was really quite sad,' she said, shaking her head. 'Patrice is so successful and busy, and Amanda gave him no support as a wife. She always put herself and her own career first, which is absurd when you're married to someone like Patrice. So selfish.'

'Amanda has been successful herself,' Anthony said, defending her. 'She's a good actress and made a hit record.'

Dita gave a derisive little snort. 'Nothing compared to Patrice. No, if you're married to someone like that, your role is to make things run smoothly for him. It would be like me trying to start some little business of my own, when of course my first duty is to look after you and make your life comfortable.'

On the night of the suicide attempt, Anthony had travelled with Amanda in the ambulance to the Brompton Hospital, and stayed with her until she was admitted (providing his credit card as security) and was settled into her room, before joining Dita, very late, at the Royal Academy fundraiser. Expecting a furious reception, he was relieved when Dita made light of it. 'Aah, here comes my favourite man at last,' she exclaimed to the table. 'Poor Anthony. His first wife tried to kill herself today. You see, she knows how lucky I am to be marrying him. Who can blame her for being jealous!'

Later, Dita said, 'I cannot believe Amanda was very serious about taking her life. You'd have thought she'd have managed that, if she'd really wanted to.'

Dita was so confident in her recent engagement, so absorbed by plans for their wedding and reception, and in her schemes for renovating the Priory, that Amanda's troubles neither disturbed nor particularly interested her. She was a worldly and pragmatic woman, not given to

introspection about the past lives of her husbands. During her time with
Goldie, and in her first marriage to Sharif Ahvazi, there had often been
complications over women: it was normal. As Dita saw it, Amanda had
no role in her future life with Anthony, and was consequently no threat.
So it would not have bothered her much, had she known about it, that
Anthony sent flowers to Amanda in hospital, and visited her from time
to time on the way home.

Morad was swimming along the bottom of the pool, trying to grab the
girls' legs and tug them under water. Jasmine had by now joined Richard,
Rosanna and the Furlong children in the pool, and became increasingly
agitated each time Morad tried to grope her. She kicked out at him in the
shallow end, but her foot was too slow against the mass of water.

'Just *stop it*, you idiot,' she kept saying. '*Stop it*. I'm trying to have a
quiet swim.'

But Morad lurked like a shark in the shallows, surfacing for breath
before returning to the bottom. He grabbed Rosanna by the ankles and
dragged her under, then rounded on Katie, who was trying to ride an
inflatable dolphin.

'Dad, can't you stop this cretin from annoying us all the time?' Jasmine
called out to her father. 'He's just being so *irritating* and juvenile.'

Wearily, Anthony walked to the side of the pool. He stood on the
coping stones, waiting for Morad to resurface.

'Morad, would you mind awfully leaving the girls alone for a bit,
there's a good chap? I think you're upsetting them.'

With an insolent sneer and a backwards kick, Morad ignored him,
pushing to the bottom and gliding up again in the direction of Katie.
Katie was holding on to the side now, trying to adjust the straps of her
goggles.

Suddenly, she was dragged under. From the surface, Anthony could
see the squat, hairy figure of Morad grappling with her on the bottom.
Caught unawares, Katie had the goggles half pulled over her face, and
Morad was spinning her round and round, apparently tugging at her
bikini with its pattern of red cherries.

'*Stop that*, Morad,' Anthony ordered. 'Stop that *at once*.' But Morad,
six feet under, did not respond.

'Honestly, darling,' Dita called out from a sunbed. 'Don't overreact.
They are only playing together.'

Through the distortion of the water, and the tangle of flailing limbs,
it was hard to see what was going on, but Katie looked terrified down
there. She was trying to fight him off, pushing at his face, and Morad was
ripping at her bikini top which finally came away in his hand. Briefly,

he rose to the surface, holding it above him like Excalibur's sword, and tossed it out of the pool onto the grass. Katie surfaced, sobbing, and Anthony shouted, 'Morad, *Morad*. I'm talking to you. Stop it this instant. *Stop it.*'

But Morad was dragging Katie back under, this time wrenching at her bikini bottoms with stubby, brutal fingers. Grasping the elastic waistband, he dragged them down around her knees while Katie struggled to tug them back up.

Tom and Richard, at the far end of the pool, now realised what was happening and hastened to the shallow end to help her. But Morad struck out at Tom with his heel, catching him on the jaw, and he winced and clutched the edge of the pool. Katie looked stricken as Morad jerked the bikini bottoms right over her ankles, and rushed to cover a delicate triangle of copper-coloured pubic hair with her hands. Suddenly furious, Anthony leapt into the pool with his clothes on, restraining Morad from behind by both shoulders and forcing him off her; it was like wrestling a full-grown bison to the ground. Anthony could feel the weight of his wet clothes – his linen summer trousers, shirt and docksiders – as they became sodden, and the sting of chlorine in his eyes. Only when he was sure Katie had got safely out of the pool did he release his grip.

He surfaced to applause from his children and the Furlongs, cowed silence from the Emboroleon children and abuse from Dita.

'You stupid man,' she was yelling at him. 'What have you done to my son? Poor Morad. It was only *horseplay*, for goodness' sake. You could have drowned him. Come here, darling, come to Mama. Poor Morad. I've never known anything like it, Anthony. Are you completely mad? You almost drowned him. Look at him, the poor boy.'

Anthony did look at Morad, who was clambering up the metal steps. Apart from looking slightly white-faced and spluttering, there didn't seem too much wrong with him. He gave Anthony an insolent glare, and patted his hair.

'Come here to Mama,' Dita urged him. 'I have a nice dry towel for you, and you can lie down here on my chair.'

'Honestly,' she said to Anthony, furiously, 'I really don't know what came over you; it was an extraordinary display. It makes me quite worried about you. I don't want you ever – *ever* – to frighten any of my children like that again, do you understand me? Poor Morad. He was scared out of his wits.'

Poor Morad lay on his back on the sunlounger, wrapped up in Dita's towel, and smirked.

37

Everyone agreed that never had a bride of a certain age looked more thoroughly soignée than Dita on her wedding day at the Grosvenor Chapel in Mayfair. Her decision to get married in floor-length white Russian fox fur, with white Cossack fur hat and matching muff, was a stroke of pure genius, and such was the scrummage of photographers outside on South Audley Street, each insisting on dozens of different shots of the high society bride, that Dita was obliged to delay her entrance for a full ten minutes in order to satisfy their demands.

Inside the church, hundreds of tiny scented candles had been placed along both sides of the aisle, and at the ends of every pew, so the nave glimmered with a wonderful, soft, Christmassy light, and was filled by the sweet fragrance of ripe figs. Anthony felt he could have done without the scented figs, which were horribly cloying, but Dita was a perfectionist, and had taken such pains over every detail of the day, he kept that small reservation to himself. The flowers, he had to admit, were spectacular: enormous arrangements of exotic blooms he had never seen before, and which he knew had been air-freighted overnight from Trinidad and St Lucia.

As he stood at the rail with his best man Archie, awaiting the arrival of his bride, Anthony could hear the excited buzz and admiring exclamations of his wife's guests. 'The flowers are to *die* for,' a voice was saying. 'I gather they cost forty thousand pounds for the big arrangements alone,' said another, which would have ruined Anthony's entire afternoon had he credited it for a single moment.

Glancing over his shoulder he saw the chapel was packed to the rafters. There must have been at least two hundred and fifty people in the pews downstairs, and a further hundred and fifty upstairs in the gallery, and more standing at the back. Although he recognised rather few of them, he thought Dita's side of the church contained the sleekest, richest-looking characters he'd ever clapped eyes on. Many had immaculate suntans, despite it being December, and incredibly white teeth. He knew from her list that half of her guests were foreign; for days, they had been jetting in to London from Athens, Nassau, Monte Carlo and Sao Paulo.

'Well, they're all in tonight, that's for sure,' Archie muttered to him. 'I tell you, we don't get many punters like these in Marshmellows.'

Anthony smiled. He was glad he'd invited Archie to be his best man, even though Dita would have preferred someone more prepossessing and social. He'd had Lex as best man at his wedding to Sandra, so couldn't do that again, and Archie always made him laugh.

'They're mostly Dita's friends,' Anthony whispered in explanation. 'I think they're what's commonly known as the jet set.'

'The second pew's full of ship owners,' Archie said. 'Four Greek billionaires in one row, it looks like.'

Anthony now understood why Dita had insisted on a London wedding. His first thought had been a low-key ceremony at Winchford, and he had even persuaded Jeremy Meek to allow them a proper church blessing at All Hallowes, despite the bride and groom having each been married twice before, in return for a large donation to the restoration appeal, but Dita was adamant only a London wedding would do. 'No one,' she pointed out, 'will travel to the countryside in December; it is not convenient.' And so Dita decided upon a 'magical winter wedding' at the Grosvenor Chapel which, being only a matter of yards from Harry's Bar, was convenience itself for her own friends, if not for Anthony's.

'Have you ever heard such a noisy congregation?' Anthony said to Archie, as they awaited Dita's delayed arrival. 'It's like a ruddy cocktail party going on back there.'

'I don't know if you ever see *Hello!* magazine,' Archie replied. 'But half the people they write about are here. All the social dukes and playboys. And those anorexic rich women.'

'Dita knows some very rum people, I've discovered that.'

Her allocation of friends, which outnumbered Anthony's by five to one, overflowed the bride's side and swamped the groom's pews as well. Mrs Holcombe and Judy, arriving late having got lost on the Tube from Paddington, found their reserved seats long ago appropriated by a swatch of society decorators. Carina Resnick, breathtakingly chic in a magenta Adolfo suit, planted herself in the second pew in the place reserved for Anthony's uncle Michael, and pretended not to understand when he tentatively tried to reclaim it.

Anthony's friends looked oddly shabby next to Dita's, bursting out of morning coats they'd worn for twenty years. He spotted Mark and Annie Plunkett in the fourth pew with the Nall-Caines, and the Fanes, Elliots and Loxtons in the row behind. All of them, he knew, had joined up for an early 'Oxfordshire contingent' lunch at Foxtrot Oscar before the wedding. Araminta Nall-Caine and Emmy Elliot, who had been bridesmaids at his wedding to Sandra sixteen years before, were sitting up in the gallery in purple and pink hats festooned with feathers. He could see his PA from the bank, Charlotte, in a pretty green suit. Lex was with his parents, Scrotum and Rosie, in the second row. Parked next to the family pews was Henrietta in her wheelchair, wearing the navy-blue three-quarter-length jacket and big family brooch she'd worn at his wedding to Sandra and to Jasmine's confirmation.

Anthony suddenly felt sad that Sandra wasn't at the wedding. He had invited her and John, as a matter of politeness, without expecting them to accept, and the Furlongs had duly declined, citing a prior engagement to visit Len and Marjorie for the weekend at a pub they were caretaking outside Worcester. Standing before the altar, awaiting the long-delayed Dita, Anthony remembered how happy he had been with Sandra at the beginning. He felt a wave of regret and shame about the way he had often taken her for granted, and finally betrayed her with Nula.

Nula, of course, wasn't at the church either, much to her annoyance. Not long after word of his engagement to Dita had gone round the village, Anthony bumped into Nula in the village shop. She looked older and more unkempt than usual, in a shabby tweed overcoat that reminded him of a coat recently stolen from the scarecrow in the kale fields behind Forge Cottage. According to Mrs Holcombe, Amanda's father, Ed, had left Nula and returned to Rome on his motorbike.

'I hear congratulations are in order,' Nula had said, without much goodwill. 'I hope you're going to ask Gaia to be a handmaiden at the wedding.'

'Goodness,' Anthony replied cautiously. 'I'll have to talk to Dita about that. I don't know what we're doing about bridesmaids and pages; we haven't discussed it.'

'Gaia's always wanted to be one,' she persisted. 'Even though I don't approve of anything churchy myself. Not when you consider all the evil that lot have brought into the world. But Gaia does enjoy dressing up, and you *are* her dad after all.'

'Look, I'll see what Dita thinks and get back to you. Let's just see what happens, shall we?'

It took Dita five seconds to declare that nothing would induce her to have Gaia as a bridesmaid. 'Even if we did say yes, which is out of the question, it would mean having to have her ghastly mother there too. Anthony, there simply isn't space. You know how crowded the church is going to be as it is. And she wouldn't know a soul there; she'd hate it.' In the end, they decided to have no attendants, and Gaia came to the church without Nula, and was looked after by Jasmine.

With swelling chords, the organist launched into 'Arrival of the Queen of Sheba' by Handel, and Dita began her slow procession up the aisle, leaning on the arm of a minor member of the Greek Royal family who ran a public relations consultancy in New York. From every part of the chapel came gasps of admiration at the first sight of the chic, vivacious bride; a cross between the Snow Queen and Cruella de Vil, as Annie Plunkett later described her. Anthony could scarcely believe that this vision of perfection, swaddled in white fur, could really be heading his way in order to marry him. Truly, he was the luckiest man alive.

From both the front pews, Anthony saw his children and future stepchildren craning their necks, and he wished from the bottom of his heart they would all be as happy with his choice as he knew himself to be. Obviously it was all going to take time; you couldn't expect everyone to get on instantly. He was sure there would be some tricky moments along the way, as there had already been with Morad, but in the end they would surely all merge into one big, extended, happy family.

Morad was lounging back in his pew, wearing the shiny new Italian suit with shoulder pads Dita had bought for him in Harrods; he had refused to wear a morning coat, saying they were uncool. He had coated his hair with gel and combed it back across his skull like a helmet. It had taken Dita several weeks to forgive Anthony for the fracas in the swimming pool. But then, shortly before the end of the summer term, Morad was expelled from Le Rosey and sent home in disgrace. It emerged that, with his friend Jonny Faisal, he had drilled a hole through the wall of the girls' shower room, through which they had been spying on them. In the flurry of recriminations, the swimming pool episode was forgotten.

Next to Morad was Ambrosia, looking dreadfully unhappy in a billowing pink meringue dress bought for her in Athens. Recently Anthony felt he had begun to get through to Ambrosia a little; she was a sweet, thoughtful thing beneath her painful shyness, and it pleased him so much that Rosanna and Katie were being kind to her. Dita had given her a complex about her weight, and Ambrosia alternated between starvation diets and stuffing herself with cake. Anthony was determined to take special care of his new stepdaughter, and was encouraging her to overcome her fear of horses and take up riding with the other girls.

John-Spiros, meanwhile, sat bug-eyed at the end of the pew, in the miniature dove-grey tailcoat he'd had made especially for his mother's wedding. Around his neck was a grey crepe de chine wedding tie held in place with a pearl tiepin.

Across the aisle Anthony could see his own four children and two Furlong honorary stepchildren.

Jasmine, he had to admit, looked absolutely ravishing in her own bohemian way. She had twisted her hair up on the top of her head, and was wearing a long black velvet dress and black lace scarf, both of which had been Amanda's. Somehow she had saved them from Sandra's purges and they fitted perfectly. Watching her standing there, in clothes he still clearly remembered on his first wife, Anthony was struck by how similar to her mother she looked. But there was an elegant, dreamy droopiness about Jamsine that was all her own, and he felt immensely proud of his eldest daughter. Considering the ramshackle way she'd been brought up, she'd turned out remarkably well. It was a shame Amanda wasn't here too, to see how beautiful Jasmine looked, but that had never been on the cards. She was still living in Elm Park Mews, so far as he knew. Since settling her hospital bill for her, he had heard not a word.

Tom and Richard were both looking very grown up. Tom was taller but Richard was broader in the shoulders and had recently started shaving. Tom was wearing his Eton tailcoat with a jazzy tie, and Richard was in his Radley Sunday suit. Seeing Tom in his tails made Anthony ponder why his own son hadn't got in to Eton, but John Furlong's son had. He could only imagine John's wife Constance had been the brains in that marriage.

Rosanna, at thirteen, wasn't looking her best, poor thing. The red crushed-velvet Laura Ashley dress she'd chosen for herself in Cheltenham made her resemble a well-plumped cushion. Katie, however, with her long copper hair, made him think of an illustration of a woodland nymph in a fairy story, dancing around the roots of a tree. Anthony had a soft spot for Katie, and was always pleased when she came up to the Priory. Exactly the same age as Rosanna, he wished some of her prettiness and lightness might rub off on his own horsey daughter.

Anthony and Dita exchanged marriage vows in firm, audible voices, and then a soprano from the Royal Opera House sang the *Ave Maria* in a setting by Verdi while the bride and groom, best man and Greek royal PR went into the vestry to sign the register. As they returned to the chapel, Anthony caught sight of Morad leering at someone across the aisle. Already he had serious misgivings about his new stepson.

The reception was held in the ballroom of Claridge's, and soon the five hundred guests were shuffling towards the receiving line while dozens of white-gloved waiters circulated with trays of champagne. The hotel's assistant general manager and banqueting manager hovered obsequiously in the shadows in their tailcoats. To Anthony, the afternoon became a blur of unfamiliar, smiling faces, as Dita introduced him to a procession of Greek ship owners and their bejewelled wives, Argentinian bankers, Lyford Cay socialites and self-satisfied French counts. Impressively, his wife knew exactly which wedding presents they'd been given by whom; for weeks, packages had been arriving from Thomas Goode, Swarovski and Asprey, full of expensive gifts Anthony couldn't envisage them ever using, such as giant crystal bowls, soup tureens painted with Bavarian heraldic motifs and a ceramic umbrella stand in the shape of a pouncing leopard. All these ostentatious luxury items came from Dita's friends. Anthony's friends, by contrast, perhaps feeling they had already given presents at his previous wedding to Sandra, were more modest with their gifts this time. He found himself effusively thanking Percy and Jacinthe for their butter dish, with its dancing china cow lid. Walter Twine, to whom the Biggeses had given a lift up to London in their car, presented the newlyweds with a basket full of home-grown winter vegetables.

Soon it was time for speeches and the cutting of the cake, and Anthony, who had sternly warned Archie to steer clear of any lewd jokes, was relieved when his best man was brief and mercifully unfacetious. Archie's few attempts at English humour were received with incomprehension by the international crowd. Anthony's own speech, larded with compliments for Dita, struck more of a chord. As he stood on the shallow platform and surveyed the sea of super-smart guests, Anthony reflected on how different this wedding was to either of his previous ones. It was as though with each marriage his life became more glamorous and more public. His old Oxfordshire friends had clustered together in one group for the speeches, and seemed a race apart from Dita's guests. From the corner of his eye, he spotted Morad slipping out of the room with a woman in a magenta suit.

It had been decided that Anthony and Dita would leave from the front of the hotel in a shower of confetti before returning through the back entrance to spend their first night upstairs in the Piano Suite. The following morning they would depart for Heathrow for a honeymoon in Mauritius at the Tousserok.

While they were checking out, there was a moment of embarrassment. 'The, er, young gentleman said you would be settling his account too, sir, for the second bedroom.'

'Really?' said an astonished Anthony. 'I don't know anything about this. Which young gentleman said I'd be settling which bill?'

'Er, a Mr Morad Ahvazi, sir. He asked us to arrange a room for him and a Mrs Resnick. He said you had approved the arrangement, and asked for the bill to be added to your own.'

38

The new Mrs Anthony Anscombe, pulsating with energy from twenty-one luxurious days in Mauritius, declared that her only priority now was to sort out the Priory. Filled with zeal, she told Anthony that she was barely even going to show her face in London, and would bury herself away in Winchford to get the house running properly. 'I've done this before on Kypsos and in the south of France. The *only way* to get it right is to be there on the spot, and supervise everything oneself. The minute you start delegating things to other people, that's when things go wrong. It's a dreadful thing to say, I know, but I wouldn't even allow a decorator to choose a light switch, not without seeing it first. Otherwise they come up with the most peculiar things and then say it's too late to change anything.'

Anthony was enormously grateful to his wife, and particularly impressed she intended spending so much time down at Winchford. He had imagined they would split their time as before, half and half between country and London, but Dita was determined to concentrate on Winchford. It slightly surprised him when she announced they would have to move out of the Priory for nine months while the renovations took place.

'Move *out*? Can't the builders do it one room at a time? That would be much simpler, surely?'

But Dita was adamant. 'The place needs rewiring and plumbing from top to bottom. There's no way we can stay here; there'll be no electricity or running water.'

'What about my mother? We can't just push her out – it's her home too, remember.'

'Ah, yes,' Dita replied carefully. 'We need to have a proper discussion about that. I'm not sure it's actually very suitable having her and all her nurses living with us in any case. She'd be much more comfortable somewhere more manageable of her own.'

'We can't banish my mother!' Anthony was horrified. 'Where could she go?'

'A nice small house in the village. I'm sure you can find one that's appropriate. I don't mean a tiny cottage, of course not, but somewhere with a pretty little sitting room and a nice downstairs bedroom for her. With some proper privacy for her nurses, so they can have their own television. Far more suitable in every way.'

Anthony exhaled anxiously. 'I don't know. She's very settled in the white drawing room, and it means she can join us for meals when we're all here as a family.'

'As I've explained, Anthony, there will very shortly be *no electricity* and *no heating* in the entire house. The place will be freezing cold and in total darkness. It will be physically impossible for your mother to remain here, even if we wanted her to. No, much better if we grasp the nettle and get her properly resettled. In actual fact, I spoke to John Furlong about it earlier on. That man is perfectly hopeless by the way; I can't believe he's the right person to be in charge of the estate office. I asked him whether there are any houses coming up, and he thinks the Lady House might become available. That's an awfully pretty little house, a perfect doll's house. I should be quite happy living there *myself*, so Henrietta can hardly object.'

'Actually,' Anthony replied, hopelessly, 'The Lady House has already been promised to a local couple. He's a computer software guy working at the Chipping Norton business park.'

'Well, you'll just have to find somewhere else for them. Surely your mother is more important than some computer person we don't even know? Really, Anthony! No, Henrietta will have the Lady House, I insist upon it. In any case, she can't stay in the white drawing room because we need the space ourselves. It's perfectly ridiculous having one old lady sleeping in one of the prettiest reception rooms in the house. It's the perfect room to hide yourself away in and read a magazine. I think it's very important in a big house like the Priory, with so much going on, to have *one place* where you can find some peace and quiet for five minutes. Agree with me, Anthony.'

And so it was decided that Henrietta and her carers would decamp from the Priory to the Lady House, just as soon as it was done up for her. Realising her mother-in-law was in no fit state to make the necessary decisions over decorations, Dita asked Carina Resnick to choose the wallpapers and curtains on a project basis, while she herself went round every room of the Priory, selecting furniture and minor watercolours that would suit the proportions of the Lady House, and which did not fit into her vision for the big one. While Anthony was away on a ten-day trip to New York, and before Henrietta got wind of the plan, her belongings were packed up in boxes. Dita had planned and executed the coup brilliantly. In no time Henrietta was installed at the Lady House with a new Magnet kitchen and new South African nurse, Chelsy.

Anthony had to spend many hours unsuccessfully pacifying her, but he was secretly rather relieved not to have to see her at breakfast any more. Anthony and Dita, meanwhile, were to make their temporary home in Steepness Farmhouse, which Carina quickly made habitable with the pick of the furniture and paintings from the Priory, new carpets and curtains throughout and a Mark Wilkinson country kitchen to replace Sandra's old pine one. Anthony, who still remembered buying the pine one in Cheltenham, asked Dita whether it was all really necessary, given that they were only going to be living at the farmhouse for nine months. 'It doesn't seem worth it to me, especially as we'll be spending a fortune on redoing the Priory.'

'Well, I'm very sorry, Anthony,' Dita replied sharply. '*You* may be prepared to slum it for months on end, but I'm not. I'd like to pull out all those ghastly avocado baths and put in some proper white ones, but I'm not suggesting doing that, since I know you wouldn't approve. But I am *not* living with someone else's kitchen. We might be here for a year, you do realise, maybe longer. We may at least *try* to live in a civilised manner.'

'A *year*? I thought you said it would take nine months.'

'The architect is saying nine months now, which means at least a year. With English builders it could easily be eighteen months. In fact, I wouldn't be surprised if we were still here in two years' time. So do let's be realistic, and try and make things as nice as we can under very trying circumstances. I would like to remind you that if your mother had maintained the Priory up to a proper standard, I wouldn't be having to do all this in the first place. It's all right for her, she's living in the lap of luxury in the Lady House, with the thermostat turned permanently up to ninety degrees. It's *poor us* who are having to camp out in this bloody farmhouse while we put right half a century of neglect.'

As Dita's plans for the Priory took shape, Anthony became increasingly alarmed by their scale and scope. In his naivety, he had envisaged rooms being repainted and essential repairs to the plasterwork, but was hardly prepared for Dita's replanning of the whole house. The very purpose of rooms was altered, as the drawing room became a library and the old library became the dining room. Having wound the local planning officer and English Heritage around her little finger, medieval fireplaces were dismantled and removed to different rooms, and walls and panelling reconfigured. Anthony could scarcely believe the number of experts that now entered his life, each issuing hefty invoices plus VAT. Stonemasons lifted and re-laid the flagstones in the Great Hall, specialist kitchen designers produced scheme after scheme for Dita's beady consideration, audio consultants installed a music system enabling perfectly-equalised sound to be piped into every downstairs room. John Cullen Lighting presented a scheme incorporating over two hundred halogen fittings, plus uplighters, downlighters and special washes of soft light to sweep the kitchen walls. Dita was troubled by the paucity of bathrooms, and soon a further five were installed, either by converting bedrooms or by the insertion of bathtubs into the corners of the larger spare rooms. Anthony was full of admiration for his wife's ingenuity, and her ability to spot architectural potential. The cost of the works appalled him but, as Dita said, 'if you don't get the basics right, everything else is a complete waste of money. The secret is to get the invisible bits done properly.'

Returning home one evening, Anthony found Dita and Jasmine engaged in a blazing row in the kitchen. Dita was screaming at her like a fishwife.

'Now, now, everyone,' Anthony said. 'Let's all calm down and perhaps someone could tell me what this is about.'

'Dita's told me I can't have my bedroom any more. And nor will Richard or Rosanna. She's taking our bedrooms away.'

'I'm sure that's nonsense,' Anthony said. 'Dita, Jasmine's still going to have her bedroom, isn't she?'

'As I've already explained to her,' Dita replied patiently, 'she will of course have the use of a bedroom. Heaven knows, we have more than enough bedrooms, and four of them are earmarked as children's rooms, so she'll have a bedroom whenever she needs one. She knows that perfectly well.'

'But not my *own* bedroom. I don't *want* to share one of those top floor ones; I want my *own* bedroom, the one I've always had.'

Anthony looked beseechingly at his wife. 'Dita, I don't know anything about this. You're not planning on moving Jasmine, are you?'

'If you had bothered to even *look* at the plans I left out for you, Anthony, you'd know all this already. I left them for you next to your briefcase two weeks ago. Really, you're impossible sometimes. I don't mind doing the whole of your house single-handedly, but it would help if you could at least read through your pile of post. The plan is for the five bedroom suites on the first floor to become guest bedrooms. Why else do you think I've been bothering to install all these damn bathrooms? When we have a houseful of friends, that's where they'll be. Your *children* are having the new, perfectly nice little bedrooms under the eaves, the ones Carina is helping me do at the moment. They're going to be lovely bedrooms, very Jane Churchilly and pretty, with a new shower room up there and everything. There's even going to be a children's sitting room, with television and a fridge.'

'But I don't want to move upstairs,' Jasmine said stubbornly. 'I like my *old* room. That's always been my room, for years. Why should I move?'

'I must say, I do rather agree with Jasmine,' Anthony said, in an anguished voice. 'Surely we don't need five spare bedrooms? It's not like we'll ever have that many people to stay at one time.'

'Of course we will. Now you're being perfectly ridiculous,' Dita said. 'Where else are people supposed to sleep when they come to stay? You can hardly invite friends to come all this way for a weekend and then shunt them away in an attic with no proper bathroom! As for five spare bedrooms, I regard that as the *absolute minimum*. Goldie has twelve on Kypsos, and that's only in the main house. Five will be awfully tight as it is. So many people are gays these days, or else single girls who haven't found husbands, and they all expect bedrooms to themselves, so one uses them up at a rate of knots.'

'All the same, I do see Jasmine's point. She is still living at home most of the time.'

'No, she isn't. She'll be away at her acting school from September. She'll scarcely be here at all.'

'Well, during the holidays. That's still four or five months a year, remember.'

'Good gracious, don't they do any work at all at these places? I thought you wanted to become a professional actress, Jasmine. You won't learn much if you keep coming back here like a homing pigeon. I thought you'd be too busy rehearsing your plays or learning your lines or whatever it is you do at drama school.'

'I *will* be, most of the time,' Jasmine protested. 'But that doesn't mean I shouldn't have a bedroom.'

'For the twenty millionth time, Jasmine, you will have a bedroom. If you really want to know, I spent an entire afternoon last week choosing fabrics for your bedcover and bedback, a very pretty little cerise check costing God-knows-what per metre, and I wouldn't have bothered if I'd known how ungrateful you were going to be. Agree with me, Anthony

– haven't I almost killed myself pulling this damned house together?'

'You have been working very hard, darling.'

'Well, then. Perhaps you could explain to your daughter how lucky she is. Those top floor rooms are going to be divine. Jasmine, Rosanna, Ambrosia and Katie, who I presume is going to be a semi-permanent fixture here in the future, as she is now, can share the girls' bedrooms, and Richard, Morad, John-Spiros and Tom can use the boys' rooms, which are going to be done in a marvellous masculine fabric from Brunswick et Fils. I find this endless fussing over who's having this bedroom or that bedroom absurd. Either we're going to have a properly organised house, or we're not. Right now, I feel very underappreciated. We cannot have children making selfish demands or it simply isn't going to work. In which case we may as well give up on the country altogether and put the Priory on the market.'

Speaking as evenly as possible, feeling increasingly exasperated, he said, 'Darling, obviously we're not going to do that, and we do all appreciate everything you're doing. You're doing a wonderful job.'

'You say that, but at the moment it feels like a very thankless task.'

'Listen, Dita,' said Anthony. 'You leave me and Jasmine to have a little talk and we'll try and work something out, OK? Jasmine's obviously feeling very emotional about her room, and I understand that. But maybe everything will seem better tomorrow. No, don't say anything, Dita. Or you, Jasmine. We're leaving the subject alone now. Jasmine and I will talk about it tomorrow.' Sometimes Anthony felt sick and tired of always having to calm everyone down.

That night Dita made it perfectly clear that her will would prevail at all costs. 'I will not be ordered about by your bloody daughter. She's so rude and obstreperous, it's completely unacceptable. I don't care if she does think I'm the wicked stepmother; she's plainly been very badly brought up and she's going to have to get used to the new regime, it's as simple as that.' For the sake of harmony, Anthony promised to talk to his daughter.

Seeing no alternative, he persuaded Jasmine to accept the new bedroom arrangements in return for the promise of a small flat in London when she began college. But the antagonism between Dita and his eldest daughter was palpable, and made him realise how skilful Sandra had been when she'd entered their lives all those years before. He found himself still feeling annoyed with Dita, and even more annoyed with himself for having supported her.

In other respects too, Dita could be ruthless in her new role as chatelaine. Even before the Priory was ready and they were living at

Steepness Farmhouse, Mrs Holcombe was summarily dismissed for dishing up lunch thirty-five minutes late and replaced by a young French chef. Anthony was so embarrassed by the manner of Mrs Holcombe's departure that, without saying anything to Dita, he sent her a cheque for £2,000 and a glowing handwritten reference, as well as a lifetime tenancy guarantee on her almshouse.

Soon the French chef, Regis, was supplemented by an Italian butler, Santos, a Spanish housekeeper, Stigmata, and a Portuguese cleaner, Victoria, who were all found cottages in Winchford as part of their contracts of employment. John Furlong pointed out that estate rents would fall that year for the first time 'with so many of the cottages bringing nothing in now, what with your mother and Nula Starling and all these new staff.' He couldn't complain too forcefully since the Furlongs were living rent-free at the Old Rectory.

In terms of comfort, Anthony sometimes had to remind himself he was inhabiting the same farmhouse in which he'd lived with Sandra for so many years. From the outside it looked exactly the same, despite Dita's clever idea of moving the front door to the middle of the house, so you no longer entered via the kitchen. Instead, you came in through what used to be Anthony's study, and the old back hall was converted into a walk-in larder for Regis's provisions. The food, under Dita's supervision, was always delicious. Every evening a three- or four-course dinner awaited him on the mahogany dining table. Returning from Kingham station, he could smell roast partridge or veal escalopes as he passed the kitchen window. Even when it was just the two of them they ate in the dining room by candlelight. The sole exception was Wednesday evenings, which was Regis's night off, when Dita served up the smoked salmon and cold lobster with mayonnaise he left for them. At least twice a week Dita organised friends to come over for dinner 'at our funny little temporary farmhouse', as she put it. She had an extraordinary gift for knowing exactly who was staying with whom for miles around, and luring entire houseparties to Winchford to make up her kind of numbers. Dinners for twenty or twenty-four people became commonplace. On Monday mornings she would sit down at her desk with her diary and address book and plan half a dozen dinners at a time, assembling interesting groups of friends and neighbours, each graded according to a precise system of her own. There were grand country neighbours who lived in Oxfordshire full-time, grand country neighbours who spent part of the week up in London (Dita's preferred group), 'amusing' neighbours who were not necessarily rich but could sing for their supper, 'duty' neighbours who need be tolerated only intermittently, and imported friends shipped in to add texture and sparkle. Into this last category fell the interior decorators, Biedermeier furniture dealers and spare men who arrived from London at two o'clock for Sunday lunch, full of insincere apologies and spiky gossip, drank the house dry, then left again in a rush without saying goodbye to Anthony. Often, as he sat at the head of his table, in the room that had once been Richard and Rosanna's playroom, eating his way through an elaborate banquet with the delicious wine Dita insisted upon, half-listening to the gossip of Dita's smart friends, Anthony remembered eating cold fish fingers and sweetcorn left over from his children's tea during his Sandra days, and congratulated himself on how much more comfortable and interesting his life had now become.

There was something awesome about the way Dita deployed her energy. Dinners, the opera, holidays, even time for sex was scheduled into a packed agenda. Every six weeks or so, a long weekend in Paris or Rome was put in the diary. In their first year as a married couple, Anthony became familiar with the best suites at the best hotels in half a dozen European and American cities. Everywhere they went Dita was greeted as a favourite client by hotel concierges, who remembered her from her Goldie days.

Having shown little interest in Winchford prior to her wedding day, and declaring it to be perfect in every respect, the new Mrs Anscombe now set about improving every aspect of her husband's domain. Satellite dishes, which had started to appear on thatched rooftops, were banned except from the Priory, where Morad insisted on one so he could watch MTV. Like some eighteenth-century chatelaine of a model village, Dita's insistence upon perfection extended to the smallest detail. The village shop was banned from displaying its freestanding Lyons Maid sign on the street, along with garish special offer posters in the window. Villagers were issued with a long list of plants and flowers they could no longer grow in their gardens, including chrysanthemums, gladioli and fuchsias. Leylandii hedges, ornamental carriage lamps and hanging baskets were similarly proscribed. Dita embarked upon an acrimonious feud with the local planning authority, which had granted permission for a carport behind one of the cottages and which Dita considered an eyesore. 'I don't even understand what *business* it is of these ghastly planning people,' Dita said to him, 'when it's *your own* village. I'm sure their attitude is class motivated; they hate the idea of people owning a beautiful place like Winchford.' When a notice to all tenants went round forbidding the use of plastic poly-tunnels in back gardens if they could be so much as glimpsed from the road, Walter arrived at Steepness Farmhouse in high dudgeon, worried he was going to have to destroy half his kitchen garden. Only Anthony's insistent intervention won him a reprieve.

Anthony came to understand that, in taking on Dita, he had chosen a wife who accepted no compromises. Even during this first flush of marriage, he found himself questioning her judgement, and wished she were less imperious.

Although 'considerate' was not an adjective most people would have applied to her, Dita was, in her own way, enormously considerate to those she deemed worthy of her consideration, which during this period included her husband. For Anthony, it was a novel experience to be viewed by his wife as a figure of stature. Sandra had regarded his job at the bank as a necessary evil – after all, men must earn their living – which interfered with the more important job of raising a family. Dita, however, understood that the deputy chairman of Anscombes and owner of Winchford was a figure due admiration and respect and she encouraged him to conduct his life more in keeping with his position; in London, they gave dinner parties for the financial community, at which his opposite numbers at American investment banks and fund managers were entertained, along with their wives. Afterwards, Dita passed on nuggets of flattery: 'Everyone was saying you're the one bright spark at Anscombes; they're all longing for you to take over from Michael.'

To which Anthony replied, 'No, that's nonsense. Michael's doing an excellent job.'

And Dita, tilting her head, would say, 'That's not what that man from Citibank sitting on my left told me. He said Michael's an awful old bumbler. He says you need to seize the helm before it's too late.'

The number and range of Dita's acquaintants never ceased to amaze him. She knew by name every waiter, manager and barman at Annabel's, Harry's Bar and Mark's Club, greeting them, 'Good evening, Bruno,' or 'Good afternoon, Eugenio.' She knew the directors of the London art galleries, who invited her to their development board lunches. She knew jewellers and auctioneers, racehorse trainers and pilates instructors, to all of whom she issued weekend invitations to stay at the Priory, just as soon as it was ready.

Anthony shuddered at the bills, which arrived in a ceaseless torrent from the contractors and decorators engaged in the renovation of his home. When his accountant mentioned that the VAT component of the works had now reached £150,000, and they had barely passed the halfway point, he started to panic. But Dita explained that the dry rot had been more severe than originally envisaged, as was the asbestos that lagged many of the pipes. 'It all had to come out, which set us back two months.

The alternative was poisoning ourselves to death. Honestly, Anthony, pour yourself a whisky and stop sweating. It isn't as if you have to pay *me* anything – all my project management is being done for love. You'll adore the house when it's done, you know you will.'

39

Anthony at the wheel of the Land Rover, Dita tight-lipped in the front passenger seat, and Jasmine sitting morosely in the back, were driving down Winchford's village street on their way into Stow-on-the-Wold, where Dita needed to collect a re-upholstered stool. They passed the hideous new bungaloid rectory, home to the vicar, and the Old Rectory next door, with its eight bedrooms and Cotswold dovecote, outside which Sandra in Barbour and headscarf could be seen deadheading a rosebush. Anthony slowed down and parped the horn, while Dita gave a little royal wave. Although the two women were studiously polite, and Sandra assured anyone who asked that she got on with Dita like a house on fire, there was a perceptible frost between them, and both would have been far happier had the other one disappeared. Well aware from John precisely how much money Dita was lavishing on the Priory, Sandra declared herself shocked. 'It's completely over the top. Such a lovely old house – there's no need for her to maul it like that.'

Proceeding along the picture-postcard street, they passed the pair of thatched cottages, home to Stigmata the maid and Victoria the cleaner, and the almshouses where Mrs Holcombe and Walter were pottering about in their front gardens. As usual, Dita sucked her teeth disapprovingly as they passed Mrs Holcombe's door, considering her bone idle and hating the circular metal drying frame behind her cottage, fluttering with the week's wash.

Involuntarily, as they passed the war memorial, Anthony glanced towards Forge Cottage where Nula and Gaia were ensconced. Soon to turn eight, Gaia looked more like her father all the time, despite the free-trade yarns and Bolivian peasant-wear Nula insisted on. Recently, Anthony had been obliged to increase Nula's monthly allowance since her reflexology and reiki venture had found few customers in Winchford and had been abandoned. Nula hadn't helped matters by telling Jacinthe Bigges that the crunchy crystals in her foot showed she was deeply repressed. Jacinthe put the word out to boycott Nula's cranky therapies for good.

Outside the pub, Anthony found his way blocked by two large removal lorries. 'God, this is the limit,' Dita snapped crossly. 'People shouldn't be allowed to move house on a Saturday morning. Hoot at them, Anthony.'

Then he saw a familiar figure emerging down the ramp of a lorry. It was Len, his former father-in-law, heaving the back end of a velour sofa. Following behind, as perky and immaculate as ever, was Marjorie, carrying a standard lamp.

'Len? What on earth are you doing here?'

'Oh, didn't they tell you?' Len replied, resting a meaty elbow on the rim of the open driver's side window. 'Marjorie and I are taking over the Plough and Harrow. Hook Norton brewery has given us seven-year tenure.'

'Really?' Anthony was astonished. 'Well, that's amazing news Len. What happened to the previous chap, Barry Sheaf?'

'Gone to work for Archie's wine bar in Moreton. He's turning the back part into a gambling club.' Len looked momentarily rueful. 'Not that I'm planning on any gambling myself, mind you.'

'And how are *you*, Marjorie? Marvellous to have you living in the village.'

'With both Sandra and Ginette living down here now, and our two grandchildren of course, we leapt at the chance when this place came up. We were very lucky to get it, but Len told the brewery people about our connection with you, and they gave us the nod.'

Dita was showing little inclination to be introduced to the matey publican and his twinkly wife, and was gazing into the middle distance.

Just then, Len stuck his big fleshy head right inside the Land Rover, thrust out a paw and said, 'No prizes for guessing who you are. You have to be Dita. Nice to make your acquaintance, Deets. I'm Len; I used to be Tony's old pa-in-law for my sins until Sandra and he did the splits. All very sad, but it happens, and there's never been a minute of unpleasantness, has there, Tone?' He gave him an affectionate rabbit punch. 'I shouldn't be saying this, Sandra would kill me, but I always preferred you as a son-in-law to the new one. Not that he's a bad bloke, but we always had a good laugh, and it's not the same with John, stiff old Charlie that he is.'

'We'd better be on our way now. We're going into Stow,' Anthony said. 'But it's lovely to see you both – and welcome to Winchford.'

'Tell you what,' Len said. 'Soon as we get this place straight, the first people we're inviting over for a noggin are you and Deets. That's a promise. In fact, we might make a bit of a party of it and ask Sandra and John too, and Jacinthe and wassisname, Percy – His Excellency – because they've been so generous to our Ginette.'

'Sounds excellent. I look forward to it.'

'Cheerio then,' Len said, with a flash of his big white Lego-shaped gnashers. 'And it was good to meet you at last, Deets, having heard so much about you. Not that I believed any of it, of course! Nice to have you in the family.'

Even before they had left the village limits, Dita exploded. Over her dead body was that ghastly common man and his simpering wife moving into Winchford. 'I insist you go straight down there this afternoon and tell them so. I'm sorry, but they simply cannot stay here. We'd be a laughing stock. We can't have friends to stay for weekends, who might very well want to walk down to the pub on Sunday morning – men do like to do that – and find themselves being served by your ex-wife's parents! Can you imagine? It's all people would talk about; I can hear them already: We went into the village inn in Anthony's village, and up popped this extraordinary man who was pulling the pints and selling those . . . those disgusting hairy snacks English people insist on eating in pubs . . . what are they called, pork cracklings?'

'Pork scratchings.'

'Vile things.' Dita made a face. 'Do you really want it said that your former father-in-law serves in a public house?'

'To be honest, I couldn't give a damn.'

'Well, I'm sorry, but it's out of the question. I cannot bear that man: he's like that awful one who runs the pub on that television soap I refuse to watch – the East End one.'

'EastEnders? No, he isn't, not at all. He's a lovely man, Len. And I love Marjorie too, both of them. One of the worst things about breaking up with Sandra was seeing less of Len and Marjorie. You like them too, don't you, Jasmine?'

Jasmine nodded sullenly. 'Len built us that treehouse at Steepness Farmhouse, the one Dita got the builders to take down.'

'We could hardly have that monstrosity bang outside the drawing room window. I hadn't realised *he* was responsible for it. No, I'm sorry Anthony, but you must speak to him after lunch.'

Anthony exhaled anxiously. He hated confrontation. 'Well, I'll talk to

Len,' he said at last. 'But I doubt there's anything we can do. The brewery can put in whoever they like as landlords. They own the lease.'

'I thought *you* owned it. It's your village. I always understood you owned the whole place.'

'The freeholds, yes, but not the lease on the Plough and Harrow. The brewery's had that for years.'

'Sometimes,' said Dita, 'I get the distinct impression this entire estate is very poorly managed. The whole place seems to be run for the exclusive benefit of your cast-off relations.'

'That isn't quite true, darling. There's only my mother, and Sandra of course. And Nula with Gaia.'

'And now these ridiculous people at the pub. I'm only surprised Amanda Bouillon hasn't moved in. I'm sure you'd say yes, if she asked.'

'Now you're being unfair. Amanda has never asked for a cottage.'

'That's not what I said. I said you'd give her one. And you would, too.'

Anthony shook his head. 'Really, Dita. Just leave it, won't you?'

Then, from the back, Jasmine spoke up. 'I'd *love* Amanda to come and live here; that's a brilliant idea. Can't you ask her, Dad? Ring her up and offer her a cottage, then I can see her all the time.'

Five weeks before Christmas, Dita announced that the Priory was sufficiently well advanced for them to move back in. 'Not all the sofa cushions will have arrived, and we *still* won't have curtains in the library because that damn fabric is taking ages to come from Venice, but I've told the builders we're taking up residence. If nothing else, it will encourage them to finish quicker.'

A few days later Anthony spent his first night in his renovated family home. The experience was disorientating. As he walked in wonderment from room to room, he hardly felt he even knew his way around any more. Doorways had been widened, narrowed, heightened or removed altogether, and corridors veered off in new directions to create entirely new spaces. Accompanying Jasmine and Rosanna on a tour of inspection, Anthony threw open the door to the Assize Chamber and found himself peering into a walk-in linen cupboard; the Assize Chamber had disappeared without trace until they discovered it could only be accessed via a different staircase. Everything in the house smelt new. Dozens of pairs of perfectly pleated Nina Campbell and Mrs Munro curtains stood stiffly to attention, as though they had been glued to sheets of corrugated metal. Scores of little round clothed tables, each with its own braided fringe, had sprung up like mushrooms in every room, topped by brand new lamps and silk lampshades, and artfully arranged with tablescapes of silver and china boxes. Almost more confusing was the rehanging of every picture, portrait, watercolour and mezzotint. Dozens of paintings had been cleaned, reframed and displayed in the little clusters Dita and her *tastemeisters* favoured. To Anthony it was almost painful to see the backdrop to his life so comprehensively remade and remodelled, as though by the sudden twist of a kaleidoscope, each piece falling into a new discordant pattern. Entering the scarcely-ever-used winter drawing room, once decorated with brocade curtains and paintings of longhorn cattle beside a Scottish loch, he found himself in a cosy sitting room, full of sofas with needlepoint cushions, and still more cushions with embroidered mottos: 'I like my husbands like my chocolate – dark and rich.' The tiny Canaletto of the Rialto Bridge, always regarded as the best picture in the house and hung since time immemorial in a corner of the Great Hall, turned up above a desk in the Judge's Chamber. Zurbaran's Flight into Egypt, Anthony's favourite, disappeared from the library to surface in a spare bathroom ('I do so hate nativity pictures,' Dita declared. 'Much too sentimental.'). Much of the furniture, too, was unrecognisable. Anthony felt sure he had never seen those elaborately carved and gilded hall tables before, nor that swaggering gilded mirror with its spears and horns of plenty. 'Oh, those,' Dita said. 'Aren't they pretty? I found them in the basement at Mallets. I can't think how your parents managed without proper hall tables.'

It bothered Anthony that he couldn't find several favourite pieces of furniture, for instance the Edwardian marble-topped table he'd previously used as a drinks table. Nor could he find his father's old desk. Eventually Dita admitted that since Carina Resnick had been unable to find a place for them in the new scheme, they had been sold at Christie's, along with half a dozen chests of drawers and bedside cabinets.

'You might have asked me first,' Anthony complained. 'Some of that furniture's been in the family for three hundred years.'

'Honestly, darling, I don't know why you're making such a fuss. They were ghastly old things. And much too big. I think we got fifteen thousand pounds for it all, which is worth having, no? Better than putting it into storage to get eaten away by bugs.'

For sheer comfort, Anthony could scarcely believe it was the same house. It was like inhabiting a luxurious country house hotel, in which everything worked and worked superbly. Finally he could appreciate the scale and perfection of Dita's vision. He had never once turned on a bathtap, or pulled a lavatory chain, without half expecting the operation to fail. Now, geysers of hot water bubbled behind every tap, and power showers thundered down on his head and back. By his bedside was a panel of switches and dimmers controlling lamps all over the room, plus special low-level, low-wattage pinhead lights for finding the loo in the night. If there was a show-house sterility to the decoration, and a surfeit of beige and taupe, Anthony hardly noticed it. Dita had been brilliantly astute in her reassignment of the reception rooms. The white drawing room, Henrietta's fetid sickbay, was almost unrecognisable, its seven sash windows draped with a hundred yards of shot silk taffeta. As he traipsed in stockinged feet from room to room (Dita had banned shoes in the house) he felt he was inspecting a magnificent stage set, ablaze with the soft glow of lamplight, with sweet-smelling poinsettias and jasmine plants protruding from cachepots on every gleaming surface.

40

It was two weeks before Christmas and Anthony was strolling through Winchford in the lichen twilight. Almost every cottage door had an evergreen wreath twined with berries and holly leaves. Many of the villagers had left their curtains open to display Christmas cribs or the twinkling Hanukkah menorahs which seemed to have been co-opted by good Christians everywhere. Through the little windows he could see Christmas cards arranged on mantelpieces and dozens of decorated trees, green, silver and tinsel-gold. For the past fortnight the estate had done a roaring trade selling spruces from the new Christmas tree plantation though, on the evidence of his eyes, Anthony guessed the local Esso garage shop had done well too with its self-assembly plastic replicas.

Tunes from the carol service, which he had just attended at All Hallowes, reverberated in his ears. Anthony adored carols, and tonight he had stood shoulder to shoulder with Percy and Jacinthe, bellowing his way through 'God rest ye, merry gentlemen' and 'Good King Wenceslas'. Almost his only dispute with Jeremy Meek had been over the choice of music at the church, the vicar favouring African native chants and 'Shine, Jesus shine', Anthony preferring the staunchly traditional. It disappointed him that not one of his children or stepchildren had accompanied him to the carol service. Jasmine was up in London seeing a play with her mother; Richard had gone to the Feathers Ball with Tom and a group of friends; Rosanna and Katie were at a pony club bop in Kingham; and Dita's younger children were spending a few days with their father at his flat in Grosvenor Square. Morad was in disgrace again, having been expelled from his new school, Milton Abbey, after only three terms, for masterminding an ambitious pornography ring. As the headmaster explained when Dita and Anthony were summoned down to Dorset to discuss the matter, 'I could have turned a blind eye if he'd just been lending out copies of *Penthouse* and *Knave*, but some of the publications aren't even legal in this country. They were perfectly revolting, involving animals and dungeons.'

Dita, needless to say, had taken Morad's side, complaining that the headmaster was small-minded. 'Don't you want to encourage enterprise in your pupils? To me, there is something impressive in sending away for these Dutch magazines. Morad's father and both his stepfathers have been very successful in business; he gets it from them.'

But Milton Abbey decided it could rub along perfectly well without Morad Ahvazi, who was even now arriving home by limousine for Christmas at Winchford. Dita was furious with Anthony for not backing her up in her battle with the authorities, and was looking for a new school for her favourite son. She had spent the morning leafing through brochures for Millfield and Bedales.

Arriving at the Priory, Anthony was overwhelmed by the chicness of Dita's Christmas decorations, which had been entirely masterminded by a young interior designer straight out of the Inchbald school, recommended by Carina Resnick. Dozens of gold obelisks and glass angels stood along the chimneypieces in the Great Hall, and crystal bowls filled with silver baubles and glass fir cones covered every surface. When Anthony emerged, rather pleased with himself, from the cellar where he'd located the nativity crib, Dita took one look and told him to put it straight back. 'I've never seen anything so hideous in my entire life.' Dita's decorations were like a window in the Tiffany shop in Old Bond Street: exuding glorious, understated good taste. But a part of Anthony was filled with nostalgia for the sprigs of holly on the Elizabethan portraits (now consigned to an upstairs corridor) and the great evergreen boughs of his mother's regime. Another bone of contention was the annual tenants' drinks. Dita declared they couldn't possibly have half the village traipsing across the new carpets 'in their great clumpy shoes'; so the party at the Priory was restricted to sixty neighbours who met Dita's approval, and whose brogues and stilettos would inflict less damage on the virgin pile.

There was one pre-Christmas fixture for which Anthony imposed a three-line whip, and this was Len and Marjorie's reopening party for the Plough and Harrow. 'We do all have to go to that one,' he announced firmly at lunch. 'Dita, Jasmine, all of us. Tom and Katie are going with Sandra and John. The Biggeses too, most of the village in fact. Apparently they're serving glühwein, and there'll be an enormous buffet, so we won't need any supper.'

Dita, who planned all the menus a week ahead with Regis the chef, began to protest that it would be far better if they came home for dinner after the party, but Anthony said that it didn't even begin until seven thirty, and it was essential they stayed for a good long time. 'Your grandfather has done a great job on the place,' he told Richard and Rosanna. 'I'm told you can hardly recognise it, he's made everything so smart.'

Flinching at the reference to 'grandfather' in the context of the village publican, Dita grudgingly consented to go along 'for as long as I can stand it, though I tell you now I shall not be touching any pub food. What do they call those frightful deep fried prawns served in a wicker *pannier*?'

'Scampi in a basket?' suggested Richard.

'How people can eat all that batter!"

'Oh, I love them,' Richard declared. 'Sometimes we get them after away-matches. With piles of chips and salt and vinegar.'

As the night of the party approached, having learnt that all sorts of surprising people such as the Hollands and the Nall-Caines were going to be there too, Dita began slightly to change her tune. For one thing, it would get the children out of the house for a couple of hours, which would allow Stigmata and Victoria an unimpeded opportunity to tidy up behind them. Already Dita was finding the Christmas holidays a trial. Richard and Rosanna had been staying at the Priory for a week, as was Jasmine, all in their new bedrooms on the top floor, which she could now hardly bear to go into, they were so untidy. To her dismay, none of her stepchildren were using the special laundry bags that she'd had made in Colefax fabrics and which dangled behind every door. Instead, they just left their old shirts and chinos strewn everywhere. At least Richard and Rosanna were moving back to the Furlongs for Christmas itself; there were far too many teenagers in the house, she decided. Morad had arrived home very depressed, poor boy, by his ridiculous treatment at Milton Abbey, which he told her was a dreadful school with no good teachers. She had had to take him clothes shopping in Oxford to cheer him up. John-Spiros and Ambrosia, meanwhile, had reappeared from their father's flat with suitcases full of dirty washing ('So thoughtless! Aleco has countless maids who could have done it!'), saying they'd had a miserable time. It turned out they were utterly exhausted, having had dinner at Cecconis every night with crowds of Greeks.

Dita had a second motive for enduring the party at the Plough and Harrow. Marjorie had sent her an ingratiating notelet, decorated with a picture of a squirrel, asking whether, as Lady of the Manor, she would do the honours by cutting the ribbon and declaring the pub open. The invitation played to Dita's vanity. The satisfaction she took in her position as chatelaine of Winchford was greater than she let on. She knew she could fulfil her role better than either of Anthony's previous wives, and the ceremony would emphasise her primacy in the village. Dita spent a long time deliberating over exactly what she would wear.

It was less than five minutes' walk from Priory to pub. Anthony insisted they should all go on foot, though Santos the butler would appear later on with the Land Rover for those who wanted to be driven home. After much fussing and hunting about for coats, scarves and boots, the family set off through the dusky gloaming: Anthony and Jasmine taking the lead, Dita picking her way gingerly along the mud-spattered lane in a mink coat and tan-coloured suede boots, then Richard, Rosanna and Ambrosia, John-Spiros in his gold buttoned double-breasted blazer, and finally Morad, a brooding, sinister presence in his new black leather, knee-length Gestapo trench coat.

As they approached the pub they could see several dozen cars already parked up on the grass verge, and the little car park full to capacity. 'Well, we won't be the only people here,' Anthony said cheerfully. 'I'm so glad for Len and Marjorie there's a good turnout.'

Dita shuddered. 'I hope it won't be unbearably claustrophobic. Otherwise Santos will have to take me straight home.'

The first indication of change was the new pub signboard, swinging from a pole above the door. The old, faded painting of a Victorian horsedrawn plough pulled by two enormous cobs had been replaced by a garish acrylic cartoon of a ploughman raising a frothing tankard of ale to his lips. The little front garden, Anthony noticed with a wince, had been stripped of its lawn and a chessboard patio with giant plastic chessmen installed instead. In the old beer garden he glimpsed a purple plastic dragon, fifteen metres tall, with a yellow plastic slide erupting from its mouth in the shape of an elongated tongue. He quickly ushered Dita inside before she spotted it too.

Just inside the entrance, radiating goodwill, meaty hand outstretched, stood Len, wearing a beige woollen jerkin with tan suede patches on the shoulders and elbows.

'Tony! And Deets! Welcome, come in, come in, it's bloody freezing outside. You didn't walk, did you?'

'Actually we did. It's only a few minutes.'

'Shrewd move, Tony, shrewd move,' Len said. Then turning to address Dita, he said, 'He does like to save on his petrol, doesn't he, Deets? Every little helps, isn't that what they say? Just kidding, Tone. And here they all come, look – Richard and Rosanna. Hi there, kids. What do you think of your granddad's new gaff then? Come on in and have some punch; it'll warm you up.'

It looked to Anthony as though every living soul within a ten-mile radius of Winchford had shoehorned themselves into the Plough and Harrow. The place was heaving. As he pushed his way to the bar to fetch a drink for Dita, he saw all the farm workers from the estate, and the tenants from the cottages, and Archie who had abandoned Marshmellows for the evening to support the new venture. John Furlong, sweating and red-faced, had locked onto Percy Bigges, whose body language suggested he was itching to get away. Both Mrs Holcombe and Judy were working behind the bar. Out of the corner of his eye he spotted Nula staring in his direction, and quickly dived back into the throng. He would have to see her over Christmas, when he delivered Gaia's present, but wasn't sure he could manage it just now.

Having secured two glasses of glühwein, Anthony looked round for any sign of Dita or the children, but they were lost behind an impregnable escarpment of heaving shoulders and backs. Walter Twine was crouched over a table playing dominoes with some of the quarrymen, and Jacinthe was addressing an intimidating semi-circle of WI ladies. The party was ramping up as the mulled wine kicked in, and Anthony hoped Dita wasn't having too awful a time out there.

Dita *was* having too awful a time. Anthony had disappeared, and she couldn't spot any of her children apart from John-Spiros, who was being infuriatingly clingy and wouldn't leave her side. The pub was everything she detested: hot, smoky and full of the most dreadful-looking people. Ambrosia had sloped off somewhere with Rosanna – she hoped not to buy peanuts – and, as for Morad, she'd last seen him heading in the direction of the bar.

Most annoyingly of all, Dita had caught sight of Sandra in the mêlée, chatting to person after person and addressing a group of children dressed as choristers. It was obvious she knew everyone in the neighbourhood. Sandra was wearing a jersey embroidered with leaping lambs, which was slightly too small for her, and had an Hermès scarf knotted around her neck. Dita shuddered. She wondered whether it reflected negatively upon herself that Anthony had shown such bad taste in women in the past. Amanda, Sandra the nanny, that mad healer . . . It wasn't the nicest feeling, knowing one was following on from those three. Now, where *was* Anthony, for heaven's sake? This was all becoming rather ridiculous.

*

'Anthony?'

Anthony turned to see a dimly familiar rat-faced man with precision-styled sideburns.

'Charlie?'

'Thought I might run into you here,' Charlie Edwards said. 'I can't have been inside this place for twenty years.'

'I remember,' Anthony replied dryly. 'You were last here with my wife.'

'Shit, and I was too. I'd forgotten that. How is Amanda? You still see anything of her?'

'Sometimes. A bit.' Once again he was struck by his reluctance to discuss Amanda with Charlie. Even after so many years, it was too raw. Spotting Jasmine heading towards him through the crowd, he said, 'Charlie, meet my eldest daughter. Her mother's Amanda, by the way. Jasmine, this is Charlie Edwards. He's a big cheese in the music business, running all the rock stars – at least I think you still are, Charlie?'

Charlie smiled a twisted little smile and said, 'Hi, Jasmine. I guess I've heard about you. Yuh, you could say I'm in the music biz. I'm chairman of Plasma-Black Cat Wardoursound.'

Even Anthony, from his careful reading of the *FT*, knew that Plasma-Black Cat Wardoursound was the biggest independent record label in Europe, recently the target of a failed takeover by EMI.

'You got any plans to go into the industry?' Charlie was asking Jasmine. 'Not planning on following in Amanda's footsteps as a rock chick?'

Jasmine's eyes opened very wide. 'I'm hoping to become an actress, but I do enjoy singing too.'

'You've got the looks, anyway. You remind me of your mum.' Was it Anthony's imagination, or was Charlie leering at Jasmine? 'How's your voice?'

She shrugged. 'I'm not really sure. I've only done singing at school. I was in the choir.'

'You should come over and have a test at the studio,' Charlie said. 'We're always scouting for talent.'

Seizing his daughter by the arm, Anthony bid a hasty goodbye to Charlie and forged back into the crowd. The last thing he was going to do was let Jasmine anywhere near him. Instead they looked around the pub, absorbing Len's numerous innovations. The public bar, so far as Anthony could tell with so many people crammed inside, was mercifully unchanged, with its original Hook Norton handpumps and display of malt whiskies and briar pipes. Packets of peanuts, cashews and pork scratchings were stapled to cardboard dispensers, which gradually revealed the figure of a topless slapper as the snacks diminished. Across the crowd, Anthony could see Morad tugging off handfuls of packets at a time to cop an eyeful of the model. John-Spiros stood anxiously behind him, sucking at a bottle of Appletise through a straw.

Next door, the old private bar and snug had been transformed into a peach-tableclothed candlelit restaurant, which represented the heart of Len and Marjorie's vision. The wattle-and-beamed walls had been ragrolled a nauseous shade of salmon pink, with brass candlesticks and guttering red candles on every table, and little brass Etruscan-style vases, just wide enough to hold a single carnation and several ears of dried corn. Presiding over an enormous buffet on a salmon-pink cloth was Marjorie, whose anxious face lit up when she saw Anthony and Jasmine.

'Anthony, you don't think people are drinking too much, do you? It's becoming very rowdy through there.'

'The punch isn't that strong, is it?'

'Half wine, half orange juice with lots of cloves and spices. So it shouldn't be.'

'Probably the heat,' Anthony said reassuringly. 'People always drink more when they're hot. Once they've got something to eat they'll be fine. And look at all this amazing food!'

The lavish buffet, offering previews of all the dishes on the new Plough and Harrow menu, ran the length of the room, with platters of chicken Kiev, deep fried breaded mushrooms with garlic mayonnaise, trout with slivered almonds, dishes of coleslaw, baked potatoes in silver foil, steaks with herb butter, and an immense array of gaudy puddings, mince pies, Viennetta ice-cream cake and a half stilton.

'You must have been cooking for weeks.'

'Not all on my own,' Marjorie replied with a little laugh. 'Ginette's been up here helping, and her lovely friend Arabella. They've both been stars. I only wish they'd hurry up and find a really nice man each; they're both such wonderful homemakers.'

Still wearing his leather Gestapo coat, Morad was making his fourth successful assault on the wine punch. Waiting until Mrs Holcombe and Judy were occupied further along the bar, he slyly lifted a bottle of vodka and a bottle of cherry brandy from the shelf and sloshed the contents into the punch bowl before thrusting the empties into a bin. Then he melted into the crowd to hunt for Katie.

Ever since the incident at the swimming pool eighteen months earlier, Morad had developed an unhealthy obsession with Katie. She, in turn, had formed an equally strong aversion to him. Lately, she refused to stay at the Priory if she knew he was going to be there too. As she was telling Rosanna, 'I was trying out the shower in that new bathroom on the top floor, and suddenly had the feeling I was being watched. When I looked up, I'm convinced I saw someone at the skylight, peeping in. It was only a split second, but I think it was Morad.'

'Unless it was Dita,' Rosanna said. 'She does like to know what we're all doing. And whether we're hanging up our bathtowels. Though Mum's just as bad.'

'I wonder which is the most annoying stepmother: Dita or Sandra?' Katie replied.

'Don't be rude about my mother,' Rosanna said cheerfully. 'She's not that bad, just boring and bossy.'

'Whereas Dita's bossy and poisonous.'

'Don't you think it's rather odd,' Rosanna said, 'that my father has married so many weirdos? I mean, he's so conventional himself, but he gets married to all these nutters.'

'I wouldn't call Sandra a "nutter" exactly.'

'No, but she's not normal either. She's always in a flap about Dad, even though they've been divorced for years. And she can't stand Dita, though she pretends to really like her. I heard her talking to John about it.'

At that moment, Tom and Richard staggered up, both the worse for wear.

'Christ, that punch has a kick to it,' Tom said. 'I've only had three or four glasses and I'm flying.'

'Hello, Richard. Remember me?' An intense-looking woman with purple lipstick and an Afghan coat was peering up at him. He recognized her, with a start, as the mad lady who'd invaded the pitch during the fathers and sons match: Gaia's mother. He hadn't seen her in ages. 'Do you know where your dad is? I need a word with him.'

'Er, last time I saw him he was in the restaurant. But that was half an hour ago.'

'If you do see him, say Nula's looking for him. And she wants to move into Steepness Farmhouse now it's standing vacant.'

Anthony didn't know if it was his imagination, but half the people in the pub appeared to be drunk. Noise levels had risen intolerably. John Furlong was stumbling about, sweat running down his face, trailed by a frazzled-looking Sandra. Even Percy looked half-cut.

Rosanna and Ambrosia, under strict instructions to have only one glass of glühwein each, and no more, had just finished their second and the room was spinning about their heads. Searching for somewhere to escape from the crush, they slipped behind the bar and ran slap into Morad, furtively tipping a bottle of Cointreau into the punch.

'Morad! What *are* you doing?'

Morad winked and carried on. 'Just livening up this graveyard binge. It's Jonny Faisal's trick. He does it all the time at home in Jeddah.'

Anthony was thinking that if he didn't find Len soon and get him to start the ribbon-cutting ceremony, Dita was going to stomp off home and the audience would be too sloshed to pay attention. Last time he'd seen her she was threatening to ring Santos to come and collect her.

Eventually locating Len in the cellar, demonstrating pump hydraulics to a crowd of captive onlookers, Anthony chivvied him upstairs and went in search of his wife. To his horror, he found her locked in conversation with Nula or, more accurately, Nula drunkenly hectoring Dita. He heard her saying, 'They must have gassed forty mink to make that disgusting fur coat of yours. How would you feel about wearing dead human skin as a fashion item?'

'Obviously it would depend on the colour of the skin,' Dita replied, coldly. Appealing to Anthony, she said, 'I would be very grateful if you could do something about this tenant of yours, darling. She's being rather a pain.'

Fuelled with glühwein, Nula was spoiling for a scrap. 'I don't know how you can face yourself, with all those dead corpses hanging off you.'

Dita replied graciously, 'I'm sure the mink are having a far happier time with me coming to the opera and ballet, than skulking about in wet grass.'

'*You*,' Nula spat, 'are repulsive. Did you know that? You're a very toxic lady, covered in make-up. If you smother your face with chemicals, it seeps through and rots your aura.'

Dita's eyes swept over Nula, taking in her droopy Afghan coat.

'Beauty comes from within, you know,' Nula said.

'Yes, I can see that,' Dita replied steelily, with an angry little sneer.

Anthony thought his wife was going to hit her. 'Ignore her, Dita. We can't have a scene in here, absolutely not.' Still fuming, Dita turned her back and moved away.

A microphone had been set up in the doorway between the bar and the restaurant, and Len was looping a length of red ribbon for the Lady of the Manor to cut. Dita was at her most dangerous: tight-lipped, icily polite and ready to detonate at the slightest provocation. Anthony longed for the whole business to be over so they could all go home. 'If I'm not out of here in three minutes . . .' Dita hissed.

It took Len several attempts to obtain silence, and even now the drinkers at the back were still talking, laughing and burping. The room reeked of alcohol and the particular smell of ingrained sweat being slowly released from the underarm linings of old tweed jackets.

'Gentlemen . . . ladies . . . my lords, ladies and gentlemen . . . may I crave your attention for just a few minutes while we complete tonight's formalities . . .' Len was in his element, welcoming everyone to his village inn 'in what many consider to be the most beautiful village in England . . . not that I'm biased or anything, even if it does belong to my former son-in-law, well known to all of you, Mr Antonio Anscombe . . .' Cheers and mostly affectionate jeers rose from all sides as Anthony gave a modest half-smile and Dita, Sandra and Jacinthe sucked their teeth in pained embarrassment.

'Before I invite Tony's latest good lady, Deets Anscombe, to perform the honours, I would first like to invite the Winchford choir to perform a selection of seasonal carols, after which I'll be asking you to dig deep, ladies and gents, for a collection for the church.' Out of nowhere, a dozen children in red and white surplices began forming a semi-circle around the microphone, and were ushered into line by Sandra.

Suddenly, with a violent stamp of her foot, Dita exploded. 'This is the *final fucking straw*!' she hissed. 'Nobody told me about any choir. I am not hanging about here any longer. I'm going straight home this minute.'

Anthony touched her arm, but she shook him off. 'Did *you* know about any carol concert, Anthony?'

'Er, no, darling, but I'm sure it won't last long. It's the village choir.'

'Well, I'm not staying for it. Pay them off at once, Anthony. Give them a cheque or something.' Then, throwing her mink coat around her shoulders in a final gesture of exasperation, she marched out into the night.

As she slammed the door behind her, Anthony found himself catching Sandra's eye, and a particular look of sympathy and understanding passed between them, such as only an old married couple can ever comprehend.

41

'Dad, have you seen the dining room yet?' It was Christmas morning in Winchford and Jasmine, more beguiling than ever in an old pair of Amanda's skintight, suede britches and a velvet coat, was walking back from church with her father.

'The dining room? No, darling. Why, has the table been decorated for lunch or something?'

'You just wait,' Jasmine replied. 'You are going to be amazed.'

'Has Dita done something special? I knew she had some ideas.'

Jasmine rolled her eyes. 'Well, you could say that.'

The format of Christmas Day, their first as a family at the revamped Priory, was already a bone of contention. Dita had been strongly in favour of a lavish dinner on Christmas Eve, followed by midnight mass, which was how it had always been with Goldie. The Anscombe children were accustomed to Christmas Day lunch as the principal focus, with turkey, Christmas pudding and brandy butter, preceded by stockings, church and presents. For once Anthony prevailed, though Dita made a point of dragging her own children to a midnight service in Moreton-in-Marsh. It crossed Anthony's mind that Dita was intentionally avoiding the village church and choir, following her outburst at the Plough and Harrow.

Christmas at the Priory was different this year, and Anthony wasn't sure what he liked about it. It wasn't simply that he hadn't got used to the new layout of the house, though, even after several weeks, he still lost his way and kept doing double takes at paintings hung in the wrong places. More disappointing were the muted decorations. Dita had banned paperchains in the study, saying sellotape would mark the new paint, and even the Christmas cards were restrained. Normally they propped them up on every flat surface, or slotted them randomly between the spines of books in the library, but Dita displayed them from lengths of gold ribbon in the Great Hall, each column of cards meticulously spaced from the next. As Rosanna pointed out, 'she won't even hang half our cards up at all. She just puts the boring ones up, not the funny ones from the postman and Mrs Holcombe.' It was true, Anthony noticed, that the only cards on show this year were Medici reproductions of the Madonna and child, scenes of seventeenth-century skaters on the frozen Thames, cards from the House of Lords and from leading regiments with views of Horse Guards Parade.

Saddest of all was the Christmas tree: not their usual bushy, gaudy evergreen with all its familiar red, green and silver balls and dangling Santas, but a prinked, anorexic spruce, decorated with crystal stars and white ribbons. Jasmine complained, 'We might as well have a Japanese bonsai tree.'

Anthony did his best to raise the spirits of his disparate family, chivvying them along with goodwill and champagne. Of his own children, only Jasmine was at the Priory for Christmas lunch, along with Morad, John-Spiros and Ambrosia, and in the afternoon they would all walk over to the Old Rectory to have tea with the Furlongs and exchange presents. At some point, Anthony also intended to sneak down to Forge Cottage with his present for Gaia, and to wish Happy Christmas to Nula, not that she celebrated it. He was anxious to steer clear of the subject of Steepness Farmhouse, which the acupuncturist still had designs on, and which Dita said would become hers 'over my dead body'.

As Christmas morning unfolded, Anthony felt himself to be a children's entertainer, or a cruise ship director charged with leading the fun for a hard-to-please roster of passengers. Jasmine, so jolly on the walk from church, relapsed into a silent sulk, brought on by Dita's presents of a fawn-coloured power suit and a book of photographs of the opera. Dita, meanwhile, was delighted by the amethyst and sapphire earrings she'd chosen for herself at S.J. Phillips, and Anthony was amazed by Dita's present of four Sulka cashmere cardigans and a leather Asprey briefcase, though he didn't need a new briefcase and wondered when, if ever, he'd wear such extravagant jerseys. Morad was hunched in a corner playing with the Donkey Kong game that Father Christmas had given him in his stocking. John-Spiros had been given a cheque for £500 by Goldie, which he announced he intended to spend on shoetrees. Ambrosia was feeling suicidal, having failed to fit into any of the tight clothes Dita had bought for her, and was quietly pigging out on crystalised apricots behind a sofa. Despite Dita's new central heating system, which meant every room in the Priory was maintained at a constant thirty degrees centigrade, Anthony found himself feeling chilly in his magnificent, sterile new home.

On the dot of one fifteen, Santos the butler announced lunch was ready. Morad refused to switch Donkey Kong off, which led to a furious standoff with Dita, who snatched it from his hands and hurled it at the sofa. 'If you've broken it, you owe me a new one, *bitch,*' Morad yelled, to which Dita hissed at Anthony, 'Do something, Anthony. You're not going to allow him to speak to me like that, are you?' So Anthony told Morad not to be rude to his mother and Morad told him to F-off. All in all, it was a tense group that sat down to eat the four-course feast Regis had prepared with such elaborate care.

Anthony could see what Jasmine meant about the dining room. Meticulously arranged down the middle of the table were two dozen pomegranates, spray-painted gold, with a pyramid of ten more as a centrepiece. Little gold-rimmed placecards had been set in front of each chair, with their names written in gold ink. Anthony didn't recognise the handwriting, and guessed a professional calligrapher had been involved. The cutlery for each setting was flamboyantly tied up in pussycat bows of gold ribbon and lace.

Having got off to a bad start, there was only one direction in which things could go, and that was down. Anthony couldn't remember a more joyless Christmas lunch, even as a child. It didn't help that there was far too much food. Dita had ordered lobster and shrimp mousse as a first course, followed by a salad of braised livers, and then, instead of the turkey, chipolatas, bacon and bread sauce he had been looking forward to, there was a capercaille with juniper berries.

'Whatever happened to the turkey?' Anthony asked, as neutrally as possible, seeing the shocked disappointment on Jasmine's face.

'Oh, nobody has turkey at Christmas; it's very common,' Dita replied. 'It's not Thanksgiving.'

'Actually, I like turkey,' Anthony replied.

'Nobody *likes* turkey. It's so bland. With Goldie, we had partridge one year. Two dozen brace were flown out to Kypsos on Christmas Eve. Now that *was* rather delicious.'

Lunch having finished earlier than usual, despite all the extra courses, the Priory contingent were ahead of schedule when they arrived at the Old Rectory. The Furlongs' Christmas lunch was still in full swing, but extra chairs were soon slotted in around the big pine farmhouse table, where John and Sandra, Richard and Rosanna, Tom and Katie, Len, Marjorie and Ginette were carving second helpings from a monstrous sixteen-pound turkey. Dita surveyed the chaotic scene with something close to pain: she could hardly bear to sit at the table, with its dripping sauceboats of gravy, bowls of chestnut stuffing, half-pulled crackers, paper hats and non-matching plates of food. Everywhere were open wine bottles with random bottles of claret and Sancerre and magnums of champagne, all plonked down between the dishes of sprouts and roast potatoes.

Everyone was slightly tipsy. John was red-faced and sweating again, explaining to Len and Anthony a new business idea he'd had for selling water coolers door-to-door in Oxfordshire. Dita thought it sounded ridiculous, and hoped Anthony wouldn't become involved. Richard and Tom had clearly been drinking far more than was good for them, and were loudly competing in reading aloud cracker jokes ('Q: Why did Eve never get the measles? A: Because she'd already Adam.'). Dita hated, too, that they were eating in the kitchen at all, with its cooking smells, jeans and chinos drying on the Aga rail and a spaniel puppy curled up on the sagging sofa.

'How amusing you've chosen not to eat in the dining room on Christmas Day,' she said pointedly to Sandra.

'We did think about it,' Sandra replied, 'but it's such a cold room, and costs such a fortune to heat, John thought we'd be better off in here. Especially as it's just us this year, not anything frightfully smart.'

Dita sniffed. Ever since the ghastly evening at the Plough and Harrow, she had sensed Sandra's disapproval, which annoyed her more than it should. How absurd of Sandra to imply they couldn't afford to heat the dining room. The Furlongs were living *rent free* thanks to Anthony's generosity. They could afford to heat the entire village if they chose!

Anthony was feeling hugely better. The warmth of the kitchen, drink, goodwill and noise, were all making him feel properly Christmassy at last. Jasmine was clearly delighted to be with the others, and gales of boisterous laughter kept erupting at the children's end of the table. Ambrosia was giggling away at Tom's jokes and even John-Spiros had the ghost of a smile on his face. Len was carving himself a third helping of turkey ('just bootiful . . . a crime to waste it') and Anthony immediately said yes when Sandra offered him a plateful with roast potatoes.

'I can't believe this,' Dita exclaimed, when she spotted him. 'You can't be hungry again already.'

But Anthony wasn't eating out of hunger; he ate out of nostalgia.

'Now, did anyone get any good presents this year?' Anthony asked.

Katie immediately told him about her puppy, a present from her father and Sandra, and the eight-week-old King Charles spaniel was brought to the table to be petted and admired.

'I'm calling him Peanuts,' Katie said, 'after the cartoon.'

'Anyone else get anything good?'

'Katie and I got some great presents from our mother,' Tom said, polishing his glasses. 'She doesn't normally get round to sending anything, so it was amazing when this big parcel arrived from Argentina.'

'What did Constance send you?'

'Incredible stuff. All to do with riding: leather gaucho whips with these really long whippy ends, suede chaps, gaucho hats. I'll get them if you like.'

Tom returned with the gear, and soon everyone was buckling the long chaps over their trousers and cracking Indiana Jones whips around their heads.

'*Outside* in the passage, if you're going to play with whips,' John ordered in a slurry voice. 'Or better still the garden.'

'Anyone want coffee? Or tea? It's all here,' Sandra said. 'Or shall we go through to the sitting room and open our presents? More presents! Goodness, aren't we all so lucky.'

From one hot room to another, with its crackling log fire and home-gummed paperchains sagging from beam to beam. Armed with a black binbag, Marjorie was stuffing it with used wrapping paper, but the floor was still ankle-deep in the stuff. Richard and Tom gathered up armfuls and fed it into the fire, so whole sheets blazed up and floated around the grate. Morad had got hold of a whip and was cracking it closer and closer to John-Spiros and Katie.

'Please stop that,' Katie yelped. 'It isn't funny!'

But each time the knotted whip-end cracked nearer to Katie's arse. She clambered over the back of a sofa to put some distance between them, but Morad forged forwards – *Crack! Crack!* – sending up dust clouds from the cushions.

Now Peanuts had found his way into the sitting room and was romping about in the drifts of paper and jumping up into armchairs. Morad redirected his attention to Ambrosia – *Crack*! – who yelped in pain as the whip caught her on the thigh.

'For heaven's sake, Ambrosia, stop making such a *fuss,*' Dita scolded. 'I can't stand it when we're all cooped up like this.' Then she hissed to her husband, 'Telephone Santos to collect us now.'

Dita and her children went home for a rest before dinner, while Anthony and Jasmine lingered at the Old Rectory. After they had gone, Anthony felt even more relaxed, and settled back into one of the comfortable sofas he remembered from the early days at Steepness Farmhouse. John poured him another glass of claret, and he was enveloped by a wonderful sense of contentment. For the first time, he felt truly surrounded by joy and merriment, and realised disloyally that the heart of his family lay here, at the Old Rectory, more than at the Priory. Looking at Sandra's kind, motherly face, he found himself wondering what sort of fool he'd been all those years before in letting her go. However could he have betrayed her with Nula? It was inconceivable. He consoled himself with the thought that at least Sandra was living close by in the village, and he'd been able to help her by lending them this house. Dear Sandra! Dear old John! On Christmas afternoon, Anthony even found himself with goodwill to spare for dreary John Furlong.

'Oh no, look at the time; we've missed the Queen's speech,' Marjorie exclaimed in dismay. 'I wanted to see Princess Diana leaving church.'

'Don't worry, I'm videoing it,' John said. 'We can watch it later.'

'Oh Christ, so that's why the video timer was set,' Tom said guiltily. 'Er, Dad, I'm afraid I changed it to *You Only Live Twice* on the other side. We always video James Bond.'

'Um, actually, I'm afraid you might not have,' Katie said. 'I changed it to record Christmas Day *Top of the Pops*. The two-hour special, with all the number ones of the year.'

Anthony took the opportunity of a blazing family row to slip quietly away on his own with the presents he'd brought along for Gaia, concealed in readiness behind the coats.

Outside felt bitterly cold after the fug of the Old Rectory, and it was already pitch dark. He made his way down the little lane, gingerly at first until his eyes acclimatised to the thin, moonless light. He loved walking through the silent village at night, with the echo of his footsteps on the road. Occasionally he heard the distant bleat of a sheep on the hill, or the coughing of a cow in a field, or a muffled explosion of canned laughter from a television showing the Christmas Day *Only Fools and Horses*. The pandemonium and booze of the Old Rectory had left him with a throbbing headache.

He arrived at the door of Forge Cottage and hesitated a moment before knocking. Were it not for Gaia, whom he loved so much, he would gladly have funked it and slipped away. Inside, the cottage was completely silent, and he half hoped they might be out, and he could leave his presents on the doorstep. He could hear no television . . . but, of course, Nula refused to have one. The only sound was the gentle jangling of a windchime in a tree.

He knocked.

A few seconds later he heard the sound of running footsteps and Gaia behind the door: 'Who is it?'

'Daddy.'

'It's Daddy!' Her little voice sounded elated.

He heard a bolt being drawn, and there she was, eight years old and barefoot, hugging at his legs.

'Hello, darling. Happy Christmas!' He kissed her. 'I'm delivering your presents.'

He followed her into the sparsely furnished sitting room where he had once lived with Amanda, now decorated with Nula's acupuncture charts and ecological posters. Above the fireplace was a black and white UNESCO poster, showing a black woman's hands extending an empty wooden food bowl while her fly-covered infant stared out through huge, doleful, imploring eyes. For some reason, the baby reminded Anthony of six-month-old Jasmine when he had found her in this very room abandoned on the sofa.

Nula was sitting on that sofa now, and he stooped to kiss her on the cheek. 'So how was Christmas? Had a happy day?'

'As you know, we don't celebrate Christmas,' Nula replied. 'Why would we celebrate the birth of a cult that brought so much bigotry and persecution into the world?'

'Well, you know . . . a time for celebration and family, goodwill to all men, that sort of thing. Even if one doesn't believe in it, it's still a nice sentiment.'

Nula snorted. 'Family indeed. I like that. I'm sure you've been celebrating with all your different families. Gaia and I are at the end of the queue, waiting for the squire's annual visit.'

'Oh, that's not fair, and you know it's not. You have an open invitation to come up and swim or play tennis any time.'

'Gaia can swim if she wants to, but I am *not* swimming in a private pool. Do you realise how much water they use? Enough for a thousand Indian villages for a year. Water's a scarce resource, you know.'

Remembering how much trouble they'd had in August, bringing home the harvest in the face of torrential downpours, Anthony was unconvinced, but said nothing.

Automatically looking round for a Christmas tree beneath which to park his presents, before realising there wasn't one, he thought how sad and cheerless the cottage looked without a single scrap of tinsel or a solitary card. His own card to them (organised by Dita with a Julian Barrow oil-painting of the Priory on the front) was nowhere to be seen.

'So, what *have* you been doing all day then?' Nula asked, accusingly.

'Well, we had a quiet lunch at home, and then dropped in for tea with the Furlongs,' he replied, purposely making it sound as low-key as possible.

'God, I hate Christmas,' Nula stated. 'It's just a conspiracy by the big retailers to sell rubbish to people they don't want or need. Gaia and I celebrated the winter solstice, which is a much more ancient and pagan tradition.'

Set out on a low table was a 2000-piece wooden jigsaw with a picture of a South American rainforest, which Nula and Gaia had evidently been working on for several days. The whole border was already intact, plus most of the canopy of trees, which must have been incredibly difficult since it was one mass of foliage. On another table, where the television once sat, was a papier mâché model of an African village, with all the huts made out of birch twigs and straw.

'I don't suppose you have an aspirin?' Anthony asked Nula.

'What do *you* think? Would I support an irresponsible pharma multinational? If you've got a headache, you should press your temples with your thumbs, just above the meridian.' Then she laughed, and said, 'Come on, I'll do it for you. Sit on the settee then.'

So Anthony sat down and closed his eyes while Gaia looked on excitedly, watching her mother doing something kind for her father for once. Slowly but firmly, Nula massaged his scalp, pressing on the acupuncture points, and the pain began to dissipate into a fuzzy, swirling numbness.

Gaia was curled up next to him on the sofa, holding his hand, and Anthony closed his eyes and did his best to relax. The silence inside the cottage was total: he couldn't hear a single sound – not the ticking of a clock nor, for once, the electronic bleeps and grunts from Morad's toys. It was the first time in months he'd known such absolute peace. After the tension of Christmas lunch at the Priory, and the noisy chaos of the Old Rectory, there was something wonderfully appealing about this simple, innocent scene. Sitting in this tiny stone-built cottage on Christmas night, having his head massaged by sympathetic hands . . . He felt his eyes begin to droop, as Nula pressed deeper and deeper on his Qi zones. He couldn't help thinking she had a point about the commercialisation of Christmas. All that elaborate food (he felt sick at the memory of the lobster and shrimp mousse), all that drink, all those presents; when was he ever going to wear *four* Sulka cashmere cardigans, for goodness' sake? Wasn't this visit to Forge Cottage the closest he'd got all day to the true spirit of Christmas, to the stable in Bethlehem? His heart went out to Gaia, thinking of her hunched over the jigsaw fitting all those fiddly bits of rainforest together. How sweetly innocent it was. He could hardly imagine Morad bothering with a jigsaw, or Richard or Rosanna, come to that.

For forty-five minutes his thoughts moved in this way until, very softly, Nula murmured that the treatment was finished, and she slipped away to fetch him 'a beaker of water'. He turned to his daughter with shining eyes and said, 'That was incredible. Your mother's brilliant at massage.'

'I know,' Gaia replied. 'She gives me two treatments every week, and I'm the only person in my whole class who's never missed one day of school this term being sick.'

Nula returned from the kitchen with the water, and Gaia asked Anthony whether it was OK for her to open her presents now. He handed her the three parcels he'd wrapped on Christmas Eve with Jasmine's help. Dita's social secretary had gift-wrapped the majority of the presents this year, but Anthony hadn't felt like discussing Gaia's presents with Dita, so had done it all himself on the quiet.

Watching his daughter unwrapping them, he wondered whether he hadn't made some terrible choices. Nula was sure to disapprove. He almost felt he was contaminating the cottage with his gifts. Gaia opened the biggest parcel first and was thrilled with the bubblegum-pink sequinned cardigan. Slyly, he glanced in Nula's direction. She rolled her eyes at him and read out 'Made in Sri Lanka' from the label. But then she laughed and said, 'OK, Gaia, don't worry, you can wear it. If you want to look exactly like everyone else at school parties, you can.'

Gaia opened the second and third parcels and was now staring uncertainly at the junior Walkman, not really knowing what it was. Anthony put in the batteries for her, and showed her how the headset fitted over her ears. Then he explained about Bananarama, and the *Now That's What I Call Music* tapes he had also given her. Gaia said she'd heard about Banarama already at school, but didn't have a favourite, having neither heard their music nor seen them on TV.

Anthony was soon doing his best to brief her about Banarama's music, and wishing Rosanna or Katie were there to help. When he'd finished, Nula said, 'You, Anthony, are a very wicked man. And I'll tell you another thing, I am *not* buying new batteries for that contraption, because batteries are non-biodegradable and poisoning the planet. So if you really want Gaia to turn into a moron listening to pop rubbish all day long, you'll have to buy them yourself, understood?' But she said it in a tone Anthony interpreted as generally affectionate.

'You know something, I've been thinking about that farmhouse,' he said as he was about to leave. 'I'd be very happy if you and Gaia would still like to take it over.'

Nula looked astonished. 'But I thought your new wife had banned us?'

'It isn't her decision,' Anthony replied sternly. 'It's mine. And I'm asking you whether you'd like Steepness Farmhouse. I'm sure the estate can provide transport and so on to help you move in.'

42

One breakfasttime at the Priory, Jasmine, who had come home for a weekend from drama school, said, 'There's something I wanted to tell you, Dad. I've been approached by a model agency.'

Instinctively suspicious, Anthony looked up from his newspaper. 'What agency? When did all this happen?'

'Last week. I was in Covent Garden, doing some shopping with Tanya from college, and this lady kept staring at me.'

'Huh, probably a fucking lesbian,' Morad said. 'Half the women in London are dykes.'

'She came over and gave me her card,' Jasmine went on. 'She seemed really nice. She asked whether I was a model already, and when I said no, she said I have great bone structure and am the right height and everything to be one.'

Morad sniggered. 'Come off it; your tits are pathetic. No way.'

'It's not that sort of modelling, actually, Morad. It's a really good agency. They represent all the supermodels for glossy magazines.'

'Yeh, *right*,' Morad said. 'Magazines like *Club International*, more like.'

Jasmine handed the card to her father, who looked at it and shrugged. 'The Lightning Agency. Well, it doesn't mean anything to me, darling, but then it wouldn't. I must say, I have my doubts.'

'The lady said I could bring my mum or dad along when I go to see them. Shall I ask Amanda?'

Thinking he didn't entirely trust his first wife's judgement, Anthony said that, no, he would prefer to come himself one evening after work, if Jasmine was really sure she wanted to follow it up. 'You don't want to do modelling, do you?'

'Dad, come on, get real. *Everyone* wants to be a model.'

Dita, who didn't regard Jasmine as nearly well groomed enough to model, said, 'Personally, I'd be very cautious. And I don't know that modelling is particularly fun, in any case.'

But Jasmine was adamant, and the following week Anthony found himself meeting her on the pavement in Brewer Street, Soho, where Lightning was situated in a first-floor walk-up. To his surprise, the agency was more reputable than he'd expected, with smoked glass doors everywhere, and chrome and corduroy sofas, and headshots and showcards of the models they represented on the walls. Jasmine said she recognised loads of them, including Adrianna Wonaçek, the Polish supermodel, and Kinshasa, a beautiful-looking African.

Anthony and Jasmine had a long talk with the talent scout who had spotted her in Covent Garden, and Anthony had to admit he was rather reassured. Soon they were discussing Jasmine's portfolio, and he found himself feeling proud, as Jasmine's father, when the booker went on and on about what a great-looking girl she was and her enormous potential. 'There's huge demand at the moment for these young English faces,' she said. 'You'll need a better haircut, but we can organise that for you.'

By the time they'd finished Anthony had agreed Jasmine could work at putting a portfolio together, and that, providing it didn't interfere with her drama course, she could take on the occasional modelling assignment, if any came up. It was in celebratory mood that father and daughter had supper together at an Italian trattoria close to the agency, and Anthony was again reminded how similar Jasmine looked to her mother at the same age. He loved having dinner *à deux* with her, finding they could talk easily about anything and everything, with the sole exceptions of Dita and Amanda. It was tacitly understood Dita's name would never be mentioned between them, and Anthony had long ago ceased trying to turn his wife and daughter into friends. As for Amanda, he hardly dared ask about her, in case he revealed too much interest, but sometimes Jasmine let slip a detail: such as Amanda's loneliness in London, or how she was missing her younger daughter since custody had been awarded to Patrice by the French courts.

Jasmine's modelling career took off instantly. The first week she did a sitting for *i-D* magazine, in which she looked like a teenage heroin addict curled up in a foetal position on a stained mattress. Dita pronounced the pictures 'utterly ridiculous and quite revolting. There isn't one single item of clothing I could possibly wear.' The following month she appeared in *Vogue* as part of a feature about new, very young, washed out, posh, bohemian English girls. Dita found it increasingly tiresome being asked at cocktail parties whether Jasmine was her stunning daughter. The next month, Jasmine was booked for advertising campaigns by Calvin Klein and Diesel jeans. The next month, she appeared on sixty-four-sheet posters advertising a new French fragrance with a phallic-shaped bottle. The next month, she was given the starring role in a low-budget movie about the life of a teenage heroin addict who becomes a model, and the resultant publicity meant features in every newspaper and colour supplement in the country. These included a joint mother-and-daughter interview with Amanda in 'Relative Values' in *The Sunday Times,* in which Amanda talked a great deal about her movie, *La Lune et Le Soleil Noir,* and her recording career, and Jasmine talked about spending weekends with her father at Winchford.

There was no mention of Dita in the interview, who took it as a personal insult and directed all her anger at poor Anthony.

43

An indication of the degree to which Anthony's life with Dita had altered beyond recognition was their joint inclusion, for the first time, in *Tatler's* annual list of 'The 100 Most Invited Partygoers in Britain', entering the charts at number sixty-three. A prominent photograph of them clutching champagne glasses at a preview at the Fine Art Society appeared with the commentary: 'New Entry! Lofty multi-million-aire financier Anthony, 43, scion of the eponymous über-private family merchant bank, and Dita, 42, striking busy-bee chatelaine of their two-thousand-acre Winchford estate in Oxfordshire, complete with medieval minstrel's gallery, recently made over by society decorator Carina Res-nick (see number 78). Handsome, three-times married Anthony is father to waif supermodel *du jour* Jasmine by first wife Amanda "Remember, remember" Bouillon, ex-squeeze of French movie heart-throb Patrice. Dita was previously hitched to perma-tanned billionaire ship owner Aleco "Goldie" Emboroleon. Kill for: a weekend invitation to Winchford Priory (ask for the Assize Chamber with Nina Campbell draped four-poster). Find them in: Chelsea, Oxfordshire, Gstaad, New York.'

When Anthony saw himself spread all over the magazine, his first re-action was one of overwhelming embarrassment. Having been brought up to maintain the lowest possible personal profile, and having always tried to avoid publicity, he felt almost sick at the thought of anyone in the village reading it. 'Multi-millionaire financier' – the words made him blush. What if the Biggeses somehow came across a copy? Or Sandra and John? Or, worst of all, Mrs Holcombe or Nula! And then he won-dered whether his uncle and aunt, Michael and Bridget, might somehow chance upon it at the dentist. Surely it was unlikely. He couldn't believe many people saw *Tatler*.

Dita was remarkably sanguine about the whole thing. Shrugging, she said that she and Aleco had been included on the list for ten years, and her only regret was that she'd slipped thirty places since marrying Anthony. 'One year they put us in at number twenty-something, ahead of Sunny and Rosita Marlborough,' she said pointedly.

'Ah well, at least nobody will see it; that's what I'm relying on,' Anthony said.

'Whatever do you mean, "nobody will see it"? What an absurd remark! Really, Anthony, of course everyone will see it. Everybody gets *Tatler*. Truly, you say the stupidest things sometimes.'

Arriving at the bank on Monday morning, Anthony's PA, Charlotte, said, 'I saw you in *Tatler* at the weekend. Nice picture.'

Anthony frowned.

At lunch in the partners' dining room, the company secretary said, 'My wife showed me a very dashing photograph of you, Anthony, in some glossy magazine.'

Anthony grunted non-committally.

'Indeed there was,' agreed Michael Anscombe. 'Bridget takes that frightful rag at home. She's always about to stop it, but she likes the bridge column. Yes, you *are* getting about, aren't you, Anthony? Do you socialise every single night of the week?'

'Not at all. Actually, I rather dislike going out. But Dita enjoys it, so needs must.'

'I don't know how you have the energy,' Michael said, 'not after a full day's work. Personally, I'm more than ready for bed after the *Ten o'clock News*.'

'Well, we are trying to have more evenings in. Dita's much firmer about saying no to things.'

Were this true, then Dita was firmer only at saying no to dinners which directly clashed with better dinners they had already accepted. As soon as she had signed off the final renovations at the Priory she felt free to spend less time down there during the week, and instead resumed her ceaseless circuit of London parties. Anthony, increasingly knackered, did his best to keep up.

To make matters worse, the more parties they went to, the more invitations they received. Their inclusion on the *Tatler* list ensured their addition to dozens of new databases belonging to PRs, fundraisers and party organisers. The tsunami of invitations was almost overpowering, and had Dita not now employed an effective social secretary, who arrived each morning at Cadogan Place to sift through the post, they might very well have drowned under the force of it all.

Not that Anthony had lost his curiosity for the ever-more-glamorous events to which they were invited. Like a nun who has passed twenty years of her life in a convent, and then discharged herself into a world of frivolity, he had a convert's passion for high society, in small doses anyway. He understood, too, that his relationship with Dita was most successful when she was busy. It was when she didn't have enough to do, or felt trapped in uncongenial social situations, that she became testy and impatient. The secret of success in their marriage lay in maintaining a high level of diversion and fun. Most weekends Winchford was filled with guests, carefully stratified into shooting weekends, business weekends and non-shooting/cultural parties. On weekdays, Dita became stir-crazy unless they looked in on two or three events every night.

Parties offered a distraction, too, from the escalating issue of Morad, who had been expelled from Millfield. Although Anthony was never able to establish precisely what had happened, amidst all the conflicting accounts, it was rumoured that Morad had been running some sort of pimp racket at the school, in which the daughter of a minister for the Cameroons and a cousin of the president of Equatorial Guinea, both fellow pupils, had been offering blow-jobs to completion for a fiver a time. Whatever the reason, Millfield booted him out, Dita was enraged, and Morad full of shifty protestations of innocence. Against this background, Anthony was only too relieved to get out of the house to a good party.

One summer evening in June, in a month already so social that Anthony felt numb with exhaustion, they went to a preview of the Chelsea Flower Show, followed by an enormously swanky dinner in a marquee in the Chelsea Physic Garden given by Cartier. Dita was in her element, the four hundred other guests being very much 'her' set, and she breezed from group to group, issuing invitations to come and stay at Winchford. Anthony noticed the social and banking heavy brigade were out in force, perambulating between beds of rare plants and clusters of waiters holding trays of champagne. More adept than he once was at identifying his fellow guests, he recognised several Rothschilds, the Conrad Blacks, the Rothermeres and the tycoon Marcus Brand, plus the young Agnellis, Prince Andrew and several prominent racehorse owners. They were about to sit down to dinner, and were circling their tables searching for their places, when he spotted a familiar, strikingly beautiful face in the throng: *Amanda*. He gulped. Could it really be her? She looked sexier than she had in years.

Dita and Anthony had been placed at a table close to the centre of the tent, betokening social gravitas and also, Anthony supposed, recognition of the size of Dita's Cartier account. In the early days of their marriage, he had questioned why Dita needed an account at the jeweller at all. 'After all, darling, it will just be me buying you things for your birthday, won't it?' But Dita protested she had always had an account at Cartier, and Goldie had never questioned it, so the account remained. Remembering that far-off dispute, Anthony now wondered how he'd ever dared challenge the account at all. He had been naïve in those days about the cost of maintaining a wife like Dita. At the time, even the £40,000 flower bill for their wedding had shocked him.

Sitting between a lardy landowning earl and a flirtatious Italian banker with a Roman title, Dita was content, knowing both of them already and appreciating the placement. Anthony, meanwhile, scanned the tent for Amanda. For a long time he couldn't spot her; there were so many tables. Adjacent to their own was the table of Cartier's managing director, a seductive-looking Frenchman named Arnaud Bamberger, seated between the Duchess of Marlborough and the Begum Aga Khan. Eventually, at a table close to the end wall, he saw her. It was definitely Amanda, no question about it, and on the same table as . . . *Jasmine*, in a tiny silver cocktail sheath sewn with sequins and pearls. It was all rather extraordinary: what were his ex-wife and eldest daughter doing at a Cartier dinner?

Dozens of white-jacketed waitresses from the Admirable Crichton catering company, each handpicked for their youth and beauty, were weaving through the tables with the first courses, a sashimi of swordfish and tuna.

'Anthony?'

Anthony turned round to see Katie Furlong in a white Nehru jacket delivering his plate of sashimi.

'Katie? What on earth are you doing here?'

'Waitressing. Attempting to clear my overdraft.'

'Good for you. I hope they're being nice to you. And Katie – help me. I've just spotted Jasmine, which is another nice surprise. Any idea what she's doing here?'

'Oh, they always invite a few starlets to Cartier dinners, apparently. Whoever's hot that year. She's brought her mum along as her date, which is sweet.'

Anthony craned his neck for another look at Amanda, but instead locked eyes with Dita who was frowning disapprovingly at him for chatting up a waitress.

He was seated next to a Mrs Charlie Crieff – Miranda – whom he'd met before with her pompous stockbroker husband. Miranda was the ideal dinner companion, capable of talking about herself and her summer plans without a prompt for hours at a stretch; which gave Anthony brain-space to ruminate on Amanda.

Seeing her again across the marquee made him realise how much he'd missed her. It was like hearing an old, favourite song that you hadn't listened to for a long, long time, and discovering it retained all its original power to move. Ever since her suicide attempt, Anthony had made a conscious decision to steer clear of her. Lex called her 'trouble with a capital T', and of course he was right; Anthony doubted Dita would be so forgiving over a second Amanda episode.

And yet . . . her presence in the tent made him dizzy with lust. Miranda Crieff was telling him about a villa they were taking in Tuscany for the whole of August, and how she was worried about the cook, and how Charlie's billionaire godfather Marcus Brand might come to stay, but Anthony could think only of Amanda. He longed for dinner to be over so he could slip away and speak to her.

Under the pretext of looking for a lavatory, he approached her table. 'Jasmine, darling! How lovely to see you . . . and *Amanda*.' Gingerly, he kissed his first wife.

'Ant!' She seemed genuinely pleased to see him, and unusually healthy. 'I thought I might find you here: the sixty-third most invited man in Britain!'

'Oh, that.' Anthony winced.

'Yes, that. Well, you never invite *me* to anything these days. According to that article, I'm supposed to ask for the Assize Chamber.'

'We should do something. Want to have lunch one day?'

'Why lunch? So you don't have to tell your wife you've seen me?'

Anthony blushed. 'No. Just that lunch is easier. How about tomorrow?'

'Can't. I'm having lunch with Charlie. Charlie Edwards.'

'*Charlie Edwards*? I thought you two lost touch years ago.'

'We re-met.' Amanda gave him a long stare. 'Charlie likes lunch too.'

Anthony wanted to say something, but sensed a presence behind him, bearing down hard. Dita.

'Good evening, Jasmine. Good evening, Amanda. I hope you've both had an enjoyable evening, hidden away over here.' She studied the place-cards on either side of them, reassuring herself they were on a dud table. 'Now, come along Anthony; it's time to go,' she said sharply. 'Some of us have things to get up for tomorrow morning.'

44

Partly as a solution for keeping Morad occupied, since no school or crammer would rise to the challenge, Anthony started a paintballing venture at the top end of the estate, in the bluebell woods beyond the cricket club. John Furlong was full of misgivings about the project, saying it would make a ghastly racket and attract exactly the wrong type of people to Winchford, but Anthony would not be deterred. He was keen to experiment in diversifying from farming into leisure, and paintballing was the new big thing. Furthermore, it would be a neat way of providing Morad with something to do, miles from London and out of doors, at which he could surely stay out of trouble.

Soon a pseudo-military club hut was built in a clearing in the woods, draped in netting and camouflage, and a hundred paintzapping guns and helmets procured, as well as scores of pairs of khaki overalls. The whole enterprise was placed under the supervision of Judy Holcombe's latest boyfriend, a burly ex-SAS sergeant named Chalkie Cliff, with Morad acting as one of his two sidekicks.

Right from the word go, Winchford Paintballing was a colossal success. Soon it was booked up weeks in advance, not only at weekends but midweek too. Rugby clubs, stag parties, salesmen from car dealerships, people were travelling from as far away as Stroud and Brackley to chase about in Winchford woods, strafing each other with paint-filled bullets. Hides and platforms were erected in trees, and the warfare zones enlarged again and again, until often there were more than a hundred and fifty people playing at one time, and even John had to accept it had become the most profitable activity on the estate, ahead even of the pheasant shoots.

Anthony got an immense kick from it all. Before they opened to the public for business, he organised a series of paintballing days for his friends, and Lex and Archie, Mark Plunkett, Bongo Nall-Caine and Beano Elliot arrived to play against a home team of Anthony, Richard, Tom, Len, Morad, Rosanna, Katie and Ambrosia plus several sharpshooters from the farm. From the Priory, only John-Spiros decided it wasn't his sort of thing. Jasmine, as so often these days, was away on a modelling assignment in Antigua.

Dita declared she had not the remotest interest in paintballing, and looked annoyed whenever Anthony mentioned its existence to her smart weekend guests. It particularly exasperated her when the most unexpected people, including a lecturer on boule furniture from the Courtauld Institute and a fabrics editor of *Architectural Digest,* both insisted on having a go, turning up again at the Priory after tea covered in slime-green paint. On the sole occasion Dita was persuaded to inspect the encampment at lunchtime, she was horrified by the frankfurter sausages and beans being served up in styrofoam boxes by Chalkie Cliff, and didn't eat a thing.

As a strategy for keeping Morad on the straight and narrow, initially at least it worked brilliantly. Chalkie Cliff, covered in tattoos and a veteran of the Falklands war, took no nonsense from Morad, keeping him busy from dawn to dusk. Some Saturdays the punters were firing off thirty to forty thousand rounds between them, at twelve quid a hundred, and Morad had his work cut out keeping them all in ammo, racing from battlezone to battlezone in a John Deere Gator.

Although the paintballing was generally viewed as a good thing by the inhabitants of Winchford, it was not universally approved of. Amongst its greatest supporters was Len, whose takings at the Plough and Harrow increased dramatically as the paintballers gravitated there afterwards. Percy Bigges was another fan; unsteady on his feet these days, he had himself driven to a treetop hide with a gun and store of ammo. His accuracy over three hundred yards was remarkable.

Opposition was led by Sandra, who complained that one of her favourite walks had been ruined. Accustomed to exercising her retrievers in the bluebell woods, she was now 'in fear of my life from these ghastly bullets. And the dogs go mad. They think it's a shoot.' However often Anthony explained that they never paintballed near the footpaths, she was not reassured.

Further opposition came from Nula, who was filled with compassion for the poor birch trees, being hit all day long by bullets. She felt a pain in the pit of her stomach, she told Anthony, whenever she saw their silver bark daubed with green paint.

It was towards the end of the fourth month of paintballing that the trouble started. Sandra was walking her retrievers, Thatcher and Tebbit, along the footpath that skirted the woods, several hundred yards from the boundary of the battlezones. Suddenly, with a sickening thud, a paintball caught Thatch full on her flank, exploding over her coat in a splatter of paint. The gun dog yelped and shot off across the fields.

Sandra turned up at the Priory, demanding an apology and help in finding Thatcher, who had disappeared. Anthony and Richard spent the next four hours striding across the fields calling for her before she finally turned up back at the Old Rectory, coat matted with the incriminating paint.

What was inexplicable was that no one had been paintballing anywhere near the footpath at the time. The battlezone had been at the opposite end of the woods. As for the guns, all unallocated ones were kept securely under lock and key. Anthony felt utterly embarrassed, and knew it had damaged the image of the venture. What bugged him was that he didn't understand how it could possibly have happened.

A fortnight later Katie was walking along the same footpath with Peanuts. This time it was a Thursday afternoon, and the paintballing had been block-booked by a private party of Thistle Hotels trainee managers, as part of a group bonding and development programme. Chalkie was lecturing them on safety procedures at the time the incident happened.

Katie and Peanuts were returning from a long circuit of the estate, which had taken them right across the valley below the Priory and up as far as the top woods. It was half term from St Mary's, Calne, where Katie had just entered the sixth form, thanks to Anthony who offered to pick up the fees. It was one of those unpredictable May afternoons when the weather changes from sunshine to milky haze from minute to minute, and the clouds of blue butterflies and purple hairstreaks that inhabited the downland appeared and disappeared with the sun. Peanuts was scampering on ahead on a retractable lead, since Katie didn't quite trust him not to chase sheep.

Katie thought she saw a movement from the undergrowth, rapidly followed by the crack of a rifle. She felt a jolt on the lead and Peanuts leapt in agony, covered in green paint. A couple of seconds later there was a second shot, this time to his head. As she raced forward to help him, she saw, or thought she saw, a dark-haired figure running off into the woods.

This time, the post-mortem was exhaustive and prolonged. The murder of a small dog by someone using a paintball gun at such short range was almost unbelievable, and mortifying for all concerned. Katie was demented by grief, and the little burial service organised by Arabella and Ginette in the garden of the Old Rectory was one of the saddest imaginable, with the vicar and half the village gathered to sing 'All Things Bright and Beautiful' and 'Bright Eyes' from Watership Down.

Anthony and John Furlong spent hours interviewing anyone and everyone who had been within half a mile of the woods that afternoon. Chalkie could vouch for the trainee hoteliers, none of whom had left his supervision, and all the guns were fully accounted for. John started to construct a theory that Peanuts might have been shot by a wandering lunatic, but no one bought into this convenient solution.

It was when they tried to establish the whereabouts of Chalkie's assistants that an alternative culprit emerged. Where, precisely, had Morad been all afternoon? Confronted on the subject, he was evasive and petulant, claming to have been in places that were easily disproved. Anthony, with sinking heart, became convinced it could only have been Morad. Certainly he matched Katie's description of the fleeing gunman.

Having no cast-iron proof, they did not call in the police. Instead, with a reluctance borne only of knowing how angry Dita would be with him, Anthony dismissed Morad from Winchford Paintballing. Still half-heartedly protesting his innocence, Morad sped off in the Gator in the direction of the Priory, to complain to his mother.

By the time Anthony arrived home, Dita was totally on Morad's side. 'Are you quite mad, Anthony, sacking poor Morad for no reason at all? He promises me he had nothing to do with that damn dog's death, and I believe him. A mother can always tell.'

Fed up with Morad and annoyed with Dita for always defending him, Anthony refused to back down and they had the biggest, most blazing row of their marriage. 'For heaven's sake, Morad's completely out of control. He'll end up in prison if he goes on like this.'

'You're a fine one to talk,' Dita spat back. 'Your first wife's a fruitcake, probably on drugs and pretending to commit suicide all the time. Your second one has a father who's actually *been* to prison. Yes, he has – in France, for reneging on his gambling debts. I know all about it. Sandra's husband is a virtual bankrupt. Jasmine's up to God-only-knows-what half the time. And you have the nerve to pick on poor Morad.'

Speechless with exasperation and not wanting to escalate the row any further, Anthony slipped away to the swimming pool. Fifty lengths later he started to calm down; the combination of the eighty-seven-degree water and the solitude of the walled garden began to work its magic.

Then Morad appeared at the pool, already changed for swimming. Anthony cursed silently. The last person he wanted to see was his stepson.

Morad padded to the end of the diving board and stood there for a moment, looking around. Then, slowly and deliberately, he manoeuvred his penis from the leg of his trunks and began peeing into the pool. As he peed, he shifted his aim from side to side, so the flow splashed across the surface in a wide arc. The urine coagulated in a yellow mist in the water, before dissolving into the greater mass. When he had finished, he slowly tucked himself back inside his trunks, smirked at Anthony, then disappeared in the direction of the house.

That night, for the first time, Anthony wondered whether he hadn't made a dreadful mistake in marrying Dita, and whether it would ruin him financially to leave her.

After another almighty blazing row, he thanked his lucky stars that at least they'd not had children together.

45

Two events now happened in rapid succession that transformed Anthony's life. Dita announced she was pregnant, and Anthony became chairman of Anscombes, following the long-overdue retirement of his uncle Michael.

The news about the baby at once pushed away any thoughts of leaving his wife, and he threw himself into the task of becoming a father for the fifth time at the age of forty-five. If he were honest, he did feel rather daunted, and even slightly foolish, at the prospect of starting all over again, and half of the handover speeches at Michael's leaving dinner included sly jokes about nappy-changing and midnight feeds. Dita took the whole thing in her stride, declaring she would be giving birth at the Portland Hospital in London ('I would *never* trust a country hospital') and Carina was hired to decorate appropriate baby and nanny bedrooms at Winchford and in Cadogan Place.

Despite having covertly called the shots at Anscombes for almost ten years, Anthony found the transition to senior partner and chairman more taxing than he'd anticipated, and he spent the first six months reorganising the internal structure of the bank. Several non-productive partners, including more than one cousin, were discreetly pensioned off, and half a dozen new, more aggressive executives brought in from outside. All of this was considered highly controversial in a family bank like Anscombes, and there was much diplomatic manoeuvring to ensure they all integrated smoothly. Dita complained that he arrived home much too late these days, but she was realistic about the investment banking world, and Anthony found her a shrewd sounding board. When he hesitated before dismissing a loyal but dozy colleague, Dita stiffened his resolve. 'If you want to turn Anscombes into something top division, you have no option.' During these early months, despite her pregnancy, Dita and her social secretary organised half a dozen work dinners at Cadogan Place, and in the private room at Annabel's and the Walbrook Club in the City, to mark the arrival or departure of significant colleagues.

Anthony increasingly felt he did not have a single minute, from one week to the next, to call his own. Every waking moment was filled with meetings, speeches, lunches and obligations at work, to Dita, to his children and to the farm. Twice a week his PA, his wife and John Furlong's part-time secretary at the estate office conducted a telephone conference in which they carved up his diary, planning his every move months in advance. Often Anthony felt he was the only person in his life not to be consulted on anything. He found it oddly depressing and almost suffocating to know that on Saturday 26 January – three months ahead – he would be shooting pheasants with a minor Italian count, then flying to Davos for the World Economic Forum, then straight home for Ambrosia's school play at Wycombe Abbey followed by a house party of guests at Winchford. He worried he was paying too little attention to his children, and far too little attention to the village. Jasmine he had hardly clapped eyes on for eighteen months. She spent weeks at a time these days in New York, where her new model agency was based. She had given up on drama school, but this hadn't stopped her from getting a string of small parts in movies, and a starring role as Cordelia in a Fringe production of King Lear in which she appeared stark naked, much to her father's embarrassment, though not apparently to hers. Richard, meanwhile, was struggling academically at Radley, and his forecasted grades at A-level were unlikely to get him a place at university. Anthony was recommending a course at Cirencester Agricultural College, since he would one day inherit Winchford, but Richard wasn't showing much enthusiasm, and wanted to go to Val D'Isère as a ski bum. Rosanna had her own problems: hating Dita, bored by school, and increasingly hanging out with rougher elements in the village. These days her 'best mates', as she put it, were Chalkie, the paintballing boss, and a pair of mechanics from Winchford Autoparts on the A44, Darren and Scotty, with whom she spent as much time as possible in the Plough and Harrow. As for Gaia, she had started secondary school in Moreton, and was as sweet and bright as ever. Anthony had raised the prospect of paying for her to go to a private school, but Nula wouldn't hear of it, saying she didn't want her daughter turning into a snob.

Tom continued to dazzle at everything he turned his hand to. An Oppidan Scholar at Eton, he won prizes for maths, history and Cantonese, and had recently been made captain of his house. He won colours for every minor sport from racquets to fives, each necessitating special jerseys, scarves and caps, all of which Anthony ended up paying for. John Furlong had joined a terrorist cell of Lloyd's names, refusing to pay his underwriting debts but losing case after case in the courts and running up legal fees larger than the original bill. Sandra confessed to Anthony she thought they would never be able to afford to leave the Old Rectory, and would he consider installing a tennis court, since she didn't like playing up at the Priory with Dita there.

Sandra also approached Anthony about giving Tom work experience at Anscombes over the summer holidays. Recently, it seemed like every teenager in Britain was looking for an internship. Some months he received half a dozen letters, all from old friends beginning, 'My lovely daughter Candida, whom you haven't seen for far too long, is in the sixth form at St Mary's, Wantage . . .' Already they'd had a young Nall-Caine and a Plunkett working in the mailroom.

When he looked reluctant at the prospect of Tom joining the growing band of surplus teenagers hanging about the bank, Sandra was insistent. 'I really don't think it's that much to ask, Anthony. Tom's awfully bright, and you *are* the chairman. You'd be lucky to have him. Anyway, it'll be good for him to see what it's like, in case he wants a full-time job with you after university.'

Dragging himself home to Winchford on Friday nights, rest was out of the question. Two weekends out of three, Dita continued to fill the house with guests, undeterred by her swelling pregnancy. If anything, the impending arrival of a fourth child increased her energy levels to new heights. Her Saturday-night dinner parties became larger and more magnificent, with ever grander wines. According to *Town & Country*, the American society magazine, Winchford Priory was now 'the most comfortable private mansion in the United Kingdom' and an invitation 'as sought-after as an overnighter at neighbouring Highgrove House'. The guest bedrooms at the Priory, it was widely agreed, provided a level of comfort and service greater than that of any country house hotel. Visitors were, of course, unpacked for, and clothes creased from the journey automatically removed for pressing. A discreet printed card on each dressing table announced, 'If you require any laundry or mending during your stay, please press 7 on your telephone.' While guests were downstairs at dinner, a bevy of maids tidied every room and dried the inside of the bathtubs with towels. The four-poster beds, with their masses of frills and ruching, glazed cabbage rose valances, down-filled eiderdowns and dozens of bow-covered show-pillows, took twenty minutes to remake to the required standard. For the boot room, Dita bought forty pairs of Royal Hunter wellingtons in varying sizes from one to fourteen, for visitors who forgot their own.

Dita also had strong views on china. As a present for becoming chairman, Dita commissioned for her husband an enormous dinner service with the Anscombe coat of arms hand-painted on every plate. So valuable, so fragile were these plates that they could never be eaten off; instead, they were placed before each guest when they first sat down, but quickly whisked away to be replaced by other, less precious china. Princess Michael of Kent, when she came over from Nether Lypiatt for dinner, declared she had never in her life seen such beautiful pieces, not even in St Petersburg. Archie got into trouble with Dita for picking up a plate and pretending to drop it on the floor before catching it again just in time.

Frequently Dita's Saturday night parties went on until two o'clock in the morning, especially when one of her musical contacts from the Festival Hall could be persuaded to play the piano after dinner. At church the next morning Anthony often felt totally washed out, and was worried he might still be slightly drunk as he read the lesson. When Dita announced her big idea of starting a country house opera festival at Winchford, like the ones at Garsington and Trafalgar Park, Anthony did his best to discourage her without provoking a scene. There was no question about it, his weekends were even more exhausting than the working week. By Sunday night he was generally too tired to eat or talk and went to bed at nine o'clock, to grab some sleep before the dawn commute from Kingham. Dita sat up in bed beside him, filling in her leatherbound Smythson dinner party book, in which she recorded the placements for all their dinner and lunch parties, as well as the menus and precisely what she had worn on each occasion. She had a phobia about being seen twice in the same dress, so carefully choreographed her appearances in Hardy Amies, Bruce Oldfield and her favourite, the dignified couture house of Saint-Simone de Paris, where she had been a customer of Hubert de Saint-Simone for twenty years.

In one area only was Dita a reluctant hostess, and that was in having the friends of Anthony's children to stay. Jasmine was away too often to care, but Richard wanted to ask several of his Radley rugby set for the night and to invite some girls too. Dita went out of her way to make things difficult, paging through her diary saying, 'No, that weekend's out – we have a houseful already, and that one's no good either; it's Chelten-ham Gold Cup week.'

Eventually, at Anthony's insistence, a date was agreed. Richard was allowed to ask six friends to the Priory, though Dita insisted that they could arrive no earlier than lunchtime on Saturday and had to leave immediately after Sunday lunch. Anthony offered to cook lunch for them all outside on the barbecue, to prevent them from wrecking the house. The whole of Saturday afternoon would be spent paintballing or, in the event of rain, watching videos in an outhouse, where a TV was specially installed. When Richard's friends were dropped off at the Priory, Anthony welcomed the three beefy young men and three rather plain girls who appeared with their rucksacks, trainers and jeans, and took them up to the top floor. He found it refreshing that, unlike Dita's guests, none showed the slightest interest in his paintings or furniture.

Anthony was showing everyone where they were sleeping when they heard a terrible screeching from somewhere downstairs, but coming closer every second. Dita.

'For goodness' sake, this is exactly what I knew would happen if we filled this house with bloody teenagers.' Dita had appeared on the landing. 'Just *look* at these tracks across the carpet,' she said. 'Everywhere, on every single carpet in the house: footprints, footprints, footprints. All left by these ghastly smelly training shoes you all insist on wearing.' She was glaring furiously at Richard's friends, who stared dumbly back. 'Who do you imagine is going to deal with these ridged tracks you've left everywhere? Poor Stigmata has got enough to do already. It's going to take her hours, hoovering every room. Richard, I blame you for this. And you too, Anthony. You should have taken one look at these shoes and told everyone to take them straight off. Well, you can all take them off now – this minute. You should know that in any case, without being told.'

46

A s her due date approached, Dita declared it was now too risky for her to travel down to Winchford in case she went into labour, so weekends were spent in Cadogan Place instead. Hating London weekends, Anthony began to feel increasingly cooped up, especially as the flat felt small for so many of them. Jasmine, at least, was living in the Pimlico basement he'd bought her when she went to drama school, and Richard was on a school rugby tour of South Africa, but Rosanna, Morad, John-Spiros and Ambrosia were all in Cadogan Place, Rosanna dossing on a sofabed in Dita's study, and in trouble for strewing her clothes across the floor. Morad, meanwhile, infuriated his mother by plugging a PlayStation into the back of the television and accidentally blowing the electrics for half the building.

Anthony insisted they accompany him on endless walks around London parks, to allow Dita some peace and quiet at home. He found it quite stressful, leading so many reluctant teenagers around Hyde Park and Battersea Park, with only the promise of hot chocolate and crisps for motivation. It didn't help that all four of them had diametrically different ideas of what constituted a good time. Morad found walks pointless and pathetic; recently, his old Le Rosey friend Jonny Faisal had moved to London and was living with some of his family and three bodyguards in a furnished apartment block on Park Lane. Morad had taken to staying out late at nightclubs with Jonny, and waking everyone up when he got back in. John-Spiros also despised walks, urging Anthony to take them to costume exhibitions at the V&A. Ambrosia would have much preferred to stay behind watching Disney videos. She had become word-perfect on the lyrics of every song in *The Aristocats, The Jungle Book* and *The Lion King,* and it seemed to Anthony she was forever crouched over one or other of them. As her tutor at Wycombe Abbey noted in her report, 'If Ambrosia put half the energy into studying her English literature set-texts that she puts into watching *Snow White and the Seven Dwarfs,* she'd be in far better shape for her impending GCSEs.' Dita's irritation with her overweight, couch potato daughter was uncomfortable to witness, and Anthony expressly forbade her from putting Ambrosia through a course of electrolysis to depilate her upper lip, saying it would make her even more self-conscious. As for Rosanna, Anthony suspected she might be in love with Scotty or Darren – he could hardly tell them apart – the Winchford mechanics. Either way, she was furious that aged seventeen she wasn't allowed to stay down at the Priory on her own, but Dita didn't trust her not to bring half the pub home, and Anthony was worried about the burglar alarm. Nor could she stay at the Old Rectory with Sandra and John, since the Furlongs had flown to Johannesburg to follow Richard's rugby tour. So Rosanna was dragged kicking and screaming up to London while her hated stepmother waited to give birth.

One November Saturday morning, desperate for an outing from the overheated flat, Anthony took Rosanna for a walk up Sloane Street under the pretext of buying provisions from the Harvey Nichols food halls. Together they carried wire baskets around the tubular shelves of designer foodstuffs, Anthony peering suspiciously at the trendy typographical packaging and exclaiming that an iceberg lettuce cost sixteen times more than at the Winchford farm shop. Rosanna insisted on choosing several bottles of exotic foreign beers from Poland and Croatia to take back as presents for Darren and Scotty, and which Anthony discovered at the checkout were nine pounds each. Anthony bought a packet of free-trade Bolivian coffee for Nula which proclaimed it had been 'harvested with respect by unindentured indigenous tribespeople and guaranteed free of multinational intervention at any point in the production process.'

Reckoning it was too soon to head back to the flat, Anthony suggested a cup of coffee in the fifth-floor bar. A waitress was taking their order when, across the room at a window table, he spotted Amanda. She was sitting alone with a drink and *The Times,* looking slightly careworn in a leopard-print fur hat.

'I won't be a moment, darling; there's someone I need to say hello to,' he told Rosanna, as he headed for Amanda's table.

'Amanda.'

She smiled up at him and kissed him hello. 'That's funny, I was just thinking about you.'

'You were?'

'There's something about your bank in the newspaper. Saying you're buying some financial company in Asia.'

'A securities and futures business in Singapore. Clever of you to spot that.'

'It jumped off the page. The Anscombe word always does.'

'Look, I'm here with my daughter, Rosanna. We're having a cup of coffee over there. Why not join us?'

Amanda stared over at Rosanna and smiled. 'I don't think I've met Rosanna. Maybe I have, I'm not sure. Yes, that'd be nice; I was feeling a bit lonely. I'll bring my drink with me.'

Anthony carried her wine glass to the table, and introduced his ex-wife to his daughter. 'This is Jasmine's mother. She's joining us for a drink.'

'In that case,' Rosanna said, 'I'll have a wine too, please, Dad.'

Anthony glanced at his watch. 'Isn't it still a bit early for that?'

'Come on, it's ten to twelve,' Rosanna said. 'The pubs will be opening in ten minutes. Normally I'm waiting outside the Plough and Harrow by now.'

Amanda laughed. 'Honestly, Ant, buy the poor girl a drink. And a refill for me while you're at it.' Then, turning to Rosanna, 'I'm glad the Plough and Harrow's still going strong. That place was a lifeline when I lived in Winchford. I used to sneak in for a quick one when your dad was out on the farm. He never knew.'

Rosanna giggled. 'It's run by my granddad now. My Mum's father, that is. He's great because he lets me run a bar tab when I'm there with my mates, and half the time we don't pay at all.'

'I don't really approve of that, you know,' Anthony said sternly, as a waitress brought a bottle of Chablis and three glasses.

'Nor does Dita,' Rosanna said. 'She hates the pub. She's only been inside once, and she had this flaming row with Nula – Dad's old mistress – and she's refused to go ever again. Which suits us fine; it means we can relax.'

'Rosanna, that's very rude and unfair.'

'No, it's not. You have to get away from her sometimes, else you go barmy. That's why we're here,' she explained to Amanda. 'To escape from Dita. She was throwing a hissy fit at the flat, screaming at everyone for making it untidy. Ambrosia – that's my stepsister – was in tears. Dita was being such a bitch to her.'

Rosanna then proceeded to tell Amanda all sorts of eye-popping information Anthony had never heard before, such as Scotty the mechanic's reputation as the best stud in the area, and how Darren had two toddlers by different women in Moreton-in-Marsh, both fathered before he was sixteen. All of them were becoming slightly drunk as the second bottle emptied, and they decided to order by the glass from then on. Soon, to Anthony's astonishment, Amanda was telling Rosanna about how she and Anthony had got together in the south of France. 'Your dad and I were screwing on this really rickety old raft, way out to sea, and there was this ruddy great storm raging at the time. But we were having such a great time, really going for it, and neither of us wanted to stop. We almost died out there, honestly. What a way to go!'

'So why did you and Dad split up?' Rosanna asked. Anthony froze, wondering what was coming next.

'Oh, that was my fault,' Amanda replied. 'I was such a stupid tart in those days. Thought I'd be better off with someone else, even though I was still half in love with your dad. He was a wonderful husband, and we'd made this pact together of undying love. Our special bond, we called it. And it *was* special, until I left him and spoiled everything. Do you know something, even on the evening before I went, I couldn't make up my mind what to do. It could have gone either way.'

'So what decided you?' Rosanna asked, transfixed by this thrilling, unknown episode of family history.

'Oh, lots of things. They seem quite trivial now. The cottage we were living in: Forge Cottage, it was called. Nobody could be happy in that place; it was so miserable and dark. It's probably been demolished long ago.'

'Actually, my half-sister Gaia lived there until recently, with her weird mum. They had these, like, wind chimes in the garden, which are meant to ward off evil spirits.'

Amanda laughed. 'We needed some of these ourselves, to ward off Anthony's mother. She was the main reason I left, actually. Couldn't stand the woman, and she couldn't stand me. Actually, sorry, she's probably your grandma or something – I've just worked that one out.'

'Granny Anscombe. Yeah, she's really scary, especially after my pony kicked her in the face when she was teaching me to jump.'

'Brilliant. Give that pony a carrot from me some time.'

'Actually, my poor mother's not at all well these days,' Anthony said. 'She's moved into a house in the village. She needs twenty-four-hour care.'

'I'd say "Give her my love", but it wouldn't ring true. You've got to admit, she was a prize cow. Maybe if she'd been different, we'd still be together.'

'You think so?' Anthony's heart lurched.

'She certainly did her best to sour things. She must have been delighted when I buggered off, wasn't she?'

'She wasn't heartbroken, let's put it that way. But, you know, she's more mellow these days, less judgemental.'

'Except about Dita,' Rosanna said. 'Granny Anscombe *hates* Dita for chucking her out of the Priory. You only have to mention her name and it sets her off.'

'You, Rosanna, are a big exaggerator. But it's true my mother has never been easy with any of my wives. Too territorial.'

'Mum says she was scared stiff of her when she and Dad were married.'

'*I* was never scared,' Amanda said. 'I just despised her.'

'If anything, my mother was scared of *you*,' Anthony told Amanda. 'She thought you were unpredictable. She's quite right about that, of course.' Then, pushing back his chair, he said, 'Christ, do you realise what the time is? Twenty past one. We're late for lunch, Rosanna. Dita will not be pleased. And I haven't paid yet.' He swayed to the till, clutching the bill.

When he returned and they were pulling on their coats, Amanda whispered, 'What are you doing later on? Come round for a drink, Ant, if you can get away. Sevenish?'

He didn't reply. But, as he and Rosanna hurried along Sloane Street towards Cadogan Place, weighed down with the carrier bags of imported beer and coffee, Anthony felt a guilty lurch of excitement.

Dita was tired and heavy from pregnancy, and said she would go to bed after tea to make a start on the Christmas cards, which she wanted to get done and dusted before the birth. This year the card was a photograph of Winchford Priory with all the staff lined up on the front steps, including three girl grooms holding hunters. Anthony found the cards cringe-makingly vulgar, but they had been presented as a *fait accompli* and he could only shrug. Morad announced he was heading round to Jonny Faisal's. Ambrosia, Rosanna and John-Spiros were watching Disney's *Fantasia* on video. Anthony said he needed air, and did anyone mind if he went out for a walk? No one minded.

A taxi dropped him at the corner of Elm Park Mews. He stood for a moment across the cobbled lane staring up at the illuminated window of Amanda's flat above the garage. He pressed the intercom.

An open bottle of wine, two glasses and a bowl of pistachio nuts were set out ready on a coffee table.

'Were you so confident I'd come?'

'I knew you'd come.'

'I might not have been able to, you realise. We're all up in London at the moment.'

'I knew you would.' She kissed him softly on the mouth and Anthony felt a shock of desire.

Amanda was wearing a kaftan in a colour Anthony thought might be peacock blue. She was smoking, and he thought how beautiful she looked, much younger than she'd appeared this morning. He supposed she must be the same age as Dita, but you couldn't compare them.

'I really liked your daughter,' Amanda said. 'Not at all what I expected. She's an absolute hoot.'

'That's what Sandra keeps saying. But she doesn't mean it as a compliment.'

'Rosanna's great. She's clearly having it away with half of Winchford.'

'Oh, come off it. She's only seventeen.'

'Exactly. And very egalitarian.'

As so often when he was with Amanda, Anthony felt he was venturing into dangerous waters. Her conversation challenged and excited him, made him feel alert. At the same time, he had a strong desire to protect her from the world.

The conversation this morning had reawakened memories and emotions long buried inside him. It pleased him Amanda remembered it all so clearly. It meant that, whatever else had happened in the interim – her marriage to Patrice, her life as a film and rock star – she had never forgotten Winchford and their ill-starred adventure. The bond had endured.

Amanda fetched a second bottle from the fridge and they drank their way through that one too. What was it about Amanda that made Anthony hit the bottle like this?

'I've been thinking about something you said this morning,' he said. 'You aren't really lonely, are you?'

'Sometimes. I don't know many people in London, not any more.'

'You should ring me.'

'You're sweet, but you're married. I don't imagine Dita would be too happy if I kept calling.'

'Ring me at the office.'

She held his gaze. 'You've been so kind already. Kinder than I deserve. I realise I hurt you in the past, and I don't want to do that again.'

'I hate the thought of you being lonely.'

'I have Jasmine; she's a star. Even though she isn't around that much. The worst thing is hardly seeing Amelie. I visited her in Paris recently; she's a sweet girl and so pretty, but we hardly know each other.' Then she asked, 'What about you, Ant? Are *you* happy?'

'Happy? Sure. Most of the time. I've got four lovely children who are all doing quite well at their respective schools. And work's going OK too,

I think. We're starting lots of new things in the Far East, opening offices in Tokyo, Hong Kong and Singapore.'

'And Dita? Rosanna sounded a bit negative.'

Anthony smiled. 'Ah, Dita. Well, she's an amazing woman, with more energy than anyone I've ever met. If you saw the Priory now – which I hope one day you will – you'll be astounded. I hardly recognise the place. But, if I'm honest, she can be tricky sometimes. She has such high standards, it's hard to live up to them. And of course we've got all Dita's gang from previous marriages living with us, so it's a bit of a bear garden.'

'She was married to Goldie, the shipping guy, wasn't she? Did I tell you he once offered me fifty thousand dollars for a shag?'

'Did you take it?'

'Excuse me! I was a respectable married woman.' She laughed. 'He's also hideous. Gold jewellery and Brioni suits . . . not my type.' Then she said, 'But you didn't answer my question. I asked whether you're happy.'

'I thought I did answer.'

'No, you skirted round it. You spoke about your kids and the bank. And your wife.'

'I'm certainly not unhappy. Will that do?'

'You are *so English*, it's ridiculous. "I'm certainly not unhappy." What sort of answer is that?'

'The truth.'

Without warning they began to kiss, quickly and passionately. It happened so suddenly that it took them both by surprise. And then, seized by the moment, they made drunken love on the sofa, oblivious to everything but their shared destiny. Afterwards they lay in each other's arms listening to the traffic from the Fulham Road while moonlight from high above the rooftops of Beaufort Street flooded into the tiny room.

It was after midnight that Anthony finally got dressed and made his way outside to find a taxi. He arrived back at Cadogan Place to a flat ablaze with lights and the children still up and dressed.

'God, Dad, where've you *been*?' Rosanna was demanding. 'We were really worried.' John-Spiros was staring at him bug-eyed in a canary-coloured cashmere cardigan.

'I've been out for a walk. Why, is there a problem?' He hoped there were no traces of lipstick on his face.

'Dita's had the baby,' Rosanna said. 'She went into labour hours ago, just after you went out. We waited and waited for you, but we had to call an ambulance. She's in hospital and it's a baby boy. She says you've got to go straight there.'

47

Seldom had a father felt more guilty than Anthony that night, as he lifted up his son for the first time.

Henry Charles Francis Anscombe, seven pounds six ounces, was the most handsome baby imaginable. He gazed up at his father with adoring eyes, or perhaps he was drunk, since Dita was feeding him Moët from the tip of her little finger.

Two hours after the birth Dita was sitting up in bed, hair and make-up immaculate, propped against her own embroidered pillows, brought in with her from home. A lofty obstetrician, famous for delivering royal babies, stood at her bedside discussing mutual friends. Half a dozen Filipina nurses in Portland Hospital uniforms bustled to and fro fetching an ice-bucket for the champagne, fresh glasses, and handing Anthony a menu in English and Arabic in case he wanted food. Having eaten nothing all evening except a bowl of pistachio nuts, he felt suddenly famished, and would happily have ordered mini kebabs or falafel – had he not sensed Dita's anger.

She waited until the obstetrician had gone before letting rip.

'For God's sake, where *were* you? You said you were going out for a short walk and then disappeared for *five hours.*'

Anthony mumbled something about having felt cooped up, and walking right along the Embankment, and vigorously rocked his perfect son to cover his confusion. Suddenly, the events of this evening felt unbearably squalid. He felt ashamed about missing the birth, even though he'd never particularly enjoyed the previous ones, and was filled with remorse about where he had been and what he'd been doing. He had let Dita down badly and, seeing her now with their tiny baby, he could scarcely believe he'd betrayed her so callously. It had never crossed his mind the baby might come tonight. Waves of regret washed over him. He was chairman of Anscombes, father to five children, owner of Winchford; he didn't know what had possessed him. When Henry clutched at his finger with his tiny, soft, pink fist, Anthony felt like crying with shame, pride and happiness. He had been insane to visit Amanda, but that was an end to it. From this moment on, it was a fresh start. His loyalty lay only with his wife and his children.

For the next seventy-two hours he shuttled between his office in Lombard Street and the Portland Hospital in Great Portland Street. Each time he returned to Dita's room, it was more full of flowers. Every surface, every windowsill, the tops of wardrobes and most of the floor was covered with vases of lilies, oleander, jasmine, orchids and dozens of roses. Enormous, extravagant arrangements arrived from all the London jewellers, from her hairdresser, even from the car service. Goldie Emboroleon sent a lemon tree and an olive tree in terracotta pots that required three hospital porters to deliver to the room. Hubert de Saint-Simone sent a wicker pannier full of white roses, all in bud, which Dita declared immensely chic. Len and Marjorie sent a bunch of yellow and orange chrysanthemums wrapped in yellow cellophane, via Interflora in Cheltenham, which arrived with a little cartoon of a champagne cork exploding from a bottle into outer space. Rosie and Scrotum Holland sent half a dozen bottles of Laurent Perrier. Carina Resnick arrived with three exquisitely embroidered baby nightgowns from the White House. Granny Anscombe sent a yellow plastic duck for the bath, which Anthony recognised from the toys section of the village shop. Sandra and John sent a framed picture of Henry's name, each letter decorated with brightly coloured balloons and teddy bears, which Sandra had painted herself with incredible care, and which was so ugly that Dita refused to have it in the room, and asked Anthony to get rid of it.

As for the other children, they heard nothing from Rosanna, who returned to Winchford to stay at the Old Rectory the minute the Furlongs got back from South Africa. Nor was there any word from Gaia, which was hardly surprising since Anthony hadn't rung Nula to tell her the news. John-Spiros arrived with a silver Tiffany rattle, and nervously held Henry at arm's length in case he got dribble on his blazer. Ambrosia turned up with a sad, fat, toy rabbit. Richard sent a letter from Radley full of news of the rugby tour and the scores for each match, and ending 'PS: Great news about the new baby'. Morad distressed his mother by not bothering to visit at all for the first four days, before dropping by for less than ten minutes, scowling and smoking. Tom and Katie sent a very friendly congratulations card, signed by them both, in which

Katie said how much she was looking forward to meeting Henry, and Tom said how much he was looking forward to his work experience at Anscombes. Jasmine, who was back in New York, couriered a knitted Peruvian baby cap to the hospital, which Dita considered common. In the card, she mentioned she was working on a recording project that might be released as a record. 'Amanda's friend Charlie Edwards is producing it, which is incredible.'

After a week in hospital mother and baby returned home, first for a month of convalescence at Cadogan Place with a pair of maternity nurses on twenty-four-hour cover, then at Winchford, which Dita was keen that Henry should learn to regard as home. More than once she said what a pity it was that Richard was the eldest son, and therefore first in line to inherit the estate, 'when he really isn't the brightest bunny in town.' Gazing at her month-old son, she implied he was already far better equipped to run Winchford than his dorkish half-brother.

Anthony adored babies, but Henry's birth could hardly have come at a worse time for him. His workload at Anscombes had reached almost unimaginable levels. The business was expanding furiously, driven by the impetus of the new executives he had hired. For the first time the bank had an office in Manhattan, and the months spent getting around America's regulatory hurdles for financial services were beginning to pay off. But it was in the Far East they were making the most dramatic progress. Already Anscombes had a seat on the Osaka Securities Exchange, and they expected to gain approval for the same thing on SIMEX in Singapore before Easter. In the past six months, they'd taken on more than two hundred new staff – futures and options traders, derivatives experts, plus all the necessary back office – and Anthony found himself making three trips to tour the Asia–Pacific tiger economies in as many months. He wondered what Michael Anscombe – or, indeed, his own father – would have made of the new people they were hiring, because they were so different from the traditional Anscombes intake. Anthony could hardly believe that all these south London yobs, with their trading floor stripy blazers and curious beards, really worked for him, or that he'd relocated so many of them to Asia, plus wives and even girlfriends, to live in expensive company flats and trade options in the pit. The language at Anscombes altered out of all recognition. These days it was all estuary accents, margin calls, put options and hedging.

At the same time the results were encouraging, and growing exponentially. In the full year before he took over as chairman, Anscombes had produced a pre-tax profit of £17 million. This year, they were on course to make £45 million. Looking ahead, the most conservative forecasts put them at £90 million for 1995, and after that, who could tell? The proportion of profit being distributed in mega bonuses to staff horrified him, but everyone assured him this was the way the market worked now. Anthony's CFO estimated that, in a few years' time, they could be posting headline profits of £250 million. Anthony found himself alternating between excitement at everything that was happening, as the family bank doubled and then tripled in size, and a creeping nostalgia for less frenetic days. Meanwhile, back in England, he had family dilemmas to resolve. Richard had left Radley with more sports trophies than any previous boy in the history of the school, but had only scraped two A-levels. Exactly what he could do next, nobody was sure, since university wasn't an option. Anthony didn't want to send him off to a ski resort with a wad of French francs, which was Richard's own preference, and Richard refused to work for his stepfather on the farm. In the end it was decided he should join Tom Furlong at Anscombes for work experience; both boys would start off in the mailroom, sorting post, and then see what opportunities arose elsewhere in the bank.

There was a similar quandary over Morad, who had been hanging out in nightspots for the best part of a year. He had spent most of last summer in the south of France, ostensibly staying at Jonny Faisal's family villa on Pampelonne beach near St Tropez, but largely spent in the Caves de Roy nightclub beneath the Byblos Hotel. Anthony was increasingly fed up with bailing him out financially. As for finding him a job, it wasn't easy. Morad was unlikely to come over well in interviews, and seemed to have no ideas himself about earning a living. At least he'd be invited to stay on Goldie Emboroleon's yacht in Greece for the entire month of August, along with John-Spiros and Ambrosia, so that would get him out of everyone's hair. Beyond that, Anthony hadn't a clue what to do with him. The only thing he felt strongly about was that Morad should never, under any circumstances, join Anscombes.

As for Jasmine, she moved from triumph to triumph. Her pop record *Luck of the Draw (Maybe Baby)*, produced by Charlie Edwards, reached number twelve in the charts and stayed on the Capital Radio playlist for nine weeks. Once again she was splashed all over the newspapers, giving interviews and handing the credit for her success to Charlie, 'one wise man and special dude'. Then, having starred as a catwalk model at the Milan and Paris international collections, appearing in four shows a day for three solid weeks, she was signed in a blaze of publicity as the new 'face' of Saint-Simone de Paris, the fashion house. According to the report in the *Financial Times*, there had been a palace revolution at the venerable old couture label. The business had been sold, two or three years earlier, to a French conglomerate owning galvanised steel plants and luxury hotels. Now they had fired the elegant designer, Hubert de Saint-Simone, who had founded the company half a century ago, and replaced him with a cutting-edge Londoner, Trevor Bratt, son of a Hoxton butcher. Judging by his photograph in the paper, Anthony wasn't sure what Dita would make of the new man at her favourite dressmaker, with his shaven scalp and prominent tattoo of a scorpion on his forehead. Almost his first act in his new position was to hire Jasmine as his 'muse', announcing that she would be appearing in all their advertising around the world. He went on to say that he'd always had 'a big thing about Jas's mum, Amanda Bouillon, the singer. She was a big influence on me, her whole style thing. As a teenager in Hoxton I had a poster of her on my bedroom wall. I used to jack off on her all the time; she was like this incredible icon.'

When Dita heard about developments at Saint-Simone de Paris, she was mortified. 'Well, they'll lose all their best clients, I can tell you that now. Everyone's leaving. All the seamstresses in the atelier have resigned in protest.'

'Maybe it won't be that bad,' Anthony said encouragingly. 'Jasmine says this new designer is supposed to be a genius.'

Dita snorted. 'That's not what Carina says. Apparently his showroom is filthy dirty, miles away in East London. Anyway,' she added, 'I don't know why he's chosen Jasmine as his house model. She's so scruffy most of the time. Heaven knows what the Parisiennes will make of her.'

The rift between Dita and her stepdaughter grew wider. Jasmine met Anthony for lunch or supper in London, but found endless excuses to avoid staying at the Priory with Dita there. One night, while having dinner alone with Jasmine at Ziani's Italian restaurant in Radnor Walk, Anthony had a brainwave. There was a spare cottage in the village – Forge Cottage – and he offered it to his eldest daughter. 'You're always travelling these days, darling, so I thought you might like a country bolthole. Somewhere to escape to when it all gets too much.'

Jasmine was thrilled. 'I'd *adore* that. Do you really mean it? Thanks, Dad, that's amazing.'

'Well, it'll be nice for me, too. I hope it might mean I'll see more of you in Winchford.'

'I've always loved that cottage, ever since I was a baby. I can remember living there, that kitchen and everything, and the bathroom downstairs; it's so cool.'

'Cool's the word. Especially in winter. I'll have to make sure the heating's working for you.'

'I've just thought of something,' Jasmine said. 'You know who'll love to come and stay with me?'

Anthony flinched. He hoped she wasn't going to say Charlie Edwards.

'Amanda. She needs to get out of London sometimes. She's going to be so excited when I tell her about Forge Cottage.'

'Well, that's a thought,' he replied uncertainly. 'Though your mother never really liked that cottage much when we lived there.'

'I bet it looked amazing in those days. All those Moroccan carpets and brocade shawls. Before Sandra came along and ruined it. I want to put it back exactly like it was then.'

At Anscombes, Richard and Tom began work in the mailroom, and at lunchtime on their first day Anthony bought them both lunch at a pub in Leadenhall market. Richard had spent the morning pushing a trolley of post around the building, while Tom assisted the dispatch clerk in sending Fedexes. There was a smoothness and intellectual confidence about Tom that Richard would probably never have. Recently, there had been great celebrations at the Old Rectory when Tom won a scholarship to Peterhouse, Cambridge, to read history and economics. The scholarship took care of the majority of his tuition fees, but Anthony had volunteered to provide an allowance to cover his living expenses for the next three years, since the Furlongs were so stretched. Richard had joined a rugby club that played two evenings a week out near Twickenham, and Dita spent her life complaining about all his dirty kit, particularly his jock strap, which Stigmata hated ironing. Despite their different interests – or even because of them – the boys got on well, and were cooking up a scheme to go and work together at a game lodge in Africa in one of Tom's long vacations from Cambridge.

Just occasionally, Anthony picked up on a slight note of jealousy from Tom towards Richard, based upon his future inheritance of Winchford. But, all things considered, Anthony felt he was incredibly lucky in his selection of children, stepchildren and honorary stepchildren, with the obvious exception of Morad.

As he remarked to Lex over a quick drink in the Plough and Harrow, 'If anyone had told me I'd end up with five children of my own plus five steps, I'd have laughed out loud. A couple of weeks ago I had to have dinner with a bunch of Chinese government officials we're hoping to start a joint venture with in Shanghai. Anyway, I mentioned to them about being responsible for ten kids and they were astonished – shocked, actually. They couldn't believe it. They all had one child each. But you know something, it's fine most of the time, a lot of fun, especially when they all get on with each other. It's not usually the children who make the problems, it's their mothers – my past and present wives.'

48

'If all the car parking is down in Repton's Field,' Dita announced, 'then that will leave the watermeadows clear for the helicopters.'

Dita had decided to give a summer lunch party at Winchford Priory to celebrate the fifth anniversary of her and Anthony's first meeting in Mark's Club. 'The garden will be at its best in July,' she said, 'and we owe so many people. We have to ask them back some time.' Determined to keep numbers down to manageable levels, they agreed that an absolute maximum of 240 would be invited, which meant twenty round tables of twelve people each.

As always when Dita became absorbed in a project, the Winchford summer lunch quickly took on a life of its own, with a support cast to match. Dita telephoned five local caterers for menus and estimates, until she decided that they would be better off with party planners from London, who had access to smarter glasses and cutlery. Then she started drawing up a guest list. Anthony was anxious to invite as many country neighbours as possible. Dita agreed, in principle at least, and added the Hollands – Scrotum, Rosie and Lex – the Nall-Caines, Elliots, Plunketts, Fanes and Loxtons. Under pressure, she added Percy and Jacinthe and John and Sandra on to her lengthening list. Beyond that she was immovable. 'I should make it crystal clear from the outset that I will *not* be asking Sandra's parents to this lunch party. I'm sorry, but it's out of the question. Anyway, I'm sure they'd be much too busy to come, serving lunches at their pub.'

To make matters worse, Len buttonholed Anthony soon afterwards in the village street. 'Just the man, just the man,' Len exclaimed when he saw him. 'I was just talking about you, Antoine. I hear you're planning some big jamboree up at the Big House, and I wanted to offer our services, best trade terms of course. We can do all the grub for you from the pub, pig roast, spare ribs, whatever you fancy. It's going to be a whole new thing for us – outside catering. We can provide all the plates and serviettes and whatnot too.'

Anthony found himself squirming with embarrassment as he explained that Dita had already chosen a London caterer.

'Not to worry, old boy,' Len said. 'It'll mean we can enjoy the occasion without worrying. I'll be interested to see what they lay on in the old tucker stakes. Could pick up some useful tips.'

Six weeks later, the great day was blazing hot and Dita, who hated cloud or rain, breathed a sigh of relief. The extensive contingency plans – which had involved removing all the furniture from the white drawing room and placing it in store to make space for the lunch tables – had proved unnecessary. Anthony, in panama hat, made a final tour of the garden, which had been prinked and buffed to new levels of perfection. Recently people had begun to describe him as looking very distinguished. He had lost a little hair and gone quite grey, but this gave him added gravitas. Thanks to Dita he was exceptionally well dressed, with well-fitting suits, polished shoes and new, expensive ties. Still occasionally diffident, there was nevertheless an air of authority about him, as befitted the chairman of the bank.

The new herbaceous borders, planted to a plan by Rosemary Verey, bristled with alliums and achilleas. Every inch of lawn had been mowed and rolled until it resembled green baize. The cliff-face edging around each flowerbed was razor-sharp. Anthony's only sadness was that his butterfly garden had been dug up on Dita's orders and replaced by a new 'white' garden of cutting flowers. 'We've got to have flowers for the house, for when people come to stay. I *know* you loved that butterfly sanctuary but, truly darling, all those bright colours are awfully vulgar, buddleia especially. One just doesn't *see* flowers like that in the country, not in proper houses anyway.'

Dita was standing on the big lawn beyond the knot garden, surrounded by caterers and organisers, directing final touches to the tables and last-minute alterations to the placement. Beneath the cedar tree an oyster bar had been erected to supply the pre-lunch snacks on trays. An extensive buffet was being set up in an open-sided marquee.

Anthony felt astonished by the sheer number of people involved in producing this lunch party. Wherever he looked there were waiters and waitresses getting changed into their white jackets, having travelled all the way from London in a chartered coach. Santos the butler, Stigmata, and half a dozen other Winchford staff were positioning themselves behind the buffet tables where they would help the guests to help themselves. Close to the garden gate, where people would arrive, a string quintet of gloomy-looking musicians was tuning up violins. Dita had cleverly secured them from the Philharmonia orchestra by pulling strings, as she put it.

Mildly overwhelmed by so much activity, Anthony strolled down to Repton's Field to check on the car parking. Here he found Walter Twine, who had been given the job of standing inside the gate and directing arriving cars to the parking lines.

'Well, it's a big do my wife's got planned for today, Walter. Thank goodness we've been lucky with the weather.'

'Oi don't know about thart,' Walter replied. 'It's too warm for me. Oi don't like it one bit.'

It crossed Anthony's mind to suggest to Walter that he remove one of his seven layers of clothing, which included tweed suit, waistcoat, tweed overcoat and flat cap, but instead he inspected the hundreds of metres of Indonesian duckboarding, specially imported by Dita in case of mud, but now mercifully redundant. As he walked back up to the house, he saw the first cars arriving and not long afterwards the judder of rotor-blades of the first helicopter landing in the watermeadows.

He reached the lawn to find a dozen guests already there and an agitated Dita. '*There* you are, Anthony. We've had search parties out. Now, stand here by me and don't wander off again.'

Soon the garden was awash with guests, many of them entirely new to Anthony, being Dita's cultural friends from her development boards and committees. He was introduced to the curators and chairmen of half a dozen galleries and ballet companies, and numerous foreign socialites he dimly remembered meeting at his wedding. As each new guest arrived, they had to walk past the string quintet – three pale men and two serious bosomy women. Nobody quite knew how to react to them, adopting an appreciative, even holy expression for a moment or two before scuttling on to where the waitresses were holding out trays of drinks.

Still feeling shifty about excluding the Pottses and Nula from the lunch, Anthony was nevertheless curious about meeting Dita's ex, Goldie Emboroleon, who had been invited with his new Russian wife, Irina. He had seen the photographs of their wedding in *Hello*, and thought Goldie had probably met his match in the stunning, spoilt-looking near-teenager draped across the pages. 'Aleco can be such an idiot,' Dita declared. 'He is led by his cock.' She insisted on calling the young bride 'Aeroflot, or whatever her name is.'

One consequence of inviting the Emboroleons was that Dita didn't feel she could say no to Amanda, when Jasmine asked to bring her along. Jasmine had her mother staying at Forge Cottage for the weekend, which had become an increasingly frequent occurrence. Anthony had several times spotted her in her leopard-print hat, stepping gingerly along in her stilettos.

'I suppose if I've invited Aleco, we can hardly refuse Amanda,' Dita said with a sigh. 'You have far too many ex-wives, Anthony. Heaven knows where we're going to seat them all. Sandra Furlong's a very dull person.'

Anthony dreaded the prospect of Amanda at the lunch, and prayed she wouldn't get drunk and give away any secrets.

Already there must have been two hundred people milling about on the lawn. Dozens of waiters in white mess jackets were weaving between them with trays of champagne and fruit cocktails in coloured glasses, while waitresses offered trays of miniature blinis with crème fraîche and caviar, tiny bunches of French beans wrapped in Parma ham, swollen prawns on skewers and bowls of Claire oysters on crushed ice embellished with fronds of seaweed. Anthony spotted his friends Mark and Annie Plunkett, with Mark's father, Sir Hector, who was looking uncharacteristically deflated, having seen his majority cut in half in the recent general election which had swept Tony Blair's New Labour to power. All around the party, guests were exclaiming about how ghastly it would be with the socialists back. 'You wait and see,' Hector Plunkett was telling everyone, 'Five years from now they'll have raised National Insurance contributions, banned foxhunting and ceded control of our borders to the European Union. Already there's talk of a camp for asylum seekers in Stow-on-the-Wold.'

Rosanna yawned ostentatiously. She felt uncomfortable at this party, with none of her friends there, and wished she was down at the pub. But Dita had bribed her thirty quid to help Ambrosia look after Henry for the day, since Henry's nannies were both assisting behind the buffet. Rosanna was besotted with her new stepbrother. At eight months, Henry looked immaculate in a perfect smocked shirt buttoned into his shorts. With his thick blond hair and dimpled pink cheeks, he was like a child in a 1950s Ladybird book, sitting on the lawn between the legs of the guests, or lugged from place to place by his two half-sisters. In a gesture of defiance, however, Rosanna was wearing her Hells Angels T-shirt, a present from Darren, and a bicycle chain bracelet twisted around her wrist.

Anthony watched his wife across the sea of heads. She looked utterly stunning in that faultless, imperious, slightly chilly way he found incredibly sexy. Since the revolution at Saint-Simone de Paris she had become a convert to Chanel, and was dressed in a state-of-chic white braided suit collected by his office driver from the Sloane Street boutique, following days of alterations. Gazing around the party, with everything running like clockwork, he knew Dita was responsible for all of it: from the perfection of the garden to the different coloured cushions on every chair, she had personally supervised each tiny detail. She was incredible. A superwoman! Her strength and energy underpinned his existence, and he was boundlessly grateful.

It delighted Anthony to have so many of his family around him. The garden teemed with smart neighbours and colleagues from Anscombes (to his surprise, every single board director and department head had accepted the lunch invitation, even those stationed in Asia, all desperate for a gawp at their boss's house) but it was his children and stepchildren he minded most about. Tom and Katie had just turned up with the older Furlongs and he had spotted John-Spiros wearing a white linen suit. His one regret was Gaia not being there, but Dita had put her foot down.

A fierce sun, practically overhead, beat down on to the lawn, and the walls of the Priory soaked up the heat, the mellow stone becoming warm to the touch. A cloud of small tortoiseshells settled on the lead pipes and window ledges, opening up their orange wings to the sunshine, while a pair of Red Admirals sucked honey from the verbena. People were gravitating towards the oyster bar, where half a ton of rapidly melting ice gave off a cooling chill.

Heading in Anthony's direction along the laburnum walk was Jasmine, closely followed by her mother, looking like a well-lived Anita Pallenberg. Jasmine was dressed head to toe in Trevor Bratt for Saint-Simone, as the label was now called, in a murky, indeterminate garment of holes, smudges and stains, with unpicked hems and frayed seams. It was the same outfit in which she had been photographed opening Bratt's seminal first show for Saint-Simone at a Paris skating rink, miles beyond the Périphérique, and which had been published on every front page. Jasmine had recently been tattooed with a tiny black butterfly just above her left ankle.

'So, Ant,' Amanda said, 'You realise I haven't set foot in this garden for ten years? It's all flooding back like a bad dream. Henrietta's not around, is she?'

'She is, actually.' He pointed to a wheelchair parked beneath the wellingtonia, in which a shrunken version of his mother was slumped, muttering malevolently. 'She's had a stroke, poor thing. I'll take you over if you like, but I'm not sure she'll recognise you.'

'No fear,' Amanda said. 'I think I'll pass on that one, thank you.'

'And how are you, darling?' he asked, kissing his daughter. 'Everything OK at the cottage?'

'Fine, I love it. The only bad thing was my mobile wouldn't work, because the walls are so thick it couldn't get a signal. But Charlie's stuck an aerial on the roof, so it more or less works now.'

'Charlie Edwards?'

'He came over for supper with Mum and me last night. He was being so funny. He's had his back lasered, so all the spots and body hair have gone. It looks great.'

Carina Resnick surfaced beside him with several unidentified women in tow. 'Ah, there you are, Anthony. We've been looking for you. Isn't this weather gorgeous? I'm heartbroken for all those poor people who flew down to Cannes this weekend for the film festival – it's ten degrees hotter here in Oxfordshire! Anyway, I want to introduce you to all these lovely ladies whose names I've already forgotten, but they work for you in your office in Jakarta. I've been telling them what a very sweet man you are. *And* the best looking, with the loveliest house. Total perfection!' And she cackled in a simpering way that Anthony found intensely irritating.

Morad, in tan-coloured suede jacket and black shirt, was spying on Katie. He was hideously randy, and it had been bugging him for months that he wasn't making any progress there. What was it with this bitch? Twice he'd invited her out – once to Tramp, then to L'Equipe Anglaise – but she kept avoiding him. He didn't know what her problem was. Ever since that episode in the swimming pool, Morad had been tantalised by the fleeting glimpse of her copper-coloured pubic hair. God, he hated girls like Katie, with her creamy white skin and glossy hair that kept catching the sun as she flicked it out of her face. Probably she was a racist, which was why she didn't fancy him . . . yet.

He could see her now, chatting and laughing with Richard. How come she never laughed like that with *him*? She looked so juicy, he felt almost sick. She was wearing a floaty, pale green chiffony top with thin spaghetti straps – how he longed to grab those straps – and what looked like several layers of petticoats beneath. Her wrists jangled with wire bangles and a braid friendship bracelet. Friendship bracelet! Why wouldn't the snotty tart be friends with him?

Long lines were forming from both ends of the buffet. Anthony could see Dita leading Goldie and Irina to the front of the queue, and people letting them jump ahead because they were richer and had arrived by helicopter. Goldie looked exactly as Anthony had imagined: small and brown with flashing white teeth. The sort of man, Anthony reckoned, who was endlessly charming and generous to his friends, and a bastard to his inferiors. Irina had incredible torpedo-shaped tits. For a fleeting moment, Anthony wondered what it said about Dita that she'd spent more than ten years of her life living with this Greek buffoon.

Edging his way along the line of food, Anthony found himself standing next to Sandra, who was piling up her plate from the dozens of different dishes. Recently Sandra had put on even more weight, and her complexion had become rather red, which she tried to conceal with a green-tinged foundation. 'My goodness, Anthony, what frightfully extravagant food,' she said, in a tone that managed to sound both greedy and sarcastic. Before setting off for the Priory, Sandra had been determined to be gracious, despite her mounting jealousy. Having arrived, she was finding it all very difficult. Wherever she turned she spotted something new to fan her envy, which she was quick to dismiss as ostentatious. The new herbaceous borders resembled photographs out of *House & Garden*; she hardly dared imagine how many gardeners it took to keep them up. Then there was the string quintet – typically Dita and over the top. And all these ghastly, flashy people arriving by helicopter! Even if she had all the money in the world, she wouldn't have a helicopter, she told herself. All she wanted was a new master bathroom at the Old Rectory, and she wondered how Anthony would react if she asked him to install one.

What irritated Sandra more than anything was how well-organised the party was. Organisation was her own great strength, but these days she had less opportunity. Well, with enough money you can organise anything, she thought bitterly.

Fifteen yards ahead she spotted her husband buttonholing some guest who looked desperate to escape. In her more clear-sighted moments she accepted that John was a bit of a bore, and wondered whether she'd made a mistake in leaving Anthony so precipitously. If she'd been less censorious, all this could still have been hers.

Ambrosia was dithering over the buffet. She would have liked to help herself to everything, but her father had just told her she was putting on weight, and her cheeks burned at the memory of it. She was starving, and could hardly believe how many delicious things there were. She helped herself from a platter of tomatoes with basil and mozzarella balls, and then from a bowl of exotic, frizzy, purple salad. Then she spotted the salsas of chopped-up mango and avocado, and the dish of little new potatoes with melted butter and chives. Really, that's more than enough, she told herself; I should go and find my place. But then she saw the waiters carving hams, and Santos dishing out cold salmon and chicken mayonnaise, and the baskets of special breads studded with walnuts, hazelnuts and rosemary.

'You should take your sweet with you now,' Stigmata told her from behind the pudding table. 'Come, Ambrosia, you like these; it's nice.' And she handed her a plate of tiny fraises des bois, tiramisu and home-made lavender ice-cream.

Everyone was seated at their tables, and the private photographer Dita had hired was up on the turreted roof, snapping away, and wondering whether he might sell the pictures on to *Tatler* or *Hello*. At ground level, the guests all seemed to be having a good time in their various peer groups – Dita had placed the smartest, richest people at the tables surrounding herself, with satellite tables allocated to fun neighbours, less-fun neighbours, Anthony's duty invitees from the bank, and a duds' table near the ha-ha. Tom Furlong, cool and handsome in white jeans and a pink shirt, was entertaining his table with stories about life at Cambridge, and the antics of the little cell of Old Etonians and Amplefordians he was part of. Leaning back in his chair, round glasses flashing in the sunshine, laying down the law on every subject, he radiated with youthful brilliance and intellectual arrogance. Watching him from the next table, Anthony wasn't surprised Tom had done well at Anscombes during his work experience there. By the end of his internship, he had found a place in the research department and impressed everyone. Poor Richard had stayed working in the mailroom for the full six months.

Morad was on his sixth glass of wine and mesmerised by Katie sitting on his left. He was giving her the hard, aggressive stare he'd heard worked on women. So far it was difficult to judge the result. Katie was totally ignoring him, or trying to, but he could tell she was rattled. Well, if that didn't work, he had Plan B in his pocket.

Sandra, whose two glasses of champagne had gone straight to her head, resolved to ask her ex-husband about installing that new bathroom in the Old Rectory. She bustled over to his table, and crouched down on the lawn beside him.

Faintly irritated by the request and its timing, Anthony said he'd be happy to have his estate manager look into it next week.

'Oh, for Christ's sake, Anthony,' Sandra snapped, the drink talking. 'John's your estate manager, remember? You've become so grand these days, it's ridiculous. And you might like to know my parents are very hurt not to have been invited today, and so's Ginette. Not that she could have come; she's got a kung-fu exam.' She flounced back to her table.

Turning away with relief from his embittered ex-wife, Anthony gazed across the garden. Suddenly he froze. Staring down at the lunch party from a thicket of beeches was an all too familiar figure, holding the hand of a twelve-year-old girl. It was Nula with Gaia. Nula was just standing there, like Saruman at the gates of Mordor, strangely witch-like in her hemp dress. Anthony's first thought was, 'Oh Lord. What's she going to do next?' All sorts of nightmare scenarios rushed into his head. He thought she might clamber down the steep bank and invade the party, or start hectoring them about ecology. The last time she'd just appeared like this had been at the cricket match, when she'd sprung the baby Gaia on him. But today she merely stood there, immobile, for almost a quarter of an hour, before retreating again into the woods with Gaia trailing behind. When he stood up, Anthony found his shirt was damp with sweat.

He was still feeling jumpy when Amanda breezed past the table with Jasmine. 'Hi, Ant. Jas is going to give me a guided tour of your house; hope that's OK.' Before he could reply, she had moved on in the direction of the Priory, evidently intent on a good snoop. Anthony looked uneasily about for Dita. She'd hate the idea of Amanda poking about.

Morad was increasingly agitated, and when he got agitated he was really mad. Who the fuck did Katie Furlong think she was anyway? More than an hour they'd been sitting at the same table, and she'd been intentionally ignoring him, talking to the loser on her other side. It was like he was invisible. He couldn't believe it: everything was the wrong way round. Here he was, Morad Ahvazi, or Morad Emboroleon as he called himself in nightclubs – it was easier to use his former stepfather's name, and more impressive – but who was *she*, for Christ's sake? Just some airhead English schoolgirl whose father couldn't even afford to pay her school fees. How dare she diss him like this?

Digging his hand into his trouser pocket, Morad carefully retrieved the little blue tablet and slipped it into Katie's glass of wine. Give it five minutes, he thought, with a smirk.

Anthony thought he really couldn't leave Amanda wandering round the Priory any longer. They'd been in there for more than half an hour now. What on earth were they up to?

Katie's head was spinning. Either that or the garden was. She guessed it must be to do with the wine, but it was very odd because she'd only drunk one glass, not having really enjoyed the taste. Perhaps she had had too much sun. She felt very strange now, like she was about to faint. She thought she should lie down for a bit, somewhere quiet and out of the sun. But she stumbled as she got to her feet, like her legs had no strength in them, and suddenly Morad was helping her, supporting her weight as she staggered towards the Priory. She had never liked Morad, but he was putting an arm around her shoulders and telling her to lean against him. She felt so dizzy.

'Excuse me a moment,' Anthony said to his neighbour, 'but I need to check on some people in the house.' He strode purposefully towards the Priory.

Entering the cool of the hall, he waited for his eyes to adjust after the glare outside. To his surprise, he heard a moaning sound coming from the television room, as if someone was ill in there.

He pushed open the door and was met by one of the most revolting sights imaginable. Poor, sweet Katie was lying on the sofa, virtually passed out and whimpering. Her dress was pulled up above her waist and her knickers yanked below her knees.

Standing over her with a hideous leering expression was Morad, vigorously masturbating over her supine body.

49

Asserting himself with Dita for once, Anthony insisted Morad be banned from Winchford for a minimum of six months. 'And I don't want to find him in Cadogan Place either, when I'm up there. I don't want to clap eyes on him, not for a long time.'

'Then where *do* you suggest the poor boy goes exactly?' Dita asked in the clipped tones she used when she thought someone was being unreasonable.

'I don't care. Not my problem. I just don't want him anywhere near me or the other children, OK?'

And so, with many conspiratorial promises from his mother that it wouldn't be for nearly so long as six months, Morad moved in with Jonny Faisal to the serviced apartment on Park Lane, and spent every night on the town at a different club. 'If you feel lonely, you can always come home,' Dita promised. 'Anyway, you will be away on Aleco's yacht for most of the summer, and then we can see.'

Anthony found himself travelling more and more frequently, as the businesses in Asia took off. He had never imagined they could perform this well so quickly. The profits they were generating in Singapore were astonishing, almost problematic, since they made the other divisions seem like backwaters in comparison. All his brightest young executives wanted a transfer to Singapore, where the beer was cold and the bonuses hot, as they put it. 'To make money in Asia, all you have to do is show up,' declared Anscombes' CFO in an interview with the *Economist*. Anthony fell into a routine of spending one week a month in the Far East, visiting two cities per trip. In the autumn, Anscombes would open an office in Seoul, and by the following spring they'd be up and running in Taipei and Sydney.

It was on long-haul flights he had most time to think and worry about work, about Winchford, above all about his family. He had a technique for running mentally through all the children in descending age order, starting with Jasmine, all the way down to Henry. Usually he did this after the second Bloody Mary had kicked in. Jasmine he knew was having a ball at the moment, endlessly written about in the papers and magazines, but still amazingly unspoilt by the attention. It was almost a miracle she'd ended up so well balanced, considering the way she'd been abandoned by her mother, and her ambivalent teenage relationship with Sandra later on, not to mention the ghastly business with Nula, which he knew had traumatised her at the time. A part of him was annoyed with Charlie Edwards for getting her into the music business, which was surely riddled with drugs. And Charlie spent an awful lot of time round at Forge Cottage. Between music and modelling, there was plenty to worry about. Each time he saw her, he hoped she wasn't anorexic or popping pills.

Richard was certainly not anorexic, nor was he interested in clothes. With his thick neck, tufty black hair and an old pair of jeans he wore every single day, he drifted through life on affability. Everyone liked Richard. He had legions of rugby mates; at the Plough and Harrow he had an instant rapport with everyone in the public bar; in the Anscombes mail room, they still asked after him. He was equally happy messing about with his shotgun or on the PlayStation, or helping out with the paintballing. But whether he had any drive at all, any ambition, was beginning to worry his father. As Richard approached adulthood, Anthony was at a loss to tell you anything his eldest son was passionate about, apart from rugby. One day he would have Winchford to look after, and Anthony was beginning to have serious doubts about whether he'd be up to it. Whenever he tried to explain anything to him about the farm, Richard nodded away while staring out of the window.

Rosanna was another puzzle. She had just left school and, as predicted, hadn't come away with brilliant academic results. Her one ambition was to work behind the bar at the Plough and Harrow. For the only time in history, Sandra and Dita were united in opposition. But what else could she do? Her main activity was persuading Len to allow 'lock ins' at the pub with Darren and Scotty, and drinking the place dry of lager. And he was concerned about her language and general stroppiness. Recently she'd got heavily into piercings, and now had three rings down the side of her ear, one in her eyebrow and one through her tongue. She said she wanted to go to Australia for her gap year, but after that Anthony couldn't begin to imagine what she would do. In the offices and businesses he frequented, no one seemed to employ truculent girls with eyebrow studs.

Then there were Tom and Katie, whom he didn't feel he had to worry about so directly, but who were both still firmly on his payroll, and looked set to remain there for the foreseeable future. Tom was clearly incredibly bright and ambitious. Nobody need worry about Tom. Sandra was already bugging Anthony about giving him a job in Asia after he left university, and for once it didn't seem like an imposition, because he'd be bound to do well out there. In many ways he was the complete opposite of Richard: wiry, driven, and behind his sophisticated facade he vibrated with a nervous energy Anthony supposed he had inherited from his mother, Constance. As for Katie, she was a dear girl. Not only was she the prettiest of them all, she was also the easiest. She had been sweetly forgiving over the latest hideous Morad episode, even though Anthony knew she had been badly freaked out by it, and had suffered from nightmares for weeks afterwards. Sandra said she wouldn't be surprised if the episode put Katie off boys for life, and she would have reported Morad to the police had the Furlongs not been living in one of Anthony and Dita's houses, which made it quite literally too close to home. Katie kept insisting that it really didn't matter. There was a vagueness and a fragility to Katie that reminded Anthony of Constance, and he felt so sorry for her that she hadn't seen her mother more than a handful of times in ten years. Sandra had tried her best as a stepmother, but really they were on different wavelengths. Katie was going to art college in September. As honorary stepfather, Anthony felt he had a responsibility to support her.

It was Dita's children who caused Anthony the greatest anxiety, and he couldn't begin to think about them without a big glass of British Airways champagne in his hand. The fact was, he found all three stepchildren a challenge in their different ways. Morad was clearly impossible, and he secretly wondered whether there was any up-side to him at all. The boy evidently had serious mental problems. In his more sympathetic moments, he was prepared to accept that Morad had had a difficult childhood, with his father, Sharif Ahvazi, dying when he was so small. He didn't trust him an inch, and suspected him of slipping some drug – probably rohypnol – into Katie's drink at the lunch party. Looking ahead, Anthony could only envisage further trouble. He hadn't said anything to Dita, but a lot of expensive claret had been disappearing from the Priory cellars, and had then abruptly stopped disappearing with Morad's rustication. Anthony found it pretty conclusive. But Dita was resolute in defence of her boy. 'Don't be ridiculous Anthony; you are imagining things.' In her opinion, Katie had been leading him on.

Anthony felt sorry for John-Spiros, because Dita so blatantly favoured Morad. With his weak, skinny frame, oversized Adam's apple that bounced around his throat like a third testicle, and big popping eyes, John-Spiros looked like an effete manservant, impeccably turned out for every occasion, but with a cringing air about him, a puppy expecting to be kicked. His great enthusiasms in life were his collection of enamel cufflinks, dress studs and ivory collar stiffeners, which he bought at West End jewellers and streetmarket stalls, and his library of architectural books. Anthony had commissioned him over the summer to put together a history of the Priory, and already he'd discovered fascinating new stuff about the medieval stew ponds. John-Spiros was so absorbed that he asked whether he really had to go to Greece and stay with this father, which he was dreading. But Dita replied, 'Of course you must go. If Aleco thinks you're not interested, he might leave the yacht to his new wife.'

And then, of course, there was Ambrosia. Anthony could never think about her without feeling perplexed, because he found her so difficult to get through to. He wanted to be a sympathetic stepfather, especially as Dita was so tough on her, forever scolding her about her weight. The whole weight thing had now become a dominant issue. Dita asked the chef to produce special low-calorie meals for Ambrosia, without cream, sugar or salt, and these were placed on the sideboard in their own pyrex dishes.

It didn't help that Dita was a perfect size ten. More than once he spotted his stepdaughter slipping furtively out of the village shop with a box of minirolls; the way things were going, she would soon resemble Sandra's sister, Ginette. He wasn't sure school helped much either. Dita had insisted she be sent away to Wycombe Abbey, to toughen her up. Perpetually miserable, she couldn't make eye contact with adults.

He fretted about Gaia for different reasons. He never felt he did enough for her, mostly because everything was so difficult with Nula. Over the summer, he'd taken Gaia for a day out to Thorpe Park, and they'd had a great time on Tidal Wave, queuing up time and again for another ride; they must have gone on it six or seven times. But when he'd dropped her home, Nula had been scathing about theme parks, saying they were cynical ploys by leisure consortiums to separate workers from their hard-earned cash.

He longed for Gaia to spend time with his other children, and become more part of the family. But between Nula and Dita it was never easy. Nula wouldn't allow Gaia to stay overnight at the Priory, and wouldn't allow her to play tennis because she'd read that tennis balls are manufactured by child labour in Malaysia. Dita had no problem with Gaia coming up to swim in the summer, but wouldn't have her mother near the house, so Anthony had to fetch and return his daughter from Steepness Farmhouse, which was logistically complicated since Nula refused to have a telephone. He worried, too, about Gaia's health. Since Nula had put her back on a macrobiotic diet, she had been whey-faced and anaemic. When he bought her a burger at Thorpe Park she devoured it in three mouthfuls.

For all this, Gaia had emerged as a sweet, inquisitive, unspoilt young girl, almost pathetically grateful for any time she spent with her father. Everything was new and fresh to her, since Nula took her nowhere. A trip to the cookie counter at Marks and Spencer in Cheltenham was a treat, and when Anthony took her out to supper, all on her own, at the Fox and Terriers in Lower Oddington, she could hardly believe the glamour of it all, and asked if she could take home the sachets of mustard and tomato ketchup from the table, because they never had sauces at home. Each time he saw her Anthony slipped her ten pounds to hide away in her pocket. A covert music fan, Gaia was thrilled that her half-sister Jasmine was a famous pop star, and said everyone at her school liked her record. Anthony made a mental note to take his first-class washbag from the flight, with all its miniature toothpastes and mouthwashes, as an extra present for her.

Henry, thank goodness, wasn't a worry. Healthy, handsome, cosseted by Norland nannies on twenty-four-hour watch, Henry at eight months was never happier than being bounced in the swimming pool by Rosanna or Ambrosia. Every afternoon one of the nannies would push him around the village in his buggy. When Rosanna took him to visit Darren and Scotty at Winchford Autoparts, he was captivated by the flying sparks from the welding torch, and now insisted on going there every day.

'I think Henry is going to be a welder when he grows up,' Rosanna announced at lunch.

'I really don't think so,' Dita replied thinly. 'I think Henry can do rather better than that.'

Anthony often felt more relaxed when he was away on a business trip than home in the bosom of his family. Checked into a comfortable hotel suite in a different time zone, here for once nobody could get at him: not Dita, exes, children, stepchildren – he was free of them all. These days the entire cast of his life was roosting in different parts of Winchford. Amanda, Sandra, Nula, Dita . . . they were all there, looking to him for financial and emotional support. He felt like the big chief of an African tribe, or a Moslem sheik, with a Number One wife – Dita – and a back catalogue of cast-offs for whom he was endlessly responsible, plus all their offspring, actual or collateral. He was currently paying five sets of school fees, plus the majority of living expenses for ten children. He was paying, directly or indirectly, for three wives, one ill mother and one former mistress. He was paying for a gardener to spend ten hours a week at the Old Rectory, four hours at Steepness Farmhouse, four hours at the Lady House and three hours at Forge Cottage. Sandra had told him the York stone on her terrace was cracking and she hoped he'd get it replaced. Henrietta wanted a log-burning stove in the kitchen. And so it went on. Sometimes, he dared himself to look back on the past thirty years and figure out how he'd arrived at his present position. He knew that, at certain moments, he was still obsessed with Amanda. It had gone on for so long now it was ridiculous, but whenever he saw her his heart beat faster. This was partly alarm, since he never knew what she might do or say next; ever since they'd slept together on the night Henry was born, he'd been haunted by their guilty little secret.

Thinking about his fourteen years with Sandra, first at Forge Cottage, then at Steepness Farmhouse, it seemed to belong to another, distant period of his life, almost predating his time with Amanda. The Amanda years stood sharper in his memory, bathed in vibrant colours; the long Sandra decade of domesticity felt grey in comparison. He could still remember how he'd first got involved with Nula, and her sympathy and compassion when he became her patient. There was still plenty about Nula he admired. She could be stubborn and infuriating, but he envied the simplicity of her life. There were no extravagant curtain pelmets, no butlers. How restful it must be to live like that. Her idealism was like a clear, hard flame, in a village otherwise short on ideals.

And then, of course, there was Dita, under whose auspices Winchford had been reborn.

'I have to hand it to your wife; she really has performed miracles,' Percy Bigges said to Anthony one evening. 'Even though I imagine she can be a handful at times.'

There was so much Anthony had to be grateful to Dita for. He admired her singlemindedness, which made her forge ahead and spend his money and get things done. She had been a godsend for his business, too. Without Dita urging him on, he might never have felt bold enough to expand Anscombes so rapidly, or to hire such good people. He understood it was largely because of her that he was a success in the eyes of the world. Furthermore, she looked fantastic and sexy, and always made an effort.

But at times, in the dark nights of his soul, he wondered whether in the end he really wanted all this. Did he need his diary filled to bursting point, and his house filled with mottoed cushions? Did he want to dress up every Saturday night, and drive miles and miles out to dinner? He found Dita relentless and judgemental, and didn't always feel comfortable with her attitude to the children. He felt treacherous thinking about Dita in this way. He'd made such a hash of things before, he couldn't even think about it happening a third time. Sometimes he wished he could just take the best bits of all his women and build them into one perfect being. Other times, he thanked his lucky stars he had Dita.

Waking in the middle of the night in a Hong Kong hotel room, still on London time, he saw the red 'message waiting' light blinking on the telephone. A recorded voice informed him he had one new message. Dita.

'Anthony? God, I do hate talking to answering machines. I *wish* you wouldn't put the damn thing on when I need to speak to you. We have a situation that I don't think can wait till you're back. Anyway, the children are home from Aleco's boat, but there have clearly been some ups and downs on the holiday. John-Spiros is in a frightful state, accusing Morad of blackmailing him over some invented story. I've spoken to Morad, who denies everything, but he does say John-Spiros became very friendly with one of the male crew. They were apparently seen coming out of a cabin on the crew deck. I don't know what to believe. It's all very trying, and I need you back here. Your secretary says she can get you on the morning flight tomorrow, so kindly be on it.'

Anthony took a deep breath and sank back into the pillows. He loved his wife, but sometimes it was just all a bit too much.

50

D ita had always had a very simple attitude to money: what was hers was hers and what was Anthony's was theirs. As the years passed, Anthony became almost immune to the cost of clothes from the Bond Street boutiques she frequented, and to the fuel bills for heating the swimming pool to Dita's required temperature. Recently she had decided to keep the pool going all year round at a permanent ninety degrees Fahrenheit, and the oil lorry was arriving fortnightly to top up the tank. Long may Anscombes continue to flourish, Anthony thought nervously, as he paid himself larger and larger dividends.

Dita's fastidiousness increased with each year. She had a fixation about cushions, which must be perfectly plumped at all times. She liked to walk into a room and preferably find it empty, with sofas and armchairs betraying no sign they'd ever been sat in. The smallest crease or indent caught her eye, and she would have to lift and shake it, or summon Stigmata. Anthony never felt quite able to relax. If he was watching racing on television and needed a quick pee, he didn't feel he could leave the study for even so short a visit without first reflating his armchair.

Similar rules prevailed over the drinks tray, or rather drinks table, since the array of bottles, mixers, ice buckets and cocktail shakers occupied a large marble-topped, eighteenth-century library bench. Dita imposed precise rules on where every bottle should be placed, beginning with the multiple brands of vodka, segueing into the gins, Martini, Cinzano and whiskies. On the extreme right of the table stood the Britvic tomato juices, Clamato, tonics and sodas; at the front, three lemons on a saucer with a serrated silver knife, bottle opener, corkscrew and mixing spoon. Santos the butler was issued with a planogram showing how the bottles must stand in relation to each other, and Dita exploded when anything was put back in the wrong place. When Richard invited his rugby friends up for a drink, she hovered over them with pursed lips.

She was a woman of passionate bêtes noires. She could not stand smoking at dinner before coffee, or anyone – women particularly – going to the loo mid-meal ('Jumping up and down like yo-yos when one's trying to have a proper, civilised dinner'). She hated clumsiness and became enraged with Ambrosia, who was always bumping into tables and was probably dyspraxic. She couldn't abide bare feet in the house, which was unfortunate since Ambrosia, Rosanna and Katie went barefoot whenever possible, as did Gaia. 'Sometimes I feel I'm going to go quite mad,' she told her husband. 'There are too many untidy children in this house, and not enough help. I'm sorry, I know how you hate spending money, but we're simply going to have to hire more people.'

Everyone believed that Anthony led an almost perfect life. At the age of forty-nine, he was tall, successful, still handsome and married to a glamorous and vivacious woman. Esteemed by his neighbours, respected by his tenants and farm workers, he uncomplainingly funded the local church, cricket club, hunt and Conservative Association, not to mention his vast army of children and stepchildren. Visitors to the Priory during this period came away declaring he must be a veritable saint, the way he put up with all those different kids sprawling around the place.

Despite the considerable size of the house, you still got the impression of colliding with children in every nook and cranny. There was invariably a PlayStation in action, with three or four teenagers squabbling over the controls while, on the screen, a car screeched through a subterranean garage. Richard and Tom would be hunched over *Grand Theft Auto*, while across the room Morad was slouched in an armchair, immovably immersed in some casino challenge on Game Boy. In the library, Rosanna and Jasmine could be found milling about the drinks table with their tongues hanging out. In summer, down by the swimming pool beyond the knot garden, the long chairs were festooned by Katie, Ambrosia and their old school friends, mobile phones clamped to ears. Even settled outside on the terrace, you risked getting caught in the crossfire of five-year-old Henry's Supersoaker. Visitors asked, 'Have you *any idea* how many children Anthony actually has? I've lost count.'

'Only four or five of his own, I think,' they were told. 'The rest are all steps, halves and what-not. He just seems to accumulate them.'

'Well, it's very public-spirited of him. A lot of men wouldn't put up with it. It's bedlam over there most of the time.'

Increasingly he saw himself as a cross between an employment bureau and a careers advisor. Richard had recently returned to Anscombes for a six-month trial in the research department. But at the end of the day it became obvious he wasn't cut out for it, and he spent the next nine months repainting some of the cottages in the village and supervising the paintballing while Chalkie was away on honeymoon in Belize with Judy Holcombe. Anthony was now pinning his hopes on finding him something at a game park in Kenya, where he knew the owners of a lodge in East Tsavo.

Tom, at least, was fully taken care of, having joined the staff of Anscombes Futures Singapore (AFS) and moved into a company flat out there with two other graduate trainees. As part of the induction programme he had spent his first six weeks touring the other Anscombes offices in the region, and a steady stream of postcards began turning up in Winchford from Hong Kong, Jakarta and Tokyo. Each time Sandra received one she rang Anthony to read him the message, and to thank him once again for being so kind to her stepson. Sandra's gratitude became rather intolerable, and the more that Anthony insisted Tom had got the job on his own merits, and it wasn't mere nepotism, the more she overdid it. 'Thank goodness for you, Anthony, otherwise I don't know what we'd all do. John's so hopeless. Without you and your generosity, we'd be living on the street.' The Furlongs were planning to visit Tom in Singapore over Christmas, accompanied by Ginette if she could get away. Recently Ginette had capitalised on her kung-fu diploma by setting herself up as a security guard-cum-bouncer, with a thriving little business in the area.

Rosanna had had a good time out in Australia, and was now back in Winchford, working at the Plough and Harrow. She seemed perfectly content, and was talking about shacking up in a cottage with Darren. Katie had started at the Ruskin in Oxford, and working as a waitress at Brown's restaurant most evenings. John-Spiros would begin at the Courtauld Institute in September, studying Byzantine art, and was in the meantime assisting in the shirt department at Harrods. Morad had moved in permanently with Jonny Faisal, and the two of them spent five nights a week in nightclubs. Anthony knew Dita gave him a larger allowance than she admitted, but it was still a mystery how Morad lived so extravagantly. When Anthony took Dita and some friends for dinner at Annabel's for her birthday, they found Morad and Jonny sitting in the bar with two highly suspect-looking women, who might easily have been hookers. Morad continued to deny point-blank he'd ever tried to blackmail John-Spiros, but it did seem there was some substance to the story; John-Spiros certainly received letters for months afterwards from a ship's steward named Yiannis. Life at Winchford Priory could be very stressful at times, Anthony felt.

He consoled himself that Anscombes Futures Singapore was having another stellar year. According to the report he'd just been looking at, Anscombes' profits from SIMEX were running two hundred per cent ahead of budget and forecast. Well, that would be nice for young Tom Furlong, who'd be in line for a jolly good bonus.

51

'I do find these luggage weight restrictions utterly intolerable,' Dita declared, as she attempted to check four enormous Vuitton suitcases onto the Twin Otter twelve-seater propeller plane from Nairobi's domestic airport.

In honour of her fiftieth birthday, Anthony was taking his wife, her four children plus Rosanna and a nanny on safari to Kenya for ten days, where they would stay at the game lodge in East Tsavo National Park where Richard had been working as assistant camp manager and guide. This great expedition, which Anthony secretly hoped might act as a family bonding exercise, had obliged Dita to assemble a whole new wardrobe of clothes suitable for Africa, and for weeks she had been accumulating immaculate beige and teal-coloured linen shirts and pretty silk blouses with jungle prints. It was this stockpile of designer safariwear that now threatened to prevent the light aircraft from taking off.

Quickly palming over a hefty tip to secure the luggage, Anthony ushered his family group towards the plane. Henry was excitedly running on ahead, binoculars bouncing around his neck and a picture book of African mammals in his hand. There had been a question over whether, at five and a half, Henry was too young for a safari, but Anthony felt it wouldn't be the same without him, and Stella the nanny needed cheering up after the long, grim Winchford winter. Rosanna had problems getting through the security scanners at Heathrow, and again this morning in Nairobi, since her tongue stud and new nose ring kept setting off the alarm, and she had been made to remove all the ironmongery at Terminal Four for the X-ray. Morad, meanwhile, had the Masai knife he'd just bought in the airport shop confiscated, and was sulking and saying he didn't want to board. John-Spiros and Ambrosia, both dubious about the whole idea of a safari and sleeping in tents, were shuffling along behind, keeping a tight grip on their hand luggage. Anthony wished Jasmine could have been there too, to jolly everyone up, but she was shooting the new Gucci campaign in Santa Fe.

Crocodile Camp, situated on a particularly scenic bend of the Galdesa river, was the most luxurious and expensive lodge in East Africa. Deceptively simple with its mud walls, polished stone floors and thatched makuti leaf roofs, it prided itself on pandering to even the most jaded tastes in the middle of nowhere. Two of the chefs came from Florence and a third from Kyoto. The thatched bandas, with their tented sides, offered views of hippos wallowing in the river, eight-foot crocodiles sunning themselves on sandbanks or, if you preferred, CNN and cable channels beamed in via satellite. Each banda had a raised viewing platform with white canvas sofas for watching game at sunset, and a private jacuzzi with piles of fluffy towels in leopard prints. As she unpacked for her stay, noting with approval the multi-speed hairdryer and Jo Malone bath essence, Dita decided that other people were generally frightfully feeble when it came to safaris, and she simply didn't have a problem with roughing it for a few days.

Anthony felt exhilarated by being in Africa for the first time. It was marvellous to see Richard looking so fit and confident. He had been working at the camp for several months taking guests out in jeeps on game drives; he seemed to have grown up, and was full of funny stories about previous tourists at the lodge. In his knee-length brown shorts, brown shirt and leather hat, he looked like Crocodile Dundee. He told his father he was having an amazing time, and had made friends with several white Kenyans who farmed upcountry. He shared a staff hut with another guide, with enough space to have friends to stay if he wished. 'Tom's flying over from Singapore at the weekend. He's got a few days leave from the old sweatshop.'

Striding around camp on that first afternoon, Anthony was awed by the physical beauty of the place. The National Park was bounded on one side by a sheer escarpment, seventy miles long, beyond which lay Somalia. He instantly fell in love with the trees of Kenya, the dom palms and euphobia and huge conifer africana with its spreading umbrella branches, and wondered how they would grow if transplanted to Winchford. On the riverbank, a yellow crested crane with plumage like an Inca headdress was picking its way carefully across the mudflats. Richard pointed out an African hawk eagle, soaring high above camp. On the way to lunch, a swallowtail butterfly fluttered across his path before settling on a jacaranda bush. As an eleven-year-old, it had been his life's ambition to one day see a swallowtail.

He arrived at the lunch mess to find a table of quarrelling, disgruntled youths. Morad was refusing to share a banda with John-Spiros, saying he'd rather die. 'Come on, I wouldn't even be able to get *changed*, not with that poof in the next bed. It wouldn't be safe!' John-Spiros, looking like he might burst into tears any moment, said he didn't want to share with Morad either and couldn't he be with Ambrosia instead? Ambrosia, who was meant to be sharing with Rosanna, said she'd quite like to be with John-Spiros, and couldn't they all just swap around, but Rosanna said, 'No fucking way am I sharing with Morad! Not if you gave me a million quid.' To make matters worse, neither John-Spiros nor Ambrosia felt happy sleeping in a banda at all, having been told that lion and hippo tracks were regularly found inside camp in the morning. 'They prowl around the tents at night and I'm *scared*,' Ambrosia wailed. 'I won't be able to sleep; they might *get in*.' The only one who seemed happy about the rooming arrangements was Henry, who adored the camp bed with mosquito netting that had been set up in Stella's banda, and told everyone he'd already farted in the jacuzzi ('You can't even tell, because of all the bubbles. You can just fart as much as you like.').

In the end, at Dita's suggestion, Anthony felt he had no option but to rent an extra banda at colossal expense, so Morad and Rosanna could sleep separately. He also managed to get John-Spiros and Ambrosia shifted to a hut next to his own, so they'd feel safer.

On the first morning, half an hour before dawn, one of the Masai warriors who patrolled the camp at night began waking the guests, calling softly at the flap of the tents: 'Sir, sir, bed tea, bed tea.' Accustomed to early starts, Anthony was quickly up and about, dressed, showered, shaved and finished in the bathroom to allow Dita her space. He loved that first hour when the mist still lay on the river, and the only sound was the occasional gloop of a hippo submerging beneath the glassy surface. Richard joined him on the riverbank, wide awake and miraculously focused in his role as guide, to point out the bird life. He's astonishingly observant, Anthony thought proudly, as Richard identified a golden-backed weaver or a bush shrike flitting about in the reeds.

Soon, a convoy of long-based jeeps was assembling at the camp gates, with drivers, trackers, naturalists and park wardens, all waiting to escort the Anscombe family on their early morning game drive. Anthony and Richard were pacing up and down, chatting to the Kenyan drivers and eager to get going. Surreptitiously, Anthony glanced at his watch: where was everybody? Dita had told him she wouldn't be long.

Henry was tearing along the path in shorts and a Ralph Lauren polo shirt, waving the Masai spear he'd borrowed from a nightwatchman. 'We won't be having *that* inside the jeep, thank you very much, Henry', said Anthony, whisking it out of his hand, before helping him and Stella up into the vehicles. Not far behind came Rosanna, yawning and wiping the sleep out of her eyes, and getting her bead bracelets tangled up in her eyebrow rings.

'Well done, Rosanna,' Anthony said. 'Now, where's everyone else got to? They're late!'

'Well, I passed Morad's tent and he's in bed,' Rosanna said. 'He's watching television.'

'Strewth!' cursed Anthony, striding towards the huts to fetch him.

John-Spiros now appeared, looking like Tintin in long linen shorts, followed by a white-faced Ambrosia. 'Are you *sure* we won't get attacked by a lion?' she asked Richard. 'I'm staying inside the jeep with the windows shut.'

Anthony arrived at Morad's banda to find him lying on top of his sheets in a pair of black briefs, watching cartoons.

'For heaven's sake, Morad, get up right now. You're terribly late. We're meant to have left twenty minutes ago.'

Morad stretched, yawned and rolled over. 'Why so *early*? It's not even half past seven, for Christsakes. Normally, I've only just got to sleep.'

'Quickly now, out of bed. There's no time for this. If we want to see any animals, we have to get going. Television off.' He grabbed the zapper out of Morad's hand and killed Homer Simpson.

'Hey, I was *watching that.*'

'*Out of bed,*' ordered Anthony. 'Now!'

By the time he returned to the jeeps, Dita was tapping her foot impatiently. 'There you are, Anthony. We're all standing round waiting for you. Honestly, there isn't any point getting us all up at this unearthly hour if you're going to disappear.' Before he could reply, Morad showed up dressed like an SAS assassin in black cashmere rollneck, army fatigues, military boots and Dolce and Gabbana shades, and clambered into the rear jeep.

'For Pete's sake, let's get moving,' Anthony said. And then, apologising to the drivers, 'Sorry to have kept you waiting, boys; we're all here now.'

The convoy of vehicles set off along a dirt track, crossed a tributary of the Galdesa via a pontoon bridge, and went up onto an endless plateau of parched brown grassland and thornbushes. 'Has anyone seen a tiger?' Henry asked, training his binoculars on the bush.

'Tigers don't actually exist in Africa, idiot,' Rosanna replied. 'They only have lions.'

'*I've seen a lion,*' Henry shrieked. 'Look – *over there,* by that tree.'

The front jeep slammed on its brakes, followed by the two other jeeps behind. Soon, all the drivers, guides, trackers, naturalists and wardens were sticking their heads through open sunroofs and peering into the bushes.

After about a minute Anthony said, 'Well, I can't see anything. Are you quite sure about this, Henry?'

Henry burst out laughing. 'Made you look, made you stare, made you lose your underwear,' he chanted, in a maddening ditty he'd picked up at school.

The convoy moved on, painfully slowly in Dita's opinion, stopping every few hundred yards to look at tiny deer, hardly larger than greyhounds. These deer, which Dita remarked were a good deal less impressive than the ones in Richmond Park, stood about in forlorn little herds, munching at grass. Each time they spotted one, the driver stopped and the naturalist whispered reverentially, 'Bluebuck. That is bluebuck.' Sometimes, he said they were gazelle, ibex or waterbuck, but they all looked much of a muchness.

'For goodness' sake,' Dita began muttering to Anthony. 'Tell them we don't want to see one more deer, can't you? We've come all this way to see lions and rhinos, not deer.'

'Point taken, Dita,' said Richard in guide mode. 'I've asked the trackers to go all out for the Big Five now. Obviously one can't guarantee anything, but I'll be disappointed if we don't find lion, rhino, elephant, leopard or buffalo this morning.'

'I'm surprised buffalo count as dangerous animals,' Dita replied sniffily. 'Though buffalo mozzarella can be terribly fattening.'

The vehicles jolted across a long veldt of scrubland beside a wide, dried-up riverbed strewn with boulders and pieces of driftwood. Anthony thought Africa was the most beautiful place he'd ever visited, and felt himself floating off into a kind of trance, mesmerised by the heat and unfamiliar landscape. In the front jeep, Rosanna was standing up with her head through the sunroof, camera poised in readiness. Each time they turned a corner, she expected to see a leopard asleep on a rock, and she repeatedly extended and retracted the zoom lens for focus. In the second jeep, Ambrosia and John-Spiros were boiling to death inside the airless cabin, with windows tight shut and doors locked. The further they ventured from camp, the more anxious John-Spiros became. Oughtn't they to be heading back now? What would happen if they ran out of petrol? They hadn't passed a petrol station all morning. So far, thank God, they hadn't seen any dangerous animals, but the thought of it made him shiver and sweat. Ambrosia was thinking how much she preferred *The Lion King* video to the real thing.

Morad was sitting on the roof of the rear jeep, mouthing into his mobile. He'd been glued to the mobile non-stop since they'd left Gald-esa. Sprawled behind him was Stella the nanny, who had stripped off her T-shirt and was sunbathing in a bikini top. Spotting her from the front vehicle, Dita was horrified. 'I can't believe my eyes,' she told Anthony. 'That girl's a disgrace. You're going to have to talk to her, Anthony. We can't have people like that working for us.'

'We can hardly sack her out here, darling,' Anthony replied softly, conscious that Henry was sitting behind them.

'It's just *not on*. You've got to back me up on this one. It's indecent, especially in front of all these black drivers. What must they all be thinking?'

Richard felt greatly relieved. Five hundred yards ahead, and clearly visible through his field glasses, was a small herd of zebra sheltering in the shade of a tamarind tree. And, better still, he could see a pair of giraffes on the horizon, snacking away at the topgrowth of an acacia bush. For a guide, nothing is more embarrassing than a no-show of animals in a game reserve, and he had several times faced the wrath of tourists who'd paid for a day's permit and expected to photograph every large mammal for their money. He felt a definite lessening of tension as he pointed out the wildlife to Dita.

Like her father and brother, Rosanna was loving the safari. It was years now since her big thing about ponies, but she felt all her old interest in animals coming back. 'Wouldn't it be wicked to have a zebra at Winch-ford?' she said to Richard. 'I could ride it in point to points.'

'They're virtually impossible to tame,' Richard said. 'People have tried, but they refuse to be saddled up. You'd be better off riding a buffalo.'

'What's the difference between a buffalo and a bison?' Henry asked. 'You can't wash your hands in a buffalo! Do you get it? Bison – like basin. You can't wash your *hands* in a *buffalo*.'

'Do shut up in the back,' Dita snapped. 'We're meant to be appreciating these beautiful zebra, not making feeble jokes.' But she was thinking: would that padded footstool in the study at Winchford look better covered in zebraskin than the tapestry material she'd just ordered?

Morad was thinking what a total waste of time this safari was turning out to be. He'd expected to see a lion bringing down an antelope, or at least springing up onto the roof of John-Spiros's jeep and scaring the shit out of the little runt. As it was, it was all just completely pointless. He'd have considered having a punt at the nanny – she was clearly begging for it – if he didn't have a few other things on his mind. Frowning, he picked up the cellphone and began punching in the code for London.

Life at Crocodile Camp had an unvarying rhythm. Up before dawn for the early morning game drive, they returned to camp at half past ten for breakfast served by half a dozen Kenyan waiters in white mess jackets. Beyond that, there was nothing planned until the evening game drive at five, except to loll around in the club room with its white sofas, giraffeskin rugs and collection of primitive witchdoctor masks, which Ambrosia found creepy and refused to go anywhere near. Anthony and Richard played chess while Morad, who was looking haggard, took his mobile down to the river to make private calls.

'Careful a crocodile doesn't get you, Morad,' Henry warned. 'They do eat people, you know.'

'Sod off, tit,' replied Morad.

Each day, fewer people showed up for the morning drive. First it was Morad who dropped out, saying he had ten thousand hours of sleep to catch up on. Then John-Spiros and Ambrosia said they'd prefer a lie-in too; Ambrosia had been having nightmares about a lion getting inside her tent and had woken her brother, so both were now exhausted. Then Stella said she'd got the runs from all the strange food. Dita announced she was fed up looking at waterbuck, and would appreciate some peace and quiet.

So by day four it was just Anthony, Rosanna and Henry joining Richard's dawn tours, while the rest stayed in bed. It was an arrangement that suited everyone, since it meant they could fit into one jeep and travel faster and lighter. On the fifth morning they watched a sleek-coated cheetah accelerate across the plain to bring down an impala, and drag it over to her cubs. The following day, having followed a trail of its dung through the bush, they found a rare black rhinoceros drinking at a waterhole.

'We ought to go back and shoot that,' Morad said when they told him. 'The Chinese pay twenty thousand dollars for black rhino tusk.'

Tom Furlong was due to arrive the next day via Nairobi from Singapore, and it was therefore decided that Dita's fiftieth birthday celebration dinner should be postponed until that evening, so he could be part of it too. Richard was excited at the prospect of seeing his stepbrother. He hadn't clapped eyes on him for a year, and had planned a big programme of drives including taking him to see the Tsavo elephants, famous for their red hides from rolling in the red dust. Anthony, too, was pleased Tom was arriving. He had a soft spot for his honorary stepson, and looked forward to hearing how everything was going in Singapore. He thought it would pep everyone up at Crocodile Camp having Tom there; after a week together, they were starting to get on each other's nerves.

Tom arrived with an embroidered jacket with a picture of a Chinese dragon on the back as a birthday present for Dita, which he'd bought in a Singapore streetmarket, and a copy of *Hello!* for Anthony. 'I picked this up at the airport,' he said, cracking open a Tusker beer. 'It's got a whole long thing about Jasmine.'

Anthony ordered a Tusker for himself and settled down on a sofa with the magazine. The feature about Jasmine went on for pages and pages, and many of the pictures had Amanda in them too. 'Supermodel Jasmine still brings her washing round to Mum,' read one caption, which amazed Anthony since he knew it was dropped off for Stigmata to take care of. The first fourteen pages had been taken at some hotel spa, with Jasmine and Amanda lying side by side on massage beds, 'being pampered' as the caption put it. These were followed by ten pages in a chintzy country hotel, toasting each other with golden goblets with a big gold candelabra between them on the table. Jasmine looked incredible in an elaborate backless balldress made of black netting and chicken wire. Amanda looked hardly older than her daughter, wearing a chainmail sheath by Trevor Bratt for Saint-Simone. Finally, there were half a dozen pictures of them at Winchford ('Jasmine's idyllic weekend haven on her millionaire father's private estate'), making lunch in the kitchen at Forge Cottage and walking across the fields with the Priory in the background.

Peering over his shoulder at the article, Dita said, 'What cheek! I don't remember anyone asking permission to be photographed in that field.'

'Ah well,' Anthony replied. 'They both look jolly nice in the photographs.'

'If you ask me, they look perfectly ghastly. Very common. Amanda's face is bright red in some of these photographs.'

Anthony could never look at a picture of his first wife without re-examining how he currently felt about her. He felt she'd become a softer, more sympathetic person than the girl he married all those years ago. Life had not always been kind to her. In some of the photographs she seemed sad and needy, and there was no denying she looked older; there were deep crow's feet around her eyes. But in others she didn't look old at all, and he clearly recognised the old Amanda from the storm-tossed raft. It crossed his mind that, if she was here at the lodge instead of Dita, they'd all be having a much more amusing time, but he quickly suppressed that disloyal thought.

*

It was a typical afternoon at Crocodile Camp. Anthony was teaching Henry to play draughts at the games table. John-Spiros was thumbing through an ant-infested picture book called *African Style and Interiors* from the library. Dita was tidying up and scolding, collecting together the numerous pairs of shoes strewn all over the place. Richard and Tom had gone off in a jeep to search for rhino. Morad was muttering into his mobile on the riverbank, and cursing whenever he lost connection.

'Be a good fellow and turn that telephone *off*, won't you, Morad?' Anthony called out. 'You've been talking on it non-stop since lunchtime.'

But Morad pretended not to hear, and moved further away from the mess banda. He was looking distinctly off-colour, and Anthony wondered if he'd forgotten to take his malaria pills.

For Dita's birthday dinner, a dining room under canvas had been erected on the banks of the Galdesa, half a mile upstream from the lodge, surrounded by a perimeter of flaming torches to keep the crocs at bay. The chefs were preparing a six-course banquet with ingredients specially flown in from South Africa. With Dita's encouragement, they had also managed to secure several bottles of French champagne which were arriving by road from Mombasa. Everyone was under instructions to change into their smartest clothes for the celebration, the high point of the holiday.

Soon they were all clambering into jeeps for the short ride to dinner, Dita dressed for the Caribbean in a long chiffon evening dress and reeking of Gucci Envy, John-Spiros in a white linen suit that made him resemble a Thirties archaeologist. Out of respect for her stepmother's party, Rosanna had agreed to remove her nose ring, but not the tongue stud in case it healed up.

It was the most romantic setting imaginable. A bonfire had been lit on the sandy riverbank, which flickered and crackled in the darkness, and the dining area was illuminated by dozens of storm lanterns. Music had been rigged up and a ghetto blaster was playing a song called 'Jambo Bwana'. Fifty yards out into the river, they heard the honeypot splash of hippos lumbering into the water. Waiters circulated with Krug wrapped in linen napkins.

Anthony's mobile went off in his pocket. Damn it, he thought, I should have switched the ruddy thing off. But he saw Charlotte his PA's name flash up on the display, and thought he'd better take it. She'd promised not to ring unless it was important.

'Charlotte? . . . No, don't worry, it's fine . . . we're all having drinks next to a river; we're having a marvellous time; all your brilliant organisation worked like clockwork . . . now, how can I help you?'

He could see Dita glaring at him for taking a phone call from the office. 'Bloody office,' she was mouthing. 'Tell them to manage without you for once.'

'We've got a bit of a problem here,' Charlotte was saying. 'Some policemen turned up at the office at lunchtime, asking where they could find Morad Ahvazi. I said he was abroad on holiday – I hope I did the right thing. And now there's something about him in the evening paper. He seems to be in a bit of trouble.'

'Oh, Christ. What's he gone and done now?' Anthony could see Morad eavesdropping on the conversation, white-faced and tipping back a glass of champagne.

Charlotte sounded embarrassed. 'Well, I'm only going on what it says here. I can fax it to you if you prefer.'

'You'd better tell us what it's about.'

'Well, some girl in a nightclub has made a complaint about him. It says here that they, er, went to bed together at a hotel, but she's saying she couldn't remember much about it the next day, and thinks she was drugged. She thinks something was slipped into her drink.'

'I see. And she's dragged the police into it?'

Dita had picked up on the drama now, and was mouthing, 'What the hell's going on?'

Anthony waved at her to keep quiet. 'Say that again please, Charlotte? The line's breaking up. The police want to talk to Morad? But you don't think they've actually charged him. What's that? Lots of newspapers are ringing Corporate Communications wanting information about him? Look, tell them to say nothing, OK? This isn't an Anscombes issue; it's a private matter, and we shouldn't be giving any statement. They should just say "No comment" to everything, please. Is that understood? And, yes, please fax everything to the camp; you've got the number. I've seen the fax machine and I doubt the line's very reliable, so you'll probably have to keep trying, I'm afraid.'

After that, the party mood was hard to recapture. Under pressure from Anthony, Morad admitted he knew what it was all about, and said the girl had invented the whole thing. 'She's only saying it because she wants money to go away. She's a professional – an escort girl – you can't believe a word she says.'

'Where did you even meet this horrible woman?' Dita asked, already siding with her son.

'Vagabonds in Duke Street. It's a club Jonny and I go to.'

'So Jonny was with you?' Anthony asked. 'Could he be a helpful witness?'

Morad shrugged. 'He'd already left. He'd met this air-stewardess from the Emirates.'

Richard and Tom did their best to jolly things along at dinner. Tom was full of stories about life in Singapore, which seemed to centre around the bar of Raffles Hotel and an English-style pub behind SIMEX, but his audience was distracted. At regular intervals Dita said, 'I just don't understand it. Why does everyone keep picking on poor Morad?' Later she said, 'This is all your fault, Anthony.'

'*My* fault?'

'You banned the poor boy from his home. No wonder he gets into trouble.'

'Darling, you know perfectly well why. In fact, it would probably be sensible if we didn't refer to that particular episode again, under the circumstances.'

'God, you can be pompous sometimes. Why are you automatically assuming Morad is guilty, when he's the one who's been falsely accused by this lying tart?'

'Dita, I am not assuming anything, I assure you. I'm trying to work out the best thing to do next. We need to find out what's been going on, what exactly this woman is saying, and then get some good legal advice.'

'Are you going to go to *prison*, Morad?' Henry asked. He found the idea hilarious. 'All you get to eat is bread and water, you know, and you'll have to dig an underground tunnel to escape.'

John-Spiros privately thought it would be a very good thing if Morad was put away for several years, and tucked into his marinated red snapper. Ambrosia sniffled into her napkin. By the time the waiters produced an enormous chocolate birthday cake with fifty candles on top, Dita barely had the enthusiasm to blow them out.

Back at camp, Anthony found the fax of the *Evening Standard* article plus some messages from the office. The article was more prominent and damaging than Charlotte had let on. A big picture of Morad stared out from the page, which described him as heir to the Emboroleon shipping empire and stepson of the chairman of Anscombe Brothers. More worrying was the photograph of the girl, who looked young and sweet, and not at all like Morad's description of a hard-bitten callgirl. Her complaint raised more questions than it answered, but she had evidently met Morad at this club, Vagabonds, where he'd bought her several drinks. Beyond that, she couldn't remember anything until waking up in a bedroom at the Dorchester Hotel. She had gone to her doctor who found traces of a strong sedative substance in her bloodstream.

The messages said that an officer from Savile Row police station had rung, asking for details of when they would be returning to the country. A second message said reporters from *The Times*, the *Daily Mail*, the *Daily Express*, the *Daily* and *Sunday Telegraph*, *The Sunday Times*, the *Observer* and the *Cotswold Journal* had all rung, leaving numbers and requesting someone call them back urgently.

Anthony and Dita sat up late, chewing over the whole affair. Anthony said he'd ring London first thing tomorrow morning and get the best lawyers possible on the case. Dita, hysterical, was filled with contempt for 'this money-grubbing whore', and wanted to file a countersuit for defamation. Alternatively, Morad should go and live in South Africa or Zimbabwe until the fuss died down, 'Since he obviously won't get a fair hearing in England. They hate people like us.'

The next morning Charlotte sent through all the articles from the day's papers, which disgorged from the fax in a long roll onto the floor. The newspapers had really gone to town, devoting almost a full page each to the story. Several new pictures of Morad had been tracked down overnight, including some unsavoury ones taken in various nightclubs and a Millfield school photograph. The *Daily Mail* had excelled itself, with no fewer than five whole pages of coverage, including a profile of Morad by Geoffrey Levy which made Anthony squirm. Somehow he'd got hold of all sorts of stuff about Morad's expulsions from Le Rosey, Milton Abbey and Millfield, and numerous quotes, all derogatory, from unnamed 'friends'. Some friends, Anthony thought. They had also very quickly made the connection between Morad and Jasmine, and there were pictures in several papers of 'Morad's stepsister, supermodel Jasmine.' A photograph of the Priory turned up in *The Times*, plus a lot of inaccurate speculation about 'the legendary wealth of the secretive Anscombe dynasty (family motto: *probity in all things*).'

Dita was enraged by the articles, snorting, 'How dare they write that!' and insisting Anthony sue all the newspapers at once. The next day was their last full one in Kenya, and Anthony looked into the possibility of flying home early with Morad to meet with lawyers. But flights proved impossible to change, so they sat out the remaining time feeling tense and glum.

Richard and Tom took Anthony and Henry out for a final drive around, to keep out of the way, and Tom told Anthony about his work as a trader. 'There's so much money to be made in Asia if you get it right,' he said. 'We have an open line between our desk at SIMEX and the Anscombes desk at the Osaka exchange in Japan. When there's a big volume of trades going through, we can make half a million dollars in margin commission in a couple of hours. It's money for old rope.'

'Well, do be careful,' Anthony warned. 'One thing I've learnt over the years is that it's never as easy to make money as people think. But awfully easy to lose it.'

'Relax,' Tom said. 'We know what we're doing.'

Charlotte faxed through the next afternoon's *Evening Standard*, which had managed to scrape up yet more on the episode. Morad was evidently now so notorious that his first name was sufficient to explain him: MORAD – DAD'S SECRET PAST. For a second, Anthony thought they'd got something on *him*, then realised it was Morad's father, Sharif Ahvazi, they were referring to. According to the article, Sharif's reputation as a casino owner had been distinctly shady. 'All his casinos were fronts for prostitution rackets and money laundering. It was well known, if you wanted a girl, or several girls, for a night or a weekend, everyone called Sharif. All the Lebanese and Iranians in Monte Carlo in the sixties swore by him,' a playboy named Taki Theodorocopoulos was quoted as saying. The article went on to disclose that Ahvazi had been married four times, his last wife being a croupier at one of his casinos: Rita Chubb, Morad's mother. She had gone on to marry Aleco Emboroleon, the shipping tycoon, and her present husband was the banker Anthony Anscombe.

'I didn't realise you'd been a croupier. Why didn't you say? It sounds fun.'

Dita had turned as white as a sheet; he had never seen her so tense. 'Aleco never liked me to mention it: he disapproved. Anyway, it was only for a short time, and so long ago I can't remember,' she said quickly. 'It's not important.'

'And your name is really Rita?'

'I never liked it. Even as a child, I wanted to change it. Does it matter so much? These days people change everything: their breasts, their faces. Why not your name?' Looking suddenly vulnerable, she asked, 'Do you suppose a lot of people will read this rubbish? Our friends, I mean?'

Anthony shook his head. 'I doubt it. You don't need to worry – most are away skiing.'

Then, gathering herself, she said, 'I just don't want my hairdresser and people like that reading it.'

'Let's concentrate on Morad, shall we? People have very short memories in any case. Whatever Morad's done or not done, there's bound to be a solution.' But he was thinking: *Morad*. It's always ruddy Morad. What did I do to deserve him as a stepchild?

The following evening they caught the overnight flight from Jomo Kenyatta airport to Heathrow. Throughout the journey, Morad watched videos in his seatback and ordered alcoholic drinks. By the time they landed in London, a light snow was falling on the runway and Morad was plastered.

"Doors to manual," announced the Captain, as the retractable gantries moved into position.

'Are you Mr Morad Ahvazi?' asked the police officer waiting at the boarding gate. 'I'm afraid I have to take you to the station for questioning, if you wouldn't mind accompanying me.'

52

By long tradition, the Heythrop hunt met on the front lawn at Winchford Priory on the first Saturday following the Boxing Day meet. Anthony regarded it as an obligation and pleasure to provide the field with mulled wine and sausage rolls, and most of the village gravitated up to the big house to look at the horses and generally snoop about.

Since Dita's arrival on the scene, the standard of hospitality had risen considerably. Her chef, she argued, was much too busy and far too grand to start making sausage rolls for hundreds of people, so a catering company in Stow was engaged instead to provide trays of honeyed sausages with Dijon mustard, mini filet mignons, spare ribs and smoked salmon blinis. As a result, twice as many hunt followers turned up, and Dita complained they were treading on the early snowdrops.

Despite having no interest in hunting herself, Dita enjoyed playing the lady of the manor, and liked to contrast the quality of food at 'our' meet to that at neighbouring big houses. The annual hunt weekend was a time for filling the Priory to capacity with guests, particularly her interior decorator friends, who lapped up the spectacle of men on horseback in pink coats. They stood well back on the terrace in their fur-collared overcoats, warming their hands around silver cups of hot bullshot, and exclaiming at what a picturesque place the English countryside is, and how they really must talk to Anthony about renting a weekend cottage.

Anthony was relieved a degree of normality was at last returning to life. It was a good eight weeks since anything about Morad had appeared in any newspaper and the case wasn't scheduled to be heard until the early spring. Already he had spent sixty thousand pounds on legal bills, and it would probably top a couple of hundred before it was over. He and Dita had spent more time in legal chambers than he cared to remember, constructing the case for the defence with a QC and his cast of assistants and solicitors. What made the whole business so soul-destroying was that Morad seemed quite ungrateful, and he was going to make a hopelessly bad witness. In the rehearsal the lawyers had made him go through, he had come over as arrogant and unconvincing under cross-examination. A part of Anthony thought, to hell with this, a year in prison will do him a power of good, but Dita refused to countenance the possibility of Morad being guilty. She was determined all his stepbrothers and stepsisters should attend court as character witnesses, even Tom and Katie Furlong. 'After all, they do live in one of our houses *entirely rent free*. It's the least they can do to help.'

It had been a grisly eight months. The bad publicity went on and on; having exhausted everything there was to say about Morad, they moved on to the rest of the family. Each time poor Jasmine was written about, they always dragged up Morad, 'her half-Iranian playboy stepbrother, recently charged on a drug rape rap.' One of the Sunday colour supplements sent a writer and photographer to Winchford to produce 'an anatomy of a quintessential English village torn apart by a rape scandal'; numerous soft-focus pictures of the Norman church, almshouses, pub and village green appeared, along with mildly irritating interviews with the vicar, Len and Walter Twine, who banged on about being given a goose for Christmas by Anthony's grandfather.

A few weeks afterwards, a second, much more distressing article appeared in the *Mail on Sunday*. This one focused on 'the colourful personal life of Morad's stepdad, multi-millionaire banker Anthony Anscombe, the much-married man who fills up his ancestral estate with his cast-off women.'

'On the surface,' the article began, 'Anthony Anscombe is a man who has everything. Fabulously wealthy, with a private estate, private village, a glamorous socialite wife and, whenever he needs money, a private bank that bears his own name. But, insiders reveal, there is another, less savoury side to the priapic squire of Winchford with its 2,000 impeccably manicured acres and picture-postcard honeystone cottages. Informed sources speak of a ruthless, manipulative autocrat who has loved and left a string of women, and whose tangled amorous history has left him supporting ten offspring, many the direct consequence of his own sexual gratification.' The article was illustrated by a glamorous photograph of Dita arriving at the Conservative Winter Ball, a picture of Amanda and Jasmine bought in from *Hello!*, an old photograph of Sandra as a jump judge at Pony Club camp syndicated from the *Cotswold Journal*, and a paparazzi shot of Nula hugging a tree.

Anthony had never seen Dita so angry as when she read that article. She entirely blamed Anthony, and said she hated being 'paraded across the newspapers next to all your exes. It's so undignified.' Anthony guessed her reaction was partly a delayed response to the exposé of Sharif Ahvazi as a Monte Carlo pimp, and the revelation she'd been born Rita Chubb. Dita had never again referred to that episode, but he knew it had rattled her. For several months afterwards, she had become nervously social, accepting every invitation as though half afraid of being ostracised. But the anxiety passed. With a hide like a rhinoceros, and an advanced sense of entitlement, Dita was irrepressible.

For weeks afterwards, Anthony found himself apologising for the article to all comers. Sandra was horrified at finding herself in the newspapers, and John drew Anthony aside to tell him how upset she was. 'You really mustn't let it happen again, old boy,' he said pompously. Nula, who didn't normally read newspapers, made a great fuss about the invasion of her privacy. Jeremy Meek referred to the article in his Sunday sermon ('We pray for all those going through turbulent times, and ask God to absolve them for all their past sins, even as they face retribution through the public prints'), which made everyone in the church gawp and stare at Anthony's pew. Len and Marjorie buttonholed him in the village shop, saying that takings in the Plough and Harrow had doubled since all the publicity. 'People drive miles on the off-chance of spotting you, squire,' Len said. 'You're a local celebrity.' Only Amanda was genuinely sympathetic, ringing him to say how unfair it all was. 'You do realise everyone in the village adores you,' she said.

It was approaching half-past ten and the huntsmen and hounds arrived from kennels and were congregating on the lawn. In Repton's Field, dozens of riders were deboxing and hacking up through the watermeadows. It was a sunny, crisp morning, with a clear blue sky the colour of duck eggs, and the waitresses from Clarissa's Kitchen, the catering company, were weaving between the horses' flanks with their trays of food. It really was the most glorious scene, Anthony thought, like an old hunting tablemat come to life. The four joint masters of the Heythrop in their pink coats and hunt buttons were welcoming the field, the hounds circling and yapping, eager to get started. The parkland with its mighty horse chestnut trees had seldom looked more alluring, the coarse grass in their shadow still bristly with early morning frost. Across the valley, the summit of Steepness Hill lay golden in a halo of sunshine. At moments like this, Anthony felt himself blessed to own a beautiful place like Winchford, and proud he could give something back by sharing it with the local hunt.

To Anthony's delight, Rosanna had recently taken up riding again and was out with the hunt, as was six-year-old Henry on his first pony. Henry looked very dapper on the chestnut gelding Dita had bought him from a stud in Northamptonshire. He had a natural seat, and in his new tweed jacket, Pony Club tie, shiny black boots and carrying a silver-topped riding crop, he was the smartest child at the meet. Dita's decorator friends had been cooing over him non-stop since breakfast.

'I think it's just *so unfair* we can't take guns with us hunting,' Henry said. 'I'd take my Supersoaker, and when I see the fox I'd squirt him in the eye.'

Out of courtesy to the hunt, Rosanna had removed her nose ring and lip ring for the day, and put her hair in a hairnet under her riding hat. Anthony could scarcely recognise her. She was living with Darren in a Winchford Estate cottage on the Moreton Road, and spending less time at the pub these days. So far as Anthony could make out, they spent most evenings together watching snooker on TV and ordering take-away curries.

Anthony was shortening Henry's stirrups when Sandra loomed up. 'Gosh, Henry, you look so grown up. You're like Little Lord Fauntleroy,' she said, nodding meaningfully at Anthony. 'I could have lent you Tom's old riding kit, if you'd asked. I've still got it somewhere.'

'I wish we had. Dita went slightly mad and bought it all new.'

'I suppose it doesn't make any difference to people like you. Money, I mean. When you have so much.'

Before Anthony could defend himself, she began scolding her new retriever, the replacement for Thatcher, which was straining at its lead. 'Will you *stop that*, Duncan. Bad Duncan. Heel, damn you, heel.' Duncan was named after the newly-appointed Leader of the Opposition, Iain Duncan-Smith, whom Sandra regarded as a great improvement on the previous two. 'We're getting somewhere at last. Blair's quaking in his boots, that's what I hear,' Sandra had said recently.

Looking around the throng of spectators, Anthony reckoned three-quarters of the village must have turned out. He spotted his mother, now so frail she could barely lift her chin from her chest, accompanied by her latest £450-a-week nurse, this one Malaysian. Average length of service for nurses at the Lady House had now dropped to less than six weeks. He didn't blame them – Henrietta was the invalid from hell – but he wasn't sure how much longer the agencies could continue to supply replacements.

'Big field today,' said Percy Bigges. 'I don't think I've seen so many people for a long time.' The towering bay buttocks of an immense hunter were reversing in their direction, and the two men moved to sidestep them.

'There are certainly plenty of foxes about,' Anthony said. 'I passed two squashed on the road this morning when I went to fill the car with petrol. Up near the Happy Eater. Two foxes and a badger.'

'Jacinthe and Bella are both mounted,' Percy said. 'There was a rumour the antis were going to make an appearance, but no sign so far, thank God.'

Anthony laughed. 'You probably heard, a group of antis turned up at the Plough and Harrow before Christmas, after the meet at Cornwell Glebe. Len sent them packing. Wouldn't serve them a drink, wouldn't even let them use the loo.'

Percy looked uncomfortable. 'You know who's become very in with the saboteurs? Your, er, friend over at Steepness Farm. The healer.'

'Nula?'

He nodded. 'I was up there the other day, dropping in the parish newsletter, and she's covered half her windows with posters. Must be difficult to see out.'

'Don't talk to me about Nula. All I can say is she's very sincere. And a good mother to my daughter, in her own mad way.'

'Well, a word to the wise. She's allowing the antis to use your out-buildings to store their placards. Not that I altogether blame her for being anti. I'm fairly ambivalent myself. But hunting does provide some badly-needed entertainment out here in the sticks.'

Up on the terrace, Anthony could see Dita with her coterie of deco-rators and art historians. John-Spiros was mingling in amongst them, trying to engage them in conversation about Byzantine mosaics, when all they wanted was to gossip about Princess Pushy and the Beauforts at Badminton. Dita was discussing her new pet project of building an orangery beyond the swimming pool in the style of Vanbrugh. Morad, thank goodness, was still banned from Winchford. As a condition of his bail, he had to stay in London at the Cadogan Place flat, where he passed his weekends watching *Gladiator* on video. Recently he had become obsessed by the movie, and had taken to quoting lines from it.

Several sharp parps on the hunting horn and the field began to move off. 'The hounds are speaking well,' said Jacinthe, as the whipper-in directed them towards the watermeadows and open country beyond. Dozens of Thelwell children in tweed jackets trotted behind on fat ponies. 'Henry, stay close to me,' Rosanna told her half-brother.

They were leaving the lawn when an ear-splitting clamour sounded from the shrubbery. Suddenly, a large group of antis, at least forty of them, appeared from the bushes carrying placards and banging on musical instruments. At their head stood Nula with a pair of cymbals, crashing them together – *Cling! Clang!* – as the din reverberated around the valley. Standing nervously next to her mother was Gaia.

'Oh Christ,' Anthony muttered. He stared despairingly at Nula. She looked absolutely bonkers in a knitted Rasta hat in the colours of the Jamaican flag: gold, green and black. Her hair hung around her shoulders in lustreless rat's tails. Recently she had given up on commercial shampoo, which she said was full of cancer-causing chemicals, and she scrubbed her head with organic soap.

Now the antis were booing and jeering the riders. Many of the others had their parka hoods pulled up over their heads, or scarves tied around their faces so it was impossible to identify them. One tossed a dead cat into the middle of the hounds, and the huntsmen fought it away from them, fearing it might be poisoned. Nula, courageous, ethereal, demented, smashed her cymbals together while chanting, 'Ban all bloodsports – let fox be! Running wild and running free!' The chant was taken up by all the protestors, faster and faster. '*Ban all bloodsports* – let fox *be*! Running wild and running *free*!'

'Oh, for God's sake just *bog off*, won't you?' Sandra shouted out from the crowd. 'Just go away, you horrible, filthy . . . *social workers*.' She spat out her ultimate term of abuse.

Other hunt supporters took up the cry. 'Yeah, why don't you fuck off. This is *private property*.' Len was rolling up his sleeves for a scrap, with a malevolent grin across his fat face.

'Do you want me to fetch the paintball guns, boss?' Chalkie asked Anthony. 'I could have 'em back here in fifteen minutes.'

'Let's not escalate this thing any further,' Anthony replied. He was worried about Gaia, who looked tiny and vulnerable surrounded by protesters and the huntsmen who were trying to corral them. If she slipped, she'd be trodden underfoot.

Nula was still crashing away with her cymbals, which were making the horses frightened. Several were backing into each other and the riders trying to steady them. Then someone lit a firework and lobbed it into the crowd of horses. It was a roman candle, which fizzled on the hard ground for a few seconds, shooting sparks, before exploding in a blaze of colour.

Horses reared up and children fell off; some were dragged by a single stirrup as their ponies bolted from the firework. Anthony was looking everywhere for Henry – where the hell was he? Then he saw him, terrified, clutching valiantly around his pony's neck while it galloped in the direction of the house. Seconds later, it lost its footing on the algae-covered flagstones, fell, and rolled on top of him. His agonised shriek was heard all over the garden.

A small crowd quickly gathered around him, wanting to help, but afraid of the pony, which was rolling about on its back, wild eyed and thrashing its legs. Only when it stumbled to its feet and hobbled off did anyone dare approach Henry. The small boy was scrunched up, bawling in pain. It was obvious he had broken his arm, and possibly several ribs.

'Nobody move him,' ordered Sandra, rushing inside the house. In no time, she reappeared with a pair of kitchen scissors and began cutting the sleeves from Henry's new hacking jacket. Dita looked furious, but was already ordering an ambulance on her mobile.

The following twenty-four hours passed in a whirlwind as Dita assumed command. Anthony watched his wife with appalled admiration as she commandeered the best private room at the Radcliffe Infirmary in Oxford, insisted upon immediate surgery, then lost confidence in the surgeon and set about identifying 'the top bone doctor in the world.' For several hours she rang everyone she knew, before settling on a surgeon at the Sloane Kettering Memorial Hospital in New York City. The specialist, it turned out, was on holiday with his family in Switzerland. Dita had him woken up in the middle of the night. Three hours later, after some mind-numbing negotiations, he had boarded a private plane to Oxford airport, and shortly after landing had reset Henry's arm.

'I still don't understand how you got him to agree,' Anthony said. 'You're an amazingly persuasive woman, Dita.'

'Believe me, you don't want to know,' Dita replied. 'Let's just say there's no point being very wealthy if you don't take advantage of it in an emergency situation like this. Poor Henry. I didn't like the look of that first doctor one bit.'

53

At some ungodly hour of Sunday night, Anthony heard his mobile ringing on the dressing table. He had come late to mobile technology, but these days all Anscombes directors were expected to be on perpetual call like doctors, so he had reluctantly capitulated. Now the damn thing was jangling away with its fairground ringtone, which was sure to wake Dita.

He swung out of bed and padded across the room. Thank goodness for the low-wattage bulbs Dita had installed in the skirting, for finding your way to the bathroom at night. Fumbling about on the dressing table, he located the mobile between his old ivory hairbrushes and dish of cufflinks and collar studs.

'Hello?' His voice sounded groggy.

'Anthony? My apologies for waking you at this uncivilised hour, but something's come up you should know about.' He heard the anxious tones of Alun Entwhistle, Anscombes' company secretary, down the line.

'Oh, it's you, Alun. I don't even know what time it is. It's pitch black outside.'

'Ten past three.'

Anthony groaned. 'Go on then, tell me. Gordon Brown has hit us with a windfall tax?'

'No, it's Singapore. We're not sure exactly what's happened – we haven't got to the bottom of it yet – but we seem to have a problem, a big one. SIMEX are saying we've breached our banking covenants and run up huge unauthorised losses.'

'Surely that's impossible.'

'You'd have thought so. I've talked to the Settlements department and they don't know anything about it either. On the face of it, the books reconcile. We can't understand what the regulators over there are on about. The most alarming part is the size of the losses they're referring to. Six hundred million dollars.'

'*How much*?' It was ridiculous, astronomical, more than half the capital base of the entire bank.

'Obviously we're stumped too. Peter Morrison has a meeting with them at noon – that's in about an hour local time. And Martin Quest is flying over later today.' Peter Morrison was Head of Anscombes Financial Products Group in Singapore, and Martin Quest was Regional Manager of Anscombes Asia Pacific, based in Tokyo.

'That's good. I'm sure they can sort it out between them.' But Anthony could hear the note of panic in his own voice. Six hundred million? It was unbelievable.

Dita had woken up now and seen the digitised time on her bedside clock. 'What on earth are you *doing*, Anthony? It's the middle of the night. Tell whoever it is to ring back tomorrow. It's twenty past *three*, for God's sake.' They had given a big dinner party on Saturday night, and a lunch party on Sunday, and were consequently knackered. Furthermore, Morad's trial was starting on Wednesday. There was a lot of tension around the place. Dita had been undergoing speech training from some man who'd coached the Princess of Wales, in preparation for her appearance in the witness box.

'Let me know the minute you hear anything,' Anthony told Alun Entwhistle. 'Anything at all.'

'There is one other rather odd development,' Alun added. 'One of our traders out there has disappeared. Hasn't been seen for almost a week. Didn't turn up for work one morning, no message, nothing. He's living in a company flat, but hasn't been there either. Not since Monday.'

'Maybe he had a holiday booked.'

'Apparently not. Disappeared into thin air.'

'Do I know him? Is it someone I've met on one of my trips?'

'I think you might, actually. I believe his parents are your neighbours in Winchford. Tom Furlong.'

'Good heavens. I know Tom very well indeed; I used to be married to his stepmother. Someone must have an idea where he's got to, surely?'

'Not so far, I'm afraid. Not at the moment.'

'You don't think the two things are connected, do you?' Anthony asked. 'I mean, Tom's disappearance and this business with SIMEX?'

'The same thought crossed my mind too. But he's meant to have been doing well out there. Tom Furlong's one of our rising stars on the exchange.'

After that, Anthony couldn't get back to sleep. The conversation with Alun was disconcerting, and he felt anxious. He was still assuming it was all a big cock-up by the Singaporean authorities, but what if it wasn't? He tossed and turned and tried not to panic. He was worrying too about Tom. It was quite unlike him to vanish; he was normally so reliable. He wondered whether a girl was involved; maybe he'd shot off on a romantic break to Vietnam or the Philippines and forgotten to tell anyone. Anthony had teased Sandra that Tom would find a Chinese girlfriend in Singapore – many of the traders did and married them too. The latest issue of the in-house newsletter contained two photographs of Anscombes employees marrying Chinese women, one a researcher on the Anscombes desk. Sandra was horrified, hating the idea of a Chinese daughter-in-law.

Thinking of Sandra, Anthony wondered whether he ought to ring and tell her about Tom. It didn't seem worth waking her. It would only worry her; he'd do it in the morning, by which time he hoped Tom might have turned up anyway. The more he thought about it, the more he felt there was an innocent explanation, or a not-so-innocent one, depending how you looked at it. Probably he was holed up with a blonde in some ritzy beach resort, blowing his bonus.

He continued to be niggled by Alun's phone call. It was just so disturbing. There were plenty of derogatory things to be said about the bureaucratic Singaporean financial authorities, but carelessness wasn't one of them. How extraordinary they'd make these sorts of accusations without any basis of fact. Anscombes had one of the biggest positions on the exchange. In fact, it was Anscombes Futures Singapore that had played a central role in opening up the exchange and bringing in business, after the Osaka exchange became too expensive. It was absurd to suggest they owed $600 million; the books were reconciled every single night, and stats sent to London for review. It was ludicrous, but troubling nonetheless.

Long before dawn he had a bath and went downstairs to make breakfast. Nobody was around and the house was completely quiet. He carried a cup of coffee into the library and sat down in a well-plumped armchair. Clearly Stigmata had been on late-night plumping duty.

Through the mullioned windows, he watched the first light of dawn rise above a mist-filled valley, the tops of the elms and horse chestnuts looming from the milky vapour. The lawn was covered with dew, and he could see the footprints of small mammals where they'd cut across from the woods. He glanced at his watch: it was six thirty, which meant it was half past two in Singapore. He was surprised not to have heard anything yet – it must be a very long meeting. He'd leave it ten more minutes before ringing Alun.

'Dad?' A small blond head was peering around the door. It was Henry in pyjamas, with his arm in a sling. His wrist and radius had been broken in two places in the hunting accident, as well as a trapezium on his hand, and he'd cracked a shoulder blade. His lower arm had been in plaster for six weeks already, and half his class at Eaton House had scrawled their autographs and get-well-soon messages on it.

'Morning, darling. You're up bright and early.'

'I'm starving. We had this really disgusting tea yesterday. Scallops. They tasted like sick or something.'

'They're Mummy's favourites. She loves scallops; they're one of her best things.'

'I'd rather eat dog poo. I'd rather eat *sushi* than that.'

'I'll make you some breakfast, if you like. Shall we do a fry up?'

Henry's eyes lit up. 'Yeah, a really, really big one, please – special breakfast. Eggs and bacon. And sausages. Everything except tomatoes.' They went into the kitchen and Anthony rootled about for breakfast ingredients. These days Dita's system for storing food in the various American fridges was so complicated, it was only fully understood by Santos and the new Indonesian chef, Maslan. But eventually he tracked everything down, and set about frying home-cured Winchford bacon.

'How's that arm feeling?' he asked Henry.

'Fine.' Henry always replied 'Fine' to every question. It was his default response. How's school? Fine. How's your birthday cake? Fine. How was the Harry Potter movie? Fine.

'Not hurting so much now?'

Henry shook his head. 'Doesn't hurt at all. Only when I use it, or try to write or something.'

The aftermath of Nula's hunt protest had been confrontational, with Dita demanding she be summarily expelled from the village. 'Why would you allow that insane woman to live rent free in one of our houses, when she's broken your own son's arm?' Of course, it was a perfectly valid question, and one which Anthony struggled to answer. But he knew that if Nula left Winchford, he would lose Gaia completely. He couldn't bear to think of her growing up in Paddington in some squalid flat. In the end, he had written a long letter to Nula, more in sorrow than anger, telling her how let-down he felt, and how irresponsible she'd been, and that Henry would probably be in plaster for ten weeks. She responded by sending Henry an Australian Aborigine xylophone made from sustain-able hardwood as a get-well present, which was far too young for him, and which Dita passed on to Lina, her Filipina maid, who shipped it home to Manila.

Henry was telling his father a rhyme he claimed to have made up himself. 'Adam and Eve and Pinch Me went down to the river to bathe. Adam and Eve were drowned, so who do you think was saved?'

'Er, now let me think about this one, Henry. Adam and Eve were drowned . . . so who was saved? Er, *Pinch Me*?' Anthony was finding it difficult to focus on the joke; he was worrying about Anscombes.

Henry darted across the kitchen. 'OK, I *will* pinch you then. There you are. Ha, tricked you! I was only doing what you said! You said "pinch me", remember. *Remember*? I was only doing what you said!'

'Oh Lord, I've been completely tricked. And you really wrote that poem all by yourself? Brilliant!' Briefly, he wondered which was older, the rhyme or the Priory. Probably the Priory, but there wasn't much in it.

His mobile rang again and it was Alun. 'You sitting down, Anthony? Not good news, I'm afraid.'

There followed the most surreal, devastating business conversation of his life. At Peter Morrison's interview with the SIMEX regulators, it had emerged that someone on an Anscombes trading desk had been concealing hundreds of millions of dollars of loss-making trades in an Anscombes Error Account, falsifying the reports and balances to London. It had been going on for more than eight months, on a bigger and bigger scale, as the culprit tried to trade his way out of the losses, ramping up larger ones all the time.

'I just don't understand how this could even have happened,' Anthony said, stunned. 'I thought we had proper controls in place.' Now he felt properly panicked. He felt a tightening in the chest, and was finding it difficult to breathe.

'We do. This was systematic fraud. The Error Account is used to manage minor trading errors. Sometimes, in the heat of the moment, small mistakes are made. A trader buys a contract instead of selling it, or vice versa. Normally the Error Account would carry mistakes totalling ten, fifteen thousand dollars max, which are reconciled at the end of each month. This time it's been used to store up losses of six hundred million, carried over from period to period.'

'And *nobody* noticed?'

'Nobody. The accounts as presented were squeaky clean. Obviously the Error Account should have been checked as a matter of routine, but it seems it wasn't. Even the internal audit missed it.'

'This is a catastrophe. I doubt we're even solvent now. The Bank of England will have to be informed, you realise.'

'I'm afraid so. I need to ask for your go-ahead to call them in. The Singapore authorities have already made it clear they'll withdraw our licence to trade. Our SIMEX desk is suspended.'

'The same will go for all the Asian exchanges, once word gets round.'

'Anthony, I have to be frank: it looks very bleak. The whole thing. I don't know how we can ride it.'

'I know. Basically, we're bust.' He felt a flash of anger, followed by a wave of dark despair.

'Dad, I think the bacon's ready,' Henry said. 'It's gone all black.'

Quickly, Anthony moved the pan away from the hob. The bacon resembled eight narrow strips of charred bark.

'And do we know how many people were involved in all this?' Anthony asked Alun. 'Sounds like a fairly sophisticated conspiracy.'

'Still too early. We know from the computer records which desk the transfers were made from, into the Error Account, I mean. Whether it was all six on that desk involved, or a single rogue trader, I couldn't tell you. However they managed it, they must have had an accomplice in the back office, or some means of manipulating the reports.'

Anthony knew the question he had to ask next. 'Was Tom Furlong ever on that desk?'

'I'm afraid he was.'

'Oh, Christ. He hasn't turned up yet, by the way?'

'No. Though we had a report of a sighting. Last Monday, the morning he disappeared. He was seen at the station buying a train ticket for somewhere in Malaysia. Alone, apparently.'

'Is there any proof he's implicated?'

Alun sounded cagey down the line. 'As I said, we really don't know anything at the moment. The Error reports were sent from various computer terminals, including Tom's, but that doesn't necessarily mean anything, since they all had each other's passwords. But, frankly, yes, I'm afraid it does rather look like he might have been.'

'Keep me fully informed,' Anthony said wearily. 'I'll be in the office at the usual time, and I'll have my mobile with me. I'll be setting off for Kingham station in fifteen minutes.'

54

Everybody remembered where they were the moment they heard Anscombes had gone under.

Anthony had been in a nine-hour meeting at the Bank of England, trying to persuade it to bail them out, when he finally admitted defeat and called in the administrators. He spent the next hour drafting an All Staff email to Anscombes' 3,100 employees around the world, explaining the situation, thanking them for their loyalty and all their hard work, and telling them they might well lose their jobs. He warned them to expect a torrent of press coverage, and asked them to say as little as possible. The administrators were hoping to sell the business as a going concern, probably to a Dutch or German bank, but nothing was certain.

After that, he rang Sandra from the office to tell her about Tom. So far, nothing had surfaced in any newspaper, but the story was about to explode and he had to talk to her first.

'I'm so glad you called,' Sandra said when she heard his voice. 'I was just about to ring you myself, actually. It must be telepathy.' In the background he could hear the first *boing* of the ten o'clock television news. He had probably only just got to her in time.

'You were?' he replied non-committally.

'It's only a small thing,' Sandra said, 'but we're starting to get some damp coming through in Katie's bedroom. On the wall above her bed. A nasty brown patch. I was wondering if someone from the estate office could come by and take a look at it. I mentioned it to John, but he never prioritises the Old Rectory. He's infuriating like that.'

'I'll make a note of it,' Anthony said. But he was thinking, with the bank bust, what will happen to Winchford? Not all of his assets were tied up in Anscombes, but most were, and he certainly wouldn't be receiving any more bonuses, or any salary, come to that. No way could he afford the upkeep of Winchford now. The farm had run at a loss for years, and the rents of the cottages never covered the maintenance, let alone the cost of the Furlongs and Nula and Jasmine and Amanda all living down there.

There was a shriek down the line and Sandra said, 'Good heavens, *Tom's on television.* I've just seen his picture. On the news. Sorry Ant, I've got to turn the sound up.'

Anthony could hear the report echoing down the telephone. Collapse of a British merchant bank . . . missing trader Tom Furlong thought to be in hiding in Malaysia . . . six hundred million dollars . . . unapproved losses . . .

After that, it became difficult to hear clearly above the sound of Sandra's shocked crying, but he could just make out some stuff about 'Old Etonian, Cambridge graduate Furlong' and a potted history of Anscombes from Ishmail's pawnbrokers shop to the present day with offices in ten financial capitals. Hearing all this on the news made it sickeningly real, and he thought of a hundred other people he should be talking to, explaining, reassuring, consoling. He should tell his mother . . . and the children . . . and *Dita.*

But Dita got in first. While he was saying goodbye to Sandra, Anthony saw his wife's name flashing on the panel of his mobile.

'Dita, I was just about to ring you.'

'So I would hope. I've just spoken to Charlotte in the office, and she said she couldn't put me through because you were talking to Sandra Furlong. So I've rung your cellphone.'

He exhaled wearily. Suddenly he felt exhausted, drained. 'It's been a terrible day. You heard the news?'

'Of course I heard. I was trying to park outside the flat, having driven up from Winchford, and there's a big crowd of photographers outside on the pavement. I was carrying this very heavy suitcase and my face-case, with no one there to help me, and they all started taking pictures. I'm afraid I was rather rude to them. I told one chap he was a nasty little prick. Horrible man in a furry anorak from the *Daily Mirror.*'

'But you're inside the flat now? You got in safely?'

'Yes, only to switch on the television and hear all this. What on earth has Tom Furlong been up to? I told you not to give him a job. I've never trusted him. He's like his father, thick as two short planks.'

'I'm afraid whatever he's done, he's caused mayhem. Anscombes has had to cease trading. We're out of business. Bust.'

'Well, Tom's just going to have to pay you back, that's all. I hope you told Sandra that in no uncertain terms. She has a ridiculously high opinion of that young man, always showing off about how well he's doing. I saw her in the lane the other day. She was pretending to be sympathetic about Morad, but really she just wanted to talk about Tom. Tom this, Tom that, and all the suits he'd had made by a Chinese tailor in Singapore. Well, she'll be feeling very foolish now, won't she?'

'I'm afraid we all will,' Anthony said sadly. 'It's just so awful. All our people losing their jobs, probably. Two hundred and fifty years of a family business – finished in one day. And on my watch too.'

Suddenly realising the implications of what Anthony was saying, Dita asked, '*We're* going to be all right, aren't we? It's not going to be *us* losing any money, I hope.'

'Anscombes is a partnership. As you know, it belongs to us and all the cousins. And now it's bankrupt. You can bet your life it's going to make an almighty difference.'

'But you haven't been so stupid as to have everything tied up in the company?'

'Not everything, no. The Priory won't be affected. And I have some other investments. But virtually all of our capital is in the bank – it's a family business, *was* – and most of the estate is held as collateral. Has been for several years, since we needed funds for expansion into Asia.' He groaned. 'I doubt we can afford to keep the village intact. Most of that will have to go, I'm afraid.'

'Well, you can start by selling the Old Rectory,' Dita said. 'That's the first thing. If Tom's caused all this mess, the Furlongs can jolly well clear out, no question.'

The next seventy-two hours passed in a blur of self-recrimination and public humiliation. Every serious newspaper in the world had the Anscombes collapse on its front page, with columns of analysis and four-page features with graphics and arrows explaining how the fraud was perpetrated and concealed. Most commentators agreed the bank had been guilty of a massive breakdown of internal controls, the responsibility for which must ultimately rest with Anthony. *The Wall Street Journal* predicted that Deutsche Morgan Grenfell or Dresdner Kleinwort Wasserstein would pick up the remnants of the business, probably for a token one pound, though everything depended on the size of the financial black hole. *The Times* had its money on the Dutch financial conglomerate ING, or otherwise HSBC. Meanwhile dozens of journalists descended on Singapore to rake over the ashes of the catastrophe. Tom's two flatmates, Eric Seow and Algy Paton-Clarke, were interviewed about the high life of young Anscombes traders 'where twenty-year-olds risk millions every day, and indulge in a white-knuckle lifestyle of cold beer and hot women, in a city where a bowl of prized abalone soup can cost up to £1,000.' Sky News sent a helicopter to swoop low over Winchford in the hope of catching a glimpse of 'fallen banker Anthony Anscombe', who was at work in Lombard Street at the time. *Time* and *Newsweek* both compiled long sterile reports, drawing on the expertise of bureau staff in eleven cities. The Londoner's Diary in the *Evening Standard* devoted no fewer than six of its seven gossip items to the unfolding Anscombes saga, with stories about Jasmine, Dita ('recently named chairwoman of the annual Royal Academy Summer Ball'), Morad, John-Spiros ('Byzantine-art expert scion of shipping tycoon "Goldie" Emboroleon and stepson of beleaguered Anscombes chief Anthony, has a new companion, I hear . . . a pedigree poodle named Oscar'), even Amanda ('One of the first people to offer support to thrice-married father-of-five Anthony Anscombe is his first love, pop star Amanda Bouillon . . .'). Matt in the *Daily Telegraph* produced a pocket cartoon of a rich banker spotting a newspaper head-line saying '$600 million bank collapse', and commenting 'Bloody hell – that's almost as much as my bonus!'. Writing in the *Spectator*, Martin Vander Weyer said he'd seen the fiasco coming years ago – it had been an accident waiting to happen, and more banks would surely follow. The *Economist* expressed amazement that the lessons of the collapse of Barings and the Nick Leeson affair had evidently still not been learnt by the financial community. *Vanity Fair* despatched four journalists to London to stay at the Dorchester to write the ultimate overview of the debacle. Walter Twine went on the early evening news to say that the Anscombes were 'highly respected in the vicinity, but had been as mean as mouseshit in the old days, only giving a goose as a Christmas box to their labourers.'

Anthony's mood alternated between anger, panic, depression and sheer exhaustion. For six days in succession he left Cadogan Place at five a.m., arrived at the office in the dark, endured fourteen hours of meetings with lawyers and accountants, and returned home shattered. Giant cartons filled with files and papers relating to the fraud soon filled his office. The days seemed so long, but when he finally went to bed he was too tired to sleep and all the problems went round and round his head in a loop. He was constantly taunted by new aspects of the disaster. What would his father have made of it all? And what would become of the loyal staff who had worked for Anscombes for so long, not so much the star brokers who would quickly find other positions, but the ladies who looked after the boardrooms, and the front desk commissionaires?

When he passed the commissionaires in the morning, he felt guilty. All day, legal and tax advisers came to tell him things, but he was almost too dazed to take it all in. Dozens of different people wanted meetings with him, but there was no time; Charlotte his PA broke down in hysterical tears from the pressure of it all, but quickly recovered and resumed work as before. 'I'm sorry, I'm sorry,' she said, 'I just flipped.' My God, he didn't blame her. He entertained a fantasy of walking out of the office himself, taking the first plane to somewhere like Fiji or the Maldives and never coming back, but of course he could never shirk his responsibilities or leave the children. If he fitted in a ten-minute walk to the top of Lombard Street and back, he was doing well.

His Anscombe cousins rang him continually, asking about developments, and furious at the prospect of losing all their money. 'Who even hired this young man in the first place, the one they think caused all the trouble?' Michael Anscombe fumed.

'I'm afraid I did,' Anthony replied. 'He's, er, the son of a family friend.'

As one meeting wound up, the next was waiting to begin. Fresh teams of lawyers and regulators congregated in readiness in his outer office. He was so tired but he could never sleep.

On the sixth night he arrived home, grey faced, at Cadogan Place to find Dita tapping her feet at the front door. 'There you are at last, Anthony. You're very late. We have to leave in ten minutes and you haven't even changed.'

'Changed?' He had no idea what she was talking about.

'You haven't forgotten we're going to the ballet this evening? For heaven's sake, you've known about it for *months*. We're taking ten people to this Frederick Ashton thing followed by dinner at Harry's Bar. Now, quickly, your dinner jacket's laid out in your dressing room.'

Scarcely able to place one foot in front of another, Anthony changed into black tie. In virtual silence they were driven to the Opera House. In the crush bar they located their guests: some very rich Asian tycoons that Dita was cultivating, Ramnakrishna Gupta and his mother Sunita, some very rich Americans passing through London, and some very rich Spaniards from Madrid. Anthony felt paranoid that everyone in the bar was looking at him – the man of the moment – which they were. He yearned to be at home, quietly in bed. Ramnakrishna's old mother, Sunita, exclaimed, 'You really are the centre of attention at the moment, Anthony. I can't open a newspaper without seeing your picture. I'd never thought of you before as a *celebrity*!'

Anthony smiled a rictus smile, and wanted to slap her. The ballet began. Anthony hated ballet. This one was some gala tribute to a famous choreographer, dead apparently, with little cameo scenes from his most famous productions. Dita laughed away as Cinderella, or was it the Sleeping Beauty, traipsed wittily about the stage. Anthony saw from his ticket stub that they had paid £500 per seat to bring everyone here, and he still had to take them all to Harry's Bar. He doubted he'd have much change from £10,000 at the end of the evening.

In the interval they had smoked salmon sandwiches and champagne. Several prominent bankers, all known to Anthony, came over to say how sorry they were about everything, and they were sure it would all work out fine in the end. But it was clear from their faces they knew it was over.

Anthony thanked them for their kindness and wished they'd fuck off and shut up. Dita hissed, 'Stop looking so long-faced, Anthony. Our being here is proving to everyone there's nothing wrong at all.'

They went back inside for the second act, and almost at once something wonderful happened. Anthony dropped off to sleep. His dreams were not untroubled ones, but it was deep, genuine sleep. For the first time in a week, his face lost some of its tension. Just then, he felt a sharp elbow in his side. 'For God's sake, wake up, Anthony. You were *snoring*. Now, pay attention and stop being so wet. Everyone has business problems, it's perfectly normal.'

Meanwhile, the hunt for Tom never left the front pages, with several newspapers offering rewards for information about his whereabouts. Sandra and John were frantic and consumed with embarrassment about the trouble he'd caused. Sandra said she was so ashamed she'd do anything to make amends, and offered to help out for free at the Priory whenever they needed her. Richard telephoned from Africa, having read all about it in the Nairobi *Nation*, asking whether he should fly over to Singapore to join the search. Katie returned home to Winchford to wait by the telephone with her family for news, and to do her best to keep Sandra calm. Constance didn't help matters by ringing from Argentina in a terrible state, having had a dream that Tom had been found dead. Katie took a gin and tonic up to her bath and was photographed in her towel by a paparazzi from the *Sun*, who must have been crouching on the high bank with his lens trained on the bathroom window. The caption said, 'Missing fraudster Tom's topless sister turns to booze.'

Sightings of Tom started to come in thick and fast. He was spotted at a hotel in Kota Kinabalu, and on a ferry in Borneo. A waiter at the Singapore Hard Rock Café next to the United Overseas Bank rang the police with a positive identification, but when three squad cars turned up, it was somebody else. Each time it happened, the whole village held its breath, and the disappointment was palpable.

In the midst of all this anxiety, Morad's date-rape trial kicked off at the Old Bailey. Anthony had planned to sit in on the whole trial to support Dita, but instead had to ricochet between bank and courtroom. The opening speech for the prosecution, which lasted for most of a full day, was lethal, and having heard it Anthony felt discouraged about his stepson's prospects. The girl bringing the charges looked sweetly apprehensive, and disconcertingly like Katie in appearance. Morad and Jonny Faisal had both turned up to court in new black *Reservoir Dogs* suits, and he'd had to tell them sharply to remove their wraparound shades. For all his expensive coaching, Morad's attitude in court was terrible, and you could see both judge and jury taking against him.

In the recess on the second day, Anthony gave him another pep talk. 'Listen, Morad. Your mother's giving evidence next. She's going to be saying all sorts of flattering things about you, what a perfect son you are, and how kind you are to small animals and to your brothers and sisters. I want you to stand up straight in that dock – *stand*, not slouch – and look like it's *you* she's talking about, OK? You've got to look serious, attentive and respectable. Do you think you can manage that?'

Morad shrugged. 'All these cocksuckers, they're just telling porkies about me. I shouldn't even *be* here, you realise.'

'Well, you are here. And you're in deep trouble. Remember that, and try to behave. Now, it's time we went back in; it's about to restart.'

'At my signal, unleash hell,' said Morad, being Russell Crowe in *Gladiator*.

Anthony could only stay for the first half of Dita's evidence, and it was hard to read how it was playing with the jury. Two of them were black, one Asian, the rest looked like supermarket checkout girls and actuaries. He prayed Dita wouldn't make one of her thoughtless, grand remarks. The court reporters' bench was packed to capacity; even those newspapers that hadn't previously elected to cover the trial were doing so now, in light of the bank collapse. It was a chance to see the protagonists at close quarters.

Dita was wearing a demure black suit with a nipped waist, and a single row of pearls. Her hair was blowdried flatter and sleeker than usual, more like a professional woman than a lady who lunches. She looked wonderfully solemn, but also haughty, as she took the stand.

Watching her, as though watching an actress on stage, Anthony found himself wondering what he really felt about his wife these days. And he realised that what he felt about her most was ambivalence. He couldn't deny that, particularly over recent days, the scales had rather fallen from his eyes. The Anscombes crisis had brought out the worst in her, and he was afraid she was even more selfish than he'd previously thought. On the plus side, he admired her strength, and the way she kept her emotions so firmly under control, but he had to admit she hadn't been very sympathetic lately, or even particularly keen to listen to his problems at the bank. She expected him to listen to her defending Morad for hours at a time, but when he tried to talk about his own difficulties, she was dismissive. 'For heaven's sake, Anthony, do stop going on about it.' Unable to sleep in the middle of the night, he had tried to cuddle up to her for comfort and bury his head against her back, but Dita had snapped, 'For God's sake, it's far too late for sex. I'm trying to sleep.' And she had moved away.

Dita's evidence was wordperfect, exactly as rehearsed. John-Spiros and Ambrosia had heard their mother's lines so many times in the past week that their own lips moved in time with hers in the gallery, as she spoke of her first husband's untimely death, when Morad was only a toddler, and how difficult life had been for them both. 'Truly, it was Morad who looked after me, as much as the other way round. Always so sweet to his mother, so considerate. He knew I was unhappy, heartbroken over Sharif; there was nothing he wouldn't do for me. Really he is a wonderful boy, like a saint on earth. Later, my maid Stigmata Corbetta will tell you more about him, in case you do not believe his mother. She will tell you what a good boy he is, always helpful in the house, never touching alcohol, not even wine. As for women, no one respects girls more than Morad. He is so chivalrous, quite the old-fashioned gentleman. My previous husband, Aleco, Morad's first stepfather, is known throughout the world for his perfect manners, and Morad learnt so much from him. The same for his present stepfather, Anthony Anscombe, who trusts Morad so much he even put him in charge of his paintballing games on our Oxfordshire estate. Morad had responsibility for more than one hundred paintguns they have there. I don't know – it's not exactly my thing – but you see how trusted he was. Anthony has a wonderful instinct for people, he believes in people . . .'

There was a furious activity of notetaking from the reporters and, feeling he couldn't take any more, Anthony slipped off to a crisis meeting with the administrators. A Japanese bank in Yokohama was interested in buying Anscombes, and their president had requested a conference call with him.

By the time he emerged from his meeting, there was a big photograph of Morad on the front of the evening paper. The headline said, 'MORAD KEPT 100 GUNS SAYS MUM.'

55

'Anthony? It's me, Sandra.'

It was ten o'clock on Saturday morning and she had rung him at the Priory. Anthony was feeling drained and wretched. The past ten days had taken their toll, as his world collapsed around him.

'Any word of Tom yet?' he asked her.

'Still nothing. We're all sitting here, waiting.' She sounded exhausted. 'I was wondering if you could possibly come over to the Old Rectory. There's something I want to say to you. It's probably easier if you come here, if you don't mind.'

Anthony groaned silently. The last person he wanted to see was Sandra. He was utterly shattered. He felt like he'd been in one continuous meeting for two hundred hours, which he virtually had, punctuated by fleeting visits to Morad's trial. He felt furious with Tom, but sorry for Sandra, who must have been going through hell. They all had. So he said, 'Give me ten minutes and I'll be right over.'

He found them in the kitchen – Sandra, John and Katie – just sitting there, watching the telephone, waiting for news. They looked terrible, like they hadn't slept for days. You could tell Katie and Sandra had been crying – their faces were red and blotchy. John Furlong was oddly shrivelled, like an old tortoise peering anxiously from its shell, as though half expecting to be hit with a spade.

'Oh, Anthony, I just don't know what to say to you,' Sandra said when she saw him. She was wearing a shapeless beige jumper with a picture of a ladybird on the front, and a big, sensible, pleated country skirt, which made her look rather broad in the beam. Anthony noticed with a shock the grey roots growing out from her dyed blonde crown. Her face looked drawn and tense. 'We're all devastated,' Sandra said. 'I don't know how to begin to apologise. We're just feeling so guilty about everything. I want to say sorry to you – that's why I asked you over. I just couldn't with Dita listening. I know I'd cry. There I am crying. What can Tom have been thinking? Your whole bank and everything . . .' She turned away to blow her nose on a large piece of kitchen roll.

'It's Tom I'm most worried about,' Anthony said soothingly. 'Is there still no news at all?'

John shook his head. 'I've been on to the Foreign Office this morning, and twice yesterday – they've given us a special number to call, but there's nothing. Not so far. We live in hope.'

'I'm sure he'll turn up,' Anthony said. 'It's difficult to just disappear with so many people looking for you. Especially these days. If he tries to withdraw cash from an ATM, anywhere in the world, they'll know about it in ten minutes, exactly where he is. The same if he books a flight. All the airports in south-east Asia have his description and passport details.'

'What's likely to happen to him?' John asked. 'He's obviously in a lot of trouble.'

Anthony looked grim. 'I think we should try and find him first, and worry about that later. He didn't set out to do any harm, and we'll try and explain that to the Singapore authorities. I mean, he wasn't trying to take any money for himself. He obviously ran up some losses, panicked and was trying to trade through them, and things went from bad to worse. I just wish he'd told somebody. Maybe he thought we wouldn't be very sympathetic, which is a bad mark against us, really.'

Sandra burst out crying again and two retrievers, Tebbit and Duncan, emerged from beneath the kitchen table to nuzzle against her thigh. Then, gathering herself, she stood up and made him a cup of tea. 'You're such a kind, kind person, Anthony. I can't bear what's happened; it's like a nightmare. I keep thinking I'm going to wake up and everything's going to be all right again. You must be *furious* with us, and all your cousins must be too. All those people losing their jobs, and their poor families. Silly, *stupid* Tom. What was he doing? And why doesn't he ring us? He must know how worried we all are.'

Anthony shuffled his feet,

'I just pray he hasn't gone and done something stupid,' Sandra went on. 'I don't think he would, but you can't be sure. I know how ashamed he'll feel, letting everyone down. He hates making a mess of things; he always has. He was dreadful about that at school – he always had to come top. I just have this terrible feeling . . .'

'No, that's enough, darling,' John said. 'It's just stupid Constance putting the thought into your head. She's been ringing us a lot,' he told Anthony. 'She's been having these ruddy dreams about Tom and rings to tell us about them. I wish she wouldn't. It isn't helping. Sandra and poor Katie were hysterical last night after she called.'

The telephone rang and everyone jumped. It rang twice more before John picked it up, and they all held their breath. But it was only Tom's old Eton housemaster, ringing to ask if there was any news.

'Still nothing, I'm afraid,' John said wearily. 'But thank you so much for ringing, Nigel. Sandra sends her love.'

'That was so thoughtful of him,' Sandra said. 'Most people haven't rung. I suppose they're embarrassed and don't know what to say. They're avoiding us. I saw Jacinthe in the post office and she pretended she hadn't seen me. Dad says a lot of people were being rude about Tom in the pub; they think they're going to lose their homes because of him. He threatened to chuck them out if they didn't shut up.'

'Well done Len,' said Anthony. 'I've always liked your father.'

'Does Dita hate us?' Sandra asked. 'I wouldn't blame her if she does.'

Anthony looked uncomfortable. 'Well, she's not very happy about anything just at the moment, to be perfectly honest. Morad's trial isn't going particularly well. He was in the witness box yesterday and didn't come over as well as we'd hoped. He got a bit rattled and swore at the judge. And Dita's hating all the publicity about Anscombes. She hasn't come to terms with it yet. She wants me to injunct the newspapers to stop them writing about us. I'm afraid she isn't being very realistic.'

'I'm just so, so sorry,' Sandra bleated. 'It's all my fault. I asked you to give Tom a job, and now all this has happened, all because of me.'

'Nonsense,' said Anthony. 'I was delighted to have him. He's a very bright boy. It's partly our fault for not supervising him properly – that's what everyone's saying. And how are you, Katie? Managing to do any painting?'

Katie tried her best to smile up at him. 'Haven't you heard, I've stopped my art for a bit.' She glanced over at her parents. 'Anyway, I'm getting a job. In television.'

'Fantastic. What are you going to be doing? Reading the weather?'

'No, actually. I'm joining an independent production company, as a kind of PA-cum-researcher. In Shepherds Bush. They make reality shows, and produce rock concerts and festivals for TV.'

'Well done you. When do you start?'

'Well, it was going to be this Monday, but . . . I told them I can't come until Tom turns up.' And her pretty green eyes filled with tears.

Back at the Priory, Anthony found Dita in a filthy strop. 'I gather you've been calling on the Furlongs. I hope you were giving them their marching orders.'

'I was asking about poor Tom. He still hasn't been found. Sandra's totally distraught, as you can imagine.'

Dita sniffed. 'You know my opinion of Sandra. Maddening creature; I can't bear her. I'd like to say I feel sympathetic, but I'm not, not after all the trouble she's caused. Now, stop thinking about Tom bloody Furlong – we need a serious talk about Morad. I'm not happy with the way this trial is going. Our lawyer's an incompetent idiot, not up to the job at all. And it's obvious the judge is prejudiced against Morad. Anyone can see that a mile off. We've got to take control ourselves now.'

'I don't know about that, darling. Seriously, we've got one of the top QCs in the country. I think he's impressive.'

'I don't. He's making a complete hash from start to finish. The person we need to get to now is the tart; it's the only solution.'

'The girl who's brought the case, you mean?'

'Exactly. The hooker. There's only one thing girls like her understand and that's money. You're going to have to cut a deal with her, Anthony.'

'*Bribe* her? You're saying I should bribe the main prosecution witness?'

'It's simply a question of working out her price. I don't know what someone like that would expect. I'd have thought fifty thousand pounds would seem like a fortune to her. If you have to go higher, then you have to. But I doubt it'll be necessary.'

'Dita, I'm awfully sorry, but I can't possibly. It's out of the question. You could go to jail if they found out. Anyway, I don't think she's that type of girl.'

Dita snorted. 'Oh, puhlease. If she was respectable she wouldn't have been hanging about in a bar all on her own, looking for punters at one o'clock in the morning. God, you're naïve sometimes. No, you must make her a nice offer. That's what she's waiting for. The whole thing's been about money from the word go; Morad's said so all along.'

'Dita, I'm sorry, but the answer's still no. I won't do it, not even for you. For one thing it's illegal and for another it's completely immoral. And that's my final decision.'

'So you're happy to stand by while your stepson is sent to prison? Is that what you're saying? Some stepfather.'

'No, of course not. I'd do anything to help Morad. I have *already* done a lot to help Morad. I think I've spent the best part of a quarter of a million pounds trying to help him. But I will not, repeat *not*, start bribing witnesses in a trial.'

Anthony stared at her, his jaw set. He couldn't remember anything he'd ever felt so strongly about in his entire life. For once he was taking a moral stand. The conversation had brought to the surface all his worst feelings about Dita: her selfishness, her complete lack of morality, her determination to win in every situation. Did she have no compassion at all for the girl whom Morad had in all likelihood raped? Dita was so self-deluded sometimes, she was almost insane. Once he had felt so grateful to her for looking after him so well; he could see now that she hadn't really been looking after him at all; she had merely been living up to her own high standards. It was always all about Dita. In ruthlessly creating Ditaworld, there was no room for anyone else.

'I'm sorry, Dita,' he said finally. 'I just won't do it. Not that.' Then he said, 'Let me ask you something. What does Morad have to do for you *not* to defend him? If he *killed* someone?'

Dita turned on him, face contorted with fury. 'You know what your trouble is, Anthony? You're wet and you're useless. You always have been. I saw that the first time I met you in Mark's Club. You always take the easy way out. I'm not surprised, frankly, your bloody bank has gone to the wall. You'd never have become chairman in the first place if you hadn't been family. And now thanks to you the whole thing's gone kaput. All because you allow people like your ghastly ex-wife – the nanny – to manipulate you. You do it every single time. No backbone. And here you are doing it again. I ask you to do *one simple thing* for my poor boy, who could very well end up in jail thanks to a racist judge, and you won't help. Well, I call it the limit. It's the final straw. As far as I'm concerned, you can fuck off, Anthony. If you won't lift a finger, I'll find someone who will, someone with some balls. I'm off to see Aleco. And I'll tell you something else. If I go now, I'm not coming back, you pathetic, uptight, English loser. I'm sorry it's been a shit week for you – first you lose your bank and now you've lost your wife.'

Anthony stared at her steelily. He was completely calm. 'OK. If that's what you want. But it won't make any difference, not to my decision. For once in my whole damn life, I'm putting my foot down.'

He heard Dita storm off downstairs and order Stigmata to pack four suitcases. And then an hour later, without saying goodbye, she departed for Cadogan Place. Anthony watched her leave from the window. Her jaw was set as she sat in the back of the Mercedes, with Santos behind the wheel.

John-Spiros, Ambrosia and Henry were playing table football in the games room with Rosanna and Darren, entirely unaware that their mother had just left the Priory for ever.

Part Six

56

'Anthony? It's Sandra. I had to ring you straight away. Tom's turned up.'

'Thank God. Is he all right? Where is he?'

'Right here, can you believe? Sitting at the kitchen table. John found him outside the back door when he took the dogs out. Katie's cooking him a huge breakfast. I don't think he's eaten properly for days.'

Anthony was relieved, but also amazed. Half the world's police and press had been searching for Tom for six weeks and he shows up in Winchford. 'But how did he get here, Sandra? Everyone thought he was in Malaysia or somewhere.'

'You can ask him yourself. He wants to talk to you. I'm bringing him straight up to the Priory.'

Fifteen minutes later a sheepish-looking Tom arrived at the house, evidently frogmarched there by his mother. 'Anthony? I'm surprised you'll even see me. I'm so sorry about everything. I've screwed up big-time. I've totally let you down.'

Anthony began to reply 'These things happen', but recognised the absurdity of the remark. It wasn't every day a world-famous bank went down for hundreds of millions of dollars. He cleared his throat. 'I'm relieved you're all right. We've been worried sick. How did you even get home?' Seeing Tom face to face was an unsettling experience. His relief at knowing he was alive was tempered by fury at what Tom had done.

Tom sounded weary. He also looked terrible. He had lost a lot of weight and his hair was long and unkempt. 'Well, it's a long story. I came overland, basically, most of the way. After I left Singapore, when I realised I had to get out because everything was about to explode, I took the first train up into Malaysia. I didn't know what the hell I was doing – there was no plan or anything. I wasn't thinking straight. Then I travelled on to Borneo, and stayed there for ten days. I only left the hotel once, and saw my picture on the front of a newspaper, so I knew the game was up. It was quite scary actually; I didn't dare leave my room. The hotel was starting to get suspicious, so I went back to Malaysia and caught a boat from Penang to Madras. Luckily there wasn't much security – they just stamp your passport without looking and that was it. In India I bought an air ticket from Madras to Delhi and on to Istanbul. I had to pay cash, because I realised I couldn't use a credit card – too much of a giveaway – so that used up most of my remaining money. After a week in Istanbul I got the train to Frankfurt in this carriage full of students, all inter-railing, and hitched to Calais. I arrived back in England yesterday afternoon on the ferry, and hitched home. I gave Dad quite a shock, because I was dossing down by the dustbins. It was too early to wake anyone up.'

'That's quite a journey. You must be exhausted.'

Tom groaned. 'I've been such an idiot. I feel so dumb and ashamed. I saw *Time* with Anscombes on the cover. I couldn't bear to read it. And there was an old *Daily Mail* on the ferry with photographs of Winch-ford and our house and everything. It's so awful. I'll probably end up in prison too. Which I wouldn't even mind that much, because I don't want to see anyone ever again.'

Anthony looked at his honorary stepson, who had single-handedly destroyed his family business. There was so much he wanted to say to him – the bloody idiot – but in the end he took the English way out and said nothing. What was the point? 'Tom, I don't know what's going to happen. I'm sure it'll all take a long time in any case. If I were you, I'd have a good breakfast and a long sleep.'

'Dad says the whole bank's being sold. Is that really going to happen?'

'Yes, it looks like we'll soon belong to the Japs,' Anthony said dryly. 'Everyone's got to learn how to bow and drink sake. There'll be geisha girls at the office Christmas party next year. Not that I'll be there to see them, of course. Whether they can pronounce Anscombes in Japanese is another matter. Their president is having dreadful trouble with it, poor chap.'

Tom chuckled for a nanosecond, then reverted to morose. 'Probably I should commit hari-kiri. It would be better than twenty years in the Singapore Hilton, as they call the local jail.'

'Don't even think about it,' Anthony said. 'I need you here to help out with the paintballing.'

'As if,' Tom replied. 'Of course I'd love to help. That's really nice of you. It'd be better than skulking around the house feeling paranoid.'

As soon as they had left, Anthony picked up an ornament and hurled it at the wall. It was one of Dita's Herend parrots, and the bone china smashed into hundreds of tiny shards. He felt furious with Tom. Genetically predisposed to be polite in every situation, he was almost shocked by the strength of his own reaction. He was reminded of how he'd felt, years ago, when Richard had run off as a five-year-old at the Moreton agricultural show, and disappeared for two hours. When he eventually turned up again he'd half wanted to hug him and half wanted to kill him for making them all so worried. It was the same with Tom. Did Tom even begin to realise the mayhem he'd caused? Anscombes was bust, the press were ringing up a hundred times a day with intrusive questions, Anthony's cousins were clearly enraged at him and kept calling for updates about the sale, and here he was trying to cheer Tom Furlong up.

The Priory without Dita felt eerily quiet. Anthony hadn't previously appreciated how much time she devoted to planning menus and supervising household decisions, and he became overwhelmed by the stream of requests from Santos, Stigmata and the rest of them, asking which linen should be put on which beds, and which dinner service he wanted for which table for supper. Dita was entirely preoccupied with the trial, now in its second week, and hadn't rung once since bunking off. From what Anthony could glean from the court reports in the *Daily Telegraph*, things continued to go badly for Morad; according to evidence given by the concierge and doorman at the Dorchester, the girl had been virtually unable to walk when Morad had brought her to the hotel, and had to be held upright while they waited for the lift.

Anthony was in any case distracted by the lawyers and accountants helping to complete the due diligence on the sale of Anscombes to the Bank of Yokohama. Ironically, he was working longer hours trying to sell the business for a token one pound than he ever had while it was generating millions in annual profits. A pall of depression lay over Lombard Street. Most of the top executives were seeking new positions at rival banks, but no one wanted to hire managers who couldn't spot a six-hundred-million haemorrhage. Big delegations of small Japanese men arrived to review the books in meeting rooms and glass-walled pods, where Anscombes staff watched them uneasily, worried about their futures. Several evenings, when it was too late for him to travel home to Winchford, he spent the night at the Connaught hotel. It occurred to him that probably he could no longer afford the Connnaught, but didn't feel like ringing Dita and begging a bed.

His personal finances were also a mess. He knew ninety per cent of his capital was tied up in the family bank, and had consequently been wiped out. The greater part of the estate, and most of the village, had been pledged as collateral against the Far East expansion, so this too was lost. The prospect of telling everyone in Winchford they stood to lose their homes filled Anthony with dismay. Some, like Walter and Mrs Holcombe, should be all right because they were long-term sitting tenants, but he was definitely going to have to put part of the farm up for sale. He hated the thought of breaking it to the Biggeses, let alone the Furlongs, and Nula, and Jasmine. His mother, he supposed, could always move back in with them to the Priory; at least he still owned that outright, so she wouldn't be homeless. When he spoke to an estate agent at Savills, however, he was cautioned how difficult it would be to sell the land without a decent-sized house to go with it, so he began to wonder whether they wouldn't actually do better to leave Winchford altogether. The idea of selling up was shocking. He had always envisaged the house passing to Richard one day, but now he wondered how that could ever happen. He doubted Richard would be able to afford the upkeep. Maybe he wouldn't even want to live there, with the land and everything gone. He was haunted by visions of what Godfrey would have said about it all. His parents had run everything so carefully, so parsimoniously, and he had blown it all in a few years.

On Saturday morning he wandered down to the Plough and Harrow with Henry, who wanted to play outside on the plastic dinosaur. For the first time in his adult life he felt uneasy strolling through the village, as though the place was already no longer his, and he imagined the accusatory stares of villagers on his back. Not only was he the Man Who'd Lost Anscombes, he was the Man Who'd Lost Winchford. A terrible weight of guilt pressed down on his shoulders. He was the Anscombe who had let it all go. If he was remembered at all, it would be as the family member who had squandered his birthright. In his head, he traced the line of events from his betrayal of Sandra and affair with Nula, which had led to Sandra's marriage to John, and to Tom's appearance in their lives, which in turn led to the fall of Anscombes. *O tempora, O mores*, the fates were surely punishing him for a lifetime of misdeeds.

'Say iced ink very fast twenty times.'

'What's that, Henry?' His son was walking by his side, blissfully unaware of everything that was going on.

'Say "iced ink" very fast. Go on.'

'Er, OK, Henry. Um, iced ink, iced ink, iced ink, I stink, I stink, I stink . . .'

'Ha, ha, you fell for it! And you do stink too, Dad. Do you get it? Iced ink turns into "I stink" if you say it fast. You said "I stink"! And you do stink. Poo-eee. You admitted it.' Henry pretended to hold his nose.

'I was completely tricked. Did you learn that one at school?' He did his best to sound cheerful, but it was hard to sustain.

Henry nodded. 'A boy in my class called Faud made it up. He's brilliant at jokes. What do you call a donkey with three legs?'

'Er, I don't know. What *do* you call a donkey with three legs? I give up.'

'A wonkey! Faud made that up too. He invents all these jokes and tells them to his bodyguards in the coach on the way to games.'

Anthony smiled at his son, and felt so guilty he had screwed up his inheritance. Len and Marjorie were behind the bar of the Plough and Harrow, which was packed with people. Anthony could see Rosanna playing pool with Darren in the newly opened games conservatory, and Walter crouched over the dominoes with Chalkie.

'Great news about the lad, isn't it, Tone? I knew it would turn out all right in the end.' Len was mopping down the counter with a cloth.

Anthony looked surprised. Tom had been lying low since his return to Winchford. John had informed the authorities his son had turned up, but so far nothing had appeared in the newspapers. 'Er, yes, it's a relief he's safe and sound. It's been a rough experience for him. For all of us, in fact.' Which was one way of putting it.

'I knew that girl was no good. Minute I read about it, I said so, didn't I, Marjorie? What annoys me is they're not allowed to print her name. She's allowed to be anonymous, making all her accusations, while the poor bloke gets splashed over the newspapers. It's bloody unjust, if you ask me. And now she's withdrawn all the charges, if you please. It makes no sense. Still, I'm pleased for Morad. His mum will be happy too, I expect!'

'Sorry, Len, you've lost me here. Are you saying there's been something about Morad?'

'On the radio news this morning. I thought you'd have known about it. The trial's collapsed. The girl's saying she can't now be sure who'd bought her the drink. She said several different blokes had been buying them during the evening. A pity she didn't think of that before, instead of causing all this trouble. Anyway, Morad's been discharged, and I'd like to buy you a drink on the house. It isn't spiked, I promise!' And he roared with laughter.

Anthony shivered. Evidently Dita's scheme to buy off the girl had worked, and she'd sabotaged the prosecution case. He wondered how much it had cost, and how exactly Goldie had fixed it, if it had indeed been Goldie, which he assumed that it was. He had a mental flashback of the tycoon and his flashy Russian wife, Irina, at the Winchford garden party, strutting about the lawn looking supercilious, and it enraged him that people like Goldie could buy justice, as though it was a commodity with a price attached. Of course he was relieved for Morad. But it irked him that, once again, Dita had used her money – or, quite possibly, *his* money – to buy her way out of trouble. He knew he ought to ring Dita and Morad to congratulate them on the result, but it stuck in his gullet.

Instead, he asked Len for a pint of Hook Norton and picked at the bowl of cheddar and pineapple cubes Marjorie provided as complimentary bar snacks. 'I should think you needed that,' Len said, watching him sink the pint. 'It must have been a rough old few weeks, what with one thing and another.'

Anthony nodded. 'Unbelievable really. I keep wondering what they'll throw at us next. All I can say is, thank God your pub's owned by the brewery, and not by the estate, or I don't know what would happen.' Suddenly he found himself unburdening to his former father-in-law who, of all the people in the village, was most likely to relate to the rough justice of business life. 'It doesn't look like we'll be able to hold on to Winchford, Len. Not the village, anyway. We'll have to put the cottages up for sale, which is a tragedy.'

'People are half expecting it, Tone,' Len said. 'It won't come as a total surprise. To be honest, it's all they're talking about.'

Anthony sighed. 'They must be very disappointed in me, and I don't blame them. If I hadn't been so impatient to expand the bank, none of this need have happened. I could kick myself. It's not even that we needed to grow. Sometimes smaller can be better; it's easy to see that with hindsight. I just feel so embarrassed for all the tenants. It's not their fault what's gone on, and there'll be so much uncertainty while it's all being broken up and parcelled out.'

'No one's blaming you, Tone. If they're blaming anyone it's . . . no, I shouldn't say. It's none of my business.'

'Tom, you mean?'

'Well, him too of course. No, I meant Dita. I don't like to point the finger. But she's not a particularly popular lady round here.'

Anthony smiled ruefully. 'I'm afraid the Old Rectory will have to go. I don't see how we'd ever be able to keep it. It breaks my heart, because I love having the children on the doorstep. Sandra and John too, of course.'

'I have to hand it to you, Tone, you've created a lovely village here, a real community. The nicest place we've ever lived in, and a lot of it's down to you, you know.'

'We're lucky, we've got some fantastic people living here. That's what makes it doubly sad. Not that some of the newspapers would agree with you. According to them, it's a den of vice. The Cotswold harem, one of them called it.'

'They're animals, worse than animals. Did I tell you, one bloke came in here pretending he wasn't a journalist, though we all saw through him straight away. He kept asking about different people in the village, you can guess who, and then started off asking me about Sandra. Did she leave you or did you leave her, and was she a looker? I waited till he'd finished, and then I said "Is she a *looker*? Well, let me tell you, matey, she looks exactly like *me*. Which is hardly surprising because I'm her *dad*. And if you don't leave my pub in the next ten seconds, your face will soon resemble a blind blacksmith's thumb, which will not be a pretty sight."'

'Well done, Len. I'm sure you did a lot for village PR there. No wonder all the articles have been so favourable, with you setting the tone.' Then he said, 'Seriously though, I'm very grateful. I'm amazed how supportive everyone's been. All this ghastly publicity has been a big pain for you all. Plus the prospect of losing their homes. It's unbearable. I wish I could see a way through it.'

'I just wish there was something practical we could do to help. That's what everyone's saying. If we could come up with something, there'd be no end of volunteers.'

Anthony shrugged. 'It would have to be a pretty big something, if we hoped to keep the village intact. I seem to remember we all worked pretty hard organising the village fete last summer, and that only raised a couple of thousand pounds.'

'You know what we ought to do, Tone? I've just thought of it,' Len said, sounding suddenly excited. 'I mean it: this could be bloody amazing. It's just the place for it, too.'

'What's that then?' For one ghastly moment, Anthony thought Len was going to suggest a village casino.

'Glastonbury. We need our own Glastonbury, here at Winchford. They had that farmer who does Glastonbury on the telly the other day, and he makes an absolute mint out of it, and he's a scruffy old geezer too, so if he can do it . . .'

'I don't know, Len. I can't exactly see us putting on a pop concert, can you? I've only been to a couple in my whole life, and that was a hundred years ago.' But then he thought: well, is it so impossible? Len was right about one thing: Winchford was the perfect location, with its wide valley below the village, a natural amphitheatre. And then he thought: Jasmine knows about music, and so does Amanda, come to that.

'You have to go for it,' Len said. 'People would come for miles if you got the right acts. When Rod Stewart played Blenheim, it was a sell-out. And I'll tell you another thing, the Plough and Harrow is having the food concession this time, no argument. None of Dita's fancy caterers.'

'OK, Len, that's a deal. If we put on a pop concert, you get to provide the sausages and magic mushrooms.'

As he strolled back with Henry to the Priory, the idea began to take hold. And, in the afternoon, he found himself walking across the floor of the valley, just out of curiosity, trying to visualise where a stage might go, and all the car parking, and how many people the fields could hold. The more he thought about it, the less absurd it seemed. He would certainly have plenty of time to plan it all. Next Friday would be his last day at Anscombes, assuming everything went through. He had already taken down his office pictures.

That evening he rang Jasmine, who was in Sharm-el-Sheik on a Top Shop shoot, and tested the idea out on her. The line was terrible, but she sounded enthusiastic. Later the same night he dropped in on Amanda at Forge Cottage. After each glass of Sancerre the concept seemed better and better, and Anthony thought how refreshing it was to be able to chat away to his ex-wife without Dita disapproving and wondering where he'd been.

'You know something,' Amanda said, as he stumbled out into the lane after midnight. 'It could be incredible, and I'd love to help. I can think of loads of acts who'd probably say yes to performing, if I called in some old favours. Go on, I dare you.'

'The last time you dared me something I ended up driving to the south of France and marrying you. And that wasn't the greatest move ever.' But then he said, 'I'll think about it. I really will. If we can somehow save Winchford, at this point I'll try anything.'

57

The first meeting of what was to become the steering committee of the Save Winchford Music Festival took place in the library of the Priory over a Saturday lunchtime.

Jasmine was back from Egypt, golden brown and swathed in orange and pink scarves. Amanda arrived from Forge Cottage, uncharacteristically efficient and armed with an Indian paper notebook, pens and a mobile phone. Anthony still found her very beautiful, though she definitely looked older these days, with rather nice laughter lines around her eyes. John, as estate manager, was distributing agendas on which items such as Date? Food and Drink? Local authority planning/entertainment licence? Numbers? AOB? had been typed out and duplicated on sheets of A4. Percy Bigges, who Anthony thought as a local magistrate would impress the council officials, had needed no persuading to join the committee. He told Jasmine he'd watched Top of the Pops last night for the first time ever, and made a list of all the best groups. 'They had this marvellous big black gentleman named Fifty Cent. He was splendid; we should definitely try to get him, don't you think?'

Santos the butler and Maslan the Indonesian chef had been cajoled into providing plates of sandwiches, though recently their willingness had markedly deteriorated, and Anthony suspected both were looking for new jobs. Santos had asked to be paid weekly rather than monthly, and stipulated cash, inventing some cock and bull story about needing to send it home to Toledo to an ill cousin with no bank account. Well, let them go, Anthony thought. Let them all go. He was fed up of Dita's retainers creeping around the house and gossiping in whispers. At least they'd come up with the crab sandwiches and several cafetières of strong coffee.

Len and Marjorie arrived with a stash of brochures of outdoor cater-ing apparatus, such as industrial-sized baked potato ovens, soup can-teens and barbecues capable of grilling hundreds of spare ribs at a time. Chalkie, the paintballing supremo, joined the group as logistics expert.

Once everyone was settled and Len had spat out his crab sandwich ('What the flaming heck's *this*, Tone? I thought it was going to be chicken!'), Anthony started the meeting. He thanked them all for coming, and re-minded them this was simply an exploratory discussion, with nothing decided, on the feasibility of holding a pop festival at Winchford. 'I think you all know why we're considering it. There's been a certain amount in the newspapers about a, er, little local difficulty we've been experiencing at my family business, which is threatening the viability of this village. Our plan is to raise sufficient funds to acquire as many of the cottages as possible, which would then be placed in a community trust to secure them for future generations. We're still working on the details but, broadly put, the village would no longer belong to the Anscombe family, but be held for the present inhabitants and their descendants, who would continue to pay current rents, which I'm told are below market levels.' He coughed. 'That's the idealistic plan in any case. Whether we can pull it off is another matter altogether. We shouldn't underestimate how dif-ficult this thing will be to do. I don't want to sound over-pessimistic, but we don't have any experience between us of staging a large pop festival – or even a small one, come to that – nor do we know if we'd get permis-sion from the local authorities. Finally, the sums of money we'd need to raise are substantial, some would say astronomical. It wouldn't be a small undertaking. And, to complicate things further, we cannot afford to take any risk. We're going to need to be absolutely certain we've got a winning proposition before going ahead. Not to make too much of it, but the last few weeks haven't been too kind to the Anscombe finances, and I can't afford to take a second big hit.' He paused. 'On the upside, looking around this room I see a lot of very clever, determined people, with a wide variety of competencies. And we are lucky enough to live in a particularly attractive part of the country, with lots going for us. Not least an almost perfect natural setting for a festival, a perfect bowl.'

He looked round the room. 'Any immediate burning questions before we move on?'

'What about toilet facilities?' Chalkie asked. 'I'm worried about drain-age since the soil round here contains a lot of clay.'

'May I suggest we stick to the agenda?' said John, officiously. 'Lavatory facilities should be discussed under Any Other Business.'

'It's a good point, Chalkie,' Anthony said. 'And one of many practical considerations we're going to have to get our heads round. I can't pretend to be a great expert on lavatories at public events. They have those superloo things at Cheltenham Gold Cup week, caravans with urinals inside.'

'You wouldn't want them at a rock festival,' Chalkie said. 'Much too smart. I could probably run you something up with old drainpiping. The pee runs off into a trough.'

'You'll need proper loos for the artists,' Jasmine said. 'If we're hoping to have Robbie Williams and Eminem and people, they expect amazing dressing rooms with private bathrooms and everything. And table tennis tables and bottles of Chivas Regal.'

'I wish we could just keep to the agenda,' said John petulantly. 'Otherwise it's anarchy and nothing gets decided at all.'

'John's right,' Anthony said, secretly thinking he was a pain in the arse, but wanting to keep him on side. 'Let's start from the top. *Date.* Presumably we need a good summer weekend when we think it won't rain. How about one of the middle two weekends in July?'

Everyone paged through their diaries, and John said, 'Glorious Goodwood starts on the twentieth this year. We don't want to clash with that. And the previous weekend is . . . no, that's all right, it's a public holiday in Malta.'

'Oh, for God's sake,' Amanda muttered under her breath. Then she said, 'How about the weekend of the fourth?'

'Passing out parade for officer cadets at Sandhurst,' noted John.

'I think Reading's that weekend. The Reading Festival, that is,' said Jasmine. 'I'd need to check.'

'Glastonbury's the end of June,' Amanda said. 'And we should find out when Party-in-the-Park is too. That's some time around then.'

'That one's up in London, isn't it?' Anthony said. 'Surely that's not a problem?'

'It is for the acts,' Jasmine said. 'If they have to choose between Party-in-the-Park and Winchford, they'll choose Party, because it gets TV. And it won't be their own decision in any case; their record company or management would decide.'

'Heavens, this is all very complicated,' Anthony said, momentarily discouraged. 'Even finding a date seems almost impossible.'

'You know who could help us on this?' Jasmine said. 'He knows everything – he does it all day long. Charlie Edwards. A lot of the artists are his anyway. We should get him involved.'

Involuntarily, Anthony found himself glancing over at Amanda. Looking for what? Some reaction?

'Charlie would be amazing,' she said. 'I don't know why we didn't think of him already. I saw him for lunch at Black Cat records recently. He's our man.'

Anthony experienced a moment of dismay at the prospect of Charlie muscling in, but had to concede he'd be a big asset. 'OK, Amanda. Could you ring him after the meeting and ask him? You really think he might be prepared to help?'

'Try and stop him,' Amanda replied. 'He'd do anything for me, and even more for Jas. He'd kill to be involved.'

For the next hour they talked security and car parking and licences, and agreed that John and Chalkie should set up a meeting with the planning people in Banbury as soon as possible, and start to get some idea of what would be required. Anthony would meanwhile liaise with the local police, while Percy investigated the alcohol licensing regulations. 'The person who'll know all about it, of course, is Archie,' Percy said. 'I knew it would come in useful one day, having a layabout son in the wine bar trade. He's thick as thieves with all the licensing bods.'

'Perhaps Archie should join the committee?' Anthony suggested. 'He'd be another huge asset.'

'I'll ask him,' Percy replied with a smile. 'He can help us get all those . . . what do they call them . . . *groupie girls*. That's right, the groupies. I'm sure we'll need plenty of them, won't we, Jasmine?'

After that, Len wanted to talk about catering, and banged on about spuds with chilli and vegiburgers for far too long until Anthony reined him in. 'It all sounds marvellous, Len; my mouth's watering already, but maybe we don't need quite so much detail at this point. It's still early days.'

'Tell you what, Tone,' Len said. 'After the next meeting I'd like to extend an invitation to the committee to join me down at the old Plough and Harrow, and we'll have a few jars together and test the menu ideas. I've got the perfect jumbo sausages in the big freezer out the back.'

'Are we ever going to talk about rock acts for this rock concert?' Amanda asked, rather pointedly. 'Because if so, I've started a list of ideas.' She proceeded to read out an astonishing page-long roster of famous acts, many of whom even Anthony had heard of before. Everyone from the Rolling Stones to Lou Reed to Dave Gilmour of Pink Floyd to Fairport Convention, one of whom lived nearby in Barford St Michael.

'That's incredible,' Anthony said. 'Do you really think some of them might agree to do it?'

'Oh yeah,' Amanda replied. 'I put in a few calls last night. I mean, you can't rely on them, because half will be out of the country touring, and the others are fucking headcases, but no one's said no.'

'Amazing.'

'We need some younger acts too,' Jasmine suggested. 'Like maybe the Black Eyed Peas. Or McFly. And Scissor Sisters.'

'Never heard of any of them,' John said. 'Are they famous? I've heard of the Rolling Stones.'

'They're all *very* famous,' Jasmine reassured him.

'What about that extraordinary woman? You know, the Madonna?' suggested Percy Bigges. 'I've always liked the look of her.'

Amanda made a face. 'Oh God, *please* not her. Anything.'

'Sandra's come up with a suggestion I've noted down somewhere,' said John. 'Here we are, look. I knew I had it. "The Spice Girls." Are they any good, does anybody know?'

'They would be if they hadn't disbanded several years ago,' replied Jasmine. 'So have the Beatles, in case you're about to suggest them.'

'Does it all have to be pop music in any case?' John asked. 'That's what I'm wondering. How about a nice opera singer? Or a choir? Much easier to obtain a licence. And quieter, too.'

Everyone ignored him.

'What about local bands?' Chalkie asked. 'The Rat Catchers are all good mates of mine. They play Friday nights over at the Sun in Splendour in Chippy. I can sound them out, if you like.'

'Talking of local talent,' Anthony said, ' I hope you're going to be in the concert yourself, Jasmine. You're a pop star. And you, Amanda. I'd love it if you'd do your old hit, "Remember, Remember".'

Amanda looked reluctant, but then Chalkie said, '*You* sang that?' He was staring at her, dumbstruck. 'That's one of my all-time favourite songs. I had no idea you were the same Amanda. It was one of the first singles I bought. I played it over and over. I had it on cassette in Belize when we were training out there. Bloody hell, this is amazing. I'm going to get your autograph after the meeting, if you don't mind.' Then he started humming the chorus under his breath: 'Remember, Remember, things past baby . . .'

'I've had one really off-the-wall idea,' Jasmine said. 'You may think this is completely mad and inappropriate. But what if we got Trevor Bratt involved in some way? He's so cool, and people love him. Couldn't he put on a Saint-Simone de Paris catwalk show or something? Maybe while someone cool is playing – a fashion and music combo. I could get all the models involved too. Kate Moss and Lily Cole and everyone; they'd be up for it, I'm sure.'

'Sounds great to me,' Anthony said. 'In fact it all sounds incredible, if we can really make it happen. One thing I'm sure about, however. It's going to involve a hell of a lot of hard graft. If anyone feels they haven't enough time, I'd entirely understand if you want to drop out now.'

But everyone assured him they were in, and they agreed to meet once a week from here on in.

As the project gathered steam, the committee swelled in numbers. Charlie Edwards came aboard, having had his arm twisted over dinner by Anthony, Amanda and Jasmine at the Fox and Terriers in Upper Oddington. By the time he'd been subjected to two hours of undiluted flattery, three bottles of St Emilion, two tequilas and Amanda's hand on his thigh for the entirety of the main course, he was fully signed up and talking about calling his old friend Sting to get him involved. 'Winchford *is* fully organic, isn't it?' he asked.

'Er, no actually,' Anthony replied. 'Not fully, though we supply organic carrots and runner beans to Tesco.'

'I'll tell Sting you're organic anyway,' Charlie said. 'So don't say anything if he asks. I need to sell this to him like it's Save the Rainforest . . .'

Archie began rolling up for meetings, always late and once with a joint dangling from his mouth.

'That isn't the dreaded weed, is it?' his father asked suspiciously.

'No way, Dad. *Would I?*' he replied, passing it to Amanda. 'Not this early in the morning, surely.'

Later, under Any Other Business, he asked whether the drugs concession for the festival had been allocated yet and, if not, could he tender for the work? John Furlong, who was struggling to obtain consent for a licence to sell lager on site, looked appalled, and Anthony had to quickly assure him it was a joke.

Had Anthony any idea how complicated it was all going to be, even to get permission to stage an event at Winchford, he would probably never have embarked on it at all. He had been unprepared for the dozens of hours of meetings with different local bodies, and the masses of hurdles to be jumped before anyone would even consider giving the go-ahead. On the other hand, it distracted him from his other worries and gave him something concrete to do; recently he'd been having withdrawal symptoms from the bank and the day-to-day structure it had provided for so long. Meanwhile, the Banbury police had issues about 'ingress and egress', and the traffic flow of vehicles leaving the site at the end of the concert all at the same time. Charlie recommended they shoot for a one-day event for a hundred thousand people, with gates opening at ten o'clock and finishing at eleven at night; the police were full of dark prognostications of four-hour traffic jams, with bumper-to-bumper queues along the narrow Oxfordshire lanes. John, meanwhile, was spending several afternoons a week with the health and safety people, and had been issued with a copy of the Purple Guide, containing rules and regulations for big public gatherings, which had become much stricter following the Hillsborough football stadium disaster. At every meeting he relished explaining in detail the nuances of the law on gates and exits, and how many would be required around the steel shield perimeter fence. 'Each gate will need four security men, and we're talking forty emergency exits at least,' he announced. 'We're looking at a *minimum* of three hundred security, and these people do not come cheap. I've been given names of various security companies and will be inviting them all to quote.'

'No need, no need,' Len interjected. 'Aren't you forgetting something, Jono? Ginette does security. That's Ginette Potts, my younger daughter,' he reminded the committee. 'Sandra's sister. She's got a great little business; she provides the bouncers for all the nightclubs from Cheltenham to as far away as Bristol.'

John looked doubtful. 'It would, of course, be marvellous to use Ginette, but do we really believe she's tough enough to handle it all? That's my worry. It's a major job.'

'Course she is, Jono, course she is,' Len replied. 'Ginette's the business. Last Saturday a bunch of louts tried to get into a club in Evesham without paying, and started threatening the bouncers with beer bottles. Ginette was on site and broke one of their arms. You could hear it snap in two, she said. They soon scarpered after that.'

There was a shocked silence.

'Well, I'm in favour. Ginette gets my vote,' burst out Sir Percy. 'She's been a great friend to my Arabella for a long time now, and Bella's always arrived home in one piece when they've been out together.'

'Good,' said Anthony. 'So that's security sorted. Only another one hundred decisions to go, then.'

Anthony had always been good at chairing meetings. At Anscombes, he'd had a reputation for keeping up the momentum, moving briskly from item to item and always pushing for a decision rather than a deferment. For his Winchford neighbours, accustomed to a gentler, more discursive Anthony, the experience of him in work mode was novel and impressive. While he was disarmingly charming and endlessly courteous, they nevertheless recognised a steely impetus they hadn't seen before. Slowly but surely the meetings became more disciplined, and the committee instinctively understood their reports should be short, sharp and well prepared. As Percy remarked to Len before one session, 'I've been up for hours mugging up on my homework. One always feels rather on the spot at these gatherings, don't you think? One wouldn't want to slip up.'

Although he initially felt Dita would have coped with the meetings so much more efficiently, Anthony found himself enjoying them more and more. For the first time in years, he was learning something new. Rock groups that had once meant nothing to him now became household names at the Priory. He bought a rock encyclopaedia in the Moreton bookshop and studied the entries on every band and artist under consideration. He wrote dozens of letters to different stars, begging them to take part. On Charlie's advice he wrote to the UK chairmen of Sony BMG, Universal and EMI to brief them on the Winchford festival, and was soon word perfect on which record company owned which act. He became accustomed to writing letters which began 'Dear Bryan Ferry' and 'Dear Coldplay'. The Winchford Rock Festival had taken on a life of its own.

By the eleventh meeting, a first stab at a site plan had been drawn up, showing where the stage would go, or rather stages, since there would need to be three of them: a 120-metre main stage, with bays either side wide enough to store several different band set-ups on rolling risers, a 'B' stage and a third, specialist, one for smaller, solo acts. Then suitable locations had to be agreed for the production village, artists' dressing rooms, luxuriously appointed Winnebagos, public car parks, crew catering marquees, raked VIP seating stands, sound desks, sponsors' tents and enormous digital daylight screens for the audience watching from the back.

'We're going to need several first aid tents and a field hospital for this many people,' John reported, having had his initial site meeting with health and safety. 'And there'll need to be full catering facilities for the St John Ambulance teams.'

Chalkie made himself an expert on lavatory facilities, reckoning they'd need 'one toilet for every five hundred men and one for every one hundred and fifty women, which means four hundred and thirty in total, if I've got it right. I think I know where to lay my hands on Portajohns at a reasonable price, and then we'll need half a dozen Portaloos – they're that bit posher – for the talent.'

Archie was put in charge of overseeing a tented shopping village, which would sell food, drinks, festival merchandise, T-shirts, bags, whistles and South Indian lassis. He omitted to mention to the committee his plans for a full range of hash cakes and hallucinatory muffins. Len otherwise had sole responsibility for the catering, including food for the hundred-man production crew who would expect full cooked breakfast, plus round-the-clock goulash and Thai curry. The artists, Charlie warned him, would put in special dietary requests nearer the time. 'It could be anything from caviar to Red Bull to Korean *kimchee*. Whatever they feel like at that moment.' John reported that Sandra hoped to run a stall selling commemorative tea-towels, having had great success with something similar at the Heythrop point-to-point.

Almost daily, fresh emails arrived from Charlie at Plasma-Black Cat Wardoursound Records asking Anthony to write more letters to potential acts: 'Dear Joss Stone', 'Dear Beyoncé', 'Dear Iggy Pop'. None ever replied, but Charlie said this was normal. 'They probably don't even *see* the letters. But you still have to write them.' As the weeks passed and no stars confirmed they'd be appearing, Anthony began to panic and wondered whether the whole thing was doomed to failure.

'Just chill, Dad,' Jasmine reassured him. 'Amanda and I are both yeses, and Amanda's calling Keith Richards over the weekend.'

'If we can get three major acts to commit, I think we can get TV,' Charlie said at one meeting. 'I've been talking to Channel Four and Channel Five, and both are potentially up for it, depending who's on the bill.'

John looked doubtful. 'Are we sure we want television? It will make it a lot more complicated, with cameras everywhere. Is there any point?'

'Well, we could be talking five hundred thousand in broadcast fees. That's for the UK rights,' Charlie replied. 'With the right acts, this could work internationally too.'

'I'll tell you what,' John replied. 'My Katie works for a TV production company somewhere in the wilds of Shepherds Bush. They do a lot of pop concerts apparently.'

'If it's the one I think it is,' Charlie said, 'they'll be perfect.'

Meanwhile, Percy and Anthony churned out letters to potential sponsors. Orange Mobile looked like a hot prospect for a while, but fell away. Virgin, Barbour, Nokia and V-water, the vitamin-enhanced drinks brand, all said they'd consider it. The Hook Norton brewery signed up as subsidiary sponsors, pledging free beer, and Winchford Autoparts came aboard as official festival welders. Initially embarrassed to be asking so shamelessly for money, Anthony soon got into the swing, even firing off begging letters to the Emboroleon Shipping Line and the Bank of Yokohama.

Home at the Priory for Easter, Anthony's children and stepchildren one by one became absorbed by the project. Rosanna and Ambrosia, both of whom had been badly shaken by the publicity surrounding the collapse of Anscombes Bank, seized the opportunity to do something positive to help, and dropped leaflets through the letterboxes of every house in all the surrounding villages, explaining the idea behind the Winchford Festival and apologising in advance for any noise or disruption. Henry did the same thing for Winchford, bicycling one-handed around the cottages, and being rewarded with Cokes and sweets by sympathetic neighbours. His arm was still in plaster from the hunting accident, and he was milking it for all it was worth. When he arrived at Steepness Farmhouse he met Gaia in the garden, who gave him a macrobiotic muffin and showed him Nula's new scented candle factory in the old stables. Aromatherapy candles were Nula's latest big thing; she was especially proud of her buttercup-scented range, made from wild flowers harvested from the hedgerows.

To Anthony's great delight, Richard came home for a month from Kenya, and promised to return again in July for the concert. He immediately hooked up with Chalkie as his logistics assistant, liaising with health and safety over the standpipes, which would be mandatory in the event of a heatwave. 'They're worried about people fainting from heat exhaustion or dehydration,' he reported after a particularly gruelling site meeting. Simultaneously, in case of torrential downpours, half a mile of backstage trackway was going to have to be stockpiled, with interlocking steel sheets to be laid across large areas of the production village. Each time a new requirement came along, John sucked his teeth and incorporated it into the budget. 'The way things are going, we risk making a million-pound *loss*,' he announced at one point.

One early morale-booster was the poster John-Spiros designed for the festival, with bold graphics and an illustration of the stage in a bucolic English valley. Large spaces were left empty to add the names of the acts. 'That's if we ever have any acts,' Anthony said grimly. 'We're getting perilously close to the point of no return. Unless a few confirm soon, we won't have any choice but to cancel the whole thing.'

Charlie advised him to stay cool ('It's always like this') and Amanda reported she'd definitely be speaking to Keith Richards the following Tuesday. 'I have a direct number for where he'll be staying in Seattle.'

Tom, meanwhile, living at home in Winchford while the Singapore authorities applied for his extradition, started work on a marketing plan for the concert. Drawing on his computer expertise, he trawled the internet for relevant sites on which to place links to a festival website, and obtained rates from the music press for advertising. As he told Anthony, selling a hundred thousand tickets at seventy quid a pop was no pushover, and the more they did now, the better.

Dita had made no direct contact with Anthony for five months when a letter arrived from her solicitors asking for a divorce, citing unreasonable behaviour and requesting an 'appropriately substantial settlement'. Shortly afterwards, Anthony read in the Richard Kay column in the *Daily Mail* that Dita was dating her friend Sir Ramnakrishna Gupta, the UK-based software billionaire listed as the third richest Ugandan Asian in Britain and a major donor to the Labour party. His Gupta Institute of Management at the University of Cambridge had been wholly funded by the Sir Ramnakrishna Gupta Foundation.

Morad, having spent several months under Dita's beady supervision at Cadogan Place, now reappeared for a weekend at the Priory, ostensibly to collect stuff from his old bedroom. Once arrived, he quickly became enthusiastic about the whole idea of the festival, and begged to be allowed to help. Ambrosia, John-Spiros and Katie all looked stricken at the prospect, and Anthony was about to turn him down but said, 'Tell you what, Morad, if you can think of any sponsors, that would be very useful. We're not doing too well in that department so far.'

Morad said what he really wanted was to work backstage, or do the mixing on the sound desks, but said he'd think about sponsorship too. The following Monday he rang Anthony in high excitement, saying that Faisal Cement and Construction of Dubai – one of Jonny Faisal's family businesses – could be interested in becoming sponsors. Seventy-two hours later, following a meeting with Faisal Corporation lawyers at an office in Curzon Street, the headline sponsorship of the Save Winchford Music Festival had been agreed at four hundred thousand pounds.

As often happens, this single breakthrough piece of good news was a harbinger of more to follow. Charlie arrived at the next meeting saying Ozzy Osbourne had ninety-nine per cent agreed to appear, and that if he confirmed it would start a chain reaction. Sting, too, was seriously considering it, and looking forward to visiting the Winchford organic wildflower meadows.

'But we don't have any organic wildflower meadows,' Anthony pointed out.

'Yeah, but *he* doesn't know that,' Charlie replied. 'I'm sure you can improvise something.'

Shortly afterwards Jasmine announced she'd managed to get Trevor Bratt to concentrate for five minutes for once, and he'd agreed to put on a catwalk show at the festival. 'He's thinking of collaborating with Björk,' Jasmine said. 'You know, the Icelandic singer,' she added, when John, Percy and Anthony looked blank.

'*That*,' said Charlie, 'is seriously, seriously cool. It could even swing it with Channel Four. If we have Trevor and Björk, Ozzy and Sting, plus you and Amanda of course, that's beginning to sound convincing. We're not there yet, but it's a definite start.'

'Any further news on Keith Richards?' Anthony asked Amanda.

'I've got a cellphone number for where he's having supper on Thursday,' she replied. 'In Hamburg.'

'Good luck.'

'Failing that, he'll be in Nevis over the weekend. I'm getting a number for that too.'

Chalkie reported he had the Rat Catchers on standby, and Jasmine said Busted could be up for it too. 'And I've got a call in to Bono, but he's been away.'

'Positive news from Sandra I should probably just mention,' John noted. 'She's come up with a design for a special festival tea-towel. A hedgehog playing the electric guitar. I've told her to go ahead and print five hundred, which we can sell on the day.'

Len reported he'd struck a deal with a frozen food wholesaler in Droitwich to buy 60,000 venison burgers for twelve pence each, which he expected to retail at five quid a throw. 'Work it out,' he said. 'It's daylight robbery, but I love it.'

Less than a week later, Anthony received two short faxes, both bringing further amazing news. The Emboroleon Shipping Line, upon the direct instructions of Mr Aleco Emboroleon, was offering to sponsor the VIP marquee to the tune of 75,000 euros, and Goldie and Irina Emboroleon hoped to drop in by helicopter to watch part of the concert. The second fax came from the Office of the President of Yokohama – Anscombes Futures Ltd, undertaking to sponsor the tented village 'with appropriate corporate branding and signage' for £250,000.

'Do you know something?' Anthony reported at the next steering committee. 'For the first time I am beginning to feel marginally confident about this event. Thanks to you all and your hard work, I think it might actually happen.'

Everybody cheered, and Len produced two bottles of champagne. 'I mustn't get too sloshed,' Amanda said as Anthony refilled her glass for the third time, 'because I've got to call Keith in a minute. He's in St Louis, Missouri, and I've been given a number where he'll definitely be.'

58

'OK everyone, cue main stage VT, cue sound and standby stage
management . . .'
From his vantage point between the turrets on the roof of
the Priory, all Anthony could see in the valley below was a sea of dancing
people, tens of thousands of them stretching into the far distance under
a blazing July sun. More than half a mile away, he had a perfect view of
the second largest of the three stages, flanked by digital daylight screens,
on which Busted were just finishing their rumbustious set. Down his
walkie-talkie, he heard the event production director issuing instructions
on the showcall channel: 'Now cue Dido . . . cue Dido to main stage . . .'

'So what do you reckon, Rosanna?' he asked his daughter. 'Think it's
going OK so far?'

Rosanna took his hand and squeezed it. 'I think we can say that,
Dad, don't you?' Then she roared with laughter. 'Actually, it's absolutely,
totally, mindblowingly amazing. Just look at it. I can hardly believe it's
happening. So many people . . .'

According to John Furlong, not only had they sold ninety thousand
tickets in advance, but a further ten thousand had been bought on the
day, pushing capacity to the limits of the licence. There were people
filling every inch of space inside the steel shield perimeter fence. Every
field for miles around was covered by vehicles, up as far as Steepness
Farmhouse.

'My God, the music's loud,' Anthony said, making a worried face.
'They'll be hearing this ten miles away.'

Rosanna shrugged. 'Don't worry, most people are here anyway. And
rock concerts are *always* loud; it's compulsory.'

'Just so long as the church doesn't collapse,' Anthony said, looking anxiously at the throbbing steeple of All Hallowes. 'I don't want an un-happy vicar.'

'He's fine. He's helping the Scissor Sisters with their make-up back-stage. I've never seen him look happier.'

Four hours into the festival and so far, miraculously, there had been very little trouble and the show was running almost to time. According to the police, there had been only two arrests, including Walter Twine who'd been cautioned for climbing over the Mojo barriers during Jas-mine's set and trying to clamber on stage.

From the roof you could see the entire festival laid out before you with all its different compounds, from the sound desks in their special fenced-off area to the sprawling tented village of sponsors' marquees, art-ists' dressing areas, crew tents, TV outside broadcast units and shopping mall of stalls. The helicopter pad on which the Emboroleons had already landed, and where Robbie Williams and Keith Richards were scheduled to land later on, was surrounded by an impregnable cordon of steel walls and a posse of Ginette's burly security men. Six acts had already been on, including Fairport Convention, the Rat Catchers of Chipping Norton and Jasmine, whose super-sexy rendition of 'Luck of the Draw (Maybe Baby)' had been the high point of the day so far.

Way below, in one of the many food enclosures, Anthony was fairly sure he could see Len and Marjorie doling out venison deathburgers and chilli jacket-potatoes to a never-ending queue that snaked round and round the mess tents. Rosanna pointed out Darren, who was assisting the lighting team behind a Wholehog console.

Already Anthony felt he'd been awake for thirty-six hours, which he virtually had, trying to solve numerous last-minute hitches. Beyoncé's people had threatened to pull her out of the concert when the antique furniture they'd specified for her dressing room failed to turn up, the re-movals van having broken down on the M40. Anthony and Richard had saved the day by carting half a dozen Sheraton tables and chairs from the Priory and lending them instead. Later, Sting had been offered a Thai green curry made with non-organic chicken, and his people had thrown a hissy fit. Meanwhile, there had been problems with the VIP lavatories backstage since there were at least twice as many people backstage than expected, and Chalkie was filling the supply tank for the stars' private loos with vitamin-enhanced V-water, generously provided by one of the sponsors.

Heat was becoming a serious issue, with the St John Ambulance teams doing brisk business rehydrating parched fans. Four teenagers had fainted, and two were on saline drips in a first aid tent. Len contacted

Anthony by walkie-talkie to say he'd already sold a quarter of a million drinks and was running out of Coca Cola, Sprite and beer. Extra supplies were being rushed in from every cash-n-carry for miles around.

Flashing their Triple A 'Access All Areas' wristbands and passes, Anthony and Rosanna returned to the arena. Just inside the main gate they spotted Sandra standing eagerly behind her stall, trying to sell a hedgehog tea-towel to a sceptical Ozzy Osbourne fan. 'I'm sure your wife will love it. What woman wouldn't appreciate a pretty new tea-towel?' Sandra was assuring him. Behind the magic mushroom stall, Anthony saw Archie with a cigar-sized joint dangling from his lips, and his arm wrapped round the waist of a very young girl.

'You take care there,' Anthony called out to his old friend.

'Relax,' said Archie, giving him a thumbs up. 'So far we've shifted twenty thousand whistles and four thousand cardamom lassis. It's an absolute goldmine.'

Dido was finishing her set with a powerful rendition of 'White Flag', which had a hundred thousand fans swaying in unison in the sunshine, and next up was Ozzy Osbourne. John Furlong, who had read somewhere that he regularly bit the heads off live bats on stage, was fretting it would all end in disaster, and had told Ginette to position several of her best security men in the wings in case he needed to be dragged off mid-act. 'Whoever it was who invited this Ozzy to be part of this concert was totally and utterly *irresponsible*,' John fumed, staring pointedly at Charlie. 'We cannot permit the slightest permissiveness on the Winchford Estate. I hope he understands that.'

'Oh, do shut the fuck up,' Charlie replied. 'I'm telling you, Cilla-ruddy-Black is more outrageous than Ozzy these days. On second thoughts, they're practically indistinguishable.'

Anthony found Ambrosia, John-Spiros and Henry sitting in the roped-off VIP enclosure with Percy and Jacinthe Bigges, and Henrietta in her wheelchair. His mother's two latest nurses had pushed her up to the arena, but abandoned her to go autograph hunting around the artists' tents. The Biggeses had found her parked next to a kebab stall. Now almost completely gaga, Henrietta had mercifully been unable to absorb the collapse of the family bank, but had somehow sensed Dita was out of the picture, which perked her up no end. Incapable of speech, there was nevertheless a deadly new gleam in her eyes.

All his children and stepchildren were having a great time, Anthony was pleased to see. Ambrosia's wristband entitled her to free food from the production village, and she was tucking into an enormous tray of frankfurters, Turkey Twizzlers and Krispy Kreme doughnuts. Inspired by his grandmother's nurses, Henry had begun his own autograph collection, and already had Jasmine, two of the Rat Catchers and several Russian models who'd be appearing later on in the Trevor Bratt for Saint-Simone de Paris catwalk show.

'Richard and Tom are both working in the logistics tent, I know that,' Anthony said, 'but has anyone seen Katie? I haven't seen her all morning.'

'She's rehearsing,' Ambrosia replied through a mouthful of doughnut. 'One of Amanda's backing singers hasn't turned up, so she's asked Katie to step in.'

'And Morad?' Anthony asked nervously. 'I haven't seen him either. Not since supper last night.'

'Oh, *we* have,' Henry said. 'He's wearing a stupid scarf thing tied round his head. What do you call it, a banjo or something?'

'A bandana?'

'Yes, bandana. He looks really gross. And he's *smoking* too – we've seen him.'

The heat had soared up into the high eighties, intensified by the cauldron-like effect of the valley. Chalkie, Richard and Tom were supervising the dozens of emergency standpipes and spraying the front fifty rows of the crowd with garden hoses and crop spray pumps. Len, who had now sold over 400,000 cans of Fanta and Sprite and was calling in favours from every local wholesaler, complained the standpipes were ruining his trade. Just as Ozzy Osbourne's act was finishing, a pregnant woman fainted in the front row and had to be passed back over hundreds of heads, until Richard carried her on his shoulders to a St John Ambulance tent. Jacinthe, who was laying out a picnic lunch on the tartan groundsheet she usually took to Glyndebourne, said, 'Haven't we been lucky with the weather? Some of this music's awfully *loud* and *brash*, Anthony. But I liked that Dido person; she has some rather pretty tunes. I might buy her cassette for the car.'

Next up was Amanda, who was to be introduced by a special guest presenter, Patrice Bouillon. The French film star had arrived in Winchford the previous afternoon and was staying with Amanda and Jasmine at Forge Cottage. To general excitement in the village, Amanda had taken him for a drink at the Plough and Harrow, where he had proceeded to down four bottles of wine and a bottle of Pernod before passing out in the public bar. Len, who had had himself photographed with the celebrity as he did all famous visitors to his pub, didn't know whether to be pleased or censorious.

Today Patrice looked very much the worse for wear as he staggered onto the stage to tumultuous applause. His film *The Count of Monte Cristo* remained one of the most-rented action movies at Blockbuster in Stow.

'Allo Weenchford! Allo Weenchford!' he hollered in pantomime French. 'Eet iz my great pleasure to eentroduce a wonderful sexy lady, and I should know that, certainly, because she was once my wife, I can say that. So I am 'appy to introduce a fantastique lady, very sexy, who still bear my nomme – my name, I should say – Amanda Bouillon . . .'

There was a further eruption of applause and onto the stage strutted Amanda, tiny and fragile but undeniably sexy, dressed from head to toe in black velvet, with Jasmine's Egyptian scarves wound round her shoulders, and wearing a big, floppy, suede sunhat. Following in her wake were two devastatingly gorgeous black backing singers and two beautiful young white girls, one dark and sultry, the other a redhead – Katie. Anthony couldn't take his eyes off the dark, sultry one, whose features seemed vaguely familiar.

At her insistence, it had been agreed Amanda would perform only two songs, since she kept saying her rock star days were well over. She began with a long, melancholy ballad, one of the songs she had written years ago in Calcutta 'at a particularly difficult time in my life.' Anthony found it eerily poignant, telling as it did the story of a young mother in a strange, exotic country, who had left her old love and baby behind to live with a 'badder bolder man' who then proceeds to find 'newer, brighter moths to flutter at his midnight lamp'. The song was evidently deeply autobiographical, and Anthony felt tears welling up in his eyes. He was standing in a group with most of his children, in a field with a hundred thousand other people, but he saw only Amanda. Every word spoke directly to his heart. 'How many times did I yearn to leave this hot land and my love's cold heart,' she warbled, 'and run back home to an old embrace in a greyer place!' When the song finished, Anthony was so emotional he could neither clap nor look anyone in the eye.

Amanda then gave an affectionate tribute to Winchford and, to his great embarrassment, to Anthony himself. 'I've lived in a lot of places, God knows, too many places, so I know what a truly special place Winchford is, the vision and heart-work of one amazing person, Anthony Anscombe. I don't know where you are out there, Ant, but I want to thank you for being such a good and loyal friend, and to tell you what an amazing privilege it is to be part of this concert for Winchford.'

Then she moved straight into her one big hit: 'Remember, remember . . . the times that we had . . . the good times were great . . . and the bad times so sad.' When she reached the chorus – 'Remember, remember, things past baby . . . Remember, remember, love don't last, baby,' the entire crowd joined in, all word perfect, all wallowing in the great anthem of lost love. Looking round the arena, Anthony could hardly believe it. Every single person seemed to know every line. He saw two of his dairymen, and the bloke who ran the farmers' market in Bourton-on-the-Water, all mouthing the lyrics and cheering Amanda to the skies. Amanda seemed stunned by the warmth of her reception, and left the stage in a trance.

Now the mood altered completely as Björk rose from the bowels of the main stage on a hydraulic lift, like some Viking scarecrow on the prow of a longboat, belting out one of her strange, discordant, mesmerising laments. As she sang, a procession of models began to pick their way across the stage in Trevor Bratt couture, trailing trains of toile and chainmail behind them, or wearing hats with reindeer antlers and rhinoceros horns. Some were dressed as Eskimo Inuits, others as Papuan tribals. Anthony had never seen anything like it; nor, judging by the awed silence that settled across the arena, had anyone else. The girls themselves were, for the most part, almost inhumanly tall with fierce Slavic cheekbones: Lithuanians, Ukrainians, Siberians and Croats. When Kate Moss appeared in an unbuttoned snow leopard trenchcoat, there was a surge of applause for the local girl. But when Jasmine came on stage in a sharkskin evening dress with a huge black fin on the back, Anthony thought his daughter looked prettier than any of them, and felt so proud of her for persuading Trevor Bratt to get involved. He was doubly pleased when Bratt bounded onto the stage, covered in tattoos, and embraced Jasmine in front of the cheering crowd.

For Anthony, the next three hours passed in a blur of stars and emotion. He wandered around the site, drinking it in from every possible vantage point, scarcely able to believe it was happening at all. Beyoncé was the star of the late afternoon, shaking her booty at the crowd as she gyrated her way through 'Crazy in Love'. Mark and Annie Plunkett, Bongo Nall-Caine, Beano Elliot and Lex Holland were all boogying at the front, directly below the stage, along with their respective grown-up children, while Lex's parents, Scrotum and Rosie, perched on shooting sticks in the VIP enclosure. Scrotum had his field glasses trained on Beyoncé's butt. Mrs Holcombe and Judy reeled about, half-cut on cider. Charlotte, his old PA from the bank, had turned up with a handsome boyfriend and a coolbox full of Pimms. What seemed like a hundred TV crew were filming the show from every conceivable angle, swooping across the top of the crowd with overhead cameras – super giant jimmy jibs – while camera assistants padded around the stage with steadycams strapped to their fronts. Anthony walked up to the top of the park and sat beneath the oak tree where he had first pledged his love to Sandra. From this place, with its distant prospect of the Priory, he got the completest view of the festival, the crowds stretching almost as far as the eye could see. It was from here he listened to Sting singing 'Walking on the Moon' and 'Roxanne', and heard his heavily amplified tribute to Winchford as 'an amazing twenty-first-century eco-sustainable village, which all of us must urgently emulate before the planet expires.' Anthony groaned and wondered exactly what Charlie had been telling him.

By the time Keith Richards and Friends, as his slot was billed, were ready to come on, it was starting to get dark, and dozens of extra vari-lites above the stage began to move on the lighting grid. All across the site, lights were being switched on around the food stalls and in the shopping village. Sandra, who had so far sold only three of her five hundred hedgehog cloths, gave a little cheer, believing that evening shopping would be more fruitful.

Then, suddenly, total blackout. Every light went off, and the PA system petered out. For a moment, the crowed sat there in pitch darkness, until people struck cigarette lighters and the field lit up with thousands of tiny flares. Down his walkie-talkie, Anthony could hear production conferring with the lighting and TV people, and Chalkie, as logistics manager, breaking in from his Portakabin. 'We have a big, big problem,' Chalkie was saying. 'The main stage generators have packed up and we're getting jack shit. Nothing's coming in to the site at all.'

'How long to fix it?' production asked via the showcall channel. 'We've got Keith standing by on three-minute call.'

'Wish I knew,' Chalkie replied. 'We're trying to restart them. They're dead as a dodo.'

'We can't leave a hundred thousand people sitting in the dark. They'll go crazy.' Already, chants of 'Why are we waiting?' were breaking out in different parts of the field.

Then Anthony had an idea. Pressing the transmit button on the walkie-talkie, he said, 'I think I know where I can get hold of some candles. Would that help?'

'Only if you have about ten thousand of them,' the production director replied caustically.

'That's how many I do have. At least I think so. I'll get back to you.'

Minutes later he was at Steepness Farmhouse and found Nula preparing to leave for the concert. She'd been down already that morning to hear Fairport Convention, and wanted to watch Keith Richards. No one else interested her. Gaia had been allowed to watch Jasmine with some friends.

'Nula, you've got to help. It's an emergency. All the lights have failed and we need candles. Rather a lot of them.'

'Then you've come to the right place,' Nula said. 'Both outhouses are crammed with them. I've done this new aromatherapy one with nettles and dock leaves.'

Soon Anthony had radioed Richard and Tom to gather up the other children and as many of Ginette's security as could be spared. Five minutes later, Chalkie and Morad arrived in the paintballing Gators, piled with kids in the back, and a human chain formed to load the vehicles with candles. By the time they arrived back at the arena, the atmosphere in the crowd was becoming mutinous.

'Any news of the generator?' Anthony asked.

'Still working on it. They reckon they've found the problem, but it's not fixed yet.'

It is surprising how quickly ten thousand candles can be removed from biodegradable packaging. Within ten minutes, the first thousand candles had been lit and positioned across the front of the mainstage. Five minutes later, there were four thousand alight, across all three stages, filling the air with the scent of elderflower, primrose and nettle. Soon they had been placed along the tops of the sound towers and the entire stage area was covered with flickering, sweet-smelling wicks. Jacinthe exclaimed it was 'quite magical,' and assumed it had all been carefully planned. The crowd began singing a Bee Gees song: 'The lights all went out in Massachusetts . . .' and disaster had been averted.

By the time the lights burst on again, there was a groan of disappointment and the arena suddenly felt too bright and glarey. Anthony closed his eyes in relief, and thanked God for Nula.

Keith Richards gave a memorable, subversive set, jamming with half a dozen old mates, some world famous, others unknown, including two members of the Rat Catchers who turned out to be former roadies for the Rolling Stones. Now there was only Robbie Williams still to go, and you could feel the anticipation in the crowd. When his helicopter tried to land during the power cut, Gaia and John-Spiros had formed the letter H from aromatherapy candles, marking the landing pad, and the chopper came to rest in the perfect place. 'Smart move,' said the pilot. 'We didn't know what was happening down here – it was like a graveyard. We almost turned round and went home.'

In the artists' dressing room area, security was heightened as dozens of fans and liggers tried to blag their way in to catch a glimpse of Robbie. Jasmine, Katie and Ambrosia took advantage of their special passes to hang around his corridor, and even Sandra made the journey, handing a tea-towel to one of his minders 'to give to Mr Williams. I think he'll appreciate the humour.' Jeremy Meek had to be frogmarched away by security when he was found peeping on tiptoe through his window.

Anthony decided to watch this final act from the VIP grandstand, surrounded by children and stepchildren. As usual, the one person nowhere to be seen was Morad, which was a pity, since he'd been helpful for once during the candle episode and Anthony wanted to thank him.

The roadies were making final preparations for Robbie's set, adjusting mikes and drumkits. And then there was a surge of applause as the star strolled on stage. By now Anthony felt so overwhelmed by everything, he could hardly focus on Robbie Williams at all, as he sauntered from one side of the main stage to the other, alternately nonchalant and supercharged, belting out 'Let Me Entertain You' and 'Feel' and taunting the audience by moving closer and closer on the projecting lip of the stage.

It was fifteen minutes into his set that a familiar figure appeared on the apron stage: *Morad*. His forehead was wrapped in the red bandana, and he was wearing the long leather Gestapo coat last seen at the opening party for the Plough and Harrow.

'What on earth's Morad doing up there?' Anthony asked anxiously. 'He shouldn't be there at all.'

Morad wandered up to Robbie Williams and, quite suddenly, snatched the microphone from his hand and bolted towards one of the PA stacks at the side of the stage. Seconds later he was clambering up the scaffolding structure. The backing group continued to play for another twenty seconds before realising what was going on, and then, instrument by instrument, the music died away.

'What the fuck is Morad doing now?' Richard was already clambering over the rows of seats, heading for the front to try and catch him.

'Ohmigod, I think he's going to say something,' Ambrosia said. She was staring, aghast, at her half-brother who was standing on the top of an enormous speaker cabinet holding the microphone to his lips. A TV cameraman with a camera dolly on a length of track was filming him as he surveyed the crowd.

'Friends, Romans, countrymen,' Morad began. His voice was unnaturally deep and portentous. 'My name is Morad Ahvazi Emboroleon Anscombe, Commander of the armies of the North, stepson to a Greek shipping billionaire, stepson to a bankrupt banker, son to an Iranian casino owner and a manipulative bitch, and I will have my vengeance in this life or the next.' He appraised the crowd with a hard Russell Crowe stare, and was rewarded by a ripple of uncertain applause as the sound team finally came to their senses and turned the volume down to zero on his microphone channel at the sound desk.

Having done his *Gladiator* bit, he now seemed unsure what to do next, so he just stood there, smouldering. He was still there sixty seconds later when Richard and the first of Ginette's security men hauled themselves up to take him away.

Robbie Williams watched the whole episode with amused detachment, making clown faces at Security. Now he reclaimed the stage with renewed frenzy; he would sing some verses of each number and turn the microphone on the audience, urging them to pick up the chorus as he belted out hit after hit. Soon, every person in the arena, with the sole exception of Henrietta, was dancing and singing along.

The roar of the crowd singing 'Angels' could be heard as far away as Stow-on-the-Wold, Anthony was told afterwards.

59

Anthony was euphoric. The concert was over and it had been an enormous, unbelievable, unqualified success. The last of the departing traffic was wending its way along the narrow lanes, and the police reported it had been one of the most trouble-free large public gatherings they'd ever experienced. Aside from the power cut and Morad's bizarre outburst, everything had run like clockwork. Wherever he looked he saw his neighbours and family fired up by their great achievement. Len was distributing free beers to the crew and security, and Ginette and Arabella were snogging openly in triumph. Sandra excitedly told him she'd sold seventeen tea-towels, which she regarded as 'really rather good, considering the very strange people who were here'. She said she'd have no trouble flogging the leftovers at the Moreton agricultural show.

Ears still ringing from the amplified music, Anthony just wanted to go round thanking everyone. It had been an extraordinary team effort, and he felt overwhelmingly grateful. Never normally demonstrative, he found himself kissing and hugging everyone he saw: Sandra, Nula, Jasmine, Jacinthe. Mrs Holcombe was so startled, and so drunk, she started kissing him back. When he saw Charlie Edwards, he enveloped him in a bear hug: 'Charlie, I can never thank you enough. We'd never have done it without you.' Charlie gave a lop-sided grin. 'The pleasure's all mine, old boy. That was one of the most enjoyable concerts I've been involved with, and I mean it too. You're a great bloke, Anthony. It was you that made it all happen.'

Anthony laughed. 'It was all of us; it was everybody.' At that moment, he felt happier than ever before in his life. He loved everyone, even Charlie – he loved Winchford, he loved his children, his wives, all of them. The Winchford rock festival had been a mega-success . . . but, better still, it was all over. He would never again need to write to another pop star, or debate safety procedures with a planning officer. Suddenly, above anything in the world, he wanted a drink, several drinks; he wanted to drink his way to oblivion. He saw Chalkie approaching with Richard and Tom.

'Chalkie, thank you. You were a complete star. You do realise we never need see those ghastly planning pedants ever again?'

'Not until next year anyway,' Chalkie replied.

'*Next* year? Over my dead body.'

'Of course there's going to be a next year, boss,' Chalkie replied. 'After today's success, it's got to be an annual event, surely.'

'You heading to the Priory now, Dad?' Richard asked. 'The party's already started.'

'Party? What party?'

'The after-party. Amanda and Jas have organised it. They've invited everyone back.'

Anthony arrived to find the Great Hall bursting at the seams. It seemed like most of the village was up there, plus half the crew, all the committee, his neighbours and several of the stars too. Across the crowd he spotted John Furlong locked in conversation with Ozzy and Sharon Osbourne, and Nula and Amanda chatting to Keith Richards. Percy was handing round the plate of cakes and muffins Archie had given him, and Walter Twine, recently released by the police with a caution, was slavering over Kate Moss. Rosanna, Ambrosia, Katie, Gaia and John-Spiros were all circulating with bottles of vodka and sparkling wine, and it was obvious everyone in the room was planning on getting massively, gloriously plastered.

John, already pickled, loomed up and said, 'Have you any idea how much we've raised, Anthony? It's unbelievable.'

'Well, I've got a rough estimate in mind, but it's only that. What do you reckon?'

'I've done some back-of-the-envelope sums, and if everything comes in as we think it will, we could hit four million. And you know me, I'm conservative by nature.'

'That's way above my highest forecast. You really think so?'

'According to Charlie, the TV will sell all round the world. He's just said that now. So that's another million, apparently. And Len and Archie both tripled their targets. And then there's the unbudgeted gate money from the extra entry tickets and car parking and . . . Sandra's tea-towels, of course.'

'If true, it's simply astounding . . . incredible.' Four million pounds would pay for the Old Rectory, Steepness Farmhouse, the Lady House and at least six more cottages in the village. He could scarcely believe it.

The atmosphere in the Great Hall became louder and more raucous. Someone had put music on – Coldplay, Anthony could identify everything now – and people were dancing. He saw Rosanna necking with Darren on a sofa, and Jeremy Meek whispering camply to John-Spiros. Lex and Archie both had different Lithuanian supermodels draped all over them, and Trevor Bratt was backing nervously away from Sandra, who was trying to sell him a half-price tea-towel. Patrice was stumbling about with a can of Stella in both fists. Abandoned wine and beer glasses, and plastic cups with floating cigarette butts already littered the surfaces of every piece of furniture, and Anthony was relieved Dita wasn't there to see it; she'd have gone insane. Tom Furlong was discreetly helping Len hand round the last of the Turkey Twizzlers and venison burgers.

Suddenly overwhelmed by bustle and noise, Anthony retreated upstairs to the minstrels' gallery overlooking the Great Hall. His father's old desk, of course, had not survived Dita's redecorative regime, and the gallery walls were lined these days with coral moiré silk, but it remained a place of refuge, to which he still liked to escape when life became too much.

People were still arriving: sound and lighting crews, make-up artists, more villagers who had heard it was a free-for-all up at the Priory.

That was when he caught sight of the girl. Her eyes were huge and black, and ringed with mascara, and her hair, also black, was long and lustrous. She glanced up to the ceiling and spotted him in the gallery, holding his stare for a moment in a way he found disconcerting and vaguely flirtatious.

He recognised her immediately: the girl from the concert, one of Amanda's backing singers, the sultry one. He knew he should look away, but found himself staring back at her. She was unbelievably attractive. Then she cocked her head to one side, in what seemed like a challenge to join her downstairs.

He returned to the Great Hall and found her easily enough. Close up, she was even more enticing than she'd appeared from above. 'What were you hiding away up there for?' she asked. 'You should be celebrating your big success.'

She had high, delicate cheekbones and luminous white skin. His heart was beating in a way it hadn't for years and his mouth was dry. He shrugged. 'It's been a long day, a long six months, in fact. I needed a moment alone.' Then he said, 'I'm Anthony Anscombe, by the way.'

'Amy,' she replied. 'I know who you are. This is your party and your place. It's a beautiful room, too.'

'Thank you. It is a lovely old house. I'm awfully fond of it.'

'I know you are,' she said, and touched his arm. Her touch shot through him like static. He noticed she had a slight accent, Italian or French, he reckoned. Suddenly unable to think of anything to say, he just stood there, dumbstruck by her beauty, wishing she wouldn't leave.

'Would you show me round your house?' she asked him. 'I've heard so much about it.' *About eet.*

'You have?' Anthony was strangely chuffed. 'Well, of course you can have a tour, whenever you want, Amy. Right now, if you like. But I warn you, it's not all that interesting unless you go in for moth-eaten old tapestries.'

He led her to the staircase and up to the long gallery with the Tudor portraits, where Amy said how much she loved Elizabethan portraiture, and how one of the pictures of a swain in a ruff reminded her of her father. Anthony flinched, not wanting to hear about any father.

As though in the pull of destiny itself, he found them heading up to the roof, Anthony striding ahead, leading the way, barely able to look at her. Amy had the most mesmerising smile; more unsettlingly, there was something so familiar about her, as though he'd known her for a long, long time.

'Are you always this shy?' she asked him.

'Me, shy? What an odd question.'

'You seem shy. But you can't really be, or you couldn't have put on the concert.'

Anthony eased the bolts of the trapdoor and they stepped out onto the roof and edged round the walkway between slates and parapet. Half a mile away, down in the valley, they could see the crew already dismantling the floodlit main stage, and loading scaffolding onto lorries. Suddenly, from somewhere far below, they heard music drifting up through the slates. More Coldplay: 'In My Place'.

Amy said, 'It is quite appropriate, *non*? "In My place". We are in your place.'

Anthony smiled. 'I promise I didn't plan it.'

At that moment it seemed natural they should dance, and so they danced together on the rooftop on that hot July night, and Anthony felt almost disorientated, as though his past, present and quite possibly his future were all converging at once, as he held on to this stunning girl who made him dumb with yearning. He suddenly felt eighteen again, not one day older than the last time he'd danced on this roof, all those years before with Amanda. He felt giddy with love. Of course the whole idea was ridiculous, absurd – he must be three times her age, for heaven's sake – and yet he was hopelessly smitten. Crazily, his mind rushed ahead, imagining . . . a future with this enchanting creature about whom he knew nothing.

'You were fantastic in the concert,' he told her. 'You have a beautiful voice.'

'It is not so special, my voice.' She shrugged. 'Nothing like my mother's.'

'Your mother's a singer too?'

'Of course.' She gave him an odd look. 'You were there today, at the concert. And, anyway, you know that.'

Before he could reply, they heard footsteps on the stairs, and a female voice calling, 'Amelie? You up here?' A moment later, Amanda's head emerged through the trapdoor. 'Ah, there you are. And Ant. Someone said they thought you were heading up here.' She stepped out onto the walkway around the slates. 'I'm glad you've met Amelie, Ant; I can't remember whether you ever did before.'

'Oh, Amelie. Of course,' he said neutrally, but his heart was thumping.

Amelie replied, 'No, it is our first meeting. But all my life I have heard about you and this village. My mother often spoke about it.'

'She did?'

'Of course. She was always speaking of Winchford' – *Weenchford* – 'and how you both lived in that little cottage, the Forge Cottage, which I finally visited last night.' She laughed. 'It was quite strange, staying there with all my family together – Amanda and Patrice and Jasmine. A nice experience.'

'Amy lives with Patrice in Paris,' Amanda said. 'Though she's getting a place of her own in September, when she starts at the Sorbonne.'

They returned together downstairs, where the party was still going strong. Anthony felt dazed, almost frozen from his close escape. No wonder Amelie had been so familiar: she was Amanda reincarnated. A teenage Amanda. Inside his shirt, he was sweating. Dizzy and breathless, he leant against a pillar, while all around him the room was heaving. Scrotum Holland was vigorously jiving with Ambrosia, to her obvious embarrassment, and John-Spiros was now squeezed on a sofa between the vicar and one of the Scissor Sisters. Richard and Katie were rock and rolling together, with Gaia hoisted on Richard's shoulders. Tom was wearing one of Sandra's hedgehog tea-towels on his head in a Morad-style bandana. Glancing at his watch, Anthony saw it was already two o'clock in the morning, and unbearably hot and clammy.

Slipping out through the side door, he escaped into the cool of the knot garden. For a moment he stood there while his eyes became acclimatised and the great cypress tree came into focus. Gradually, he became aware that someone else was close by.

'Anthony?' It sounded like Charlie's voice.

'Charlie? That you?' He could see him now, sitting alone on a garden bench, smoking what looked like marijuana.

'I'm trying to come down,' Charlie said. 'I still get overhyped by concerts, even now, and then I can't sleep. Stupid, really.' Then he said, 'I saw you with Amelie. She's cute, isn't she?'

Anthony flushed in the darkness. 'She reminds me of her mother. Exactly like Amanda was.'

'Just not so dangerous.'

'You don't think so?'

'Amanda was deadly. The ultimate heartbreaker. But I don't need to tell you that, I'm sure.'

Anthony chuckled ruefully. For the first time he saw Charlie as fellow victim rather than enemy. It must be a sign of maturity, he reckoned.

'I feel I owe you an apology for nicking your wife.' Charlie said. 'I never said anything before, but I should have. I know it was all a long time ago, but still.'

'Thanks, but don't worry about it. I suppose I nicked her from you when she was your girlfriend. We were both obsessed. I cared at the time, and for a long time afterwards, but the strange thing is, I don't think I do any more. Must be getting old.'

'I felt guilty when she ran away with me from you and Jasmine,' Charlie said. 'But you know how it is with Amanda: you find yourself being drawn into things, until you can't help yourself. She has that effect on people.'

Anthony grunted. He wasn't sure he wanted to hear any more.

'She made me promise; it was like this dare,' Charlie said. '*Accept my dare*, that's what she used to say. She dared me to come with her to Paris. She was one powerful chick in those days.'

Anthony didn't reply.

'I nearly topped myself when she broke it off the second time,' Charlie said. 'You probably don't remember, but you caught us in the pub together – you were meant to be doing the harvest or something. It was just after that Amanda finished it. No warning, nothing. She said she was pregnant but had chosen to stay with you.'

'That's what she said, was it?' Anthony asked, suddenly horribly alert.

'I almost feel I owe you a big cheque or something, for the amazing way you looked after Jas,' Charlie said. 'You were like this perfect model father, so I always knew she was well cared for and everything. But I still felt bad about it, like I was dodging my responsibilities. That's why it's been so great getting to know her properly. It's like I've been making up for lost time.'

'Charlie, this may seem a very strange question, but I'm not sure if I'm hearing this right. Are you saying Jasmine is *your* daughter?'

'Sure,' Charlie replied, sounding surprised. 'I thought you knew that. Amanda said she told you years ago, when it first happened. She said you knew all about it and were cool about it.'

The garden started spinning around him, and an acrid sickness rose up from the pit of Anthony's stomach.

'Oh my God,' he said. 'I had no idea.'

Then he stumbled into the darkness beyond the cypress tree, and threw up all over its roots.

60

Five months after the concert, Amanda moved the first of her belongings into the Priory. It all happened so haphazardly and so gradually, you could not actually say for sure when or how it happened at all. It was more that she stayed over for a night after a party, and then for a weekend, and then another weekend, and soon it made sense to keep some of her clothes in Anthony's bedroom cupboards.

Over time, it became understood that Anthony and Amanda had got back together again, and she now spent thirty or so weekends a year at the Priory, and sometimes whole weeks at a time, when she wasn't away travelling or recording. After her appearance at the Winchford festival and the massive international exposure it brought, her career enjoyed a revival, and a new album, *My Bruised Heart,* was released on Black Cat's Legends label, showcasing all the Calcutta period ballads. After she performed 'Badder, Bolder Man' on the *Michael Parkinson Show,* the album made a brief appearance in the charts, which gave her her biggest confidence boost in years and she even began writing again, much to Anthony's delight.

Anthony tried his hardest not to get too excited by Amanda's reappearance in his life, but found it impossible to disguise his joy. The fact was, he adored having her there. Each day was a blessing though a part of him remained wary, because he knew his Amanda, and that she was still capable of disappearing again. He asked nothing of her and expected nothing of her, and knew himself to be as profoundly happy as it was possible for him to be. By now, God knows, he recognised her shortcomings: she was late for everything, she missed trains, she forgot about important arrangements even when he'd repeated them half a dozen times. But he felt more content, and most himself, when she was there with him, and his neighbours commented they'd never known him more relaxed, with no bank to worry about and a shrunken estate, and Amanda padding barefoot about the Priory with her guitar.

In many ways she was exactly the same person now as before. In other respects she was calmer and less elusive, and consequently much easier to live with. She had lost some of that edge of danger, and no longer reminded Anthony of a flighty wild-eyed horse, always preparing to bolt.

To his great surprise she had turned into an instinctive cook in the intervening years, and spent hours in the kitchen making huge, generous salads and bowls of pasta with pesto for everyone to enjoy. Another speciality was her North African tagines, which she'd learnt during her many trips to Morocco and Algeria. 'When you've been hanging about film sets for as long as I did, you *have* to teach yourself to cook,' she said. 'Anyway, I was a French housewife for God knows how long, and it's kind of expected.' Unlike Dita, Amanda never planned a single meal even one day in advance, buying aubergines, tomatoes and garlic at the market, or whatever caught her eye. From the day she moved into the Priory they never again ate in Dita's soulless dining room, not even at Christmas, and the kitchen was always filled with neighbours, his children and their friends, the sound of corks being drawn and much laughter.

Little by little, Dita's makeover of the house was softened and subverted by Amanda touches. Rajasthani tablecloths and Moroccan kelims started to appear in the Great Hall and in the library, and the stiffer button-backed armchairs were swapped for comfortable, slightly battered ones from a local auction house. The bottles on the drinks table stood no longer in height order, and had Anthony not been too well trained by Dita to altogether change his ways, the whole drinks area would quickly have become a shambles of unfilled ice buckets and dirty glasses. Upstairs, however, she at least no longer left her unpacked suitcases all over the bedroom floor, and some of her clothes even found their way onto hangers in the wardrobe, though most were draped permanently across chair-backs. In the garden she directed the gardener to soften Dita's rigid planting, and some of the lower terraces were allowed to revert to wilderness, which increased the butterfly population no end.

To Anthony's great relief, Amanda's reappearance played well with all his children and stepchildren, who stayed at the Priory more frequently than before, gravitating there every weekend unless something better came along. Jasmine, of course, was thrilled that her parents (as she still regarded them) were back together, and although Anthony came to accept he wasn't Jasmine's biological father, he found it didn't change anything in his love for his daughter, or in hers for him. Following some anguished debate with Amanda, who seemed genuinely remorseful she'd never told Anthony the truth, they decided they should make a clean breast of things to Jasmine. Initially she was furious with her mother and stayed shocked and tearful for several months. But, as time passed, she too became more accustomed to the idea. 'I'm still calling Dad "Dad" and Charlie "Charlie", you know,' she announced to Amanda defiantly.

'One day you're really going to have to tell me why you left me,' Anthony said to Amanda while they were walking hand in hand through the bluebell woods (the paintballing having packed up for the evening).

Amanda sighed. 'All those years ago from Forge Cottage, you mean? God knows, I've thought about that a lot at different times, and I still can't work out what was going on in my head. I was young and selfish then, and the drugs probably didn't help much either.' Seeing his face, she said, 'Not that I was ever a big user, but they were around. Charlie always had some.' They clambered over a stile at the top end of the woods and out into the open meadows beneath Ironstone Hill. For several minutes they walked in silence. Eventually Amanda said, 'You know what it might have been, Ant? I never felt I quite deserved all that devotion. From you, I mean. You were so good and kind – whatever I asked for you always said yes, and whenever I took you for granted you forgave me. You were the perfect husband. And I couldn't handle it. I was on such a self-destructive path, I needed you to save me from myself, but you always forgave me, every time. And then I got re-involved with Charlie and just lost sight of everything. I became so muddled about what I really wanted . . . and needed. Then I became pregnant. I knew it was Charlie's child; I knew exactly where and when she'd been conceived – on the top of Primrose Hill after a party. There's like this little clearing up there with a water fountain, and a trough for dogs to drink out of. So I was having this baby and I didn't know what to do or who I could even tell. Stupidly, I told Charlie. That was a complete waste of time, because he totally freaked and refused to have anything to do with it. This was all just before Christmas. I was up in London, Charlie wouldn't talk about it, so in the end I came down to Winchford – do you remember, you collected me from the station? It was Christmas Day, and we went to your parents for lunch and I told everyone I was pregnant. I *was* going to tell you the truth; I really did mean to. All the way there on the train, I'd been planning how to break it to you. But then I couldn't bring myself to. Not when you were so excited and everything, not to mention your parents and their friends. All that champagne! So I funked it. I just didn't want to wreak any more havoc in your life. You probably won't understand, and I wouldn't blame you, but that's how it felt at the time. I felt so uncomfortable, a big fraud. I didn't even feel comfortable with Jasmine when she was born; it wasn't supposed to be like that. And the kinder and more considerate you were to me, the worse it got. I didn't *want* you to be that kind. I was undeserving. I just got more and more paranoid until one day I knew I had to get out. It was a question of survival. And it was so difficult to force myself to do it.'

'Leaving Jasmine, you mean?'

'No, you idiot. Leaving *you*. My one true love. The person in the world who adored me more than anybody else. We had that special bond – it did mean something, you realise. I'd never loved anyone that much before, and I never did afterwards either. Not Patrice. *Definitely* not Patrice. Definitely not Charlie. None of the others either . . . you don't need to know about them.'

Anthony laughed, and his eyes filled with tears. For the first time he no longer felt any jealousy, present or retrospective.

'You see,' Amanda said, hugging him on the footpath that led back to the Priory, 'I've run back home to an old embrace in a greyer place. That's what the song says.'

'So it must be true,' Anthony replied, taking her gently by the hand.

A couple of days later Anthony attempted to repeat some of this to Lex while they were having a quiet drink at the Plough and Harrow. He wanted to explain Amanda's state of mind when she'd walked out. Lex listened to it all with an increasingly sceptical look on his face. Privately he thought it sounded like a load of old tosh. But he said, 'Well, as long as she doesn't disappear for another forty years, or get back on drugs, or sleep with too many other people, I'm sure you'll both be very happy.'

Richard and Rosanna both got on fine too with Amanda, saying they greatly preferred her to Dita. 'Whatever turns you on, Dad,' Rosanna said, shrugging. She was so involved with Darren these days, helping him build the business at Winchford Autoparts, which had diversified into selling second-hand quad bikes, that Anthony felt she hardly noticed in any case. Katie formed a particular rapport with Amanda, with whom she discussed painting and sculpture, and Tom too spent a lot of time up at the Priory these days while his case slowly worked its way through the legal system. The Bank of England had set up its own investigation into the fall of Anscombes, which looked set to last for another two years, with everyone giving evidence to Financial Services Authority regulators. Anthony had been interviewed three times already and was co-operating fully, though he did rather wonder what the point of it all was, so long after the event. Tom's extradition to Singapore had been twice resisted by expensive lawyers, paid privately by Anthony, and there was a chance he might now be tried in Britain instead, which was his preferred option.

As for John-Spiros, Ambrosia and Henry, they clicked with Amanda straight away, and the Emboroleon children made it clear they still loved coming to Winchford, regarding it as their home. In fact, this became something of a bone of contention with Dita, who felt they should all be spending weekends with her and her new boyfriend, Ramnakrishna Gupta, at his enormous mock-Regency mansion on the Wentworth estate near Sunningdale, overlooking the golf course. Henry now spent every third weekend at Greenviews, which had an Olympic-sized indoor swimming pool surrounded by golden Ganeshas and pergolas. He reported back that his mother was completely redecorating the house from top to bottom, 'even though I don't think she likes the area or the house that much.' He also said Dita's new lover was 'a bit fussy and strict. He gets really stressy if we use the wrong towels in the fitness centre.'

Letters continued to arrive from Dita's solicitors, demanding a divorce and a substantial settlement. These made Anthony feel depressed, and also furious, as they became greedier and greedier in tone. In the end he demanded a meeting with her at the flat in Cadogan Place. It was the first time he'd set eyes on her since the day she'd left the Priory after the collapse of Anscombes, and he found himself feeling nervous at the prospect. But when she started demanding money he became un-characteristically angry and assertive. He informed her that since she was far richer than he was these days, with her Emboroleon divorce settlement, he intended to petition the courts for half her assets, plus a share of any future assets from Ramnakrishna. Dita turned white as a sheet and told him he wouldn't dare. 'Wait till I tell the court you've shacked up with that whore Amanda Bouillon. She's slept with half the men we know.'

'What horrible language, Dita. Wherever did you learn it? In the casino? Does Mr Gupta know about all that, I wonder?'

Twenty minutes later they agreed to a no-blame divorce with no money changing hands either way.

In Winchford, Amanda's reinstatement in Anthony's life led to a subtle realignment in village hierarchy, particularly when it was understood she wished to undertake no village responsibilities at all. To her great satisfaction, Jacinthe quickly filled the vacuum left by Dita, reassuming the presidency of every local institution from the Young Farmers to the Brownies, as well as Lady Chair of the annual fete and flower show, dog show and national garden scheme in aid of the nurses. Sandra became her invaluable deputy, and often commented on what a pity it was

Amanda didn't do her bit for the village, because it meant she missed out on so much. 'It's *her* loss.'

Where Amanda came into her own was at the annual Winchford Music Festival. She helped Anthony secure headline acts year after year and invited them all to stay at the Priory. In fact, her rock weekend houseparties over the festival became an important draw, as word got round about how much fun and how outrageous they were. For all his efficiency and growing experience of the music industry, Anthony never developed an instinct for what was hot, and it was Amanda who talked Missy Elliott, Franz Ferdinand and Keane into playing Winchford, as well as the legendary jam session with Mick Jagger, Bono, James Blunt and Chris Martin of Coldplay.

Some people thought the secret of Anthony and Amanda's happy relationship was that they never remarried, and that Amanda spent twenty weeks a year doing her own thing, well away from Winchford. After Jasmine opened her 'Jas' boutique on Westbourne Grove, selling pretty, ethnic, boho clothes at fantastically high prices, Amanda became one of her daughter's principal buyers, regularly touring India and Indonesia to source silks, brocades and beaded slippers. Whenever she returned to Winchford after a long absence, she and Anthony were so pleased to see each other that those around them found it incredibly touching.

As for Nula, her aromatherapy candle business took off like a rocket after the publicity of the first festival. Within weeks she was supplying Liberty, Fenwicks and Space NK, and soon had more than a dozen different eco-friendly products, none tested on animals, nor indeed tested at all. So brisk was demand she had to take on more than thirty people, all working from Anthony's outhouses at Steepness Farm. Since she felt strongly that illegal asylum seekers were unfairly victimised, Nula made a point of hiring only Albanian, Sudanese and Chinese workers, who dossed down in the barns at night and, being illegal, commanded low wages. Before long, the business was turning over such a fortune that she stepped back from day-to-day management and returned to her first love of healing. She bought a rather natty electric car and drove all over Oxfordshire, channelling heat from her clammy, healing hands.

After Richard returned from Kenya, he said he'd been thinking a lot about life, and what he wanted more than anything was to get involved in the farm. He began work as John Furlong's assistant in the estate office, where there was still plenty to do, even though Anthony had sold off many large fields and the quarry. In due course, John was persuaded to take early retirement to make way for Richard, who duly became manager of Anscombe Estates. He was full of bright ideas, and very popular with all the workers, the suppliers and the customers. John remained heavily involved in the rock festival, liaising with the local council, and also taking on Chalkie Cliff's responsibility for toilets after Chalkie's girlfriend, Judy Holcombe, ran off with one of the Rat Catchers – a great village scandal – and Chalkie decided to leave the area. Sandra, meanwhile, became a part-time house-guide for Knight, Frank, the estate agents, which suited her down to the ground, enabling her to snoop round all the local manor houses and barn conversions for sale. The only drawback, as John often remarked, was that it gave his wife extravagant ideas: she was forever returning from a viewing fired up with desire for new quarry tiles in the kitchen or a hydrotherapy bath.

Rosanna was the first of Anthony's children to marry, when she tied the knot with Darren at a civil ceremony in Chippy, followed by drinks on the Old Rectory lawn. Sandra confided to Anthony that she 'wasn't exactly over the moon' about their daughter's choice of husband, 'but what can you do these days?' Six months later, their first grandson was born: Rio, named after the Manchester United footballer.

Tom's trial lasted eleven weeks, and was heard before a judge on the grounds that the case was too complicated and technical for any jury to understand. In his summing up, the judge noted that, while Tom had behaved reprehensibly and employed systematic deception, much of the blame must rest with his immediate superiors for inadequate supervision. Numerous critical observations were made about the quality of Anscombes management, all gleefully reported in the newspapers. Tom was given a three-year suspended sentence and five hundred hours of community service, which he elected to take in Oxfordshire, in the form of digging Mrs Holcombe's and Henrietta Anscombe's front gardens.

After so much negative publicity, it was obvious Tom could never get another job in financial services, or probably in any large corporation, and John and Sandra became quite worried, wondering what he could ever do in life. 'Goodness, this whole business has been one long nightmare,' Sandra declared to Anthony, almost accusingly, as if it had all been his fault, rather than Tom's, that the bank went bust. Sandra, for one, had taken the judge's words to heart, and was inclined to blame the system more than her handsome stepson.

In the end Tom came up with his own solution for his future, moving to Shanghai on a tourist visa and starting a software company on the Bund. Within two years he was employing four hundred Chinese staff, had permanent domicile, and had married an Australian girl from Melbourne named Jodie. According to his stepmother, he was well on his way to making his first ten million. Anthony and Amanda decided not to travel out to China for the wedding, but John and Sandra went of course, as well as Katie, Richard and Tom's mother, Constance, and her husband Gracido Menendez who flew in from Argentina. According to Richard there had been an amazing wedding reception at the China Club, a four-hour banquet with about twenty courses, including shark's fin soup, and Tom had worn his old Eton tailcoat which Sandra brought out for him.

Poor, fat Ambrosia had got married too, to a thirty-nine-year-old Greek shipping heir, Manoli Andros, whose father was a close business associate of the Emboroleons. Anthony and Amanda were full of reservations about the match, which had clearly been cooked up by Goldie, but Ambrosia seemed resigned to it and said she didn't really mind that much. Everyone flew out to Greece for the wedding, which was held on the Emboroleons' private island of Kypsos, and lasted for four whole days of extravagant partying. All the guests were accommodated in a flotilla of magnificent yachts moored in the bay beneath the Emboroleon villa. It was unfortunate the yacht on which Anthony and Amanda had their cabin was anchored quite so close to Ramnakrishna and Dita's private gin palace, which had been crewed over from Cannes for the event. It meant they heard every word of their constant arguments, and Dita's complaints about the closet space in her stateroom being totally inadequate.

Against all expectations, Ambrosia looked really rather beautiful on her wedding day, as she exchanged vows under a golden canopy with numerous Greek Orthodox patriarchs in attendance. Anthony didn't think a lot of her husband or his mirrored sunglasses, but if he made Ambrosia happy, that was fine by him. Goldie made a long and tedious speech that scarcely mentioned his daughter at all, but plugged his newest, biggest container ship, which was bigger than anybody else's container ship. John-Spiros, fired up with vin santo, then gave an unscheduled speech of his own, full of affection for his younger sister, about how they had formed an amazing bond as children since neither of their parents was ever around much for them. The pathos was lost on nobody.

The unspoken spectre at the feast was Morad, who wasn't there of course, being incarcerated in Belmarsh Prison, Thamesmead. The latest Morad scandal had been all over the newspapers, which must have been pure torture for Dita, and said a lot too about the toughness of her new husband. Morad had organised a break-in at the Gupta mansion at Wentworth, waiting until his mother and stepfather were out of the country, and according to the tabloids 'filling three vans with priceless paintings and valuables'. A downstairs window had been smashed, suggesting the means of entry. Later, however, Morad's personal number was found on the computerised keypad of the burglar alarm entry system, at the precise time he had been claiming to have been asleep in London. Three accomplices were also arrested.

Dita had, as usual, done everything to have the charges dropped, but Ramnakrishna refused point blank, and insisted the prosecution go ahead. Morad had been sentenced to eighteen months. It spoke volumes about the balance of power in the Guptas' relationship that Dita hadn't got her own way for once. Having seen Ramnakrishna at close quarters, Anthony reckoned nobody messed with the tiny, strutting, Asian martinet.

While Ambrosia began a new life with Manoli in Athens, her brother began a new life in London with another older man, Adrian, an interior designer who had once worked in the Islamic department at Christie's. Without fanfare, they moved into a flat together in Albany, where they entertained very privately and exquisitely, and started a collection of rare Iznik ceramics. Not long afterwards they jointly launched an exclusive concierge service called Exponentially, aimed at cash-rich, time-poor millionaires; they could obtain opera tickets, valet suits, book holidays and Gulfstream jets and walk your dogs, whatever you wanted. Everyone agreed John-Spiros had found his perfect métier, and his advice on every subject, from bed linen to flowers, was faultless. Under John-Spiros and Adrian's painstaking supervision, all the pictures at Winchford Priory were rehung, and Anthony was even allowed to have some of his favourite Elizabethan portraits back on display in the library, which delighted him.

Henrietta Anscombe died at the age of eighty-nine, surrounded by Thai nurses, some of whom had known her for a fortnight at least. Two days later, Walter Twine keeled over in the Plough and Harrow. Nobody knew his precise age, but he was believed to be one hundred and eight. An immense congregation turned out for his funeral, which contrasted poignantly with Henrietta's sparse gathering earlier the same week. Anthony presented a cheque to the church for a plaque in Henrietta's name and a small electric organ in Walter's memory. Richard subsequently moved in to his grandmother's old home, the Lady House, once it had been replumbed and rewired, and it also became home to his wife of two years, Sara, a white Kenyan, and their year-old daughter, Molly.

Eighteen months after her wedding to Manoli, to no one's real surprise, Ambrosia reluctantly separated from him, citing her husband's serial infidelity. Apart from the honeymoon, where her adored baby daughter Olympia had been conceived, Ambrosia had been ignored and bullied throughout her short marriage. Too much in awe of her father to end it, Ambrosia was devastated when Manoli left her. She returned to England where she divided her time between Dita's flat in Cadogan Place, Winchford Priory and the other Priory, the Roehampton clinic, where she was treated for depression and low self-esteem. She swung between hysterical tears and a zombie-like catatonia. Anthony was seriously worried about her and Amanda suspected she was being prescribed far too many drugs.

One weekend, in desperation, Anthony sent Ambrosia to Nula for a healing session. Apparently it did wonders and Ambrosia went back for a whole course. Slowly she regained her equilibrium and, after a stressful Greek court case, Olympia too. For a year, mother and daughter lived in a serviced apartment near Marble Arch, until Ambrosia announced she was missing the sunshine and wanted to live in Greece. She took Olympia to Kypsos, and moved into a converted oil press on the Emboroleon estate, seeing practically nobody from one month to the next.

Three years later, however, she suddenly exploded out of her self-imposed purdah, announcing ambitious plans for a holistic health farm on Kypsos, the Aphrodite Spa, where women could discover their inner beauty and self worth. Several million dollars later, all bankrolled by Goldie, the spa opened to rave reviews, much helped by John-Spiros, who knew the editors and health and beauty writers of all the glossy magazines. In its first full year of operation, the Aphrodite Spa was named Best New Aegean Retreat in the annual *Condé Nast Traveller* Spa Awards.

Arabella and Ginette gave everyone something to talk about by announcing their engagement and issuing very formal, engraved invitations to a beach wedding at a Caribbean hotel. The invitation card began 'Sir Percy and Lady Bigges have great pleasure in inviting you to the marriage of their daughter, Arabella, to Miss Ginette Potts, daughter of Mr and Mrs Leonard Potts . . .' Jacinthe, who had known nothing about it, went into shock for several days at the thought of all their friends opening the envelopes.

According to Sandra, the ceremony had been 'really surprisingly unembarrassing, given the circumstances', and Bella and Ginette had worn matching morning suits. Percy had given his daughter away, and so had Len.

The Plough and Harrow, unaffected by the Anscombes crash, went from strength to strength, and was always packed. If you wanted a table for dinner in the dining room, you were well advised to book a week ahead. A skittles alley had recently been installed behind the car park, and Marjorie had started a collection of commemorative mugs in the public bar, celebrating the marriage of the Prince of Wales to Camilla Parker-Bowles. Len's pub quiz nights and speed-dating events caught on big-time, with people driving from miles around in the hope of finding their ideal partner. In the opinion of Archie, now fat and fiftyish, who went along a few times to watch, the standard of women was truly shocking: 'a complete dog show. I'm telling you, Ant, you've never seen anything like it.'

Anthony hadn't felt like discussing women with Archie at that moment, because he was still furious with the old roué for having an affair with Gaia, who was less than half his age. She had been doing some waitressing at Marshmellows when Archie had moved in on her. Anthony was genuinely outraged at the thought of his daughter with that old reprobate, and forbade them to see each other, which only made matters worse. Fortunately the affair burnt out quite quickly, well before Gaia went up to St John's College, Cambridge, to study archaeology and anthropology.

The girls who spent most time at the Priory these days were Katie and Amelie. Katie led rather a solitary life in London during the week, having returned to her first love of art and working at her sculpture studio in Edith Grove; at weekends, her beautiful copper hair was always spattered with clay. She had recently held a small exhibition of her work at an adult education college near the studio, where Anthony had bought a plaster cast of a woman's hands, mounted on a bronze block. Since the incident with Morad at Dita's lunch party, Katie hadn't had a steady boyfriend, and Anthony hoped it hadn't put her off for life. On the other hand, she seemed perfectly happy without one, in her vague, arty way.

Amelie had taken to coming over for weekends from Paris every couple of months, and she and Amanda had never got on better. After leaving the Sorbonne with a degree in international relations, she had joined Canal Plus, the television station, as a documentary researcher. Two years later she was anchoring a late-night current affairs programme, specialising in African music and race relations. She was undeniably beautiful, like her mother, and very focused, unlike her mother. Anthony found her earnest tortoiseshell spectacles sexy.

Henry continued to spend most weekends at Winchford, especially after Dita's split from Ramnakrishna, so Greenviews was no longer an option. Anthony spent a lot of time on the M4 at weekends, collecting and delivering him from school leave-outs, but Henry was off to Brown University in the States soon, which would be sad for everybody. Henry was still a golden boy, still blond, adored by everybody in the family.

'It'll be difficult to see so much of you when you're at Brown,' Anthony said. 'Though Amanda and I are planning on a trip to Rhode Island once you're settled in.'

Henry smiled. 'I really will miss you, Dad. I'll miss Winchford too. I really love this place.'

'Well, maybe you can go and visit your mother one weekend. There must be an airport close by to fly to.' Dita had recently married an eighty-nine-year-old American department store heir, Marshall Pretz III, and was busy renovating his home in Hilton Head, South Carolina.

Henry rolled his eyes. 'Maybe. I'll think about it. I haven't seen Mum since the wedding. I hope she's OK. Marshall is awfully old, you know. He had to say his vows sitting down.'

'None of us are getting any younger,' Anthony replied dryly. 'And it's nice for Dita being married. She prefers being married.'

'Speak for yourself,' said Henry, teasingly. 'You're hardly one to talk. One of my friends asked me the other day how many different wives you've had, and I had to stop and think.'

'Only three, so there's no need to be cheeky. Anyway, I'm not even a married man at the moment. I'm old, free and single.'

'Yes,' Henry said. 'And if I were you, I'd leave it that way.'

'You don't think Amanda and I should remarry then? You do approve of Amanda, don't you?'

'Yeah, Amanda's great. She's perfect for you. She's the best you're ever going to get. Just don't screw it up by getting married. Face it, Dad, you're not the marrying kind.'